THE GODLESS KINGDOM

THE LOST GOD BOOK FOUR

SHEILA MASTERSON

THE GODLESS KINGDOM

THE LOST GOD BOOK FOUR

SHEILA MASTERSON

Ebook ASIN: B0CV85H95F

Paperback: 9781960416124

Hardcover: 9781960416117

Cover Design and pine flourish: Andrea Laguer

Hardback Case and Map Design: Mike Sisak

Editing: Erin at EKB Books

Proofreading: Tabitha Chandler

To all those still struggling to write their own stories.
It's never too late to reclaim the narrative and find the words
that will lead you back home to yourself.

A NOTE FROM THE AUTHOR

Dear Reader,

THE GODLESS KINGDOM deals with some difficult subjects including violence, grief, post-traumatic stress disorder, panic attacks, anxiety, death, fertility issues, threat of sexual violence, loss of a parent (historical), consensual explicit sex, and light BDSM. I've attempted to treat all sensitive topics with the utmost care, but this content might still be challenging for some readers. Please take care of yourself.

Happy Reading,
Sheila

THE G⊛DS

Olney Gods

Clastor - God of All Matter

Adira - Goddess of the Sea

Aelish - Goddess of Truth

Desiree - Goddess of Love and Beauty

Sayla - Goddess of the Hunt

Devlin - God of Wisdom and Reason

Cecilia - Goddess of Mind and Memory

Neutral Gods

Grimon - God of Death

Samson - God of Lust

Aurelia - Goddess of Fertility and Harvest

Argarian Gods

Endros - God of War and Discord

Cato - God of Manipulation and Influence

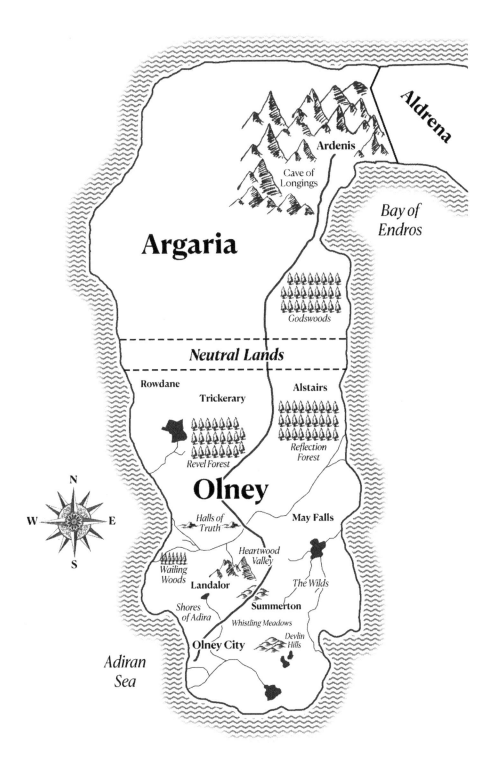

BEFORE

RAINER - 18 YEARS AGO

R ainer watched his favorite book of Olney history burn in the fire.

Raymond McKay loomed over him like an angry shadow. "It's for the best. Clearly, the book was distracting you from practicing."

Rainer nodded, turning his gaze back to the book as the pages charred and the ink bubbled. For the first eight years of his life, his adoptive father had barely given him a second glance. Raymond frequently traveled for weeks at a time for work, but recently things had changed. His father was home more often and spending more time at court—and he'd taken a sudden interest in his son. While Rainer had always wanted the attention, he wished it didn't come with so much expectation.

It started with an assessment from a master swordsman who spent a full afternoon testing Rainer's ability to learn and move fluidly. Rainer had trained with other children with basic weaponry at the Little School, assuming that even if he eventually took over his father's business, he'd first have a military career of some sort.

Within a week, he went from a routine of school and afternoons reading or swimming in the sea to a vigorous schedule of training every daylight hour he wasn't in class.

"When you want to be the best, you can't afford distractions," Raymond said.

"But I came in first for archery. And second place in swordplay is still really good," Rainer said helplessly.

"Second place is first loser, Rainer. It means you could have won with a little more effort. I don't understand why you'd be content to be good when you should be great," Raymond said, his voice stern. "Your lineage should give you a huge leg up on all the other boys."

A lineage Rainer knew by heart but read constantly anyway in the book that was now roasting in the fire. His father didn't know the book was rare. Didn't know Rainer had stolen it from the Olney Castle library.

Just once, he wished Raymond would be proud of him. It wasn't clear if he didn't have the patience for children or if his expectations were such that he expected Rainer to live up to the abilities of his birth father, Zelden Novaris, at only eight years old.

Rainer had read every single thing he could about Zelden Novaris. He'd read about how Zelden was on the front lines of the Olney-Argaria conflict for years, how he'd led the battle to hold back Endros's men to give Olney time for a counterattack, and how he'd fallen in battle when Rainer was just two years old. He had no memories of the man, or of his birth mother, who'd been bonded to his father—a detail that was left out of the histories since romance between a witch and their guardian was no longer permitted. Rainer had searched high and low for any additional details about their relationship, but they were difficult to find, especially since he needed to conduct most of his research away from Raymond's prying eyes. His birth mother had died just after having him, and his father had died in battle when Rainer was so young that he had no memory of either of them.

His earliest memories were of the warm voice of his adoptive mama, Maura McKay, reading him stories and taking him for walks along the beach.

Rainer wished he could use his birth father's surname, but Raymond insisted that coming up through the ranks with such a name would be a curse. Better to claim the name once he'd already proven himself. Rainer was always torn between the humiliation of knowing he was falling short, the desire to belong to something, and the need to prove that he could make his way on his own.

Deep down he knew that Raymond was right. If people knew who he was, he'd always be measured against the standard that the greatest hero in Olney history had set. Still, he wished that Raymond could at least recognize how hard he was trying.

No warmth in Rainer's life had ever come from Raymond McKay. He was the one man eternally disappointed in Rainer's progress, no matter how many compliments and accolades Rainer received from his tutors and swordplay trainer in the few months he'd been training. It didn't matter what progress he'd made; it never seemed enough for the man whose love he was desperate for.

Rainer tried to push the thoughts away because they made his chest feel tight and his eyes burn. Mama said it was brave to let himself feel all his feelings, but Rainer had been around enough of his peers and read enough stories to know the truth. Warriors didn't cry, especially over hurt feelings.

For so long, all he'd wanted was to see his father look at him with pride, the way so many of his peers' fathers did. But Raymond only showed up to training sessions to talk business with other fathers. No matter how well Rainer fought—even when he'd bested all of his opponents, including those the next class up—he'd turn and find his father's attention elsewhere.

It wasn't until they were home that Raymond would lay into Rainer for every minor mistake he'd made. Or, like with the book, he'd break or ruin distractions to help Rainer stay focused.

Perhaps Rainer shouldn't have been happy to have negative attention, but it was better than being ignored.

"Now we have an appointment. Let's leave this mess behind us and remember to stay focused and win next time," Raymond said.

Rainer nodded, following his father out the front door of their estate. He waited for an explanation as Raymond turned away from town instead of toward it.

Rainer's father tugged his arm as they hurried along the trail toward the woods.

"Hurry. You've already messed up once today. This is *not* an appointment we want to be late to," Raymond McKay barked.

"Why not?" Rainer asked, stumbling to keep up with his father.

"Because today you have an opportunity to make a good first impression with the huntmaster."

Rainer had seen the huntmaster many times. Leo Reznik was an imposing man, a fierce fighter, and the leader of the Olney military. He was a war hero, like Rainer's birth father, and everything that Rainer hoped to be someday.

"How do I do that?" Rainer asked.

He would do whatever his father asked and one day it would be enough. If all he needed to do today was make a good impression on the huntmaster, he could handle that.

The din of town quieted as they moved farther from the heart of Olney City. The estates grew larger and more elaborate, and the trail opened to denser forest. His father sighed impatiently, tugging his arm so he'd move faster.

"Where are we going?" Rainer asked.

Raymond sighed heavily. "To the seer's suite in the woods."

Rainer said nothing else, trailing behind his father, trying to ignore the swell of nervousness that turned his stomach. Finally, they reached a cozy cottage with a wooden fence and a large herb garden.

Raymond stopped before the gate and knelt in front of Rainer. He'd never lowered himself to Rainer's level before.

Nervous tingles spread through Rainer's limbs. He was startled by this gesture—something so normal he'd wanted for so long.

He tried to memorize everything about the moment. As hard as Raymond was on him, Rainer liked being spoken to like an adult— like he could handle the responsibility. Each chance Raymond gave him filled him with equal parts dread and excitement.

Raymond looked him in the eye, running his fingers through

Rainer's hair to smooth it. "Rainer, this is very important. When you go in there, the huntmaster, the ancient seer, and Lady Reznik will all be waiting for you. It is extremely important that you be kind to the young lady. Make a good impression on her and the huntmaster. She is a very young witch, so do what you can to be friendly, and if the seer decides you are a good fit to be her guardian—"

"I could be a guardian for a witch?" Rainer interrupted.

He couldn't help the outburst. Zelden Novaris had made his way through the Olney army ranks as a guardian in the prince's guard before being promoted to the king's guard, and then, when they saw his eye for defending a target, to lead the front lines of the army. He'd been paired with Rainer's birth mother, who was a talented earth witch. They were a fearsome pair who helped win many battles with their quick leadership and harmonious fighting styles.

This was Rainer's chance to be not just all the things he wanted to be, but all the things that would make his adoptive parents proud. On top of that, he'd seen Lady Reznik shoot her bow at a tournament months before and he'd been stunned by her composure and astonishing accuracy, as well as a creeping feeling of familiarity—as if he somehow knew her already.

His father gripped his arms. "Yes, you could. But only if you're a good fit for Lady Reznik and only if you accept the bond if it's offered."

Rainer nodded. "I won't let you down, Father."

"I'll be very proud of you if you can do this, son," Raymond said.

Something ached in Rainer's chest at the words, but he bit his lip and nodded to keep any weakness from showing on his face. He tried to imitate Raymond's curt nod, then turned to face the cottage.

He opened the garden gate and walked up the pathway. With every step, he felt as if something was calling to him from inside the small building. As he drew closer, his heart pounded in his chest and his palms grew sweaty. He took a breath before knocking on the door.

It swung open, revealing a dark-haired woman with violet eyes. She smiled widely at him. Raymond had called the woman ancient, but she didn't look much older than Rainer's parents. Still, her presence loomed large, making the hair on the back of his neck stand on end.

"Rainer McKay. Come in, dear. We've been expecting you."

Rainer's stomach twisted. His mouth went dry. He followed her inside, hoping she wouldn't notice his racing heart or clammy skin.

The room was dim. As his eyes adjusted to the scant light, he spotted the huntmaster pacing the room and Lady Reznik sitting in front of the seer's desk, her back to Rainer. Her feet swung back and forth, her braid bouncing each time her heels hit the chair legs.

Rainer's heart thundered in his chest, the echo of it whooshing so loudly in his ears he worried everyone would hear it. Even looking at the back of her head, he felt drawn to her—pulled in by some invisible force. It made no sense. And yet he had the strangest sense that he'd feel better if he could just see her face.

Then, as if she felt his wish, she turned to look at Rainer and the world stood still.

PART I:
BRAVE WITH
THE HAND

1

RAINER

A beautiful woman slept in the chair next to Rainer's bed. Her dark, curly hair was pinned up neatly, her silk dress immaculate as if she was going to a formal dinner instead of sitting by the bedside of an ailing warrior.

According to King Vincent, she'd been at his side from the moment he was hurt. Eloise Spellman had led Rainer out of the dark of his mind with the words of a fairy tale. It was her insistent voice that had reached him in the dark.

Something about seeing her now didn't resonate with what he'd felt and heard when he was half-conscious. Her voice, while lovely, did not feel familiar, but then everything about waking up was disorienting.

Rainer didn't understand why the daughter of the wealthiest landowner in Argaria would waste any time on him. He wanted to say something profound, but he did not know how to express gratitude to someone who'd saved him from the turmoil in his mind.

He wanted to ask her to tell him the fairy tale about the village where it rained stars again. Or maybe he just wanted to feel the comfort of her body pressed against his, or her hand gently brushing his chest, though none of that was appropriate, and mentioning it might embarrass her.

An unwed lady shouldn't share a bed with him. That Eloise had risked her reputation only showed her commitment to helping him. But now he missed the certainty that touch brought him. The only other times someone had touched him since he'd woken were in a clinical way.

Rainer kept searching for the warm tingling feeling, but he hadn't felt it since waking. Maybe he just wasn't close enough to her.

"Lady Spellman?" he rasped, his voice stale from lack of use.

She jumped, her eyes snapping open. She was on her feet in a moment, smoothing her dress and hair before bringing him a cup of water.

He smiled at her. "I wasn't waking you so you could wait on me. You just looked uncomfortable."

She handed him the cup. "How did you sleep?"

"You don't have to keep watching me while I sleep. I have had no issues waking since the first time."

A blush rose on her fair skin. "I know. I just didn't want you to be lonely. You must feel so disoriented without your memories."

Rainer studied her. "Why are you so kind to me, Lady Spellman?"

"Eloise," she said insistently. "I'm kind because you once comforted me in a bad moment and I feel compelled to do the same for you."

"And if I were to absolve you from the responsibility?"

Eloise frowned. "You don't want my company?"

Rainer scrubbed a hand over his face. "I'm finally back to full training today. I hardly need a babysitter."

Eloise winced, wounded by his words.

"I'm sorry. I shouldn't take it out on you. I just hate that you're wasting your time watching me sleep, even if I appreciate it," Rainer sighed.

Eloise nodded, her smile tight. "I understand. I'll leave you to it."

She turned on her heel and left him alone with an apology on his tongue.

Great. Now he'd lost not only his memories but also his tact, good manners, and the company of the person he wanted most—or at least the person he was pretty sure he wanted most. There was a wrongness about her, like he'd expected her to look or sound a certain way and upon waking she was someone new.

He threw his legs over the side of the mattress, his back and limbs stiff from time spent in bed. They'd finally moved him out of the healer's suite to his bedroom, but after weeks spent in bed, he was dying to get back to active guard duty. He couldn't remember much of his life, but he was certain he'd not had a month off from workouts since he began training as a boy.

The healer, Magdalena, had him on bed rest for almost a month, only allowing him up to stretch and take his meals. She released him from the clinic when he agreed to nap both in the mornings and afternoons. She said that he'd suffered significant damage to his brain and he needed time to heal. But he couldn't stand all the sleeping. Every time he closed his eyes, he was afraid he'd be trapped once again. His body was constantly buzzing with nerves. For years, he'd kept the persistent, creeping anxiety at bay with a relentless training schedule. Now, with nothing to burn it off, the agitation was twisting him in knots.

He splashed water on his face, pulled on a clean tunic, and looked in the mirror. Neatly combing his sleep-tousled hair, he studied his face, searching for something that would illuminate a memory.

He ran his fingers over the scar on his neck, trying to call up the memory of how he'd received it. The injury must have been harrowing. It looked like an arrow wound. The longer he looked, the more frustrated he became. Finding his body littered with scars was like living a history written by someone else. He couldn't connect any of the marks with the events that had created them.

He ran his thumb over the crescent-shaped scar on the outer edge of his left palm. Warmth bubbled in his chest, like his body had a fondness for that particular scar. Still, nothing came to mind.

He scrubbed a hand over his face, turning away from the mirror, rubbing his sternum. His tunic dragged over his most mysterious scar. The gold line over his heart looked to be a mortal wound and yet he had no recollection of receiving it.

He'd spent an hour the night before staring at it in the mirror, his body rolling through so many emotions: fear to grief to relief and joy. Every failure to make sense of the havoc in his body only left him more frustrated.

A knock on the door interrupted his daydream. A moment later, King Vincent Savero walked in.

Rainer waited for Grant to appear. Vincent's right-hand man was always lurking and something about his assessing gaze and silent smirking made Rainer furious.

"Your Grace," Rainer said, bowing to the king.

Vincent waved him off. "That's not necessary when we're alone. Please just call me Vincent."

Rainer's gaze darted to the door again. "Where's Grant?"

"He's giving us some privacy," Vincent said. "How are you feeling, Rainer? I understand you are very close to being cleared for training."

Rainer nodded. "I can't stand the sight of these four walls much longer."

Vincent grinned. "That's very good. Can you tell me what you remember?"

Rainer sighed, trying not to sound like a petulant child. It was all anyone asked him these days, and each time he failed to remember more, he felt worse.

"King Marcos sent me here to help ensure a peaceful transfer of power from Xander to you. I remember Xander handing over power to you and that he was relieved about it. He prefers to play the role of prince and the aristocracy didn't take him seriously. He was exhausted and overwhelmed. I remember there being an attack just after Xander's wedding. The wedding itself is foggy. I only remember pieces of it. But rebels who wanted to reinstate Xander attacked the castle and we were trying to get the staff out safely—and then it all gets foggy again."

Vincent placed a reassuring hand on his shoulder. "That's great. You have all the important bits."

Rainer swallowed the lump in his throat. "But I have this feeling like something went really wrong. I know I was hurt and a bunch of my memories were stolen by a slayer, but there's something more and it's just a black hole in my brain. I feel—"

Shame. Rainer felt shame that he didn't understand at all.

Vincent held up his hands in surrender. "I know you're frustrated, but I need you to take your time. As happy as I am to have you back, the last thing I need is for you to have a setback when you're doing so well. I am counting on you, Rainer." He hesitated, his brow pinching. "Listen, there's something I wanted to talk to you about. I know you've been feeling bad about the attack, but I would like to promote you. Between you and me, Grant is a good soldier, but he's not a leader and he doesn't have your talent or warmth. You know how to inspire loyalty."

Rainer frowned. "But I was bested. I was hurt—"

"By an army of men, Rainer." The king shook his head. "Even you are not above being overwhelmed by a large group of well-trained hunters."

There was one last nagging question Rainer had been too afraid to ask since waking, but the anxiety of not knowing was driving him mad. "I know that I'm a guardian. Where is my witch?"

Vincent's eyes darted down to the floor and he swallowed hard. "I'm afraid that she was a casualty of this fight."

"No—" Rainer gasped, breathless.

He'd failed at his most sacred duty. *From this day to my last day, I promise my sword and my strength.* That was the guardian vow and he had failed. He could not even recall her name, her face, or her magical affinity, but he felt her absence like a limb that had been hacked off. Suddenly, the empty feeling inside him made so much more sense.

Vincent placed a gentle hand on Rainer's shoulder. "I can't imagine your grief, as confusing as it must be with no memory. But you fought valiantly against an army of men and you protected someone very important to me."

Rainer straightened. "I did?"

Vincent nodded. "I know you were only visiting to help with the transition and acting a temporary member of my king's guard, but I see a permanent place here if you want it—a chance to redeem yourself. I know you have a life back in Olney, but I also know how a family name and expectations can follow you like a shadow."

Rainer swallowed hard. He knew Vincent was speaking from his own experience, but the words hit close to home. All that waited for him back in Olney was a father who was never satisfied and an empty house full of memories of his late mother. He'd miss his morning swims in the warm sea, but what Vincent was offering was the opportunity to make a name for himself away from expectations. He was offering a way to overcome the monumental failure of not protecting his witch.

"You could be my top advisor on all things."

"What do I need to do to prove that I'm ready?" Rainer asked.

Vincent's grin grew wide. "I knew you'd be interested. The first thing we need to do is root out the traitors who helped organize the coup attempt. I suspect that there are still spies within these walls waiting for their next opportunity. We need to find every single one and rip the entire organization out by its roots so that the people of this court and kingdom are safe again. Discord serves no one."

Rainer nodded solemnly.

"While you were convalescing, we ran raids and patrols of every known rebel hideaway in Ardenis, but for all the extra manpower I haven't seen results. I'm pulling back on daily patrols to hopefully lull the rebels into a false sense of security. If they think it's safe, they might make a mistake and we will be ready." He met Rainer's gaze. "You will be my eyes and ears."

"I can do that." Rainer sounded pathetically eager.

Vincent gave him a pat on the back. "I know you can. I will also need you to monitor someone for me."

"Like spying?"

Vincent shook his head. "More like guard duty."

Rainer nodded. "That's not a problem."

"I know. It's what you've been doing for years."

Rainer frowned. It was. That's what guardians did, though he could only vaguely remember guarding a particular person.

"Finally, I'll need you to settle down."

Rainer choked on his surprise.

Vincent shrugged. "I know it seems archaic, but both men in the council and in the army appreciate knowing their leader has roots here. A family man is one that everyone trusts."

Rainer nodded slowly. He'd always wanted a family, and he had a strong recollection of imagining how he'd raise his children differently than his father had raised him—with praise and empathy and kindness. He'd never make them feel like love was something they had to earn.

"I'm inclined to agree with you, sir, but I imagine courting someone will take some time."

Vincent nodded. "I understand that might be overwhelming, but I assure you there are plenty of ladies who are interested in a hero. I expect you'll be breaking a lot of hearts when you finally settle down. You were always quite popular at court."

Rainer tried to call up memories and saw a parade of women, though none seemed like a significant relationship. He supposed he would have to reform his casual ways and court someone properly. Still, settling down felt right, like it was something he'd been planning to do but hadn't quite had the time.

Vincent wasn't just giving him the opportunity to redeem himself; he was offering a pathway to success. Instead of constantly moving the finish line, Vincent was offering Rainer a few simple steps to garnering the recognition he'd always wanted. After the attack, Rainer had as much to prove to himself as he did to the rest of the world, but if he became the king's second-in-command, not only could he ensure peace for both kingdoms, but no one would be able to deny his value not just as a soldier, but as a leader.

Rainer wrung his hands in his lap as he considered it.

"I can do that, Your Grace," he said finally.

Vincent grinned, clapping a hand on his back. "I'm counting on it. I know you won't let me down." He nodded to the nightstand. "Your latest carving is in there. I hear you haven't picked it back up since you've woken, but I know it used to settle your nerves."

Rainer slid open the nightstand drawer. Inside was a wooden blob that very vaguely resembled a flower with star-shaped petals. Beside it were two other wooden star flowers, more finished than the first. The vaguest hint of a memory tugged at the corner of his mind, but it was just an argument with his father and his hands carving away at a similar flower.

"I made these?" Rainer asked.

Vincent nodded. "A skill you picked up to help with dexterity and to still your anxious mind." He patted Rainer's shoulder. "You and I both know an active mind is great in the field, but it can be hard to settle that vigilance when we're at home. It will be good for you."

Rainer was flattered the king cared about him enough to know his hobbies and talents and to remind Rainer of something that might help him get his mind and hands back into shape.

Vincent Savero wasn't just a good king. It seemed he was also a good friend.

Rainer smiled as he watched the king depart. For the first time since he woke up, he could see the path forward out of the dark and doubt in his own mind.

2

CECILIA

C ecilia swallowed the Godsbane the same way she swallowed her contempt—reluctantly and with the vicious promise of vengeance in her eyes.

Godsbane itself tasted like weak earthy tea, but the feeling of being cut off from her magic made Cecilia feral with rage.

She slammed the empty glass down on the table by the fire. The guard was entirely unfazed by her tantrum, swiping it up and leaving her alone in her room.

Every day for the last month had been an echo of the one before it. She'd wake to cold, gray light streaming through the windows, dress in the heaviest clothing she could find in her closet, and then a guard would show up with her daily Godsbane. She'd ask to see Rainer and she'd be ignored.

Twice she'd managed to sneak out to help Xander escort servants beyond the castle walls. Twice she'd watched them flee to safety while she returned to the castle under cover of darkness with Xander by her side. Twice she'd been certain that the chill in her bones upon returning was not from the cold but from the fear of what could still happen to her within those castle walls.

Once again she was a prisoner in Castle Savero, confined to her sitting room, bedroom, and the few places she could reach via passageways that Vincent didn't know about.

She walked to the window and leaned her forehead against the cold glass. Her breath fogged the view of the city of Ardenis below, clearing for longer stretches as the panic settled to low-grade anxiety in her chest.

From what she could tell from the few conversations she'd been able to sneak in with Magdalena and Mika, most of Xander's allies had fled. The rest had stayed and were either loyal to Vincent, hedging to see who truly came out on top, or trapped by the fear of retaliation. It was an unbelievable mess that they'd only begun to sort through, and one made more difficult since Vincent had taken to parading Xander around like they were the best of friends. It was rare that Xander could escape to talk with her alone. It was also a blessing because it meant that he was always there when Vincent came to see her.

She pressed her hand to her sternum, sending a surge of peace through her bond with Rainer. She hadn't been permitted to see him for one month. *One month.* She hadn't been there when he woke up, and she was crawling out of her skin with worry. Missing him was one thing, especially when she could feel through their bond that he was okay, but she knew the sight of him would calm the riptide of dread and panic that pulled her under out of nowhere. He didn't know how to control what passed through their bond because he didn't know the bond existed. That meant Cecilia had spent the better part of a month getting hit with every bit of anxiety and frustration he felt.

The door to her room flew open, and Cecilia was instantly on her feet, brandishing a hairbrush in front of her like a dagger.

Vincent stalked into the room and chuckled. "Going to brush me to death?"

She gripped the handle until her knuckles turned white. She tried to settle herself with the weight of it in her hand, its smooth texture—anything to distract her from the fact that the man who attacked her was standing in front of her, close enough to strike again. She looked at the door, waiting for Xander to appear.

A moment passed but he didn't arrive. Instead, Grant walked in.

She stepped back instinctively. She hated Vincent for the joy he'd stolen from her. Touch had always grounded and calmed her. Once a lush landscape of desire, lust, and longing, Cecilia's body was now a wasteland. Everything warm had gone frigid. Everything that was once soothing was suddenly terrifying.

He'd infected her with fear. Now, where there had once been a seemingly endless reserve of courage, she found her fingers scratching at the bottom of an empty well. She could not force her body into action—could not fight off this new type of memory that lived in her bones and held her frozen in place when the waking nightmare took over.

"Calm down, Cecilia. I'm not here to hurt you. I'm here to make a deal," Vincent said. He stepped toward her.

Her eyes darted wildly, looking for a weapon. Most objects she could use to defend herself had been removed from her room. Her gaze caught on her own wild eyes in the vanity mirror next to her. Her face was thinner, a clear sign of her lack of appetite from both fear and the effects of the Unsummoner bracelet. Shadows bloomed under her eyes from lack of sleep, and so full of fear, she looked like a stranger.

Think, Cece.

She could break the mirror and use a piece of glass in the worst-case scenario.

Cecilia shuffled closer to the vanity as she turned her attention back to Vincent. A smirk drew up the corners of his lips.

"I just said I'm not here to hurt you," he said as if reading her mind.

Cecilia gritted her teeth, trying to settle her nerves and stop her knees from shaking. "You'll have to forgive me if I don't believe you. What do you want?"

Vincent crossed the room, sitting on the edge of her bed. It was a power move—meant to intimidate her. She hated that it worked. The sight of him on the bed where she'd been struggling to sleep since he attacked her would give her fuel for her nightmares. She forced her body to face him squarely, her hips poised on the edge of the vanity, the brush still in her hand and ready to smash the mirror into shards if necessary.

"Rainer is safe and healthy. He's been taking it easy, but returned to full training today. Unfortunately, losing so many of his training memories has put him a little out of sync, but the muscle memory is all there. He will be back up to speed in no time. I'm sure you'll be thrilled to hear that he's terrible with a bow now. It seems he learned a lot from you."

It should have made her feel better, but the words filled her with grief.

Rainer's voice burned bright in her mind, a beacon that she needed to see in the dark. *"Do you really think my heart could forget you when you've been wrapped around it for more than half my life? Do you think I wouldn't feel you the moment you're close to me? I could never forget you. You and me...we are infinite."*

Cecilia wished she shared Rainer's certainty. She thought of his face when he said those words. He had told her she could borrow his confidence if she didn't feel it because he was so certain he wouldn't forget her. She took a shaky breath.

Get it together, Cece, she scolded herself. *This is not the time to fall apart. Rainer hasn't even seen you yet. He might remember you on sight. Just be patient for once.*

"It appears that you did a sufficient job. He thinks that I'm king, and he hasn't asked for you once," Vincent said. He took obvious pleasure in the words that were like a knife in her side.

Cecilia had made a deal with Cato to remove herself from Rainer's brain and she'd done a good job of it. Still, some part of her hoped that even her memory witch and goddess powers weren't a match for his love. It was the stupid hope of a fairy-tale-obsessed girl, but she couldn't help it. There was so little going well, she couldn't stand to let go of it.

She placed the brush on the vanity and clasped her hands to keep them from shaking. She stroked her thumb slowly over her inner wrist.

"So, what more do you want from me?" Cecilia asked. "It's not like I can tell him anything. Cato made sure I couldn't."

Vincent sighed. "Yes, but I can't exactly have you running around without an explanation for your presence. Your bond is still intact, no?"

Dread pooled in Cecilia's stomach. "Yes."

"I assume he will feel it if he's around you, so I need to make sure that our good little soldier stays in line. You have two options. First, you can choose to be a traitor I keep chained in the tower until I need you."

The words were so heavy with innuendo Cecilia thought her knees would give out.

Vincent smiled at her horror. "Let me see it."

"See what?" she gasped.

"Let me see how you're healing," Vincent said, nodding to her leg.

Cecilia stood frozen, her chin jutting out in defiance even as it trembled. Her eyes snagged on Grant Marzen. Her father had taught her to know her enemy, and Grant had taken pleasure in holding her down so Vincent could slice up her leg.

In the past month, she'd learned a lot about Vincent's right-hand man. Grant was slightly shorter than Rainer, but equally broad, which meant he was still nearly a foot taller than her and close to double her weight. He preferred short swords and was formidable with them and with his fists. He had smooth, tan skin, pale blue eyes, and short, dark hair that he clearly wanted to seem effortless but was too perfectly tousled to be believable. He was handsome enough to get away with being mean his whole life.

A gentleman would have looked away. But Grant didn't even bother pretending not to look as Cecilia bunched her skirt and slowly drew it up. She was relieved at least that one of Magdalena's healers, Grace, had gone over the glamour on her thigh again this morning to make it appear *almost* healed. Beneath the glamour, her skin was smooth and perfectly healed, but Vincent didn't need to know that, and as long as he didn't touch it, he wouldn't.

She drew the skirt high enough that Vincent could see. He made to move closer, and she pushed herself back onto the vanity, clenching the brush defensively in her fist again.

Vincent chuckled. "You wear it well. What does my cousin think of it?"

Cecilia looked at the floor. She felt guilty for not telling Xander what had truly happened when Vincent attacked her, but every time she tried to speak about it, the words tangled between her brain and mouth. Living through the experience itself was isolating, but she felt just as isolated in the aftermath, as if the pain was trapped inside of her with no way out.

Since the attack, she'd been tended to by Xander's spy friend, Mika, and the castle healer, Magdalena. They both tried to get her to speak more, but the words slipped off the tip of her tongue and floated away like smoke on the breeze. Sharing her experience and how it affected her now seemed simultaneously like it would make her less alone and also like others' reactions would remind her just how solitary she was in her pain.

"Ah, you haven't let him see." Vincent clicked his tongue in mock disapproval. "And here I thought you were still so close. No wonder he looks so sullen all the time."

"You said there were two options, but you only mentioned one so far," she snapped. "What's the second option for me—the one that doesn't require being locked away in the tower?"

Vincent's grin grew wider. "You'll act as my fiancée. We'll formally announce our engagement soon and you'll help me interrogate Xander's men to figure out where his wife and spymaster are. I'm certain you'll be useful in ways I haven't even thought up yet. I'd prefer to keep you close to make sure you're following the rules. Plus, Cato's bargain has had some less-than-desirable limitations."

A surprised giggle burst from her lips, the tension in her body snapping at once. Cato was such an asshole, but at least he was equally horrible to everyone. She'd have to figure out exactly what that meant.

Vincent frowned. "As long as you do as you're told, you'll have my protection."

"And who will protect me from you?" Cecilia hated the way her voice shook when she said it. She wanted to be strong, but if he stayed in her room much longer, she would crumble.

"Cecilia, I'll admit I'm curious considering that performance you put on in the library, and the hold you seem to have on my cousin, who's never been one for monogamy. But if we're being honest, dallying with you would be purely for sport and the enjoyment of watching you break. You do make it fun and having you close makes it easier to manipulate both you and Xander. Long term, I'm much more interested in Lady Brett."

The words sharpened Cecilia's mind. He was testing her, waiting for a reaction to see if Sylvie was still close.

She wanted to threaten him with a slow, painful death if he touched Sylvie, but she had no weapon and no way of hurting him since he valued nothing but power. If Vincent even breathed in Sylvie's direction, Cecilia would rip him apart with her bare hands.

"Why are you like this?" The question slipped out unbidden, but she could not fathom how someone became so cruel.

"Why don't you ask Xander? Now what will it be?"

She hesitated. She wasn't sure what keeping her close would do for him.

Vincent sighed, waving his hand impatiently. "I see you turning this over in your mind. Remember, one of these options allows you to lay eyes on your precious guardian occasionally. The other keeps you locked away in the tower as an enemy of the kingdom for my personal use."

Cecilia swallowed the bile that crept up her throat. She shook her head, trying to rid herself of the memories that haunted her day and night. The violence had etched them into her mind in a constant, torturous cycle that she didn't need her power to summon. She longed for access to her memory witch powers so she could pull up any pleasant memory. She wanted to lose herself in the past so she could forget the horror of the present and the man sitting across from her.

"Take off the Unsummoner bracelet," she said.

"Cecilia, you're not in a position to bargain."

"It makes me sick to be cut off from my power. Xander's probably having the same issue. We'll both keep getting physically weaker."

Vincent shook his head. "No. You're both just foolish enough to think that you can overpower me. I don't trust you not to try something."

Cecilia clenched her fist around her hairbrush in frustration.

"You'll act as my fiancée in ceremony only," Vincent continued. "You'll stay in your own rooms when you're expected to. You'll be present at events and look pretty and assure everyone that things are running smoothly. When I choose to let you, you can forgo your daily Godsbane and use your goddess powers to help the kingdom and solidify my rule. As long as you behave, you'll be treated with respect."

Cecilia shook her head. "Will I truly be expected to marry you?"

"Eventually, yes."

She shuddered, spinning her engagement ring from Rainer around her finger—the same ring her father had given her mother. "What would be the point? It's not like I can give you heirs."

Vincent frowned.

"You didn't know." The surprise nearly knocked Cecilia over.

It was a day for ripping open old wounds. Though she'd grown used to tending to this one—going back to it whenever she needed to settle into her grief—ripping it open for someone who'd already taken so much from her felt especially sickening. A deep ache settled in her chest.

Vincent furrowed his brow. "Know what?"

She shouldn't have been surprised. Cato kept secrets when it suited him and he was the type to hold on to them until he ensured their reveal would have maximum impact.

"In order to access my full powers, I had to give up my ability to have children. The witches of Olney could see Cato coming. They knew he'd want to use the Lost Goddess to continue his lineage and create more gods, so they made it so he couldn't. They forced me to exchange my fertility for my goddess powers."

Vincent stared at her, the tic in his jaw the only sign of his frustration. He stood suddenly.

"Fuck!" he shouted as he closed the distance between them.

Cecilia slammed her brush into the mirror and grabbed the first large shard of glass as it shattered. It bit into her palm, but she thrust it out in front of her, warding him off.

He stopped short, watching the blood drip from her palm, down her wrist, and onto the floor. "Is that your decision?"

"Does that admission change your offer?" she countered.

Vincent scrubbed a hand through his dark hair, his gold-flecked onyx eyes sharpening on her. "No. It's a minor setback. We can figure out children. You'll just have to lay claim to them. Does this mean you'll choose the second option?" His gaze fell to her trembling, bloody hand.

"Yes. I'll play make-believe."

Vincent pursed his lips. "Very good. Grant, take her down to the healer."

Cecilia took a step back. Pieces of broken mirror crunched under her boots.

Vincent laughed. "I'll expect to see you out of this room and more active in everyday events from now on, *dearest*. I'll see you tonight."

Grant gestured toward the door, and Cecilia brushed by him, following Vincent into the hallway. She waited for Vincent to disappear around a corner before she let out a breath of relief.

Grant lingered. His hand clamped down on her arm and she fought not to scream. Suddenly she was back in the dining room, pinned helplessly to the table while Vincent carved his initials into her thigh.

Her head spun, and she barely caught herself on the wall.

"What's wrong with you?" Grant barked.

She spun, brandishing the shard of mirror at him. "Do not touch me."

His eyebrows shot up. "I've seen you eyeing me up."

She huffed out a breath and started down the stairs. "You never test your oatmeal before you take a huge mouthful in the morning. That's bold of you, considering how adept witches are with natural poisons."

Over her shoulder, she watched Grant blanch. *Good, let him stress over his food.* When her father taught her sleight of hand, he'd been adamant that it was really just the art of attention.

"*People look where you look and they pay attention to the first place you touch, Cecilia. Make sure they're not looking where you'll actually strike, and play into their prejudices,*" Leo had said.

She wanted Grant wearing himself down with worry about his meals until she decided how she'd take him out. He, like Vincent, thought that women were weak. She looked forward to teaching him how wrong he was.

They continued down the hall and a staircase leading into the corridor that led to the healer's suite.

"You put up a valiant effort, but you didn't stand a chance then, you know," Grant said. "You don't now, either. So whatever little idea you're thinking up, just forget it. Fall in line and I won't have to deliver any more punishments."

Cecilia spun on him. He was to Vincent what Evan was to Xander, she supposed, and in his own way he mirrored her friend. The serious set of his jaw; the assessing, narrowed eyes. Though that was where their similarities ended, because even when Evan hadn't liked her, he'd never been cruel.

"You touch me again and I will gut you," she gritted out. Her hand trembled, the glass cutting deeper into her palm as she squeezed.

"You need to understand that you aren't in charge. You won't be anytime soon and the only way forward is to fall in line and—" He reached for her and the second he moved, she plunged the glass into his neck.

She didn't even realize she'd done it until she felt his blood warm on her hand. The impulse had completely taken her over. For a moment her body was not her own. It belonged to the panic.

Grant's eyes went wide in shock as she pulled the shard out. Blood spurted from the wound and he pressed his hands to it to staunch the flow. He crumbled to his knees, looking at her in disbelief.

"I told you not to touch me," she rasped.

Grant's wide, pale eyes locked on hers.

"It's unpleasant to feel so helpless, isn't it?" she whispered.

Vincent had cracked her open, and it seemed all she had left was cruelty. Maybe his cruelty had festered in her over the past month. Before, she couldn't have imagined enjoying making someone feel as powerless as she had, but now she found she was shockingly comfortable with it.

"It's a shame I have this stupid bracelet on or I could fix you if you asked nicely," Cecilia quipped. "Perhaps someone will wander along and find you in time. Or perhaps if you scream, someone will hear you."

A choked gurgle bubbled from Grant. Cecilia turned and dashed down the hall into the healer's suite, torn between righteous anger and guilt.

Magdalena's jaw dropped when she saw the blood all over Cecilia.

"It's not mine," Cecilia started. "Well, most of it isn't."

"Whose is it?" Magdalena countered, waving over a healer from the other side of the room.

Cecilia looked down at the ground. "Grant's. He's dying in the hallway," she said casually, throwing the mirror shard into a washbasin and holding her bloody palm out to Magdalena.

Magdalena nodded at the young healer who was staring at Cecilia. "Grace, go fix him there and I'll have someone join you so you can bring him in here."

Grace nodded and rushed out into the hall.

Magdalena gestured to the cot, and Cecilia sat down on it. The healer pulled out some alcohol and cleaned the wound.

"What would possess you to do such a thing? Your position is very precarious," Magdalena said. Her voice was calm, but her face pinched in fear.

"He touched me. I reacted. I don't even really remember doing it. He grabbed my arm, and I was suddenly back in the dining room. It happened so fast," Cecilia whispered. Tears sprang to her eyes.

"Where was Xander?"

Cecilia shrugged. "I don't know. Vincent must have shaken him off. He offered me two options, and I don't think he wanted Xander's interference."

She explained the options as Magdalena's tingling healing power knitted her skin back together until there was no sign of injury.

"I'm sorry. I screwed up," Cecilia said, blinking away tears.

Magdalena cupped her face in her hands. "There, now, dear. It's all right. I should be able to wipe the memory from him so he doesn't remember what happened and we will put him to sleep, so he wakes up in his bed."

Cecilia nodded, but she couldn't stop shaking. "What's happening to me? Am I losing my mind?"

Magdalena shook her head. "No, it's just a reaction to the fear. We see it sometimes after an attack like yours—see it in some of the hunters after a bad battle as well. It will pass. Just try to take slower, deeper breaths."

Cecilia shook more violently, her breathing so shallow her vision turned spotty. No matter how she tried, she could not turn the tide of fear in her body.

Only a moment passed like that, with Cecilia certain she was dying, but it felt like an eternity before a gentle healing tingling wove through her. It soothed her heart to a slower rhythm, and she recognized it.

"You know Xander's soothing spell," Cecilia croaked.

Magdalena smiled. "I do. It's the only thing he's ever taught me, but he's good enough not to brag about it."

Cecilia calmed and turned her attention to a commotion on the other side of the room. While she was panicking, Grace and another healer must have brought Grant in. The two healers were bent over him, blocking Cecilia's view of his face.

Grace caught her looking. "He's going to be fine," she said. "Maybe a little weak and confused about what happened because we'll need to wipe the memory."

Magdalena nodded, turning back to look Cecilia over. "I will help once I'm finished here."

Cecilia dried her clammy hands on her dress, looking away from the healer's kind eyes. She knew what was coming. The same thing that she always asked when Cecilia had one of these episodes.

"Would you like to tell me about it?" Magdalena asked.

Cecilia shook her head.

As much as she wanted to speak it aloud to reclaim it and call back the power it held over her, the words for the pain vanished the moment they hit her tongue, leaving her with a mouth full of sighs.

"All right, well. I'll be here when you're ready."

Cecilia appreciated that there was no pressure to do it, but found comfort knowing someone was waiting for her to heal in her own time.

3

RAINER

Eloise sat by the windows in the sitting room, sipping tea and chatting with several other ladies. She looked stunning in a purple gown with silver embroidery, and Rainer felt woefully unprepared for how to even approach her.

Relax, McKay. It's a thank-you walk in the garden, not a marriage proposal.

He looked at the bouquet in his hand. The royal gardener had assured him that the pale pink roses, zinnias, and pansies were an appropriate thank-you gift, not just a sign of romance, but Rainer still worried they weren't right.

His heart raced, anxiety rearing up thanks to the workout he'd skipped to be standing in the doorway like an idiot. He considered postponing, but then Eloise looked up, and her face brightened.

"Guardian McKay, it's so lovely to see you," Eloise said.

Rainer thrust the bouquet toward her, clearing his throat. His mouth was suddenly dry and his tongue twisted with words that seemed trite. "I wanted to thank you for sitting with me while I was lost. You—" He cleared his throat, straightening his stance. "You helped me find my way out of the dark, and I appreciate it."

Eloise took the flowers, breathing in their scent before looking up at him.

"I was hoping that you would take a walk with me," he said.

Eloise smiled widely. "I'd love to. Let me just get my cloak."

She breezed by him, leaving him standing awkwardly with the other ladies in the room whispering and casting glances at him.

Finally, Eloise reappeared in a dark plum-colored cloak.

"I put the flowers in water in my room. They're so lovely. You didn't owe me any thanks. I was happy to be there."

Her face was so earnest, and it was a relief to have one person who didn't look at him like he was weak.

Rainer held out his arm. She threaded her gloved hand through the crook of his elbow and they fell into step as he led her out the side door into the garden.

The morning was chilly but clear. The sky was finally blue, smeared with big fluffy clouds after days of miserable gray. Snow melted, dripping from leaf to leaf in the garden, adding a soft staccato to the sound of their footsteps on the garden trail. They passed patrols and groups of ladies who, upon seeing them, began whispering furiously to each other.

"It's quite awkward when it feels like everyone is talking about you," Rainer sighed.

Eloise grinned up at him. "Guardian McKay—"

"Rainer."

"Rainer, you must know that ladies are helpless for a hero. I suspect you'll be popular at court for a very long time," Eloise said.

Heat rose on Rainer's cheeks, and he looked away. A pleasant silence settled between them and the tight ball of anxiety in Rainer's chest unraveled ever so slightly.

"You'll forgive me, but I'm afraid I still don't remember everything from before the attack. Did we know each other well?" Rainer asked.

Eloise smiled at him, her pale green eyes sparkling in the sunshine. "We didn't know each other well, though I must admit that I had a bit of a crush. You were very kind to me when I found myself in a hard moment and that comfort has stayed with me."

Her cloak parted as she brought her hand to her chest over the swell of her breasts, as if to show the weight of his comfort. He quickly averted his gaze, taking in the roses around them that still bloomed brightly despite the frigid weather.

"How are you feeling?" Eloise asked.

Rainer sighed. "Still a bit at a loss for where I belong. I am a guardian who failed his witch."

Eloise frowned. "You mustn't be so hard on yourself. The king would not offer you a place here if he didn't have faith in you."

Rainer rubbed the back of his neck. The king might have had faith in him, but he didn't have much in himself. "I'd feel better if I could remember anything. I hate being so confused."

That was putting it lightly. He remembered pain and grief. He remembered fear so sharp and biting that it still left him feeling shaky on his feet. But he could not summon a vision of the moment leading up to the attack, or even anything since he'd arrived in Argaria for Prince Xander's wedding.

Rainer was frustrated with himself for being bested and furious at the slayer who had stolen his memories. It was a mercy that Vincent and his men had reached Rainer in time or he might have had nothing left. But all of that was too much to burden Eloise with.

"I'm sure you'll figure it out. Right now, you have a blank slate. That's overwhelming, but I'm sure it's also thrilling. Not everyone gets to reinvent themselves," Eloise said. She looked wistful.

Rainer shook his head. "Look at me complaining to you about a lack of choice when you're at the whims of your father. I'm sorry."

Eloise's eyes widened. "How observant of you to notice. I certainly don't fault you for your overwhelm. I'm sure if I'd lost my sense of self, I would find it unsettling. Even now when I know myself, if someone were to offer me an open path to do as I wish, I'd probably be at a loss for where to start."

Rainer smiled at her. "Well, what do you want for yourself?"

"Love." Eloise blushed. "Apologies. I'm not sure why I said that."

Rainer placed his hand on hers atop his arm. "I think that's a nice place to start. Why love?"

"It's what we all want, isn't it?"

Rainer frowned. Was that what he wanted? It didn't seem so. He just wanted to understand where he belonged in this new world. He wanted to honor his lineage as a warrior. He wanted to be known for being brave and strong and a fierce fighter. But love seemed a foreign concept. It wasn't as if what he remembered of his life had shown him much love. His father was adamantly opposed to love, and while he held little affection for the man, Rainer knew he had a point. He'd only seen love make fools of men. The last thing he needed when he had the king's ear and attention was to waste the opportunity on some silly love affair.

Love would mess up his routines, set his entire world in chaos, and that was the last thing he needed when he was trying to settle into who he was now, and who he might be if he never remembered the before.

"I suppose, in a way. I hadn't given it much thought," he said finally.

"I'd imagine not. Tough warrior like you," Eloise teased. "But I'm sure you want a family at home waiting for you at the end of your long days. A wife to keep you company. A home of your own."

That sounded oddly comforting. He imagined a cottage by the sea, taking his children down to the beach to play in the sand, teaching them to fight and shoot and swim, and coming home to a wife who was sweet and thoughtful. He imagined her blue eyes—the same shade as the sea out their cottage window.

The specificity of the daydream stopped him in his tracks. He tried to cling to it. But like a dream before waking, the glimpse was there and gone. The longer he waited for a face to form in his mind, the more certain he was that it never would.

He shook himself from the confusing daydream.

"Are you well?" Eloise asked.

"Yes, I thought I remembered something, but it never focused." Rainer sighed. He suddenly felt woefully wrong out in the garden—as if he was late for an appointment or had forgotten something critical. They'd reached the far end of the garden and Rainer paused, looking at the tall stone wall and the iron gate that led beyond the castle boundaries. The stone was marked with bright red paint, drawn into a symbol that Rainer didn't recognize.

"What is that?" He nodded at the symbol. "Did one of the rebels vandalize the castle?"

Eloise followed his gaze. "That's a ward, to keep out any meddling gods."

Rainer frowned. "Why would you want to keep out the gods?"

Eloise chewed on her lower lip and rubbed her gloved hands together. "Not all the gods. Just the ones who assisted the rebels. I'm sure you'll see Cato in the castle. He's helping to root out the rebels."

Rainer glanced down the wall and spotted a red smudge in the distance by the gate that led toward the stables. He ran a hand through his hair.

"You seem agitated," Eloise said.

"I'm sorry. At the strangest moments I get glimpses of memory, but the moment I try to drag them closer they slip through my fingers and I'm left with nothing but the sensation that I'm missing something critical, and looking at these symbols feels like I should remember something."

Eloise smiled sadly. "I'm sure it feels unbearable to know you've lost important things. I hate to see you so gripped by the loss. Perhaps it would be a good exercise to focus instead on who you want to be and what you want to achieve."

Her advice was sound, but Rainer couldn't shake the pervasive sense of wrongness in his life. Since he'd woken up after his incident, he felt completely out of place. The healers told him it was normal. They said he would feel disoriented in his life, but Rainer truly felt no connection to the details of his life that the people around him explained. What he could remember clearly felt strange and out of sync with the rest of his memories that existed lifelessly in the back of his mind.

They finished the loop of the trail, and Rainer led Eloise back inside.

"Forgive me for saying so, but you seem far away." She flushed and looked away. "I'm sorry, it's rude of me to press."

Rainer was messing this up and she was being so insistent in trying to help. He was supposed to be thanking her for her care but instead he'd only made her worry more.

"I'm terrible company these days. Often lost in my own thoughts."

Eloise smiled sympathetically. "I am here, even if you just need quiet company."

Her kindness made him feel worse, his body practically vibrating with the need to blow off steam.

Rainer bent to kiss her hand, then immediately stalked off toward the training room.

All of his memories were jagged edges—nothing fitting neatly together. There were only short bits of time he could remember at once. No long-form memories except the recent ones of him trying to uncover the rebellion, though those memories were hazy.

He removed the dagger and sword from his belt and stowed them out of the way in the training room closet. Wrapping his knuckles, he turned toward the straw-and-grain-stuffed dummy hanging at the center of the room.

Rainer didn't understand the fury and bitterness inside him. Every bit of his body felt leaden, slow, full of poison. His movements were violent. Although he'd been cleared for light duty a week ago, he'd been hesitant to push. Now he could tell it had been far too long.

Constant rest had stoked his frustration into an inferno. He pummeled the dummy as if he could beat his damaged memory into submission. His lack of progress with remembering his former life and a sinking feeling of incompetence plagued him.

He used to be someone else, but no one would help him remember. The healer had advised the king that it was best to give Rainer minimal information and let him remember naturally. Sharing too much too fast would do more harm than good. But as the person with half a memory, it felt like a punishment to Rainer.

He was certain he was forgetting something enormous.

Remember, the voice taunted him. But when he probed the places in his memories that were incomplete, he found nothing but questions.

Rainer felt hollowed out. As if something had sucked all the light out of his memories. Every single memory of childhood until the present seemed full of shadow where something significant should have been.

Had his world really been so dark?

He punched the bag harder, faster. Finally, when his chest burned for breath, he stopped.

Rainer unwound the bloody cotton from his knuckles. As he walked down the hallway toward the stairs to his room, he realized he had forgotten his favorite dagger and sword—the ones with the crescent moon on the hilts—in the training room closet.

He crossed the room, grabbed his weapons, and was about to step out of the closet when a woman wandered into the training room.

Rainer wasn't sure why he paused, but something about her stopped him in his tracks. The moment he laid eyes on her, every thought in his head ground to a halt, settling on one word: *Mine.* The word clanged off the empty walls of his mind like a coin in a jar.

He could not place her—couldn't call up a single memory of her face. And yet something about her stirred a familiar possessiveness in him.

The woman lifted her arms overhead, then folded forward over her legs. Rainer was frozen in place as she moved through a stretching routine that looked familiar to him, but like everything else in his life, he couldn't place it. He felt strange watching, especially as she moved through a series of somewhat suggestive positions. She knelt, bringing her chest to the mat, and Rainer sucked in a breath at the sight of her perfect ass tipped up in the air.

"Praise Clastor! This stretch routine is truly a gift from the gods."

Rainer had been so mesmerized he didn't notice Prince Xander appear at the training room entrance.

The woman laughed and slid onto her stomach, pressing her hands to the mat and lifting her chest as she looked over her shoulder at the prince. "See something you miss, Your Highness?"

"I don't have to miss it so much when I get to watch this," Xander said. "Maybe tomorrow you could do it in your undergarments and torture me like you used to every morning."

The woman giggled, wholly unbothered by his crudeness. "To what do I owe the honor, Xan? I'm surprised you're allowed near me."

The nickname startled Rainer almost as much as the casual way she spoke to royalty. She didn't bow or use his title. She simply rolled over and hopped to her feet.

"I understand you've been beating the crap out of your guards. The *king* had some complaints, so he sent me to remind you of your place," Xander said.

"As if I could forget," she grumbled.

She was small next to the prince, nearly a foot shorter than him. Still, he approached her with wariness, as if she was someone to be feared and respected. Xander handed her a wooden practice sword from the rack on the far wall. Rainer was surprised to see she knew how to hold it, weighing it and checking its balance before demonstrating a few practice strikes.

"I thought you'd be too busy," she said.

"I'm never too busy for you."

She started through a footwork and swordplay routine. It was the same one Rainer did daily. They must have trained in the same program, but she didn't look like a guardian or a hunter.

In her tight black pants and black and gold tunic, she didn't dress like a lady either. The only giveaway of her status was the elaborate style of her hair and the green ribbon woven through it.

"You look exceptionally lovely this morning," Xander said. The prince leaned against the far wall, watching her.

The woman smiled but said nothing. She moved fluidly through each movement. The only sound in the room was her breathing and the soft padding of her boots on the practice mats.

Xander let out a sigh. "You move just like him. You've even inherited the same mistakes."

She sighed and paused. "Horseshit! I'm flawless."

Rainer almost laughed at how casually she swore in front of the prince.

"Your weight is too far back on your heels on your third turn," Xander said. "Stay on your toes, especially when you're pivoting... here—can I touch you?"

The woman froze, then nodded. Rainer couldn't see her face, but he swore he could feel how nervous she was. She seemed comfortable with the prince until he suggested touching her.

"Just your arm and your left calf," Xander said softly. She nodded and he approached her like she was a wounded animal. He adjusted her wrist and her stance and stepped back. "Try it again."

It was only when Rainer watched her repeat the movements that he realized he made the same mistakes in his practice.

"I don't know why I still do this every day. Do I really think if I do this, it will somehow help? Like my actions and routine will bring back normalcy. It's so stupid," she said.

Xander smiled sadly. "I know swordplay isn't your favorite anyway, love."

The term of endearment stopped Rainer from breathing. She wasn't the new princess, that much was clear, but it was obvious that this woman and the prince were close. Perhaps Xander had a consort that no one had told Rainer about. It would be unusual so close to his wedding, but not impossible. Royal weddings were more strategic alliances than love matches. Still, he couldn't understand why a mistress would be trained in combat.

"Would you like to spar?" she asked.

The prince grinned at her. "As much as I enjoy any time I can get my hands on you, I worry it might be too much. Are you sure you're ready?"

She placed her hands on her hips. "I'm sure I'll mop the floor with you."

Xander laughed, but her face grew serious.

"Honestly, I don't know," she whispered. "If you tell me where you're going to touch me, it's fine, but I don't know how I will do without knowing. But I have to get over it. I have to be able to defend myself and not freeze."

"Well, perhaps it's better to test it out with me than wait to find out. You say the word and we'll stop."

She nodded.

"What do you want to try?"

She hesitated. "I want to break out of a hold. Xan, what happened —" She took a shuddering breath that felt like it shook through Rainer's chest. "It can't happen again. I need to be able to fight."

The words were a stone in Rainer's stomach. He swore he felt her anxiety and panic from where he hid in the closet. He wasn't even sure why he was hiding when he had every right to be here. Though if he came out now it would be obvious that he was eavesdropping.

Xander held up his hands. "All right, let's just go over the basics. I'm going to grab your wrists from the front."

He did, and she easily broke away after two tries.

"Okay, from behind now," she instructed. "I'm going to bend over that table and I want you to—" Her voice cut off as soon as Prince Xander stepped up behind her where she was bent over the table.

She straightened with a start. For a second Rainer worried she'd seen him, but then he realized she was shaking violently.

The prince stood perfectly still. His brow scrunched; his hands flexed in panicked grief. He looked at the woman like his heart was breaking.

"Tell me what to do, love," he said.

Rainer could not make sense of the scene. His mind fought to pull together the pieces, but he could barely remember anything besides Xander's panicked face in flashes.

"I don't know." The woman wiped tears from her face. "I keep expecting to turn around and see him. I keep reaching for his hand like a habit."

"I want to hold you, but I know—" Xander didn't finish. He held his arms out wide and the woman curled into them and began to cry.

Rainer waited for the prince to hug her, but he kept his arms wide as if afraid to touch her.

"Can I touch you?" Xander asked. She mumbled something and he wrapped his arms around her, gently rubbing her back. "I know, love. I'm so sorry."

"Don't be sorry," she said. "You did the right thing. I'm so proud of you."

The moment felt much too intimate for Rainer to bear witness to, but he was trapped in his hiding place. If he came out now, they'd know he'd been spying the whole time.

"But I should have—"

"No. Xan, look at me." She cupped his face in her hands and stared into his eyes. "You are *not* to blame. I will not have you take this on. I wanted to help you and I have never been more proud of you, your integrity, or the leader you've become than I was in that moment. Even when I was terrified. You have become who I always knew you could be—who you were always meant to be. Don't let any of this take away from that."

Her fierceness stole Rainer's breath. Even as tears streaked down her cheeks, she was a force. She electrified the entire room with her will.

The prince stared at her and nodded. He cupped his hands over hers on his face.

"More than that, it wouldn't have gone any differently if you'd simply given up what he wanted," she said. "It would have been a different series of events, but I'm almost certain the result would have been the same."

Xander leaned his forehead against hers, squeezing his eyes shut. "I wish I could take away everything that hurts you, love."

She pulled back slightly, putting distance between them. "No one can do that, and if they could, I wouldn't want the fear in my body to be a mystery."

"I know it doesn't feel like it. And it's not right now. But it's going to be okay. I know what you've lost."

The words made her cry harder. "Your life is at risk."

Xander shrugged. "What else is new?"

The prince was so casual about the attack. Was he really cocky enough to think he could defend himself against rebels that had sneaked into their midst?

"It's going to be all right," the prince continued, his voice soothing. "I've still got a few tricks up my sleeve. I'm going to do what I do best—"

"Flirt?"

Xander grinned. "You mean charm people with my undeniable wit and good looks?"

She laughed. The sound rang a chord in Rainer's chest, rousing joy he hadn't felt since waking.

"And you—you're going to do what you do best," the prince said.

She wiped her eyes on her tunic sleeve. "Act out and cry a lot?"

Xander laughed. "No—you're going to be you and he's going to fall in love with you. He won't be able to help himself."

Rainer wished they would say who they were talking about.

The woman looked at Xander skeptically. "I've never had to seduce him before."

Xander smiled. "Is that what you're self-conscious about? You have always had a way about you that is compelling without having to try. It's quite maddening, if I'm honest."

"But I don't know how to flirt," she said.

"Lies. You've flirted with me plenty and even if that weren't the case, you learned from the master," he said, gesturing to himself.

The woman rolled her eyes. "I suppose."

"Do you remember when I lost my mind, love? When I was lost to you?"

Rainer had so many questions. His memory drew up bits and pieces of a crueler version of the prince, but he couldn't put them together.

"I never lost you completely. Remember why?" Xander started. "You told me once that memory lives in more than the mind. It's in the body; it's emotion. Even when I hated you, I loved you intensely. Even when I was furious, I couldn't stop touching you like you were the most precious thing I ever held. Because my mind didn't know what to make of you, but my body did—my heart did."

"I was careful. The goddess power is more precise. I had to take a lot. My brain is so full, but how could I bear to lose more?" she whispered.

Rainer could not make sense of their conversation at all.

"Dance with me," the prince said.

"Now?" she asked. "It's a ridiculous time to dance."

Xander winked at her. "Nonsense. The best thing that ever happened to me started with a dance."

She grinned at him.

"Put your feet on mine, wrap your arms around my waist."

She followed his instructions.

"Good. Now, can I wrap my arms around you?"

"Yes," she said, leaning her head against his chest.

Rainer was certain he'd be more comfortable if they were simply having sex. What was between them felt infinitely more intimate. The prince hummed a low song, and the woman closed her eyes as he moved with her.

Rainer didn't understand his irrational jealousy. Was he jealous of the prince? Of what the two of them had? He couldn't tell.

After a few moments, she pulled back. "I should go."

Xander laughed. "All right, love. Be careful."

She turned and left the prince standing there, reaching after her. He sighed heavily in the silent room before leaving in the opposite direction.

Once Rainer was sure that the prince was gone, he wrapped his knuckles and punched madly at a hanging grain bag. He thought of the haunted look on the woman's face. He drew on the bottomless well of rage inside him and unleashed all of his energy into a barrage of punches.

4

XANDER

It wasn't the first time fate had taunted Xander Savero.

He'd been thrust into the role of king when Cato had made him kill his brother Davide a year ago and he'd spent almost every moment since shirking his responsibilities. But the moment he'd stepped up and finally accepted the role, his cousin Vincent had stolen it out from under him.

Now the place that was just beginning to feel like home was a prison once again. The unsettled feeling squirmed under his skin as he paused in the hallway outside the war room, trying to summon the strength to go inside and play a part he loathed.

Xander squeezed his eyes shut, trying to use the moment of quiet solitude to think around the problem. He had no ideas. There had been many closed-door meetings with Vincent, Xander, and individual members of the council over the past month. In each one, Vincent worked to ingratiate his way to support and Xander acted as if he was glad to have someone to take the responsibility off his hands. Today was the first full council meeting and Xander needed to be impeccable.

The first few weeks after the attack, security was so tight and Xander and Cece were still learning the rhythms of the new patrols.

They had only just begun to smuggle servants out of the castle last week. Any mistake Xander made now would put their smuggling operation and the safety of all the castle staff at risk.

Xander hoped to the gods this first meeting would go smoothly, though it was foolish to pray for their help with Cece on a daily dose of Godsbane and the rest of the gods unable to enter the castle. Once Vincent figured out how Xander's friends kept Cato out of their heads, he'd had the entire castle warded so that gods couldn't simply drop in. They had to be invited at his behest and could only stay as long as he wished them present. It meant that they wouldn't be getting much help, communications or otherwise, from Grimon inside the castle walls. Even Cato wasn't free to wander. He was only allowed in once a day to reinforce his magic bargain so that no one could share what had happened during the coup, and he was always accompanied by two armed escorts.

Vincent was being exceptionally careful.

There were too many balls in the air, and Xander was terrified of dropping any. One false move and his wrongs would be taken out on Cece.

Xander couldn't bear it. He could still hear her screams in the other room when Vincent's men dragged her away.

Xander had only contained his rage that night because of Cece. Because she gave him the slightest shake of her head. Her eyes told him to stay calm, to not make things worse. He'd seen the crestfallen look on Rainer's face—the shame. She'd needed Xander to stay calm not just for her, but for Rainer. In Rainer's mind, he had failed her not just as his fiancé and the love of his life, but as her guardian. He'd let her be hurt in a devastating way. Worse, Rainer had felt it all.

He'd struggled harder than Xander thought he'd have the energy to with the amount of blood loss and pain he'd endured. He thought Rainer would be in shock, but the guards had to pin him to the floor after he tipped and broke his chair, trying to get to Cece. Xander saw his brutalized back as they held him down. Still, he struggled and called out to her. It was heartbreaking.

Xander had always known how much Rainer loved her. He'd seen it a hundred times since the three of them had entered this frustrating dance. But he'd never seen anything like the way Rainer fought for her then. He'd never seen him look so crazed and desperate—not even when Cece died. Because Vincent wasn't taking her life. He was taking her soul—the part of her she'd fought so hard to get back. The part that Rainer had fought so hard for.

That day broke something in all three of them.

For Xander, it broke his heart and his fight. He knew he'd made the right decision, but his heart never stopped warring with his head. He knew down to his bones that Cece would have been hurt even if he'd told Vincent what little he knew. It all came down to Cece, and she kept her mouth shut because she was truly the bravest person he'd ever met, and also the one with the worst sense of self-preservation. Xander loved her for it, but it wounded him in a way he still didn't understand. Both Rainer and Cece bled for Xander's kingdom that day, and he'd been unharmed. Because Vincent needed him.

Which was why he forced himself to play along for now.

His family tree had been hacked down to just two gnarled limbs. Both he and Vincent were ruined in their own ways. Xander was terrified that would be his legacy—the accidental king who'd let a maniac take over. He took a deep breath with his hand on the doorknob before pressing into the war room.

All the men at the table looked up at him before looking back at Vincent, who stood at the head of the table.

Xander's gaze clashed with Reese Reynolds and Chris Lamotis, across the table. At least he still had two of Evan's spies at his disposal.

Vincent tapped his knuckles on the mahogany table.

"Those of you in this room are the only ones in this kingdom who know the truth. You have options," Vincent began. "I've already apologized to you for hiding myself as William Arvato, but I needed to earn your trust without the scourge of my father's history. You've already watched me make countless decisions in Argaria's best interest. Now, under my true name, Vincent Savero, I am here to right the sinking ship of the Kingdom of Argaria. Some of you may not agree with my methods, but I'm here to make things better for all of you at this table by correcting the mistakes Xander has made with the nobles and commoners of this kingdom. I do not blame my dear cousin, Xander. He spent most of his life in an enemy court. But beyond that, he was a second son. He was not raised to rule. He was raised to fight, which is why he's the best Savero warrior in generations. Unfortunately, he's turned out to be the worst king."

The council members shifted in their seats. Even some of the older members seemed nervous, their eyes shifting to Xander for a response. He kept his face placid.

"Even Xander will admit his shortcomings. Won't you, cousin?" Vincent said, looking at him.

Xander swallowed hard. He wanted to gut Vincent right there with the letter opener on the table. But that was the kind of rash instinct Vincent was telling the council to expect. Lashing out would only prove his point. If Xander wanted to be king, he had to be a patient strategist like Evan. He had to think like a king and play a longer game.

Xander stood reluctantly. "I think you all know that we haven't always seen eye to eye on this council. I have tried my best to do what is right for our kingdom, but it's no secret that many of you have been disappointed with my rule."

The words felt like a betrayal to everyone who had sacrificed for him. Cece would tell him becoming a spy again was his sacrifice—patience instead of swift vengeance.

Xander cleared his throat. "I've done my best, but I'll admit that in this case, my best has not been enough. I will concede the throne to Vincent, who has been raised to rule and who has proven himself—" Xander could barely grit out the last words. "Who has proved himself a better strategist and a more qualified king. The truth is that I never wanted to be king. I did it for the sake of our people after a fierce war. I only want what is best for Argaria and I'm willing to accept that isn't me. I will work side by side with my cousin to ensure a smooth transition."

The group stirred quietly, nervous glances passing between them.

"What of the unrest with the common folk?" Edward Spellman asked.

Vincent's eyes narrowed on him. "What of it?"

Spellman pressed on, leaning forward in his chair. "If I may suggest—the farmers on my lands had a record season of crop production. We could quell their angst with a bit of free food."

Xander fought a smile. It was a small mercy that Spellman seemed as content to be a thorn in Vincent's side as he had been in Xander's. A man whose loyalty could be bought with power could always be purchased by someone else.

Vincent's jaw ticked. "Fine. I will do as you suggest and provide some food to them for these harsh winter months. But I'm increasing nightly patrols until the city settles down and if the food and oversight don't settle them, I will raise their taxes again. Let's make that known." He smoothed his tunic. "Now, if any of you feel that I'm incapable of handling this position, I will be happy to relieve you of your post and send you on your way."

From anyone else, the words wouldn't have sounded threatening, but the way Vincent menacingly eyed each person at the table let them know that compliance was survival.

Richard Chavers, one of the longest-serving council members, who'd served King Damian and was known for his leadership in their war with Olney, stood with a start. Xander's heart leapt into his throat. Days ago, when he and Vincent had met with Richard, he'd been stoic and said almost nothing.

"This is outrageous!" Richard snapped. "The boy might need some polish, but I will not stand by and let some usurper take the throne with violence. I knew your father. William Savero was a thief and a manipulator and it's clear you're made of similar—"

Vincent moved so quickly that Xander didn't have time to shout a warning. His blade was in Richard's heart before he'd even finished his sentence. Vincent twisted the dagger before pulling it out, the sucking sound deafening in the silent room.

Richard was dead before his body hit the floor.

"Clean that up," Vincent said calmly to his guards. They bent and

47

retrieved the body as Vincent wiped his blade on a handkerchief. "His family will be stripped of its title and it will be awarded to someone more suitable for our new vision for this kingdom. I'm not without a heart, though. They can keep their land. Any other takers?"

No one dared move.

Xander's gaze flicked back to Reese and Chris. He wasn't worried about Vincent noticing, since they'd always been his allies on the council. He gave them both a nod, letting them know to go along.

Reese clenched his jaw but nodded back and Chris sighed.

"Speak now or I'll assume that you're truly ready to steer this kingdom in the right direction," Vincent said.

Xander held his breath, but no one spoke up. Relief and betrayal warred in his chest. He found it hard to believe that all of the men on his council were content. Still, they were wise enough to assess the threat before they made a move.

"Very well. I just wanted to be certain we were on the same page. We can continue tomorrow, once this mess has been removed," Vincent said, sneering at the blood on the floor.

Chairs scraped against the floor as the council rushed to escape the room. The door clicked closed behind them, leaving Xander alone with Vincent.

"We need your wife," Vincent said.

"Jessamin fled during the attack and she won't be back, unless she returns with the Novumi army," Xander said.

Jessamin hadn't actually fled to Novum, but Xander wished she'd return with her army in tow as much as he wished she was safe and far away. Their relationship was brand new, and more friendly than romantic, but he'd grown fond of her quickly. They had shared a very special wedding night with the hopes that they'd soon have an heir. The best place for her was nowhere near Vincent.

"I need you to write to her and get her back here to help smooth things over," Vincent said.

"I will not invite my wife to her death."

Vincent cocked his head to the side as if he were regarding a child. "I promise not to harm Jessamin. I simply want to ensure our alliance for the time being. When you cease being useful, you'll die, which of course will be a terrible and hopefully gruesome accident. I will invite your lovely wife to stay."

Xander shook his head. "You're going to try to marry her?"

Vincent grinned. "Oh no, haven't you heard? I already have a fiancée. I'll be marrying an ex-goddess and former princess, Lady Cecilia Reznik."

Xander felt like he'd been plunged into the Bay of Endros in midwinter. He was frozen with fear.

"It's just that you spoke so highly of her talents and, after having a taste, I want more." Vincent's taunt made Xander feel sick with rage and grief. "I want *so much more*. I want to spend my time taking more and more from her and watching you know that's exactly what I'm doing. Who knows, your misery is so delicious to watch it might even help you live longer."

It was hard to believe Vincent was the same cousin Xander had chased around as a boy, but desperation changed people. Xander might have spent most of his life undercover in an enemy court, but he had joy. Vincent spent his life in the eastern wastes between Argaria and Aldrena. It was desolate and cold and the people there were survivors but not the kind who prided themselves on community. They were the type to stand on the backs of the weak to move up in the world. He'd never known anything else.

"She won't agree with that," Xander mumbled.

"She already has. The only thing that foolish girl cares about is her guardian and maybe you. She wouldn't leave now, even if she could. So, the last piece to slide into place is your new princess wife."

"Why are you doing this? Why are you so cruel? I was just a child when you left," Xander said.

Vincent leveled him with a furious look. "Of course you don't know." He barked out a cruel laugh. "You really have no idea what your father has done. His lack of thought for his people is the least of his crimes. He saved a special cruelty for anyone who threatened his throne."

Dread pooled in Xander's chest, making it harder to breathe. His instinct was to deny it, but he had a sinking suspicion that he'd only seen hints of what his father was capable of.

"He had my mother killed, you know," Vincent said.

Xander swallowed hard. He didn't have many memories of his Aunt Ophelia. She'd been a great warrior before she married his Uncle. Xander only remembered that she had been a beautiful, kind woman who loved to ride horses and kept to herself.

Vincent's dark eyes drilled into him. "One minor disagreement with my father and he was written off after years of loyal service. He went from ally to threat in the blink of an eye. Your father started by killing my mother. He said he wanted to control threats to his legacy and if my father didn't get to the eastern wastes without argument, he'd kill me too."

Xander shook his head. He searched for a denial but he had none. "I didn't know."

"Of course not. You were too busy being treated like a little prince," Vincent said. "But we only made it a few days' ride from Ardenis when Damian must have decided that wasn't going far enough. His men chased us into the forest. My father made me hide and when they caught him, he wouldn't tell them where I was, so they made sure that he couldn't grow his legacy. They made him pay."

Xander frowned.

"They killed most of his men and made very sure he could not have any more children, Xander. He would have died if he hadn't left a few guards with me, including one of his hunters who was also a talented healer. He saved my father's life, but the damage was done. Damian counted on us withering. Easier to wait for one Savero nephew to die than to allow my father to create more children. That really got into my father's head. I think that was the last sane moment he had, but it was the moment that forged me."

Xander was speechless. His mind spun. He didn't want it to be true. He thought he'd made peace with his father's faults and cruelty, with the damage he'd done to the working-class people in Argaria, the people who'd been hurt most by his endless warmongering, but he'd only seen the tip of a horrifying iceberg.

He willed that to be the end of it, but Vincent spoke again. "I'd expected you to be more self-righteous, but I can see from the look on your face that you saw *your father*, Damian, for who he was."

The emphasis on the words "your father" was not lost on Xander. He didn't know how Vincent knew the truth. Perhaps he was just bluffing, but Xander forced himself not to react.

"We are all driven to survive and I have no problem getting down in the muck," Vincent said. "I like the challenge of dominating an opponent. You'd be surprised how just a little bit of cruelty inspires it in other men. I suppose we all have some kernel of bitterness inside us and when one of us is bold enough to nurture it, it stokes that same boldness in others. I seem to have attracted followers with similar proclivities."

Vincent's voice was so calm, his face strangely stoic. "Your Cece. *Gods, she struggled.* I can still feel her squirming against me. I can still hear the way she begged me not to. She has such a lovely scream. Makes me hard just thinking about it."

Xander's fists clenched. He ground his teeth together so hard he thought they'd shatter.

Vincent smirked. "It's the spirited ones that are the most fun to break. I don't think I need to remind you that you had your own chance at breaking her and, from what I've heard, you did a pretty good job."

Shame unspooled in Xander's mind. He hated the reminder of the way he'd hurt Cece, taken away the autonomy she fought so hard to hold on to.

"I would never do something like that to her."

Vincent shrugged. "You'd be wise to remind her to fall in line. What I did that night is the least I can do and, frankly, I can do that again as many times as I like, wherever I'd like, in front of whomever I'd like, and I'm not afraid of sharing if I'm too tired or bored."

There would be no getting through to his cousin, no reasoning with him. And even if Vincent's madness was King Damian's fault, Xander's legacy wouldn't be paying for the sins of a father who wasn't even his to claim. He refused to let his people be terrorized by yet another horrible king.

Xander wished for a weapon. He could hear Evan's voice in his head, reminding him he couldn't act until he knew where all of his people stood. Spellman was powerful, but if Xander simply killed Vincent now, he wouldn't have a chance to root out the poison under the surface.

"Now write your letter to your new wife and ask her to come to the table to negotiate," Vincent said.

There was no way Xander was letting Jessamin return to the castle while Vincent and his men were there.

Xander sighed. "I will write to Jessamin, but she's a strategist. I doubt she will come."

"Then tell her I'll kill you if she doesn't," Vincent said.

"You'll kill me anyway."

"Yes, but she doesn't know that."

A guard burst into the room. "Your Majesty, I apologize for the interruption—"

"I said I was not to be disturbed!"

"I know, Your Grace, it's just—"

"Spit it out, man!" Vincent yelled impatiently.

"There's a woman at the gates who claims to be Princess Jessamin Orum."

Xander's stomach dropped while Vincent's face lit up.

"Look at that! She's saved us the trouble. Bring her in at once!" Vincent said. He sat back in his chair, gazing at Richard Chavers's blood seeping into the cracks in the floor.

"It's awfully late for a royal to expect to be seen," Xander said. The wind howled outside the windows as if agreeing with him. "It could be an assassin in disguise."

Vincent rolled his eyes.

Xander stood, brooding awkwardly off to the side. Castle Savero was the last place he wanted his new warrior queen. He paced nervously, tapping his thumb to each fingertip.

Finally, the doors opened and the queen walked in, followed by two of her guards decked out in lavender garb. Xander froze, forcing the confusion from his face. She looked at him, her brow pinched with concern.

"Xander," she purred, closing the distance between them and kissing him on the cheek.

Xander couldn't help but smile back at the beautiful woman standing in front of him. "Darling, what are you doing here? I wanted you to be safe and far away."

"I know, but they assured me that power had transferred peacefully to your cousin, and I wanted to come back for you. I cannot run from a fight," she said. She turned to Vincent, curtseying. "Your Grace."

Vincent stood and crossed the room, tracking bloody footprints in his wake. He kissed her hand. Jessamin's two guards, Freya and Nicholette, shifted nervously behind her, their hands poised on their blades. A creeping suspicion grew in Xander's mind.

"Your Highness, I'm sorry that we were not formally introduced before," Vincent said. "I was quite busy during your wedding with all of my men who were acting as security."

Xander's heartbeat kicked up, and he held his breath, trying to remember if Jessamin and Vincent had ever been closer than across the room at a party.

"I'm happy to be of service to the kingdom, but I came back to ensure the safety of my husband. I've sent word to my mother, and she hoped that I would visit by month's end with my new husband. She was quite insistent since the wedding was so rushed and she hadn't met him yet. She's hoping to have a Novumi ceremony to celebrate there," she said.

"That sounds festive, but I'm afraid you might have to postpone a bit since there's so much to do here. We will make sure that happens as soon as possible," Vincent said, slipping back into his old accommodating William Arvato voice.

How easily Vincent had played Xander, his friends, and the entire Argarian royal council.

"I hope Your Majesty will forgive me and my guards, but I'm quite tired from our travel," she said. "I hoped my husband could escort me to our room so that I might wash and rest."

"Of course. Xander, go spend some time with your wife and please don't forget all we've talked about," Vincent threatened.

Xander nodded and held out his arm. She took it and walked with him through the halls all the way to their room. Her scent hit him as they walked, tugging at a memory he couldn't quite call up without his magic. He waited until the bedroom door was closed and her guards were stationed outside before he turned to the woman.

"I don't know who you are, but you're certainly not my wife," Xander said.

She grinned at him. "Ah, but you do know me."

He could see it now in her expressive eyes. "Isla?"

She smiled and Xander knew he was right. When he'd met her before, he'd only seen her eyes, the rest of her shrouded by a veil.

"Queen Jessamin's cousin and royal decoy at your service. Let's hope that the new king didn't make me as easily as you did. Now sit down. I have so much to tell you."

Xander's relief was so strong his knees almost gave out. "So Jess is fine?"

"Yes. She's with Maren, Evan, Cal, and Sylvie, but she was losing her mind being trapped there, so they decided they could send me as backup."

Xander's gaze passed over her, assessing the slight difference in appearance between Isla and his wife. Isla's skin tone was a bit lighter, with a dusting of freckles across her nose, and her eyes were closer to amber than Jessamin's warm brown, but their height and build were almost identical.

"It's uncanny. Even your mannerisms are the same," he said.

Isla nodded. "I've studied Jessamin since we were girls and part of my testing as a decoy required passing for her at several court events. I've spent as much time studying her as I have studying weaponry and battle strategy." She sat in the chair by the fire, an eerie shadow of Jessamin.

"Don't you ever miss being yourself?" Xander asked. The question slipped out and Isla looked shaken by it.

"Can I not be both? You see, I've instantly switched out of character now that we're here and while I'm sure you haven't challenged your wife in combat, I assure you that you'd notice our differences there."

Xander fought off a grin. "And which of you would win? I was under the impression that my wife is the fiercest warrior in Novum."

Isla scoffed. "You can't be serious, Your Majesty."

"Xander," he corrected. "Or *darling*, if you prefer."

Isla bit her lip and smiled at him. "Xander," she said. "She'd like to think she'd win, but she's gone soft from time spent princess-ing." Isla unpinned her elaborately braided hair. "Plus, you and I have sparred once before. You should remember looking up at me from your back."

Xander smirked. "A view I'll not soon forget and perhaps one we could revisit."

Isla pressed on. "I accused you of being a pretty face surrounded by pandering idiots. Turns out I was wrong. You were surrounded by traitors."

"But you feel the same about my pretty face?" Xander asked.

She ignored the question, continuing to unpin her hair before removing several blades from her bodice. Without warning, she hiked up her billowing skirt, offering a flash of her long legs as she untied one of her boots. She glanced up like she was testing him.

Xander crossed his arms, leaning against the wall to watch her. When she was satisfied with his attention, she started on the other boot.

He pulled off his own boots before tugging off his tunic and undershirt, tossing them in a basket in the corner as Isla stood and looked at him. Her eyes went wide as they passed over his bare chest, her gaze lingering an extra moment on the scar over his heart.

"Well, I suppose you could have saved me some energy with the undressing you just gave me with your eyes," Xander said.

Isla huffed out a breath, but her cheeks and the tips of her ears turned dark pink as she stalked across the room, placing her dagger on the nightstand. "If I had known, I would have turned around," she said.

"I'll sleep on the sitting room couch," Xander said.

"Nonsense," Isla said. "I'm quite certain that we're both mature enough to sleep in the same bed and we don't need servants noticing and starting rumors. You and Jess need to appear to be a united front."

"I will keep my hands to myself," Xander assured her.

She studied him for a moment, holding his gaze as she slipped out of her dress and tossed it on a chair. Xander tried not to stare at her ass in her lacy underwear as she crossed to the closet to change into a nightgown, but Isla caught him looking.

"See something you like?" she teased.

He shook his head and looked away. "Sorry, I—"

"I'd be more insulted if you didn't look. I'd be disappointed that the notorious royal flirt, Xander Savero, didn't think me worthy of his attentions."

"Notorious royal flirt?"

"I wanted to know what all the fuss is about," she said with a grin.

Xander couldn't help but smile. "Oh, I assure you that any fuss you've heard is probably underselling my skill."

"Really?" Isla said, her eyes lit with amusement.

"Certainly. Just let me know when you'd like me to prove it."

"When? Not if?" Isla asked. "Cocky."

"You have no idea," Xander said, unbuttoning his pants.

"We'll see," she said.

"I normally sleep naked, but I don't want to show everything at once. I wouldn't want you to get too attached too quickly," Xander taunted.

"That won't be an issue," Isla said.

"And why not?"

"Because one man has never held my attention long enough for attachment to form."

"I suspect that will change," Xander said.

Isla laughed. "It's a shame I don't find you as compelling as you find yourself."

"You wouldn't be the first woman to be mistaken about that."

"And you wouldn't be the first man I've met whose opinion of himself rivals the gods," Isla countered.

Xander laughed. "The gods aren't so great, trust me. I've met several and most of them are assholes."

"Well, in that case, perhaps your opinion is more self-aware than I realized," Isla said, rolling away from him.

Xander laughed as he climbed into bed and blew out the candle on the nightstand.

"Good night, *darling*," he whispered. He smiled up at the ceiling and for the first time in months, he fell asleep as soon as he closed his eyes.

5

EVAN

The pub was full of cackling barmaids, raucous music, and the scent of stale whiskey and wine. For a hunter with heightened senses, a crowded bar was an affront—the music and flirting too loud, the cloying scent of perfume and sweat overpowering, and the drinks always warm and watered down.

Evan pulled his hood up higher, glancing at Cal, who sat in a darkened corner of the bar with a clear view of the door. Evan met Sylvie's nervous gaze across the table.

"He's late," Evan said softly.

Sylvie nodded, tugging her hood lower, as if anything could hide her loveliness. Evan hadn't wanted her to come—not because she couldn't handle herself, but because Sylvie was quite literally too eye-catching to be a clandestine spy. Her grace made her stand out as upper-class. Her face was too memorable for her to slip in and out unnoticed. But trying to argue with her after she'd been cooped up for weeks at the Temple of Aurelia was hopeless. She was worried sick about Cecilia, Rainer, and even Xander. And Evan was worried sick about her.

Sylvie did not speak any more about what had happened to her years ago, but every time Evan thought about it, his fury grew wilder inside of him—the kind of rage that made him hungry for a fight, searching out violence in any minor slight. Thinking of her hurt that way, of the grief in her eyes when she'd told him—like she'd thought he would love her less—filled him with rage so poisonous he worried it would bleed out into everything else in his life.

Evan came to attention as a figure in a dark cloak shuffled out from the back room of the pub, where many men disappeared with whores for clandestine meetings. Evan held his breath, afraid to hope it was who he wanted it to be. The figure darted to their table, staggering side to side before slumping onto the bench beside Sylvie. Evan was about to jump to his feet when the man's hood tipped, revealing a grinning Reese Reynolds.

"Sorry I'm late. I'm eternally being followed by Vincent's men, since he hasn't decided if he trusts me yet."

Evan stuffed down his panic. "Where does he think you are?"

"At the brothel across the street with Chris Lamotis. He's covering for us for the moment."

Evan sighed and shook his head. "What news do you have?"

"Krysk, and allegedly Jeset, are both willing to come to the table to negotiate with Vincent. Obviously Marcos is still holding out in Olney, and he was so bold as to send an inquiry to Vincent requesting the status of his ambassadors given the sudden transfer of power," Reese said, winking at Sylvie.

"Smart of him," Sylvie said. "Better that Vincent thinks we aren't in contact. Also smart of him not to let on more about his personal relationship with Cece."

Evan nodded. Vincent obviously knew Cecilia was valuable, but if there was yet another person who cared about her safety who Vincent could manipulate, it would only make things worse. He didn't need to know that Cecilia was like a sister to the king of Olney.

Evan shook his head. The way that woman could wrap princes around her finger was supernatural.

"I'm sure you've seen the unrest in town from Vincent's tax hikes," Reese continued, his hushed whisper barely audible under the music. "He's maxed out guard patrols to try to manage the civil unrest, which means that there have been fewer guards in the castle. Xander should be able to communicate more directly going forward."

Evan nodded. "That's a relief."

"How's Cece?" Sylvie asked.

Reese swallowed hard. "There's been an interesting development there. I have not seen her because she stays in her rooms most of the time, though I expect we will see more of her now that Rainer is up and about in the castle. I've only seen him once, but he's definitely different—"

"What's the development?" Sylvie asked.

Evan took her hand. Sylvie hadn't slept well since they'd heard Cecilia screaming during the attack. There was a darkness in her eyes like she was reliving her own experience.

Reese hesitated, running a hand through his hair. "Yes, they are telling the story that she and Vincent are engaged."

Evan choked on his whiskey. "What?"

His mind spun in different directions. If Vincent thought that would gain him favor with the Argarian court, he was foolish. What possible motivation could he have?

"He wants to keep her close." Sylvie's voice was a breathless rasp, her eyes growing glassy.

Reese cocked his head toward Sylvie. "Xander says that it's part of her plan and that we should trust that she knows what she's doing, but I haven't seen her with my own eyes to read her state of mind."

Sylvie looked unconvinced. Evan gave her hand a reassuring squeeze.

"This is a bit of good news, though. Vincent is also still trying to interrogate guards he suspects of treason, but with no luck thanks to Cato's bargain. The trickster created a mess, as usual," Reese laughed. "It's lucky that some piece of it worked out in our favor."

Evan frowned. Was it possible that Cato had known that? According to the information Xander had passed along about what happened after Evan and the rest of the group made their way out of the castle, it was Cato who'd intervened to keep Rainer from being killed. But the trickster god only did things that were in his own interest. Evan couldn't figure out why Cato would care if Rainer lived or died. Especially when he'd been content to try to kill Rainer himself a year ago.

"Are you sure that you and Chris shouldn't get out while you can?" Sylvie asked.

Reese shook his head. "We're in this up to our necks. We won't leave Xander and the lot of them at Vincent's mercy. Vincent is already pandering to the nobles. It will undo all the work we have done this past year to try to promote equity between classes."

Evan had been turning over the beginnings of a plan in his head. Vincent's strategy had been perfect in how multifaceted it was. They had to find a similar way to strip him of noble support while riling the common people to their cause.

"Have you had any luck figuring out who in the council you can trust and who are the traitors?" Evan asked.

Reese took a long drink of his ale and scowled. "Gods, that's wretched stuff." He drank some more. "We haven't had much luck yet. Chris and I are working on it but it's slow going. It's going to take time to do this right. If we rush it—"

"We risk not catching all of the traitors," Evan finished. "We risk doing this again in a few months."

Sylvie was quiet, staring into her ale. "I'm more worried about leaving them in there too long. Cece is strong, but everyone has a breaking point."

"But how will she feel if we tell her that we can't be certain that we've rid both kingdoms of all those who could hurt her?" Evan asked.

Understanding bloomed in her eyes. "Like it's not safe to sleep."

The words sent Evan's stomach tumbling. *Was that how Sylvie felt before Cal took care of the man who'd hurt her?*

He shoved the thought away. Her fear and pain made him so irrational, and he needed to think clearly to strategize.

"We are going to get every last one of them. We just need to be smart, and that means moving slower than all of us would like," Reese said.

"Why are you so committed? Why risk yourself?" Sylvie asked, her words sharp with accusation.

Reese had always been a pragmatist, but since his brother Teddy's death he'd become more of an idealist. Evan had a feeling he knew the reason. Though Reese hadn't tipped his hand, there were subtle hints he'd found a love of his own.

Reese arched an eyebrow. "I see that your fiancé has yet to share his suspicions with you. Chris and I go back a long way—to before his father, who was raised common and elevated to nobility when a distant uncle died. I've only known him to be a person with tremendous honor. It disgusts me that people look down on him because of where he came from."

Sylvie shrugged. "I still don't see that being enough."

Evan grinned. He loved her suspicion because it was a reflection of his influence on her.

Reese's grin grew wider. "You're wise to be skeptical, my lady, though you only need to ask yourself what you might do if someone wanted to keep you from being with your fiancé."

Sylvie's eyes went wide as saucers.

Reese waited for her to say something, clearly aware that aristocracy defined such behavior as deviant.

A smile stole over Sylvie's face. "Well, aren't we all just fools in love?"

Reese shrugged. "I've found that being smart is overrated where love is involved. If you risk nothing, you gain nothing."

"I couldn't agree more. I practically had to die to get this man to commit," she said, jerking her thumb at Evan.

Reese laughed. "I don't know. I think he was pretty committed right away. He got that ring out of storage the month after you came to Argaria."

Evan glared at Reese. "You sellout."

Sylvie's laugh rang out. "I knew it! I knew I had him!" She clapped her hands in delight and Evan smiled despite himself.

"Do you have anything else related to saving this kingdom to tell us, or are you content to share all my secrets with my fiancée?"

Reese shrugged. "That's all I have for now, and I should be getting back soon. Chris hates when I leave him alone with the whores too long. They're much better than him at cards and they clean him out. If I have anything else, I'll leave word for the high priestess at the Temple of Aurelia."

Reese pulled his hood up before making his way out of the crowded bar.

"We should go, Syl," Evan said. He reached across the table to take her hand, but before he could, someone stumbled over to their table and slumped into the seat beside her.

Evan had his dagger out and pressed into the man's groin before his gaze met familiar silver eyes.

His face had been manipulated. His hair was lighter, his skin more olive, and the scar over his eye was so faint Evan could have missed it, but it was undoubtedly Cato.

"Is that any way to greet your greatest asset?" the trickster god asked with a grin.

Sylvie shifted away from him.

"I trust you about as far as this dagger is from your balls," Evan gritted out.

Cato's grin grew wide. "Honestly, you try to kill one prince and suddenly—"

"You killed Davide and tried to kill Xander," Sylvie said.

Cato shrugged. "Xander killed Davide. Plus, I knew that Cece would save Xander. That woman is stupidly loyal to people who absolutely do not deserve it."

Sylvie rolled her eyes. "Fine. But you stabbed Rainer."

Cato cocked his head to the side. "Rainer stabbed Cece and everyone likes him just fine."

Sylvie bristled.

"I know. We all like to pretend that's part of a great love story and not a man stabbing the love of his life in the chest because she tricked him. That Little Dove does know how to work those two men of hers, I will give her that. I can appreciate her talent for manipulation."

Evan shook his head. "Give me one reason not to kill you right now."

Cato's grin turned feral. "I walked into this pub and picked out you and Cal over there immediately. The way I see it, your little street gang is not so well hidden and you could use some help from a master of disguise," he said, gesturing to himself.

"We would never accept your help," Sylvie snapped.

"Lady Brett, never say never. *Never* is a challenge. I think we can all agree that desperate times call for desperate measures," Cato said. "You all stand out and you really do not need that right now, as Vincent's guards are going tavern to tavern looking to hunt you and your friends down."

Sylvie gripped the edge of the table, her knuckles white.

"I can help you all hide, but even better, I can get you into and out of the castle with relative ease when the moment is right. For now, we have work to do out here, and I can help you all blend in."

Evan wanted to argue, but the notion spun a new idea into his mind. If they could move about freely, they could use Vincent's tactics against him. His mind flew to the day he and Xander had happened upon the town crier disparaging Xander in the market. In his short time as king, Xander had become a darling of the common folk. They were more likely to rally, especially now that Vincent had reinstated the previously very heavy taxes.

"Are you seeing things my way for once, Farlan?" Cato taunted.

Evan held up a hand. "Let me think for a second."

"You can't be serious," Sylvie hissed.

Evan met her eyes. "We can use this, Syl. You know we need help."

"We can't trust him. Vincent could have sent him out here just to mess with us. You are smarter than this."

"So are you. We're outmatched and our only hope is to be able to blend. Sometimes war makes strange allies." Evan glared at the god. "What's in it for you, Cato?"

All the earlier humor disappeared from the trickster's face. He looked down at the table, either putting on a front of guilt or actually feeling it. "I may, possibly, have taken things a little far this time."

Sylvie huffed out a disbelieving laugh and said, "You think?"

At the same time, Evan said, "Just this time?"

Cato held up his hands. "I know, but this time was different. It's just not *fun* anymore."

"Ruining lives?" Sylvie asked.

Cato shook his head. "I unknowingly crossed a line. You have no reason to believe me, but even I have boundaries, which I realize now I don't want to cross. Pulling strings has always been fun, but it was a game of finding a worthy adversary and besting them. I do not condone violence like that—it's unoriginal."

"Unoriginal." Sylvie glared at him, venom in her tone.

Cato pursed his lips. "It's common and boring. I don't like violence for violence's sake, especially the brutish type that takes advantage of an uneven playing field. I may have gone too far this time and done some damage that can't be undone."

Sylvie's face went ghostly white as Cato met her eye.

"I know you both have no reason to believe me and many reasons not to. I can't promise we want the exact same thing, but I can promise that we don't want any more collateral damage," Cato said.

Evan had never seen him look so serious, but they'd been burned enough by the gods to not trust any olive branches he extended.

Cato ran a hand through his hair. "I realize that you don't want to, but I'm counting on you being smart enough to know that you have to trust someone now and it's easier to rely on other people if I help you hide."

Evan leaned his head back and groaned. They were out of good options. They'd sent Isla to the castle to help, but there was no telling what she would be able to accomplish. Xander wouldn't leave his people in a lurch. Cecilia wouldn't leave without Rainer. And Rainer, by all accounts, had no idea who he was.

Disguises would help Evan, Sylvie, and Cal move much more freely. Especially since Cato could make them look different every day.

"I have limited power now, much like Cece. I have to use it daily to walk through the castle to enforce my bargain to keep Cece and Xander from reminding that big amnesiac guardian who he is. By the way, I can no longer enter the castle without Vincent's invitation thanks to the wards." He nodded at Sylvie's angry face. "Yes, Lady Brett, he stole your idea and is using it to keep us gods out."

Evan tried to find the lie in Cato's offer. He knew better than to fully trust him, but they also only had bad options and at least if they worked with him, they could keep an eye on him. "How would it work?"

"I'd have to regularly see each of you. But it would allow you to stop hiding out so much. You could do some real damage," Cato said.

Suddenly a barmaid appeared at their table. "Hey luv, a handsome blond gentleman up front says to tell yas that there are wolves in the henhouse next door. Says he'll meet ya in the usual place."

That was the code from Cal, letting them know the tavern was about to be raided by Vincent's men.

"Is there a back door?" Evan asked.

The maid nodded her head to a dark hallway to their left.

Sylvie's wide eyes met Evan's as he handed the maid a few coins and she disappeared into the crowd.

They ducked down the dark hallway, but Evan shoved Cato against the wall before they stepped outside.

"Fine, you can help, but you have to start right now. Hide us so that we can slip out of here without a problem," Evan said.

Cato turned toward Sylvie. The air filled with the leather and pine scent of his magic as Cato took her hand. She flinched but didn't pull it away. Evan watched as her face transformed. Her cheeks grew fuller, rounding out her face, her eyes shifting from icy blue to emerald green and her hair from golden-blonde to dark auburn. It was startling to see her look so different, though her mannerisms were the same. While Evan didn't consider himself particularly romantic, he was certain he'd recognize her no matter what.

Cato took Evan's hand next and Sylvie let out a startled giggle as his hair lengthened to skim his shoulders, woven through with gray.

"Instant aging," Cato said with a grin.

Sylvie smirked. "I like it."

Evan arched an eyebrow. "Do you?"

She nodded. "Very distinguished."

Cato rolled his eyes as a pounding sounded from the front of the tavern. "Shall we?"

The trio stood and made their way down the dark hallway and out the back door of the tavern as a commotion rose from inside. They paused in the alleyway.

"We'll meet you at the night market tomorrow at dusk at Graylen's. It's the ale stall in the market with the little green moth on the banner," Evan said.

Cato sighed heavily. "Fine. That's fair. I'll be there."

Evan ushered Sylvie away, weaving through the crowded streets, careful to avoid Vincent's men despite their disguises. Evan wasn't totally willing to trust Cato, but he was willing to use the god until he figured out what he really wanted.

6

RAINER

The woman who'd danced with Prince Xander was in the training room again.

Rainer stared at her from the doorway, knowing he should leave but unable to force himself. Her slumped shoulders betrayed her grief but did nothing to take away from the grace with which she moved. The smoothness of her exercises suggested she was a trained fighter, but she wore the fine dress of a lady.

He couldn't take his eyes off of her. She was beautiful, but it was more than that. When he saw her, his body was a symphony of sensations. His heart raced, his mouth went dry, and there was a sharp tug in his chest. Rainer may not have remembered who exactly she was, but his body seemed to.

Mine. Again, the word sliced through his mind like a sword, leaving him wincing in pain. He shook it off.

It felt impossible that he knew so little about her—like he recognized her on sight, but could not make sense of the context of her.

From the first moment he laid eyes on her, she seemed to pull the light in the room, as if some unseen force was trying to highlight her. He had to have known her before, but when he searched his memories for her, he found nothing.

She turned suddenly, and her bright cerulean eyes met his. She blinked up at him, her lips parted in a gasp, which he'd realized too late was because he'd crossed the room and touched her arm.

It was as if his feet had a mind of their own.

"Sorry," he mumbled, but he didn't step back.

"Hello," she said.

"I'm Guardian Rainer McKay," he said dumbly.

"I know."

A wave of frustration surged into his chest. It must have been his own, but it was so strong and sudden it confused him. He could swear it belonged to her because it matched her expression. Did he offend her by touching her?

Her brow softened. Suddenly the frustration turned into such a sharp longing it stole his breath. He could not figure out what he wanted, only that he felt the yearning intensely.

She smelled like the childhood he couldn't remember—a haunting combination of lemons and lavender. He fought the impulse to hug her. He was a fighter trained to defend himself, yet he automatically opened up his stance to make room for her. That alone made him feel like he was losing what was left of his mind.

Everyone said the memory loss was normal, but he wanted to remember this woman very badly.

Tearing her gaze from his, she looked down to where he touched her arm. A curl fell in front of her eyes and he instinctively tucked it back behind her ear. Her eyes went wide. It was *far* too familiar. He'd made her uncomfortable.

She pulled away from him, clasping her hands and running her thumb over her inner wrist. The light caught on a ring on her finger.

"You're engaged," Rainer blurted out.

She looked crestfallen as she met his gaze again. "I am."

She belongs to someone else, Rainer—stop ogling her.

"And you love him?" He couldn't stop his stupid mouth from asking the question.

Her eyes were glassy. "With all my heart."

Rainer felt such a sharp pain in his chest that he brought a hand over his heart. He couldn't seem to take a deep breath. A moment later, the feeling was replaced with an incredible rush of warmth and love. He closed his eyes and took a deep breath. When he opened his eyes again, there were tears streaming down the woman's face.

He had to know her, but how could he have forgotten that face?

A flurry of footsteps interrupted them as King Vincent and Prince Xander entered the room.

"Rainer! I see you've met my fiancée," Vincent said.

"Your fiancée, Your Majesty?" Rainer asked.

The woman discreetly brushed away her tears before turning to face the king.

"Of course, you've met many times before—Lady Cecilia Reznik," Vincent said. "I'm very happy to say that you saved her life during the attack."

Vincent swept across the room and kissed the Lady Reznik's hand. Her whole body went rigid when his lips touched her skin.

Rainer felt an unnatural rage rise up in him. He was furious the king had touched her, but that didn't make sense. His allegiance was to the king, not to this woman.

Prince Xander's eyes were also on Lady Reznik. His gaze was full of sadness. He did nothing to hide his feelings for her, even in front of King Vincent. It had been one thing to witness Xander's flirtation when he thought he was alone in the training room with her, but to see the open adoration on his face in front of everyone was strange.

Xander raised an eyebrow, but Lady Reznik shook her head. The two seemed able to communicate through a look. The strangest surge of jealousy twisted in Rainer's chest.

Vincent studied Rainer seriously. "You seem frustrated."

"I just hate that I can't remember simple things like this. How can I do my job and protect you if I don't even know who your threats and allies are?" Rainer huffed.

"Rainer, you are one of a kind. Don't be so hard on yourself. It will come back to you eventually, and if it doesn't, we will form new, better memories. You're like family to me," Vincent said.

Rainer flushed with pride.

"We all have suffered with this attack. But we will root out our enemy and I will have vengeance for my beautiful fiancée."

Rainer looked from Vincent to Lady Reznik. Her gaze was cast down to the floor and her hands shook where they were clasped in her skirts. Rainer thought back to the way she'd panicked in the training room the day before with Xander and how the prince had asked before he touched her.

Someone had hurt her badly, and that filled Rainer with rage so potent he could barely see straight.

"Come, dear, we'll be late for tea with the court," Vincent said, sliding his arm around Lady Reznik.

The prince might have been delicate with her, but the king didn't seem nearly as concerned with her comfort.

Rainer shook his head. It was none of his business.

The king led Lady Reznik away. Rainer wanted to follow, but he forced himself to walk in the opposite direction. He needed time and space to process all he'd learned.

Lady Reznik. The name was so familiar. He scoured his brain but found no memory of it. What had she suffered during the attack?

King Vincent said that Rainer had saved her, but she still seemed traumatized, skittish—like a wounded animal. The fact that she didn't like to be touched was all he needed to know, especially after Rainer had seen the obvious intimacy between her and the prince, but she'd still struggled to let him touch her.

The thought of her being hurt twisted Rainer's gut. He knew well enough that some men looked at a wild woman and saw only something to be broken and tamed.

Rainer walked down another hallway toward the stables. Fresh air might do him good. He was about to round a corner when he heard her name on another man's lips. He paused and waited to hear more.

"You should have seen Lady Reznik in those lace undergarments. She's petite, but she has a fine ass," the guard said.

Rainer's whole body went rigid.

"And those perky tits," a second guard sighed. "Only someone who was asking for a good fuck would wear such scandalous lacy undergarments."

The words ignited a strange knowing in Rainer's body. He could not remember what exactly he'd saved Lady Reznik from, but now he wasn't sure he wanted to remember. If the guards had seen her in a state of undress, it could only mean that at the very least she'd been humiliated during the attack on the castle. Rainer could hardly contain the fury that built in him. It burned like a wildfire.

"I wish I could have had a chance to give her some discipline myself," a third guard added. "It was nice to see that snotty little witch get what she deserved."

"I'll tell you what, I wouldn't mind seeing our queen-to-be on her knees with my cock in her smart mouth. That'd shut her up right quick. I'd teach her to like it. I'd fuck the attitude right out of her," the first guard laughed.

Rainer saw red. He tore around the corner. His hand shot out and pinned the man to the wall.

"What the—" The guard choked and clawed at Rainer's fingers.

"Are you talking about Lady Reznik?" Rainer gritted. "The king's betrothed?"

The guard stared at him with wide eyes and nodded.

"You think it's funny to enjoy a woman's terror?" Rainer asked. "To talk about what she looks like in her undergarments when she was powerless because *you* didn't do your job and protect her?"

Rainer barely had a chance to register the confusion on the guard's face. He pulled his fist back and punched him. Rainer smiled at the satisfying crack of his cheekbone. The other men were frozen in place and did nothing to help their friend. Rainer punched the man until his face was a bloody pulp and he slumped lifelessly to the floor.

Rainer turned to the other two startled guards.

"You!" He grabbed the guard who suggested that Lady Reznik's undergarments meant she was asking to be assaulted. He shoved the man into the wall, holding him there by his neck. The guard squirmed, but Rainer was bigger, stronger, and blind with rage.

"Tell me: if I use your logic, I could say that you're asking to be punched in the face by saying such idiotic things, no?" Rainer taunted.

"Vern's not breathing," the other guard whispered, having checked on their friend.

The man in his grip struggled, but Rainer just smiled at him.

"Please," the guard begged.

"Is that what she said while you were busy looking at what she was wearing instead of protecting her?" Rainer asked.

The guard's gaze darted around like he didn't know the right answer.

"Answer me!" Rainer shouted into his face.

"No, she didn't beg. She didn't scream until he made her," the guard said shakily.

Rainer couldn't think through the rage of imagining someone making Lady Reznik scream. He slammed the man's skull into the wall repeatedly until his head was a bloody mess.

Finally, he turned to the last man. Clearly, Rainer had failed the future queen, and she'd paid a heartbreaking price.

He took the dagger from the last guard's hip sheath. The man had the sense to fight, but he was no match for Rainer's rage. Rainer slit his throat and dropped him on the floor like garbage.

He watched the blood pool on the floor dispassionately. His memory hadn't returned, but his body knew it all at once.

He was a thing that men knew to fear. He was a force they knew not to reckon with, and for the first time since waking, Rainer felt satisfaction in that.

He stormed down the hall, taking turn after turn until he finally stumbled outside, hoping the cool air would calm his mind.

Rainer was still a bit lost on the castle grounds, and it took him a moment to realize he was in the royal gardens. The smell of roses blended with the cold mountain air. He bent over with his hands on his knees, taking deep breaths. His mind spun wildly. He felt panicked and so unbelievably angry. As his breathing settled, he finally stood and looked around.

The king and several prominent members of his court were gathered in a sitting room in front of large glass windows, looking out to the garden where Rainer stood. Rainer searched the room, looking for Lady Reznik, finally spotting her standing apart from everyone else, sipping a cup of tea in the far corner of the room by the door that led outside.

He stared at her through the glass. She radiated loneliness. He could feel it even from where he stood. In a room full of bright scarlets and deep plums, her black dress marked her as the only mourner in a sea of revelers.

Suddenly, Lady Reznik's eyes connected with his and went wide. She dropped her teacup and the whole room jumped, turning to look at her.

She pushed through the glass door into the garden.

"Are you all right?" Lady Reznik asked breathlessly.

Rainer looked down. He hadn't realized he was so cold. The blood was turning tacky on his hands. "It's not my blood."

She let out a breath, her shoulders relaxing. They stood there staring at each other in silence for a few moments, but it wasn't awkward. Instead, the tightness in Rainer's chest started to unwind and the rest of the world seemed to go quiet.

Finally, they were joined by the king. Lady Reznik flinched as his hand slid to the small of her back.

"Rainer, Rainer, Rainer...what am I going to do with you?" Vincent said with a grim smile. "I understand that you killed three of my guards. I appreciate your fierceness, but I can't have you taking out your anger on my men."

Rainer nodded. "I apologize, Your Majesty. They were—"

Vincent looked at him expectantly.

"They were saying crude things about Lady Reznik and the attack. It was disgusting and conduct very unbecoming of your royal guard," Rainer said.

Lady Reznik looked like she wanted the ground to open and swallow her up. Prince Xander appeared beside her and lightly brushed her arm with his own. If Rainer hadn't seen them the day before, he wouldn't have thought anything of it, but he knew it was the prince trying to offer what little comfort he could publicly.

"Is that so?" Vincent asked.

Rainer faltered slightly, but Vincent seemed to appreciate the conviction. "Yes."

"You seem to have a lot of rage," Vincent said, more to himself than Rainer. "Seems that my trickster delivered as promised."

Lady Reznik bristled next to him.

"Come with me," Vincent said. "You too, Xander."

Rainer had no choice but to follow. He had no idea if he was being marched to his own doom or someone else's.

He followed as Vincent wove through the hallway and up a staircase until they approached the heavy wooden door of the tower lockup.

Several guards sat in separate cells. They wore the scarlet regalia of the rebels that supported Xander Savero, unlike the black and gold that Vincent's men wore.

"Rainer, I'm happy to see that you have so much energy to expend," Vincent said. "I've had a particularly hard time getting information out of these guards."

Rainer's eyes passed over the guards warily. They were already bloodied, several fingers on each of their hands broken.

"You want me to get information out of them?" he asked.

"Yes, of course. I'm sorry, I keep forgetting you need reminders. Forgive me. This was one of your former jobs as my top guard. It should come as an instinct," Vincent said reassuringly.

Rainer looked at the prisoners again. Nothing about this felt natural to him.

"If it helps, these are the men that allowed my Cecilia...and you... to be hurt," Vincent said.

That was all it took. These men were just like the ones downstairs who thought that a woman's terror and humiliation were fodder for jokes. Rainer relished the opportunity to dissuade them of that notion.

"Xander, you'll supervise. I advise not getting in his way. If you'd seen my guards, you'd understand," he said.

Vincent left the two of them there. All three guards looked at Xander, though Rainer couldn't understand why. They'd waged a rebellion in his name that had led to violence against Lady Reznik, whom the prince was clearly fond of.

One by one their faces fell when they realized the prince would not be their salvation.

Rainer unlocked the first cell.

The man stood helplessly at the center of the chamber. He was filthy and bloody and the smell of him was nearly enough to make Rainer's eyes water.

"Tell me what happened during the rebellion. How did you assist the rebels?" Rainer asked.

The man opened his mouth to speak, but nothing came out. He gasped and choked. Finally, he sighed helplessly, tilting his head back.

Rainer didn't hesitate. He punched the man in the face. The guard stumbled back.

"I swear. I can't say anything about it. I would if I could," the guard panted, trying to breathe around the pain of the blow.

"McKay, he seems like he's telling the truth," Xander said.

Rainer paid him no mind. "I'll stop when he tells me what the king wants to know."

7

CECILIA

The Castle Savero training room, with its stony walls and hay mats, was a far cry from Cecilia's cozy cottage in Olney, but she made do. The few pieces of routine that she held onto kept her going.

She'd held on the the irrational hope that Rainer would know her on sight. But that hope was dashed when he'd only been mildly flustered, with none of the usual warmth in his eyes.

Cecilia could not make Rainer remember her, but she could move as she always did in the morning and hope to quiet her mind. Her body, however, remained agitated, waiting for a blow that never arrived.

Each morning, she stretched, testing the borders of herself, prodding the tender places in her soul to see if her body, made foreign by fear, was a home again. But most days she still felt shipwrecked on the shores of a nightmare, unable to let down her guard.

When her muscles felt pleasantly warm and limber, she sat with her back against the wall on the side of the room with no windows or doors so she could see every approach. Her new vigilance made it impossible to meditate if she sat anywhere else. She closed her eyes and breathed deeply, trying to sense the confidence in herself that once felt like a reflex and now eluded her.

Her survival now relied on her ability to lie, and she'd always been a terrible liar. Rainer used to tease her, saying that she had a face for telling the truth because she was too expressive to hide her true feelings.

Now, her contempt had taken on a life of its own. Seething anger burned through her like a fever that refused to break, waiting for the slightest push to send her over the edge. She was furious at Vincent, at the Spellmans, but mostly she was furious at herself—for not doing more in the moment to save herself and Rainer. It was easier to live with the anger than it was to embrace the relentless fear that lived beneath it.

The idea came to her in the quiet, as if summoned by her desperation. Taking a page out of Sylvie's book, Cecilia would rely on her beauty and stature to fool people into forgetting that she was strong. Better that Vincent's men think she was a lovely, helpless lady than a powerful goddess with a seemingly bottomless well of rage to pull from. After all, there was nothing weak men loved more than seeing a powerful woman humbled.

For the first time, Cecilia was happy to be seen as a soft flower when she knew herself to be a wild, feral thing. How far she'd come from resenting her position as a lady.

No one looked at her and saw a beast born of thorns. Instead, they saw someone small and timid, with a smile that inspired apathy. She couldn't wait to rip apart everyone who had betrayed them.

Memory loss might have made Rainer meaner, darker, more vindictive, but betrayal and hurt did it for her. She'd pour every ounce of it into taking revenge on those who swept a victory out from under them.

Grant walked by the training room door, pausing to give her a menacing glare. She was sure he wouldn't remember how he'd gotten that nasty scar on his neck, but he looked at her like he didn't trust her anyway.

Look at this beautiful face while I slice you apart, she thought.

The guard leaned against the wall, his eyes narrowing on her. He couldn't possibly know that she'd slipped an herb into her usual guards' morning tea that would keep them all in the bathroom for the day. But he distrusted her all the same.

Grant shook his head but left her in peace.

Cecilia shivered. It was impossible to stay warm in Argaria. Back home, the winters were mild, but Ardenis was frigid, the wind biting, whistling through every fissure in the castle's walls and leaving her chilled even after exercise.

She brushed her thumb over the crescent scar on her hand.

She'd lost Rainer—thankfully not to the god of death, but to a hole that she'd created in his mind. It had been a special kind of suffering to pull herself out of him one memory at a time. She had relived each tender moment while he lost it.

Worst of all, she knew memory was the base on which personality was built. Removing herself from Rainer's memory might have made him different to begin with, but she was woven into most of his developmental memories. She had no idea what would happen to the very core of the man she loved.

The questions remained. Who would Rainer have been if he'd never met her? If he'd never been bonded to her? If he hadn't grown roots that wrapped around her own? The bloody scene she'd seen the day before terrified her. He'd looked like a beautiful, bloody god of vengeance. She should have been horrified, and part of her was, but another, darker part of her was satisfied that he'd viciously killed two of the guards who had held her down while Vincent scarred her body and soul. Still, she worried that he'd lost all the sweetness that made him so unique and wonderful to her—a warrior who was better suited to caretaking.

The truth was that she'd never realized how desolate her life was without him. Through everything that happened, every trial and challenge, Rainer had been beside her, in one way or another. Suddenly, she was on her own.

If Vincent thought he could take Rainer away from her, he was in for the fight of his life and she had no problem playing dirty.

Cecilia was woven into Rainer like vines and roots, and no one would be able to pull them apart. It didn't matter if Rainer remembered her. She would remember for both of them.

She'd become accustomed to sensing his proximity as she moved about the castle, praying for any glimpse of him she could get. She felt him growing closer, the bond wrapped around her heart humming. Even without his knowing it was there, the connection felt like an anchor, holding him to her, grounding her so she wouldn't float off into fear.

Scrambling back onto the mats, she went through her stretch routine. She paused when she felt Rainer's eyes on her as she slid her chest along the ground, keeping her backside high. A rush of surprise and desire shot through their connection and she bit back a laugh. Rainer not remembering the bond meant he didn't shield his emotions from her at all and now that he was close she could sense him stronger than ever.

"Guardian McKay, if you stare at my ass any longer, I'm going to have to charge admission to the training room." Cecilia glanced at him over her shoulder.

Rainer cleared his throat, shifting from foot to foot. "Your guards are sick, or else they refuse to watch you."

Cecilia smirked. She'd beaten up the three guards Vincent sent the previous day and although he'd threatened to throw her in the tower, getting away with it in the first place let her know she was too valuable to him to be locked away. It emboldened her to sneak an herbal laxative into her guards' breakfast.

Now Vincent had sent Rainer to watch her as some sort of test.

That information was interesting. Vincent saw her as a way to strengthen his image to anyone at court who was hedging their bets. According to word they'd received from Evan, the announcement of her engagement to Vincent had not been received well by the common people. They were still starry-eyed over her fairy tale love story with Rainer, and they would not be so easily swayed.

"The king has assigned me to keep an eye on you today," Rainer said stiffly.

"On me?"

"Yes."

"But not on my ass specifically?"

He bristled, narrowing his eyes. "Is your ass not part of you?"

Cecilia grinned at him. "Yes. You seem to find it my most compelling attribute."

"Isn't that better than being compelled by your ability to drive all of your guards away? I'm just here for the day on a temporary assignment—to keep you in line."

"Keep me in line?" She hopped to her feet and turned to face him. "And how do you think you'll do such a thing?"

He swallowed hard, his eyes focused on her lips as her teeth dragged across them. She was determined to do anything she could to capture his attention.

He shook his head as if trying to rid himself of a bad idea. "We just need to get you on a regular schedule. There is no problem a bit of discipline can't solve."

Her sweet rule-following Rainer—that was apparently who he would have been had she not been in his life. Her mind briefly flashed to the sight of him covered with blood after he'd killed three guards with his bare hands the day before, but she pushed the memory away. He could be both things: rule-following and explosively angry.

She trailed her fingers down the front of his velvet tunic. "So if I misbehave, you'll be in charge of...disciplining me?"

Rainer went rigid. "I think you mistake my meaning."

"I don't think I do," she said. "I must warn you, punishment from you will likely only serve to inspire naughty behavior."

Rainer's eyes went wide. "What sort of queen speaks in such a way?"

"I'm not a queen," she said plainly. "I'm just a lady."

"A lady with a filthy mouth."

"Indeed. I'll have you know speaking is the least filthy thing it does. Perhaps if you punish me you'll find out firsthand."

Rainer took a step back and she nearly burst out laughing at how wide his eyes were. Years of Xander's flirting had taught Cecilia a thing or two.

"Guardian McKay, are you afraid of me?"

He stood up straighter. "You're being terribly inappropriate."

"According to who?"

Rainer scowled. "According to basically any rules of decorum for how to behave in court as a betrothed woman—as a future *queen*."

"I find that behaving and following rules is a terrible bore. It's much more fun to break them, but if I've violated some rule, then I submit myself for punishment." She walked to the table and bent over it dramatically, leaving her ass poised on the edge. She propped her head in her hand so she could watch him.

"What...what are you doing?"

"Preparing for my punishment."

Rainer finally laughed, more in disbelief than amusement. "Is this how you scared off your other guards?"

"Is there something scary about me bending over to take my punishment for being a naughty girl?"

"No, there's something scary about the king's betrothed trying to seduce anyone stupid enough to have a death wish. Get up."

Cecilia turned so that she sat on the edge of the table, swinging her legs. "Does this mean I'm not being disciplined? That's disappointing. Things were just getting interesting."

"You are a lovely menace," Rainer said, shaking his head.

"So you think I'm lovely?"

He sighed heavily. "You seem overly familiar with me. We must have known each other before."

"Or perhaps I'm just trying to embrace my role as future queen by making sure that everyone feels at home in my castle."

"Well, you're making me uncomfortable."

Cecilia cocked an eyebrow. "Really? The good kind? Or the bad kind?"

"There's a good kind of uncomfortable?" Rainer asked.

"Of course. The bad kind of uncomfortable makes you want to shrink away, hide, pull back. But the good kind—" She hopped off the table and walked toward him. She drew her fingers down his chest and circled him. The scratch of her nails on his velvet tunic deafening in the silent room. "The good kind makes you want to push forward, keep going. It excites and inspires. It makes your heart race."

She met his gaze and desire slipped through their bond.

Thank gods. He's still in there.

He leaned down, his cheek nearly brushing hers, and she went perfectly still. His breath danced over the shell of her ear.

"The bad kind," he whispered before drawing back and stepping away from her. "I'm not interested in your body other than to keep it from harm."

It hurt to hear even if desire surged from his side of their connection.

"What about my sparkling personality?" she asked with a grin.

He shook his head. "You aren't easily discouraged, I'll give you that."

"Nothing would discourage me from trying to win you over, Guardian McKay. I think you're worth the effort."

"Come. We have to go to lunch with the king," Rainer said.

She shook her head. "No, I don't think so. I think I'd like to go outside."

"You're not allowed outside."

"Not allowed?" She scoffed. "I'm the queen-to-be and a grown woman. Why would I not be allowed to go outside?"

Rainer's brow furrowed. He clearly couldn't think of a good answer, which meant that Vincent hadn't figured out a good way to contain her. It was perfect because if she could get to the stables, she could drop off a message about the new guard patrol timing with the only stable hand they knew they could trust. The man had been taking care of stashing messages behind a loose stone in the outer courtyard wall—a place that Xander and Cecilia couldn't consistently get to without raising suspicion. It was one of the places where Evan and Xander had hidden messages to each other growing up and it was far enough removed from the gates that Evan could easily reach it undetected.

"I have a purpose," Cecilia said. "I heard there are new wild horses that they brought in to be broken by the stable master. I'd like to see them."

"You like to ride?"

"No, I *love* to ride. But I also know horses and I want to make sure they're treated properly."

Rainer faltered. "I don't know—"

"Guardian McKay, if you need to be at that lunch with the king, please don't let me delay you. I'll be but a few moments late."

He rubbed the back of his neck. "I'm going with you. It's my job to be your shadow."

"Lucky me to have such a handsome man trailing me," she said as she brushed by him.

She didn't bother with a cloak as she dashed down the hallway, through the heavy wooden door, and out into the sunlight. The icy air stole her breath momentarily. Having not been outside in days, the cold was a welcome change from the stifling castle.

She tilted her chin up to the sun, hidden behind gray clouds but still bright, her breath rising like tiny puffy clouds.

She turned abruptly and started toward the stables with Rainer on her heels. Instead of going inside, she cut around to the side fields, attracted by shouting.

As they approached, they saw a man lying in the dirt and a wild horse running around agitatedly.

"What's wrong?" Cecilia asked.

"My lady." Both of the stable hands bowed. "The stable master was kicked and we can't get to him because the horse is so agitated."

Cecilia stared at the beautiful black and gray mare pacing behind the fence as if daring them to come near her.

"What's her name?" Cecilia asked.

"Tempest," the man said.

"All right then."

Rainer reached for her, but he was too slow. She jumped the fence and walked toward the horse. Rainer shouted her name, but she ignored him.

Tempest let out a whinny and bucked. Cecilia picked up the rope the stable master had dropped.

"There, there, girl, it's okay. Tempest, right? That name suits you," Cecilia said.

"Lady Reznik, come back here right now. It's not safe," Rainer hissed.

"Guardian McKay," she said in a singsong voice, "please stay calm and keep your voice low. Horses sense fear and anger."

She took another step toward the horse. Tempest stilled, allowing her another step.

"They want to keep you in this little space. I understand. It's not fair when you're meant to be wild. But do you know what? You just have to play the game. Give them what they want for now. But as soon as you get the chance, you can run off. You just have to play the game for now, girl."

By the time she finished talking, she was close enough that she could touch the horse. She gently ran a hand down Tempest's neck and the horse let out a discontented whinny.

"I know. It's dreadfully cold. I hate it, too. We can get you a blanket, you know. Just let me get you on this lead, okay?" She carefully looped the rope around the horse's neck. "Good girl," she soothed, rubbing a hand down the horse's neck slowly. "All right, let's go."

She led the horse gently away from the stable master, who was struggling to his feet. The two stable hands rushed in and one helped the stable master away.

A third stable hand stepped toward Cecilia. She recognized him by the scarlet ribbon slipped through the buttonhole in his tunic. She slipped the note from her pocket and tucked it into her hand with the rope as she passed it to him.

"She needs to be in a larger field. This is much too small. Let her spend a week running there before you try to bring her back here and then let her run here for a week before you try to do more. She's too wild for these walls," Cecilia said, blinking away tears.

The stable hand nodded. "Message received, my lady."

She turned and walked back to the fence against which Rainer leaned, a hand on his head as if struggling with a headache. When she finally climbed back over and looked at Rainer, his face was inscrutable.

"That was very reckless," Rainer huffed.

She forced her face into a smirk. "Don't be such a fun-sucker. I knew she'd be okay. You, on the other hand, look a little worse for the wear."

"Just a headache," Rainer said, waving her off. "You've done that before."

She was certain he meant for it to be a question, but it came out like a statement and she wondered if it was possible that he was remembering something from their youth—a day when she'd hopped into the pen with one of her father's wild horses and Rainer had been similarly outraged. Her father had lectured him for an hour afterward.

She tried so hard not to hope. She knew she needed to be patient. But hope was a reckless thing that grew in even the most inhospitable environment.

Rainer looked down at her horse-shit-covered boots. "You'll need to change."

"Don't be ridiculous," Cecilia said with a wink. "We shouldn't keep the king waiting."

8

XANDER

Xander drummed his fingers on the dining room table. Beside him, Isla's posture was perfect, but her assessing gaze passed over each man in the room, looking for weaknesses.

Since the first night, she'd been all business, but Xander was relieved to have any ally, especially since he couldn't stop thinking about the way Rainer had laid into those men in the interrogation. He'd delighted in beating the prisoners to a pulp.

Xander had fought bloodthirsty hunters his entire life, but the current version of Rainer McKay scared the shit out of him. It was clear that Cece had smoothed Rainer's rougher edges, and without the memory of her, there was nothing to blunt his anger. This was the first time he'd ever thought that Rainer might actually beat him in a fight.

The false memories Cece planted about Xander abdicating to Vincent combined with Cato's added manipulation had stoked Rainer's anger. Clearly the helplessness he'd felt during the attack had turned him into a ruthless weapon. Rainer had killed three men for simply joking about an event he couldn't even remember.

Then, during the interrogation, he'd beat Xander's guards within an inch of their lives. Xander had needed to rush Magdalena up to heal them. He was walking an incredibly dangerous line, but he wouldn't give up on the people who put their faith in him. He would find a way to get everyone he could out safely and then he'd find a way to beat Vincent at his own game.

Across the table, Vincent droned on to Edward Spellman about their plans to break the Olney-Argaria alliance and rule over both kingdoms.

"Obviously we can't outright let the council know we plan to break the alliance with Olney, but we will require something of King Marcos that we know for sure he won't do so that any aggression after that is warranted," Vincent said.

Spellman nodded. "Of course. Most of the nobles don't see the benefits of an alliance anyway. Old grudges die hard and it's easier to justify taxing the working class at higher rates in wartime."

The strategist in Xander knew that the fact that they thought they were untouchable meant they'd be more likely to underestimate resistance, but their audacity to discuss it so openly irked him, especially with Isla there.

Vincent grinned at Xander, lifting his wine to mimic a toast to the destruction of his life's work. Xander clenched his fork in his hand until Isla's warm hand softly closed over his.

He'd been trying to ignore the attraction he felt toward her—trying to forget the way she'd curled against him in her sleep. He had not expected the vicious princess guard to be so cuddly or such a heavy sleeper. The longer he watched her out of the corner of his eye, the more certain he was that she hadn't realized she'd been so familiar.

Perhaps she already had a lover and was used to sleeping with another body in her bed. But Xander hadn't had that comfort in a year. Even his first night with his new wife, he'd gone back to his own bed afterward. Last night he'd stared at the ceiling as Isla threw an arm and leg over his body, her face buried in his neck. He could still smell her faint vanilla and jasmine scent on his skin, and he'd forgotten how much he liked that.

Isla squeezed his hand. It had been so long since someone soothed Xander like that on instinct. He met her gaze and she offered an indulgent smile, as a newlywed queen might, and just for a moment he wished this wasn't a lie. That they weren't in danger. That he could start over and get to know her without the complication of a rebellion and his marriage to her cousin. He wished his life could be simple.

But wishing wouldn't save his people, so he settled back in his chair and focused on Vincent.

Vincent lowered his voice as he and Spellman began to discuss Eloise. Xander tried to pick out their hushed words, but it was hard with the scrape of forks and knives and the commotion of Cece entering the room with Rainer on her heels.

Xander expected Cece to react to Isla, but instead her gaze locked on the table and he knew immediately that something was wrong. A look of terror flashed through her eyes—there and gone. He didn't understand what set her off until Vincent grinned at her and gestured to the seat next to him at the head of the table.

"Lady Reznik, I saved you the best seat in the room. I wanted to remind you of your place of honor," Vincent said with a menacing smile.

Cece's face was placid as she crossed the room, but Xander could read the tension in her gait as she sat down in the seat next to Vincent. Her back was rigid, her eyes focused on divots in the tabletop in front of her.

The revelation hit Xander like a bolt of lightning. This was the room where Vincent had dragged her. The room where Vincent had put his hands on her and made her scream—on this very table. Xander's stomach turned violently at the horror of it.

Cece had only recently started attending meals with the court, electing to eat in her rooms until Vincent insisted she show herself.

Xander had been wrong to think things couldn't get worse than Cato's manipulation. They were in an entirely new game of chess, one in which none of them were cruel enough to anticipate their opponent's next move.

Cece's eyes flicked around the table, narrowing at Grant standing in the far corner before settling on Isla. A slight smirk tipped the corner of her lips as she met Xander's eye, then she averted her gaze and stared at her soup. She clasped her hands neatly in her lap and her thumb brushed over her inner wrist. Her breathing evened out and her heart slowed.

On the far side of the table, Rainer's hand rested on his chest, his brow furrowed in concern. He looked puzzled—likely by whatever panic Cece was feeling.

Isla leaned closer so that her lips were right next to Xander's ear. "What am I missing, dearest?"

Xander glanced at Cece and then back at Isla. "This is the room where it happened."

Isla's eyes widened slightly, her jaw tightening as she sat back in her chair. Her face remained calm and serious, but beneath the table, she gripped the arms of her chair tightly.

Vincent sniffed loudly and made a sour face. "Cecilia, you smell foul."

A smile tugged at Cece's lips. "Not sure how you can tell over your own rotten stench," she whispered, only loud enough for Vincent and Xander to hear.

Vincent's jaw clenched as Cece's gaze darted to a very confused Rainer. Xander understood impulsivity well, but he worried she was walking a dangerous line, testing how Vincent would handle conflict in front of Rainer. It wasn't the worst strategy. It was clear Vincent wanted Rainer to be his good soldier, but if Vincent wanted to play the good guy, he'd need to behave in public at the very least. Xander's concern was what he would do when the guardian wasn't around.

"Lady Reznik saved the stable master after there was an accident with one of the new mares," Rainer said.

"And what were you doing outside, dearest? You know I don't like you going out without me. I worry about your safety with such a recent rebellion," Vincent said.

Cece clenched her fist in a white-knuckled grip on her fork—

she'd been offered no knife. "I was very careful and in capable hands." She winked at Rainer.

Vincent pursed his lips. "Cecilia, are you forgetting our deal?"

She leveled him with a glare. "I haven't forgotten anything about our deal or the debt in the ledger between us."

"I'll put more guards on you again if you insist on sneaking out," Vincent threatened.

"You'll do so at your peril," Cece said, slamming her hands on the table.

The entire room went utterly still, the guards frozen in place at her show of defiance against the king.

Vincent ground his teeth together, his hand flexing at the edge of the table. "You'd speak that way to the king?" he asked, tilting his chin toward Rainer.

Cece settled back into her rigid posture. "You're right." Her gaze flickered to Xander. "Apologies, Your Majesty." Her eyes slid back to Vincent. "I forgot my place."

Isla blew out a breath, looking genuinely impressed.

"I'll remind you later," Vincent said.

Xander swallowed hard at the exchange, but Cece didn't look concerned.

As they ate, he caught Cece's eye across the table. He tapped his pointer finger on the table twice. They'd created a set of nonverbal signals to communicate with each other. Two taps was a check-in.

Are you okay?

She kept her eyes on her plate and gave a quick nod as she picked at her food. She tapped her fork on the plate twice and looked at him.

He sucked in a breath. For a moment he could see all the fear and pain in her eyes and it left him feeling breathless and lost. She narrowed her eyes and he realized he hadn't responded. He nodded back.

I'm okay, Cece. Just worried sick about you and everyone else.

He brushed his fingers back and forth across his eyebrow three times. The signal meant that more stowaways needed to escape the castle. Over the past two weeks, they'd assisted in leading thirty-three people to safety. It took them weeks to establish a system, but now that Vincent was increasing nightly patrols, the window had narrowed and required more creativity. Xander wasn't sure how they'd pull it off tonight.

Most servants who remained in the castle were there because they wanted to be, but there were a few stragglers who had needed some time to get their affairs in order before they could flee.

Cece's blue eyes widened slightly as she took a sip of her water. She made a fist, then opened her fingers, her palm facing up toward the ceiling, asking how urgent the timing was.

He flattened his palm against the table as he picked up his glass of wine with his other hand. *As soon as possible.*

"I'm suddenly feeling quite ill," Cece said, standing so abruptly she nearly knocked the chair over.

Vincent's suspicious gaze narrowed on her. He looked like he wanted to force her to stay but realized he couldn't do that without making Rainer suspicious. "Very well, *dear.* You may go."

Cece dipped into the shallowest curtsey possible and left the room.

Grant moved to sit next to Vincent. They spoke in hushed tones about unrest among the common folk around the outskirts of Ardenis. Xander tried not to look excited at the prospect of his people rising up in support of him. He knew that Evan intended to use Vincent's own tactics against him from what little information they'd been able to exchange. He was pleased it seemed to be working enough for Vincent to be concerned. It also ensured that he would need Xander alive longer.

Xander forced himself to wait five minutes before he pushed his plate away. "I should go write that letter you've asked me to pass along to Marcos."

Vincent nodded, waving a hand dismissively.

Xander turned to Isla. "Shall I escort you back to our room?"

She shook her head, her eyes flitting to Vincent and back. "I'm finishing up, but my guards will see me back and I'll catch up with you then."

Xander glanced to Nicholette and Freya, Isla's two vigilant guards stationed by the door. They both nodded.

"Should I still be following Lady Reznik?" Rainer asked as Xander made his way to the door.

"She'll likely just be in her rooms for the afternoon, but you can go check on her in an hour or so," Vincent said.

Xander quickened his pace. They had an hour. He walked down the hall and ducked into the alcove where he found Cece waiting.

"Who is that woman pretending to be your wife?" she whispered. "The resemblance is uncanny."

Xander grinned. "Jess's cousin, Isla."

"It should be illegal for there to be two women that beautiful in the world," Cece said, shaking her head.

Xander laughed. "I agree, but what a fortunate man I am to have had both of them in my bed."

Cece's eyebrow shot up and she grinned. "Really? Do tell."

Xander grinned. "Isla was only there to sleep, love. Don't be jealous."

She rolled her eyes. "Don't flatter yourself. We'll talk about your new crush later. For now, just tell me how many people we need to sneak out."

"There are about fifteen ready to go. They're hidden in the pantry, but we don't have much time," Xander whispered.

"Fifteen!" Her eyes went wide and she chewed her bottom lip. "I can create a diversion. Can you lead them to the meeting point? It takes the guards an extra minute to make it around the far wall of the castle on that route. Then, meet me by the old hunter training grounds? That should be far enough out of the wards to get a message to Grim. Two birds, one stone."

"Love, are you certain you're up for this? We don't know what the reaction might be," he said.

She crossed her arms. "Don't assign me your peace of mind. I have my own to manage."

The words were brutal and efficient in their honesty. Xander tried not to wince.

"I'm in charge, right? I get to at least choose what risks I'm willing to take. For fifteen people, I'm willing to take the punishment." Her confidence didn't waver but he saw a hint of fear in her eyes.

"I hate to even ask, but—"

"Xan, we should talk later. I need to tell you something important. I promise I can handle this. Do you trust me?"

He nodded. "Of course."

"Okay. Give me until dusk. I have an idea."

Xander couldn't help but smile. "Of course you do."

"I aim to annoy," she said, patting him on the shoulder and ducking out of the alcove.

Xander stepped into the light and found Isla waiting. Her eyes narrowed on him.

"You two aren't as discreet as you'd like to think."

"Jealous?" Xander asked.

He was delighted by the way her eyes narrowed. "Hardly."

Several guards' footsteps echoed down the hall, startling both of them.

Xander grabbed Isla and pulled her into the alcove so they wouldn't be spotted scheming when he was supposed to be writing to Marcos. Isla shifted, her chest brushing his in the small space, the scent of vanilla and jasmine wafting off her skin like an invitation.

As the guards' footsteps retreated down the hall, he leaned in closer to explain their plan, but paused when Isla drew in a breath, her gaze dropping to his mouth.

Xander had the surprising and possibly insane impulse to kiss her.

He hadn't felt truly compelled by anyone since Cece. Now he felt desire where he'd not expected it.

It wasn't that Isla was any lovelier than the princesses that pursued him just weeks before during the courting festival, but she had an intensity about her. Attraction only became more of a mystery to Xander the harder he tried to pin it down. Isla had dropped her guard while they were sleeping. Now his curiosity was getting the best of him and he wanted to see her ruffled.

He let his gaze linger on her bust and the elaborate beadwork on her bodice. The craftsmanship of gowns from Novum was impressive. "This is a pretty dress. I bet it's as deadly as it is beautiful. How many blades are hidden in it?"

Isla huffed a soft laugh. "If you can find them all I'll let you cut it off me when we get upstairs."

Xander ran his hand up from her hip to the notch just below her ribs. "One." He run his fingers up and few inches and tapped the next blade. "Two." He lifted his hand higher so it rested just below her left breast. Her breath hitched and a familiar thrill zipped through Xander's blood.

"Three. And I'd wager three in the same positions on the other side. So that's six."

He brushed his fingers across her ribs to her back and slid his hand down to rest just above her ass. "A seventh here, and an eighth on the other side." He grinned at her. "How did I do? Will I be seeing this dress shredded on our bedroom floor later?"

She shook her head.

"I missed one?"

Isla cocked her head to the side. "You missed five."

The woman had thirteen blades in her dress—probably more in her boots or strapped to her thighs. Just thinking about it made him want to continue his scavenger hunt.

Up close, Xander couldn't stop staring at the differences between Isla and her cousin. Their builds were similar, but Isla had a prickly fierceness that settled around her like a warning not to get too close —the exact kind of warning that had always felt like more of an invitation to Xander. Old habits died hard and even after all of this time, he still loved the rush of a challenge.

Isla was tall. All it would take was a slight tilt of her chin to bring those full lips to his. Logistically it opened up a whole new set of opportunities that he hadn't had with Cece. Not that he was complaining about what he and Cece had. Part of the fun with her was that she was small enough that he could throw her around a little bit.

95

Isla's height and strength, however, meant she could easily meet him where he was. Standing as they were now, he could hike up her dress, hook her leg over his hip, and be inside her with ease.

As if reading his mind, her gaze dropped to his mouth again.

He stroked Isla's cheek and her wide eyes flew to his. "Looking for something, *darling*?"

Her eyes narrowed in determination. "Just assessing a threat."

Xander grinned, leaning closer so that they breathed the same air. She didn't cower.

"What's your assessment?" he asked.

Falling into a flirtation tactic was reflexive, but the moment the words were out of his mouth, they felt unnatural. Perhaps it was a result of how many surprises he'd suffered as of late, or maybe it was something larger.

"My assessment," Isla said, pressing her chest against his, highlighting once again how well their bodies fit together, "is that even you don't believe your games anymore."

She couldn't throw down a challenge like that and expect him not to take it.

"Who said it was a game?"

Xander tilted her chin back and pressed his lips to hers. A shiver went through her body, like she was electrified by the kiss. Xander felt fluttering in his chest as if something long asleep was waking.

The kiss was soft and slow—a lover's kiss—not at all right for a light flirtation. She sighed into his mouth, pulling him closer.

He had kissed Jessamin on their wedding night, and it was lovely, but it had been so long since he'd kissed someone out of pure desire. Kissing Cece had been a consuming thing—a rhythm he knew by heart. Now the strangeness of kissing someone new out of passion after so long without left him testing the boundaries of the kiss, looking for differences in the way she responded.

She pulled away suddenly.

"I'll not be an experiment, *Your Grace*," she rasped breathlessly, her brown eyes full of frustration.

Xander swallowed hard. "I don't know what you mean—"

Isla rolled her eyes. "You started kissing me, but you finished kissing someone else. I'll not be in competition with a memory. Nostalgia is compelling, but I have the benefit of being real and right in front of you. I'm too good to lose out to some fairy tale in your head."

Xander was bewildered and utterly put in his place. He searched for an explanation that would soothe her but found none. When had he become so bad at this? Charm had never failed him before. It was easy enough to figure out what a woman wanted and turn himself into that. But Isla didn't seem to be lacking anything, leaving him no easy way to approach her.

He wasn't even certain what he was trying to do. He didn't need a love affair right now and he certainly didn't need to be chasing after his wife's decoy. What would Jessamin think?

Shame was like a wave of ice water washing over him.

"So what are you two planning?" Isla asked impatiently.

"I have a large group of servants I need to smuggle out of the castle at dusk tonight."

He waited for her to insist it was too dangerous or foolish, but she just nodded. "How can I help?"

"Cece is going to create a diversion. If you and your guards could watch the door we come out of to make sure none of Vincent's men notice my expedition, that would be very helpful."

Isla studied him quietly. "You've been doing this the whole time— helping your people escape?"

He nodded. She pursed her lips but said nothing else.

"Just before dusk I'll come and walk you down to the side door by the kitchens while Cece sneaks out to create havoc."

"How will we know when it's time?" Isla asked.

"Cece is about as subtle as a sledgehammer. I'm sure it will be clear." Xander smirked.

Isla rolled her eyes. "I'll say. That was quite a performance she put on at lunch."

Xander felt ill remembering the look on Cece's face when she entered the room.

Isla's intense brown eyes softened and she swallowed hard. "He's a monster to make her sit there and relive that. He enjoys it."

Xander frowned, running a hand through his hair. There was no doubt in his mind that Vincent's behavior was monstrous, but King Damian had made him that way. It was hard to reckon with Vincent's violence without reckoning with Damian's. Everything twisted together, making it impossible to cast judgment without Xander forever altering his already-damaged opinion of the man he'd always looked up to.

Xander worried what it said about him that he was raised by a man who embraced such easy violence. He'd never questioned the way violence came second nature when he was in hunter training, but now he worried that, even without Damian's blood, he could still fall into his habits.

Maybe the only true difference between them was the length of time they'd been king. Perhaps in several decades, apathy would make Xander equally cruel and the reflex for brutality was simply lying in wait.

Looking at Isla, he found himself wishing he could find the words to speak the haunting thoughts aloud, though he wasn't sure if she would reassure or taunt him.

Instead, he held out an arm and led her back to their room so he could write a warning letter to Marcos.

―――――

Ever the overachiever, Cece managed to cause full-out chaos the moment the sun ducked below the tree line. Shouts came from outside and one of the guards ran back inside sporting an arrow wound. He claimed that the king's betrothed was perched in a tree by the old training grounds, shooting anyone who got close.

Xander laughed from his spot outside the kitchen doorway. Isla turned away from her guards and looked to him for direction. He nodded his head toward the hallway behind them.

"I'll need cover when we get outside, but I have no idea how hard it will be to get weapons—"

Isla hiked up her gown and drew out a dagger. She reached behind a nearby bush and pulled out a bow and quiver full of arrows.

Xander grinned at her. "I like a woman who's always prepared to fight."

"How original," Isla quipped.

He winked. "Maybe later I can finish my scavenger hunt for those last five blades."

Nicholette and Freya smirked and looked at each other. Isla ignored her guards and Xander as she walked toward the kitchen doors. It was frustrating that she was so completely unfazed by his flirtation.

"If you stand on the other side of this door, it's a natural choke point. If you can't kill a guard, at least try to knock them out and I'll have someone wipe their memory later," Xander said.

Isla nodded and ducked behind the door.

"Isla?"

She peeked her head out, her two guards poised behind her.

"Please be careful," he whispered.

Isla smiled and Xander had seen her grin so rarely that warmth pooled in his chest.

Xander stepped into the kitchen and nodded at the cook. The cook knocked three times on the pantry door. It creaked open and a group of terrified-looking servants filed out. The group of fifteen shuffled through the kitchen, following Xander out the door.

"Keep close to the castle wall so the overhead patrols don't see you. Stay quiet," Xander said.

Distant shouts from the old hunter training grounds drew the eyes of several in his group. Xander snapped his fingers, urging them along.

It took a few minutes to reach the gap in the garden wall. He helped the children through before helping their mothers. Finally, he squeezed through and gazed down the hill. A torch flickered half a mile down the road.

Though he couldn't see Evan, that was the meet-up point his friend had agreed to. The fact that Evan was so close inflicted an ache in Xander's chest. He ignored it, leaning over to the closest maid.

"See that torch?"

She nodded.

"Stick to the side of this road so you can hide in the shadow of the trees and make your way to the torch. When you get there, you'll find help to get wherever you're going and shelter if you need it."

She smiled at him, her eyes glistening with unshed tears. "Bless you, Your Majesty."

He shooed them on, watching for only a minute before he turned back toward the castle. He darted back through the gap in the wall and deposited branches in front of it.

Shouts rose from the direction of the old hunter training grounds. As he drew closer to the commotion, he heard several guards shouting to each other, perplexed as to how she'd acquired arrows. Cece's laugh rang out like a bell. Xander smiled instinctively at the sound. He watched as several guards carried a hunter with an arrow buried in his kneecap. The other two had hand wounds. She was using them as target practice.

Xander loved that woman, but she was definitely going to get herself into serious trouble. Still, her courage was magnetic.

The cold air burned his lungs. Snow crunched underfoot. He hadn't been outside much since Vincent took over. He'd need to start taking training more seriously again, especially now that it was winter, a season that demanded acknowledgment with its harshness and the way it could freeze the air in your lungs.

He heard footsteps and turned to find Rainer a few paces behind him.

"McKay?"

"The king has sent me to retrieve Lady Reznik," Rainer said dutifully.

"Yes, of course. She seems quite content to be retrieved."

Rainer slowed slightly. "You think she'd shoot me?"

Xander slowed alongside him. "I'd approach with caution. She's the type to shoot first and ask questions later."

Rainer slowed his pace, walking a step behind Xander.

"My love? Are you enjoying your evening of sport?" Xander called as Cece came into view.

She was poised a good fifteen feet up a tree on the edge of the training grounds, bow in hand and a smile plastered on her face. "Moving targets are more fun," she said.

"Your talent is unmatched as always, love. I do worry that perhaps you're causing a world of trouble for yourself. Make no mistake, though, you look exceptional doing it."

She grinned at Xander and, for a moment, he felt as if no time had passed. Even in the dark he saw the mischief sparking in her eyes and he could do nothing but try to breathe around the ghost of love that stirred in his chest.

"Nonsense. I'm just having some fun. No one has been irreparably maimed. I just need some personal space." She smiled brightly at Rainer. "Good evening, Rainer."

Rainer glowered beside Xander. "*Guardian* McKay."

"So formal," she teased.

"Lady Reznik, please come down," Rainer pleaded.

"Cece," she corrected. "You asked so nicely but I am so enjoying the view. Xan, I believe there's a stag over there. You should shoot it," she said, gesturing toward a heavily wooded area to their left.

"*Cece*, please come down," Rainer insisted.

"Why don't you come up here and retrieve me yourself, Rainer?" she said suggestively.

Xander laughed as he ducked behind the trees. He glanced back at the warded stone wall several yards behind them.

The smell of smoke and cinnamon filled the air and Grimon stepped out from behind a tree.

Xander felt the press of his magic instantly. The sharp scent filled the air as Grimon put up a sound damper with his magic.

"I need this to go to Marcos," Xander said, handing over the real communication for his Olney counterpart. No doubt Vincent would be sending the fake version soon.

Grimon rolled his eyes. "Sometimes I think you forget who I am."

"Sometimes I think you forget that if you insist on smelling like a bakery, it's hard to take you seriously," Xander said, arching a brow.

"How is she?" Grimon asked.

Xander jerked his head to the side. "See for yourself. She's having a great time flirting with her fiancé and he's desperately trying not to be charmed."

"Any luck with his memory?"

Xander shook his head. "Not so far but she's only just started to actually spend time with him."

Grimon sighed. "Have you been able to make progress with rooting out the opposition within your walls?"

Xander shrugged. "Slow going when you're trying to figure out who the good guys are and everyone looks the same."

Grimon nodded as Xander handed him correspondence for Evan and King Marcos. "You'll make sure Marcos gets this?"

Grimon sighed. "I live to play courier."

"That's why you're my third favorite god," Xander said.

"Third?" Grimon challenged, sounding genuinely offended.

"Cece is my favorite, for obvious reasons, and then your brother."

Grimon threw up his hands. "Samson! Seriously."

Xander laughed. "I'm joking. You'd be first if it wasn't for my lovely ex-wife and, of course, if you didn't dislike me so much."

Grimon frowned. "You've grown on me."

Xander could hardly contain his glee at the admission. "I knew it!"

Grimon held up his hands. "Don't let it go to your head. It's been nice to see you grow up." The edges of his body began to flicker. "I have to go, but keep Cece safe."

Xander nodded solemnly. "I'll do my best, though you know how she loves to make it a challenge."

Grimon evaporated in a puff of smoke with a smirk on his lips. Xander waited for Cece to finish her flirting.

9

RAINER

It was official. The king had assigned Rainer the most difficult task in the kingdom to prove his worth. What Rainer expected to be a simple guard assignment had turned into chaos. Lady Reznik was more wild woman than lady. He was beginning to understand why the king didn't like her going outside. The snow between the castle and the tree in which she perched was specked with bright red blood.

Rainer approached the tree where she was waiting, bow in hand. They were beyond the wards that kept out the gods and that meant Lady Reznik was at risk. Rainer still didn't have clarity as to what exactly the gods had done to aid the rebellion, but he'd read enough histories to know that the gods loved to meddle in human affairs. He glanced back at the courtyard walls where the line of protection around the castle ended. His heart kicked up.

He turned his attention back to his charge. Lady Reznik clung to the trunk of the tree high above, grinning down at Rainer. Her eyes were bright even in the fading daylight. When she smiled at him, he felt a rushing sensation in his chest.

She gazed out at the horizon as if looking for something. Maybe she felt as on edge as he had since the rebellion and she was looking for danger. At the moment, however, she was the only pressing danger to her own well-being.

"Please come down from there, Lady Reznik. There are no more guards coming. The king sent me instead."

"Please call me Cece." She made it sound as if *he* was being the exasperating one and not the other way around.

"Please come down from there, Lady Reznik," he repeated through gritted teeth.

"Why don't you come up? The view is spectacular," she said, still squinting into the distance.

Rainer placed a hand against the trunk, trying to position himself so he could break her fall if she slipped. "Because I'm not sure this tree could bear both of us."

She leaned forward, putting too much weight on a branch that looked as perilously close to snapping as Rainer's nerves. Then she grinned and shifted back to grip the trunk of the tree.

"Fine. But make sure you're in good position to get a nice view of my ass as I climb down," she said as she turned and hooked her bow across her body to descend the tree. "Perhaps the view will stop you from being such a fun-sucker all the time."

Rainer had tried very hard not to notice the way the tight black pants clung to her backside, but now that she'd called attention to it, he couldn't look away. His heart leapt into his throat as he watched her slip and then regain her footing. Once he saw she was sure-footed, his eyes were indeed glued to her ass.

She fumbled for her grip when she was just a foot off of the ground and stumbled into his arms. He caught her and she grinned at him.

"So gallant."

He quickly set her on her feet. "You'll go back inside now?" He meant for it to sound more commanding, but it came out like a plea.

"I'll do no such thing. What an absolutely preposterous sugges-tion. It's a beautiful evening," she said, the puffy white cloud of her breath brushing over his cheek.

"It's freezing and you don't have a cloak," Rainer griped.

"I'd be happy to keep you warm," she said, winking at him.

"Are you always this—"

"Charming? Adventurous? Exhilarating?"

"Maddening."

"I suppose madness is in the eye of the beholder." She tossed her bow and quiver aside, plopped down in the snow, and stretched her arms and legs wide, sweeping them up and down as if swimming in the snow.

"You'll catch your death," Rainer said.

Lady Reznik was awfully free-spirited for a lady of the court, and especially for a queen. Vincent was so stern, it was hard to imagine the two of them happy together. Harder even to imagine how they'd ended up together.

"Oh, relax. Lay down here. You'll see what I mean," she said, patting the snow next to her.

"If I lay down, will you come inside?" Rainer asked.

"We can certainly discuss it. Lay down."

"No."

"Don't be such a fun-sucker," she sighed, flopping back in the snow.

"You keep calling me that. What is a fun-sucker?"

"Someone who sucks the fun out of all situations with his handsome brooding."

He hesitated. He couldn't remember a time when he'd seen snow, though that didn't mean he never had. A sort of childlike wonder had grown in him when he watched the storm through the window the previous night, observing the whorls of snow whip through the castle courtyard.

Rainer didn't want to lay down in the snow and be cold and wet, but he needed to get her safely inside.

"You're overthinking it," she said. "This is a win-win. You get to lay down and relax for a moment and when I get up there's going to be a perfect imprint of my ass in the snow for you to gawk at."

The snow crunched as Rainer laid down next to her. "You are so crude."

"Yes, but I'm also fun."

"Your kind of fun is the kind that ends in everyone else getting in trouble."

She shrugged. "I'm sure I'll be in plenty of trouble myself."

A comfortable silence stretched out between them. The fresh snow seemed to muddle all sound in the forest behind them. Court life was so loud, but here it was almost soothing, even with the wet snow melting into his pants. A breeze swept through the trees behind them, making the branches groan with the effort of moving while weighed down with heavy snow.

"I've only seen snow a few times in my life and when I have, I've never been able to stop and enjoy it," she said. "It smells so fresh, like it's sharpened the scent of these pines. Even the sky seems clearer now."

It *was* beautiful now that the sun had given way to darkness and the sky was scattered with stars.

"We should be getting back—" Rainer started.

"Rainer—"

"Guardian McKay."

"*Rainer*, you worry too much. A few more minutes won't matter. I'm already in trouble. Let me have another minute before I go back in there."

"Why do you seem so unhappy?" Rainer asked.

"Because I am." Lady Reznik hesitated, clearly trying to figure out what she could say. "I lost someone dear to me."

Rainer went still. "In the rebel attack?"

"Yes." She held up her hand, her gaze fixed to the ring on her finger.

"I'm very sorry," Rainer said. "Is he the one who gave you that ring?"

"Yes. It was my mother's ring. It means a lot to me. So I kept it even when the king—"

"Even when the king asked you to marry him," Rainer finished for her. "What was he like? The man you lost?"

She smiled sadly. "My fiancé was kind and thoughtful. He could be incredibly stubborn. I had to basically force him to face his feelings, but once he did, he was a dream come true. My best friend, the steadiest person I've ever known. He was an incredible fighter, but he didn't have the heart for it. He was too sweet for this world. Also too much of a martyr."

Recognition tore through Rainer. "He saved you."

Her lips pressed into a grim line. "He did."

Rainer couldn't remember ever being in love, but he was certain if he cared about someone like that he'd happily lay down his life to protect them. "I doubt he'd regret it."

"I don't think he thought about the fact that *I* would. That was his thing. Always making decisions for me," she sighed, her eyes lit with pain and anger. She was so mercurial.

Rainer swallowed hard. "I lost someone too."

Lady Reznik's eyebrows shot up. "Oh?"

"My witch."

She pursed her lips. "I'm sorry for your loss."

Rainer huffed a sigh. "Might be harder if I remembered her."

"It will come back. Memory is a strange and complicated thing and grief can make us more hesitant to recall what we have forgotten." She glanced at the bow she'd cast aside. "Until today, I hadn't shot a bow in more than a year."

If that was true, her skill was remarkable. Rainer's curiosity got the better of him. "Why?"

"Originally, I thought I was just tired of violence, but the truth is that I think of my late father every time I touch a bow. I swear I can still hear him critiquing my form." She brought a hand to her heart.

"When did he pass?" Rainer asked.

"It's been nearly two years, but it still takes the air out of me at the strangest times, over the simplest things."

"You were close?" He was no longer just making conversation to get her to go along with his plans. He truly wanted to know about her.

She paused as if struggling for words. "Yes, we were very close. I was his only child, and he was very good to me. He cultivated my curiosity and my fighting skills, but most of all, my skill with a bow."

"I'm sorry for your loss," Rainer said. Too late. He was always a beat or two off with her—always a little bit disoriented.

She smiled faintly. "Thank you."

"What would he say if he were here?" Rainer asked.

"That is a very good question. He'd probably say something about how I hunt down trouble like it owes me a debt. Then he'd remind me who I am and who trained me and to stop being—" She sighed. "He'd tell me to stop being so hard on myself."

"He sounds like a good man."

"He was." Her smile was strained. "Grief is a strange thing. At times it seems distant, but it's always waiting to pounce in moments of weakness, like a starved beast perking its head up at the prospect of being fed."

That beautiful smile of hers that made his heart race was really just a shield behind which she hid all the things that hurt her most. Somehow, he seemed to feel the pain and grief that lived in her heart just by looking into her eyes. He'd never felt anything so intense as the strange rush of emotions that blew through her like fierce storms coming down from the Argas Mountains.

Her eyes told stories that didn't have a beginning or an end. They went on and on and he didn't know half the words. He felt like he was trying to translate some coded message without a cipher, but he wanted so badly to know exactly what it all meant.

"Why did you hurt the king's men?" Rainer asked.

Her brows pinched together. "Because they were trying to retrieve me and I wished to be free."

"You hurt them."

She waved a hand. "Flesh wounds. I'm an excellent shot." She glanced toward the heavens. "Look."

The evening was so dark, some of the stars even seemed to have their own distinct colors. Rainer had never noticed that before.

"See. If we'd gone inside, we would have missed this," she whispered. "Let me tell you a story—"

"We don't have time for that."

She blew out a breath. "Don't be ridiculous. There's always time for a story. This is a good one. It's about a spirited young lady and a grumpy old guardian. They sprawled out in the snow, looking up at a night sky that was sugared with stars."

"*Sugared with stars?*" Rainer said skeptically.

"You mustn't interrupt," she chided. "I'm telling the story and I reserve the right to take poetic license."

Rainer smothered a smile as she continued.

It *was* a beautiful night. A restless feeling stirred in his chest when he noticed her studying him out of the corner of her eye as she spoke.

Rainer counted the stars, trying to place them in constellations though even in his memory constellations contained holes. Her tale reminded him of the story that had led him out of the dark of his mind, and the voice whispering it to him as he tried to wake. He was told it had been Eloise's voice, but she sounded so different now that he was awake.

A falling star shot across the sky.

Lady Reznik gasped. "Did you see that? We get to make a wish. Here, let's do it together."

Without asking, she grabbed his hand and squeezed her eyes shut. Her skin was cold and soft except for the calluses on her fingers. Her hand felt so delicate in his. Sadness sank in his chest before it lifted and warmed as if he were lying in sunlight on a hot day.

Rainer mimicked her, closing his eyes to concentrate. He had no context for making a wish because he didn't remember who he was enough to want something other than his memory.

When he blinked his eyes open and looked at Lady Reznik, her face was unreadable again.

"Make a wish. Don't just humor me," she sighed.

"I wish you'd behave yourself and not sneak out of your rooms to play target practice with the king's men. I wish you weren't such a pain in the ass to keep track of. I wish you'd do one thing I ask without argument. I wish you'd stop calling me a fun-sucker."

"That is a wish only you can grant," she countered. For the first time, her shoulders relaxed.

"We should go in. It's getting dark and it's very cold, Lady Reznik."

"*Cece*."

"It would be inappropriate for me to be so informal."

She rolled her eyes and looked back at the sky.

"Will you go inside now?"

She let out a belabored groan. "I suppose, but only for you, Rain."

He bristled at the nickname as she stood, brushing snow from her pants. She helped him up and grabbed her bow and quiver. She turned to make the trek back to the castle.

A hunter in scarlet—Savero rebel regalia—darted out from behind a tree to her right. He swiped at her with his sword. Rainer's heart jumped into his throat as she threw her bow up to block the blow. She spun away, brandishing an arrow from her quiver as a makeshift weapon.

Rainer was frozen in fear and confusion, scanning the tree line for any other attackers.

The man swiped at her and she blocked again, slashing his arm with the arrow.

She fought well. She was fast, practiced, smart. She knew how to use her speed to make up for the disadvantage of her size. Her moves were taunting until she slipped in the snow and the man caught her across the stomach.

Pain lanced through Rainer as she crumpled in the snow. Prince Xander darted out of the tree line to Rainer's right and drove his blade through the man's chest and the guard collapsed into the snow.

Panic raced through Rainer's blood as he knelt beside Cecilia. The prince stood over them, checking the woods for any other threat.

Rainer pressed his hands to her stomach. "Lady Reznik—"

"Will you at least call me Cecilia?" she asked.

"Cecilia."

She smiled weakly, wincing as he pressed his palms to her bloody shirt. "Finally. Don't fuss now. It's a flesh wound." She glanced over Rainer's shoulder. "Is all well, Xan?"

The prince nodded. "All quiet out there."

Of course. The prince had hunter's hearing. So why, then, had he waited to come to their aid until after the man had wounded Lady Reznik? Suspicion snaked through Rainer's chest.

Xander Savero did not seem like a power-hungry person. Rainer knew the type, having been raised by Raymond McKay. But the prince seemed content to blend in. Still, it was a bit too convenient that he'd appeared just in time to play hero against a rebel who wanted him on the throne.

Perhaps it was just an elaborate setup to convince Rainer to trust him. If so, it had failed.

Blood seeped from the ragged cut in Cecilia's stomach, turning the snow beneath her pink.

"You need to take me to the healer," she said.

Rainer stared at her. "You can't do it yourself?"

Vincent said she was an incredibly powerful witch. She should have made easy work of the wound.

She held up her wrist, which bore a silver bracelet that looked more manacle than jewelry. "It's an Unsummoner bracelet."

"Why?"

Her lips parted, then closed, and she cleared her throat. "I sleep-walk." As if that explained everything. Her eyes fluttered closed and she winced.

Rainer hooked an arm around her shoulders and one under her knees and scooped her out of the snow, casting one last suspicious glance at Xander. The prince trailed behind Rainer as he carried Cecilia back to the castle and into the healer's lounge.

Magdalena greeted them. "Guardian McKay, it's good to see you on your feet again. Who do you have there?"

Cecilia turned her head and smiled at the woman weakly. "Hi Mags."

Magdalena tutted and nodded to a cot. Rainer laid Cecilia on the bed. He stood to leave, but Cecilia grabbed his hand.

"Stay with me," she pleaded.

When he saw her eyes, he realized for the first time that she was shaking from fear and not the cold. Her terror chilled his blood as if it were his own. This much empathy wasn't healthy. But for some reason, he could not seem to block it.

He sat down next to her, allowing her to hold his hand. But when the healer lifted her tunic, he stood abruptly and excused himself, leaving a frowning Xander to sit with her.

It was just her stomach, but it wasn't appropriate for the king's guard to see so much of the future queen.

She belongs to Vincent. The thought chafed. Her independence seemed larger than life—it felt more like she belonged to herself.

He rounded the corner, heading toward the training rooms to blow off some steam before bed, but instead came face to face with Grant and King Vincent.

Grant's assessing eyes burned into him, as if he could read that Rainer had seen more of the future queen than he should have.

Rainer bowed. "Your Grace."

"I hear you were successful in getting my betrothed to stop maiming my guards and come inside. You really seem to have a way with her," Vincent said.

Rainer fought off a smile. "If I have a way with her, Your Majesty, I'd hate to see what it looks like for someone who doesn't."

King Vincent chuckled. "She is a complicated woman indeed."

"I think she just needs a bit more time to adjust," Rainer said. Right away he knew it was the wrong thing to say.

Vincent's face grew serious and Grant's eyebrows shot up.

"Rainer, I, of all people, understand how charming my Cecilia can be, but do not let her trick you into thinking she's not an exceptionally strong woman," the king said. "She needs to be met with an equally strong partner. If you coddle her, she will continue to act out."

Anxiety buzzed in Rainer's chest. His fingers itched for something to carve to burn away the stress. He was grateful Vincent had reminded him that carving quieted his mind. He supposed Cecilia was right when she said his body might remember things even if his mind didn't, because he'd been whittling away at a new carving and it was starting to resemble the finished star flowers he'd found in his nightstand.

He wondered if the king would punish Cecilia for acting out and hurting so many guards. Rainer couldn't afford to care. She'd hurt people and stirred up trouble when the court desperately needed stability.

Still, something about the suddenness of her little rebellion struck Rainer as odd. If she was a good enough shot to maim the guards in spots that would hurt and disarm them, but not seriously wound them, she could have hit them as soon as they'd made it a few feet from the courtyard walls. Instead, she'd let them get closer. Almost as if she was trying to draw them away. It didn't make sense.

Rainer rubbed a hand over his face. His lack of memory had made him suspicious of everyone and that kind of paranoia would be just as dangerous as being relaxed around her. "I take full responsibility for her behavior today—"

"Why would you do that?" Vincent asked, patting him on the shoulder. "You weren't assigned to watch her at the time, though I think perhaps you should be going forward since she didn't use you for her target practice."

Rainer was certain that was a bad idea. He was too easily swayed by her, eternally on his heels.

Vincent's face softened and he squeezed Rainer's shoulder. "You're too hard on yourself. Don't worry so much. I have big plans for you."

That should have felt comforting, but Rainer only felt a surge of anxiety that he'd somehow fall short of such expectations.

10

RAINER

Two days later, Rainer knocked on Lady Reznik's bedroom door. He hadn't seen her since she was injured, so he was immensely relieved when she opened the door, looking completely done up. Her hair was twisted back into a neat updo and woven through with a golden headband spotted with little white star flowers. She wore a black woolen dress with gold buttons that fastened all the way up to her neck. Though she was far less pale than she had been after her injury, the inky black of the dress was a bit too harsh against her fair skin.

"You've been summoned by the king, Lady Reznik—"

"Cece," she interrupted, her brow pinched.

It was a bad idea to be so familiar, but she didn't seem the type to let it go. "*Cecilia*. If you aren't up for it, I can tell the king you're still tired from the attack the other day and need to rest."

She held up a hand. "Nonsense. I'm good as new. Let's go see what he needs."

"You'll need a cloak."

She darted across the room, ducked into the closet, and reappeared a moment later in a dark green cloak.

Rainer led her down through the castle. The cobblestone courtyard had been cleared of snow, but ice formed between the cracks. It crunched under their boots. Rainer glanced at Cecilia out of the corner of his eye. Though her dress was made of heavy wool and her cloak lined with fur, she was already shivering against the cold.

She caught him looking. "Admiring the scenery?"

Rainer's cheeks heated as he searched for an excuse. "Just wondering how long it will take for that big pile of snow to melt." He nodded to the far side of the courtyard.

She cocked her head to the side and kept walking.

They cut down the path to the field behind the stables. An unforgiving wind whipped across the castle grounds, stealing Rainer's breath for a moment.

Cecilia shivered beside him, pulling her cloak tighter around her body and tucking her gloved hands within its folds. Her footsteps became quicker and her shoulders hiked higher as they moved closer to the pen where she'd helped the wild horse days before.

Vincent stood by the fence, speaking with the stable master. Xander leaned against the fence beside the king, his eyes narrowing on Rainer. Behind him, the same wild mare from days before was trotting in the pen as if she'd been fully trained. Cecilia drew up short, her cheeks growing pink, her eyes full of fire.

"Dearest, I'm so glad you could be here to see this," Vincent started.

Cecilia dipped into the shallowest curtsey Rainer had ever seen. He wasn't even sure it could qualify as a curtsey.

"It's such a pleasure to give an animal the attention it needs to be properly broken," Vincent continued. "I've seen to her training myself, you know."

Seeing the wild horse trotting circles in the smaller pen, a rider atop her back, filled Rainer with sadness he couldn't explain.

To Rainer, Vincent said, "You see, my fiancée thought that she needed more space to run." He gestured to the horse. "But you and I know that Tempest just needed some discipline. No one wants to be the bad guy, but I'll do it because it's my job as king. I need to know what's best for everyone even when they don't."

He turned, guiding Rainer away from Cecilia and offering a conspiratorial smile. "As my advisor, I need you to know the same. I need to trust that you can be firm with Cecilia. She's been floundering since the rebellion. She's frightened and wild, like a wounded animal. She's quite angry with me because I let her get hurt, and she's right. It's my responsibility as king to keep everyone safe, and while I was saving my people, she was harmed. I take full responsibility for that. I need you to get her back on track. Can you do that?"

Rainer nodded solemnly. It was a relief that the king understood that she was struggling. It wasn't that Vincent didn't see her fear; it was that he believed in a firmer approach. The knowledge settled Rainer's unease.

Cecilia climbed up on the fence and Vincent turned his attention to her. Her gaze was fixed on the horse as if her will alone could make the beast wild. Tempest stopped and turned, charging toward where Cecilia stood at the fence before rearing up and tossing the man from her back.

Cecilia turned back to the king, challenge in her eyes. "It looks like not every beast is so easily broken."

The king's nostrils flared. "Lucky I have the fortitude to keep trying." Vincent smiled indulgently at her. "I'm glad you're here for this, Cecilia. I know you're fond of your new guard, and how badly we could all use some good news." His smile grew wider as he turned his attention on Rainer. "Rainer, I am so grateful for your commitment to your service with me, and especially for protecting my dearest Cecilia during that dreadful attack on the castle. Now that things are settling down, I would like to reward you for your loyalty and commitment. I'm very excited to share that I think it's time for you to have the kind of love and recognition you deserve. I have chosen a wife for you."

Cecilia gasped. The blood drained from her face. She opened her mouth to speak but nothing came out. Her shock matched Rainer's. He'd done nothing to deserve such a thing, but it rankled that the king wouldn't ask him to choose for himself. Then again, a politically advantageous marriage would help his standing with the king and maybe it would stop everyone from looking at him like he was damaged.

Rainer chose his words carefully. "I thought that was a longer-term plan."

"If you want to be my top advisor, you need to look stable and settled here. Nothing will do that better than a good wife. Lady Eloise Spellman would be a wonderful choice for you. Her family is incredibly wealthy and loyal to me. They own some of the best lands in Argaria. She's a stunning woman. But Grant has made his intentions known. If you're not interested, I can't justify denying him, and it will put him in a more advantageous position to remain my top advisor."

For some reason, Rainer wanted to rebel against the idea—everything the king said was enticing, yet the offer felt more like a curse than a blessing. But he was not about to let Grant sweep this opportunity out from under him when he was so close to winning Vincent's trust.

"Your Grace, surely a choice like this should be up to Guardian McKay," Prince Xander said. He had been so silent during the exchange, Rainer had forgotten he was there.

Vincent sighed. "Quiet, Xander. Don't fill his head with your romantic notions of marrying for love. Honestly, you, of all people should be supportive, having had a recent political marriage yourself. I'm bestowing a great honor. Don't you agree, Rainer?"

Rainer nodded emphatically. "Of course, Your Grace. I apologize for my reaction. I'm just surprised. I hardly know Eloise."

Vincent chuckled. "Don't worry, you'll have a chance to get to know her. You'll make a handsome couple and she'll give you many beautiful children."

Cecilia made a choked sound. The king gave her a cutting look and she quieted herself. She looked down at her feet as her tears dripped into the dirt.

Rainer wanted to see her eyes, certain he'd be able to ascertain some unspoken sign that she was okay and just grieving the recent loss of her fiancé. The king said something, but Rainer couldn't tear his eyes away from Lady Reznik. Her shoulders curled in. He seemed to feel her deep grief as if it was his own.

"If you agree, we can begin by having the two of you spend some time together this afternoon," Vincent continued. "As long as you're both agreeable, there is no reason why we can't have you married by the end of the month."

"So soon?" Xander interrupted. "Surely Lady Spellman would like to have a say, and she probably has family who would need to make arrangements to attend." The prince's gaze met Rainer's. He looked furious, though Rainer didn't understand why.

"Alliances are more important now than ever if I'm to hold the throne. Lady Spellman's family holds great wealth and sway with the nobles. It would be a favor to me, Rainer, but you've seen the woman. You wouldn't exactly be suffering. She's stunning and very agreeable."

"Then why don't *you* marry her?" Xander asked.

Vincent smirked at him. "Because I'm already betrothed, of course."

Rainer cleared his throat. "I'll do whatever I must to secure your crown, Your Majesty."

The king clapped him on the shoulder. "That's my boy."

Cecilia turned and stormed away from them. Little white star-shaped flowers blossomed from the cracks in the ground where her tears had landed.

"Her tears make flowers," Rainer said, meeting the king's eyes.

Vincent's gaze trailed after his fiancée. "She's an incredibly *talented* woman, yes."

For some reason the innuendo in the words enraged Rainer. He wanted to remember so badly why he felt that way. Xander looked equally furious. Rainer strained for any hint of a memory, but his mind remained stubbornly blank.

"I need to go check on my lovely fiancée, but I'll arrange for Eloise to meet you this afternoon for tea," Vincent said, patting Rainer on the shoulder.

Panic clenched in his chest. It was all happening so soon. He needed to go back to his room to calm down.

The king turned to leave. Xander lingered.

"Why was she so upset?" Rainer asked. "Please, if you know something I've forgotten, please tell me, Your Grace."

The prince shook his head. "For the love of the gods, stop using my title, McKay. It's weird. Just call me Xander. And please stop asking. I can't tell you, even if I want to."

"Please." Rainer couldn't keep the desperation out of his voice.

"Why do you care?" Xander snapped.

Rainer didn't understand his fury. He couldn't find the words.

Xander's mouth formed a grim line. "I wish I could tell you, but the healers have forbidden us from doing so." His speech was stiff, devoid of affect—as if he'd rehearsed and repeated someone else's words.

"I want to remember," Rainer persisted.

"If you wanted to, you would." Xander's face fell. "Cece has been through a lot recently. She was hurt. She has been forced to give up a lot and it's unfair because she puts everyone else first."

Rainer felt an irrational surge of jealousy that the prince knew her so well. The pressure in his chest was almost unbearable.

"I think I need to go to her," he said.

Xander shook his head. "That's not the best idea. The king is a very possessive man. He might not take that in the best way, and it likely wouldn't be you that paid the price for it."

Rainer's eyes went wide. "He'd hurt her?"

"I've spoken out of turn. I have to go," Xander said, turning to dash back into the castle.

A sinking feeling settled in Rainer's stomach. He didn't truly believe that Vincent would hurt her, but he wanted to find Cecilia to ensure that she was all right.

That conviction floated away as he made his way back to the castle. Vincent held the keys to Rainer's whole future. In Olney, Rainer was constantly under his father's thumb, but here he could make his own way and finally prove himself not only as a great warrior but also as the king's right-hand man. In Olney, his birth father's legacy was a constant shadow looming over him, but here in

Argaria that pressure felt far away and he could more clearly prove his value.

He walked into the castle, relieved to be out of the wind. He was not sure how he knew where she would be, but his feet had a mind of their own. They carried him down the hallways to a sitting room with the door cracked open. He heard her before he saw her and pressed himself against the wall by the door to her rooms.

"This was not part of the deal! You cannot do this!" Cecilia said, her voice shrill.

Vincent's impatient voice cut through her sniffling. "You're being hysterical. This is exactly the deal we made."

A sob rang through the silence. "This is not what I meant!"

Rainer could feel her agony and desperation even though he couldn't see her. He fought the irrational desire to burst into the room and comfort this woman he hardly knew from an argument he didn't understand.

"You should have learned already to be more specific in the deals that you make," Vincent said. "But I don't think that's what's bothering you. You're worried that someone else can provide the things you can't."

The room grew unbearably silent.

A memory stirred, but when Rainer tried to grasp it, it slipped through his fingers like a dream after waking. He cursed his broken mind. He tried again. The memory was fuzzy at first, but it sharpened after a moment.

A girl, perhaps six years old, stood in front of a roaring crowd in a fancy dress. The hem was caked in mud. Then the memory cut, leaving him with a headache like someone had rang a bell inside his skull.

Rainer leaned his head against the cool stone wall and tried to focus on the conversation in the bedroom.

"Accept this or I'll consider this defaulting on our deal," Vincent said.

What deal had they made? Rainer's head throbbed; he was so confused.

"Fuck you." Cecilia's voice was a whisper but the hurt in it sliced through Rainer.

A loud crack split the air and it took Rainer a moment to realize the king had slapped her.

"Watch your tongue and fall in line, Cecilia. Fight me all you want behind closed doors—you know how I like to fight. But do not take this recklessness outside these doors anymore."

Rainer took a step toward the door. He stopped and clenched his fists. Throwing away his chance to prove himself because of a lovers' spat between the king and his fiancée would be foolish. He certainly didn't approve of a man raising a hand to a woman, but Vincent was the king and he could make Rainer's entire future. He couldn't risk it when he was so close to redeeming himself for failing his witch.

Vincent wasn't just offering Rainer a chance to redeem himself. He was offering him a chance at the glory he had always dreamed of.

Rainer ducked around the corner just as the king left the room. Rainer waited until Vincent's footsteps faded before he walked down the hall and into the room.

Cecilia sat on a chair by the window, her face buried in her hands. Sunlight streamed through the large windows, highlighting dust motes that swirled and shimmered around her.

"My lady?" Rainer said softly. "I wanted to make sure you were all right."

Her head snapped up to look at him. Her left cheek was bright red. It was dark enough it looked like it might bruise.

Anger burned through Rainer, but he said nothing. Instead, he stared at her, waiting for her to speak about the violence—to give him an entry point. But she just wiped away her tears and smiled as if nothing was wrong.

Maybe she thought he hadn't overheard. It wasn't his place to force her to talk about it, and what could he even say? *I'm sorry I didn't stop a man from putting his hands on you when I know better.* The shame made Rainer sick, but he knew it would be worth it to bide his time.

She stared at him as if searching his face for something hidden.

"Can you see me to the healer's suite?" she asked, her voice emotionless as she wiped away her tears.

Rainer nodded. She wove her arm through his, and he led her down the corridor.

Cecilia was uncommonly quiet as they walked, and he longed to break the silence, but his tongue stayed twisted and tangled with words that felt trite.

When she got to the healer's suite, she turned to meet his gaze. "I'll just go back to my room after this to rest. I wouldn't want you to miss your tea with Lady Spellman," she said in a way that suggested she very much would like him to miss it.

Cecilia closed the door in his face without waiting for his response.

11

RAINER

Lady Spellman poured tea with the same meticulousness Rainer brought to his swordsmanship routine. He had not realized that so much went into the perfect cup of tea. He felt like a brute for normally gulping his down as soon as it finished steeping.

Rainer studied her, willing himself to stop picking at his raw cuticles—to stop fidgeting altogether. As far as he could remember, he had never courted someone, and that made him more nervous. He had no recollection of his interests, which meant he had no idea what to talk about.

Lady Spellman looked gorgeous. Her dark curls were pinned up, several tendrils skimming her elegant neck. Her elaborate, dark purple dress accentuated her figure and made her breasts impossible to ignore.

She caught him staring and smiled.

Rainer quickly looked at the teacup she held out to him, his cheeks heating. "Sorry."

"I hardly need you to apologize for giving me a good look, especially if we're going to be spending time together."

"I didn't mean to stare, Lady Spellman."

"*Eloise*," she said. "Let's not be so formal. I'm fine with you staring, as long as I can stare back."

Rainer was surprised by her forwardness. "Do you want to get married?"

"I was hoping for better when it came to a proposal," Eloise said.

Rainer choked on his tea. "I didn't mean—"

Her face brightened. "I'm just teasing. Yes, I want to get married. I've waited a long time to find the right partner. I thought perhaps it would never happen."

Rainer frowned. "But why? You're so beautiful and kind and, clearly, very thoughtful."

Eloise smiled. "I'm sure you know that I'm at the whims of the men in my life. My father and older brothers. We're very wealthy and although there have been several interested suitors, so far they've only been interested in my wealth."

Rainer shook his head. "I have no interest in your fortune. I have family money."

Eloise sipped her tea. "I understand your father made his fortune in the garment trade."

Rainer nodded. "Yes, he's hoping to retire soon and sell the family business."

Although Olney was a kingdom away, Raymond McKay's disapproval was a constant voice in Rainer's head. He looked at Eloise and wondered what she would say if she knew who his real father was. Would she be impressed? Or would she, like Rainer, only see the ways he was falling short of Zelden Novaris's legacy?

Rainer had the distinct impression that he used to be better at this—like the ghost of charisma still inhabited his body but wouldn't fully settle in. He could vaguely remember charming women but had no sense of how to do it now.

He picked at his nails, wishing for his blade and the half-carved star flower he'd left on his nightstand. He could only vaguely call up disjointed, frayed memories of learning from a carpenter, yet somehow, when he picked up the carving and blade, his hands seemed to miraculously know what to do. The relief was instant because the scrape of metal on wood dulled the anxious thoughts in his head to a dull hum.

Eloise looked at him expectantly. He'd let the silence go on for too long.

"I'm much more interested in getting to know you," he said.

"Well, I'm an open book. What do you want to know?"

Rainer's teacup clattered in his shaky hands as he set it too hard on the table. He was making a mess of this. "How do you picture your life? What do you want out of it?"

Eloise's eyebrows shot up.

"Is that the wrong kind of question?" He rubbed a hand over the back of his neck. "Gods, I hope you'll forgive me, but I'm afraid I don't have much experience with courtship."

"Your nervousness is charming," she said. "I'm just surprised you want to know about my desires. Men usually prefer to talk about their vision for the future than to hear mine."

Rainer shrugged. "Would you prefer that?"

Eloise shook her head. "I always enjoyed dressing up and going to court parties, but I find that it gets tedious with age. I've been doing it for so long that I don't mind playing the game, but I'd like to have something real—away from court. I'd like to have a family of my own and a husband who comes home and actually wants to share his burdens with me. I want partnership. It would be nice to have someone who sees me as an equal at home, even if not in the rest of the world. Obviously, I'd also like to have a connection with the person so that we genuinely enjoy each other's company."

Rainer liked the picture she painted. He could imagine himself coming back after a long day to a quiet home with her. He'd been so focused on achieving, he hadn't really thought about what came after or what reward he wanted beyond the recognition of a job well done. He could have a life and home, a place where he was always wanted and valuable.

Deep down he'd always wanted to be a father, his heart clenching each time he imagined looking into bright green eyes like his own and having the chance to prove he could be more compassionate, encouraging, and loving than Raymond McKay. Rainer would never treat his children like currency to be traded for social status. He'd shield them from court life and let them be whomever they wanted to be.

"Rainer?"

Eloise's voice startled him from his revelry. He shook his head. "Apologies, I was imagining the life you described."

"And you found it compelling?" Her voice carried a note of apprehension.

Rainer nodded. "I think I hadn't given myself much time to consider anything beyond my ambition, but a life without more than my work would feel empty."

Eloise's face lit up. She was truly striking, her beauty seemingly supernatural in its symmetry—as if someone had taken a collection of lovely features and fixed them just so.

Rainer knew he'd been with quite a few women, but he felt suddenly out of his depth.

She ran her fingers over her collarbone. He tracked the movement as her finger trailed down her chest, then sipped his tea, his mouth suddenly parched.

"I'm sure you hadn't anticipated getting married so soon, but I think we'd be a good pair and I certainly suspect we'd enjoy ourselves behind closed doors," she said with a smirk.

Rainer sputtered into his tea.

"You disagree?" she challenged.

Rainer shook his head. "No, I—you're obviously very lovely—"

She leaned closer, her gaze fixed on his lips. She smelled faintly sweet—like vanilla and honey. He liked that—that she smelled like things you could find in the kitchen. It made him think of baking. Though he couldn't remember how he'd learned his way around a kitchen, he could call up a lemon cake recipe and several pasta dishes from memory.

"I suppose there's only one way to find out," he said.

He didn't allow a moment of hesitation. He cupped her cheek and pressed his lips to hers.

It was clearly not her first kiss, but Rainer wasn't one to judge a lady for experience. The power shifted between them quickly. She climbed into his lap as she deepened the kiss. She tasted sweet and astringent, like tea and honey biscuits. It was so inappropriate, but it was a relief that she had let her guard down.

It felt good to have her soft body pressed against him. He pulled her closer, tangling his fingers in her hair as she whimpered. He'd had no intimate touch at all since his accident and he'd almost forgotten the pleasure of a woman's warmth.

Her hands came to the button at the top of his tunic and all at once, he regained his wits. He pulled away.

Panting, he met Eloise's eye. "Seems you were right."

She grinned. "Such a gentleman to stop me. You could have more if you want."

Her eyes lit with lust, and he was half-tempted to do just that.

But good sense won out. They were in a sitting room, and although the door was closed, someone could walk by the windows outside or come in through the unlocked door without notice. Lord Spellman had given them a surprising amount of freedom considering he'd left them with no chaperone, but the man was conniving enough that it might have been intentional.

Rainer scrubbed a hand over his face. He lifted Eloise off of him, setting her back in her chair. He was so confused. He wanted affection, but kissing her felt a strange mix of pleasant and wrong.

"I wouldn't ask a lady of your stature to risk her reputation."

Eloise's face fell. "Is this because you're not certain?"

"We've already gone further than we should have, and you've certainly made your point," he replied.

Eloise nodded. "Such a gentleman. If you change your mind or have a stroke of ungentlemanly notions, I hope you'll find me."

Rainer's jaw dropped.

A knock on the door startled them and her father appeared in the doorway. He had a pinched, disappointed look on his face.

"Eloise, you have to run along. We have other suitors vying for your time and attentions," Edward Spellman said, narrowing his eyes at Rainer. "Unless Guardian McKay has something he'd like to say."

Rainer opened his mouth and closed it, unsure why he couldn't just commit to what the king had asked. He planned to, but everything was happening too quickly. He wanted to make such a critical decision with a clear head.

Eloise gave him a flirtatious smile as she joined her father.

"Eloise, would you join me for a walk in the gardens tomorrow?" Rainer asked.

Her grin widened. "I would love to."

"Perfect, I'll meet you here after lunch."

She nodded and took her father's arm, leaving Rainer alone in the sitting room with his thoughts.

Eloise certainly wasn't subtle, but Rainer liked a woman who went after what she wanted. He'd prefer someone assertive over a wilting flower. Still, he felt like something wasn't clicking into place.

He couldn't start a life with someone when he wasn't even sure who he was. What if he became someone else when his memories returned and Eloise didn't like that person?

If his memory loss was permanent, then this seemed just as good a place to start as any, but something tugged in the back of his mind. Kissing Eloise had felt wonderful—warm and soft and soothing—but there was also a hint of wrongness, like he was trying to wield an unbalanced blade. He was uncertain if it was simply that he shouldn't have been kissing a woman he wasn't promised to, or that his body was expecting someone else. He stood and left the room.

He couldn't remember being with anyone before the attack, though he couldn't remember *anything* in the days leading up to his visit to Argaria. He could remember glimpses of things—speaking to Xander at a party, as well as conversations with Xander's traitor spymaster, Evan Farlan, the very man who had led the rebellion. Rainer had flashes of Xander's wedding to Jessamin and walking into a room where wisteria grew from pots as vibrantly as it grew in the wild. In that memory, a woman stood with her back to him and no matter how many times he tried to focus or how urgent the memory felt, he could never hold it long enough to get a good look at her.

He tore down the hallway toward the training room but stopped short when Xander ducked in the side door of the castle, brushing snow from his dark hair. He looked startled. Rainer's gaze narrowed on the box in his hands tied in twine.

"Sweet tooth?" Rainer asked.

Xander shrugged. "Jess is still getting used to life here and I ran out for sticky buns from my favorite bakery."

His demeanor had shifted too quickly. Rainer was certain he was hiding something.

"Can I see?"

Xander's hand tensed on the box for a moment before he nodded. "Of course."

Rainer pulled the twine before tipping back the box's lid. The scent of warm butter and sugar hit him as he looked down into a box that was indeed full of sticky buns.

Xander followed his gaze and let out a breath. "Want one, McKay?"

Rainer frowned and shook his head. "I'm on my way to training."

Xander rolled his eyes. "Of course. Perfect little soldier. How did your date with your future wife go?"

Rainer swallowed hard. "Eloise is a lovely woman."

"Quite opportunistic as well. But I suppose you and I have always had similar taste," Xander mused.

There was a challenge in his eyes that Rainer did not understand, and he didn't like his tone. Eloise was only doing what any woman in her position would and she seemed to be genuinely interested in Rainer.

"Am I permitted to carry on in my family castle or will I receive a pat down as well?" Xander taunted. "I'm sorry to disappoint, but if that's the case, I'd prefer a female guard."

Rainer rolled his eyes and stepped away. He retreated down the hallway to the training room. The prince was hiding something, that much was clear, and it was possible that Vincent had given him an assignment of which Rainer was unaware, but ever since the day Cecilia had been wounded, he hadn't trusted the prince.

Vincent seemed to doubt Xander, but the prince had resigned his power with ease and, if Rainer wasn't mistaken, relief. In the few memories he had from before, Xander had seemed anxious and apprehensive—even contemptuous—about ruling. Now he seemed more in his element skulking around the castle, and apparently sneaking out for pastries for his new wife.

Rainer shook his head. The more he tried to pull at the strings of his old life, the more unraveled he felt. He yanked off his tunic and wrapped his knuckles when movement outside the window caught his eye.

A young boy in plain, dirty clothes swung a practice sword. His form was sloppy but it was clear he was following a hunter training protocol. Rainer recognized it from watching the Argarian army warm up. He'd watched them working out for a month before he'd been released from his room in the castle.

The boy paused, smacking his head and chiding himself as he started over. Rainer was reminded of himself as a boy and he couldn't help but smile.

He cracked the door open. "Hey!"

The boy jumped, his wide eyes settling on Rainer. "Sorry, my lord. I swear I was going to put the practice sword back. I just wanted to try it out," he said softly, the tips of his ears growing red.

"That sword's too big and heavy for you. You need to start with something lighter."

The boy frowned. He couldn't have been older than seven.

"I can hold it just fine," he said, jutting out his chin.

Rainer grinned. "Sure, you can now, but after fifty repetitions your arm will be ready to fall off." He shook his head. "A sword should be an extension of your body. You need a blade you can hold onto. There are only two reasons a warrior lays down his sword: when he's dead, or when he's lost the will to fight."

The boy's eyes bulged. Rainer remembered the first time he'd heard an instructor say those words. He'd probably looked equally startled. But now he could only ever imagine laying down his blade in death—perhaps because that was the only way he could match his father's legacy. Rainer was certain he'd meet his end before he ever lost his will to to the one thing he excelled at. Quitting any earlier felt like succumbing to the poison Raymond McKay had spewed at him for years.

Rainer jerked his head to the side. "Come on in here and let's get you properly outfitted."

The boy hesitated, his eyes darting around the yard.

"What's your name?"

The boy looked up at Rainer sheepishly. "Michael. My mother works in the kitchen and she told me to stay out of trouble."

"Well, I won't tell if you don't tell and I hardly think training to become a warrior is trouble."

The boy grinned as he darted inside. He followed Rainer to the rack of weapons, his eyes wide as saucers as he took in the many different types and sizes of practice swords. Rainer picked one out and handed it to him.

"Try that one. Hold it out in front of you."

Michael held the sword out.

"Perfect," Rainer said.

He picked up his own wooden practice sword and walked to the middle of the room, Michael on his heels. He led the boy through his morning warm-up routine step by step. The kid was a fast learner. Though he was young, he quickly memorized the steps so that he could work on making them flow together seamlessly.

Rainer led him through the sequence several more times until it was like second nature. Then, he stood back and watched Michael, calling out corrections to his form.

When he was finished, the boy grinned up at him. "When do I get to fight?"

Rainer remembered that feeling well—the eagerness to prove yourself. The actual fighting was so woefully different. He'd quickly come to loathe the violence he'd been eager for.

"Hopefully not for a very long time, if ever," Rainer replied.

The boy frowned and dragged his toe across the floor. "Yeah, Ma says we might have to leave soon. She says the castle isn't as safe as it once was."

Rainer's stomach dropped. "Were you here for the attack?"

The boy nodded, his expression tightening with fear. "We hid in the pantry, but that's why I want to learn. Next time I want to be sure I can protect my mother."

Rainer swallowed hard. The boy was a kindred spirit, and Rainer remembered well the feeling of wanting to protect his mother. Raymond McKay's abuse had never turned physical, but his sharp words did their damage, and Rainer had done what he could to shield his mother.

"All right, I'll see you back here same time tomorrow. If anyone gives you a hard time, you tell them that Guardian McKay said that it was okay."

Michael grinned and nodded before darting out of the room.

It wasn't the workout Rainer had been counting on, but he felt relieved. Since waking, he'd been restless. Helping someone else recover in their own way made him feel calmer than he had in days. Strangely, it was the caretaking that left him feeling more at peace than his best training session.

He walked back to his room and bathed, then climbed into bed, listening to the wind rattle the windows of his bedroom.

Rainer stared at the shadows dancing across the ceiling. He should have felt settled after his interaction with Eloise. She was smart and kind and beautiful—everything he'd hoped for in a wife.

Still, he tossed and turned until sleep finally took him.

———

Orange sunlight streamed through large glass windows, painting shadows on the bedsheets. Waves crashed somewhere nearby. The salty scent of the sea blew in on a warm breeze.

Rainer's fingers threaded through Cecilia's, pinning her hands to the bed above her head. Her pale green dress was unbuttoned, giving a tantalizing glimpse of her cleavage. He dipped down to draw a line of kisses over the curve of her breasts and she whimpered.

Her legs were wrapped around his hips, her skirt bunched around her waist. The softness of the skin of her inner thighs against him was driving him out of his mind as he thrust into her. Neither of them was completely undressed—too desperate for each other to be bothered.

She felt divine, tight and hot, and so wet for him as she lifted her hips to meet each thrust. She panted in his ear, "Rain."

He pulled back and paused, meeting her gaze. Her cheeks were flushed with exertion and her blue eyes sparkled as she smiled up at him.

"Say it," he whispered.

"I'm just for you, Rain," she said.

He moved faster, more frenzied. Wanting to make the words true. Wanting to prove to himself that she was all his.

She writhed beneath him, struggling to meet his rhythm, her breathing quickening until her fingernails dug into his hands and her back arched and she gasped. She clenched around him as she climaxed.

Rainer never wanted it to end. He bit his cheek to keep from going over the edge with her because she felt fucking perfect.

He wasn't ready to be done with her yet. He needed more of her. He wanted to make her react that way over and over.

When her body finally relaxed, she looked up at him with a huge smile on her face. She opened her mouth to speak—

———

Rainer woke to a loud whistle of wind through the windows. For a moment he was disoriented. The dream had been warm and bright, but the room was cold and dark. The fire burned low in the hearth. His head was pounding. Sweat soaked his skin and sheets.

He groaned.

A dream. It was just a dream—a shockingly realistic one.

He could practically taste the salt of her skin, smell her lemon-lavender scent, feel the heat of her body. He was painfully hard.

He tried to think of something, anything else, but he could only think of Cecilia—how good she'd felt beneath him, how perfectly in sync they were.

"The king's fiancée," he reminded himself.

Still, the logic did nothing to spoil the desire he felt.

He took himself in his hand roughly, stroking his cock. The bite of pain reminded him what wanting someone like her could do to him.

He tried to ignore that it wasn't the sex that had turned him on as much as the warmth that pulsed in his chest when she smiled at him, the possessiveness of the words "just for you." The way she trusted him. The way he felt connected and loved and whole. He came fast and hard, bright stars bursting behind his eyelids as he collapsed back to the bed, panting.

Rainer was fucked. Both literally and figuratively.

It's a one-time thing—to get her out of my head. It will never happen again.

But as quickly as the thought arose, Rainer knew it was a lie.

12

EVAN

E van stood off to the side of the square, watching as a town crier made his way to an elevated platform.

The long hair Cato had given Evan tickled the back of his neck and got in his way all the time, but the disguise had proven effective. Vincent's patrol hadn't given him a second glance.

Sylvie threaded her arm through his elbow and leaned in close. "Do you think people think you're my husband or my father?"

Even with her hair red, her eyes green, and her face slightly rounder, Evan knew Sylvie's smile. He missed her usual face, but he was happy she was disguised and safe.

"Hear, hear!" the town crier shouted. "The false king has infiltrated our castle. His men have terrorized the castle staff, and imprisoned our true king."

Gasps rippled through the crowd.

"Vincent Savero, who was long ago banished by King Damian, has managed to get his grip on the king's council by making promises to Lord Spellman and several traitors. They attacked King Xander in a vulnerable moment. He lives but is under duress in the castle, trying to keep even worse violence from breaking out. He has fought hard for the peace we have now, and he's doing his best to keep it."

More murmuring went through the crowd, but they were clearly riveted.

"Where is Queen Jessamin?" someone shouted.

"The new queen is at his side. She will help make this right, but she's still spreading her goodwill through town," the crier shouted.

"It's true, we received food and new clothing at Aurelia's Orphanage," a woman on the edge of the square shouted.

Murmurs of approval for Jessamin rose from the crowd and Evan blew out a sigh of relief. Sylvie squeezed his arm a little tighter.

"Vincent has claimed that he's the true king," the town crier continued, "but we know that isn't true. His own father once tried to usurp King Damian and the good king was gracious enough to banish him and his son to the eastern wastes instead of killing them, and this is the thanks he gets for it—a coup."

Evan sighed. This part was a little false history. Xander had shared exactly what had happened to Vincent and his father. The more Evan learned about Vincent's history and his fierce desire to survive, the more terrified Evan felt of his violence. For years, everything that surrounded Vincent had been veiled in mystery. In the past, when he'd asked Damian about the threat, the late king had insisted it was nothing. Evan knew better than to have taken him at face value, but he had. Still, they couldn't win by playing fair. Not when Vincent had no problem playing dirty.

The crier puffed out his chest. "Vincent's sudden tax hikes have crippled our city. Families are being forced from homes they built with their own hands, and too many of us are struggling just to feed our children. King Xander has tried to give power back to the people, and that means we are responsible for the future of our home. We must do something before Vincent Savero destroys our kingdom."

"How can we help King Xander?" a man shouted.

"What can we possibly do? We don't know how to fight," a second voice yelled.

"We can march on the castle and protest!" the crier declared. "We can spread the word and let King Xander know that the people of Argaria won't be ruled with lies and force. We can spread the word that Vincent poses a danger to us all. It's common practice for his men to pillage the farms and burn everything they can't take with them as they go. They hurt the women, too. You've seen the refugees flooding the city."

An uproar tore through the crowd, which seemed half-horrified, half-disbelieving.

"It's true. My sister's family was in Gladens, in the east, and his men rolled through and left no one alive but women who ended up wishing they were dead," a woman called, her eyes wet with tears as two women next to her squeezed her shoulders.

Sylvie shifted beside Evan. He reached for her hand, but she stepped away, walking over to the woman who'd just spoken up. Evan resisted the urge to follow her and make a scene. She was safely disguised, but ever since she'd been stabbed and nearly died, he felt panic when she was out of reach.

He watched as she spoke to the women in a low voice. Then the woman who'd spoken pulled Sylvie into a tight hug.

A moment later, Sylvie came back to stand beside him.

"What was that about?" Evan asked.

"I think I have an idea for when we know who to trust. There are a lot of women who have a score to settle, and I think we might have a surprising army of our own that we never considered. Especially with the castle losing so much staff. There will be vacancies."

The crowd grew more uproarious as one of Vincent's guards chased the crier from the stage. The crowd shouted in outrage and obstructed the guard from catching the crier as he fled. The shouting grew louder, the people coming together to demand an end to the cruel reign of the false king. The mob marched up the street toward Castle Savero's walls.

Part one of their plan was sliding into place, and Evan felt the first dangerous seeds of hope take root.

———

The air in the brothel was so thick with perfume, cheap wine, and sweat that Evan cringed as they stepped into the foyer. Though the lighting was dim enough to hide the dinginess of the space, Sylvie looked woefully out of place, even in her disguise.

Made You Look was a higher-end establishment, not as sleazy as Veli's Shadow Lounge several blocks away, where witches tended to clients with more extreme proclivities for fire. But even the nicest brothel in town didn't come close to paralleling the luxury in which Sylvie had grown up.

The madame perked up from her place behind the counter. She leaned forward and her scarlet dress gapped, offering a scandalous view of her ample cleavage.

Sylvie squeezed Evan's arm. She was practically vibrating with delight.

"Good evening. I'm Madame Jamie. Welcome to Made You Look, the finest brothel in Ardenis with the loveliest and most talented whores in the city. We can cater to any preference." Madame Jamie tossed her sleek, dark hair over her shoulder. "What can I interest you in?"

"Company," Evan said.

Madame Jamie looked from Evan to Sylvie. "You'll be bringing your—"

Sylvie coughed to cover a laugh. The changes to Evan's appearance made him appear older, and Sylvie was delighted that wherever they went people couldn't help but notice the clear age gap between them.

"My friend," Evan said. "We have an appointment, with Belle."

Madame Jamie smiled knowingly. "Of course. You and your lovely friend. That will cost extra. A bit more tit for a bit more tat, if you know what I mean."

Evan nodded, handing her a few coins, wondering how exactly Sylvie had convinced him it was a good idea to bring her to a brothel. She was calmer now that she had something to focus on. She had been restless without that sense of purpose, but with it she bordered on reckless, treating every outing like an adventure.

"Upstairs, third room on the right for you," Madame Jamie said, shooing them toward the narrow stairwell. She patted Sylvie on the backside as she walked by. "Good girl."

Once they were upstairs, Evan led Sylvie into their room.

She looked around the space, her gaze sliding from the four-poster bed to the dingy, sheer curtains.

"Oh, Ev, you take me to the nicest places," Sylvie teased.

A shadow stepped out from behind a dressing screen. "If the clients who come here are looking at those hideous curtains, I haven't done my job," Mika said. "Just be glad for the low light so you can't see how truly disgusting it is." She pulled Evan into a hug.

"You work here?" Sylvie asked, her eyes bulging.

Mika shrugged. "Only when I want to. Turns out Vincent is even more of a whoremonger than his uncle was, so we spend plenty of time at the castle entertaining his soldiers. Sadly, since his little rebellion, he's not allowed me close to him."

"He has in the past?" Sylvie said, her eyes wide.

Fury descended on Mika's face. "If I'd known—gods, I would have ripped his throat out with my bare hands. I expected I would know him when I saw him."

Guilt formed a lump in Evan's throat. He'd failed her like he'd failed the rest of his friends.

Evan knew Mika's history. She'd lost the woman she loved to one of Vincent's attacks two years ago. That was when she'd first contacted him and told him she'd work for him if he ever needed a female spy. He'd been all too happy to have someone with such a gift for making men part with their secrets without them realizing. Men of the court thought whores were stupid. The more they had to drink, the more their lips loosened. Mika had long been one of Evan's most productive and talented spies. He had immense respect for her and all she sacrificed in the name of vengeance.

"I'm sorry," Evan said. "I should have paid more attention to the money trail."

Mika held up a hand. "We all missed things. It's not your fault."

"How is Cece?" Sylvie asked. "What happened to her?"

Mika sighed and shook her head. "I won't tell her story for her. You'll have to ask her yourself. Physically she's fine, but mentally she's struggling. Rainer seems determined not to remember her."

Sylvie's face fell. She looked pale in the firelight. Evan placed a hand on her shoulder, and she leaned into his touch. He couldn't imagine what was going through her mind. He still felt so angry every time he imagined Sylvie in that same scenario. It might have been years ago, and she seemed as at peace with it as she could be, but it was still fresh for Evan. Nothing had made him feel such pure and helpless hatred and rage. Since the attack on Castle Savero, Sylvie had tossed and turned, dark circles blooming beneath her eyes even in their disguise.

"So, what's the latest?" Evan asked.

"Vincent is irate with the lack of staff around the castle since your most recent smuggling mission," Mika said. "He's started having guards take over some tasks, which is making the remaining staff understandably tense and, of course, it makes our sneaking around harder."

Evan sighed heavily. That was a recipe for disaster. Even though those who remained had agreed to stay in place to help Xander, Evan didn't want them taking any unnecessary risks. He and Xander had taken pains to get to know every last servant in the months before the attack to ascertain who they could trust and who might be a spy.

Mika sat in front of the vanity, brushing her hair as she spoke. "He's more suspicious of people coming and going now. Faces the guards are familiar with, like mine, are easy. But even with your modifications," she said, waving a hand at their magically altered faces, "I'm not sure how easy it would be for you to infiltrate without some sort of obvious reason for being there."

Evan nodded. It was too risky for them all to be inside again until they knew exactly who their allies were.

"Both of your council members are working on figuring out where allegiances lie, but it's difficult considering Vincent's brutality," Mika continued. "No one is terribly willing to fess up to wanting something else."

"It makes sense," Sylvie said. "It's not like the two of them can ask who wants things to go back."

"And even if they could, how could we trust that after our past mistakes?" Evan added.

Mika nodded, studying Sylvie's face. "Don't lose heart, Lady Brett. The rest of us have been doing this a long time now and we are figuring it out, just at a slower pace than we'd like. But a longer game is safer right now with so many moving parts. Vincent had Jess write to her mother asking for a meeting to discuss more favorable trade terms."

Evan ran a hand over his face. The real Jessamin was going to be furious about that. She was already upset enough that they had sent Isla into the castle in her stead.

"That said, he seems none the wiser about the decoy." Mika hesitated. "He also wrote to Marcos under the guise of negotiating a more solid truce and better trade terms as well."

Evan frowned. "What do you think he actually wants?"

Mika met his gaze. "To kill Marcos and take the two kingdoms for himself."

"Lovely," Sylvie huffed.

"The last letter from Marcos said that he's worried sick about all of us and his people, but he's wise enough not to take the bait of a private meeting," Evan said. "He offered us any assistance we might want, including a faux delegation or warriors made to look like diplomats for a surprise attack, but he defers to us on the best tactic."

Mika nodded. "Until we know exactly who we can trust and until Rainer remembers what's going on, we could just as easily end up in the same place with more lives lost. It's best to stay the course for now. We will keep the lines of communication open."

"We can't just do nothing," Sylvie said, her voice tight.

Evan rubbed the back of his neck. "Trust me, I know how you feel, but when we do this, it will be for good. We have to be sure we have cut all the poison out of this kingdom so that we can finally have some peace."

Sylvie sighed, leaning back in her chair and staring into the fire.

Evan knew she was frustrated, but they were doing their best. They were fortunate to have the alliance with Olney and the convenience of Grimon delivering messages faster than any messenger service.

"What about Aldrena?" Evan asked.

Mika laughed. "They haven't even responded, though it's unclear if they're worried it's a trap after the fake Princess Clare tried to kill Xander. They could be concerned about retaliation, or they might be doing what they've done the past twenty years and keeping to themselves." Her eyes darted from Sylvie to Evan.

"What is it?" Evan asked.

"The boy who leaks me Vincent's correspondence told me that his letter to Marcos also requested the presence of Raven Whitewind," Mika whispered.

"The seer?" Sylvie asked, eyes wide. "What would he want with the seer?"

Mika shrugged. "Unfortunately, that was not included with the letter."

Dread washed over Evan. It was possible Vincent wanted to stay a step ahead of any adversaries or was searching for the best time to kill Xander, but he doubted an ancient witch like Raven Whitewind would subject herself to the whims of a king who usurped his throne.

"I'm sure we have nothing to worry about," Evan said. "As we learned last year, even when Cato thought he'd kidnapped her, she made sure he knew that he very much did not. She is a seer; she's likely already aware that he wants to see her. And as she told Cato, she doesn't go anywhere she doesn't want to."

Mika looked lost in thought, like she was trying to solve some complicated puzzle. "Still, it seems an interesting choice for a man who is dying to hold on to his power. I can't help but wonder if granting him access to her is wise."

Evan frowned. "I am certain that she won't offer anything that isn't in Olney's best interest and, now that there's an alliance, Argaria's as well."

Sylvie looked less certain.

Evan turned back to Mika. "You'll let me know if she arrives?"

Mika nodded. Voices rose in the hallway and the three of them stilled to listen. A door opened and closed. Footsteps faded down the fall.

"You should head out," Mika whispered. "I have another client coming soon."

Evan helped Sylvie to her feet, and they made their way to the door.

"Wait," Mika called. She crossed the room to them, quickly unbuttoning and then rebuttoning Evan's shirt wrong before mussing his hair. Then, she shook her fingers through Sylvie's hair until it was believably tousled and ran a thumb over her lips to smudge the berry stain Sylvie wore.

Evan liked seeing Sylvie like that—like he'd just had his way with her and kissed that sweet berry taste right off her mouth.

"Now you're perfect. Stay safe, you two. I'll be back here same time next week for more," Mika said loudly as she shooed them into the hall. She winked at Evan before turning back and leaving them in the dim hallway.

As they stepped out into the cold evening air, Sylvie smiled at him. "Thank you for bringing me with you. It feels good to be doing something instead of sitting around worrying." A giggle burst out of her. "I can't believe I'm thanking my fiancé for taking me to a brothel."

Evan laughed, pulling her closer. "Well, if you liked it, I'm sure Mika would be happy to have us back for real once this mess is dealt with."

Sylvie arched an eyebrow. "You think I want to share you?"

"How do you know I don't want to share you?"

Her face lit up. "Really? You'd like to watch us together?"

The question brought up a compelling mental image that Evan shook off, his eyes darting around as if the one moment of distraction would be enough to bait any waiting attacker.

"Don't be distracting when we're out in the open, Syl," he whispered.

She giggled as they wove through side streets and alleyways, taking a winding path back to the Temple of Aurelia when someone in a cloak burst from a side street.

Evan had his dagger out in a second, corralling Sylvie behind him. But when the man tipped his hood back, Evan was met with familiar gray eyes.

"For fuck's sake. What are you doing here, Cato?" Evan asked, trying to keep his gaze from the temple across the street where their entourage was hiding.

They weren't supposed to meet him until the next morning to reinforce their disguises with his limited godly magic. They'd been so careful to keep those meetings far from their base, but now Cato was mere feet from their hideout.

The trickster grinned. "I told you I wanted to help, but you insisted on playing spy thinking I didn't know where you were. I've known since the beginning, but I haven't given you up. I want a chance to help."

Evan ran a hand through his hair. "Go away."

Cato held up his hands. "Listen, I know you think you don't need me right now, but I suspect when you get back to the temple you're going to want my help."

Evan froze. "What did you do?"

Sylvie took off across the street and Evan followed. He was tense as they approached the large temple doors. Shrill voices inside had Evan drawing his dagger as they pressed the door open.

"You simply cannot, Jess. I will not allow it," Maren shouted, her eyes wild, her hands clasping Jessamin's shoulders.

Evan lowered his weapon but remained frozen outside the temple.

The queen's jaw was tense. "I am in charge, Maren. Not the other way around. I may be a queen outside her castle, but you still promised me your allegiance."

"Not when you're being irrational," Maren snapped.

Evan was unsure how to navigate a lovers' spat, but Sylvie brushed by him. Cato leaned against the doorframe, looking amused.

"What's going on?" Sylvie asked.

Maren turned to Sylvie. "Finally, someone rational. What's going on is that your queen wants to march her ass behind enemy lines to talk to her husband."

Jessamin threw her hands up. "You say it like it's so unreasonable. Like I'm being chaotic and irrational when I want to have a very important conversation with my new husband face to face. Every man deserves that."

"It is out of the question," Maren said fiercely. She met Evan's gaze, her eyes pleading. "Tell her it's crazy."

Evan sighed. "It is crazy, Jess. I promised Xander I would keep you safe and I cannot do it in there. There are too many unknown factors."

Jessamin paced the center aisle. "I have done everything you've all asked of me. I've sat and stewed in my rage and worry but I cannot continue to do so simply because I'm important. These are my people now too and I need to help. Beyond that, I need to talk to Xander face to face."

"If only there was a way to do that," Cato said smugly.

"Why?"

Evan was afraid of the answer. There was only one thing he could imagine would make a pragmatic strategist like Jessamin so insistent —the same thing that would make her equally unsafe no matter where she was. The same thing that would put additional pressure on their timeline to take back the kingdom. It would also explain why Cato was so certain that they'd need his help.

Jessamin met Evan's gaze. "Because I'm pregnant."

13

XANDER

Xander stepped out of the passageway and into his room, relieved to see Isla sleeping soundly in his bed. He tucked the wooden box he'd retrieved under his arm and slid the bookcase back into place, checking that she hadn't woken. Her breathing remained steady and even.

He crossed the bedroom as quietly as possible. Isla had heightened hearing, and he needed privacy for what he had to do.

The place above the hearth looked empty now without Cece's mother's painting. It had been a comfort in his weakest moment, but it didn't belong with him anymore.

He hoped Cece wasn't offended by him returning something that had once been so precious to him, but it occurred to him when he was lying awake beside Isla that making room for someone else in his life required some changes.

He'd started with the painting, but now it was time to let go of the letters he'd hoarded. He flipped open the lid and stared down at the loopy handwriting. It felt strange to burn the very thing that had kept him going in the most desolate year of his life, but there was a rightness in it, as if in letting go of this desperate story, he was rewriting what was possible for him moving forward. He could not be who he was before the joy and loss of the last two years, but he could rebuild himself into something new.

He imagined this like a spell, and burning each message could sever the last ties between him and Cece. In his heart, he knew he didn't need them anymore. It was as she'd said when they said their final goodbye: what was his was no one else's. What was hers was hers alone. Surrendering the physical symbols of their love didn't make it less real and made it no less valuable to him. His love for her was slowly changing form, and he felt at peace with it.

One by one, he fed the letters to the fire, releasing a little more of their history as the paper curled and burned.

"A little late for a ritual."

Xander jumped, turning to face Isla. Her voice was husky from sleep. She propped herself on an elbow, her eyes fixed to the last letter in his hand.

"Better late than never in this case, I think," he said, his voice hoarse.

Isla swung her legs off the bed and crossed the room to meet him. She moved with such effortless confidence. Her burgundy silk night-dress hugged her body, leaving little to the imagination. Not that Xander needed help imagining.

She was free with her body—profoundly unselfconscious. Even having just woken up, her face creased from the sheets and her hair still wrapped in silk, she was completely unbothered by him looking at her.

Isla's confidence made him feel out of his element. Cece had been so innocent and fiery when they first met, it was easy to bait her. It was always easy to read her because they were so alike.

But Isla was so self-possessed. She did not need a single thing from Xander, and he was married to her cousin. Even if it was an unconventional marriage, it felt wrong to pine after Jessamin's decoy.

Isla sat on the floor beside him, glancing from the ashes of his letter in the fire to the last one in his hand. "Why did you keep them so long?"

Xander looked at the letter. It was the one he'd read the most, the edges mangled, the creases nearly torn through from folding and unfolding it so many times. He knew every line of it and every place where the ink was smudged with tears. He could even imagine the expression on Cece's face when she had written it.

He swallowed. A sudden knot formed in his chest. "In the beginning I just wanted to feel like I meant something—like I still had some part of the person I loved so much. But then—" He blew out a breath, trying to master the surge of love and grief in his chest. "Have you ever felt completely alone in the world and then you hear a story, or a poem, or some line from a play and you know that there was someone out there who understood that exact thing you are feeling in this very moment?"

The serious set of Isla's brow softened. "I have."

He held up the letter. "This one made me feel so understood. And when I read how much pain she was in, I didn't feel vindicated or satisfied. I felt relieved that I wasn't alone in the memory of what we had. Everyone was looking at me to have the answers for a kingdom of people, and there she was, a world away, feeling the same things, hurting the same way, and understanding what I was going through even though I never responded to any of her letters."

He leaned over to toss the letter in the fire, but Isla caught his hand. "Maybe you save just that one."

Xander held her gaze. "I don't think so. For a long time, I needed it—" He relinquished the letter to the flames before he could second-guess. "But I don't now."

Isla took his hand in both of hers and they watched the letter burn.

"My brother, Davide, once told me to name the fear and it would lose its hold on me. I used to be afraid I'd never have someone who understood me like that again." He met her eyes. "I'm not afraid of that anymore."

She watched as he pulled the chain out of his shirt. His gold wedding band clinked against the links, shining in the light of the fire.

He'd worn it there since he returned from Olney. He couldn't stand to see the reminder so clearly on his finger day after day, so he'd taken to wearing it on the chain around his neck, where he'd only notice it when it shifted against the scar on his chest.

"Will you burn that too?" she asked.

He shook his head. "I don't think this fire is enough to melt it down. Feels wrong to even try until I know what to do with it."

Isla smiled softly. "You'll forge it into something new."

He nodded. "As it forged me."

Her entire demeanor was softer than he'd ever seen it. He wondered if she'd let him kiss her, but thought better of it.

"We should get some sleep. We have a long day tomorrow," he said.

He stood and helped her to her feet, walking her back to the bed. He tucked his ring into the drawer in his nightstand beside the box that held his mother's sapphire ring, which Cece had recently returned. He stared at it for a moment before shutting the drawer.

As he and Isla climbed into bed and laid down, facing each other, the wind howled, rattling the balcony doors.

"Storm blowing in," he whispered.

Isla looked past him toward the balcony doors. "What does it sound like?"

He grinned. "So, you did hear the storm song I hummed for you the night we met. You acted so unmoved."

She rolled her eyes. "Yes, I liked it. Must I pay for it now?"

"Of course not, darling. I'll hum you a storm song anytime you ask."

He hummed along with the rhythm of the storm until his eyes grew heavy and she slid her hand into his.

She didn't let go until morning.

———

Xander was done sitting on his heels, waiting for Vincent to do his worst. He'd already proven that he had no problem punishing Cece for getting out of line when he'd had a hunter in fake rebel regalia attack her days earlier. That stunt was clearly meant to give Rainer a chance to play hero and send Cece the message to stay in line.

She'd fully recovered but Xander had a plan to try to expedite the process before one of them was hurt again. They needed to be more discreet moving forward.

The afternoon was unseasonably warm, which meant that most of his councilmen were out and about in the gardens. If Xander was going to figure out which side his remaining nobles were on, he'd need to test each of them.

Isla's gloved hand rested on his arm, and he was trying to act natural. She studied him in a way that made him inconveniently nervous. In the light of day, he felt uncomfortable with the vulnerability of the night before. He wanted her to think he was charming and clever, so much so that he couldn't remember how to hold his arm properly. It was as if he forgot how to do the most common movements around her.

"Are you well?" she asked, gripping his arm tighter.

"Yes, I'm fine."

He continued to watch her out of the corner of his eye as they walked. She wore a deep burgundy cloak that parted to show off a gown of the same color with an intricately beaded bodice. He stared at it, not just because of the heart-shaped neckline that gave a tantalizing view of her full breasts, but because he was certain it contained some sort of weaponry, like all of her dresses seemed to, and he wanted to know where.

Her hair was braided around her head, a ruby tiara tucked atop it. The jewels glistened in the sunlight, bringing out the warmer tones in her skin. He knew better than to underestimate any woman, but looking at her in that dress, she didn't look like someone who could have you on your back with a blade to your throat in a second.

Perhaps that was the appeal.

"If you're done with your gawking, I think I see someone up ahead." Isla's gaze narrowed on the path before them. "Is that him?"

Xander nodded, unbothered that she'd caught him admiring her. "Corin! Lord Archer!"

Corin Archer turned and walked toward them, a younger man beside him who looked too much like him not to be his son. "Your Graces. It's good to see you out making the best of the fair weather." His eyes flashed over the castle. "Especially with it being so stuffy inside."

His tone sounded like he sincerely didn't like Vincent, but there was only one way to know for sure.

"Happy to hear you say so," Xander said. "Jessamin and I were just saying how respite can be found for those who prefer more open discourse and radical positions at Liar's Kiss. I'm sure you've heard of the most famous brothel in Argaria."

Corin's eyes widened, as did his son's, the not-so-subtle meaning of Xander's message dawning on him. "Respite, Your Grace?"

"Indeed," Xander said. "In fact, if you wanted to see for yourself, or if you know anyone who is in need of respite after recent events, that would be a good place to find it at dusk on Thursdays."

Corin's mouth twitched. "That's good to hear, Your Grace. I think perhaps some were worried that you were as comfortable as you let on with your new occupation."

Xander almost laughed. The man was so expert at double talk, no doubt from his time managing his shipping business, that Xander prayed he was on their side and not Vincent's.

"Well, we won't take up any more of your time," Corin said. "My son and I have a meeting with the king."

Xander patted him on the shoulder. "Be agreeable and safe, Lord Archer."

The men bowed and left.

"One down, two to go, darling," Xander said.

Isla pursed her lips. He'd noticed she did that when she was trying not to smile at his flirtation.

They repeated the exercise when they found a second council member, Felix Bidell, by the garden sitting room, telling him a similar tale. Xander named the gambling hall and fighting club, Death and Fortune, as the location.

Finally, they found Vaughn Salvatore, who droned on about the future of the grain trade in Argaria for a good fifteen minutes before Xander had a chance to feed him the same tale of a burgeoning rebellion, only substituting the matchmaker's studio, Heart of Chaos, for the meeting place.

In three days, he would have their friends on the outside keep an eye on each location at dusk to see if any of the men sold them out. It wasn't a foolproof plan, but they might get lucky.

Xander led Isla back into the castle and up to their rooms.

"That man's incessant chatter should be considered treason," Isla said, rubbing her temples as they cut down the hallway.

"A queen's job is to listen to all her subjects and give equal weight to their complaints, darling."

She rolled her eyes. "I suppose it's a good thing I'm not queen."

Xander felt a surprising pang of hurt at the words. He knew she meant it less about him than the tedious requirement of hearing out loyal subjects, but he couldn't help noticing the way she kept reinforcing the space between them.

"So you gave them three different locations and you'll wait to see which, if any, are raided?" Isla asked.

He nodded.

She gave him a strange look. "I'm not sure I like how easily you perform. It makes it impossible to tell what's real and what is illusion. All those clever words coming out of your mouth, and yet I can't tell which are you and which are the lies."

"The mark of a seasoned spy," Xander said.

She frowned. "And what will you do with such a skill when your spying days are over?"

"I assume I'll use this clever mouth for more satisfying endeavors."

"Are you ever serious?" Isla huffed, rounding the corner toward his suite.

Xander sighed, shaking his head. "I am serious all the time, but if you joke when you're worried, it makes the burden feel lighter. I've been through too much these past few years not to find the humor in the little things."

She gave him a sidelong glance. "You know, in Novum we have a god for this?"

"For jokes?" Xander asked, arching a brow.

"No, for espionage. The god of lies. He helps those who request his aid lie smoothly, though you seem to have a silver tongue, so perhaps you do not need his assistance."

"I promise lying is the least interesting thing my tongue can do," Xander said.

Isla fought a smile.

"Tell me more about your gods. Are they like ours?"

She shook her head. "They're less disruptive, that's for certain. We more see their influence in the world—the god of stories speaking through the royal storytellers' mouths. The goddess of the stars and the god of the moon, lovers who spend the whole year reaching out to share light, until the summer when their love for each other creates rainbow auroras in the sky."

"You sound quite devout."

Isla smiled. "I suppose we all have to worship something."

"Ah, but that which I'm most devout to can only be worshipped in private," Xander said.

"You're a relentless flirt, but I'm not interested." The dark flush that crept up from the neck and her dilated pupils suggested otherwise.

"Then why do you look so turned on?" Xander taunted. "You know, I'd be happy to show you what I mean. Do you think you'd like being worshipped by a king?"

The look in her eyes suggested she'd like that very much, but she cocked her head to the side in challenge and glanced down the empty castle corridor. They had paused around the corner from the hallway that led to his room, and though it was usually bustling with guards this time of the day, it was strangely empty.

"I imagine it would be much the same as any overconfident man who's *worshipped* me," Isla said. "It would only serve as a very sloppy and very quick prologue to a mediocre main event."

Xander loved the challenge she presented. "Darling, I assure you that's not what I mean. I have no problem spending hours on my knees simply because I enjoy giving praise. As far as I'm concerned, that is the main event."

Isla swallowed hard. Her gaze dropped to his mouth, and she shook her head. A slight smile passed over her lips. "Gods, you are nothing but trouble."

"I think you mean fun."

She shook her head. "No—fun I can handle. You are trouble."

"How do you figure?" Xander asked.

"Because you act like a cad, but you're really sweet underneath."

"I assure you, Isla. I have nothing but the worst of intentions."

She laughed. "You don't. And that is exactly why I will be keeping my distance. Plus, you're still hung up on your ex-wife and you're married to my cousin."

He crossed his arms. "I hardly think it's my fault that I fall for exceptional women."

Isla rolled her eyes. "Of course not. You're helpless to your whims. Poor, tortured Storm Prince."

"It's Storm King now, actually," he said with a grin.

Isla shook her head. "You are incorrigible."

Xander stepped closer, stroking her cheek. "I suspect that you like that."

Before he could stop himself, he'd pinned her to the stone wall. He waited for a breath to see if her instinct was to pull away or if she felt the static pulse between them too.

He kissed her. Her whole body arched into him, as eager for the contact as he was. She moaned into his mouth.

Desire tore through him like wildfire. He hadn't felt that sense of new reckless wanting in a long time. It felt like a lifetime ago, and yet the moment he touched Isla it came rushing back.

His love for Cece had been fierce and consuming, leaving room for nothing else. He'd expected that would be the case forever, that he'd live a lifetime on the memory of what they'd had and simply go back to his old ways for physical needs. He'd never struggled to find creative and willing bed partners in Olney or Argaria. Now, as

Isla opened up to him, he felt strangely unprepared for something more.

He'd been afraid he'd never find that feeling again, that he'd forever be bored, unable to work backwards to casual relationships after Cece. His first love had nearly killed him in every sense of the word. Now a new possibility opened before him.

It frightened him that he could see more with Isla. Because he didn't just want to take her to bed. He wanted to know her—to peek inside her mind and understand how to make her laugh, how to surprise and delight her, how to make her want to do the same with him. He didn't just want to go through the motions and perform a version of himself. Isla's intensity could match his.

She tugged him closer, her leg hooked over his hip, her fingers digging into his ass, encouraging him to grind against her. Even the way she kissed was confident and demanding.

He slid a hand up her side, cupping her breast, and she whimpered against his lips. It had been so long since he'd felt the driving need to connect with someone that way, to look into her eyes and see her fall apart in his hands.

He drew a blazing line of kisses down her neck, and she dropped her head back against the wall, a hand coming to the back of his head, her fingernails digging into his scalp. He ran a hand up the slit in her skirt, pulling back to meet her eyes.

She nodded and he slid his hand higher, brushing over the lace of her undergarments. Xander groaned along with her when he felt how wet she was.

"What are you doing to me, Isla?" he sighed, sliding the material to the side and brushing his fingers against her.

She moaned, arching into his hand, equally electrified by the touch, her eyes locked on his. He couldn't think about how fucked up it was that he was fingering his wife's decoy and that she was the first person who made him want to move on from a history of hurt. Perhaps he'd always been destined for complicated relationships because of his standing as a prince, but just once it seemed startlingly simple.

He liked Isla. She liked him. And, right now, it was just the two of them and no one else needed to know.

A new relationship didn't banish the ghosts of the old, it just took up residence in the same house. His heart might always be haunted, but it didn't mean he couldn't have love in his life.

"Please say you want more," Xander panted.

"More," she rasped, nodding eagerly.

He slid a finger inside her and she let out a sensual moan that Xander felt all the way to his toes. His cock strained against his pants. It couldn't be helped. But this was about Isla, the woman who was protecting her queen all while driving him out of his mind slowly.

He slid another finger inside her, brushing his thumb over her clit as she panted, dropping her face into the crook of his neck to stifle her moaning as she rode his fingers. He quickened his pace, feeling the first flutters of a climax in the urgent way she clung to him. Then her teeth dug into the place where his neck met his shoulder and she moaned, bearing down hard on his fingers as she quivered against him. It was so sexy. He slowed his movements as she twitched against him.

She leaned back against the wall, panting as he withdrew his fingers, lifted them to his lips, and sucked them clean. Her eyes lit with lust as they tracked the movement.

"Take me to bed," she panted.

Xander smirked, victorious. "As my queen commands."

She untangled herself from his arms, grabbed his hand, and tugged him down the hall. He couldn't wait to get her out of that dress and splayed out on the bed. He could only imagine how wild she'd be with his mouth on her. He glanced at her out of the corner of his eye as they rounded the corner to his room, her lips swollen from kissing, her hair coming loose from its updo. She was so meticulously put together all the time, it was nice to see her undone.

Making a mental plan for exactly what he was going to do, he burst into the bedroom only to find two people waiting for them.

Xander went rigid. He looked from the woman in front of him to the redhead beside her. "Jess?"

Isla went rigid next to him. Could Jessamin tell he'd just been making out with her cousin? That he had every intention of bringing Isla back to this very room and doing a whole lot more than that?

Jessamin grinned. "Hello, darling. I'd been waiting so long my disguise wore off." Her eyes passed over Isla's disheveled hair and Xander froze, waiting for her reaction.

A grin tugged at Jessamin's lips. "Could we speak alone, Xander?"

He nodded dumbly and Isla and Maren walked to the sitting room and closed the door behind them to give the illusion of privacy.

Xander cleared his throat, trying to calm his racing heart. Jessamin's gaze dropped to his pants, where his cock was still very obviously hard. The shock of seeing his wife should have been like being plunged into an ice bath, but Xander still felt so wound up. He was disappointed that the moment Isla had finally given him a glimpse of her, her cousin had shown up to ruin their fun. The timing couldn't have been worse.

"Having fun in my absence?"

Xander shrugged. "Yes, I was."

She smirked at the emphasis on the past tense.

"What are you doing here? I made Evan promise to keep you safe outside of this place."

She held up her hands, crossing the distance between them before taking his face in her hands and kissing his cheek. "I am glad to see you looking so well. Despite your correspondence, I have been worried sick."

Xander pulled her into a hug, relieved she wasn't furious at him. "Am I doomed to marry women who are too courageous for their own good?"

She tilted her chin up and laughed. "You married a warrior in a pretty dress, darling. You should have expected nothing less. Now sit, we must speak."

Xander sat in the chair and Jessamin stood before him, looking suddenly nervous.

"I could not bear to stay away longer, but once I explained the changed circumstances Evan was forced to agree with me. It would be bad if I was caught in a cell of rebels."

"Why? What changed circumstances?"

Jessamin smiled. "It seems we were successful on our wedding night attempt. It's very early, but I'm pregnant."

Xander felt breathless. His entire lineage had been almost eradicated and now, all at once, he was going to have a family again. Beyond that, he'd become so accustomed to the idea of not fathering his own children when he'd been with Cece that he'd put the idea out of his head altogether. He'd believed he could convince himself not to want it, even if deep down it was the one thing he'd always wanted.

He was going to be a father. Argarian tradition considered a wedding night baby to be a very good omen of more blessings to come, but it was hard to tell if he was seeing the sun on the horizon or was simply in the eye of a larger storm.

He'd always been the outsider in his family, and he wanted the opportunity to belong to something, to be the kind of parent who would accept his children's differences as unique and lovely parts of them instead of things they should be trained out of. He'd be more like his mother.

"Say something," Jessamin said, looking more uncertain of herself by the moment.

Xander jumped to his feet and swept her into a hug. "I'm at a loss for appropriate words, but please don't take that as anything other than my being overwhelmed with joy," he said, placing her back on her feet and tilting her chin up to meet her eyes. "How are you feeling? And why come back here now?"

Jessamin smiled. "I'm well. I was very tired and a bit nauseous, which is what tipped me off, but I'm otherwise fine. I came back because I can't stay in hiding out there. I'm much more likely to be noticed in Ardenis than I am here in the castle surrounded by Vincent's men. The common people know me now. Not to mention the fact that it would be much harder for me to have consistent oversight by a healer in town without being found out, and that could destroy everything our friends are working for out there."

Xander nodded, his head spinning. "But isn't Freya a healer? She could have helped you."

Jessamin shook her head. "Freya is fantastic in battle. Healing wounds with no scar, tending to poison, even. It's why she's one of my guards. But she has no experience dealing with pregnancy beyond her basic training. She could not do for me what Magdalena can."

Xander ran a hand over his face. He knew she was right, but there was so much at risk. "How did you even make it in here and disguise yourself?"

Jessamin frowned. "That's the part you're not going to like. Cato has been helping us disguise ourselves so we can cause havoc in town."

Xander dropped his head back and groaned. "You must be joking. Evan approved all of this?"

"Your trickster god can be very compelling."

Xander shuddered at the memory of just how compelling Cato could be. "But what's his angle? What does he have to gain?"

"I suspect he's bored, so perhaps just entertainment," Jessamin said.

"That's what I'm afraid of."

She shrugged. "Regardless, he's offered to fix my disguise daily when he does his castle walkthrough to enforce his bargain with you and Cecilia and the rest of the staff."

Xander nodded. He was afraid to believe it because he'd made enough mistakes when it came to Cato in the past. "Did you make a deal with him?"

Jessamin shook her head. "No deals. He offered."

Xander frowned, rubbing the bridge of his nose. "Okay, but you have to be so careful. You'll stay in my rooms, and we will have Magdalena come to you."

Jessamin grinned as he dropped to his knees and kissed her stomach.

"Jess, thank you. I didn't think—" His throat constricted, choking the words. "I thought I might never have a family of my own and it means a great deal to me that you were willing to do something untraditional."

She squeezed his hand. "It means a lot that you were willing to as well. I always wanted to be a mother. Motherhood is revered in Novum. My own mother will be delighted. She will be truly insufferable. Best we hold out telling her until this whole mess is figured out or she'll have the entire Novumi army on our shores in a week and I'm not sure that kind of force will keep the peace we're hoping for."

Joy and grief warred in his heart. The news was welcome but so overwhelming.

Jessamin ran her fingers through his hair. "You look a bit sad, darling."

Xander swallowed hard. He wasn't sure if it was stress, relief, or joy, but the words spilled out without his permission. "I think that I had a vision in my head of what my life was going to be and then I met Cece and it shifted so abruptly and I was on this new path, and I was so used to it. I hardly had time to settle in before it was ripped away. And now I have this new vision of my life and I should feel joyful. Instead, I'm terrified someone's going to rip it away again and there will be nothing I can do."

"Don't feel bad about that. Fear just means you still have something worth losing," Jessamin said. "It's about what you do with the fear."

Xander nodded. Like his brother Davide had said: *Name the fear and it loses its power.*

She ran her hands over her bodice. "Plus, if someone comes near me, I will gut them with my bare hands to protect this child."

Xander grinned. "I believe you.

Her eyes narrowed on him. "It's not just fear, is it?"

Xander shook his head. "The first thing I thought is that I wanted to tell Cece. I know she'll feel genuinely happy for us. I know that's true, but it doesn't mean that it won't hurt her. We've been through so much together. When I have good news, she's the first person I want to tell."

"Are you so sure that she can't take it? It seems to me she could use some good news too."

Xander sighed. "You're right. As always."

"The four best words a man can say to his wife," she said with a grin. "Now, would you like to tell me why my cousin looked so disheveled when you two walked in?"

Xander froze. "I don't know—"

Jessamin waved a hand. "Spare me. I'm not the least bit upset or surprised. You deserve some joy. I just want to know what I'm walking into."

"Isn't it weird?"

"I'm honestly surprised it took you two this long. I think she's had a crush on you from afar since we were children. Isla loved stories about the Storm Prince, so when we were invited to court for you to choose a wife, she was clearly torn between wanting me to win your heart so we could stay and hating that idea because it meant she couldn't win it herself," Jessamin said.

Xander stared at her. "I'm certain you're not supposed to be sharing this with me."

"I'm certain she never will if I don't give the necessary push. Isla is stubborn to her core. I want you to have what I have. I know you weren't ready before, and maybe you're still not now. First love is brutal. But I think you deserve to be someone's first choice."

The words sliced through him. She'd named the deepest longing in his heart so casually.

Jessamin took his hands in hers. "You've given me so much. Allowing me to be a partner and rule beside and be with Maren. It's okay to trust someone again, to let someone see you for real. I get the impression you didn't the first time around."

Xander swallowed hard around the swell of grief and longing in his chest.

"It would be okay if you stopped punishing yourself, Xander. You're a good man and you deserve love."

He looked away, focusing on the roaring fire so he'd have an excuse for the burning in his eyes. Jessamin came to stand beside him, threading her fingers through his and leaning her head on his shoulder. Sometimes love was holding someone's hand in the silence and waiting for the storm to pass.

14

RAINER

Ice-cold fear spread through Rainer's chest, ripping him from a heavy sleep. He sat up in bed, his stomach tied in knots.

For no reason he understood, he raced down the hall to Cecilia's room. There were no guards in the hallway. Vincent's hunters seemed to only be vigilant when the king was watching. Often, they left their posts in favor of playing cards in the stables or huddling in dark corners with whores.

Rainer didn't bother knocking; he threw the bedroom door open, somehow knowing he wouldn't find her inside. The sheets on her bed were a swirled mess, but there was no sign of her.

"For fuck's sake," he sighed.

The king's fiancée was going to be the death of Rainer.

He took off down the hall, checking unlocked closets and rooms. The longer he searched, the more fear crept up on him.

Rainer breathed deep, trying to summon an idea of anywhere else to look. He took off in the opposite direction. He finally found her in a dark hallway in a nearly abandoned wing of the castle. If Rainer remembered correctly, this was the wing that belonged to the former king and queen of Argaria. Xander had explained that Vincent hadn't wanted to use the former king's quarters because he was superstitious about sleeping in a room where a king had been killed.

Cecilia stood, staring down a long, dark hall at nothing in particular.

"Lady Reznik, you scared me to death. What are you doing out of bed?" he asked.

She didn't move—didn't even seem to hear him.

Rainer looked at her more closely. She wore only a red silk night-gown. Her feet were bare, and goosebumps covered her arms. It was incredibly inappropriate for him to see her in such a state of undress, but she didn't even seem to notice him.

Cecilia continued to stare. Rainer stepped up beside her, finally seeing her tear-stained face.

"Please," she whispered.

"Lady Reznik?"

She still didn't acknowledge him. He reached out to touch her arm. She flinched and drew away. She gasped and looked around wildly, backing away from him.

"No, please," she begged.

"Cecilia, it's just me—Guardian McKay," he said, trying to take her arm again.

She struggled against his grip and took a swing at him. He barely ducked in time to avoid getting punched in the face. Her eyes were blank—not a hint of recognition on her face.

She's sleepwalking. She'd told Rainer that was why she wore an Unsummoner bracelet—so that she wouldn't hurt anyone when she was lost in a nightmare. But he hadn't thought to ask how to help her wake up. He didn't even know if that was the right thing to do.

"Don't touch me! Please, please don't!" She kicked and scratched at him and started screaming. He tried to restrain her so she wouldn't hurt him or herself, but she flailed wildly.

"*Cece*, it's Rainer. It's okay. I've got you," he said.

She stopped struggling at once, as if the name broke the spell she was under. Her eyes cleared and she looked up at him. "Rain?"

His heart clenched. She looked so helpless and truly terrified.

"I'm going to let you go now, okay? I know you don't like to be touched, but I was afraid you were going to hurt yourself." He pressed a hand to her forehead. "Are you feverish?"

She looked around, trying to get her bearings. "No," she mumbled. "I just sleepwalk sometimes since—"

Rainer felt like an ass for assuming the worst. Vincent had mentioned it in passing that it was the reason she wore an Unsummoner bracelet. If she used her magic against someone while she was sleepwalking, she could easily kill them, and the king needed to protect both her and his people.

Rainer started to release Cecilia, but she clung to him. Her body shook violently. To his horror, she buried her face in his chest and started sobbing. He stood helplessly as she cried, not knowing if it was better or worse to hug her. She didn't like to be touched, but she was so distraught that not holding her felt cruel.

"Can I hug you?" he whispered.

"Yes," she mumbled.

He wrapped her in his arms, and she leaned heavily against him.

"All is well now," he whispered. "It was just a bad dream."

She just cried harder. Rainer cringed. He was so bad at this. Her tears filled him with intense panic.

"We should get you back to your room," he soothed. "You're shivering."

He started to pull away so he could give her his robe, but she clung to him desperately.

"Please, just a little bit longer," she whispered.

Rainer knew he shouldn't coddle her. Vincent had warned him not to, but it would have been cruel to lead her back to her room and leave her alone.

So, he held her. He tried to ignore the profound calm that came over him as Cecilia relaxed against his body. He tried not to notice how holding her was as much a comfort to him as it was to her—how her body seemed to fit with his, her head tucked perfectly against his chest. Her hands slid up the hem of his shirt, her cool fingers moving idly on his waist as she settled. It wasn't appropriate, but he let her do it because it felt nice, and it seemed to calm her more than anything else had.

Cecilia's sobbing quieted to sniffles, and she looked up at him. "I'm sorry. Did I hurt you?"

He shook his head. "I'm fine. You didn't know what you were doing. Let's get you back to your room."

He pulled off his robe and wrapped it around her. The hem dragged on the floor, but she pulled it tight around her.

"Why are you always so cold?" Rainer asked.

"Olney is much milder. I'm not used to winters this harsh," she said.

"Then why do you wear so many lighter dresses to court events?" Rainer asked.

"Because the king likes them, and the king gets what he wants... one way or another." The bitterness in her tone made Rainer uncomfortable. "When I'm alone in my room I usually wear a sweater, but I must have taken it off in my sleep."

Though Rainer could understand the importance of appearances, especially after the recent attack, he wondered why Vincent wasn't more concerned with her comfort. Rainer would be. Every time he took Eloise to walk in the gardens, he made certain she had a warm enough cloak and always paid close attention to be certain she wasn't getting too cold. It seemed that Cecilia resented putting appearance above comfort, but Rainer supposed that was the price of being queen.

When they got back to her room, Cecilia dug an oversized sweater out of her tangled sheets and pulled it over the nightgown. It was clearly not her size. The hem hit her mid-thigh. He wanted to ask whose it was. He'd never seen Vincent in anything but fine clothing and armor. But it was none of his business whom it belonged to.

She handed his robe back to him. He put it on and caught a hint of her lemon-lavender scent on the fabric. He didn't understand how she smelled so good all the time, or the way the smell of her drew up all the blank spaces in his memory.

"I'm okay now. I probably won't do it again," she said as she pulled the blankets around her and laid back in the bed. She didn't sound certain at all.

She grabbed a green ribbon from the nightstand, but instead of using it to tie up her hair, she tied it around her wrist, her lips moving silently, as if in prayer. Perhaps it was some sort of superstition that witches had to banish bad dreams.

"Why the ribbon?" he asked.

Cecilia met his gaze. "Sometimes you just want to know you're not alone when heading into battle."

She said it so casually, as if he should know exactly what she meant. And some twinge in his chest made him feel for a moment like he might. But the feeling was fleeting.

Cecilia shifted, and for the first time Rainer noticed a stack of pillows next to her, as if mimicking another body. For some reason, seeing her lying in the bed curled against a pile of pillows made him feel incredibly sad.

"Lady Reznik?"

"*Cece.*"

"Cece, what happened to you? Can you just tell me, please?" he asked.

Her eyes met his. She opened her mouth to speak, but nothing came out. Her brow furrowed and she sighed. "I wish I could."

Rainer tried to quell the frustration that surged. All he wanted was for one person to help him remember. The healers knew best, but they didn't know what it was like to have lost all the context in his life and be surrounded by people who could fill in the gaps.

"Do you dream about losing the man you love?" Rainer asked.

She shook her head. An uneasy understanding settled into him.

"You dream about what happened to you—during the rebellion." He couldn't bring himself to say the words—to think of her being hurt that way. "You don't feel safe still?"

She nodded, her eyes gleaming with unshed tears. "What a pair we make. You can't remember and I can't forget."

There was forced humor in her voice, but he saw a glimpse of the grief beneath. So often their goals seemed at odds, but now he saw that they were both just trying to heal.

"How should someone approach you if you sleepwalk like that again?" Rainer asked.

She looked like she was about to cry again. "I don't know. It used to work for someone to just guide me back to bed and then hold me there, but obviously, you don't want to do that."

Rainer was a little startled to find that was actually his exact impulse. The few moments he'd held her in the hall were the best he'd felt since waking up after his accident. It was best not to think too hard about that or how quickly he had slipped into calling her Cecilia not just aloud, but also in his mind.

"I know you said that you won't do it again, but why don't I just sleep in this chair in front of the door?" he suggested.

She sat up. "You'd do that?" Her eyes filled with tears again.

"Oh, please don't cry," he whispered. "I don't know what to do when you cry. It makes me feel panicked."

She laughed through her tears. "Sorry. I've just felt very—" She didn't finish, but somehow Rainer knew she was going to say "lonely."

Maybe that was why she spent so much time driving him crazy. She was isolated and eager for any interaction. He supposed being the future queen was a lonely experience. Vincent was busy all the time and Rainer had seen the way the ladies of the court treated her like an outsider—though she *was* one, it was unkind of them to make it so clear on a daily basis.

He didn't understand how Cecilia seemed to surprise him a little bit every day. Each time he thought he had her figured out, he learned something else that startled him.

"It would be very nice if you stayed, but I don't want to get you in trouble. You need your sleep, too," she said.

"I don't mind, and I don't sleep well anyway. I'll go back to my room before dawn." He moved a plush chair in front of her bedroom door and slunk into it to begin his vigil.

———

By his eighth loop around the winter market in downtown Ardenis, Rainer had memorized the four most convenient exit routes that had the quickest path back to the castle, as well as six less ideal options if things were especially dire.

With fewer people milling about and several of the stalls closed, it was easier to keep track of everyone. So far, the only excitement Rainer had encountered involved one runaway baby goat named Luther, who took to stealing apples from a neighboring farm stall.

Rainer reached the end of the row of stalls and nearly bumped into a priestess of the Temple of Aurelia, who was carrying an extraordinarily large box of sweet buns. She met his eye and winked. "A treat for the women in our outreach program."

Something about the explanation felt forced. Rainer didn't know what program she was talking about, but he'd confirm it with Vincent later.

Bells rang out in the market. Three chimes. Three o'clock.

Rainer had dropped Cecilia at Threaded Dressmaker's Shop two hours ago. What women did in a dress shop that took so much time was beyond him, but the seamstress, Mariah, had shooed him away. She pointed out the female hunters stationed at the entrance and claimed that a big, brooding guardian would scare off her clients.

He'd tried to stand down the street, but the seamstress's hunters ran him off, so he was forced to do laps of the market, passing by the shop's windows every fifteen minutes or so to ensure nothing was going wrong.

Ardenis was particularly agitated. When Rainer had escorted Cecilia down from her room that morning, Grant was waiting for them. A rebellious town crier had shown up at the market at first light, spreading rumors that Vincent wasn't the rightful king and stirring the people into a frenzy. People had gathered to protest for hours outside the castle walls, their number swelling in the morning light. Rainer had no doubt it was the work of the rebels that still hid somewhere in town.

He'd had to take Cecilia the long way around the back of the castle to avoid trouble. It made him uneasy that he was the only one guarding her. Maybe it was some kind of test from the king, but Rainer couldn't help the fear that crept in when he thought about her sobbing in his arms.

She'd been uncommonly quiet and disturbingly agreeable on the walk. He was fairly certain that she was embarrassed by her emotional scene the night before. He'd just pretended like it never happened. Now, as he walked through the market, trying to focus on the goods in the booths, he couldn't stop thinking about the way she'd clung to him—the way he'd liked feeling like a safe place for her to hide.

A stiff wind blew a scarf loose from the booth beside him. Rainer grabbed it and carried it back to the woman manning the tent.

"Thank you. These winds are brutal today," the woman said, her gaze settling on the emblem on his sweater. "Ah, you're an Olney guardian. We don't get many of those around here. Are you bound to a witch?"

Shame unspooled in Rainer's gut. He fought the urge to defend himself to this woman, but there was nothing to say. He could not even summon the face of the witch he'd failed.

"No," he said. "Not all guardians are bound to witches. Some just protect royalty."

The woman nodded earnestly, but Rainer could not bear to hold her gaze.

"You don't seem the type to be shopping at my booth," the woman said. She nodded to a stall at the end of the row with daggers and light leather armor. "Thought you'd be down there shopping at Warsword's Way with all the other warriors."

Rainer pulled off a glove and ran a hand over a teal sweater hanging from the rack in front of him. He could picture Cecilia in something like that. She was always shivering, and while Rainer hoped that the seamstress would make her some dresses more appropriate for the northern chill, he doubted she would go against the king's wishes. She pushed boundaries, certainly, but after hearing

Vincent and Cecilia the other day, she must know not to continue to push him.

Maybe if Rainer bought her the sweater, it would help him shake the tightness in his chest that hadn't relented since he found her sleepwalking.

"That's a lovely choice," the woman manning the stall said. "Is it for a lady friend?"

Rainer hesitated, then nodded. He knew the woman was asking if it was a courting gift, but Cecilia was a lady, and a friend of sorts.

"You have excellent taste. Fine local wool, very warm for a lady who's always chilled. I also have it in gray and red if that would complement her better," the woman said.

Rainer shook his head. "I think this will do. She has blue eyes."

The woman smiled at him as if she saw something he didn't. "That's a perfect color. She'll love it." She wrapped the sweater in paper and string and finished it off with a pale pink rose and a wink. "The pale pink is for courting."

Rainer's cheeks warmed as he handed her the payment and slipped the package under his arm.

He turned and crossed the square. Snow turned muddy underfoot, melting between the cobblestones. People rushed by with little regard for their surroundings, as if they hadn't all been under attack just weeks before. While it was good that they had short memories—or were at least resilient from years of living on the edge of war—it unnerved him how something that had broken his mind left no mark on everyone else's.

He turned down the seamstress's street yet again. Cecilia was waiting for him. The seamstress's hunters looked relieved to be rid of him.

Rainer almost scolded Cecilia for not waiting inside, but he stopped himself when he saw tears on her cheeks. Her eyes were closed, but her chin was tipped up toward the sky like the sun's rays might be enough to heal her.

Her quiet grief stole the air from his lungs. He stayed where he was, a few doors down, waiting for her to compose herself. Finally, she wiped her cheeks and blinked her eyes open before turning toward him.

"You're back," she said, forcing a smile.

For a moment he considered if it was better to ask her to talk about it or let it go. She hooked her hand through his arm and started to walk.

"How was it?" Rainer asked.

"As fun as getting poked and prodded for hours for a bunch of dresses you hate can be," she grunted.

"Why would you get dresses you hate?" Rainer asked.

"I didn't design them. They are to Vincent's taste, and we apparently disagree on everything when it comes to fashion," she grumbled.

"Well, if you behave yourself, perhaps you'll get a surprise that you like better than those stuffy dresses," Rainer said.

She paused and turned to look at him, noticing the package in his hands. Her face lit up, her eyes shining. "Rainer, did you buy me a present?"

He rolled his eyes. "Don't make a big deal about it. I was hoping it would be good motivation for you to head back to the castle without arguing."

She grinned broadly. "You're so handsome when you blush. I see it so rarely."

"Should I take it back?" Rainer asked, arching an eyebrow.

She slumped and started toward the castle. "Fine, be a fun-sucker. I was just excited about my present."

Rainer sighed, following her. "I wish you'd stop calling me that."

"I'll stop calling you that when you stop acting like such a fun-sucker."

He looked at the booth to their left, which advertised a variety of love potions and hexes.

"See something you need?" Cecilia teased. "Perhaps a spell for Lady Spellman."

"Hardly."

Cecilia pursed her lips. "I suppose you're right. She's not one to need convincing when it comes to you."

Rainer didn't like the way she spoke about Eloise, that hint of knowing in her voice—as if Cecilia knew more than he did about the woman he was courting.

Cecilia paused in front of the booth of love spells. "It's utter nonsense anyway. No one has the power to make someone love them. All magic requires an exchange, and what could possibly purchase something as valuable as love? It's a shame so many people waste their money, thinking that love spells are real."

"If I didn't know better, I might think you were trying to stall returning to the castle," Rainer said.

She grinned. "I promise that I only need one more stop."

True to her word, she only made him stop once so that she could buy a lemon cake, which she ate half of before looking at it wistfully and offering him the rest.

"You don't want it?" Rainer asked. "I thought they were your favorite."

She stared at him. "How did you know that?"

Rainer frowned. How *did* he know that? He couldn't remember her saying so. He must have heard it in passing. He shrugged, and she looked so disappointed that he felt guilty.

She held up her wrist, the one with the Unsummoner band. "When a witch is cut off from their magic, it ruins their appetite, and makes them tired. Being without magic makes us sick—like losing something vital."

Rainer frowned as he followed her. Why did she have to wear it all the time if it made her unwell? Couldn't she take it off during the day? He'd have to discuss it with Vincent during his daily briefing on Cecilia's well-being. Vincent had asked him to continue acting as her personal guard. He claimed none of the other hunters wanted to risk being maimed, but Rainer suspected it was a test of his loyalty—one Rainer was determined to pass. He'd failed Cecilia once by not getting to her until she'd been hurt. He wouldn't do it again.

"Did we know each other in Olney?" Rainer asked. If he'd

known her before coming here, it would make sense that he'd have some remnant of her likes and dislikes in some far corner of his memory.

Cecilia paused, clenched her jaw, and blew out a breath.

"You can't say, but I'm assuming we did," Rainer said. He wanted to ask where her guardian was. She was a witch from Olney, so she must have had a guardian. But he couldn't stand to ask another question and be met with her frustrated silence.

Once they were back in the safety of the castle, Rainer relaxed. He saw Cecilia to her room, where she said she'd open her present before taking a nap.

She stepped behind the changing screen. Rainer tried to look away—a better man would have—but the screen was backlit by the fireplace and as she took off her dress, the shadow of her figure showed through. Rainer's mouth went dry. His heart raced as she bent over to pull up her pants. It was a luxury to watch Cecilia without her teasing. She was petite, but the curve of her ass was slightly disproportionate to the smaller swell of her breasts, and the effect was mesmerizing. Lust bubbled up in his stomach. He couldn't look away.

Cecilia stepped out from behind the screen. She walked to the looking glass on the far side of the room and pulled her hair free from the neck of the sweater. She didn't just look good in it; she looked incredible, effortless, and sexy, especially with her hair loose down her back. For some reason, seeing her in casual attire undid him more than any of the lovely dresses she wore. The teal made her eyes stand out a vibrant blue, and when she smiled at him he felt his heart squeezing. It slunk off her shoulder, revealing creamy skin and three freckles. Rainer had the irrational urge to kiss that perfect constellation.

The sweater was an enormous mistake—bachelors did not buy gifts for unavailable women. It sent the wrong message. Vincent would be upset if he found out.

"This has to stay between us," Rainer said, glancing at her reflection in the glass.

She smirked. "Of course. It will stay between us. Unless you wish to remove it."

He crossed his arms. "I thought we'd moved on from that tactic of yours."

"It's a perfect fit, and so soft." She smiled and turned to face him. "Thank you, Rainer. It's beautiful."

He shrugged, but he could see in the mirror that he was blushing again. "It looks very nice on you. I'm sure Vincent will like it."

She froze. The reminder of the king was enough to throw cold water on both of them.

"Well," Rainer said abruptly. "I'll leave you to your rest, but I'll be back in an hour to wake you for lunch."

Cecilia nodded, frowning as he turned to leave.

He made his way down the hallway, scrubbing a hand over his face to focus himself. He was happy to have training with Michael to distract him from his idiotic behavior. The kid was getting better, but, more than that, he was eager to learn, attentive, and took mistakes in stride.

The hour flew by. Rainer didn't even realize it until he heard clapping from the corner of the room.

He turned and saw Cecilia grinning. She looked flushed and lovely in the teal sweater, her hair braided over one shoulder.

"Bravo, excellent work, young man. We'll make a warrior out of you yet," she said.

"My lady," Michael said, bowing.

"My lord," Cecilia said, dropping into a curtsey.

Michael's cheeks went bright red, and he looked down at the ground. Rainer knew how he felt.

"Are you Guardian McKay's new trainee?" Cecilia asked.

Michael nodded, finally meeting her eye, his ears glowing red at the tips.

"You could not have a better teacher. How fortunate that he's made time for you," Cecilia said, her eyes catching Rainer's.

"I thought I told you I would get you when I was finished," Rainer said dumbly.

"I tired of waiting and thought I'd save you the steps. I figured you would be here, though I admit the new recruit was a surprise."

"It's okay, Guardian McKay. My ma will be worried if I'm not back to the kitchens soon. Thank you for my lesson," Michael said, placing his wooden practice sword on the rack with a reverence typically reserved for a priceless relic.

"Keep practicing your footwork and I'll see you tomorrow," Rainer called as the boy darted to the door and ducked out of sight.

"If you're not careful I'll begin to think you've gone soft," Cecilia taunted.

Rainer rolled his eyes. "He's just a bored kid and it's best to keep him off the street now with so much unrest in the city. I've not gone soft."

Her eyebrow arched. "So, you're hard, then?"

"You seem in better spirits after your nap," Rainer said.

She grinned. "Oh, nonsense. The nap had nothing to do with it. I just thrive in the company of men who are entirely unmoved by my charm."

Rainer shook his head, wishing those words were true.

15

CECILIA

C ecilia stood at the edge of the fighting ring, watching as Rainer took down yet another opponent. The hunter had to have had twenty pounds on him, but Rainer made it look easy.

She'd always thought his name suited him. Rain like springtime. Like renewal. Like droplets poised on delicate petals. But now she was reminded of a different kind of rain—a destructive force that flooded and churned and raged in rising river tides.

Rainer fought with a viciousness she'd never seen in him—not like a guardian defending a charge, but like a weapon of pure death who wanted to inflict pain for the triumph of it.

This was who Rainer would be if it weren't for her: a brutal sword, waiting for a hand to wield him.

She didn't want it to be true, but she needed to accept the possibility. If he could accept her as the fiery goddess who shattered every bone in Davide Savero's hand, as the broken version of her who came back from death, she could accept the vicious warrior version of him.

She'd always loved his nurturing side and his gentleness. It was still under the surface, prompting him to buy her that sweater. But seeing him like this heated her blood. Her Rainer held so much back. This Rainer was wild.

Her reckless nature made her curious to know if he'd be the same or different than the last time he lost his temper with her. The memory of that day in the library was burned into her brain even without her goddess magic.

She hadn't felt remotely interested in anything physical in weeks —since before Vincent attacked her. But as Rainer stepped back from his cowering opponent and stripped off his shirt, the coiling in her lower belly wound tighter.

Sweat glistened on the strong planes of his chest, dripping down the lines of his abdomen. His skin steamed in the cold air.

"Fuck," she breathed, the word rising with a little white cloud of breath that carried her curse away.

The next opponent stepped up and Rainer went to work. She felt the telltale crackle in the air behind her. Xander couldn't sneak up on her anymore. Even though the Unsummoner bracelet cut him off from his magic, the Storm King still sent the smallest swell of energy through the air when he was close. It made the hair on Cecilia's neck stand on end.

"You look hungry," Xander whispered.

"Maybe I am," she murmured. "Maybe I'm starving."

Xander grinned. He was clean-shaven, his cloak and clothing neatly pressed and his hair looking freshly cut and neatly combed.

"You clean up nicely," she whispered. "Is that the work of your wife?"

He quirked a brow. "Which one?"

Cecilia laughed in spite of herself. "How long have you been waiting to use that line?"

"Since the second one showed up."

Xander's face and easy charm opened doors. Cecilia wondered what it was like to always have such an advantage. Then again, she had glimpses of it. Men had always taken notice of her pretty face, but beauty was a blessing and a curse for women. A blessing for the way it meant that people smiled at her on the street and trusted her.

A curse for the way it drew unwanted attention and left her in constant fear of standing out too much.

"What do you think of him?" she asked, nodding at Rainer.

"I think he's finally fighting at his potential. Why? Does he frighten you?"

She shook her head. "He never frightens me."

"He should."

"Well, he doesn't."

Cecilia watched Rainer take another man to the ground.

Xander turned to face her head-on. "He doesn't know you, Cece."

"His body does. Watch this." She tugged hard on their bond and then let all the lust she felt watching him fight flow through it.

Rainer went rigid and turned to look at them. He licked his lips and scrubbed a hand over his face, taking a slow glance at Cecilia from head to toe.

"What did you do to make him look at you like that?" Xander whispered, leaning so close that his lips were almost brushing her ear.

"I let him feel how much I want him. Just like how you're trying to make him jealous now."

"Didn't have to try very hard. He looks a bit confused," Xander chuckled.

Cecilia grinned at him. "Wouldn't you be confused if you suddenly got super horny in the middle of a fight?"

Xander shrugged. "Not really. Fighting always makes me horny."

Cecilia rolled her eyes. "You are truly ridiculous."

"Is it okay to touch you?"

She nodded and Xander ran a hand down her neck and tugged a curl that had escaped her braid.

"You play the part so well, but I have to assume that you returning my mother's painting means you're not nearly as enamored as you look right now," Cecilia said, pressing her hand to Xander's heart.

When she'd returned to her room after sleepwalking several nights ago, she noticed the painting tucked next to the passageway in her room. She knew it could only be from Xander, but she hadn't had a chance to discuss it with him since.

"I hope you're not offended," Xander said, his voice tender. "I'm not trying to erase you, but it felt a bit like all the things I held on to for comfort have started to weigh me down. I still love that painting and what it means that you sent it home with me, but I think perhaps it's time to make space in my life for someone else."

He slid his hand to her waist before allowing it to drop to her hip. The movement was so practiced and casual, and his body language was so overtly sexual, no one watching would have guessed their conversation was so serious.

Xander sounded so nervous. But the admission thrilled her. She had to swallow a lump in her throat.

"I'm happy for you, Xan. She better know how lucky she is."

Xander's cheeks pinked.

Cecilia couldn't shove down the delight. "Alexander Maxwell Savero, are you blushing?"

He cocked his head to the side and bit his lip. "First time for everything."

Cecilia laughed. "Oh, you are in so much trouble."

Xander leaned closer, his gaze on her lips. To the untrained eye, he might've looked interested, but Cecilia felt the difference between this performance and his genuine attention.

He dropped his hand to her backside and squeezed. "Looks like Rainer still prefers you in pants."

Cecilia whipped her head around and caught Rainer staring at her backside.

"Guardian McKay, do you want to go a round?" she called.

He narrowed his eyes. "That's hardly appropriate."

She shrugged. "I don't see why not. You've insisted that I report to you when I wake each morning. No reason you can't give me a workout."

Rainer looked only mildly startled by her innuendo. "Fine. Let's go. No weapons," he huffed, stepping back into the center of the ring.

Cecilia grinned as she tied off her braid and pushed up her

sleeves. She did a quick stretch, trying to warm her muscles, but they were aching from the constant chill.

"Enough messing around. Do you want to fight or not?" Rainer asked impatiently.

"Perhaps I'm just looking to roll around in the dirt with you," Cecilia said.

Rainer sighed heavily. He shook his head, but she caught a hint of a grin.

"Oh my gods, did you just consider smiling? Xander, mark the calendar so we can remember this momentous occasion when—" Rainer's fist flew, forcing her to spin under his arm.

She elbowed him in the kidney. Rainer stumbled forward and she shoved him with her boot, sending him to his knees.

He spun to look at her, his eyes wide. She grinned at him, gesturing for him to try again. Satisfaction bolstered her. This version of Rainer didn't know all her moves the way she knew his. She could probably take him down another time or two if she tried.

She let him get set again, waiting for him to strike. When he swung, she darted close to his body, catching him in the chin with the heel of her hand, then punching his stomach before spinning to the side to stop his counter.

Either Rainer was tired from fighting so much, or he was holding back. She rolled her eyes as she crowded him to deplete his advantage. Some things never changed.

She swung her leg and he caught it. She brought her other leg up and wrapped it around his waist. Rainer froze as their eyes locked. His hands came to her hips as he tried to wrench her off. She used his momentum to lean back, flipping him onto the ground and straddling his chest.

"You seem tired, Rainer," she said breathlessly, grinning at him.

He easily tossed her off and spun her so fast she didn't see him coming. She landed on her stomach, the wind knocked from her lungs. He pinned her hands behind her back and sat on her hips.

Cecilia was helpless against the panic that seized her body. She froze and her muscles tensed, and began quaking violently. Her mind crowded with an unwelcome memory. Hands holding her against a cold wood table, a knife biting into her thigh. She couldn't breathe.

"Lady Reznik?" Rainer whispered, all hints of aggression gone from his voice.

A moment or maybe a lifetime later, he was wrenched off of her back and Cecilia spun, hands up, ready to fight. She came face to face with Xander.

"Hey, it's okay, love. It's just me," he said, turning a murderous gaze on Rainer. "Gods, McKay, you've got a foot and a hundred pounds on her. Take it easy."

Rainer held up his hands. "I'm sorry. I wasn't thinking. Are you well?"

Her lip trembled. She would not cry in front of all these guards. She dug her fingernails into her palms and dipped her chin in a quick nod. Rainer looked unconvinced but stood to retrieve his shirt, giving her a glimpse of his scarred back. The sight of it punched the air from her lungs.

Even without her memory powers, she felt transported back to that room watching him get whipped nearly to death. Magdalena had told her that violence could imprint a living memory that clung to the body and made you believe you were back in the moment. It was visceral, sickening, disorienting. For a moment, she was in both the cold, fresh air of the training grounds and the dark sitting room with the smell of sweat and copper in the air and Rainer's blood splattered all over her dress.

"Cece?" Xander's face came back into view, sending the mirage up in smoke.

"I'm fine," she snapped, climbing to her feet. "Don't go soft on me now, Your Grace." Her gaze darted to the guards on the periphery of the ring.

Xander nodded and stepped back to give her space.

"Come with me," Rainer said abruptly. His guilt had been wiped away by a sullen, angry expression.

She followed him away from the watchful eyes of Vincent's men, trailing him through a hallway, up staircases, and down long corridors until they reached the door that opened to the castle wall.

"Where are we?" she asked. "Even I don't know this part of the castle."

She took in the view of Ardenis far below. From above, she could almost imagine she was living a fairy tale—a princess looking down on her kingdom from a safe distance.

"It's certainly a nice view, but what are we doing here?" Her eyes came to rest on bloodied grain sacks stacked against one of the walls.

Rainer shrugged awkwardly. "This was stupid." He looked embarrassed, his cheeks flaming in the bright sunlight as he turned toward the door.

"No, wait," she said, catching his hand. He yanked it away. "Tell me why you brought me here."

"When I'm having a bad day or feel overwhelmed, I come here." His words were rushed. "No one else knows about it. No one from ground level can see you. No windows have the right angle to see you if you stay close to the building. It's quiet. It's one of the few places I can think."

Cecilia looked around again and pointed to the grain bag. "Also where you work through your frustration?"

He looked suddenly self-conscious. "Occasionally."

They were quiet for a moment.

"When you're having a bad day, you can come here and have some alone time."

She smiled. "I'd love to, but if I disappear, my watcher will probably be cross with me."

Rainer bit his lip and a surge of pleasure hit her through their bond. "If I can't find you, I'll check here first."

"What if I want a break from you?" It was silly, but she was trying to keep a hold on her emotions, and she was perilously close to tears.

"Then you can tell me when you see me. I know it's probably stupid, but—"

"It's not stupid," she interrupted. "It's actually very thoughtful. I can see why you like it. This castle can be so loud and claus-trophobic."

He smiled and she wanted so badly to throw herself into his arms and make him hold her for hours. She missed the way he woke her up slowly in the mornings, the way he let her shove her ice-cold feet on his legs at night, and the way he was always ready with a story when she needed to escape reality for a while.

"Thank you, Rainer," she said.

He grinned widely.

She was getting used to this angry, brooding version of her love, but his grumpy demeanor meant that the few smiles she wrung out of him caught her so off guard she felt her self-control evaporate immediately.

"You need a haircut," she said, reaching to pinch one of his waves.

Rainer stilled. It was too familiar, but their intimacy was inex-orable, even with Rainer not knowing who he was.

He nodded his head toward the door. "Come on. I have one more thing to show you."

She followed him back through the winding hall to their wing and into his room.

"Guardian McKay," she said in a mock-scandalized tone. "This is hardly appropriate for an unwed lady."

"It's only for a moment," he said too seriously.

She turned in a slow circle, taking in his neatly organized books and weapons. A jar full of wooden star flower carvings on the night-stand caught her eye.

"Those are very good. Have you been carving much?"

He ran a hand through his hair. "A bit, yes. It's the strangest thing. I don't really remember learning how to, but if I relax and stop thinking so hard about it, my hands seem to remember the things my mind does not."

He pointed to a small cupboard next to his bed and opened its doors. "Can you fit in here?"

"What?" Cecilia said.

"Can you? I want to see something," Rainer said.

She climbed in and Rainer closed the doors, securing her inside —but just for a moment.

"If something goes wrong again—if there's another attack—you come right here and hide, okay?" Rainer said. "I promise I will come find you. Just stay hidden until I get here. I've even tucked my dagger in here—"

"That's my dagger." She ran her finger over the crescent moon on the handle. She was shocked her bargain with Cato allowed her to say it.

Rainer froze, a crease forming in his brow. "Yours?"

She licked her lips and nodded.

He grew silent, a mix of confusion and frustration blooming through their bond. She wanted to comfort him, and to have him comfort her, but he'd be baffled if she threw herself at him. Cecilia was beginning to worry she'd done too good a job of removing herself and burying his most precious and most painful memories behind a magical wall in his mind.

She cleared her throat. "Is this about the other night—the sleep-walking?"

Rainer nodded. "That and today. Clearly, you're still scared, and I wanted you to feel like you had the means to hide or defend yourself if you need to. You're clearly capable." He rubbed the bridge of his nose. "Cecilia, why does this dagger match the inlay on my sword?"

"I had them both made." The words came slowly, as if the bargain was trying to decide if admitting it broke a rule. She held utterly still, but nothing happened. No thunderclaps. No burning pain in her blood. She supposed the words were not necessarily related to Rainer remembering and not a clear enough hint to count against her bargain. Saying more, though, would have consequences. She could feel her throat starting to tighten and a subtle burning in her blood as she thought about what she'd like to say next without breaking her bargain with Cato.

"How will you tend to me in another attack when you have Eloise to worry about?" she asked, deflecting before he could ask more questions.

Rainer frowned at her. "Eloise has her own guards. My responsibility is still to you. The king's will comes first."

"Above your love?" Cecilia challenged. It was petty, but she couldn't stop herself from saying it.

"I don't love Eloise," he said.

Relief crashed down on Cecilia in a great wave. "Then why are you courting her?"

"Love is easily the worst reason to court someone. It serves no purpose," Rainer said.

She was torn between laughter and tears. This Rainer could be so completely pragmatic, but her Rainer had always been a romantic at heart. Even when he would roll his eyes at her for turning all their stories into romances, he waited to see how they ended, a smile on his face when the lovers found their way back to each other.

But this wasn't one of their stories. This was more like the horrifying tales he used to read her when they were young and she was annoying him.

"What about comfort, joy, affection?" she pressed.

Rainer shrugged a shoulder. "I'm courting her because my king bid me to do so. She's from a good family. If I want to become the king's top advisor, marrying into the Spellman family is an easy step to advance my future."

"So, you'll treat a woman's future as a means to an end? She certainly doesn't look at you like that's what you are to her." Cecilia couldn't keep the judgment from her words. She hated to see this version of him that was so shaped by his father.

Rainer swallowed hard, his face full of guilt. "It's what the king wills. I don't have a choice," he said quietly.

"And if the king bid you to jump off the castle wall, would you?"

"No," Rainer said gruffly.

"What if he bid you to kill me?" she asked.

The thought horrified her, but she wouldn't put Vincent above it, especially if she continued to mess with his plans. If he knew that the reason he couldn't find good help in the castle was because she, Xander, and Isla had sneaked most of the staff to safety in the dark of night. If he knew how she was working to sabotage him at every turn.

Rainer closed the space between them and brushed his hand to Cecilia's cheek. The intensity in his gaze startled her. She flinched ever so slightly.

Recognition lit in his eyes as if he was realizing he'd touched her without permission. He immediately backed away a step, but she moved so that he was touching her again.

"I will never hurt you. It's my job to keep you safe. You're engaged —why would the king want to hurt you?" Rainer asked. "What are you both not telling me? I know there's something and please don't say you can't tell me."

"Rainer, watch me. It's not that I don't want to," she said. She tried to say more but the burning in her blood left her gasping for air.

Rainer gaped at her. "You can't tell me. You're spelled not to."

She nodded.

He sighed. "I promise I won't hurt you, Cecilia. I will keep you safe. If something else happens, you hide here and the dagger will be waiting for you. I'm trusting you with this. If the king finds out I've given you a weapon, I could be in trouble."

"Of course. Gods forbid I defend myself," she snapped.

Rainer frowned.

"I'm sorry, I'm being rude and invasive and you're trying to be kind to me. Forgive me."

She looked away and swallowed the knot of emotion in her throat. Even without knowing who he was or what they were to each other, Rainer was doing what he'd always done—making sure she felt safe.

———

Cecilia walked down the hall toward the healer's suite. She was so tired of being forced to talk to Magdalena and Mika. She knew that they knew more about recovering from the type of violence she had endured than she did, but she wanted to be done with it. To never think of it again. To not feel the constant, insistent press of it on the back of her mind.

She paused in the hallway, glancing at the dining room door. Stepping closer as if a moth to flame, she pressed the door open, peering into the space.

The dim light of evening cast shadows on the walls that gave the effect of dark hands reaching toward her. She stepped inside anyway, walking toward the table. She ran her hand over the cool wood surface.

Her throat contracted. She thought she was ready, but she was not.

Before she could reach the door to the hall, the scene pressed in from all sides. She drowned in sensation. It was not the first time it had happened, but it carried no less surprise or terror.

Breath locked in her lungs, her heart tried to burst free from its prison. Not a memory of the mind but a memory of the body.

Her ears filled with the sound of her wheezing breaths.

Hands forced her down, holding her still—helpless. Her mind said *fight*, but her body said *freeze and they won't see you. Freeze and you will be fine.*

And then, blade to skin, a warning grumbled, a hand pinning her neck to the table, nothing but her own humid breath bouncing off its cool wood.

Screaming—screaming like losing something she could not get back—the sound of losing a self. Screaming like her soul depended on the sound to keep it from floating off, cut from her body like a wraith. And then blood and sweat and her vision prickled white with stars—stars that guide back her love.

Finally, breath arrived; the vision cleared; the ringing in her ears lessened.

Cecilia gasped, wiping tears from her cheeks as she took heaving, sobbing breaths. There was no magic needed to bring that memory back repeatedly.

Magdalena called them "echoes," but Cecilia had only heard an echo get fainter. For her, the body memory seemed to grow louder and more insistent each time—as if the constant vigilance it forced would prevent the violence from recurring.

Cecilia ran her hands over the hard wood of the door where her forehead rested. *I'm still here in this room.* She picked three objects from the room: a wooden dining chair, an hourglass, the iron fire poker.

I am still here. My body is still here. I am okay.

Her breathing slowed and the dizziness abated. Time found the proper pace.

She straightened, rushing out of the room and down the hall to the healer's suite.

"It happened again," she said as she breezed into the back room of the suite.

Magdalena looked up from the tea she was pouring. "An episode?"

Cecilia nodded and the healer's gaze flashed to Mika.

"Perhaps it's because you refuse to talk about it," Mika said. "If you shared, you might take some of the pressure off."

Cecilia frowned, clasping her hands together, rubbing her thumb furiously across her wrist. "Fine, what do I say?"

"Why don't you start by talking about your first sexual experience? Was it a positive one?" Magdalena asked.

Cecilia shook her head. "This can't possibly work."

Mika sighed. "It does, but you have to trust us. It took us a long time to get here and no one experience is the same, but we've found a process that works for a lot of women."

Cecilia chewed her lip, considering. She sighed, dropping her head back. "Fine. My first experience was good. It was great, actually. Xander—oh gods, I really shouldn't talk about the king's sex life, should I?"

Mika burst out laughing. "As if he wouldn't delight in the rumors."

Cecilia giggled. "It was wonderful. Xander was so focused on making sure I was comfortable. He was careful and then he—" Her cheeks heated and she looked away from the other women.

"He what?"

Cecilia shook her head, fighting off a giggle. "He basically tutored me on how to find my own pleasure, so I wouldn't have to rely on him or any other man."

She glanced back at her friends, both of whom were wide-eyed.

Mika shook her head in disbelief. "He must have been very much in love. I have met a lot of men, and not one would take such care to make himself superfluous."

Magdalena tipped her head back and cackled.

Mika shushed her. "You don't want anyone to take notice of us," she scolded.

"It was honestly a better experience than I could have imagined for myself, and of course I've heard the rumors, and in my opinion, they undersell his talents," Cecilia said.

All three of them burst out laughing.

"Okay, maybe this isn't so bad," Cecilia said upon catching her breath.

Magdalena smiled, sipping her tea. "And what about your more recent experiences, with Rainer?"

Cecilia smiled, looking into the fire and shaking her head. "It's hard to put it into words. With Xander there was this instant unstoppable attraction, something magnetic. But there is nothing like what it is to be with Rain. To feel what the person you love feels, to know that they feel you. He anticipates every need, and he stays so open and connected. I miss it. I feel like if I could have that sense of touch and grounding, I would finally be able to shake this panic."

She sipped her tea, trying to rid herself of the lump in her throat.

"Have you tried on your own?" Mika asked.

Cecilia nearly dropped her teacup. "Touching myself?"

Mika nodded. "Fantasizing about something and seeing if you can give yourself that comfort."

Cecilia picked at a loose thread on the hem of her dress.

"Just try it, Cece. What do you have to lose?" Magdalena said.

Cecilia was afraid to find out. She could hardly stand to bathe without fear that someone would tear in and find her naked. Her body felt strange to her for the first time—like something shameful. She wasn't sure pleasure was something she could summon on her own, at least not while she was trapped within these castle walls.

PART II:

DAWN IN A
DARK MIND

16

RAINER

Cecilia Reznik was the most maddening person Rainer had ever met. He'd arrived to retrieve her for the training session she insisted on every morning, only to find a note tacked to the door—the first in a series of riddles that sent him all over the castle.

That had been hours ago. She'd somehow managed to write enough riddles and clues for a scavenger hunt that he spent the better part of the day looking for her. He was a warrior, not a fucking child, and yet he'd played her silly game. In fact, he'd been more into it than he wanted to admit, not that he'd let her or anyone else know that. Rainer liked puzzles, liked learning how her brain worked—but he did not like how long the game went on.

It was clear that she wanted him distracted. Dread pooled in his stomach when he considered what she might be up to. He'd noticed the way she acted like a blank canvas in public, allowing the people of the Argarian court to paint her however they liked. She wore her black and gold dresses, neatly tucked her unruly hair into elaborate updos, and listened attentively—perhaps suspiciously attentively—at social events. He'd chalked it up to vigilance after the attack on the castle, but now he wondered if there was more to it. Perhaps the attack out past the wards had been orchestrated to lull him into a false sense of trust in her. Perhaps she was helping the rebels.

Rainer paused inside the stable doors. The answer to the most recent clue had been Tempest—the horse Cecilia had calmed days before. As he watched the horse trot properly around the field, something tugged at his memory.

The day after Cecilia had stolen a bow and then been attacked out beyond the castle walls, Vincent had complained about servants fleeing the castle. Originally Rainer had assumed that the staff no longer felt safe and wanted to be somewhere else until the transition of power was resolved. Now he wondered if there was more to it. If they wanted to leave, couldn't they have asked Vincent? Why smuggle themselves and their families out while the guards were distracted?

He frowned as an ache pressed behind his eyes. The headaches were getting worse, but he refused to tell anyone for fear they'd send him to the healer and have him bedridden for days.

The stable hand pulled back on Tempest's reins and grinned. "I suppose you're here for your clue."

Rainer sighed and shook his head. "She gave it to you?"

The man tugged on his vest, reached into his coat pocket, and handed Rainer a slip of paper. "Good luck. Your lady is a clever one."

"She's not my lady," Rainer said, too quickly judging by the hike in the stable hand's shoulders.

"My mistake."

Though Vincent seemed above her influence, the future queen had an impressive ability to charm everyone else. Rainer's stomach turned when he remembered the sound of the king hitting her—the way she'd been so calm about it when Rainer wanted to rage.

Rainer shook off the memory, unwilling to look too closely. The rules had always served him well, but his mother had drilled into him from the time he was old enough to understand that he was to always respect a lady's boundaries and never, ever was he allowed to raise his hand to a woman.

He unfolded the note.

———

"In my halls, secrets and mysteries roam;
find the answer among volume and tome."

———

He sighed walked back to the castle. He turned down the hallways, getting lost once before he finally remembered where the library was.

The room smelled like ink and parchment and a warm fire lit swirling dust motes as he made his way through the ceiling-high shelves of books. Why hadn't he come here sooner? He loved stories. He'd been so wrapped up in his duty, he had forgotten how much stories soothed him.

He rounded a corner and his eyes fell on a long mahogany table. A knife-sharp vision sliced through his brain. He winced. As soon as his eyes closed, he saw a pale back bent over the table, dark, curly hair pooled around her and her dress shoved up to her waist as he moved behind her.

He blinked his eyes open and met Cecilia's concerned gaze. She lounged with one leg tucked under her, the other dangling over the arm of the plush chair.

"Rainer, you found me!" Cecilia grinned, placing her book in her lap.

A flicker of a vision returned. He closed his eyes, trying to chase it.

———

Cecilia sprawled in that same chair, her eyes bright with lust and locked on his. He knelt between her legs, shoving her dress up. He placed a book in her hand.

"Keep reading, Cece," he whispered before lowering his mouth to her.

———

As fast as the vision arose, it evaporated, leaving him breathless, aching, and much too warm. All the blood in his body rushed south. He tried to call it up again, to examine its edges, looking for proof that it was his imagination when it felt so real. His fantasies were deeply specific and unrelenting, interrupting him in the least opportune moments. Now the vision refused to return.

Anxiety swirled in his chest. His mind might have been getting worse instead of better. It was becoming difficult to distinguish memory from fantasy, and it felt like there was something supernatural drawing him to Cecilia.

A soothing calm spread through his body, as if in answer to his nervousness.

"I don't appreciate being given the slip," Rainer said.

"You don't enjoy scavenger hunts that end with a beautiful woman?" Cecilia challenged. "What a fun-sucker." She flipped a page in her book. "I don't know what you're so grumpy about. I told you exactly where to find me."

He tried to maintain his scowl, but a half-smile broke through. Her face lit with victory. Truthfully, his anger had fizzled the moment he saw her curled up in a chair in the back of the library.

She looked adorable and more relaxed than he'd ever seen her. Her hair was piled in a bun on top of her head, curls as wild and untamable as the woman herself.

"Are you expecting me to believe you've been in here all day and not causing trouble?" Rainer asked.

Cecilia's eyes ignited with mischief. "Of course not. Obviously I was up at dawn to set up your scavenger hunt."

It was a deflection, but he'd get nothing out of her by asking questions outright.

"What are you reading?" he asked.

She held up the book. *Myths and Fairy Tales of Olney.*

Rainer fought a smile. "What's your favorite?"

A strange expression passed over her face. She tried to say something and was surprised when she couldn't. She shook her head and cleared her throat. "It's hard to pick a favorite, but most of these I've read hundreds of times. Why?"

"I like fairy tales too," Rainer said, sitting down in the chair beside hers.

He was grateful that she seemed so calm today. Even if he found her sudden docile nature unnerving, he was glad to not be chasing her.

"What's your favorite?" she asked.

Rainer sighed. "I can't remember."

She looked sad for a moment.

"I do know this one. I can never tell if it's a memory or if it happened while I was unconscious. Lady Spellman read to me often while I was ill, so perhaps it was her reading it, but I keep remembering parts of this story about raining stars."

Cecilia's eyes brightened. "Would you tell it to me?"

He shouldn't have. He should have taken her back to her room for dinner and sleep, but she had an uncomfortable pull on him.

Cecilia leaned her head against the chair. As he spoke, her eyes fluttered closed. He paused, surprised by her fatigue. She rarely stopped moving. She'd taken to napping most days, but it was strange to see her tired so early. It wasn't even dinnertime yet.

"Keep going," she said softly without opening her eyes.

Rainer continued. He was surprised by how much of the tale he remembered. It must have been from his childhood.

When he finished, she smiled, her eyes still closed.

"I love that one," she said. "I wish I could go there and collect wishes." She sighed dreamily, her head lolling against the chair. "What do you think Jack was saving his wish for?"

Rainer swallowed hard. The question made him so sad, though he didn't completely understand why. "I don't know."

She looked too pale in the firelight, her skin porcelain against the red velvet chair.

"Are you feeling well?" Rainer asked. Without thinking, he leaned over and touched the back of his hand to her forehead.

She jumped. Her eyes shot open and she gasped.

Rainer jerked his hand away. "I'm sorry. I forgot you don't like to be touched," he whispered, silently scolding himself for making her uncomfortable.

Her eyes went glassy and she swallowed hard. "It's not the touching as much as it is the surprise." She blushed and looked away and he was glad for it because her humiliation made him feel ill. "I'm fine. Just tired. Will you tell me more stories?"

Rainer sighed, leaning back in the chair next to hers. "I don't know any."

"Then make one up or read me one. I like listening to you."

He looked at her skeptically. "We both know that's not true."

She giggled. "I like listening to you when you're not bossing me around. You're a good storyteller."

The compliment and her sincerity made Rainer flush with pride. He hadn't felt like he'd been good at much of anything since waking. "All right—give me a moment and I'll make one up."

Rainer started a story about a young woman who ventured into the wild to save her father and twin brother and ran into powerful elemental beings who changed her fate. As he spoke, the story unfolded in his mind in rich colors. Occasionally Cecilia spoke up and made suggestions, most of which added romance to the story—a questionable topic in the company of an unmarried lady, but he figured all fairy tales needed their happy ending. He went on longer than he expected to and when he stopped he realized Cecilia was asleep in her chair.

"Lady Reznik?"

She didn't stir. Rainer repeated her name louder, but she still didn't wake. He could leave her, but he needed to get dinner soon and he didn't like the idea of leaving her vulnerable in public. His stomach was growling loudly after running all over the castle grounds hunting down her clues. He needed to get her to bed, but it didn't seem like she would wake.

"I'm going to carry you to bed," he whispered. He carefully slid one arm under her knees and the other under her shoulders, lifting her into his arms.

She tensed.

"It's just me," he whispered into her hair, and she relaxed.

"Rainy," she muttered sleepily.

A bolt of pain ricocheted through his head and he froze in place. Was it a memory? He tried to call up something familiar, but nothing came.

He sighed as he started to walk. Cecilia snuggled against him, tucking her face into the crook of his neck. She let out a contented sigh that filled his chest with warmth.

She smelled so good. He couldn't explain why he found it so comforting. When she was so close, things didn't feel quite so heavy. All the icy darkness that he'd found himself floating through since waking after his accident was warmed by her nearness.

He must have known her before. That was the only explanation.

He took the servant stairways, hoping that no one would notice the king's guard carrying the sleeping future queen. Rainer wasn't sure how Vincent would react if he found out.

When he finally reached Cecilia's rooms, he carried her to the bed, removed her boots, and tucked her under the covers. When he tried to draw away, she grabbed for his hand.

"Don't leave yet," she whispered. Her eyes cracked open and pleaded with him. "Please don't leave me alone yet."

Rainer felt like a chord reverberated through his chest at the sad look on her face. She was lonely. Of course she was. She didn't have any friends that he had seen, other than Xander, and from what little he could remember, she'd been taken away from her life in Olney. There were pieces missing, too many of them to fully understand.

All he knew was that at that moment, she was achingly lonely, and it was so clear on her face that he felt it in his own heart.

He didn't understand it. For days she'd been driving him out of his mind, stoking his fury as if it was simply a game. Why did he feel utterly compelled to take away anything that hurt her?

"Just until you fall asleep again," he relented.

She sighed and pulled his hand close, snuggling it against her chest. He pulled it back, compromising by holding her hand and rubbing his thumb back and forth over her inner wrist.

After a few minutes, her breathing turned light and even. She looked so innocent in sleep—a far cry from the chaotic wild woman she was during the day. He forced himself to look away.

She was Vincent's. Rainer shouldn't have been in the bedroom of an unmarried woman, especially this one. He was about to leave when he realized there were tears sliding down her cheeks.

He checked her breathing, but she was still asleep. Witnessing her loneliness was one thing, but seeing her so distraught sent such heavy grief into his chest he almost doubled over.

"Rain."

Rainer startled. She was still asleep.

"I miss you so much," she rasped.

He froze, studying her, trying to figure out if she was messing with him, but she was heavily asleep.

It was as good as confirmation that they'd known each other before. Well enough that she missed him. Well enough that she felt comfortable falling asleep on him.

Rainer could hardly breathe around the cold ache in his sternum. He gently extracted his hand. Standing abruptly, he left the room, tearing through the halls, his hunger forgotten. He was confused and disoriented.

The farther he got from her, the more furious he became. Furious at whoever had attacked him. Furious at himself for being a victim. Furious at his mind for not remembering. Even furious at Cecilia for making him feel twisted in knots when his life was working out the way he had hoped.

———

Rainer still couldn't shake the previous night's fury as he made his way to the tower to meet Vincent.

The large door creaked open and he found Grant inside sneering at him. He wondered if the guard knew that Vincent was planning for

Rainer to replace him. That might explain his disdain. Then again, Grant didn't actually seem to like anyone.

Behind Grant, Vincent stood, tapping his knuckles on the bars of a cell as he smiled at Rainer's approach. For some reason, the grin made Rainer more nervous than at ease.

"Your Grace," Rainer said, bowing.

"Rainer, I have excellent news this morning. We conducted a raid last night of a known rebel location."

Rainer frowned. Why hadn't he been made aware they were even doing a raid? Did Vincent not trust him?

Grant glared at him from over Vincent's shoulder like he was thinking the same thing.

"And we found this man inside. We believe he is one of the rebel spies in our court. I need you to work your magic and get whatever you can out of him," Vincent said.

Rainer looked into the cell and, despite the smear of blood on the man's face, he recognized him.

"I don't mean to question you, Your Majesty, but he isn't just a guard or commoner. Shouldn't we get permission—"

"You need more permission than mine?" Vincent asked, narrowing his eyes.

Rainer swallowed hard and the king's face softened.

Vincent clapped a hand on Rainer's shoulder. "I'm sorry. That was harsh. I'm under tremendous pressure to root out these traitors as fast as possible. Please forgive me—" He swallowed hard. "Last night there was a report of violence similar to that which befell my sweet Cecilia at the location we raided." He shook his head and blew out a breath. "I could not live with myself if I didn't do everything in my power to stop it."

That was all Rainer needed to hear for his fury to return in full force.

Vincent put his hands on Rainer's shoulders and looked him in the eye. "I'm counting on you to resolve this for me. I believe that you are the man for the job, but I do have a backup plan in case you're unsuccessful."

It wasn't a threat. His ego was less important than a traitor being found out, but the idea that someone else might be the one to do it lit a fire under Rainer's ass.

"I won't let you down," he said, turning back to the cell.

"I'll give you a half hour before we try a different strategy," Vincent said.

Rainer kept his gaze on the man in the cell as Vincent and Grant filed out.

Pulling the key from his pocket, he unlocked the door, stepped into the cell, and locked it behind him.

Finally, he turned to look at the man tied to the chair.

"Good to see you, Rainer. Wish it was under better circumstances—"

Rainer's fist hit the man's face before he could finish his sentence. That one blow opened a release valve on his rage. It all poured out in a torrent, replacing everything Rainer was with fire.

17

CECILIA

The moment Vincent burst into her room unannounced, Cecilia grabbed the wooden chair from her vanity, brandishing it against him. She was certain she'd been found out for spying on one of Xander's council members, Vaughn Salvatore, the previous day while Rainer was on his scavenger hunt. Xander and Isla had set a trap and Cecilia had been tracking Vaughn to see what he would do with the information he'd been fed.

She'd been careful, but it was possible that Rainer read more into her antics than she'd expected.

Vincent rolled his eyes. "No need to make a fuss. I need your help."

"My help?" She glanced at Grant's looming figure in the doorway and dread uncoiled in her stomach. "With what?"

"Does it matter? You know the price of disobedience and if you think I'm done taking from you, I'll be happy to free you of that notion," Vincent said.

It was too optimistic to assume that the absence of her daily delivery of Godsbane had been an oversight. While the Unsummoner bracelet on her wrist kept her cut off from her witch magic, Vincent's diligence in ensuring she took a daily dose of Godsbane was the only thing that kept the remnants of her goddess magic at bay. Occasionally, in the mornings, right before her dose arrived she'd feel the faintest hint of her power returning. But it always drained away as soon as she swallowed the tonic. Without it, she'd thought she might be able to cause some havoc at court, but it seemed Vincent had other plans.

She stood a little straighter, trying to ignore the shaking in her knees. "Will this outfit do?"

Grant rolled his eyes, but Vincent just nodded. "Pants are fine for your room, but in the future I'd prefer if you wore the dresses I had made for you. It's important we present a united front."

Cecilia tried not to laugh at that notion as she followed him out the door. Stumbling along behind him and Grant, she scoured her brain for reasons Vincent might urgently need her. "Where are we going?"

"To the tower," Vincent said. "I'm tired of playing around. Cato made it impossible to tell who is helping my castle staff escape and conspiring against me. If people can't speak their sins, I'll have you dig around in their minds instead."

Cecilia attempted to stall, terrified of who might be waiting for her in the tower. "But the Godsbane—"

"I intentionally skipped your dose today for this purpose," Vincent said, grabbing her arm to drag her along faster.

She tried not to wince at his touch, but it was impossible to feel his hands on her and not also feel the acute terror in her body. She'd tried so many things to get over that fear. She'd attempted to watch Vincent train—tracking his weaknesses so she'd know how to find her opening if she faced him one-on-one—but he mostly trained privately with Grant in a windowless room, so her opportunities were few and far between.

Vincent glanced back at her. The sadistic glimmer in his eye made her blood run cold.

She tried to mentally prepare herself for seeing one of her friends behind the tower door, but once it was ripped open and she was led into the cell, she was rendered speechless.

The combined smell of blood and mold made her gag, and Reese Reynolds sat strapped to a chair, his face a mess of swollen bruises, cuts, and blood. She gasped, taking a step back, because the person standing in front of him who'd dealt the beating wasn't one of Vincent's minions. It was Rainer.

His eyes went wide when they landed on her. Surprise, anger, and shame bubbled through their connection.

Rainer's clothes were splattered with blood, his knuckles torn open. Cecilia had to remind herself that she couldn't heal them as long as the Unsummoner bracelet was on her wrist.

"What's the matter, McKay? Was I so tough you had to bring a lady to break me?" Reese taunted. It was a relief that he was so spirited for how crumpled his body looked. Reese turned his attention to her. "Well, if it isn't the queen-to-be."

Reese's tone was taunting, but she knew he was trying to remind her to wipe the alarmed look off her face. Seeing him covered in blood transported her back to the moment Teddy had died. Shaking her hands as if she could shake the panic from her limbs, she fixed her face into a frown, despite the growing incessant hum of death whispers.

"Cecilia, we need you to search his mind for signs of treason," Vincent said. He leaned closer and lowered his voice so just she would hear him. "Rainer's methods, while compelling to most, have not made any progress. I'm beginning to see how the trickster's bullshit deal may have kept people from sharing all secrets, not just those secrets I meant to bind."

Cecilia found herself in the strange position of being mildly grateful for Cato. She immediately dismissed the thought as temporary insanity.

She turned to face Rainer, gesturing to Reese's bloody body. "Honestly, how can you be so patient all these years and so short-sighted now? How am I supposed to get anything out of him when you've beat him to pulp?"

Rainer stepped back, looking horrified and chastised. "She

shouldn't be here. It's not an appropriate place for a queen," he mumbled.

"How many queens do you know?" Cecilia snapped.

Rainer winced at her sharp tone.

She knelt and took Reese's bloody face in her hands. *Think, Cece. Get it together and come up with a plan.*

She turned back to Vincent. "He's barely conscious. How am I supposed to get anything?"

Vincent grimaced. "That's very much your problem, dearest. Need I remind you the price of failure?"

She arched a brow at him and nodded toward Rainer.

Vincent seemed to remember himself. "The fate of the kingdom is in your hands, Cecilia. Time to rise to the occasion again and keep our people safe." He turned to speak in hushed tones with Grant in the corner of the cell.

Rainer retreated to the other corner to wipe his hands on a towel.

Cecilia stroked Reese's cheek.

He smiled weakly. "I hope I look better than your face suggests."

"Vanity won't save you," she murmured.

"Says the pretty witch," Reese whispered.

"This face has cost me plenty," she said, sounding more bitter than she intended. "How did you get caught?"

Reese winced as she shifted her hands. "Wrong place. Wrong time. He just suspects and it doesn't help that he's never liked me."

She squeezed her eyes shut, trying to think of a way to save him. She turned back to Vincent. "What exactly am I looking for? Reese is on the council and is privy to plenty of insider information. How will I know when I've found the right memory? It helps if I can narrow in on something."

Vincent sighed heavily. "Just find out if he's somehow feeding information to the common folk. I've heard rumors several of the Reynolds family soldiers have been helping to feed the crowd at our gates."

"Is feeding the hungry a crime, Your Grace?" Cecilia asked.

Vincent scowled at her. "It is when they're actively committing treason."

"And if I find nothing?" she pressed.

"You'll find something. I'm certain," Vincent said. "When you do, I want to see the evidence and then I want you to wipe his memory."

Cecilia turned back to Reese. She felt Rainer's heavy gaze on her and panic clenched in her chest. Sensing his agitation through their bond, she watched Rainer out of the corner of her eye, wondering if he was putting it together that the only person he'd seen resort to memory erasing since he'd woken was Vincent.

She would not make Reese a mindless husk. The days of vengeful Goddess Cecilia were over, at least when it came to allies. She'd consider revisiting that part of herself for vengeance against Vincent.

An idea hit her like a lightning strike.

"Lord Reynolds, I need you to stay conscious so that I can search your mind," she said aloud.

Then she closed her eyes and plunged into his memory. He strained against her magic for a moment before letting her in. She created a false memory like she had many times before when she was a full goddess. She was rusty after weeks without practice, but it was all she had.

In the memory, she told Reese he was going to have to carry on as if she was stealing memories and it hurt a great deal.

She pulled out of his mind and waited for his eyes to clear. When they did, he gave her a small nod.

"It's probably going to take a while," Cecilia said, hoping Grant and Vincent would leave.

She turned to look at them and saw nothing but determination in Vincent's dark eyes. It didn't seem likely that they'd leave her alone with Reese. She turned back and settled in to do it the hard way—to try to save the brother of the man who'd once saved her. She owed that much to Teddy.

She dug her nails into Reese's bruised face and he let out a yelp as if she was savaging his mind. It was impossible to tell if it was better to pretend she'd found something or nothing at all.

For his part, Reese did a great job of acting, though he was probably already in so much pain it likely wasn't acting at all.

She turned back to Vincent. "I've only seen him around the castle and running errands in town."

Vincent narrowed his eyes at her. "Well, if you don't find anything of use, then simply wipe his mind."

Her jaw dropped. "He's a member of your council and one of the major landowners of Argaria, Your Grace. Surely you don't mean to cause a stir."

Vincent turned to Grant. "Are there others in the family line?"

"Two more boys, the oldest eighteen," the guard said.

Cecilia scowled at Grant, planning his death for the hundredth time since the day he'd held her down while Vincent carved up her leg.

"Eighteen is plenty old enough to take over and he'll be easily managed," Vincent said.

Cecilia felt Reese go rigid behind her. "You must be joking. Wiping Reese's mind will raise a lot of questions."

"And I welcome those questions." Letting out a belabored sigh, Vincent took a step toward her. "Dearest, I'm sure you don't want to give me a reason to doubt your allegiance."

"Not at all, my sweet," she said. "I simply wondered if Lord Reynolds might have some knowledge worth holding on to. Once I take his mind, it will be lost."

"Can't you store it?" Vincent asked, eyes narrowed.

She shook her head. "Not the entirety of someone else's memory."

Vincent pursed his lips. "Well, I guess we'll have to risk losing it."

She turned back to Reese. "I'm sorry to say this will be quite uncomfortable, Lord Reynolds."

Bringing her hands to his cheeks, Cecilia pushed her goddess power into him, and he let her in immediately. She planted a memory for him to act as pained as possible before sitting there like an empty husk.

He played it very well, but by the time his shouts turned to whimpers, Cecilia's nerves were as shot as if she'd actually done as Vincent requested. She felt sick and exhausted, and she called up every bit of grief from the past few weeks to bring tears to her eyes as she turned back to Vincent and Grant.

"Happy?" she asked.

Vincent poked Reese's shoulder. Reese sat slack-jawed, staring at the wall.

"You really did it."

"Of course I did," Cecilia huffed.

Vincent sighed as if this was an enormous inconvenience to his day. "Very well. I'll have Xander send word to the family first thing tomorrow. Rainer, you'll lock up. Grant, with me."

Vincent and Grant left Cecilia in the cell with Rainer and Reese.

Cecilia bent low so Rainer wouldn't hear her and whispered, "I'll be back soon. Hang in there and keep up the act."

Then she brushed past Rainer and walked out the door. He pulled the bars closed and turned the key in the lock and she followed him out of the tower. Rainer locked the heavy wooden door behind them with a resounding click.

He turned to face her with a coldness in his eyes that made Cecilia both angry and terrified for him.

"Lady Reznik."

"Cece!" She only came up to his chest, but it didn't stop her from giving him a shove. "Is that what you are now? A big man who tortures people nearly to death? You'll make yourself a weapon because you don't know what else to be? Are you so proud of what you've done?"

Rainer crossed his arms. "I'll do as my king commands."

"And if your king commands you to jump off the top of the castle, will you do that also?"

"If it will save my kingdom," Rainer gritted out.

"How far you've come in just a few days. Eloise must be really compelling."

Rainer crossed his arms. "She is, actually."

Cecilia could not catch her breath. She'd heard so little about their courting over the past week, she'd hoped that it had fizzled.

Cecilia stared up at Rainer, searching his face for the man she loved—the man who had been horrified when she'd broken a few bones in Davide Savero's hand. But there was no sign of that Rainer. Was it fair of her to not accept him like this when he'd always accepted all parts of her?

"There's no part of you less lovely than the whole," he'd said.

It wasn't that Cecilia was frightened of his violence; she was more terrified that it would chase away what sweetness Rainer had left. Her heart ached for how lonely and angry he felt now. It was easy to underestimate your effect on someone when you were around them all the time. Now that he had forgotten, she could clearly see how much damage unrooting herself from Rainer's memories had on his personality.

"What do you want from me?" Rainer asked.

"I want you to think for yourself for once. Why is the king having you torture his own council members? Does the rest of the council know?"

Rainer frowned.

She arched a brow. "Does that seem like protocol to you? Does it seem like the kind of thing that will garner good will?"

He said nothing. She saw the doubt in his eyes, but it wasn't enough. Rainer couldn't be trusted to do the right thing as he was now. He was too driven by the need for approval and Vincent was the perfect surrogate for Raymond McKay. The king hadn't stopped singing Rainer's praises and rewarding him for his good work.

She shook her head. She'd need to use Rainer if she wanted to get Reese out in one piece.

"Come here," she snapped.

Rainer frowned but walked toward her and gasped when she tugged him into a hug. She called up her power of hope and pressed it into him. He shivered, then relaxed against her as the tingling power pressed into him.

"What is that?" Rainer asked.

"It's called a hug. Gods, that slayer must have really done a number on you if you don't remember basic affection," she teased.

Rainer sighed. "I mean the magic that smells like your skin and feels like sunshine."

"It's hope, Rainer," she said, reaching her fingers into his pocket to steal the tower key.

Leo Reznik had taught her to pickpocket when she was seven years old, and she'd perfected it with years and years of practice. She'd only ever used it for silly things, like leaving notes in Xander's pockets or sneaking biscuits from Aunt Clara's kitchen. These stakes were considerably higher.

She craned her neck to meet Rainer's eyes as she drew away, carefully dropping the key in her own pocket.

"Why do you look at me like that?" Rainer asked.

"Like what?"

"Like you're waiting for me to tell you something important."

Cecilia sighed, patting his chest. "Maybe I am."

Then, she brought her hand to his cheek and sent him a memory that he needed to abandon his watch and go to the library to read the entirety of *Fairy Tales of Novum, Volume One*.

Once he disappeared down the hallway, she dashed down the hall to a passageway that led to Xander's suite.

She popped out of the passageway into Xander's room without warning and nearly took a punch to the face from a woman she'd never seen before. She ducked and spun away.

"Cece?"

Cecilia stared at her, trying to place the familiar voice. "Jess?"

"Goddess bless, you scared me to death," Jessamin said, and Cecilia pulled her into a fierce hug.

"I scared *you*? You're not supposed to be here. Do I want to know why you're wearing someone else's face? I can see a bit of you in there, but gods, you surprised me." Cecilia laughed, looking over the woman who had Jessamin's eyes and voice, but much shorter hair and much darker skin.

"Never mind. We can talk about it more later, but right now we need an immediate extraction," Cecilia said, meeting Xander's eye across the room. "Reese Reynolds is in the tower and he's in very bad shape. I had to pretend to steal all his memories and I don't know how long he'll be able to hold up the ruse before they just try to kill him."

Xander looked panicked. "Can he walk?"

Cecilia shook her head. "Not without a healer. Rainer did a number on him."

Xander cringed. "If you can sneak Magdalena in to heal him enough to walk, Isla and I can get him beyond the wards once it's dark. He just needs a way to let the outside team know to come pick him up."

"What about Chris?" Cecilia asked.

Running a hand through his hair, Xander considered it. "He could leave word at the brothel, but it's risky. If Vincent suspects Reese, no doubt Chris will be close behind."

Cecilia shook her head. "I think he needs to get out too. He and Reese have done enough. We need them safe, or they'll become a tool that Vincent can use against us."

"He won't like hearing that."

"He doesn't have to like it. He just needs to get out," Cecilia said. "I used the lack of Godsbane today to send Rainer to read a whole book of fairy tales and bought myself some time to get Magdalena up there, but I don't have forever, so I should go."

"We'll be ready by the time he's done." He grabbed Cecilia's hand before she could duck back into the passage. "Do be careful, love?"

She nodded and disappeared down the narrow corridor. She made her way downstairs to the healer's suite, the constant brush of cobwebs on her face setting her nerves on edge as she fingered the heavy metal key in her pocket.

When Cecilia stepped out from behind the tapestry in the healer's suite, her gaze landed on Mika and Magdalena huddled in the corner by the fire.

"What's wrong?" Magdalena asked, hopping to her feet.

Cecilia looked down at herself, realizing how much of Reese's blood had transferred to her clothes. "It's not mine, but I need you to come heal a prisoner so we can get him out."

Mika shook her head. "Mags, you can't keep doing that. It's too dangerous and you're too important to this movement."

"I would do it myself if I could," Cecilia said, holding up her wrist.

Magdalena met Mika's gaze. "We do what we have to, dear. You know this. We are at a critical moment and we can't be selfish. I'll be fine."

"I'm going to be with her and I have my goddess power now," Cecilia said.

Mika handed Cecilia a dagger. "Take this too and be back in no less than thirty minutes. Any longer and her absence will be noticed."

———

It took Magdalena a half hour to heal Reese enough that he could stand and walk on his own. She mended broken ribs, fingers, internal bleeding—every injury a reminder of how brutal Rainer had been. When she was finished, she slathered Reese's wounds with a salve to prevent infection until he could get to safety and have Sylvie take care of the rest. The pungent smell of the salve hung in the air of the cell.

Reese was exhausted and, after such a long day, struggled to keep his eyes open, prompting Magdalena to burn some morning root under his nose to help jolt him awake. As embers from the burnt roots dropped to the prison floor, Cecilia stamped them out.

Finally, Xander and Isla entered the tower, helping Reese out of the room and into the passageway. Cecilia locked the door behind them, sending Magdalena down to the healer's suite. She turned to go find Rainer and return his key when she rounded a corner and slammed into his chest.

"Lady Reznik."

She frowned at him. "Guardian McKay."

He winced as if it hurt to hear her using his formal title after weeks of insisting on calling him Rainer.

"What are you doing up here still?" Rainer asked.

"Looking for you. I thought perhaps you'd be around here brutalizing another member of the king's council."

He crossed his arms. "I was doing what was required of me."

"And you're back for more?"

Rainer's hands flexed on his biceps. "I'm back because I'm supposed to be on guard duty, but I seem to have misplaced my key."

"That sounds irresponsible," she taunted.

"I was disoriented after a tiny witch yelled at me for being a brute," he said.

Cecilia looked past him and gasped, and Rainer turned. She launched into a coughing fit to cover the noise as she dropped the key on the ground.

"What was that about?" he asked.

"Thought I saw a ghost, but it was a shadow from a guttering candle." Cecilia shrugged, her gaze angling toward the ground. "Is that the key?"

Rainer picked it up, trying it in the tower door, which groaned open. Cecilia held her breath, hoping he wouldn't go in so Xander and Isla would have more time to get Reese out.

"Rainer," she said. "Do you like to hurt people like that?"

He kept his back to her, his hand poised on the door. Shame surged through their bond. "You don't have to like your duty to do it. I do what's required, Lady Reznik. I do what my king asks of me." He sighed, hanging his head before turning to give her an exasperated look. "You should try it sometime."

"Oh, did I not just do that? Wipe the mind of a council member who did nothing wrong and risk losing support of a small region of Argaria so that Vincent could feel powerful? Didn't you watch?"

Rainer looked down at the floor. His jaw clenched, then he pulled open the tower door and marched into the cell. She followed, trying to think of a way to slow him down. Her brain was too frozen in panic to be of much assistance.

Rainer barked out a curse as he tore the cell door open and ran inside. She could lock him in, but then she would definitely give herself away as an accomplice. Using her goddess power was a possibility, but she felt so guilty for using it on him for something minor earlier that the thought of taking away more of his memory made her nauseous.

"Where the fuck is he?" Rainer asked.

"Reese?" Cecilia marched into the tower, her eyes widening as they fell on the empty cell. "He couldn't have escaped on his own. I wiped his whole mind. He'd be lucky if he remembered how to walk, even if you hadn't beat him to a pulp."

Rainer sniffed loudly. "What is that smell?"

Panic tightened Cecilia's chest. *The scar salve and morning root.* The cell still reeked of them.

Cecilia should have stalled him longer. Rainer tore around the cell, checking under the cot and even peeking out the small window as if a man Reese's size could have fit out of it. Finally, his eyes came to rest on the crumbled herbs on the cell floor. He picked them up, eyeing them carefully before bringing them to his nose to smell.

"Do you know what this is?" he asked.

Cecilia crossed her arms. "Just because I'm a witch doesn't mean I know every herb in the two kingdoms, Guardian McKay."

Rainer frowned, his eyes narrowing on her, but instead of asking anything else, he stormed past her and out of the cell to sound the alarm. Once he was gone, the breath rushed out of Cecilia. She didn't know if the gods could hear prayer from within the wards, but she sent up a silent plea that Reese and her friends would be safe.

18

XANDER

Though Xander had tried to prepare himself for the violence of Reese's face—a face that looked so much like his late best friend's—seeing it rendered him an absolute wreck. Grief ripped the air out of Xander's lungs the moment he laid eyes on Reese.

Isla noticed, of course, because she didn't miss anything, but there was no time to waste. They'd dragged Reese through the passages, out into the snowy night, and beyond the castle's walls, concealed by the blinding snow.

"How did this happen? How were you caught?" Xander asked.

"An honest mistake, Xan. I have a contact at Death and Fortune, so I go there to gamble and watch the fights at least once a week to check in," Reese said.

Xander clapped a hand to his head. It was *his* fault Reese had been hurt.

"Don't blame yourself," Reese said. "I should have made sure you knew all my hangouts the way that Evan does. That's on me. It was bad luck that I happened to arrive when they were watching," Reese said. His voice was almost lost in the howling wind. "Besides, it clears up where Lord Bidell's loyalties lie. Good news is he's so old he might die before we get to take a crack at him."

"Reese, I'm so sorry. If I had known, I never would have risked it." Xander shook his head. "Evan was probably watching you get dragged away."

Reese shrugged. The gesture was an eerie echo of Teddy. "I accepted the risks when I signed up for this job years ago. The fact that I've made it this far without running into any issues is miracle enough. Don't beat yourself up. You should know better than anyone after your years in Olney how we take on the risks and live with the consequences."

Reese might have forgiven him, but Xander wouldn't forgive himself as easily. "It's a lot to accept that I could have lost another Reynolds brother," he said.

Reese met his eye. "Isn't the loss of one punishment enough? Don't take this on."

They were all soaked to the bone by the time they made it to the meeting point where Chris Lamotis was waiting. He took one look at Reese and his posture withered.

Reese held up his hands. "Don't fuss. It looks worse than it is, but gods, am I glad you're coming with me," he said thickly.

Chris tucked Reese into a dark cloak, the movement reverent—almost tender. He leaned his forehead against Reese's and blew out a shuddering breath. "I was terrified."

The words were barely a whisper but Xander could tell from the way Isla shifted beside him that she'd heard it too.

Xander couldn't believe he'd missed it before when it had been right in front of his face. He'd not seen either of them do more than mildly flirt with the women at court. Xander had always wondered why two wealthy and handsome men on his council weren't at least courting when they were clearly so popular with the ladies.

But the way Chris tended to Reese, slowly helping him up onto the horse, so careful not to touch any wounds—it was the way one tended to a lover.

Chris turned back to Xander.

"You could have told me," Xander said.

Chris shrugged a shoulder and smirked. "It never came up."

Xander cleared his throat. "All the same, you would never find judgment from me. I'm just happy you'll both be safe."

"I can't thank you enough for getting us out, but we'll be mighty worried not being inside to have your back," Chris said solemnly.

Xander reached out and took his hand. "You two have been invaluable and courageous this whole time, but I won't risk you any longer. Besides, I'm sure you can still do plenty of damage from out here. You know where you're going?"

Chris nodded, pulling Xander into a hug before mounting his horse.

Isla stood next to Xander, watching as the men were swallowed up by the dark. The wind was beginning to slow, the cloud cover giving way to splotches of starry sky.

Xander wished he could feel the storm instead of just hearing it—like he could when he had access to his magic. He still had a sense of it, could feel it strengthening. It had always been like that for him—as if the wind was a language he could speak from the moment he was born in the heart of a storm. It wasn't the same when he couldn't feel the magic of it like it belonged to him.

He rubbed at the bracelet on his wrist.

"Do you miss it?" Isla asked, gesturing to the sky.

"Like an old love," Xander sighed, turning to meet her warm brown eyes.

"I know what it sounds like, but what does it feel like to you?"

Xander frowned, trying to think of a way to describe something so numinous. "Have you ever heard a symphony play?"

Isla nodded.

"It's kind of like I imagine it would feel to direct one. There's this disharmony when it starts, like all of the instruments tuning up before the first piece begins. The clouds that clash together, the change in temperature, the wind that barrels through as two discordant sounds connect, and then it starts and it's this perfect harmony, rain calling to wind calling to lightning and thunder or, when it's colder, to snow. And when I have my magic, it's like I'm conducting. I can bring it to this great, roaring crescendo, or I can keep it small and temperate. There's a beauty and grace to a storm and I can feel it in my whole body, like I'm part of the song."

He'd never spoken so openly about his connection to magic.

Isla's breath came out in puffy white clouds. "That sounds beautiful."

He nodded. "I've never been without it. It's one of the few constant things in my life. Even when I was young and didn't really know what I was doing, I could work with it. I got better so quickly. It was so natural I never even tried to reach for any other power, never thought I could until Cece taught me. It's fun to try new things, but there's nothing quite like the storm."

"I'd like to see it," Isla said with a grin.

"You will." He said the words with certainty, but he was beginning to doubt himself. "We should sneak back before someone important notices our absence. If we're caught, say you've never seen a snow-storm and I took you out to walk in it."

Isla nodded, weaving her arm through his. He led her back toward the castle. As they neared the entryway, Xander felt oddly vulnerable, like he'd revealed too much of himself.

Clearing his throat, he guided her back inside. They walked down the long corridor into the grand hall, where they found Grant waiting. He frowned at them, his eyes narrowed in suspicion.

"Just going for an evening walk?" he asked.

Xander shrugged. "I am the Storm Prince. Should I not enjoy a storm with my lovely wife? Especially when I have no access to it myself."

Grant rubbed his chin, still eyeing the two of them with suspicion. "Vincent wants to see you."

Xander nodded. "Very well. I just need to take Jess upstairs."

Isla's arm tightened on his as he turned and led her up the stairs. "I don't like that man."

"Join the club," Xander huffed.

They rushed down the hall and into their room. Xander helped Isla out of her dress, letting his eyes linger an extra moment on her lower back. She strutted into the closet for a change of clothes. They'd given Jessamin the neighboring suite, which was connected to Xander's by a passageway. She needed her own space to rest, and Maren was always on her guard, ready for any attackers.

Isla had stayed with Xander in his rooms, and he was starting to get used to it. It was nice to have someone sharing his space again.

He changed into drier clothes and Isla reached to smooth his hair.

They both froze, as if realizing the intimacy of the movement at the same time. She drew her hand away but remained close, breathing the same air.

"I should—"

Isla stepped away quickly, putting space between them to dispel the tension. "Of course. Just be careful."

Xander nodded, stashing his dagger at his waist. He darted into the hallway and down the hall to the grand staircase.

A shadow darted behind him. Hands shoved against Xander's back. The world slowed. His eyes went wide, and his body tipped forward.

Vincent's threat of a gruesome accidental death surged in his mind.

Of all the ways Xander thought he'd die, falling down the stairs had not even made the list, and yet there he was, panicking as he tried to assess the safest way to tumble down the long staircase.

If he had his magic, he would have summoned a great gust of wind to break his fall. The Unsummoner bracelet made that impossible.

At the very last second, a hand snatched at his tunic, dragging him backward. He landed on his back with a thud. Behind him, Isla sprang into action.

Xander hopped to his feet as she plunged a dagger into the man's chest.

"Who sent you?" Isla growled.

The guard's eyes darted to Xander. "He knows."

Isla yanked her dagger free and pushed the man hard, sending him careening down the stairs. She rushed to Xander's side, cupping his face in her hands. "Are you all right?"

Xander nodded. "Thanks to you."

He looked at the crumpled body at the bottom of the stairs, his heart still pounding, and something that had been growing between him and Isla seemed to overtake them both at once.

He pulled her into a kiss. It was savage, desperate, as if a kiss alone could shake the fear from their bodies.

Xander pulled away only long enough to guide her to the first room he could find at the top of the stairs. By the grace of the gods, it was empty. He closed the door behind them, locking it as Isla tore at his clothes.

Whatever sense of decorum had been holding them back was gone. She yanked off his tunic and undershirt. She ran her hands over his skin, her callused palms leaving a rush of goosebumps in their wake as she reached the button on his trousers.

Dropping to her knees, she pulled him free of his pants. Xander couldn't catch his breath as she stroked his cock. It was a practiced motion, as if she'd done it enough to know exactly what she was doing. A groan burst from his lips at the first swipe of her tongue, and his head fell back against the door, his body completely in her control.

He took a shuddering breath, looking down at her. She held his eye as she took him deep, hollowing out her cheeks.

"Fuck," he grunted, trying not to thrust his hips.

She moaned, bobbing her head as she pushed him toward a climax at an alarming speed.

"Isla." He brought a hand to the back of his head. "You have to stop or I'm going to lose it."

She pulled back, grinning up at him.

"Take off your dress and get in the bed right now."

"Take off your pants and fuck me right now," she countered.

So that was how it was going to be—a battle of wills. Xander had become so accustomed to losing that he was delighted for a fight where both of them could win for once.

It was only a moment before Isla was naked, but it felt like an eternity. She backed toward the bed, sitting on the edge as he knelt in front of her. He drank in the sight of the fullness of her breasts, the strong lines of muscle on her stomach, and her full hips.

He ran his fingers up her inner thighs, following each line with a trail of kisses, before swiping his tongue over her clit. Her hips lifted off the bed as she moaned. He pressed them back into the mattress, holding her in place as he slid his tongue over her in slow, lazy licks, relishing the impatient whine that burst from her mouth. Her hand came to the back of his head, urging him on. Xander chuckled as he picked up his pace, devouring her until she was panting, fingernails digging into his forearms. Her toes curled into his back, and she gasped as she climaxed.

Gods, he liked that sound almost as much as he liked feeling her at his mercy for once.

He climbed up her body, barely waiting for her to catch her breath before meeting her warm brown eyes.

"You are beautiful." The whispered admission was reckless and accidental.

The moment stretched out, the silence between them heavy with unspoken things. He was torn between levity and honesty because he felt so much that he could not find words for.

"Xander, please," she rasped.

He rubbed his cock over her slowly, teasing. He wanted her to beg, but he was also impatient to get inside her.

"Xander." Her voice was more urgent, her hands on his hips, pulling him closer.

Without warning, she rolled him onto his back and sank onto him in one swift, practiced motion.

"Fuck!" Xander's hips flexed instinctively.

Her pussy clamped down around him. She paused for a moment,

her fingernails raking down his chest, her hands coming to rest on the scar over his heart.

She rolled her hips and Xander gripped her tighter, pulling her down farther, grabbing at her as if touching more of her was the only way to possess her.

She moved fast, frantically, rocking against him, chasing another release. Her gaze locked with his. He couldn't catch his breath, couldn't stop his hands from shaking because he could see in her eyes that this was not some fleeting attraction. For a year he'd been alone, but he wasn't alone in this—in the terror of surprise affection. Isla felt what he felt.

Xander knew the feeling brewing in his chest acutely, the way all hunters had an instinct for danger. How many times had he stood on the edge of some dark forest, wondering if he'd enter and find victory or ruin? He'd hoped his days of risking oblivion were over and yet here he was about to do it again. If he went in alone and she wasn't there to help guide him back out—he didn't know if he'd survive that.

Pushing the thoughts away, he focused on her, moving in rhythm with her until her whole body tensed, her back arched, and she cried out, carrying Xander over the edge with her.

They stared at each other, breathless and fearful in the afterglow, until finally Xander drew away.

He lay beside her, tracing a finger over the lines of her stomach. "Why did you follow me out of the room?"

She was quiet so long he thought she might not answer. "It didn't feel right letting you go alone after the day you'd had. I was worried about what Vincent had planned. I don't—" She sighed shakily. "I don't know how you bear the constant threat."

Xander frowned. "But you've guarded the princess of Novum your entire life. How do you not understand the feeling of eternal vigilance?"

Isla shook her head. "All women know. The understanding of Vincent's kind of violence is so instinctual it's perhaps the first thing any woman understands as she comes of age. But to see someone like him relish in his cruelty, take pleasure in the mental warfare as well as the physical..." She shuddered. "I was never under the impression that the world was kind. Even in a queendom such as ours, you come to understand the brutality of nature. I think that's why my cousin has come here. Sometimes you need to be in a place where you can do something about that cruelty. But that's also why I couldn't let you walk into that—to face a man like that—alone."

Xander swallowed thickly. "Why?"

Isla ran her fingers through his hair. "Because you hold on to your loneliness like it will save you, when really it's a boulder that will drag you down to the depths."

"My whole life relied on instinct and these past couple years have made me doubt all of them. Before I met Cece, I was eternally an optimist—always able to talk myself out of problems. I did not know how to risk my heart. I did not even acknowledge that I had one."

Isla propped herself on an elbow, running her fingers over the scar over his heart. "Why did Cato stab you?"

"Because I tricked him. I hid Cece's weakness from him to keep her safe—or rather to keep Rainer safe. I knew what an impossible task I'd set before myself with her. But I live for the rush of a challenge. And so, I saw her look at Rainer that way and I wanted her to look at me the same. I really thought I was charming enough to have that. But I learned better. I learned when he nearly died and she screamed like she was dying too. And so, I protected that weakness of hers from Cato. I let him twist me in knots and ruin my love for her to protect the love of her life. But I'll never know if I did it as some self-sabotage or to atone for being the selfish enough to manipulate her."

Isla stroked his cheek. "You learned from a mistake, Xander. People cannot expect a king to be perfect. All they expect is that you will learn from your mistakes."

A lump formed in his throat. "I also didn't know the extent of my father's mistakes until this whole ordeal with Vincent." He met Isla's gaze. "I worry that I'm more like Damian than I would like to be. If I was taught to think in the same extremes, what's to keep me from being just as harsh?"

She pressed her palms over the scar on his chest. "We are not our parents. For better or worse, we make our own way in this world. Even us royals."

He hesitated, but he wanted so badly to tell her the secret he'd been holding on to most of his life. The same one that had left him with an eternal chip on his shoulder and something to prove.

"What if—" he started but his chest was so tight he could hardly speak. "What if I was only half a royal?"

Her eyes widened slightly. "If you're saying what I think you're saying, then you're quite reckless with your pillow talk."

"It's not pillow talk. I've made quite a few mistakes in the past. I thought maybe I'd try starting with honesty and see how it goes."

Isla was silent for a moment, studying him as if she was trying to solve a riddle. "How do you know for sure when there are no records of it?"

Xander sighed and flopped back on the bed. He closed his eyes, trying to summon the memory and failing thanks to the bracelet on his wrist. "Before I left for Olney at fourteen, my mother, Juliana, pulled me aside. I assumed she was going to try to talk me out of it. She and the king had been arguing about it for weeks. Instead, she brought me into her private sitting room and told me the truth. That my true father was her consort, Arthur Randal. I insisted that she was mistaken; that there was no way to know for sure, but—"

His voice broke as he remembered the look on his mother's face —sheer desperation. She had been so afraid for him.

Isla tucked his hand between hers. "But?"

He blinked his eyes open and turned to meet her gaze. "But she told me how, despite the fact that there was magic in her family line, my grandmother and her family were mostly earth witches, but Arthur, though he didn't have magic himself, came from a long line of talented storm witches. And it explained so much—why Damian hated my magic so much and wouldn't let me use it. Why I had nothing of his temperament. Why I'd had such a knack as a hunter, and why Arthur Randal had paid special attention to my training, not directly training me himself, but making sure I had men he trusted to work with."

Isla squeezed his hand. "I'm sorry that you found out that way."

Xander took a shuddering breath. "Do you remember the first day you felt grown up? That was how I felt. Like I'd gone from being a child one moment to an adult the next. Because then my mother got on her knees and begged me not to spy in Olney because if anyone discovered who I was and I was caught, King Damian would dismiss me for what I was and let them do whatever they wanted with me. It wasn't the first time in my life I'd known that no one was coming to save me. The Storm Prince story is true, after all. But it was the first time I wished my mother would have lied to me about it."

What he left out was that his mother had brought in Arthur Randal after that, and he had pleaded with Xander as well. But Xander hadn't listened. He was young and angry and so certain he could make it on his own. Then, they'd summoned Magdalena, who had taken the memory of what had happened from him so he would forget it all and no memory witch could pry the truth from him. It wasn't until he had looked into the truth mirror that Xander had remembered it and there was no one left alive to aim his fury and hurt at.

He had left for Olney early the next morning without even saying goodbye to his mother.

"You are the only one who knows this."

He watched the understanding wash over Isla. He'd given her something entirely personal and valuable. She wanted to know that he'd moved on, and he was trying to offer her something he had never given to anyone else.

Isla ran her fingers through his hair. "I'm so sorry that the man who raised you was an ass, but you are not him, just like you are not the man who didn't bother to raise you. You are not their neglect or their mistakes. You are what their secrets forged you into, which seems to be a flawed man with a good heart."

Warmth spread through his chest, the feeling of acceptance both wonderful and terrifying. He kissed her.

Isla pulled back and leaned her forehead against his. "In my experience, perfection is boring and overrated. We all have a past, but if we aren't careful it can become an anchor. I think you should be sure you've made peace with it before you charge into the future."

The message was clear. He'd had his closure with Cece, and he'd made his peace with it, but now the memories remained, filling him with fear and confusion when Isla wanted certainty.

Part of him wanted to surrender. How nice it would be. But a bigger part of him couldn't stop remembering the year after Cece, when he'd felt so lost, so heavy with unspent love for her, he'd barely survived. He wasn't certain that he could let himself love again at all.

For the first time he understood Cece's conundrum. Xander had always been second. Deep down, he'd always known Rainer was first, and it frustrated him to no end. How could she want them both? How could she not remove that part she reserved for Rainer and give it to Xander when he'd been her husband?

But now he was the one who felt haunted by something unfinished. He did not want to put Isla second, especially to a memory. His love had been so stubborn, slow to shift into a new form, but he was learning it was okay to be haunted as long as he didn't force Isla to banish those specters for him. He felt he'd lost some piece of him to Cece; that although he was healing, he would never quite be the same.

For the first time since he'd left Cece in Olney, he wanted to give himself to someone else. But a woman like Isla did not seem the type to be satisfied with less than all of him, or maybe she was not convinced that she had it yet.

He'd been far less aware of what was happening with Cece, having never been in love before, having been completely swept away by the inevitability of loving her.

Now he felt himself treading water, waiting to be sucked out to sea in the undertow. So much about love was still dangerous and unknowable.

His timing, as always, was terrible. The last time he'd felt this, he'd been about to accomplish his life's work. This time he was trying to save his kingdom from a maniac. Everything he'd learned about love was messy, wrought, filled with chaos—and yet he wanted it again, like a dog who couldn't stop returning to a master who did nothing but kick him.

Perhaps Xander had learned nothing at all and was cursed to forever be reckless when it came to matters of the heart.

Falling in love was an unbelievably foolish thing to do, but he'd never been terribly wise.

19

CECILIA

Anxiety twisted in Cecilia's stomach as she walked down the castle hallway. Two hours ago, Vincent had sent her a sudden and ominous invitation to a court party. She felt marginally more confident about walking into an unknown event with Xander and Isla at her side, however tremulous that semblance of safety felt after the attempt on Xander's life the previous evening.

Vincent's impatience was making him volatile.

Cecilia watched Xander and Isla out of the corner of her eye. Their posture was more natural than it had been previously. Xander's hand rested on hers and Isla's eyes scanned the hallway like she was ready to protect him from any adversary. Something had clearly shifted between them, but Cecilia wasn't about to bring it up.

"I have to make Rainer remember before Vincent sends someone else to finish the job," she whispered.

"He will, Cece," Xander said. "You haven't had much time. I'm capable of looking out for myself and when I'm not, my lovely wife does it for me."

Isla rolled her eyes and Xander's face lit up, his gaze lingering on her lips.

Cecilia fought a smile. When Xander was courting the princesses, she had felt so jealous, but now, it was good to see him look at someone else that way. It was what she wanted for him.

When they turned the next corner, the sound of voices and clinking glasses echoed through the hall. A small girl who couldn't have been more than six stumbled out of the doorway in front of them. She paused, looking up at Cecilia with wide eyes.

"Are you a princess?" the little girl asked, taking in her jeweled headband.

Cecilia grinned and lowered to her knees so she was at eye level with the girl. "Do I look like a princess?"

The girl nodded, her raven curls bouncing. Her wide, pale green eyes darted over Cecilia's shoulder to Xander and Isla.

"Want to know a secret?" Cecilia whispered. "I used to be a princess."

The girl's eyes went wide.

"But you see that handsome man over my shoulder?"

The little girl's eyes fluttered to Xander, and she gave him a shy smile. "Yes."

"He's a prince and that lady next to him is his wife, the princess," Cecilia said.

The little girl's lips parted in a gasp and she dipped into the most adorable curtsey Cecilia had ever seen.

"Your Graces," she said, lifting her eyes to look at them.

"And who are you, my lady?" Xander asked, bending to kiss her hand without missing a beat.

"Lady Isabella," she said, her cheeks growing pink.

"Well, Lady Isabella, do you think you could show the prince and princess to the party?" he asked.

Isabella's face lit up and she took his hand, dragging him down the hallway to the sitting room as Cecilia and Isla followed. Cecilia stole a glance at Isla and saw her gaze was glued to Xander's backside.

"See something you like?" Cecilia teased.

Isla looked away. "I don't know what you're talking about."

"Can't say I blame you. Did something happen between you two?"

Isla glared at her.

"I only ask because I've suffered the same disorientation."

Isla cleared her throat. "And how did you right yourself?"

"I didn't. I surrendered to it."

Isla scoffed and Cecilia laughed, but the laughter died on her lips as they entered the sitting room.

She wasn't sure what she'd expected when Vincent told her about the party, but it wasn't this. It looked like he'd invited half the kingdom.

"Ah, dearest, you're finally here. Thank the gods. You know she does take such pride in her appearance, but it makes her late so often," Vincent said to the men beside him. He slid an arm around Cecilia and guided her toward the windows.

She tried to keep the tension out of her shoulders as her eyes landed on Isabella again, who was standing beside a woman who looked to be her mother. The little girl kept stealing furtive glances out the window and giggling and whispering things to the child next to her, who must have been a slightly younger sister.

"What is this about?" Cecilia whispered.

Vincent squeezed her arm hard enough to bruise and leaned in so close his lips nearly brushed her ear. "I know you had something to do with Reese Reynolds escaping. I'm not a fucking idiot."

Cecilia held her chin high, trying to ignore the panic in her chest. "I don't know what you mean. I've done everything you've asked of me. Especially since you've been so clear about the consequences."

He eyed her skeptically. "I was so certain I'd found the proper place to apply pressure, but you've forced me to reassess."

"How could I compel a king?" Cecilia said, her voice barely taunting enough to hide her terror.

"There is a price to pay for treachery, so allow me to remind you that I can always find more to take from you if you insist on defying me," Vincent whispered, menace in his tone. He released her arm and grabbed two glasses of bubble wine from a servant, handing one to her.

"I want to make sure you have a good view of the happy occasion," Vincent said.

"The gardens look lovely with the fresh snowfall, but what are we celebrating?"

Vincent's grin widened. "You'll see any moment now."

Dread pooled in Cecilia's stomach. She sipped the bubble wine to try to soothe her anxiety. Her eyes met Xander's, but she saw the same confusion in them as he whispered to Isla.

She was about to try to subtly make her way toward them when movement in the garden caught her eye. Warmth pulsed in her chest as she took in Rainer. His hair was still a bit too long, but it was neatly combed, showing off the waves she loved so much. She wanted to run her fingers through it.

All her fantasies were shattered when she realized that Eloise was on his arm. Cecilia's stomach lurched; a dizzy, sick feeling spun through her.

Rainer stopped, turning toward Eloise, holding both of her hands in his.

Cecilia wished she could hear everything he was saying even though she knew the words would probably hurt. She knew that look on his face. He looked utterly smitten with Eloise and she looked just as delighted by him. Of course she did—Eloise had been after Rainer since he had returned to court.

Cecilia brought her hand to her heart as if that could shield her from feeling hurt.

Then, Rainer went down on one knee and held up a ring and Eloise nodded. He jumped to his feet, picking her up in a hug before kissing her. The room erupted in cheers. The two of them turned toward the sound, both looking embarrassed and delighted.

Cecilia felt faint. She tried to keep her face placid, but she knew by the triumphant grin on Vincent's face that she had in no way succeeded.

Before, when it seemed that Eloise was just a responsibility that Rainer thought he needed to fulfill to get the recognition he so desperately chased, it was easy to believe that they'd never get to this point. But now, faced with the possibility that Rainer might actually be happy with Eloise, Cecilia felt breathless.

She was so certain fighting for him was the right thing. Her gaze settled on little Isabella and Cecilia instantly recognized her resemblance to Eloise. They must have been her nieces. Was that what Eloise's children with Rainer would look like? Perhaps their eyes would be greener.

Cecilia was sucked down and down and down into a vortex of doubt.

Rainer and Eloise came in through the glass doors to another round of applause. Vincent rushed forward to speak with Grant. Cecilia stayed where she was and drank her entire glass of wine in one gulp, ignoring the burn of the bubbles that made her eyes tear up.

Her heart felt like it was being squeezed in a fist, but she pasted a smile on her face as several ladies' glances lingered on her. Half of the room knew her history and half didn't, but clearly everyone was expecting a scene that she had no intention of giving them.

Xander appeared at her left shoulder with Isla beside him.

"Cece—"

She held up a hand. "I should have known. This is who Rainer would be. He follows the rules. He does what he's told, and he'll do anything to prove himself."

Xander frowned. "How do you figure?"

"If you take away me, you also take away my father's influence in his life, and a lot of the best memories with his own mother. All he's left with is Raymond McKay."

Xander sucked in a breath.

"What was wrong with his father?" Isla asked.

"He treated Rainer like nothing he ever did was good enough," Cecilia said. "He traded Rainer's success like currency all while never once telling him he was proud."

Isla wrinkled her nose in disdain.

Cecilia sighed. "Who knows who his birth parents were and how much of that driving force to achieve something comes from Raymond McKay and how much of it he was born with. I'll probably never know."

Xander frowned, a flicker of recognition lighting his eyes.

"What? Do you know who his birth father is?" Cecilia asked.

"Of course I do," Xander whispered. "I was a spy behind enemy lines and my guards made a point to know everything about the most skilled warriors in Olney." He cast a darting gaze around them to make sure no one was listening. "I'm shocked that you don't. I thought you two knew everything about each other."

"It was such a closely guarded secret. I never pried about it, but I was always curious," Cecilia breathed.

Xander exhaled heavily. "Zelden Novaris."

"The warrior?" Isla said, her eyes wide. "Women in the Novumi army talk about him like he's the epitome of valor."

Cecilia couldn't contain her own shock. Zelden Novaris was even more revered than Leo Reznik in Olney history. His hard work on the front lines had given Clastor and Leo enough time to prepare for Endros's onslaught during the War of the Gods. He'd fought with just one battalion, beating back thousands of Argarian hunters at a choke point in their front lines. Zelden was one of the last three men standing. He'd sent one of the men to warn the rest of Olney that he'd fallen and then he and his last warrior held off Endros's men so he could escape. He was a legend.

So many things about Rainer suddenly made sense. Originally, Cecilia had thought he'd become a guardian because Raymond McKay wanted the prestige of a son who was important. Now, she saw it as a more personal choice to honor Zelden's legacy. Still, she couldn't help but ache for the man she'd loved her whole life, who never felt good enough and never stopped striving to prove himself even to her.

Cecilia swallowed hard and glanced back at Rainer. Eloise met Cecilia's gaze and arched an eyebrow, her lips pursed as if to say, "*Your move.*"

The hurt gave way to anger. Cecilia was so furious at Eloise she thought she might breathe fire. Cecilia had seen Rainer kiss plenty of other girls in front of her over the years, though not since they'd been engaged, and certainly not so joyfully at a public event. At least

Rainer had the sense to look embarrassed, while Eloise looked thrilled. Cecilia wanted to pounce on Rainer, drag him into another room, and remind him how he *should* feel.

But what if she had staked her whole future on a man who was in love with their history? What if he couldn't love her out of context? What if she was only as compelling as the folklore they'd written together and without it there was no magic?

Cecilia shook out her hands as if she could rattle all her fears loose. She focused on Eloise. The look of triumph on her face wiped away any doubt that she was a victim of circumstance.

Vincent walked toward Cecilia with another glass of bubble wine in his hand. "Dearest, shouldn't we go wish our congratulations to the happy couple?" he said, trying and failing to contain his glee.

"Of course." Cecilia smiled, hoping it didn't look as tense as it felt, and took Vincent's arm, allowing him to corral her toward Rainer and Eloise. The crowd parted to make room for the king, several eyes lingering on her face as if waiting for her to break.

"Rainer, what happy news! I know this is just the next step in you claiming your rightful place at my side. Family is so important," Vincent said, squeezing Cecilia's waist.

Rainer looked shocked to see Cecilia. Guilt bubbled through their connection, and she sent peace and calm back. His face relaxed, but he rubbed his sternum, his brow pinched.

"Congratulations to you both. Rainer, I have no doubt you will be a wonderful, attentive husband. And Eloise, I hope you get everything you deserve," Cecilia said sweetly.

Eloise arched a brow. "I intend to."

"I do hope you'll excuse me from the merriment. I'm so exhausted these days," Cecilia said.

She knew Vincent wanted to argue, to make her stay and suffer longer, but he also knew how bad it would look if the queen-to-be fell asleep at the banquet table. The more people became aware of the Unsummoner bracelet's effects, the more questions they would raise —questions that Vincent wouldn't want to answer.

Cecilia turned on her heel and left the room. She didn't take a full breath until she'd rounded the corner and heard Xander and Isla's footsteps behind her. She ducked into a sitting room to catch her breath.

Panic swelled in her chest, her heart thundering like it might escape her ribcage. The air in the room seemed too heavy to draw in. Her vision narrowed.

Not now, she begged her body. But the sensations didn't relent.

If Rainer was there, he would hold her against his chest and make her breathe with him to slow it down. But he was in another room down the hall, kissing his new fiancée.

Cecilia struggled for air.

"Cece." Xander's voice sounded muffled and far away. He repeated her name louder, stepping in front of her, his hazel eyes wide with worry. He took her hand and brought it to his chest. "Breathe with me."

She squeezed her eyes closed and imagined Rainer soothing her. Her palm lifted as Xander took a deep breath and she tried to mimic it. It took several tries and all her concentration to slow and deepen her breaths. After a few minutes, her breathing matched Xander's and the darkness cleared from her vision, her tense muscles relaxing.

"I'm sorry. I'm so embarrassed," she said.

Xander shook his head. "Don't be. They happen to me too—ever since the day I almost died."

"They do?"

Xander chuckled. "You'd love to hear that the first significant interaction I had with Jess was when she found me having one in my room. It was when I knew I'd have to pick one of the princesses. She rubbed my back and sang a song until it passed."

Cecilia stared at him, slack-jawed. Isla looked equally shocked.

"I know it's hard, but you are going to get through to Rainer. He's putting on a show now because that's the only part of himself he remembers, but he *will* remember you," Xander assured her.

She felt far less certain than she had at the beginning of the ordeal, but she held on to what hope she could the same way she held on to Rainer's certainty in that final moment. *"I will always know you, Cecilia."*

"I know you're relying on me, but I'm not a lifeboat, Xander. I'm just out here treading water beside you, trying not to drown," Cecilia said.

He leaned his forehead against hers. "I know."

"You should tell her," Isla said. "We need her in on everything."

"Tell me what?" Cecilia asked at the same time Xander said, "Does now seem the best time?"

"If not now, when?" Isla asked.

Cecilia looked between the two of them, picking up a distinct tension that accompanied a lovers' quarrel. The two of them had fire in their eyes.

"Does this have something to do with why Jess is back inside the walls of this castle instead of far away where she'll be safe?"

Cecilia hadn't had a chance to ask Xander about it while they were busy trying to hustle Reese to safety, but the thought had been nagging at the back of her mind. The last thing they needed was another royal target for Vincent. Isla wouldn't be able to efficiently serve as a decoy if Jess's disguise wore off. And the fact that the plan relied on Cato's help made her even more anxious.

Finally, Xander's shoulders sagged, and he turned to face Cecilia. "I'd hoped for better timing—to tell you once we'd figured all of this out. I thought we would have by now, but with us still not certain who we can trust and Rainer getting sucked into Vincent's grip more each day, it's become necessary to keep her close."

Cecilia narrowed her eyes on him. He was sweating, wringing his hands. She had rarely seen Xander look so nervous.

"Necessary why?"

He chewed at his bottom lip. "Jess is pregnant. That's why she's back here and hidden. It's dangerous here but more dangerous if she's caught in a den of rebels. And she'll need more regular access to a skilled healer, preferably one who has delivered royal babies."

Xander stared at Cecilia, not moving, as if he expected her to throw a fit.

She could hardly contain her surprise. She knew that they'd reached an agreement, but she didn't realize that Xander had actually slept with his new wife.

A shocked laugh slipped out of her mouth. "Oh my gods—"

"It was obviously a big surprise, and it's still very early—"

Cecilia's eyes blurred with tears. She blinked them away to see a concerned pinch in his brow. "Oh my gods, Xander. You're going to be such a good father." She pulled him into a fierce hug. "You must be so thrilled."

Xander rubbed her back. "I am."

"Gods help us, that baby is going to be so cute," she said, blinking away a whole new flood of tears. "What about Jess? How is she feeling?"

Xander caught her face in his hands, studying her like a puzzle. "Cece—"

"I know you didn't want to tell me because—" It was hard to say, and not just because Isla was watching them, but because Cecilia was torn between joy and grief. She didn't know how to explain herself.

Isla stood frozen, as if she'd accidentally walked into a snake pit and only now realized.

Cecilia placed her hands on Xander's chest. "You didn't want to tell me because you know that I can't have children and you were there when my heart broke about it. But breaking your own heart won't heal mine. You never need to hide your joy from me. I'm *so* happy for you."

Xander's face softened and he squeezed Cecilia's hand.

She sighed. "You have to stop looking at me like that."

"Like what?" Xander asked.

"Like you're waiting for me to fall apart, and you feel personally responsible. You have to release the guilt about being happy and the guilt about what Vincent did to me."

"How can I forgive it when I could have stopped it?" Xander asked, his eyes full of grief.

"I don't know how to absolve you more than I already have," Cecilia said. "It wouldn't have made a difference if you'd agreed to help Vincent. I would have been hurt all the same without him ever touching me. Let today be proof of that." She shifted, holding up her wrist with the Unsummoner bracelet. "All I want is to pull up something good because the memories are fresh and burned on the insides of my eyelids, so I see them each time I close my eyes—they're all bad. Vincent hurting Rainer. Vincent hurting me. Me begging you with my eyes not to give in and screaming in my heart for you to save me from something all while knowing it's inevitable. I want my power back not just so I can destroy him, but so I can stop destroying myself, Xan."

"Cece," he rasped.

Cecilia blew out a shuddering breath. "Vincent didn't do what you think he did."

Panic tore over his face and he held up his hands. "You don't have to—"

"I do," she interrupted.

Isla took a step toward the door. "Maybe I should leave—"

"No, stay." Cecilia met Xander's eyes. "It's hard for me to talk about. Like there's a block between my brain and mouth, but I have been trying to find the words. Vincent didn't rape me."

Xander let out a breath in a rush. He still looked doubtful.

"He threatened to. He wanted you both to think he had. But he cut his initials into my thigh and told me that he would do worse if I didn't scream. So I did. I wanted to tell you right away, but I was so terrified it was like I was trapped under water. I wasn't even present in my body until I realized he was going to try to kill Rainer and then I was so panicked. I just—" Tears burned Cecilia's eyes. "Xander, he didn't hurt me how you think, but the fear of it still lives in my body and I'm just trying to get it back. Not to mention that the only reason he didn't do it then is that he wanted to be able to continue to use it as an effective threat."

Isla looked sick. "He's disturbed."

"Every time you look at me, you look so guilty, and I just want you to stop feeling responsible for another man's violence," Cecilia said.

"I don't," Xander said, closing the space between them. He held his arms out and she curled into him and let him hug her. "Love, I have been so worried about you because you haven't said anything about it, and I just wanted to know that you're all right."

"I'm all right. But if we don't stop him, he and his men will continue to spread this violence and I refuse to let that happen," Cecilia said.

To her surprise, Isla came in behind her, wrapping the two of them in a hug.

"No one deserves to feel that terror. We are going to make him pay for this," Isla said softly.

"I have no doubt about that, but what if I lose Rain anyway?" The words slipped out without permission, the fear too large to contain, and Isla and Xander had no reassuring words to offer. "I thought I was getting through to him. He'd even started to smile...and now he's proposed to her."

Cecilia drew away, spinning her engagement ring on her finger.

Brave with my hand.

She wasn't feeling particularly courageous, but she pulled the ring off and held it up to the light to see the engraving inside the band, reminding herself of the second part of her spell for courage.

Brave with my heart.

20

EVAN

Evan tried to roll the tension from his shoulders, but seeing Reese beaten within an inch of his life brought back the memory of Teddy bloody and lifeless. Evan squeezed his eyes shut, trying to rid himself of the memory.

Reese had been such a mess when Chris brought him in that Evan worried some of the damage might have been permanent. Sylvie had done an expert and meticulous job healing every cut, leaving only one faint scar that Reese insisted gave him a roguish mystique.

Reese was fine and he'd had a full day to recover and be doted on by Chris and the priestesses. But Evan still felt rocked.

Now Reese leaned casually over a pew, finishing a joke that had Cal laughing until he cried. It was a relief to see him joking again.

Chris crossed the temple to where Evan stood leaning against the marble wall.

"Thank you for hiding us," he said.

Evan nodded. "Happy to have you. Sorry that Reese had to take a beating to get here."

Chris shrugged a shoulder. "I think he's more upset that his wanted poster doesn't do him justice."

Reese held a paper high in the air. "I'm a little offended that someone drew my nose so big. Aren't they supposed to have memory witches do these wanted bulletins?" He angled the poster toward the crowd of priestesses and gestured to his nose. "While I admit it's hard to capture this perfection, I don't think this was a very good attempt. Wouldn't you agree, ladies?"

The priestesses giggled.

"I know we had a lot of urgent fires to put out before now, but I received word that Raven Whitewind is in town," Chris said.

Evan shook his head. "Why on earth would she respond to Vincent's summons?"

Chris rubbed his chin. "I can't imagine, truly. But Vincent was confident she was coming right before I escaped and I asked one of the hunters who works for me to keep an eye out. He sent word along a few minutes ago that it's official."

Evan's gut roiled. Vincent working with an ancient witch was dangerous. He tried to catch Sylvie's eye, but she was too distracted by the news. "It can't be for anything good. You weren't able to get Vincent to spill his plan?"

Chris gestured to Reese. "Neither of us were. It was clear from the beginning that he didn't trust us. He knew already from Spellman that we were Xander's most loyal supporters. I think he was just waiting for his moment. It's very lucky that Cece was able to make it look like she'd wiped his mind to keep him from being killed."

Reese scoffed as he sidled up beside them. "I resent that no one is congratulating me for my excellent acting skills."

Chris rolled his eyes and threw an arm over Reese's shoulder. "Yes, you are an unparalleled talent, but we have a bigger problem. Whitewind is officially in town."

Reese frowned. "We can't let her help Vincent figure out how to keep power. If she sees all the different paths forward, she could show him how to get rid of Xander. She could show him how to get rid of all of us."

"You're all looking at this the wrong way."

Cato's voice made all of them jump.

Evan turned and found the trickster lounging across the altar as if it were a chaise. Evan's fingers brushed the dagger at his waist.

Cato cocked his head and gave Evan a patronizing look. "As the only one of us that has truly dealt with that wretched hag in the recent past, I can guarantee that no one manipulates Raven, not even me. I doubt some traitor king with little impulse control is going to be able to. If she's here, it's for a reason that has nothing to do with giving him what he wants."

Sylvie arched an eyebrow and Evan startled. He couldn't get used to seeing her expression on the face that Cato had given her. The differences were subtle, but he knew every inch of her face like the back of his hand.

"Maybe you're just losing your touch in your old age," Sylvie said.

"Easy, witch, or I'll consider feeding you to that vicious king who seems to have taken a fancy to you," Cato said with a wink.

Evan bristled. He had suppressed reacting to Sylvie being in danger for so long. Since she'd been wounded, he'd completely lost his composure. Evan loved and hated caring because it gave him a vulnerability, and the last thing he wanted was someone hurting Sylvie to get to him. She'd been through *enough*.

"Watch what you say. You're on thin ice in another god's temple," Evan said.

Cato grinned, holding up his hands. "Oh, calm down, boss. I'm joking. Honestly, you've all been in hiding too long. You're far too serious these days. Makes me miss Cece. She may have stabbed me in the heart, but at least she has a sense of humor."

"So, you think the seer is here to help us?" Sylvie asked.

"I think that ancient witches serve one master: balance. I should know." It was amazing how condescending Cato could sound while talking about his own mistakes.

Sylvie seemed satisfied with that response, but Evan needed to know more. "How could she help?"

Cato sighed exasperatedly. "Gods, you're thick. What does Raven Whitewind do most of the time—or rather, what *did* she do?"

"Bond guardians and witches," Sylvie said. "You think she's here to help Rainer and Cece."

Cato shook his head. "No, I think she's here to pass along cryptic riddles that might aid Cece—but she knows a lot about memory magic, so it's possible she might help by accident. She seems to have a soft spot for Cece."

"She was friends with Cece's birth mother, Selene Carrick. She and Raven and two other witches helped create the Gauntlet. Or do you pretend to forget the time the ancient witches of Olney tricked you at your own game?" Sylvie taunted.

Cato glowered at her.

"Regardless, if there is anyone who knows about memory recovery and the complexity of giving and taking and storing memory, Raven would know," Sylvie said.

"Exactly!" Cato swiped a finger over the altar as if testing for dust before jerking his thumb toward the statue of Aurelia on a raised platform behind him. "You ever met her?"

"*Goddess Aurelia*?" Chris asked, wide-eyed.

Cato shrugged. "A bit high-maintenance. She's known for her neutrality, but she's actually much like Goddess Sayla when it comes to men who commit violence against women."

Sayla, goddess of the hunt, Cecilia's half-sister, was known for inflicting vengeance upon sexually violent men. When Evan had met her, she'd been both enigmatic and terrifying, but he'd never heard tales of Aurelia avenging women in the same way.

"She understands how to manage her image," Cato continued. "You could take note, Farlan. But she's been known to help women avenge themselves." His gaze raked over a group of priestesses clustered in the front pews. "Isn't that right, ladies?"

The women eyed him suspiciously, then went back to whispering amongst themselves.

"You mean to tell us we have been hiding among Aurelia's avenging army?" Sylvie asked.

Cato threw his head back and laughed. "I hardly think they function in the way you're thinking." He narrowed his gaze on the women in the front row. "Unless something has changed."

Evan looked to the high priestess, Kenna, who'd stepped forward from the group. "Is that true?" he asked.

Kenna looked at her peers, and they all nodded. "Yes. Most of the women here have either been witness to or victims of violence by men. When they arrive, part of our program, if they choose to participate, is to empower them to defend themselves. We are hardly an avenging army, but we have some basic skills, not to mention a talent for poisons as our goddess is of the harvest, which includes many herbs that can be both medicinal and poisonous."

Evan stared at Kenna. He'd known her for a long time and the temple had served as a hiding place for any of his spies that had been discovered over the years, but the omission of that information made him see their relationship in a whole different light. He knew that the place was a haven from violent men, but Evan hadn't thought Kenna put him in that category.

As if reading his sudden doubts, Kenna turned to look at him. "It's not about you, Hunter Farlan. Healing is paramount here, and part of that requires the ability to defend oneself."

"I would have helped train them if I knew," Evan said.

Kenna cocked her head to the side. "I'm sure you can understand the need for discretion. We make decisions collectively and on the basis of what information is critical. Until now, this information has not been something you needed to know to work with us."

Evan wanted to defend himself, but then thought of how Sylvie had kept her own secrets about the violence that had been inflicted on her. It wasn't about him. It was about women needing to be able to share in their own time in order to heal.

"Well, now that we've settled everyone's hurt feelings, we know where to get our little army. Now we just need to figure out when to use them," Cato said.

As if it was truly as simple as that.

Kenna conferred with the priestesses in the front row before turning to look at Evan again. "We are willing to help, but I am responsible for these women. I won't approve a plan that puts them in steeper peril than necessary. You'll need a good way to be certain which side everyone is on, because I won't have them pay a price for your mistakes."

Evan nodded, nervousness churning in his gut. Distinguishing friend from foe was exactly what they were trying to do, but his failure to see what was right in front of his face for months had left him doubting his ability to do so. He didn't want these women to suffer any more than they already had.

Sylvie's soft hand slid into his and squeezed. She leaned her head on his shoulder.

"Is this a good idea?" he whispered.

"Don't take on the responsibility for them, Evan. They chose to help —don't be another man that underestimates their ability or takes away their agency. Let them help, and trust them to tell you where the line is," Sylvie said. "Allowing them to help gives us the advantage of surprise because Vincent is too much of a pig to suspect women. He would certainly notice if we tried to sneak in a battalion of our own men."

Evan looked around as more priestesses flooded the temple. "I'm sure they know basics, but this is a lot of women to train in a very short period of time."

"Then we better get started and come up with a plan," Sylvie said.

Cal joined them. "You really think that we can train all of these women to take out Vincent's men? I'm all for evening the battlefield, but Vincent's hunters have years of combat training."

"I think it's the only viable option we have," Evan said. "Sylvie is right. Vincent will suspect something immediately if he gets a bunch of male staff hired at once, but if we manage to sneak women in, he will think nothing of it."

Cal sighed. "What about our friends still inside?"

"Yes—are we concerned at all that our resident brainwashed guardian is set to marry another woman in a few weeks' time?" Sylvie asked.

Evan sighed. Word of Rainer's engagement to Eloise Spellman had reached them earlier in the afternoon. It was a complication they did not need, and no doubt Cecilia was beside herself. She wasn't known for her even temper. That concerned Evan the most.

"You're looking at this all wrong," Cato said. "A wedding is a great opportunity for outsiders to get into the castle. You should know that by now, all things considered."

Evan sighed, rubbing the bridge of his nose. Cato seemed just as keen to antagonize them as he was to help.

"You think Vincent won't be ready for that?" Evan challenged.

Cato shrugged. "I don't think he'll be ready for much. He's frustrated he can't get information out of any of your people. He's even more frustrated that the common people are protesting at the castle gates. But where he really loses focus is when it comes to taunting Xander and Cece. His penchant for psychological warfare distracts him from rational decisions. If he was thinking rationally, he wouldn't be rushing an event that invites a bunch of strangers into the castle so soon after the transition of power."

Loath as Evan was to admit it, Cato had a point. Shaking his head, he wondered what the world was coming to with the trickster god making sense.

"What if we train any of the priestesses who volunteer and have them come in for the wedding?" Sylvie suggested.

"Can we rely on them?"

Sylvie glared at him.

"Syl, I'm not doubting that women can do it," Evan said. "I'm acknowledging the considerable grief, fear, and anger that they would need to manage to do so. Is it more damaging to send them into an environment where we can't guarantee their safety?"

Sylvie's face softened. "Don't you think we should leave it up to them? By empowering them to decide for themselves, we're giving them the opportunity to make things right."

"We will have the element of surprise on our side," Cal added.

It could work, but there were so many variables. Still, it might be their best option to get inside with minimal casualties. They could always abandon the plan if it was too dangerous.

"We already know the basics," one of the women said. When Evan turned to look at her, she took a tentative step closer. "We certainly aren't warriors, but we are quick learners. Some of us also have magic. We can be a resource. Please, at least give us the opportunity to stand up for ourselves and our kingdom."

Her conviction was compelling. Evan had relied on the talent of female spies for years. He didn't doubt their ability to unearth valuable information or their cleverness and strength. What concerned him was the brutality of Vincent's men and their willingness to scheme and play dirty.

Sylvie grinned at the woman, looking thrilled at the prospect of leading an army of ladies against Vincent's men. Still, Evan worried it wouldn't be enough. The problem with Vincent's meddling was that it had stripped him of his confidence, and he had much more than his own bruised ego to contend with. He knew things were bad. It was Evan's job to understand how the changes Xander was making to Argaria's deeply ingrained classist systems were affecting the overall mood in court and in town.

"Cal, can you sit with them and figure out what they know? That will give us a good place to start. We can try to come up with a plan that gives advantage to the skills they already have," Evan said.

Cal nodded and crossed the room to Kenna and her priestesses.

Sylvie hooked her arm in Evan's and led him to a quiet place at the back of the room. "So, Cato's turning out to be more helpful than expected. I don't know whether to be skeptical or grateful."

"Do we have to pick one?" Evan asked.

"You're tense," she said, rubbing her fingers over his jaw.

"Is there another way to be right now?"

Sylvie grinned. "I could take you in one of those meditation booths and we could find out."

Evan laughed, pulling her into a kiss. "That sounds good right about now, but it's strange to think about being with you when you look like someone else. It feels like cheating."

"I don't know, I kind of like this gruffer, older version of you," she said, playing with his hair.

Evan sighed. "I can't stop going over how this might work and what other resources we might be able to get access to."

"Always so responsible, though I suppose you wouldn't be the man I fell in love with if you didn't consider all the angles," Sylvie said.

"That's how I got you, after all."

Sylvie rolled her eyes. "You got me because I took a dagger to the chest for you."

"That seems to be a theme for our group of friends, doesn't it?" Evan teased.

She shuddered. "Here's hoping that trend ends."

"What else do you think we should do, Syl? You've been so quiet."

She worried her plump lower lip with her teeth, a maddeningly distracting habit that drew Evan's mind back to sneaking her into a meditation booth for alone time.

"I wonder if our friends in Aldrena would like the opportunity to pay Vincent back for using their princess's name to commit crimes against another kingdom. Now that we know those fake princesses were just Vincent's plants, I have to think this is an opportunity for alliances," Sylvie said, startling him from his dirty thoughts.

"You think they'd work with us to help hide some of our people in their delegation for the wedding?" Evan asked.

"It doesn't hurt to ask. If we know they haven't responded to Vincent's correspondence, they're probably at a loss for what to do, but it doesn't take a genius to know that Xander makes a far less volatile neighbor," she said.

Evan smiled. That was his Sylvie—always seeing all the political angles of things.

"Sure," she continued, "it would be a risk to them if Vincent finds out and our plan doesn't work, but no more of a risk than waiting to see what he does when they don't want to work with him."

He kissed her.

"You're brilliant," he whispered as he drew away. "Marry me."

Sylvie blew out a startled breath. "I already said yes."

Evan squeezed her hand. "No, marry me before we charge into one more dangerous situation."

He braced himself for teasing or for her to say she couldn't possibly find the right dress while they were in hiding.

Instead, she smiled brilliantly and said, "Yes."

21

CECILIA

Alcohol was the simple answer to a complicated problem. Cecilia should have thought of it herself. Drunk Rainer was always so snuggly and sweet, and he likely did not remember that particular bit of information.

She'd almost laughed out loud when he showed up at her door with a bottle of whiskey and a deck of cards. Unfortunately, he had much higher tolerance than Cecilia, and in order to get him to drink she had to do the same.

"To what do I owe this surprise, Rainer?" she teased, sipping the whiskey and savoring the warmth that spread down her throat to her chest. "Are you here to celebrate your engagement?"

Rainer looked chastened by the question. He shrugged. "I thought you might want some company since you've been shut up in your rooms for the past day. And I brought you something to read." He pulled a book of Argarian fairy tales out from under his arm.

Cecilia didn't buy his explanation, but she went along with it because being with him away from prying eyes, she felt pleasantly light for the first time in weeks. Rainer only intentionally sought her out to guard her and her only plan for the evening was to sneak down to see Magdalena and Mika, but his sudden presence led her to believe she was missing something.

She took the book and placed it on her nightstand. "Will Lady Spellman be joining us?" she asked.

Rainer frowned and guilt swelled through their bond. "No."

"If I didn't know any better, I might think that you were trying to distract me from something," Cecilia said.

Rainer shook his head. "Can't you just enjoy the satisfaction that I consider you a worthy adversary?"

She grinned at him. He was a terrible liar. As she shifted and the teal cashmere sweater he'd bought her dipped off her shoulder, his eyes tracked the movement.

"Why did you answer dressed like that?" he asked.

"Like what?"

Rainer gestured to her nightdress. She had been prepared to act as if she was going to sleep when he did his nightly check-in on her and had slipped the sweater on for warmth. Still, it wasn't an appropriate outfit for anyone but a lover to see her in.

"If you thought it was inappropriate, why did you come in?"

Rainer's cheeks pinked. "Because I knew if I suggested you put something else on, you'd likely find something more scandalous to spite me."

"So, you're saying you think I look appealing?" Cecilia asked.

Rainer frowned, dealing the cards. "I'm saying you look like trouble."

"That's exactly what I was going for!" she exclaimed, delightedly clapping her hands. The whiskey had gone straight to her head, and she felt giddy.

They played several hands. Cecilia let him win five times in a row. When they were younger, he used to let her win after she lost too many times because he felt guilty. It took him a long time to put together that she intentionally threw the first few hands to lull him into a false sense of security.

She sprawled lazily on the bed, looking over the edge of her cards to where Rainer sat on the floor, leaning against her nightstand.

Since waking up after the attack, he'd been clean-cut, but tonight stubble dusted his jaw, and she fought the urge to reach out and brush her fingers over it.

"You have a terrible poker face," Rainer teased.

"Maybe that's just what I want you to think," she countered.

"It's not. You're refreshingly expressive," Rainer said.

She sat up, feeling the pleasant lightness of the whiskey in her limbs. Sitting across from him as they drank and played cards, she could almost forget their circumstances. She could almost ignore the chill of the castle, the terror constantly cresting and receding in her body.

Rainer looked so relaxed. He hadn't looked like that since before she stole his memories.

"So, have you assumed all of the duties that you had before the attack?" Cecilia asked, pretending to nurse her drink. "Other than just guarding me, of course."

Rainer sipped his whiskey. "I'm not sure since I don't remember everything I did before and since you seem delighted to make keeping you out of trouble a full-time job."

"Nonsense—it's part-time at best. I sleep late and go to bed early."

Rainer arched an eyebrow like he didn't believe her. Did he suspect she'd been sneaking around? He could easily be the one to rat her out to Vincent since he had forgotten what side he was on.

"The king still seems tentative to put too much responsibility on me, but I think that he's coming around," Rainer said, a hint of pride in his voice. "He's been progressively bringing me in on some of the high-profile prisoners and has tasked me with figuring out if there are any more people in our midst who might be a threat to his reign."

Cecilia sighed. "That sounds like more than a little responsibility. I'm sure he wouldn't let just anyone know which prisoners are where or what the king's daily schedule is."

Rainer frowned. "How did you know I know his schedule?"

She giggled. "I didn't until now."

That was certainly information worth having. Cecilia only had the basics of Vincent's daily schedule—not enough to know when he was most vulnerable.

Rainer looked back at her with amusement in his eyes, glancing briefly at the door. She needed to suck him back in and get him talking or he would leave. If Vincent was actually letting him in on important information, she might be able to get it out of him.

"Care to make this more interesting?" Cecilia asked.

Rainer arched an eyebrow. "What could be more interesting than playing poker with the future queen?"

Cecilia tipped her head back and laughed. He liked to remind her of her position when she was making him nervous. "Finish that glass and I'll tell you."

His glass was nearly full, but he didn't hesitate to knock it back. The last few drops clung to his lips. Cecilia wanted to kiss them away.

Rainer's eyebrows shot up, making it clear that sentiment was written all over her face. "See something you like?"

Cecilia grinned. "Actually, I only see things I like."

The tension between them seemed poised to snap if either of them moved. Gods, she wanted him to touch her almost as badly as she was afraid to be touched.

Rainer shook his head. She almost had him.

"My idea is that whoever loses the next hand also has to lose an article of clothing," she said. Rainer's eyebrows nearly shot up to his hairline. "Don't tell me you're going to say something about that being inappropriate. You're already corrupting me with your alcohol and gambling."

Rainer laughed. "I figured it was nearly impossible to further corrupt you."

He narrowed his eyes, considering her proposition. She watched him go through a whole host of emotions. He clearly wanted her pliant if he was even considering her request. As much as she wanted to see him naked, she'd have to throw the next few hands so that she ended up in a state of undress that was enough to entice him to tell her what was going on. For today, spying had its benefits.

Just a few hands later, she sat in just her silk nightgown and thigh-high wool socks. If Rainer noticed her sudden losing streak, he must have chalked it up to drunkenness. He shuffled the cards, dealing for both of them. She reached for hers and the strap of her nightgown slipped.

He sucked in a breath and their gazes clashed. She paused, her fingers brushing his.

Rainer drew his hand back like he'd been burned, looking suddenly extremely interested in his cards. She was losing him.

"It seems things are finally calming down with the common folk," she said.

Rainer shrugged a shoulder. "There have been less of them gathered at the gates." He sipped his whiskey and played his cards.

He was like a stone wall. She'd have to try harder.

She leaned forward more than necessary to reach for her cards and her strap slipped again. "I know Vincent is livid that he hasn't found Reese Reynolds yet," she said. That was her best guess. Vincent would be the last person to share valuable information with her.

"We'll find him soon."

Cecilia laughed and reached for her drink, allowing her strap to slip for a third time.

Rainer shifted, trying to look anywhere but at her chest, where her gown was hanging scandalously low. "I don't see how it could be so hard to find one mindless man, but it doesn't bode well for finding the rest of the rebels."

"But you have no leads," Cecilia said.

Rainer cocked his head to the side and she worried she'd pushed a bit too hard. His face softened. "I won't let anyone hurt you, Cecilia. You don't need to worry."

She shifted to the floor. The stone was cold, even through her thick socks. The roaring fire had chased most of the chill from her room. But with just her nightdress, she was cold enough that her nipples pressed hard against the silk.

Rainer's gaze dropped to her lips and then her chest. She wished she'd worn a more low-cut nightgown so he would see the golden scar on her chest. That wouldn't expressly be helping him remember, but surely he'd wonder why her scar matched his.

Rainer licked his lips and looked away.

Cecilia reached over their glasses and the cards to take his hand. "I won't let anyone hurt you either."

At first, he smiled like he thought she was joking, but then the creases around his eyes softened and he looked almost startled.

"I should go after this hand," he said, taking another long gulp of whiskey.

Cecilia let him win one more time. She brought her hand to the hem of her dress and Rainer's eyes went wide as saucers.

"Just kidding," she said with a wink. She pulled off one of her socks and tossed it at him.

He laughed, though she couldn't tell if it was at her or himself, then he stood and pulled on the sweater he'd shed.

Cecilia crossed the room, sitting atop a short chest of drawers by the door. "Do we have somewhere to be?"

"I have somewhere to be. The only place you have to be is here," he said softly.

"What if I want to come?" she asked, lacing every word with innuendo.

Rainer swallowed hard. He crossed the room, stopping right in front of her. His hand came to rest on her thigh. The only barrier between them was her high wool sock that reached almost to the edge of the slit in her nightgown.

Immediately Rainer met her eyes, searching for permission. He was so good about acknowledging that boundary, so understanding, even without his memories.

She held his gaze as she shifted so that his fingertips slid to the gap above her sock. He hesitated before brushing his fingers over the skin of her thigh.

Rainer leaned in close so that his breath danced over the shell of her ear. She tilted her head back, eyes closed. She was so overwhelmed by his closeness, the smell of him like salty air and clean linens and lilac. She wanted to crush him against her and bury her face in his chest, but she knew he would see that as inappropriate.

"Cece, you don't want to come with me," Rainer soothed. His cheek brushed against hers, stubble pleasantly scraping her skin. "This is the boring stuff you hate. Stay here and read. I brought you that book. Can you do that for me?"

Cecilia barely registered his words because his thumb was gently stroking her inner thigh. She felt wild with desire—a feeling she thought long dead. Now she wanted to rub her body against his.

"Hmm?" she asked dumbly.

Touch had been so difficult for her since the attack, but Rainer's touch was so soothing she didn't ever want it to stop. She snapped her eyes open and met his gaze, praying he wouldn't stop touching her.

"Cece, can you stay here and not cause trouble? Be a good girl?" he asked.

If anyone else had said the words, she would have rolled her eyes, but the second they rolled off Rainer's tongue, she wanted to purr. He made it sound filthy and it was the first time since everything had gone so wrong that she felt actively turned on. Everything she worried had gone to sleep forever in her came roaring back to life at his closeness, at the way he breathed the words in her ear and the sensation of prickly hot desire surging through their bond.

"You'll do that for me, right, Cece?" Rainer asked, meeting her eyes. "Be a good girl?"

She gasped, high with lust. Her teeth dragged over her bottom lip as she nodded. He smiled. He was so close to her face and so handsome she thought she'd die if he didn't just kiss her. She forced herself not to reach for him.

"Yes," she breathed.

Rainer sighed, his nose grazing up the column of her throat. "How do you always smell so good?" He seemed momentarily distracted—as lost in her as she was in him.

"Magic," she mumbled, willing his lips to press to her skin.

"You'll stay here in your room and not try to escape and cause trouble, right?" He nuzzled her neck, and she dropped her head back against the wall, practically moaning.

She hadn't felt so turned on in weeks, and suddenly her body was flooded with tension, heat, and heady lust.

"Yes you will, won't you? You'll be such a good girl for me," he murmured, his lips grazing her skin.

"Fuck," she mumbled.

He chuckled and the vibration of it pulsed through her whole body. "Stay here. Be good."

Then his warmth fell away, the door closed, and the key turned in the lock. Cecilia snapped out of her daze as the lock clicked.

What. The. Fuck.

How had she been so dazed that she didn't realize what he was doing? He used her own distracting seduction techniques against her.

"Rain!" She pounded on the door. "Come back!"

When it was clear he wouldn't return, she sulked and slid down the door to the floor. "Asshole."

But she couldn't deny that, for the first time since Vincent had put his hands on her, she finally felt the familiar warmth spreading through her body. Before, she'd wanted Rainer's comfort and his affection, but now she wanted his body. She wanted his mouth and his hands all over her skin and she definitely wanted him telling her what a good girl she was while he did it.

The words sparked an idea. She climbed into bed and closed her eyes, imagining him touching her, whispering in her ear. *"You're such a good girl."*

The words were like a match to tinder. She touched herself tentatively and then more urgently, chasing something that stayed frustratingly out of reach, no matter how much she reminded herself that she was safe in her body behind a locked door.

She gave up after a few minutes and sat with a huff. At least she felt something. Part of her was worried that what she'd felt before would only return in fits and starts, but now that familiar warmth felt within reach.

Rising from the bed, she pulled on her boots. They still smelled faintly of the stables from a prank she'd pulled on Grant that afternoon. She smiled as she ducked into the passageway leading from her room to meet with Magdalena for her healing session.

The healer's suite was quiet this late at night, the candles burning low in their holders. Fragrant smoke burned in a dish of dried lavender. Magdalena sat in her chair by the fire, a patient, soft smile on her face.

"Is it necessary for me to be here for these sessions this often?" Cecilia asked.

Mika crossed her arms, tapping her foot impatiently. "Was it necessary for you to wear the same boots you wore to stables this afternoon when you went to get horse shit to smear under Grant's bed? I'm going to smell like a stable when I go to Rainer's bachelor party."

Cecilia frowned. Her Rainer would have been entirely uninterested and probably adorably disoriented by a bunch of scantily clad women dancing for him, but this Rainer was different—edgier. Perhaps he would enjoy it after all.

She glanced at Mika's low-cut red gown. Most men would enjoy the view.

"I used gloves and washed my hands five times, but I can't help what's left on my boots," Cecilia said. "And thank you for noticing the excess of my antics. Systematically ruining Grant's day is hard work and I've put a lot of effort into creative ways to do it."

Mika shook her head.

"You're deflecting," Magdalena said, her gaze piercing Cecilia even through the steam of her tea. She sipped slowly, waiting for Cecilia to speak.

"I know you want me to talk about things, but it's not helping. I can't forget what happened even though it wasn't as bad as it could have been. I'm not getting over it, so what I need to know is how to live with it."

Magdalena gestured to herself and Mika. "This is how we live with it. Women have been doing this for centuries: sharing our grief, carrying it for each other when we lack the strength to bear it alone.

It's part of the legacy of women in this world. Men think they're strong because they take, but it takes much more strength to endure, to hold back and strike at the right moment. To bottle your rage and use it when you need it instead of spreading it around like it's your right."

Cecilia watched her friend's face. This little room in Magdalena's suite was one of the only places in the entire castle where she could take a deep breath.

"This is how we take care of each other. Generations of women leaned on other women to hold the hurts only they could understand. The weight is unbearable alone. It's hardly bearable together. In witness we save each other," Magdalena said.

Love was many things, but at that moment, it was understanding and empathy.

"I know I'm okay, but I can't get over the fear that at any moment I'm going to be just as powerless. It's like I'm constantly on edge, constantly waiting to have to fight my way out. Does that go away?" Cecilia asked.

Mika sighed, taking Cecilia's hand. "I think it goes away at times and at others it comes back all at once." She shook her head. "I cannot believe that I was within striking distance of him when he was unprotected for months, and I didn't end him."

Cecilia squeezed her hand. "So was I. How could we have known? I was supposed to be able to sense his emotions and I never got even a hint of resentment from him."

Magdalena shook her head. "You're both being too hard on yourselves. He has had years to plan this. We did the best we could with the information we had. All of your feelings are valid, but I refuse to accept that either of you should have or could have done more. We know better than to go down that road. It won't undo anything. It won't bring Ivy back. Now, Cece, did you do your homework?"

Cecilia huffed out a breath, her cheeks heating. "I tried. It didn't work."

"What happened?" Magdalena asked.

Cecilia squirmed in her chair. "I could touch myself, but I can't finish."

Her cheeks burned. She'd never discussed anything like this with Rainer or Xander other than in the context of dirty talk. Talking about it so plainly made her feel raw and vulnerable.

"It will come back," Magdalena said. "You're still in an environment that feels chaotic and unsafe. When you feel safe again, it will come back."

"And when will that be?" Cecilia snapped. She sighed, regretting the hardness in her voice. "I'm sorry. I know you're trying to help. I can't help feeling that if I could get myself over the finish line I'd be less cranky."

Mika laughed. "On that note, I have to be up in the bachelor suite for the festivities. You two will be all right on your own?"

Cecilia nodded and Mika paused in front of the mirror to check her hair and makeup before rushing out of the room.

"Have you been practicing coming back to your body in those moments of panic?" Magdalena asked.

Cecilia nodded. "I start with the texture of my dress, like you suggested. Then, I look around the room and describe three objects to myself. Usually that's enough to get it to abate, but not always."

She did not know how to untangle her tongue so the words might flow. She felt like she'd boil inside from the frustration of it.

How could she express what it was to still feel phantom hands on her skin—to feel pinned down and unable to move at random moments? Would the world look at her the same if his hands had left permanent burn marks on her skin the way they had on her mind? She did not know how to point to where it hurt because it was nowhere and everywhere, and it could have been worse.

But then all the ways it could have been worse shredded through her mind like claws. Because those things could still happen. She was in a prison of her own mind inside of a prison of her own choosing, but she refused to leave Rainer behind, and she'd worked too hard for peace to allow Vincent to destroy it.

"Maybe I just need to be more stubborn than the fear."

"I wish it were that easy," Magdalena said. "I think perhaps you have to forgive yourself."

"Forgive myself?" Cecilia said, baffled.

Magdalena nodded. "I think you blame yourself. You think you should have or could have done more. You must forgive yourself for any weakness you felt in that moment."

The words were sobering, confronting. Any hint of relaxation from the whiskey she'd had earlier was gone now.

"How do I do that?"

"If I could give you a shortcut, I would," Magdalena said. "It might simply take time for you to find the entry point into forgiveness, but it will happen. You have to have faith in yourself. You never doubt your ability to heal others, but now it seems you have nothing but doubt about your ability to heal yourself."

Cecilia stood. "I think I need some air."

"Don't be so hard on yourself. You've been brave to try what we've suggested. You've come a long way already and I'm here for you when you need to talk," Magdalena said.

Magdalena's warmth made Cecilia miss Aunt Clara. It wasn't lost on her how fortunate she was to have so many women who lifted her up when she was hurting.

Cecilia hugged Magdalena and left the healer's suite. The candles guttered, sending shadows scattering over the wall as she walked down the hallway and shoved the heavy door open. She stepped into the cold night air. The guards shifted at her presence outside, but none tried to stop her. Rainer had probably scared them all to death.

Fresh snow crunched beneath her feet, dulling the sounds of the garden. There was a pervasive stillness that settled into the evening now that the storm had blown out.

She walked along the path, taking in the flowers that looked as if they had been sprinkled with powdered sugar. Finally, she came to a bench. She sat, ignoring the way the snow seeped into her dress, chilling her backside, as she tilted her head up to the clear night sky.

Sometimes there was little left to do but make a wish and hope it came true.

22

RAINER

It was Rainer's bachelor party, but he seemed to be the only one uninterested in female company. All around him men delighted in the displays of skin, but Rainer's mind was singularly focused on the fresh memory of the sliver of pale skin on Cecilia's thigh peeking out from the top of her sock.

He hadn't wanted to stop and, judging from the way she'd shivered at his touch, she hadn't either. She'd gone from teasing to pliant so quickly, and he'd forgotten himself as well, nuzzling into her neck like he had any right to touch her. Like he had any right to even think about another woman that way when he'd just proposed to Eloise.

Shame suspended him in the doorway to the boisterous sitting room. The heat in the room, which was already full of too many writhing bodies and the strong smell of whiskey and ale, made his stomach turn. This was not what Rainer had in mind for a last party before marriage, though he supposed he'd had enough of an idea to lock Cecilia in her room so she wouldn't witness it.

No one had seen him yet. He could still escape to his room, make his excuses tomorrow, try not to think about the way Cecilia had gasped and arched into him when he called her a good girl. If he'd known that was all it took to make her cooperate, he would have done it day one.

But it hadn't occurred to him that she would find him as compelling as he found her. She liked to flirt and tease, but it wasn't until she'd given him a genuine smile over her cards that he'd thought perhaps all her flirtation had been about more than just getting a rise out of him.

"Rainer! You're late to the party. Pull up a chair and grab yourself a girl. The dances will start soon and that's when the real fun begins," Vincent said, clapping a hand on Rainer's back as he walked by.

Rainer crossed the room and poured himself a whiskey. The air was suffocating, thick with the smell of strong wine and perfume. A drummer, a fiddler, and several other musicians sat off to the side, tuning up their instruments, and several women were costumed as Olney goddesses. He recognized the pink diaphanous gown meant to represent Goddess Desiree and a woman wrapped in some strategically placed leaves who seemed to represent the goddess of the hunt.

Rainer fought to hide his discomfort. It was a bit sacrilegious for whores to be dressed as goddesses, but no one else seemed the least bit bothered by it.

He searched for a friendly face in the room but was a little embarrassed to realize he hadn't made any friends since waking up. He kept waiting for someone to pop up and tell him they were old friends, and the more time that passed without that happening, the more Rainer wondered why he hadn't made more time for friendships before the rebellion. Had he been so focused on advancement that he hadn't the time for anything else?

A grimmer possibility came to life in his mind. Perhaps all his friends had died in the attack. He ran a hand through his hair. It should have occurred to him to ask someone before now because this was humiliating.

Xander sat across the room by the fire, a lovely blonde woman poised on the arm of his chair. The prince smiled at her indulgently as she played with the collar of his shirt.

Vincent had two scantily clad women perched in his lap, both blondes with full breasts and wide hips. They looked nothing like Cecilia—but then again, maybe variety was the appeal of looking outside of one's relationship for company.

Although Rainer had a vague recollection of being with women in Olney, he was fairly certain he'd never sought company outside of a relationship. He didn't understand the purpose. Why commit to someone if you couldn't really commit? It was greedy and unnecessary—not that Rainer had any room to judge when he'd just been all over a woman who wasn't Eloise.

Still, Rainer looked at the king in a new light. Vincent was someone who'd always had everything but felt the world owed him more. He'd never be satisfied, and he was saddling beautiful, wild Cecilia with the burden of his endless wanting.

Immediately, Rainer knocked back the rest of his whiskey. That was none of his business. He was there to protect her body from harm but had no such responsibility to her heart.

"You disapprove?" Vincent's question startled Rainer from his racing thoughts.

Rainer recognized the challenge in the words. Of course he disapproved. It was disrespectful to a future queen to act that way so publicly. Plenty of kings had lovers, but they kept them privately.

"I don't, Your Grace," Rainer said, looking around the room with faux wariness. "I just wonder if all of these women have been vetted and if there aren't safer means of entertainment."

"We don't pay because we can't get it elsewhere, McKay," Vincent said. "We pay to walk away without complication. We pay for a woman who knows what she's doing."

Rainer crossed and uncrossed his arms.

"Are you suggesting this is something I should be getting from my betrothed?" Vincent challenged.

His gaze burned into Rainer as if he could smell Rainer's attraction to Cecilia. Xander had warned him that the king was jealous. The last thing Rainer needed was to get the most unavailable woman at court into trouble because of foolish lust.

Rainer swallowed hard. "Of course not. I just wonder if making it such a public event could lead to gossip."

Vincent smiled. "Always the strategist. I can appreciate that, but I assure you, my men understand the value of discretion." He leaned closer, his dark eyes burning into Rainer. "I know you have your wholesome values, but I've seen what an animal you can be behind closed doors when you're questioning those traitors. Just let go for the night."

Rainer cringed. It wasn't that he didn't believe in his duty, but he wasn't proud of the way rage overtook him when he was trying to get answers from traitors. Every time, he couldn't help thinking of the people who had been hurt and killed in the attack—at least that was what he told himself to pretend that there wasn't a direct line between his uncontrollable rage and the thought of someone laying a hand on Cecilia. He had no right at all to feel so protective of her, but ever since he'd witnessed her fear and vulnerability right after he woke up, he felt possessed by a need for justice that could only be exorcized with his fists.

Rainer nodded, trying to casually make his way to the corner of the room. This was not what he'd had in mind when Vincent said he wanted to reward him for his hard work.

Music swelled and several women began to dance. Vincent's guards looked on with interest, clapping along with the beat and shouting encouragement for the women to shed more clothing. The entire event made Rainer feel sick.

It was perfectly respectable work for these women, but the energy in the room set Rainer's teeth on edge. Vincent's men didn't seem to respect boundaries, despite the dancers swatting their hands away, and they were just as handsy with the servants pouring their drinks, though it was clear they were castle staff and not employed by the brothel. He watched a server twist a man's wrist back. It was a basic defensive move he learned in the first year of his own training, but he was surprised to see a servant knew it. The guard held his hands up as if mockingly chastised and the servant scurried away.

Rainer tried to get swept up in the music and merriment, but he felt awkward and out of place, even as his peers offered him toasts and women offered him dances that he politely declined. The room felt claustrophobic. Rainer was staring down a future that was coming at him too quickly. He needed more time.

He walked to the window, threw it open, and welcomed the cold winter air as he waited for the tightness in his chest to abate. The snow that had blanketed the kingdom in white all day had subsided, muffling the din of the city below. Moonlight shimmered on the snow, making it sparkle like stars had fallen to earth. It reminded Rainer of the fairy tale that had led him out of the dark. It reminded him of Cecilia lying in the snow, talking about a night sky sugared with stars. He huffed a laugh. What a ridiculous way to describe the sky.

His breathing slowed and his heart settled into a steady rhythm.

Movement in the castle gardens caught his eye. At first he thought he'd imagined it, but then a small shape wandered out of the shadow, a cloak pulled over their head. Between the slight stature and the familiar gait, he knew before they brushed back their hood that it was Cecilia.

He groaned, running a hand through his hair. *How did she escape that room and why is she outside?* She was an absolute menace. He could stay where he was and hope she found her way back to her room alone, but he felt compelled to go make sure she was safe.

A blonde woman appeared at his elbow, startling him from his staring.

"Guardian McKay, are you well?" she asked.

Rainer turned to look at her. She'd been sitting with Prince Xander earlier.

"Mika Notte," she said, recognizing that he didn't remember her name.

"Apologies, my memory is not what it once was," he said.

Her bright red lips turned up into a smile. "So I've heard. Are you not enjoying the festivities?"

"I'm not sure they're to my taste."

"You don't like to feel aroused?" Mika challenged, brushing her sleek blonde hair behind her shoulders, giving a tantalizing glimpse of her full breasts in her black lace slip.

Rainer shrugged. "In a group setting? No. But that's not the problem. I don't like what these women make me feel."

"What do these women make you feel?" Mika asked.

"Nothing, Lady Notte. They make me feel nothing at all. Meaning no offense. You're obviously all very lovely."

Mika smothered a laugh with an elegant hand. Her gaze followed Rainer's to the garden far below where, despite the chill of the evening, Cecilia sat on a stone bench in the open air, staring at the roses. She tipped her chin up, looking at the night sky. Making a wish, no doubt.

"And what does *she* make you feel?" Mika asked.

"Chaos," Rainer breathed. He hated that he'd said it aloud and revealed a weakness so easily, but the word tumbled out of him like he'd been holding it back for a lifetime.

As much as Cecilia calmed the endless droning rage he felt, as much as she calmed everything in him, she also brought forth complicated, overwhelming emotions. He had no control of himself around her and he desperately needed discipline right now. She systematically stripped his defenses away with her antics—with her reckless wandering—with her lack of regard for her own safety—and, gods help him, with her laugh that made him feel like the ground had dropped out from beneath him.

Cecilia was the worst kind of trouble and yet he could not stop seeking her out. He wanted her with a hunger that could consume the stars, the sun, the moon, the whole world if he let it.

She lived down the hall, but it might as well have been across the sea or among the night sky for how unattainable she was to him. Still, her impossibility did nothing to take the edge off his wanting.

Mika's lips drew up in a knowing smile. "Well, I suppose that would be terribly appealing to a rule follower such as yourself."

Rainer frowned. "I hate it."

"And also, you don't," Mika said with a grin.

He smiled back in spite of himself. "And also I don't," he agreed. "But that's not what I want."

"Sometimes we think we want something, but the fates give us what we need instead."

Rainer wanted to argue with her, but he certainly didn't belong in that room. "And what did you want?" he asked.

Mika's eyes lingered on Cecilia in the courtyard. "I thought I needed vengeance."

"And now?"

"And now I think maybe what I need is a friend. Maybe it's greedy, but I aspire to have both."

Rainer frowned as Cecilia laid back on the bench. "She's supposed to be locked in her room."

"Doesn't seem like she's hurting anyone."

"It's my job to keep her safe, and she makes it impossible."

"Perhaps she's content to live with a little danger for the sake of gaining peace," Mika murmured.

Peace. What a foreign concept. It felt as if Rainer had been fighting his whole life. He couldn't imagine putting down his sword for good when it had been his purpose for so long.

"Maybe you should go talk to her," Mika offered.

Was that what he needed? Permission?

"There are warriors who are strong and brave physically, but it takes a different kind of fortitude to be gentle—to coax someone out," Mika said.

Rainer was torn between staying and leaving as quickly as possible. Surely Vincent would notice if he excused himself too early, but Rainer already knew that Cecilia wasn't safe after she'd already been attacked beyond the castle walls. It was possible she was in danger from those in the rebellion, like that guard who'd attacked her in the snow, but it was also possible that she was part of it. Rainer couldn't begin to reconcile the vexing, lonely witch with someone who would help support the rebellion, and if she had, he'd assumed she would have been spared their violence. Though Cecilia did love to rebel against expectations and social norms, he could not imagine her being a part of such a dangerous fight.

That thought disturbed him. Holding on to feelings of any kind for the king's fiancée would do nothing for him. Rainer needed to get his head on straight.

Raymond McKay had given Rainer so little wisdom over the years, but some things stuck, and genuine affectionate feelings for someone who was unavailable would bring nothing but ruin to Rainer's life.

Still, the pull to Cecilia was relentless.

The room broke into roaring laughter as the men delighted in a new dancer, who hopped onto the table at the center of the room. She had a flower crown in her hair and wore a translucent green dress, a quiver of arrows strapped over her back. She pulled out a bow and an arrow.

Rainer tensed as she drew the string back and loosed an arrow. It hit a man on the other side of the table in the chest. He gripped the arrow and winced, his face twisted in a pained grimace, but then he drew his hand away and held the arrow high. The tip had been replaced with a strawberry, which the man bit. The men burst into calls for berries in all sorts of innuendos and the dancer started to twist her hips and fire berry arrows around the room.

Rainer set down his drink and sneaked out of the party while the men were distracted. He charged down the stairs and out into the garden. Beneath his feet, fresh salt crusted the cobblestone path, melting the snow into slushy puddles. He turned down the main trail and then made a left, finding Cecilia where he'd seen her sitting moments before.

"Lady Reznik?"

"Cece," she said, keeping her gaze on the sky.

"Do I want to know how you managed to make it out of a locked room?"

She shrugged. "I imagine you'd love to know, but the real question is would it be wise of me to tell you? Can't you simply accept that I'm an unparalleled talent and there's not a room or cell in the two kingdoms that could contain me if I wished to be free?"

Rainer sighed. "What could contain you?"

She blew out a slow breath, white vapor curling out of her mouth. "Love."

Rainer swallowed hard, at a loss for words. Wind blew through the garden, bare branches scratching together like claws. "We should go inside. It's not safe for you out here alone."

"I'm not alone," she said, finally pushing up into a sitting position to look at him.

"You know what I mean."

She waved a hand upward. "I just wanted to see the sky."

Rainer looked up. "Look at that. Sugared with stars."

She huffed a startled laugh. "Sugared with stars. Well said."

They fell into silence. Rainer wasn't sure what to say, but he felt calmer now that he was away from the noise of the party. The night was cold, but her presence was a comfort.

"What are you doing here?" Cecilia asked. "I thought you'd be too busy with your whores."

Rainer raised an eyebrow. "So you saw that?"

"Surprised to see the bachelor straying from his party."

"As surprised as he is to see you straying from your locked bedroom."

She pursed her lips. "Okay, I'll go back to bed and won't sneak out again if you do one thing."

Rainer groaned. "What one thing?"

Cecilia's eyes sparkled in the moonlight. "Make a wish."

Rainer shook his head, but he gazed up at the night sky. "What if I don't see a shooting star?"

"Then just pick the star you like best," she whispered.

Making a good wish seemed like something you needed to know yourself in order to do, and Rainer still remembered so little of his past.

"You're a memory witch, Cece. How do you think losing memories affects a person?" he asked.

A flash of anger, grief, and confusion ran through his chest.

"I've restored a lot of memories. People forget how much memory is tied to emotion and personality. When you lose your memories, you lose the context of your own personality. I imagine it feels like you don't know who you are at all. That must be frustrating—to be an adult and have to reinvent yourself without having all the puzzle pieces to do so."

Rainer nodded. Frustrated hardly covered it. "I'm finding it hard to make a wish since I don't know who I am or what I want."

She studied his face intensely, as if looking for some hidden depth in his words. "Don't be a perfectionist, Rainer. Wishes are about what the heart wants, not the head."

Cecilia made it sound so easy. He tipped his head back, waiting for the stars to scatter and offer him hope. Her hand slid into his and the gentleness in her touch made him feel suddenly fragile.

Rainer hated how soft he felt every time she touched him. Soft was weak, and he could not afford to feel weak when the world around him and especially the king demanded he be strong. It didn't matter that he felt the familiar warmth spreading in his chest when she was close, it didn't matter that she looked at him like he was the best thing she'd seen all day, and it certainly didn't matter that he wanted to know what she might have let him do if he'd skipped the party and stayed in her room.

He could not need her. He couldn't need anyone. To need was to be weak. They were the only wise words that Raymond McKay had ever drilled into him. *Show love when you need to but never when you feel it.*

As if they sensed his doubt and indecision, the stars refused to move and grant him a wish. Rainer picked one anyway and wished for his memories back. It seemed as safe a wish as any, not that it mattered. He'd already made the wish a thousand times a day.

"All done?" Cecilia asked.

He nodded, leading her back to the castle and up to her room. She was surprisingly quiet, as if she could sense how spent he was.

When they reached her rooms, the key was in the door where he'd left it. Cecilia opened it and paused in the doorway, turning to face him.

"Why didn't you stay at your party?"

"There was nothing there for me. I have no interest in women who aren't my betrothed."

The lie made him feel guilty, but not for the reason it should have. He felt bad for lying to Cecilia, but for the fact that he did in fact have an interest in someone who wasn't Eloise.

"How gallant of you not to be tempted." Cecilia pressed her hand to his chest, right over the golden scar. "What did you wish for?"

He closed his eyes, trying not to twitch as her thumb shifted, pressing his tunic against the scar. Rainer hadn't realized how sensitive it was. Goosebumps rose on his skin.

"I thought you said I can't share what I wish for, or it won't come true," he said, finally meeting her eyes.

Cecilia smirked, holding his gaze as she whispered, "I think you remember more than you think."

The door clicked shut before Rainer could tell her she was wrong.

He wanted to pound on her door to demand she tell him what she meant. Why did she have to be so cryptic and vexing all the time?

Rainer turned and stormed down the hall. Cecilia's words had crawled under his skin, burrowing deep and making him itch. Was he remembering her? Did he have the same sort of magnetic pull to her before the attack? Did he have a fucking death wish?

He needed to end the madness and stop the endless turmoil in his mind. He needed Eloise to set him straight. He needed to spend more time with her. If he spent as much time with her as he did guarding Cecilia, surely he would feel equally compelled.

Rainer turned down hallway after hallway until he made it to Eloise's wing. It was late and wildly inappropriate for him to show up unannounced. All of her ladies had likely already gone to bed.

He drew up short. It would be wiser to turn around and go to sleep alone in his own bed, but he knew that he'd just wake up from yet another visceral dream of Cecilia and he'd had enough of them in the past two weeks to drive him insane. He needed to blot out thoughts of her with thoughts of someone else.

He continued down the hall, knocking lightly on Eloise's chamber door. He listened for stirring inside. His stomach churned with guilt as he knocked a second time, holding out hope that she was still awake. Just as he was about to flee, the door opened and Eloise stood there, looking startled in a midnight-blue velvet robe, her hair unbound and hanging down her back in raven curls that looked soft and freshly combed.

She was so poised, so neat. Even answering the door this late at night, she was put together, unlike Cecilia, who had answered her door in a slip and a sweater, her hair wild and unbound.

Eloise's brow pinched in concern. "Rainer? Is all well?"

His cheeks warmed as he met her gaze. "All is well. I just—" He stumbled over his words, unable to voice why exactly he was there. It was disrespectful and inappropriate. "The king threw me a bachelor party and I know I was supposed to like it, but I found my mind was elsewhere the whole time."

Eloise's face lit with a smile, her eyes darting past him to check the hall before she grabbed a handful of his tunic and dragged him inside. That was all the invitation Rainer needed. As soon as the door closed behind him, he pulled her into his arms, kissing her with all his pent-up frustration.

She pressed closer, untying her robe to reveal a beautiful silk nightgown with delicate lace that highlighted her full breasts. Rainer shoved the robe off her shoulders as he drew a line of kisses down her neck, dipping between her breasts. She moaned and he pulled back to meet her eyes.

"Is this okay?"

"It's more than okay," she said, pulling off his shirt. "You have no idea how much I've thought of this." She ran her hand over his chest, pausing to stroke the golden scar, noting how it made him shiver.

Instantly, his mind flew to Cecilia brushing her thumb over his scar through his shirt as if she knew exactly where it was. Rainer needed to banish her from his head—even now he couldn't help feeling like he was letting her down in some way, as if she was watching, knowing this was happening. Guilt and dread pooled in his chest.

Eloise pulled him toward the bed and his focus was back on her. He slipped the straps of her nightgown off her shoulders, revealing her breasts. He bent and sucked one of her nipples into his mouth and Eloise let out a breathy moan. Her hand came to the back of his head as she arched into him. He dragged his teeth over her peaked nipple and she twitched.

"More," she begged, urging him toward the other breast.

He gave equal attention to both until she was panting, her eyes hooded with lust, her cheeks flushed.

"I want to see you fall apart for me," he rasped against her skin.

"Yes," Eloise said urgently.

His hand swept up her inner thigh, coming to rest on the silk between her legs. He rubbed her through the delicate fabric and she whimpered into his mouth. Dragging the damp silk aside, Rainer brushed his fingers over her and she moaned his name.

"How do you like to be touched, El?" he taunted, rubbing her slowly with a featherlight touch.

"Harder," she said breathlessly.

He rubbed his fingers against her harder before thrusting one inside. She arched into him, her fingernails digging into his back.

"Like that?" he asked.

"More," she whimpered.

He grinned at her as he pushed another finger inside her, sliding them in and out as he rubbed his thumb over her clit. She twitched and writhed, meeting each of his thrusts.

This was what he needed. Rainer needed another beautiful woman coming undone for him. Eloise squeezed his fingers, already close to giving him exactly what he needed to clear Cecilia Reznik from his mind completely.

"I want to taste you," he whispered.

"Yes," Eloise gasped.

He withdrew his hand and she whined until he slid her undergarments off and hiked her nightdress up. He shoved her legs wide, dragging her to the edge of the bed, and held her gaze as he knelt. He licked her and she shuddered.

She ran her fingers through his hair as he went to work, alternating between his tongue and fingers. Eloise's soft moans became louder, more insistent. Her legs tensed, toes curling as her heels dug into his shoulders. Rainer quickened his pace until she was panting. He was tempted to draw it out, but her fingernails dug into his arm and he gave in. He curled his fingers and Eloise gasped as she sailed over the edge, her hands clenching in the sheets.

Still, he didn't feel satisfied. It felt mechanical. Like he was going through the motions to prove he could.

He wiped his mouth on her inner thigh and she smiled at him, her eyes still hooded with lust as he rose to his feet.

"Rainer, I want you inside me," she said, fumbling with the button on his pants.

She was so tight and wet, that would be just what Rainer needed to banish Cecilia for good. But for some reason, he couldn't commit to it. He pulled Eloise's hands away and her eyes met his in the dark, searching for the answer to his hesitance.

If he did this now, he'd be taking something he didn't deserve. His heart wasn't in the right place. He couldn't in good conscience sleep with Eloise for the first time—for what was probably her first time—when someone else was still in his head.

"We should wait." He brushed Eloise's hair back from her face tenderly. "El, it's not that I don't want to, but I'd like to save something for our wedding night. Tonight was about you. I just wanted to make you feel good—to make myself feel good, really."

Her bottom lip kicked out in a pout. "But I want to please you too."

"Believe me, you did," Rainer said, tugging his shirt on.

She grinned at him.

"I should sneak out before someone gets suspicious, but thank you for letting me be wildly inappropriate for the night."

Eloise sat up, shrugging her nightgown straps back into place. "Feel free to be wildly inappropriate with me anytime. You fully live up to the hype."

Rainer gave her a good-night kiss before checking that the hall was clear and making his way back to his room, praying he was back in control.

23

RAINER

The morning was miserable, cold and rainy. It made Rainer homesick for the beaches of Olney and morning swims he could hardly remember. Sheets of rain pounded the stained-glass windows in the corridor, the wind rattling the panes like a thief eager to get inside. He walked faster, trying to shake the nagging memory of the previous night.

Rainer was most certainly not back in control despite his best efforts with Eloise. As if to prove there was no escaping Cecilia, he'd dreamt of her all night in all manner of sexual scenarios, on her knees before him with a look of challenge in her eyes, on her back at the edge of the bed looking wanton and needy, up against a wall with her legs wrapped around his waist as he moved inside her. The dreams chased him from sleep and left him aching and frustrated.

He rounded the corner, nearly crashing into Magdalena. The healer righted the stack of towels and basket on her arm before anything spilled.

"Forgive me, my lady. I didn't mean to barrel into you," Rainer said, straightening the bundle of towels in her arm.

The healer grinned at him, the faint lines around her eyes crinkling. "Nonsense, it's good to see you charging around these halls feeling better, Guardian McKay."

"Thank you. And thank you again for all your hard work. I'm sure it took a lot out of you," Rainer said, his mind flying to the mess of scars on his back.

Her face grew serious. "I wish I could have done more."

Rainer shook his head. "You did brilliantly. I understand it was quite a mess."

She nodded. "You've not stopped in for a while to check in on the recovery of your memories. Have you been well?"

"I have. Unfortunately, I've had little luck recovering what I've lost. It's frustrating but I'm hoping in a little more time I'll be ready," he said.

Magdalena's face fell. "Pity to lose so much of oneself. Many of my past patients who have had memory issues have found that emotion ties to memory more than we think. Some memory lives in the heart and the body. Perhaps paying attention to that might serve you."

Rainer nodded. "While I have you, I wondered if I might ask a favor. As you've probably heard with the king making such a fuss about it, I'm marrying Lady Spellman shortly. I know it's not in Argarian tradition, but I was hoping to surprise her by including something personal in our ceremony. When I was still unconscious, Eloise read me a fairy tale about a village where it rained stars. It calmed me when I was agitated and helped guide me out of the dark."

Magdalena frowned. "I'm afraid I can't help with that."

Rainer sighed. "I was hoping, since you were there, you might remember the name of it."

Magdalena held up a hand. "No, that's not it. Lady Spellman wasn't around until after you woke up."

Rainer stared at her. If Eloise hadn't been there, who had calmed him with her urgent whispers? Whose story had pulled him out of the chaos in his mind? When Eloise had asked him to repeat it back to her the other day, he'd assumed she wanted to test his memory. Now he saw the request in a different light. She hadn't known the story at all. It was a minor lie, but she could have just as easily told the truth.

"The story you heard was spoken word—told from memory. As I understand it—" Magdalena hesitated, her mouth opening as if she was uncertain the words would come out. "It was your story that—" She cleared her throat, frowning. "Someone was recalling the story for you."

"Who?" Rainer pleaded. His head throbbed as if just talking about the memory was rooting it back into his mind. He could still feel the warmth that spread through his chest, the magic that tingled like the starlight in the story.

Magdalena pursed her lips. "It's slipped my mind. I wish I could help."

Rainer let out an exasperated breath. "You remember the rest with such specificity but not that?"

"I apologize, Guardian McKay. I've offered what I can remember and some practical advice for getting your memories back. Follow those emotional threads. Don't be afraid of the things that carry the heaviest emotional weight. They might just be what weaves your mind back together."

A pungent scent hit Rainer's nostrils.

"What is that smell?" he asked.

"Anti-infection salve. I'm afraid it smells wretched, but it works wonders. You would know," Magdalena said.

The memory snapped into place but it wasn't from his own healing journey.

When Rainer had entered the cell after Reese Reynolds disappeared, that exact smell had hung in the air.

He eyed the healer skeptically. Magdalena was the Castle Savero healer and had been for decades; could she really be a spy betraying Vincent?

Magdalena shook her basket so the bundles of herbs inside fell back into place. He squinted at them and realized it was the same dried plant he'd seen on the floor of the tower cell after Reese escaped.

"What herb is that?" Rainer asked.

Magdalena frowned. "It's morning root. It's to help energize weary patients who are at risk of passing out."

Rainer nodded, his mind whirling. If Magdalena had been in the cell, she could have revived Reese enough for him to escape. There was a spy right under their noses the whole time, in a prominent place in the castle.

Vincent had trusted Magdalena, and she used that trust to turn his own people against him.

Rainer had been lauding her for healing him when she'd been the one who'd set into motion the very events that left him without his memory. It was unacceptable. He wanted to apprehend her right then, but figured Vincent might want to root out exactly who else was involved.

"Thank you," Rainer said.

Magdalena smiled, turned, and left him staring after her as if she had nothing at all to hide. He stormed down the hall toward Vincent's war room, frustration boiling through his veins. It was bad enough that each time he grasped some hint of his old self it only seemed to bring more questions than answers, but now they were going to have to reckon with the fact that one of the most talented healers in the kingdom was a traitor. Vincent was going to be livid.

Rainer paused outside the war room doors when he heard loud voices inside.

"I know you're not telling the truth." The hardness in Vincent's voice set Rainer's teeth on edge.

"I suppose you're an expert at lying," Cecilia's voice taunted.

"You'd really tempt me to follow through on what I started? Do you have so little survival instinct?" Vincent barked.

Cecilia laughed bitterly. "If you're going to do it, do it. Let's end the suspense of waiting for the executioner's blade to fall."

"Who is helping you?" Vincent said. "I'm not stupid enough to think that you're not involved in this."

There was a shuffling and a choking noise. Panic swelled in Rainer's chest, but he had no idea why. The sounds of a struggle held him frozen in place.

Cecilia sputtered. "Just because people are on to your games doesn't mean I'm to blame. Your problem is that when you ally yourself with traitors, it's hard to see whose blade is coming at you until it's buried in your back."

The sharp sound of a slap split the air and pain welled in Rainer's sternum as if he'd been hit. The room went silent.

"Is that all, or do you want to smack me around some more?" Cecilia asked, her voice laced with venom. "Would you prefer I lie? Is your paranoia so profound?"

Why did Cecilia provoke Vincent when he was under so much strain? Rainer was torn between running inside and intervening and keeping things simple by letting them settle whatever marital spat they were embroiled in.

"You're dismissed," Vincent said.

A moment later Cecilia tore out the door, her eyes falling on Rainer.

"Perfect," she huffed, brushing by him.

Rainer followed at her heels. "Are you well?"

She laughed and kept walking, bringing a hand to her sternum. It was only then that Rainer realized how badly she was trembling.

Rainer raced alongside her. "Tell me what's wrong. Lady Reznik, talk to me."

"Cece!" she nearly screamed.

"*Cece*, slow down. You have to tell me what happened. Why were you fighting?"

Her eyes met his and the angry, fearful look in them drew him up short. She turned and stormed away. "I can't stand the sight of you."

"But why?" Rainer asked, following her. He reached for her shoulder, forgetting how she hated to be touched.

She quickly pushed him against the wall, sliding something out of a pocket in her dress. The tip of a sharpened wood stake pressed against his throat. Despite the fury on her face, her body shook violently in what was definitely fear. She wasn't allowed to have real weapons, so she'd made one of her own and now she looked ready to plunge it into Rainer's throat.

"I'm sorry," he said.

The pressure on his neck increased slightly as she gasped, "For what?"

"For touching you without your permission."

"*That? That* is what you're sorry for." Her shoulders slumped as if the words broke her.

Rainer struck fast, knocking the stake from her hand and trying to duck away from her. She caught him with a knee to his stomach. She came at him hard. She was all attack—all fury—reckless and foolish. He blocked the series of vicious blows until he struggled to do so without hurting her. She looked to be a moment away from breaking down. He had to do something.

"I'm going to touch you now," Rainer said.

He ducked, hefting Cecilia over his shoulder. She kicked and punched at him madly as he carried her.

"What the fuck are you doing?" she screeched, but he ignored her and stalked to the end of the hall, taking the two turns that led to his favorite spot.

"You need to cool down," he said.

He pressed through the door onto the castle wall where he liked to hide and train. Ice-cold rain poured down on them in torrents and Cecilia let out a shrill flood of curses as he lowered her to the ground.

She came at him again quickly, fists flying hard and fast. Rainer easily dodged her, blocking each furious swipe of her hands.

"Why are you so angry with *me*?" Rainer asked breathlessly.

Cecilia was small, but she was surprisingly fast, and she hit harder than she ever had before. It was clear that she'd been holding back when they previously fought.

"Because you're supposed to—" She faltered, pausing as if surprised she could speak the words. "Because you're supposed to protect me."

All at once her anger evaporated under the chill of the storm, the icy rain cooling her rage to sadness. Her ruined dress hung limp. The wet black silk left almost nothing to the imagination, clinging to her breasts and stomach, highlighting the curve of her hips. It took all of Rainer's concentration to keep his eyes on her face.

"I am protecting you—mostly from yourself," he rasped.

Cecilia laughed and dropped her head back in frustration. In the gray, stormy light, Rainer saw the first signs of bruising on her cheek and around her neck. He froze, staring at the marks.

It was easier to pretend he didn't know that something was wrong between her and the king when he didn't have to look directly at the evidence of it. It would have still been simpler to ignore it, because to get involved meant he'd have to choose a side and his honor and his duty required two different choices. Now that Rainer stared at confirmation of what he'd heard, he wasn't certain what to do with it.

"Why do you look surprised by violence you've already heard?" She pushed past him, pacing through the torrent of rain. "It's not the first time you've heard him strike me." She studied him. "Perhaps it's fine to you as long as there are no visible bruises. It's the most common violence in the world, you know? The violence that disguises itself as love."

Rainer had nothing to say. She stopped suddenly, turning to look at him again. Her expression contorted, grief and frustration warring on her features.

"Oh, I see," she said. "You don't think there's anything wrong with a man disciplining his property. I suppose you're just like him now. Such a good little pawn for the king. Delivering his beatings to whomever he bids you. You know, Reese Reynolds's brother once saved my life. He has been nothing but a loyal member of this kingdom." She paced back toward the door they'd come through, then turned to look at him again.

Rainer advanced on her until her back was against the stone wall next to the door. "That's bullshit! I do not think it's okay, which is why I killed those soldiers who spoke about you with my bare hands. Don't presume to know me, Cece! You're always walking around here talking like you know better than me—than everyone, really. It's exhausting. Maybe if you didn't act like such a know-it-all, the king wouldn't—" He couldn't even finish the sentence because the wrong-ness of the words made him feel sick.

The truth was Rainer wasn't okay with it. Seeing the marks on her pale skin filled him with the most potent anger he'd felt so far, which only succeeded in making him more confused and, therefore, more furious. This reckless, infuriating woman was driving him crazy. She was the worst kind of trouble, yet he couldn't stop seeking her out. He thought of her all the time, worrying, wanting to spend every moment with her.

He was so tired of fighting it—so exhausted from trying to pretend that the only time he felt even a hint of familiarity in his life now was when Cecilia was close.

"You're right," she snapped. "I don't know you at all. But if I did, I'd say you're a pathetic sheep who can't think for yourself. I honestly don't know why you even—"

"I'm going to touch you now," Rainer said.

She squeezed her eyes shut as if waiting for a blow, which only made him more furious with himself, the king, and her.

He cradled her face in his hands and kissed her.

Just once would be enough. Just to get it out of his system—to rid himself of the relentless magnetism of this woman he hardly knew. Just to exorcise her from his mind so that he could move on and marry Eloise like his position demanded.

Cecilia tensed, but then her fingers clawed at his shirt, pulling him closer, parting her lips so he could deepen the kiss.

She tasted sweet—like black tea and sugar and lemon and mint. Somehow Rainer *knew* she'd taste like that, and it wasn't just that he'd seen the way she heaped sugar into her tea every day. A deep sense of knowing left a trail in his mind that led him to nothing but darkness that smelled like her skin.

The feel of her was so familiar. The more he kissed her, the more he felt right on the edge of remembering—like he was on the precipice of waking and grasping for the frayed edges of a pleasant dream.

From the first airless moment of the kiss, he knew with certainty it would never feel like enough. Enough was a lie he'd been telling himself to make his life simple. But as soon as his lips met hers and she'd sighed with the same relief that he felt so acutely, he knew he was done for.

Cecilia wrecked him. Because even though she'd been furiously yelling at him the moment before, as soon as he kissed her, she climbed his body, fighting her soaked dress to wrap her legs around his waist. She clung to him. He was completely lost to her. The way she leaned into him, the soft whimpers she made against his mouth, the way she seemed to coax all the warmth in his chest to life.

Rainer didn't want to touch her and risk her stopping, so he pinned her against the wall with his hips. Her desperation matched his as she grinded against him. He met the rhythm of her movements instinctively, swallowing the moan that burst from her lips.

The kiss blew open the doors of his life, a knowing settling into his bones. He might not have had memory on his side, but he seemed to read exactly what she needed, his tongue chasing hers, his touch inspiring hers in a dance he wanted to both lead and follow.

The rain and wind were brutally cold, but everything between them steamed away the chill. Rainer needed more. Cecilia was infuriating, but kissing her was the first time anything seemed to make sense.

When he spent time with her, he felt furious and scared and frustrated and exhausted and a whole host of other things. She blew through every room like a mountain storm. But now that she opened to him in a different way, he seemed to intuitively understand the rhythm of her.

She was so maddening and sexy. Kissing her was like breathing. Cecilia had somehow become as necessary as air and Rainer had sentenced himself to a swift death by daring to press his lips to hers. Because she was not for him, no matter how much it felt like she should have been.

This is the king's fiancée, you idiot. You have a fiancée of your own.

Still, in another life, Rainer was certain Cecilia would be his.

It was not like kissing Eloise. Eloise's kisses were insistent, expert, lovely. But kissing Cecilia was consuming in the way it felt to give in to sleep after an exhausting day or to find comfort by the heat of a fire on a cold night. Rainer wanted Cecilia to take him over. Her closeness made him hyper-aware of the vast emptiness he felt when she wasn't in his arms. It was something he didn't know he lacked until then, and there was no way to fix it.

All the anger he'd felt before evaporated until he only felt desire and joy and a painful longing. Nothing had ever felt as good as kissing Cecilia Reznik, at least nothing he could remember. Her fingers slid through his hair, pulling him closer. She was full of the same desperate abandon. Rainer struggled to keep his hands in place and avoid touching her anywhere that would make her uncomfortable. Her hips rolled against him harder, and he wished he could hike up her dress and give her the relief she was seeking. Instead, he kept his hands on her face and neck so she wouldn't pull away.

The cold rain mixed with warm, salty tears. She was crying.

Rainer pulled away and the spell was broken. He set her back on her feet.

He hated that he'd done that. It was the most idiotic thing in the world. He was risking his position, his honor—his very life—to kiss a pretty girl when his own fiancée was downstairs. He was risking his entire world to touch a reckless, wild woman who had no respect for authority and a sharp tongue that ensured trouble followed wherever she went.

She stared at him, wide-eyed. "Why did you do that?"

He shook his head. "To get you to shut up and stop hitting me."

"That's the only reason?" she asked, one eyebrow cocked.

"Yes," he gritted out.

"Then why are you so hard?"

Rainer's cheeks heated. He was painfully hard, and he hated that she'd noticed his total lack of control.

She crossed her arms. "Why go on so long if you were just trying to startle me? Seemed to me like you were a moment from hiking up my dress and fucking me right up against the wall."

Rainer shook his head, trying to loosen the image from his mind. He forced himself to focus. "You have a filthy mouth."

"As I've said before, dirty words are the least filthy thing about this mouth." She winked at him.

His cock twitched as his mind filled with visions of her on her knees. He needed to calm down. This conversation would not go anywhere good.

Rainer scrubbed a hand though his hair, slicking back rainwater. The storm had settled to a drizzle and the wind had died down to an occasional gusty breeze.

Magdalena's words echoed through his mind. How was Cecilia the one person he seemed to have no memory of and yet made him feel so much, so intensely?

"Fighting with you is infuriating and exhausting," Rainer started. "And also it's the best part of my day. Better than winning a sword fight. Better than receiving accolades from the king. Better than walking in the garden with Eloise while she holds my hand and kisses me so sweetly. She doesn't make me feel like I'm going to lose my mind. She doesn't make me feel like I'm going to make nothing but bad decisions. She doesn't keep me up at night wondering if she's all right."

"Why is it the best part of your day, then?" Cecilia looked as hopeful for his answer as Rainer was terrified of it.

"Because fighting with you feels like home. No matter how mad you get, how hard you hit, how cutting your words are—I can't help feeling like I'm right where I'm supposed to be—like I've done it a thousand times. I don't get tired of it. I don't want to stop. I only find myself wishing I was fighting for you instead of with you."

"Then do it! *Fight for me*, Rainer." The anguish in her voice chilled him.

He stared at her, suspended between what he wanted and what was required of him. How did she make him feel so endlessly balanced on a knife's edge? When would it stop? Why couldn't he surrender to it?

"Why don't you leave him?" The question slipped out without Rainer's meaning to ask it.

She looked down at the city of Ardenis far below the castle walls. "This kingdom needs stability. A lot of people are relying on me to fix what is broken here."

Rainer didn't understand it, but he could not seem to separate himself from the path that was laid out before him. He could not hurt Eloise. He could not threaten his standing with the king. He felt responsible for Cecilia, but he could not protect her when she didn't even seem to want to protect herself.

He had suspected Cecilia had stolen the key to the tower from him, though he had no real proof. But Magdalena had clearly been the one to help Reese heal enough to escape. If Cecilia was helping her, she was placing herself directly in the path of Vincent's wrath. Even if she believed Reese was innocent, her loyalty should have been to her fiancé. As Rainer's should have been to his.

Guilt slid between his ribs.

No matter what feelings Cecilia stirred in Rainer, the woman was nothing but trouble.

She wrapped her arms around herself, her teeth chattering. Her presence was always so large and boisterous it was easy to forget that she was small and delicate. He looked at her then, really looked at her.

She was thin. She'd lost weight since they first met. Her ribs were visible through the wet silk of her dress. He had noticed her pushing her food around at meals, but rarely eating it. Something seemed to be consuming her. He desperately wished he could remember what.

"Please leave him. Leave here. Go somewhere safer." Rainer tried to be gentle, but his words were edged with desperation. He needed her away from danger and away from him. "Don't you miss Olney? You could go there and find someone who deserves you. Sometimes it's better to survive than to win."

She shook her head and glared at him. "Coward."

The word was barely a whisper but sharp as a blade.

Rainer froze. "What was that?"

"I said you're a fucking coward!" The intensity of her eyes burned through him. "This is survival, Rainer. Surviving is *ugly*. It takes something you cannot get back, but I would do anything for the people I love. *Anything*. So don't judge me while you stand there and do nothing."

"Nothing?! I'm saving you from yourself," Rainer huffed.

"No, you're saving yourself from me. From having to make a hard choice. From knowing that you'll stay safe even while I hurt. From having to admit that I make you feel too much and that makes you uncomfortable."

Rainer hated that she saw him. He hated that she was right so often, hated how she seemed to know what he felt. How she looked right at the shame he tried to hide and dragged it out into the light. She was so unnerving.

"You make me feel *nothing*," Rainer said coldly.

The moment he saw the flicker of hurt in her eyes, he knew that wasn't true. Because that wounded look on her face left him feeling sick.

She made him feel too many powerful, confusing things. He tried not to recognize the way she made his heart race. He tried not to acknowledge the way he constantly found himself staring at her lips. He tried not to understand the inexplicable way she felt like home—the way the only time he felt the ravenous anger inside him settle and make space for light was when she was close. His body, his mind, his very soul were on the precipice of remembering her and the need to do so settled into him like a great wave of panic.

The woman was more forbidden to him than anything else. That must have been the appeal. It was the only thing that explained the persistent urge he felt to draw Cecilia away from the castle, to hoard her to himself, to hold her close forever. It was more than just an impulse of desire, though that was there and sharp as ever—it was a deep longing that settled into him each morning when he woke, reaching out on the bed beside him for something that was lost to him.

"You look at me like I need to be more than I am," Rainer said. "But I'm a guardian. A protector. This is what I am here for—*to fight*."

The words sounded so foolish. But Rainer had only ever known one thing: how to be a sword in someone else's hand.

Cecilia closed the distance between them and pressed her palm reverently to his heart. "You are not a weapon."

The words hollowed Rainer out. Or perhaps he'd always been hollow, and she simply threw open the door to show him how he was made of nothing but an empty ache that no accolades could fill.

Cecilia looked at him with the sort of conviction he could not ever remember having. Rainer was humiliated by the sheer desperation he felt. He wanted so badly for someone to ground him in the truth, but this woman confused him to no end. Looking at her then, he felt certain her words could cast a spell that would give him back his sense of self. Removed from the expectant gazes of the court, he could be exactly what she wanted him to be.

"Then what am I?" he asked.

"A shelter." She looked at him like she could will him to remember who he was, and he wished she could. "You are not a tool for someone to use. You are the harbor to turn to in a storm."

With that, Cecilia left him standing in the rain—alone with his lies.

He stood there for a few long moments, watching the clouds of his breath dissipate. Then he turned and tore into the castle. If Cecilia wasn't going to look out for her own best interest, Rainer would cut off her ability to put herself in harm's way by removing the rebels in their midst.

His skin warmed as he charged down the candlelit hallways.

The way Cecilia Reznik took up every free space in his head was disorienting. Rainer needed to avenge himself against his lack of control by recommitting to his original goal.

He found King Vincent in the throne room, speaking with Grant in hushed. Rainer didn't like the man, mostly because he held the role that Rainer coveted. He also didn't like the way Grant leered at

Cecilia or the way she seemed on edge whenever he was near. Now Rainer had the chance to surpass his rival.

"Rainer? Has my lovely fiancée already scared you off today? She can be quite trying," Vincent said, effecting a sympathetic tone.

Rainer bit the inside of his cheek, trying to put the bruising on her neck and cheek out of his head. "I'm not here about Lady Reznik, Your Grace. A different matter has come to my attention."

Grant crossed his arms, leaning back on his heels, his gaze burning into Rainer. "We have enough to attend to as it is with the growing crowd of commoners outside our gates."

Vincent held up his hand. "Nonsense. I'm sure that Rainer wouldn't be here if it wasn't important."

Rainer nodded. "I think I have a lead on who allowed Reese Reynolds to escape."

24

CECILIA

Cecilia stumbled down the castle hallway, her soaked dress clinging to her chilled skin. She barely reached the healer's suite before she collapsed into a fit of tears.

"Oh dear," Magdalena said, helping her to a chair by the fire and pulling out a blanket to wrap around her soaked dress.

"He's never going to remember," Cecilia sobbed.

"There now, love," Magdalena said, gently brushing Cecilia's damp hair back from her forehead and handing her a handkerchief. "Now, do you want to explain why you're soaked to the bone and shivering?"

Magdalena tipped Cecilia's head up, taking note of the mark on her cheek and the bruises around her neck.

"Those aren't from Rainer?" Magdalena said tentatively.

Cecilia shook her head. "Vincent. But Rainer heard him hit me and he did nothing."

Magdalena went to work, the tingling of her healing magic buzzing over Cecilia's skin. "You know, he's quite confused. I ran into him this morning. He seems just as committed to remembering."

"He kissed me," Cecilia rasped.

Magdalena's lips curved into a smile. "Sounds like he's remembering something."

"So I thought, but then he just gave up again. It's like he doesn't want to remember—and I know—I know how unfair it is for me to say that when I'm the one who buried his memories behind his grief and failure." She swallowed hard around the lump in her throat. "I know I can't be angry at him for being the man that I love, but it breaks my heart a little bit every time I can feel him right on the edge of remembering but he chooses to turn away."

Magdalena rubbed Cecilia's back in slow circles. "He seems desperate to remember, and I'm sure you are a big part of that, but to remember his life is also to remember your pain and his own."

Cecilia knew that was rational, but she wanted to rage against it. Vincent hurting her was no more Rainer's fault than him being whipped was hers. Still, it was impossible to watch someone you loved suffer and not feel responsible for erasing all of their hurts.

The scrape of the passageway door cut through the room and they both turned to see Mika duck out from behind the tapestry on the far wall, her eyes narrowing on Cecilia.

"What happened to you? You look like a drowned rat," Mika said.

"Rainer kissed her," Magdalena said, pouring tea into three cups.

"Was it good?" Mika asked, taking a sip from the cup Magdalena handed her.

Cecilia glared at her. As if she could forget what it was like to be turned inside out by a kiss from the person she loved most. "Of course it was. He's still Rainer."

"So what are you doing here instead of in his bed?" Mika said with a grin.

"I'm glad you're in the mood for jokes," Cecilia said. "He told me he feels nothing for me and he was quite adamant."

"What a liar," Mika laughed. "That man has his heart in his eyes every time he looks at you, just like he always has. The difference is that now he's too stubborn to realize. You can hardly blame him after you worked so hard to empty his head."

Tears burned Cecilia's eyes.

"Cece," Mika said, "I'm kidding. He's going to remember. He's right on the edge now. The kiss is just proof that you're winning him over."

"Let's not forget that he's still engaged to Eloise," Cecilia grumbled.

"Only because he's trying to empty his mind of you," Mika said.

"I suppose that's as effective a way as any," Cecilia said bitterly. "What's the word?"

Mika's face brightened. "Our friends on the outside have come up with a brilliant plan."

"It's about time we had some good news. How can we help?"

Mika nodded. "Well, as the king's betrothed, they were hoping you could hire some new attendants and even some new kitchen staff."

Cecilia was relieved to have something to focus on. "It shouldn't be a problem since Vincent has been complaining about the lack of staff all week."

"Maybe we can have one of our hunter friends let it slip to Grant that the Temple of Aurelia trains some of the most attractive maids," Mika said.

Cecilia scrunched her nose. She hated Grant, but that was the type of thing he'd take note of.

"Think about it," Mika said. "Now that Vincent is giving Rainer so much responsibility, Grant must be feeling the pressure to secure his place."

"These women know what they're getting into?" Magdalena asked. "They will need to be okay in close proximity with the man."

"I'll be sure that we only bring in those who can handle the pressure and we will be here to keep an eye on them," Mika assured her.

Cecilia felt a surge of anxiety in her chest. "Rainer is close. You should get out of here, Mika. I have an excuse to be here, but you don't."

Mika nodded, ducking into the passageway behind the tapestry.

Cecilia turned her eyes back to the door just as Vincent and Grant walked in. Grant sneered at her, but Vincent's gaze was focused on Magdalena in a way that sent Cecilia's heart racing.

"What are you doing here?" Vincent asked.

"Just having some violence erased from my face and neck," Cecilia said tightly.

Vincent looked almost lovingly at the bruise on her face. "It is such a lovely face, dearest. You should be more mindful of your surroundings. The world can be quite perilous when you least expect it."

Cecilia's gaze darted over his shoulder as a somber Rainer appeared in the doorway. He'd changed into dry clothes and his hair was neatly combed. There was no sign of their earlier kiss, though she could still feel the phantom touch of his lips on hers. How could he be so calm when she was so rattled?

Vincent's eyes narrowed on her. "Why are you all wet?"

"I got caught in the rain," she said absently, her attention focused on Grant, who was circling the room like a shark, his eyes lingering on the cabinets and herbs that hung from nails along the wall.

"You should be more careful, Cecilia. I wouldn't want you to catch your death out there," Vincent said as Rainer began to circle the room as well.

Cecilia was suddenly glad they'd shooed Mika away. The hair rose on the back of her neck and the faint hum of death whispers skittered around the room.

"Can I help you with something, Your Grace?" Magdalena asked.

Vincent grinned. "I think you can. Guardian McKay had a question for you about some herbs."

Magdalena turned to Cecilia, a warning in her eyes. "I'm happy to heal you later, Lady Reznik. You may go, but do be more careful."

Cecilia crossed her arms. "I'd prefer to stay here by the fire for now."

"Lady Reznik, you'd be warmer if you changed into dry clothes," Rainer said.

She glared at him. "I'm sorry, I don't remember asking for a guardian's opinion."

Vincent's eyebrows flew up at the exchange. "Throwing your royal weight around, dearest?"

"I learned from the best," she said.

"Here it is," Rainer said.

They all turned to see him holding a handful of morning root.

"Did you need some morning root?" Magdalena said breezily. "I would have been happy to bring it up to your room, Your Grace."

Vincent pursed his lips. "No. Guardian McKay found some morning root in the cell that Reese Reynolds recently escaped from, and clearly the man didn't have mind left to use it himself."

He was about to say more when Xander entered the room with Isla on his heels.

Xander frowned, his gaze passing over Cecilia's damp clothing and bruised face before he turned to face Vincent. "Why have I been summoned?"

"Were you aware that your family's long-standing castle healer has been conspiring against the Savero reign?" Vincent asked.

Xander's shoulders tensed as he looked at Magdalena. "I'm certain that's not true. Magdalena has served this family for decades. Her talent cannot be overstated, nor her commitment to my family," he said.

"Yes, *your* family," Vincent said, his smile menacing. "It makes sense. She has magic and the ability to come and go from the castle at will to gather herbs and supplies from the market. She has every opportunity."

Cecilia could barely breathe. She didn't know how to help or deflect attention away from Magdalena without implicating herself or Xander. Isla's hand lightly brushed her skirt. She clearly had some type of weapon hidden in her pocket. Cecilia didn't have anything that could take out Vincent and Grant, but even if she tried, she wasn't certain how Rainer would react.

Xander shook his head. "What you're suggesting is impossible.

Magdalena would never betray my wishes that way. She brought me into this world, for the love of the gods. Plus, any healer in this suite knows what morning root does. Don't most witches know basic herbs like morning root?"

Cecilia nodded vigorously.

Vincent gave Xander a pitying look. "I can understand your loyalty, cousin. It's very admirable. But Guardian McKay has proof. When Reese Reynolds escaped, the scent of one of her healing salves was left in the cell, as well as some burned herbs that we just found in here."

Xander barked out a disbelieving laugh. "That's hardly definitive proof. Any of the healers could have helped him escape, or anyone who has been the beneficiary of Magdalena's services, for that matter. Isn't that right?"

"It's true that I give that salve out to many of our hunters, Your Grace. It helps with infection and scarring, and many a soldier use morning root to stay awake on long shifts. Some smoke it, but others prefer to just burn it and breathe it in," Magdalena said.

Vincent frowned, turning his attention to Cecilia. She tried to keep her face placid, but she knew the determined look on Vincent's face meant he wouldn't be satisfied until he'd hurt someone.

"Well, I could always bring all of the healers in and question them one by one until we find the culprit," Vincent suggested.

"Or you could bring in all your guards and question them. Maybe start with those who have the most access," Cecilia said, her eyes narrowing on Grant. "I could always take a peek inside Grant's brain first thing tomorrow since I've already had my medicine for the day."

Vincent grinned at the challenge in her voice. "That won't be necessary. Grant's commitment to the cause is above reproach."

"Is it, Grant?" Cecilia said, walking across the room, brushing her fingers over the guard's tunic, daring him to lash out at her in the way the threat in his eyes promised he would if Vincent wasn't watching. She trailed her finger up to the scar on his neck.

This was dangerous, reckless, but Cecilia could not help herself.

She refused to sit by and watch more of Vincent's version of justice carried out.

"This is quite a scar," she said. "How did you get it?"

Grant jerked away, his hand flying protectively to the vicious-looking scar she'd given him.

Cecilia pressed on. "You don't remember? What a curious thing. I would gladly help you, but alas." She gestured to her Unsummoner bracelet.

"Enough nonsense," Vincent barked.

She turned her pout on Vincent. "Dearest, are you telling me that you're not the least bit curious how this happened and why he mysteriously can't remember? What a convenient excuse to avoid suspicion of treason."

Grant's eyes went wide as he realized the doubt she was trying to cast seemed to be working.

"Who could have had more access? More familiarity with your schedule as well as that of the other guards?" Cecilia continued as she circled Grant. Her heart pounded so loud in her ears she could hardly hear her own words. She was vaguely aware of Rainer rubbing his sternum, likely feeling her anxiety and fear.

"You want me to believe that the man who has been my second-in-command for nearly a decade chose this particular moment to betray me?" Vincent said.

"Is there a better moment than the one where you trust him blindly?" Cecilia countered. "If there is a thing I know, it's well-timed betrayal."

Vincent frowned. She could see doubt in his eyes for the first time. She was starting to learn that logic was less important to Vincent than a perceived threat. All he cared about was holding on to the power he'd stolen.

As if he sensed the shift in the room as well, Grant turned to face Vincent. "Your Grace, you can't seriously believe what she's saying. We've worked for years for this moment for you. Why would I throw it away now when we've finally achieved what we wanted?"

Vincent stepped in front of his guard. The entire room stilled, everyone holding their breath to see what he would do.

"It seems like my lovely fiancée wants to cast doubt on you, Grant. What could you have done to make her so suspicious?"

"Your Majesty, I swear—"

Vincent held up a hand and Grant instantly shut up.

"Magdalena, do you want to admit to helping the prisoner escape or should we go through your healers one by one?" Vincent asked.

"Your Grace, I'm certain none of my staff would have gone against your will and mine. They have strict instructions that you are the head of the Savero line now and should be treated with the respect owed you," Magdalena said.

"And you?" Vincent prompted.

"And I wouldn't be foolish enough to betray my king," Magdalena said flatly, her gaze darting to Xander, who looked frozen in fear.

Cecilia wanted to scream at Magdalena to lie. It was not the time to lay down and accept fate. It was time to fight.

"I knew your mother—tried to save her when Damian's men attacked her," Magdalena said. "She was a good woman. It was the one time I went against King Damian because the job of a healer is to help everyone who needs it, and your mother was nothing but a bystander in a fight between two power-hungry men."

"Don't speak of my mother," Vincent snapped.

"I was too late. I did what I could to relieve her pain, but she'd lost too much blood," Magdalena continued. "She was a good mother. Do you know what she said to me as she lay dying?"

Vincent took a threatening step toward her, but Magdalena stood her ground. Cecilia willed her to back down, to bend a knee just to save herself.

"She said, 'Get my boy away from that monster.' But by the time I helped her cross over and came to find you, your father had already spirited you away. There are few things in my life I've regretted more than that. Especially seeing what damage you've done now."

Vincent's jaw twitched, his hands clenched at his sides. "How dare you lie to your king? We need look no further." He looked to Rainer. "McKay, take care of her."

The death whispers rose to a thunderous roar. Cecilia stood frozen in shock because Rainer didn't look horrified. He looked resigned, hesitating for only a moment before stepping forward, drawing his dagger, and slitting Magdalena's throat.

The whole scene seemed to unfold in slow motion. Cecilia charged forward to catch Magdalena, aware only of the healer's body and her own thunderous heartbeat.

"No," Cecilia rasped, cradling the healer against her body, trying to staunch the flow of blood. She looked up at Vincent. "You've made your point. Now take this bracelet off so I can heal her."

The crazed look in Vincent's eye dissipated and his lips tipped into a smile. "I'm afraid not. The punishment for treason is death."

"Vincent, she has *decades* of healing experience. Keep her in chains if you must, but she is invaluable," Cecilia said, frantically holding the hem of her already-soaked dress to the wound.

Vincent stood over her, unmoved, his gaze focused on Magdalena's eyes. He didn't even react when the light went out of them.

Cecilia's blood felt like it was boiling in her veins. It took every ounce of self-control not to try to kill him immediately. Killing Vincent wouldn't root out the traitors in their midst. If she took him out, it would just create a power vacuum for another villain to fill. They needed to cut out all the poison for the kingdom to survive.

She took a deep breath and stared down at the woman who'd been so focused on making Cecilia feel safe in her own body again. Her anguish twisted her stomach in knots, her grief like a well with no bottom. Nowhere was safe anymore.

Cecilia carefully laid Magdalena's body down and closed her eyes before standing and turning to Xander. "You'll see her buried properly?" she asked, hiding her trembling hands in her dress pockets.

Xander nodded, his face pale and drawn.

"I think I'll rest for the afternoon." Cecilia left the room without turning back.

She didn't need to look to know Rainer was following her. Her anger burned hotter with every step. She was shaking by the time they reached her rooms.

The war was supposed to be over and yet Cecilia was still losing people she loved. She could not stand to lose any more.

She'd spent years learning to bleed without flinching—walking into dark caves and cutting her palm like her pain was nothing but a currency casually spent on power. But this violence was different, and she couldn't summon the same fearlessness. Not when it was Rainer running her through.

It wasn't Rainer's fault. Vincent had used him as the exact weapon he would have been if he and Cecilia had never met. It was unfair of her to be so angry at him—to keep waiting for him to be the man she loved before when she'd promised to love every version of him.

Rainer followed her into her room, and she spun on him, finally ready to lose her temper.

"I can't stand the sight of you," she said. "Magdalena is the most talented healer I've ever met, and you just killed her like she was a common criminal."

"She was a traitor."

Cecilia wanted to scream. "She was helping me. She has listened to me talk for hours. She's the only person who could help me after—"

The crease between Rainer's eyes disappeared as recognition stole over his face. "I'm sorry."

"An apology feels a bit ridiculous now, doesn't it? What can I do with those words? They are so flimsy when there's no action to back them up. What shall I do when you're the villain, Rainer? Who will save me from you?"

Rainer looked as bereft as she felt.

"Should I run and hide in your room?" she asked. "Should I use my dagger against you? I suppose if I kill you, I'll just apologize to your corpse and all will be well."

He opened his mouth, then closed it. "I didn't realize she was important to you."

"Would it have changed anything?" She turned her back on him.

He hesitated. "No. I would have done as the king commanded." He grew quiet. "Cece, you need to consider how it looks that you spent so much time with her and she was a traitor."

"Tell me this, Guardian McKay—if I come under suspicion for being a traitor, will you ask any questions or simply show me the business end of a blade? I wonder how His Majesty would feel knowing that moments before you shared your suspicion about the finest healer in the two kingdoms, you had his betrothed pinned to the castle wall while you dry-humped her like a horny teenager."

"Cece!" Rainer snapped. "Keep your voice down or I'll be the one meeting the business end of a blade."

"What are you doing? When will you decide which side you're on?" she asked. "How long will you play to me one moment and Vincent the next? How can I feel safe when at any moment someone might decide I'm the enemy and you'll be sent to dispatch me?"

"I want what's best for Argaria."

"You're not even from here. Have you ever questioned the fervor of your loyalty?" she snarled, surprised the words were allowed.

Rainer frowned. "I'm from Olney but I didn't have the same opportunities there, at least not without my father using my accomplishments to launch him into higher social circles. Here I have an opportunity to make my own way. I can prove my value not just to the king but to two kingdoms' worth of people."

"And so long as your ego is served, who cares who gets hurt?" Cecilia scoffed.

Rainer crossed his arms. "What do you know about it, Cece? You're a powerful witch."

Cecilia laughed bitterly, shaking her head. "Of course, what would I know about struggling with identity? Just a girl who didn't know who or what she was her entire life only to find out that everyone who loved her knew before she did and let her walk into a trap. How could I possibly understand wanting to prove myself? Wanting to make my own way?"

Rainer stared at her, bringing a hand to his head and wincing. She wanted to say more but when she opened her mouth to speak nothing came out thanks to the deal with Cato. She threw her hands up in frustration.

"What happens when Vincent decides Olney is the enemy? When Marcos Teripin won't bend to his ever-changing will?" Cecilia asked.

"You're worried about your kingdom," Rainer sighed. "Of course you are."

He said it like it was such a simple thing. Like she hadn't crawled back from death to banish the god who brought on all of this havoc.

"You forget everything. You have no idea what this peace has cost me. It is so delicate, and it cannot ride on the whims of this king who can't control his temper enough to keep his hands off me," Cecilia said.

Rainer's eyes lit with fury. "I'm trying to protect you as best I can. Why are you so insistent on making it difficult?"

"Why are you so intent on being a murderous, stubborn ass?"

It was easier to hold her anger so she wouldn't feel how afraid she was, so she could ignore the way her knees were shaking, the way her heart ached.

"Cece—" Rainer's voice was suddenly soft as he reached out and stroked her cheek.

Normally she would have felt grateful for the touch, but now she was only reminded of the way Rainer's gentleness had the ability to break through all her walls.

"You'd touch me like you care while my friend's blood is still on your hands."

Rainer drew back as if she'd punched him in the gut. He stood frozen in place, staring at her. "You didn't actually erase Reese's memory, did you?"

She stared back at him, afraid moving or saying anything would have him sending her to a swift death. She'd never been afraid of Rainer, but for the first time in her life, Cecilia wasn't certain that he'd protect her. She wasn't certain he wouldn't be the one to send her back to the grave. The only thing she knew for sure was that she was entirely at his mercy because she would not fight back.

"I suspected that day in the tower," Rainer continued. "I only found the key after I found you. I just couldn't figure out why you'd be working against your fiancé."

Cecilia kept her mouth shut. It was likely no mystery at all to Vincent that she was involved, but it was one thing for him to suspect and another for Rainer to admit he knew. So far Vincent was content with his performance art because he seemed to get a sort of twisted thrill out of making her watch him corrupt Rainer. But if Rainer figured things out, Vincent would have no reason left to perform.

Rainer ran a hand through his hair and cleared his throat. "I killed her to protect you, Cece. If Vincent was satisfied that he'd found the spy, he wouldn't keep looking."

Her relief felt like a betrayal to Magdalena, but Cecilia couldn't help it. She was eager to cling to any hint that Rainer could still come back from this.

"Why do you protect me?" Cecilia asked, embarrassed by the desperation in her voice.

Rainer arched an eyebrow. "Why do I feel it here?" he asked, placing a hand on his chest. "Like I need to protect you. Like I'm drawn to you always. Like I can't take my eyes off you when you're in the room."

Cecilia chewed her lower lip, opening her mouth and closing it, unable to say anything.

"You make it impossible to be rational. I cannot think around you," he said, taking a step closer. "My heart has not slowed to a normal rhythm since I kissed you."

"I thought I made you feel nothing," she bit out.

"I lied—"

Before she could argue, he'd swept her into a kiss and she melted into him, her body boneless with relief and confusion and grief. For a moment there was nothing but the two of them, the kiss a familiar push-pull, an exchange in which she lost herself and found new depth she didn't know she could reach in loving someone.

In her weakness she allowed him to steal her breath. His hands gently unpinned her hair as they had so many times before, until at last strength rushed up to meet her in the form of rage.

She shoved against his chest, startling him so much he stumbled back, the spell between them broken.

"And I suppose you don't consider this treason?" Cecilia asked.

Rainer frowned. "The only treason is that which my heart commits against my will."

Cecilia stared at him, speechless, her breath still quickened from his touch. In that moment, Rainer was both the man who'd been endlessly patient with her and the vicious, volatile man he'd become. It hurt and helped to see them both at once, like a warped reflection in the murky surface of a pond.

He waited, his eyes fixed on her.

When she said nothing, he backed away and slipped into the hallway. The door closed behind him and the lock clicked, and Cecilia was left with her grief.

Her quiet was short-lived. Not a moment after he left, Mika burst in through the passageway.

"He killed Mags and you're kissing him!" she said in a harsh whisper.

Cecilia turned her teary eyes on her friend as guilt twisted in her stomach. "What would you have me do? What if it was Ivy?"

"Don't you speak her name! Ivy was all that is good in this world—"

"And so is he!" Cecilia wiped the angry tears from her cheeks. "You think I don't feel it? That I'm not furious with him? That it doesn't kill me to know how he will hate himself if he ever remembers? Magdalena saved my life—more than once. I was drowning and the two of you saved me, but before I ever met you Rainer saved me. He saved me a thousand times in a thousand little ways, and he may not know who he is, but he will always be mine. Do not make me choose between him and vengeance because if I can only have one, I will always choose him."

Mika's pain was raw on her face and in her voice. "Vincent has taken everyone I love. He has taken the only real family I have ever had."

"And he will pay, Mika. I swear he will. You can be the one to do it and I will clap while you drive in the blade, but we cannot allow ourselves to be broken by loss. She would not want it for us."

It was hard to believe they'd all been joking together just a half hour ago and now there was one less of them in the world. It was harder to believe that Rainer was responsible for that.

Cecilia pulled Mika into her arms, trying to act as a buffer between her and her pain.

25

EVAN

Evan leaned against an evergreen, glancing from the god of death to his wife-to-be. The night was cold, but the stormy weather had broken earlier in the day, leaving the old castle training grounds blanketed with snow.

"What did Xander say when you told him?" Evan asked Grimon.

"He said 'Evan really wants to put all of us in one location at the same time. Isn't he supposed to be the strategist?' and honestly, Farlan, I'm inclined to agree," Grimon said. "You're not usually one to make impulsive decisions."

Evan sighed, meeting Sylvie's eye. "We've had too many losses. I refuse to go into another dangerous situation without officially making Sylvie my wife."

"I don't blame you. If you give her much more time, she'll realize she's too good for you," Grimon teased.

Sylvie giggled and winked at the god of death.

Evan shuddered, remembering the moment during Xander's engagement announcement when Sylvie had been stabbed in the chest. It had been weeks, but the memory was as fresh as if it happened yesterday. She'd said nothing to Evan about her time in between life and death, and he hadn't pressed. He hated to admit that it was fear that kept him from asking, not a lack of curiosity. He was just happy to have her back.

Evan had never considered himself particularly romantic. He'd never even considered getting married before meeting Sylvie. Settling down had been the farthest thing from his mind. His entire romantic history was a series of casual flings, but the moment he met Sylvie, he saw a future where he was more than just a spy for the first time ever.

Sylvie's blonde hair was curled and pulled back from her face, cascading down her back. Her lips were bright with the berry stain she loved to wear and her pale blue eyes were lined with kohl that made them look even more radiant. The priestesses at the temple had spent hours helping her primp, not that she needed help.

She was so clever and beautiful and, for some reason Evan still didn't understand, she was marrying him.

Sylvie smiled at him as if she could read his mind.

"I can see you looking for something to worry about. Cato is disguising everyone else so that the two of us can look like ourselves during the ceremony and he'll be there to help us escape if anything goes wrong," Sylvie said.

"And what if this is just an elaborate game to him?" Grimon asked.

Evan shrugged. "Then he'll be dead before his body hits the ground. I don't think he's keen to be as reckless now that he isn't immortal."

Grimon sighed, shaking his head.

Samson sidled up, throwing an arm around Sylvie. "It's a shame that you're taking this man off the market, but I hope you'll give me a call if you ever decide you're willing to share."

Evan shook his head. He had no idea why the god of lust had latched on to him, but he wasn't easily deterred, and his interest delighted Sylvie.

"I promise you'll be the first god I reach out to," she said, patting the god of lust on the shoulder before turning to Evan. "I have to go get changed into the dress I had made, and Cece is meeting me on the other side of this hill. I'll see you soon," she said, kissing him on the cheek.

He was tempted to follow her, but Cal trailed her, waving him off.

"Bad luck," Cal said with a grin.

Evan watched her disappear over the hill, then turned back to the god of death.

"How is the training going?" Grimon asked.

Evan had hoped to avoid thinking about it too much today. It was hard to put the constant worry out of his head ever since Sylvie had shared what happened to her. He felt responsible for keeping all of those women safe.

"They're better trained than I would have expected but mostly with defensive moves," Evan said. "They've made a lot of progress for such a short time, and I couldn't ask for more attentive students. They're quick studies, but I've also not trained many women. We have some in the Argarian army but I'm less familiar with the differences in fighting style."

"Don't you have a tiny goddess who could give you some pointers?" Samson asked.

Evan nodded. "Cece has been very helpful, but it's one thing to read instructions and another for the women to see them demonstrated, and unfortunately Vincent would notice if she was gone for an extended period of time. Plus, she's more valuable to Xander on the inside. She's the one who figured out that Vaughn Salvatore is also working for Vincent."

Samson shook his head. "That castle is full of more self-serving traitors than ever. What a spectacular mess."

"Hopefully soon it won't be full of any," Evan said.

The fading sunlight cast the shadows of the forest longer. Soon Sylvie would walk down their little woodland aisle. Mika had taken it upon herself to prepare the space. She fussed with the ivy along the makeshift aisle. Thanks to Grimon, Sayla—goddess of the hunt—had shown up and was working with Mika to make the old hunter training grounds beautiful. She'd pulled natural elements from the forest to make it look more like a woodland fairy tale, with a trellis made of ivy and snowdrop flowers.

Sayla turned her intense gaze on Evan, pulling her red fox fur tighter around her as she shivered. "Every time I visit Argaria I remember why I chose to be a goddess in the south."

Evan bowed. "Goddess, thank you for being here and for making it look so lovely. I know Sylvie will love it."

Sayla waved a hand like it was nothing to claw spring from the depths of winter.

Evan repeated the words he wanted to say over and over in his head, patting his jacket pocket to ensure he still had the piece of parchment with his vows. He did not have a way with words, and it had taken hours for him to come up with something worthy of Sylvie.

The soft crunch of boots in the snow to their right had all of them turning as a man in a black cloak stepped out of the tree line. They all drew their weapons, but he put his hands up.

"Stand down, it's me." It was Xander's voice, but his skin had been turned ghostly pale, his hair black and streaked with gray and the angles of his face made harsher. "I brought Isla."

A woman who had to be Isla but looked nothing like her with lighter skin and light brown hair stepped out behind him. Her eyes narrowed on the area, looking along the edges of the forest like she was assessing threats.

"We should move quickly. It was hard for us to sneak away, and we need Cato to put us back to normal before we go back inside," Xander said, pulling Evan into a tight hug. "I'm excited for this. I think we all need it. Though I must admit I didn't expect grand romantic gestures from you."

Evan rubbed a hand over the back of his neck. Xander had always possessed an ease when it came to expressing himself, but Evan had no gift for it.

"I've learned my lesson," Evan said. "What we're doing is danger-ous. You saw that with Magdalena." He swallowed hard and Xander nodded solemnly.

Grimon had passed along the news to them that morning and

Evan still felt winded by it. Even in disguise, he could see the grief in Xander's posture.

"I wanted to make it official while I had the chance," Evan said.

Isla shifted the bag from her shoulder and glass clinked softly inside as she set it on the ground. "We brought bubble wine for a toast."

"Thank you. It's nice to officially meet you, Lady Orum," Evan said.

She smiled. "Just call me Isla."

Evan's gaze lowered to their intertwined fingers, and he arched a brow. Xander smirked in a way that Evan would have recognized no matter how Cato disguised his best friend.

"Will the queen be joining us?" Evan asked.

Xander shook his head. "I'm afraid she's having another vicious bout of nausea, but she sends her love. She also sends a brilliant idea. She thinks the best time to strike is during Rainer's wedding." He looked to Isla for approval and she nodded.

"Jess is so bored and sick stuck in our rooms, but it's given her time to come up with a strategy. We already have the element of surprise with our little army, and we have access to the Temple of Aurelia. We could easily hide our warriors in the crowd right under their noses."

"That's only a week to come up with a good plan," Evan said. He was apprehensive. A wedding for a wealthy family like the Spellmans would bring more security than most and more scrutiny.

Xander held up his hands. "I know there are so many angles to consider, but this is a good place to start. If we push much longer, we risk all of our safety anyway."

"What if Rainer remembers before then?" Evan asked.

"Then he'll pretend until we're ready," Isla said.

It wasn't ideal, but Jessamin's idea had merit. Their success relied very heavily on the element of surprise. If they could figure out a few more details about the wedding logistics, they could have a plan in place in a few days.

A throat cleared behind them and they turned to see a petite woman with dark red hair and a narrow face. On stature alone she could have only been Cecilia.

She clicked her tongue. "No plotting on your wedding day," she scolded. "Now everyone get in place. The bride is ready." She walked back into the tree line.

Isla took her place beside Cal, Grimon, Sayla, and Samson. Xander walked to the front of the aisle, standing beside Evan.

Evan's heart pounded in his chest as he turned. He suddenly felt not nervous, exactly, but overwhelmed, surprised to find himself in this moment. He wished for the parents he'd never had a chance to know, but even more than that, he wished Teddy was there. His friend would have gotten the biggest kick out of seeing him so in love.

Even in death, Teddy had gotten his way. It seemed both Evan and Xander had done exactly what their fallen friend had hoped and fallen in love.

Cecilia and Sylvie walked out of the tree line arm in arm. Evan and Sylvie had agreed to blend the wedding traditions of their two kingdoms, and he was happy she had a woman who cared about her to walk down the aisle with her.

The sight of Sylvie, her scarlet dress bright against the white snow, stole the air from Evan's lungs.

The bright red silk dress accented her fair skin and hugged her curves. She wore a matching cape that billowed before her as she walked. Beside her Cecilia was all smiles, whispering something to Sylvie, likely about the stupefied look on Evan's face.

Evan straightened, clearing his throat.

Xander patted his back. "You're a very lucky man, Ev. I'm happy for you."

Evan nodded, his chest tight with surprising emotion as Sylvie stepped up beside him. Cecilia kissed her and Evan on their cheeks and stepped aside to huddle with the rest of their friends.

"What a wonderful thing to be here in the middle of the chaos to see two of our dearest friends profess their love to each other. It seems that chaotic weddings are our thing," Xander said, grinning at

Cecilia. "I'm delighted to be here tonight to marry Evan Balor Farlan and Sylvie Rose Brett."

Evan could hardly hear Xander over the beating of his heart. He gripped Sylvie's cold hands in his, and she anchored him to the moment. The calm in her eyes seemed to bleed into him, his shoulders settling, the vigilance in his body replaced by love for her.

Xander had made up the ceremony on his own, insisting that as the king of Argaria he could blend their traditions with Olney's while keeping it short and sweet since such a gathering was dangerous.

"It's in moments of great joy that we pause and remember great grief as well. Let us take a moment of silence for all those who aren't with us here today," Xander said.

They bowed their heads and Evan thought of Teddy, of the parents he'd never known, and even of King Damian, who was flawed but gave Evan a good life. Finally, he thought of Magdalena, the healer who'd also known him his entire life, who'd healed his wounds when he was injured in training. Where joy walked, grief followed, but that was the price of caring about people.

Without Xander and Teddy—without Sylvie, Evan would be sleepwalking through his life, blindly listening to whatever the king told him to do. That was no way to live a life. Especially now that he knew there was something better.

"As is done in Olney tradition, the couple will speak their own vows," Xander said.

Sylvie met Evan's gaze, her eyes already glassy with tears. "Evan, men have looked at me my whole life—admired, complimented, tried to woo me—but you are the first man who has ever actually seen me underneath. You have loved me for my mind. You've allowed me to grow. You've encouraged me to be my most confident and strategic self, and rather than feeling threatened by it, you've been delighted. I'm lucky to be the person who gets to try to make you laugh when you're being too serious, come to bed when you're working to late, and make your codependent king think for himself so that you can have a life of your own."

Xander chuckled quietly.

Sylvie squeezed Evan's hands as she continued. "I'm very happy to be your partner in life, like I have been in everything else so far. I love you very much. I promise to love you when you're broody and worried. I promise to help you strategize and work through problems as often as I make you laugh and have fun."

When she finished, Evan swallowed hard. His words suddenly seemed too small for the moment.

"Sylvie, I'm a man of few words so I hope you'll forgive me for having so few to express what you mean to me. From the first moment we met, I was taken with the way you assessed everything around you, and when I saw your fury for the first time, I think that's when I really fell in love, though I much prefer when it's not directed at me."

Sylvie blew out a breathless laugh.

"I've not had many good examples of love in my life. I didn't grow up with a family of my own, but I know what it is to choose a family, and I choose you. Today and every day after. I choose you for your mind that is as complex and beautiful as your heart. I choose you because from the first time I saw you trick a man into thinking your idea was his, I didn't think 'I need to stay away from that woman.' I thought, 'I need to keep her close.' You are beautiful and kind and I'm to be the man you choose as a partner. I love you and I can't wait to spend the rest of my life beside you."

He brushed tears from her cheeks. "I promise to love you as much when you're angry as I do when you're happy. I promise to always listen to your wise advice, even if I don't always take it. When I don't, I promise to let you say you told me so."

Sylvie laughed.

"Most of all I promise to love you in every moment of growth, for all that you are now and all you will become."

Sylvie's smile lit up her whole face. Evan's relief was profound. She deserved the world, but what he'd given her was clearly good enough.

"What you have joined here together today, let no man or god tear apart. By the power of—well, me—I pronounce you married. You may kiss," Xander said.

Evan pulled his wife into a kiss, dipping her dramatically as their little crowd cheered.

When he set her back on her feet, she grinned at him, flashing her rings to the crowd.

Isla handed out glasses and the group of them stood in a circle, passing the bottles of bubble wine until everyone had some in their glasses.

Evan looked around the circle at his closest friends, shivering in the moonlight, breath coming out in puffs of mist. They were quirky and strange, but they were a family. Not the one he was born with, but the one he chose for himself—the one he'd learned to make time and space for outside of his duty—and he had Xander and Teddy to thank for starting it and Sylvie to thank for keeping it going.

"Before we depart I thought we could all give some well-wishes to our happy couple with a group toast. I'm king, so I go first," Xander said. "I wish you both more good days than bad, more love than you know what to do with, and a lifetime of peace after all of our struggles."

He elbowed Isla, and she held up her glass. "It's Novumi tradition to wish a couple long memory for the good times, short memory for the bad times, and a tongue made for telling stories so they'll be passed down for generations to come."

Isla looked warily to Goddess Sayla, who was standing beside her.

"I wish you fruitful hunts, quiet evenings, and that your every arrow pierces the heart of your enemies for clean killing," Sayla said, gulping down her whole glass of wine before reaching for the bottle again.

Cal looked from Evan to Sylvie. "I wish that you both take joy and hold on to it as much as you can. Syl, you are my best friend and you have been through so much. I hope that you'll teach him to be less serious," Cal teased.

Grimon held out his glass. "I wish you a long and happy life and a swift and painless death. I hope I'll not see either of you in my realm for a very long time." He elbowed Samson in the side.

Samson grinned, holding up his glass. "I wish you a prolific sex life behind closed doors or out in public, wherever you fancy—"

Sylvie giggled.

"—and I wish that should you decide to invite outsiders, I'll be your first request," Samson finished.

Evan shook his head, but Sylvie looked delighted. The laughter of the group grew quiet as their gaze fell on the next guest.

Cato lifted his glass. "I wish you the ability to always sort a truth from a lie and I wish you tricks that bring laughs, but never hurt feelings." He turned toward Cecilia.

She pretended she didn't notice as she lifted her glass. "I wish you patience with each other, but also with yourselves so that you can keep learning to love better," Cecilia said, blinking away tears. "And if Rainer was here, he would probably say something like he wishes you a lifetime of good stories and that all your wishes come true."

She wiped tears from her cheeks as they clinked glasses and drank.

Evan threw an arm around her. "You okay, Cece?"

"Gods, aren't we all just fools in love?"

Evan laughed. "I guess I was the last one to fall."

Cecilia rolled her eyes. "*Please.* Sylvie was the last one to fall. You were absolutely out of your league the moment you met her outside Olney Castle."

Evan sighed. "Awkward that this is a rare occasion when you're right."

Even without memory magic, that moment when Sylvie had narrowed her curious gaze on Evan, he knew that if a woman like that could be interested in him, he might risk a relationship.

"Someday you'll learn that I'm always right." Cecilia turned to Xander and Isla. "We should get back. We've already been away too long."

"So soon?" Evan asked.

Cecilia sighed. "It's hard to shrug him, and he can find me, remember?" She tapped her chest. "He doesn't realize why he can find me, but he does it on instinct."

Normally Evan would be strategizing, but he needed just this one evening of happiness with his wife before he went back to the task at hand.

"It's okay to relax for a night," Cecilia said, following his gaze to Sylvie. "The moment we stop living our lives is the moment Vincent wins. I refuse to give him any more ground and you should too. We're doing all right on the inside. A little more time to sort out the traitors and we'll be ready." She pulled Evan into a tight hug. "I know you'll take good care of her, but maybe let her do the same from time to time."

Evan smiled as he pulled away. "I'll try."

Cecilia wandered over to speak with Sylvie while Xander took a step closer to Evan.

"Believe it or not, I always knew you'd end up here eventually," Xander whispered. "No man is so self-contained. Not even you. I'm happy for you, Ev."

A lump formed in Evan's throat. Xander had been the closest thing he had to family his whole life, and it meant the world to Evan that he'd taken the risk to be there.

Xander pulled him into a hug, and Evan's gaze flicked to Isla, who stood behind the king, her eyes scanning their surroundings like a sentry.

"Picked up a new watcher?" Evan whispered.

"Picked up more than that." Xander laughed as he pulled away looking genuinely charmed. He held out his arm to Isla. "Come, darling. My body needs guarding."

Isla rolled her eyes, but she took his arm and walked toward the castle with Cecilia and Cato on their heels.

Evan watched them go, feeling for the first time since they'd been surprised by Vincent that they might just stand a chance.

26

XANDER

After Cato restored their appearances, Xander and Isla walked back toward their room. Xander was silent, trying to process all he'd lost and all he'd gained. His mind was a mess of memory and longing. The past few days twisted together in an impossible tangle.

He had one week to plan their attack and it felt like both an eternity and the blink of an eye. There were so many moving parts to consider.

Xander had seen the death of someone he loved up close too many times. Between one blink and the next, the woman who'd brought him into the world made her way out with nothing but Cece's soft gasp to mark her departure.

Magdalena left a vicious hole in their lives. There wasn't one of them whom she hadn't touched. Evan had been stoic about her death, but Xander knew how close his friend was with the healer, who'd been one of the only true caretakers in his life.

When Xander was a child, she'd let him indiscreetly spy on her when he was curious about his magic. She had always seemed like a fixture. He had thought that Magdalena would bring his child into the world as she had him, but now she was gone and Xander felt helpless in the tide of chaos Vincent had brought to Argaria.

Grief tore away pieces of him each time it sank its claws in. Losing Magdalena was a surprising and unexpected blow, and her death brought the reminder that violence could come for any one of them at any moment.

It wasn't that Xander hadn't felt the pressing anxiety of that fact since Vincent's takeover, but each day, it felt more urgent. Between Magdalena's death and Reese's narrow escape, Xander felt adrift.

All of that combined with Evan's wedding and the joy of watching his best friend marry someone wonderful made Xander want to cling to anything that might offer solace.

He knew not to treat Isla like a life raft when he was lost at sea, but old habits died hard. The moment his bedroom door closed behind them, his hands were already reaching to tear off her dress.

Some feelings were too big. It wasn't just that Xander lacked the language; it was that there were no words to sum up the feeling of grief and failure and joy all at once. There was nothing to describe the potent terror of recklessly falling for another beautiful, dangerous woman.

Just once he wished he had a thing for timid, docile women who wanted rapt attention. Instead his heart was set on falling in love with every fierce, independent woman who very much did not need him.

His thoughts were a tempest. He itched for the relief of magic.

The only thing that brought him back was Isla's touch, her breath in his ear, the way she moved with him like the two of them heard a melody that no one else could. He wanted to be lost in her for whatever short moments he could carve out of the chaos.

They stumbled across the room, pulling off the last of their clothing. Xander laid Isla back on the bed for the fourth time that day.

The danger around them all the time had stoked his desire to a fever pitch. He could not get enough of Isla, of being had by her. Her appeal was unique. Her strength and confidence meant she very much did not need him to know what she wanted. She'd demand and she certainly knew how to make his knees weak with her displays of flexibility and dexterity.

It was strange how quickly their movements had become practiced. In such a short period of time he'd come to know her body, its rhythm. Their attraction had a heartbeat of its own.

What was between them was surprisingly soft, passion easily shifting to tenderness without warning in a way that left him feeling like he was trying to sail on unseasoned legs.

Isla lay beneath him, her hair splayed out around her in a halo.

He was so overcome by the swell of affection in his chest. He'd always been too much and holding the words back felt like holding back a flood.

"Gods, you're so beautiful. Be my consort."

All of the momentum between them ground to a halt. She froze, staring up at him.

"Excuse me?" Isla choked out.

"Be my consort. It's a position of great respect and it's meant for the king's lover."

She frowned. "You'd have me be your prized whore?"

Xander shook his head. "No, you don't understand. Our people recognize the king's consort. She's second only to the queen and you already know that my relationship with your cousin is purely a friendship."

"Can we not have this conversation while you're inside me?" Isla said, pressing him away. She sat up, crossing the room to the closet and wrapping herself in her robe. She stood for a moment in front of the hearth before returning to the bed.

She looked so beautiful backlit by the firelight. He waited for her to speak, his heart in his throat.

She crossed her arms. "This request—more a command, actually —is not as romantic as you think."

Xander brushed his damp hair back from his forehead. "I'll admit my timing was poor—"

"Do you think I'm the type of woman who is happy to be a backup plan?"

Xander pressed his hand over the scar on his chest. "But you're not a backup plan. You would be first in my heart."

"And yet the world would look at me like I'm a consolation prize," Isla snapped. "Do I seem like the kind of woman whom one makes a mistress, Xander?"

Xander frowned, suddenly seeing the immensity of his error. "No, I don't think that. I'm sorry. I was only thinking of myself."

"I should be leading a godsdamned army. I am an elite warrior. I can't believe you want me to be your backup plan."

The conviction in her voice hit him like a gut punch.

"I don't," he said. "I swear. I care for you—so much that I wish I could make a selfish decision and abandon my responsibility to be with you. But every decision I've made in the past year has been for the best of my kingdom and I have made big sacrifices—so have the people I care about. Being king means that I'm always giving up what I want in service of what my kingdom needs. I wish I were someone else so I could put you first, but I don't have that luxury."

Her arms remained crossed in front of her chest like a shield. "Then perhaps this affair has run its course. It was fun while it lasted, but I don't want either of us to be confused about what this is."

"Isla—"

She held her hands up as if to ward against his affectionate tone. "Please don't argue. I was happy to be a place for you to temporarily bury your worries, but I can't be what you need. Once Jessamin is safe and settled and Argaria is at peace, I will return to Novum and take up the mantle of leading the Novumi army."

Xander stood, letting the covers fall away, ignoring his nakedness. He closed the space between them and took her hands in his.

"Lead my army, then. Just stay a while and be with me. Let us see what this can grow into."

Isla's face hardened. "I understand that you are king and perhaps you are unaccustomed to hearing 'no,' so allow me to familiarize you, Your Grace. My answer is no."

Xander sighed and shook his head. "You'd be surprised to know that I have heard that quite often in my life, but I should warn you the last woman who said that to me ended up marrying me."

A smile ghosted across Isla's lips, but it was quickly chased away by a frown. "That is my final answer. I had plans before you and I have no intention of changing them on the whim of a king who was in love with his ex-wife until a month ago."

Xander swallowed hard. He wanted to argue with her, but there was nothing to say. It wasn't Isla's responsibility to sacrifice being someone's first choice just so that he could have happiness in his life. He was hardly the world's safest bet.

To an outsider it might seem that he jumped from love to love like he was swinging between branches in the forest. In reality, he'd loved once and now that he recognized the feeling again—the possibility of it ending in real happiness—he didn't want to lose a chance at that after everything else he'd lost.

He saw all of his mistakes so clearly now. Losing Cece had been a brutal price to pay to learn it, but he finally felt like he actually had something to offer in a relationship, if Isla would just give him the chance to prove it.

"I've done this all wrong," Xander said. "I know I can be rash and excessive in my affections. Having overwhelmed people with my intensity most of my life, I'm aware that it makes me seem less serious. But I come on strong because I know what is between us is rare. The foolish way I asked you was wrong, but I swear my heart is in the right place."

She turned away from him, crossing to the door that led to the room where Jessamin was likely already asleep. Turning back to meet his eyes, she shook her head.

"There's no room for heart in what's between us, Your Grace. I'll see you in the morning."

The finality of the door closing behind her rang through Xander's bones. He'd given it his best shot and he'd failed. He was proud at least that he'd risked it, however foolish his approach might have been. But none of the best things in his life had been easy, and he had no intention of giving up without a fight.

27

RAINER

Rainer had never been so simultaneously certain that he had done both the right thing and the wrong thing. Cecilia had avoided him for three days, choosing to stay in her room instead of dragging him all over the castle. Time dripped without her antics, which had somehow gone from making him crazy to being the only thing that made him laugh.

He felt so guilty. He never would have guessed that Cecilia had been sneaking around for counseling instead of spying. When he killed Magdalena, he'd robbed Cecilia of the opportunity to heal her mind. He was just doing his job to keep the kingdom safe, but more and more often it seemed that doing that job meant hurting Cecilia.

Perhaps Rainer didn't deserve her forgiveness, but he wanted to try for it anyway.

The memory of their kisses echoed through his body, reverberating in every moment when he could not busy himself with some activity.

Unsure how to apologize for murdering someone, he bought a bouquet of two dozen white roses in the market and made his way to her room after dinner when there were fewer servants in the hall to gossip. The last thing he needed was for word of this to get back to

Eloise. He hesitated outside Cecilia's door, suddenly tongue-tied. He took a bracing breath and forced himself to knock.

After a few moments of silence, he thought perhaps she was still freezing him out and refusing to answer as she had all week—only sending short, curt replies from the other side of the thick wood door.

Rustling came from the other side of the door and Cecilia appeared, wrapped in a dark blue silk robe, her hair pinned up on top of her head.

"I apologize. Clearly you were getting ready to sleep," Rainer mumbled.

Her gaze raked over him, coming to rest on the roses in his hand. "Doing some gardening?"

"They're for you. May I come in? I'll just take a moment of your time, I promise."

He didn't just want a moment. He wanted all of her time, all of her attention, all of her humor and every wild thought in her head. He'd tried to will away the wanting, but the more he wished it would pass, the more it rooted into him.

She opened the door wider and he hurried inside, closing the door behind him.

He thrust the bouquet toward her. "I surrender. I'm certain I was wrong, though I'm uncertain what I should have done instead. Still, I'm sorry that I hurt you and took away someone who was helping you heal."

Cecilia took the roses from his hands, taking a deep breath of their scent before placing them in a pitcher of water sitting on a side table in her sitting room.

"Thank you. They're beautiful." She leaned against the table; the distance between them seemed cavernous.

Rainer took a tentative step toward her. "What else can I say? I've turned myself inside out searching for the words."

She pursed her lips. "And yet you found so few."

He froze. "What words could take the place of a life?"

"None," she said. "But you can't just give me roses to make up for killing someone."

The blue silk robe brought out her eyes. Even in the harsh orange firelight they were radiant as the sea. The empty, cavernous feeling that had settled in his chest over the past few days finally warmed in her presence.

"What do you want from me?" Rainer asked.

She turned away from him, running her fingers over the roses. "I didn't want to talk to anyone about what happened to me. No one tells you the way that pain can tie your tongue in knots—how you can feel so much and have no words for it."

Rainer held his breath, afraid even the slightest disturbance would stop her from speaking about the rebellion.

"It felt like it was all trapped inside me. I thought that speaking about the—attack out loud would make it truer, or at least it would make it more true to everyone else. I was so busy protecting everyone with my silence that I didn't realize I was hurting myself by carrying the burden of it alone. If Magdalena hadn't forced me out of my comfort zone, I wouldn't have realized that."

Rainer wrung his hands, wishing for something to carve, but all he had was the star flower in his pocket and it was already finished, or as finished as he could make it.

He pulled it out and handed it to Cecilia. A faint smile broke over her face as she held it up in the firelight.

"It's beautiful." She crossed the room and set it on her nightstand. "It's your best one yet."

Rainer froze, the words cutting through him. *Your best one yet.* Meaning she knew that he'd made others. They'd known each other well enough before the rebellion that she was aware of his hobbies.

Cecilia turned back to face him, seemingly unaware that she'd given him a crumb of their history as she crossed the room with a small vial in her hands.

Rainer lowered himself to his knees. "I'm truly sorry. How can I make you believe me?"

Her eyes burned into him. "Will you think for yourself the next time he bids you do something?"

Rainer frowned. "He's my king."

She sighed, tilting the vial in her hand from side to side. The liquid inside glowed yellow. "When will it be enough, Rainer? What are you trying to prove, and to who? Wouldn't you like to be worthy of someone's love and respect without having to earn it, or does it only feel worth it if you're constantly having to prove yourself? Have you ever wondered why that is?"

The words crawled under his skin, growing itchy the more he considered them.

She pulled a dropper from the vial and dribbled some of the yellow liquid into her palms, set the vial on the table beside them, and rubbed her hands together. Then she reached out and took his right hand between hers, massaging his callused palms with the oil. An earthy herbal smell hit him as she gently worked on his tense hands.

"What would you do for yourself? Just because you wanted to— not because you had to prove something?" she asked.

Rainer climbed to his feet and stared at her. She was incandescent with conviction, and she made it look so easy. But he had no context for his past and relied entirely on proving who he was now. The only conviction he had was that which he'd gained since waking up.

"What would I do?" he asked.

"Yes. If you stopped thinking about pleasing everyone else."

He closed his eyes, considering. Lust rushed through his chest as he imagined it.

Eloise was stunning, poised, honest. She was everything a lady should be. She was an easy woman to want, and she'd spark desire in any man who laid eyes on her. It wasn't that he didn't find her attractive. He just didn't find her distracting.

There were things he knew in his head and things he knew in his heart. But wanting Cecilia was a thing he knew in his soul.

Before he could think better of it, he opened his eyes, cupped her face in his hands, and kissed her. She gasped in surprise, then slowly relaxed into him.

Rainer felt simultaneously relieved and angry that it felt so good to kiss Cecilia. How could kissing perfect Eloise feel so wrong and kissing the king's fiancée feel so incredibly right?

He fought to keep his hands from wandering too far, only moving them to lift her onto the table so that she was closer to his height.

Everything in his body begged him not to ever stop. As if removing his lips from hers would break something fragile inside him that he'd just excavated.

She tilted her chin, parting her lips to let him take the kiss deeper. He wanted to devour her. The sweetness of her mouth, each quick breath she took. He swallowed up every sigh and whimper, wishing he could touch more of her but not daring for fear he'd scare her away.

She had no qualms about touching him, though, her greedy hands sliding up his tunic, raising goosebumps on his skin. Leaning back, she hooked one leg over his hip and drew him toward her. He ground against her mindlessly. He wanted to look right into those bright blue eyes and see what she felt reflected there.

The pulse in his chest became a living thing, separate from him, wrapped around his heart. It stretched and throbbed. It ached for the woman he was kissing, as if it connected directly to something that lived in her, too.

They fought for control over the kiss. It was a brand-new type of battle for Rainer. He gained the upper hand by using his height and her surprise to his advantage; Cecilia wrested it back by touching him anywhere.

After dreaming of it for so long, he could perfectly picture her smiling up at him, the flush of her cheeks and the sound of her soft sigh. He was as curious to know what it would feel like to hold her while she slept as it would be to wake up to her smiling face.

Her fingers moved idly against his sides. Soothing, intoxicating, familiar. Everything about her was so godsdamned *familiar*.

Living that way was maddening. He was eternally on the precipice of remembering something terribly important, certain he'd forgotten something that would ruin him.

As if sensing his thoughts, one of her hands trailed downward, seeking out the painful, rapidly growing bulge in his pants. She rubbed him with startling confidence, like she knew exactly what he liked. He pressed hungry kisses down her neck, and she let out a moan that nearly made him lose his composure. Her robe had come untied and slipped off her shoulders, revealing a lace and silk nightgown beneath, her nipples pressing against the delicate fabric. He fought the urge to touch them as he kissed his way back to her mouth.

She sank her teeth into his lip and tugged and he groaned into her mouth. It was nearly impossible not to hike up her nightgown and bury his face between her thighs. He wanted to taste her, to hear what sounds she'd make when she climaxed, to know if she'd be soft and quiet or passionate and loud.

She finally broke the kiss, her hand moving faster, and Rainer realized she had pulled away to watch his face as she stroked him.

"Fuck," he whispered, and she grinned.

He wished he could touch her back, but he didn't want her to stop, so instead he gave her hair a slight tug. That was all the encouragement she needed. She unbuttoned his pants and pulled him free, wrapping her hand around him. She held his gaze the whole time.

Her hands were small and soft except for a few calluses on her fingers. Her gaze was a fire burning through him. He couldn't stop wondering what kind of filthy things would come out of her mouth if he could get inside her.

Cecilia worked him faster.

"You make me so fucking hard," he rasped, the words strained. "I wish I could touch you. I'd go down on you until you were too exhausted to stand."

A sly grin tugged at her swollen lips. "I'd prefer you only touch my face and hair and neck."

Then, to his immense surprise, she hopped off the desk, turning him back so his hips rested against it, and lowered herself to her knees.

Rainer cursed, nearly falling over from surprise as she took him into her mouth. He brought a hand to her hair. She looked so sexy, and he was mesmerized by the wet slide of her tongue. She licked and sucked his cock like she knew exactly what he liked, torturing him with her perfection.

The more often she seemed to read his mind, the less convinced he was it was supernatural. He had to have had some sort of relationship with her—and if the way she'd mastered his pleasure was any indication, it seemed to be an intimate one. That explained why she was so flirtatious with him. But it didn't explain *when* they'd had a relationship since she'd been engaged to a man who died in the attack, and was involved with the prince, and had since been engaged to Vincent.

If Rainer had any sense at all he wouldn't be standing there like an idiot, letting the king's fiancée suck his cock, but he was lost to her. Cecilia was fully in control, and the triumphant look in her eyes suggested she liked him powerless to her whims.

She swirled her tongue before taking him deep again.

He groaned. "How are you so good at that?"

She let out a soft moan around him, sending a bolt of pleasure up his spine. She was getting satisfaction out of pleasing him.

"Gods—" he groaned.

Cecilia drew back and smirked up at him, sliding her hand over his cock. "There are no gods here, Rainer. They've all been cast out of this castle. If you're going to beg for mercy, it better be my name on your lips."

Cecilia was so sexy and Rainer was entirely at her mercy. She took him deep again before he could even catch his breath. She bobbed her head and hollowed out her cheeks, her eyes locked on his. Rainer fought the urge to thrust his hips forward, seeking more of her hot mouth.

As if sensing his desire, she raked her fingernails over the backs of his thighs and his hand fisted in her hair.

"Fuck, Cece! I'm going to—"

But Cecilia seemed to know that would do it and was already taking him deep, not allowing him to pull away as he groaned out his release.

When she was finished, she looked up at him and licked her lips.

Rainer stared at her, panting, speechless. Cecilia looked like a lady, fought like a warrior, but sucked dick like she could read his mind. He had no idea what to make of her, but he was pretty sure he was falling in love with her. Maybe he already was. Maybe he always had been.

Maybe was a lie he told himself to make his life less complicated.

But he'd felt the flicker of it in that moment she'd pressed her hand to his chest and said, "*You are not a weapon.*" He couldn't remember anyone ever looking at him like he was worth more than his violence, more than the blood he could spill, more than his ability to turn the tide of a battle.

Since he'd woken after the attack, he'd only been aware of all the ways he was lacking and all there was to strive for. But Cecilia's desire for him to remember seemed born entirely out of wanting him to be at peace.

He helped her back to her feet and she grinned at what was surely a truly idiotic look on his face. She was an absolute marvel and Rainer was in over his head.

"What?" she asked.

He shook his head, trying to force himself into silence. He didn't know what finally made him say it, but it might have been the look in her eyes, bottomless and blue and so expressive.

"I think if I'm not careful I could fall in love with you," he said breathlessly.

She smiled and joy pulsed in his chest.

He leaned in closer, brushing his lips against hers. "I think if I'm not careful I could fall in love with you over and over again, every day, for the rest of my life."

She grinned as she pulled back and met his eyes. "Maybe you should."

"Maybe I should," he repeated.

His gaze dropped to her lips again. He needed to leave the room. If he stayed, he didn't know what would happen, but it was already impossible to keep his hands to himself. He wanted to make her come fourteen different ways, but he couldn't bear the thought of making her uncomfortable.

"Can I—"

She shook her head. "It's not that I don't want to. I just don't know if I can yet, and that was so nice. I don't want to spoil a good time."

He wanted to say something clever, but he had nothing to offer but hatred for whoever had made her so afraid. He realized what courage and trust she'd placed in him just then. He swallowed around the lump in his throat.

The realization made him certain. They had to have been together. She wouldn't have been able to do any of that if she didn't already trust him. She had to have known him well enough and had enough of an established relationship to feel comfortable doing something scandalous to begin with.

When he met her eyes again, he knew the thing he'd felt the first time he'd seen her up close. He knew the space around his heart buzzed to life around her because he was in love with her.

As if sensing his attention, that same space in his chest buzzed to life with a pulse of warmth. He closed his eyes and brought his hand to his heart. He could live in that feeling, but it might get them both killed.

"I should go back to my room, though I admit I feel silly that I came to apologize and you did all the work."

Cecilia smirked. "Pleasant dreams, Rainer."

He almost laughed, but she gave him a look that said she knew exactly what he'd be dreaming about. She winked as she closed the door and left him in the hallway with his bewilderment and unspent desire.

28

CECILIA

The last thing Cecilia wanted to do after her first sexual victory since the attack was go see Vincent the following morning. But she had no choice but to appease him for now. She smoothed her hands down the bodice of her wool dress and paused in the hallway, trying to steel herself to face Vincent.

She hadn't been aware Castle Savero had a throne room. Guards bracketed the large, intricately carved wooden doors. Cecilia recognized the scene cut into the wood only because she'd seen the moment illustrated in artwork back in Olney. It depicted the fall of the front line, the battle where Rainer's birth father, Zelden Novaris, had fallen. For Olney the scene depicted courage against all odds, but in Argaria it was clearly meant to be a monument to victory. Cecilia glanced down the hall, wondering if Rainer had glimpsed this art.

She didn't know why he'd never told her who his birth father was. She wouldn't have thought of him any differently. There were so many things that made sense now that she knew. Rainer always made a point to stop and look at the art of this scene in Olney. All their lives Cecilia had assumed it was born of an aspirational commitment to being a good warrior. Now her heart ached because Rainer was probably just looking for signs of himself.

All her life she'd felt so isolated and strange until she'd learned who she truly was. All that time she'd thought Rainer fit in so easily. Now, she wondered if he'd felt just as lonely and had hidden behind a cheerful, gregarious exterior. It hurt even worse that if he didn't remember, she might never know.

One of the guards cleared his throat. "My lady?"

Cecilia nodded and the guard opened the door.

She walked into the throne room. The crowd of pandering nobles all seemed to stop speaking at once. They stared at her, parting as she crossed the room to the dais where Vincent sat. She dipped into a shallow curtsey.

"Your Grace, you summoned?"

Vincent leaned back in his seat, looking much too comfortable on the throne he'd stolen, his eyes raking over her menacingly. "You look lovely today, dearest."

Cecilia said nothing, holding perfectly still under his appraisal. She did not look lovely. She looked washed out in the ugly gold dress, but she didn't care because she'd secretly had a spectacular dress made for Rainer and Eloise's engagement party that evening.

"Thank you," she said with the fakest smile she could manage.

He smoothed his tunic. "I want you to spend some time with Eloise this afternoon. She was hoping you'd be one of her maids in the wedding and I assured her you'd be delighted. She'd be so honored to have the future queen in her wedding party."

"You want me to attend her?" Cecilia forced her face into a neutral mask, but Vincent's grin let her know she'd done a poor job.

"Yes. She was hoping for some pointers on Guardian McKay, and since you've known each other for so long, I thought you would be the best person to offer her counsel."

"I'm afraid I'm quite busy this afternoon."

Vincent frowned. "Surely not too busy to bestow wisdom on a bride."

Cecilia clasped her hands together. There was no way to avoid Vincent's cruel games. Emotional warfare was his chosen method, and he was so skilled at it that he didn't need to deliver the punishment himself anymore.

"Of course," Cecilia said reluctantly.

Vincent clapped his hands. "Marvelous. She's in her rooms awaiting you for tea. You may go."

Cecilia curtseyed and left the room, ignoring the gawking of the various lords and ladies who were clearly hoping for a more dramatic show, most notably Edward Spellman, who stood by the throne room doors, grinning and holding court with several other council members.

She breezed out of the throne room and up to Eloise's rooms. Her mind spun. She wanted to believe that Eloise wasn't inherently cruel —that she was just another woman being told what to do by men who controlled her future. But Eloise had admitted she was attracted to Rainer even before the attack. While Cecilia didn't want to give in to the paranoia that became stronger by the day, she couldn't overlook the possibility that Eloise had been in on it since the beginning.

There was only one way to find out and at the very least Cecilia could try to excavate some more critical details they would need for the wedding.

Cecilia knocked and was summoned inside.

"Lady Reznik, you have perfect timing," Eloise said.

Cecilia considered leaving until she spotted a seating chart for the wedding ceremony. She took a few steps toward the table where two copies of it were laid out. She tried to appear casual as she glanced at Eloise. "Perfect timing for what?"

Eloise gave her a triumphant smile. "My fiancé will be visiting my bedchamber tonight for the first time. I could use every insight you have."

Cecilia's heart hammered in her chest. "I think you mean *my* fiancé."

Eloise rolled her eyes, dismissing the servant who had been fluffing a dress hanging from a hook by the closet.

When they were alone, Eloise turned her green eyes on Cecilia. "I hope you don't blame me. It's not my fault you didn't marry him while you had the chance."

Eloise's words stung. Cecilia had kicked herself so many times. She'd been so foolish ànd stuck in her own grief and now she might really lose him.

"He's quite the catch," Eloise continued. "He's handsome, strong, intelligent, charming. He has those beautiful green eyes. And he's very well-endowed."

It took every ounce of self-control for Cecilia not to take a swing at her.

Eloise pursed her lips. "No, I haven't seen it yet, but I have felt it when he had me in his lap and he was kissing me. And my gods, the way he made me scream with his tongue."

A wave of nausea surged through Cecilia as she forced herself to sit in a chair by the window. Eloise had to be lying, but doubt crept into Cecilia's mind.

She'd felt so confident when she woke that morning, thinking about the desperate way Rainer had groaned her name, how he'd been entirely at her mercy, and how she'd felt powerful for the first time since Vincent had held her down and carved his initials into her thigh.

Now, Eloise was ruining the vision.

Maybe Cecilia was just a conquest to Rainer. Just one last dalliance before he settled down. She couldn't read any dishonesty in Eloise's expression.

Eloise plopped down on the chair beside hers as if they were the best of friends. "Now tell me everything."

Cecilia frowned.

Eloise laughed. "Your petulance was amusing in the beginning but it's exhausting now. You should want your love to be happy. I can give him what he wants most. I am one of six children, Cecilia. Imagine his joy at having that many children. Imagine them with his beautiful green eyes."

Cecilia blinked away the burning in her eyes. She did want

Rainer to have that. It was the one thing she couldn't give him, and it broke her heart.

Eloise blew out a breath. "If that's not motivation enough, the king said to warn you that if you don't help me, he will make you perform every act you don't talk about with him tonight."

Cecilia recoiled at the thought of Vincent touching her.

"You knew better than to fall in love with someone you couldn't satisfy. Now tell me how to make him happy," Eloise said.

Cecilia met her eye and for the first time she could read Eloise's insecurity. "He'll never love you like he loves me."

Eloise frowned. "He will if I give him time. He doesn't even know you."

Cecilia shook her head. "You'll never have what we do."

"Nothing?" Eloise taunted.

Cecilia swallowed hard and stared into the fire, forcing herself to hold her tongue.

"Fine," Eloise said. "If you want to be that way, I'll tell the king that you weren't cooperative."

Cecilia tipped her head back and sighed. "Why are you helping Vincent? Surely you must know he's a monster."

Eloise wavered. "We are all the monsters the world makes us, Cecilia. All of us are just trying to survive."

She may have called herself a monster, but for the first time Cecilia saw Eloise as a scared girl who'd been the victim of a monster, rather than a villain herself. She might have felt pity if she wasn't so jealous.

Cecilia gripped the arms of her chair. She sent a surge of love through her bond with Rainer. She knew he wouldn't know what it was, but she wanted him to feel loved anyway.

"I've never had anyone be so gentle with me," Cecilia said. "He's respectful and careful. He probably won't feel comfortable sleeping with you before you're married."

Eloise gave her a skeptical look.

"I know," Cecilia said. "I'm sure you've heard that he was prolific back in Olney, but that was an illusion. He hasn't been with as many women as he'd led people to believe. He has a lot of honor. I think he will tell you he doesn't want to shame you, and that he wants to do things the right way. He can be a bit superstitious sometimes, especially when he's anxious. Right now, he's very anxious because he doesn't remember things."

"How do you know?" Eloise asked.

"Because I've known him most of my life. I know every look on his face. I know every tic, every sigh, every shadow that passes through his eyes."

Eloise swallowed.

Cecilia laughed. "I'm jealous of you too. Rest assured the feeling is mutual. Rainer is the best man I've ever known. He will respect you because you're his wife. I wouldn't count on him staying the night, even if he wants to."

Eloise brushed her hair over her shoulder. "I can be persuasive."

Cecilia bit her tongue.

"Tell me what he likes," Eloise commanded.

Cecilia nodded and took a deep breath. "He's an amazing kisser. He likes to be thorough, so he'll kiss for a very long time, but you probably already know that."

Cecilia couldn't help someone else please the man she loved. She didn't care about the consequences. She switched strategies.

"He can be shy at first, especially since it's your first time together and he doesn't want to pressure you. It's best if you take the lead. Truth be told, he likes a little aggression, so the more forward you can be the better."

Eloise looked at her doubtfully, but Cecilia continued without missing a beat.

"He takes consent extremely seriously. If he has a hint that you're not on board he will bail out. He can't stand to feel like a woman is uncomfortable."

Eloise sat back, considering. "What if I'm too aggressive?"

"You?" Cecilia laughed. "The first time we were together, I was a goddess. I don't think there's such a thing as too aggressive for him."

She failed to mention how Rainer had still been incredibly slow and gentle with her.

Eloise was satisfied with that explanation.

"He likes when I use my mouth on him, although as you can imagine, it's a challenge. You have to really go for it and not be tentative."

Eloise raised an eyebrow. "I won't be."

Cecilia pressed on. "You can't treat him like things are transactional. Sometimes he likes to give just because he wants me to feel good and he doesn't want anything but that. But you can't treat him like he needs to earn love. He's always been treated that way—" Her voice broke and she cleared her throat. "Rainer is worth much more than what he can give me."

When Rainer had said those words to her—"*Cece, you are worth more than just what you can give me*"—it had healed something that had been broken in her for so long.

Eloise frowned. "Keep going. What positions does he like?"

Cecilia couldn't tell all lies or Eloise would realize and start doing the opposite of what Cecilia suggested. She had to slip some truth in.

"He likes to take me from behind because he loves looking at my ass. I doubt he'll feel the same way with you since you're just a lady."

Eloise balked. "What do you mean?"

"I've spent my whole life training as a hunter, working my ass into shape while you've been sitting on yours at tea. That's one place you can't compete."

Cecilia smiled at the recognition on Eloise's face. She was pissed but she knew it was true.

"He also loves to have me in his lap because he has his hands free to touch me. He likes the closeness but he's also in love with me, so he might feel uncomfortable with that kind of intimacy with you."

"*Was* in love with you. It's important that we all stop living in the past." Eloise scowled. "I'm sure we'll get there."

Cecilia smiled as a wicked thought came to mind. She shook her head and Eloise took the bait.

"What? What is it? You must tell me, or I'll tell the king."

Cecilia sighed as if it hurt to give away such a secret. "Eloise, I can't. It's the one thing that's still just between us."

Eloise grabbed Cecilia's hand and squeezed. "Please, just tell me. I don't want Vincent to hurt you."

Cecilia wanted to slap her—to tell her he already had, to say if she knew what he'd done she'd never threaten to tell him. She wanted to tell Eloise if she didn't want him to hurt her, Eloise and her family wouldn't have helped him come to power.

Cecilia looked down at the floor and forced tears into her eyes before meeting Eloise's desperate gaze.

"Please don't make me—" Cecilia begged.

"It's for the best." Eloise sounded so sincerely conciliatory.

Cecilia's shoulders slumped in faux defeat. "I told you how much he loves my ass—"

Eloise shrunk back, stunned. "You've done that."

Cecilia hadn't, but Eloise deserved to feel a little bit nervous. She was helping hold Cecilia captive with the man who had assaulted her. A few nerves were the least Cecilia could inflict upon her, but it was enough to assuage her more violent fantasies of what she'd do to Eloise.

"I love him. If it isn't already clear, I would do anything for him," Cecilia said.

Eloise stared at her, and Cecilia held her gaze. She could practically feel Eloise trying to find the lie in it. A worried crease settled into her brow as she sat back and took a long drink of wine.

"Wine helps," Cecilia said with a sad half-smile.

Eloise's eyes went wide for a moment, but she nodded.

It was almost impossible for Cecilia not to laugh. She was worried she oversold it, but Eloise still looked terrified. Maybe it would be enough to scare her off from rushing into things.

Cecilia looked away, biting her lip as if trying not to cry. "Is there anything else, or have I poured enough of my heart out?" she asked curtly.

Eloise remembered the position she was in and fixed her face into a mask of indifference. "Does he like to cuddle after?"

"He does with me. He likes to lay in bed and kiss me for a long time. He whispers how he loves me over and over while he kisses any skin he can get to. Then he holds me tight to his chest and strokes my scar." Cecilia brought her hand to her chest. That was all true. "But as I recall, that wasn't the case with other women he was with, so don't be disappointed."

Eloise rolled her eyes. "He may not be there now, but he'll get there."

Cecilia raised an eyebrow in challenge. "We'll see, I suppose. Anything else?"

Eloise looked suddenly self-conscious. She looked down at her lap and then back up at Cecilia. "Do you think he could get there with me?" she asked.

Cecilia held her gaze. She wanted to scratch the eyes out of Eloise's perfect face. She wanted to kill her for helping Vincent. She wanted to hurt her as badly as possible.

She kept her face placid. "No, I don't." She meant it. "You don't stand a chance. He might do what he has to, but he won't lie to you. And even if he did, you will never know for sure that he would have chosen you if it wasn't about his duty."

Eloise stood suddenly. "You don't know that. You'll see at the party tonight."

Cecilia shrugged. "Maybe I will, but I doubt it."

The truth was Cecilia wasn't sure that was true. Rainer might fall in love with Eloise. There was no way to know for sure.

Eloise clenched her fists at her sides. Fury burned through the air around her. "He will love me."

Cecilia laughed as she stood, pausing in front of the table with the seating arrangements for the wedding. She studied the layout, memorizing as much as she could. "I suppose it's a shame your rich daddy can't purchase that love, huh?"

Eloise huffed out a disbelieving laugh.

"You want to know what Rainer wants?" Cecilia taunted, giving the seating chart one last long look. "What will truly make him happy? What will satisfy him in bed like nothing else?" She glanced at Eloise over her shoulder. "It's me."

Eloise gave her a wicked smile. "Then I'll just have to settle for satisfying him in life with the only thing he's ever wanted. Our children will be so beautiful and for that he will love me more than he ever loved you."

Cecilia crossed the room in a huff and slammed the door behind her as she left, trying not to feel the truth of those words.

29

XANDER

Cece sauntered into the library, a wide grin on her face as she sat across from Xander in front of the fire.

"You look like the cat that ate the canary, love," Xander said.

Truthfully, she looked pale and exhausted. Her eyes were shadowed with dark circles and her cheeks were hollowed. She looked how he felt being cut off from his magic, but it seemed the stress had made her lack of appetite worse than his.

Xander had spent hours trying to figure out how the temple would be set up for the wedding so they could strike with minimal casualties, but he was frustrated that all he could really do was guess where Vincent would seat his supporters.

"I brought a present." Cece bent down, slipped a rolled-up paper out of her dress pocket, and handed it to him.

Xander unrolled it and stared at the crude drawing. For a moment he couldn't make sense of the boxes and names. Then he saw the aisle and the altar and it clicked into place.

He stared at Cece. "This is the seating map for Rainer's wedding."

"It is."

"How on earth did you get it?"

345

"Long story and I might have missed a name or two. I had to do it from actual memory, not enhanced memory, but I think I got everyone who we suspect might be working with Vincent. Can you find a way to get it to Evan?"

The tension in Xander's chest relaxed ever so slightly. He hadn't realized how much he needed a win after royally fucking up with Isla.

"You're brilliant. I don't know what I'd do without you," he said. "We are so close. We just need to know if Corin Archer is an ally. Just because he didn't share the location we gave him with Vincent, doesn't mean he's on our side."

"We might have to take a gamble," Cece said.

Xander scrubbed a hand down his face. He had hoped they wouldn't. "I suppose you're right. Now what did you get up to today and why do you look so pleased with yourself?"

"I may have been forced to share all of Rainer's sexual preferences with Lady Spellman." She smirked and stretched. "I may have oversold some and undersold others."

"Is that all?"

"I may have suggested that he has a very strong preference for anal," she said smugly.

Xander lost it. He laughed until his stomach hurt. He could not remember the last time he'd done that.

"I also may have had her fiancé's cock in my mouth last night," Cece said.

Xander shook his head. "You are a menace with a filthy mouth."

"I am." She grinned. "But aren't you glad I'm a menace who's on your side?"

"Never more than at this moment. Where did you find the time? Was this after the wedding?"

She nodded. "Don't get too excited. He still doesn't remember anything from before, but he won't soon forget last night."

Xander chuckled. "Gods, I needed that laugh."

He was relieved to see her looking more like herself. It was good to see her smiling. The look on her face that night weeks ago still haunted him. Sometimes he hardly recognized this Cece as the woman he'd first met on the dance floor at the Godsball years before. Back then she'd been so uncertain of herself and so afraid to ask for what she wanted. But sometimes he saw flashes of mischief in her eyes, joy in her smile that brought him right back to that moment. The woman who sat before him now had earned her conviction.

Cece leaned back in her chair, eyes narrowing on him. "Why do you need a laugh? What's on your mind?"

"You mean other than the fact that the woman who brought me into this world, who has served my family for a generation, was killed? More than me getting yet another person loyal to me hurt?"

"Xan." Her face softened and she placed her hand on his. "We all know what we are risking, and we are doing it for the same reasons you are. You cannot take it on—"

"I'm king. It is my job to take it on. I can't help feeling—" A lump in his throat choked him. "I can't help feeling responsible, but beyond that I can't help feeling that I'm not worth it. I was never under the illusion that my father was a nice man, but I thought he had limits. Now I find myself about to become a father and terrified I will be the same."

Cece didn't know the truth of his parentage, but not sharing blood with Damian didn't keep Xander from worrying about how his attitudes might have bled into Xander's subconscious. And one too many times in the past year he'd thought about just running away, which was essentially what his birth father Arthur Randal had done.

Xander had the blood of an absent father and the nurturing of a callous one. He wanted to forge his own path, but he was worried that he could easily slip into the well-trodden path of either of those men.

"Oh, Xan." Cece pulled him into a tight hug. "You are a better man than your father could have dreamed of being. You are not just him. You are also your mother. Never once have I seen a hint of your father in you, but I have seen her almost daily. In your kindness, in the fierce way you love, in your protectiveness and loyalty. Do you remember what you said to me when I was afraid I'd be a brutal, careless goddess?"

He frowned, trying to recall the moment, wishing he had access to his magic to watch the memory.

"You said not to judge myself for mistakes I made when I was still learning how to be in that role. You said the fact that the fear of becoming that brutal kept me up at night was a clear sign that I had learned something from my mistake. What happened to Mags—" Her voice broke, her eyes glassy with tears. "I feel it too. I feel responsible too—like I traded one life for another. But I know she wouldn't have it any other way. Sometimes the best we can do when we are the person with the most power is trust that the people we love deserve the same agency over their lives to decide what is worth sacrificing for."

Xander sighed.

She shook her head. "Do you have any idea how many times I wanted to collect all of you and hide you somewhere safe when Cato was after me? Daily, hourly—every single minute, Xan. But at some point, I had to admit I couldn't do it on my own and none of you would let me. I thank the gods you didn't. What a beautiful thing to have people who won't let you be alone even when the risks are terrifying."

Xander wrung his hands. "But how do I live with it?"

"You remind yourself it's not about you. It's about everyone else. I came here for answers and to finish what we started and because I owed it to everyone who sacrificed. Because I'm a woman of my word and I promised your mother that I would protect you. And because when I stood in that temple with you I promised to fight with you and for you." She squeezed his hand. "We endure because the work is not done."

He nodded. "Love, you can be very compelling."

She flipped her hair over her shoulder. "Yes, well, I've had the practice of giving myself pep talks in the mirror each morning." She patted his hand. "Now, do you want to tell me what's really wrong?"

He laughed, shaking his head. "How do you do that?"

A satisfied smile split her face. "Do what?"

"Read me in that unnerving way of yours."

"Well, I had to make a quick study of you since you had a head start. Couldn't have you keeping the upper hand for long." She gestured broadly to his face. "This face says, *Cece, help. My wife's decoy is not impressed with my nonsense.*"

Xander ran a hand through his hair. "I fear I may have ruined things with Isla."

Cece smiled at him knowingly.

"You aren't jealous?" It wasn't that he wanted her to be, but he'd struggled so much with jealousy that it felt like if she didn't feel it, then what they'd had wasn't as equitable as he'd remembered.

"I suppose part of me always will be a bit jealous," Cece admitted. "But it's selfish not to want the absolute best for you. You deserve someone wonderful. How did you mess up?"

"I asked her to be my consort and she was insulted."

Cece frowned. "She was insulted that you asked her to take a place of privilege?"

Xander frowned and looked away.

"How *exactly* did you ask, Xander?"

He sighed. "I may have asked when I was overcome by a particularly intense moment in bed."

Cece clapped a hand to her forehead, looking horrified. "Xander!"

He threw his hands up. "I know, I know! I panicked. I barely had any blood flow in my head—at least the thinking one. I can't be held responsible for the things I say when I'm overcome with lust."

"Don't I know it," she said. "You are so fucked."

The curse startled him. She swore so rarely outside the bedroom, but on this occasion it was appropriate.

"I am. She is incredibly self-assured, and I am out of my element. How do I fix it?"

"You tell her what an idiot you were. You tell her that you care for her. And you would like the opportunity to make her a better offer when you're inside her. A respectful one, befitting the station of a consort, especially one who I'm sure has no intention of sitting around like a pampered lady."

Xander sighed. "I think she's upset that I can't love her like I loved you."

Cece smiled sadly. "Every love is different. Instead of telling her what you can't give her, why don't you focus on what you can?"

"Like what?"

Cece shook her head. "I can't tell you. You have to figure it out for yourself. You can give her grown-up love. You can give her what's left. You can give her respect, attention, humor, companionship—romance if you pull your head out of your ass and stop thinking with your favorite appendage."

"Your favorite too, if I'm not mistaken," he said with a wink.

"Your new favorite is going to be your right hand unless you get your shit together," she taunted. "Isla wants to be won over—not by a performance. You're clearly taken with her. Just be honest. Be vulnerable. Don't fuck this up, Xander. She's good for you."

Xander nodded.

She kissed his cheek and turned to leave, pausing in the doorway. "Also, it never hurts to show up with flowers or jewelry, though in her case, I'd choose something heartfelt and not just flashy. And you have unique access to her closest family member. Use it."

His mind instantly flew to his mother's sapphire ring, the same one he'd once given Cece.

"Love, you are brilliant."

She turned, pinning him with those big, blue eyes. "I know."

Then she ducked into the passageway and out of the room.

Xander tucked the scroll she'd delivered inside his tunic and left through the passageway that led back toward his rooms. After the assassination attempts, Isla had made him agree not to leave his room without her unless he was taking the passages. She'd made herself scarce since their fight—still appearing beside him in an official capacity, but she'd barely said a word to him and had slept in the adjoining room at night.

Xander walked down the darkened passageway until he reached the bend and took a narrow, uneven staircase up to his floor. He walked the rest of the way in silence, trying to figure out how to start this conversation with Jessamin. She'd seemed open to the idea of him and Isla, but being amicable and being enthusiastic to help were two very different things.

Xander pushed open the door and entered the room. It felt lonely, the fire burning low, the space nearly absent of Isla's scent.

Xander crossed the room and knocked on the door to the princess's quarters and was beckoned inside by his wife's voice. He entered and searched the room, at first disappointed to find that Isla wasn't there, then worried.

"Where's Isla?"

"Training," Jessamin said. She and Maren locked eyes, some unspoken conversation passing between them.

"She felt like she was getting too soft without her daily workouts, so she went down to your private training rooms via the passages," Maren said.

Xander had noticed that, though his wife's consort had her fiery moments, she was quick to comfort and spare someone's feelings. Perhaps that was why Jessamin had fallen for her in the first place.

Xander couldn't get used to Jessamin's disguise and it startled him to hear her voice come from someone else's face. Still, he was happy for the safety of her disguise.

"How are you feeling this afternoon, darling?" He crossed the room and placed his hand on her shoulder.

Jessamin smacked him away. "I'm feeling fine. Just tired and nauseous, like every other day. And sick of all of you constantly asking how I'm feeling." She pressed a palm to her stomach. "He's going to be strong. I can tell."

Xander grinned. "He?"

Jessamin nodded. "Just a feeling I have. Perhaps he'll be a Storm Prince like his father. And hopefully not an incessant worrying gnat, like his Auntie Maren."

The redheaded guard rolled her eyes at the barb, returning to her perch by the window.

"Does the thought of a baby boy please you?" Jessamin asked.

"It pleases me that it's a healthy baby. I could care less about gender," Xander said.

Jessamin clapped her hands. "I suspect it would be best for you if it wasn't a girl. I think she'd have you wrapped around her finger in a second."

Xander grinned at the thought of a little girl with his hazel eyes and his wife's smile. "Gods help us both if it's a girl. She'll be as charming as me and as beautiful as you, and as deadly as the both of us. The world won't be ready."

Jessamin's laugh rang through the room, relaxing the tension in his shoulders.

"What's on your mind? You've been wandering around like a lost child since Evan and Sylvie's wedding," she said.

Xander hesitated. She'd probably already heard Isla's side of the story.

"I made a mistake with Isla that I am eager to fix, but I wanted your opinion, and before I tell you what I did, Cece already berated me for my idiocy, so I promise I don't need to hear it again. I just need to know what to do to fix it."

He regaled Jessamin with his supreme foolishness, but she just laughed when he was finished.

"Look how you are tied in knots for my cousin," Jessamin chuckled. "Goddess bless, I never thought I'd see the day after how lovesick you were over Cece when we first met."

"I want to give Isla this," he said, handing Jessamin the ring box. "And I want to ask her to be my consort. I like how I feel when I'm with her. I like that she challenges me. I like that she doesn't care who I am. And gods, I know that it's difficult to take me seriously because I fall fast and hard, but I want her to stay with me always and not just at the whims of your mother. I want to make promises to her that go beyond what you and I have promised, if she'll have me."

Jessamin smiled warmly. "Isla has always been stubborn and competitive. She doesn't like to feel she's second to anyone, but you and I know that there is no accounting for first love. Tell her how you feel, what you can offer, and be willing to accept that it might not be enough. But also, be willing to hope that it could be. Put yourself at her mercy and just be yourself. Not the performing Xander, though he is very charming. If you want her, you have to let her see you weak."

Xander scrubbed a hand over his face. "Have I ever been weaker?"

"Many people would say I traded a position of power for one of weakness, you know," Jessamin said.

Xander frowned. "Who? Why?"

"Warriors at home saw that I surrendered a position leading the Novumi army to come here and be some man's wife. They look at me and think I traded myself into a kingdom where my only power comes from my husband. They see what is in front of them—not all the possibilities." Jessamin looked across the room at Maren. "At home I could not be with the woman I love. I could lead an army that would likely never see any action. The life I saw in front of me was small and stifling. Coming here opened up so many possibilities. What people at home can't see is that here, I can change the world for women. I can have a huge impact on two kingdoms' worth of power structures. I can help you strategize."

Xander liked the sound of that.

"I could have stayed safe on the shores of my home," she continued. "But I would have never met you and I wouldn't have known that I could be my full self. I have the love and the family I always wanted, and the opportunity to make a difference in this world. Our partnership has changed the course of my life for the better and I have every intention of making waves."

Xander nodded. "Much-needed waves, Jess. My storms are at your disposal."

Jessamin patted his hand. "What I'm saying to you is that you can stay safe where you are, or you can take the risk and know that you are heading into completely uncharted territory. I seem to remember finding you in a panic over your broken heart shortly after we first met. Have you let her see more than your brave face?"

Xander sighed. Could he really go there again? Lay himself bare on the altar of vulnerability and hope that Isla liked what she saw?

He'd already offered her a secret no one else had; what more could he share?

He remembered how he'd felt with Cece. Torn open, raw, living every day like he was daring love to wound him. It was terrifying to think of risking it again. It still felt too soon, but if he didn't act now, he might miss his chance and he'd never forgive himself if he didn't at least try.

PART III:
UNLIKELY HEROES

30

CECILIA

The dress was a rebellion. For weeks, Cecilia had worn nothing but black, like she was in mourning. It only took one early slap for her to know that Vincent requesting she wear his colors was not a request at all.

Now, as Cecilia stood poised to descend into the ballroom in her sparkling white gown, she felt radiant, a bright star in a sea of dark gowns. The seamstress, Mariah, swore Cecilia to secrecy to preserve her and her family's lives. Cecilia was happy to keep her secret in exchange for the most spectacular and personal dress she'd ever worn.

Her breath hitched as she descended the stairs, the whole crowd turning to look at her. The song the small orchestra was playing ended and the only sound in the room was the soft patter of her silk slippers on the marble stairs.

Before Cecilia could reach the bottom, Xander rushed up a step to meet her. She placed her hand in his and he bent to kiss it.

"Love, you're so beautiful it hurts to look at you," Xander said. "Half the men in this room are staring at you and the rest are trying not to in front of their wives."

Cecilia looked over his shoulder, searching for Rainer in the crush of people. "I don't need them to look at me. I need *him* to."

Xander led her toward the dance floor. "Trust me. He is."

"Different than the way he looks at Eloise?"

Xander smirked. "Yes. When he looks at Eloise he looks happy, but when he looks at you he seems miserable, starving, wrecked. I know that look well."

"Xander," she chided.

"What? It's true."

"That is a decidedly un-friendly thing to say," Cecilia teased.

"Perhaps you don't have the right kind of friends."

She laughed. "You are impossibly charming."

"I know." Xander sighed as if it was a great burden to bear. "We all have our lots in life. How do you feel?"

"I feel more like myself than I have in weeks."

"And who are you?"

Cecilia grinned at him. "Vengeance."

"Well, you look incredible. That dress should be illegal."

The compliment bolstered her, a sense of warm satisfaction settling in the body that hadn't quite felt like it belonged to her since the attack. Mika and Magdalena had assured her that it was all normal, but for Cecilia it was strange to feel so closed off. She'd dressed more conservatively than she ever had before, preferring pants over dresses, and heavy wool gowns that buttoned up to her neck over the scandalous ones she used to wear.

Tonight was the first night she'd worn anything even remotely revealing since the attack and she'd done it all to capture Rainer's attention and to stick it to Vincent, who insisted that she wear his colors all the time. She hoped it made the statement *"Don't fuck with me."*

"The question is *why* do you look so exceptionally stunning?" Xander inquired.

She grinned. "Black doesn't suit me. Vincent can keep me captive, but he does not own me. I won't wear black as if I'm mourning. I won't perform as some sort of doll. There are parts of me that even he can't touch." Even as she said the words, she didn't feel as confident about them as she had in the past. Vincent had created fractures in a psyche she had only just begun to heal.

Xander's brow softened. "I simply worry you're provoking him. Even if you do look like a goddess in this dress."

She smiled at him. For a moment she forgot the past two years. All the war and loss and pain between them disappeared and there was just the beautiful, magnetic eyes and smile of the man who swept her off her feet. Though her love for him had shifted, perhaps even faded, it simmered beneath his gaze, as if ready to boil over with the proper attention. Perhaps that was the nature of old love. Maybe some love stories were short, some were long, and some had endings that would always feel a little raw and unfinished. If she thought too hard about it, it simply hurt.

Xander leaned close, his cheek brushing hers. "I'm not the only one who has noticed."

She followed his gaze to where Rainer stood across the room. Eloise was next to him, chatting animatedly to her friends. She looked gorgeous in a scarlet dress, but Rainer's gaze was set on Cecilia.

"Honestly, his pining now might be worse than it was when you and I first got back to Olney after the Gauntlet. And that was truly a pathetic time for him," Xander said.

Cecilia shot him a warning look, but Xander's gaze dipped to her chest.

"Now that I'm closer, I'm starting to see a story on this dress."

"Thank you for noticing," Cecilia said.

Xander smiled suggestively. "I particularly like your little doves."

She slid her hands to the place just above her breasts where two doves were stitched, diving down toward the golden scar on her chest. "Yes, they're a reminder to keep hope alive. To always return to courage in action and emotion."

Xander's lips parted and he nodded. He looked like he wanted to say more, but something across the room caught his eye. He left her alone for a moment, darting over to the small ensemble of musicians.

He whispered something to them before he rejoined her on the dance floor, pulling her into his arms.

"Where's your wife, love?" she asked.

He nodded toward Eloise. "One is over there, staying in earshot of the couple of honor. The other is tucked safely in our suite as it seems she's a bit under the weather."

Cecilia grimaced. "Still? Did you give her the ginger tea I made?"

Xander nodded. "She says that Novumi women believe it's a good sign, that the child can steal strength from the mother. She expects it will abate soon."

The music shifted, sounding the first few chords of a Reldan.

Xander grinned at her. "For old times' sake? May I touch you?"

He was so good at reminding her that she might have no control over the situation she was in, but that she'd always have control over when and how he touched her.

"Yes."

Xander's fingers skimmed her bare back, just above the dip of her dress, before coming to rest flat against her skin. He drew her body against his. She held his gaze.

"Making Rainer McKay insanely jealous is one of my favorite and most practiced talents," Xander whispered. "If we want to draw him in, we need to raise questions in his mind. We need to prey on his jealousy. He still seems to have the instinct to protect you. Let's stoke that fire, love."

Xander pulled back and Cecilia gave him a wide, adoring grin before pushing her hips flush to his. Xander spun her into a dramatic dip.

She moved with him easily as she had so many times before, his touch familiar. She drew her leg out of the slit of her dress, hooking it over his thigh as they leaned to the side and took several steps back. She circled Xander, caressing him seductively before he pulled her back against him.

He dipped her low as the song ended before lifting her to her feet. He stepped back and took her hand to kiss it. Instead of kissing her knuckles as usual, though, he flipped her hand over and pressed his lips to her inner wrist and the crescent scar on her palm, the exact places Rainer loved to kiss.

Anger shot through her connection from Rainer and Cecilia smiled indulgently.

"You're still a wonderful dancer, Cece," Xander said with a wolfish smile. His gaze darted past her shoulder. "Guardian McKay, what a pleasant surprise."

Cecilia whipped around and found Rainer standing right behind her. Anger and confusion slid through their bond.

"Your Highness." Rainer offered the smallest perceivable bow. His gaze lingered on where Xander still held Cecilia's hand.

Xander remained wholly unbothered. "My love, you are a vision in white. Is she not, McKay?"

Rainer's gaze raked over her appreciatively. "Yes. You look lovely, Lady Reznik."

"*Lovely*," Xander scoffed. "She looks like a goddess and there's not a man in this room who can keep his eyes off of her."

Rainer's eyes narrowed on the prince. His jealousy thrilled Cecilia but she couldn't tell if it was born of lust or something more substantial.

"Did you need something?" Xander asked. "I was just going to ask Cece to have a drink with me in the courtyard where it's a bit less stuffy—away from prying eyes."

Xander's words were so heavy with innuendo that Cecilia almost laughed.

"Shouldn't you be dancing with your wife? I'm not sure if the king would like Lady Reznik—" Rainer started.

"Don't be such a fun-sucker, Rainer," Cecilia said. "The king is busy, so unless you require my partnership for the next dance, I'm inclined to join Xan for a cocktail."

Rainer frowned at the nickname. He sighed in resignation. "Actually, I *was* hoping you would dance with me." His cheeks pinked slightly.

"And here I thought you'd be busy with your fiancée," Cecilia said.

Rainer appeared pained by the word. His eyes darted around the room.

"Oh, put the poor fool out of his misery, love," Xander said.

Rainer blushed again and Cecilia had to stop herself from reaching up to touch his heated cheeks. She'd seen him blush so rarely.

"I would love to dance with you," she said.

Relief shot through their bond and a smile broke over Rainer's face as he took her hand. He led her away from Xander—away from the crowd—to a quiet corner of the room.

"May I touch your back?" he asked.

She nodded and he wrapped an arm around her, pressing her body against his as he started to move her around the floor. There were fewer eyes on her than when she danced with Xander, but she felt Eloise's gaze like daggers in her back.

"Prince Xander was right," Rainer whispered. "Lovely is too small a word for how beautiful you look in that dress. You stole my breath when you walked into the room. You look like a star to wish on."

"And what would you wish for?"

He smiled tightly. "Restraint."

She brushed her fingers up his neck, running them through his hair, which was starting to curl.

"What would your wish be?" he asked.

"That yours didn't come true," she whispered.

Guilt and lust rushed through their bond. Cecilia could practically feel her back scald under Eloise's burning gaze.

"You look very handsome," Cecilia whispered.

She continued to play with the hair at the back of his neck. They'd danced that way hundreds of times, but she kept waiting for him to be uncomfortable with the intimacy and pull away.

Instead, Rainer pulled her closer, his gaze dropping to her lips as his thumb grazed the skin just above the top of her dress. It was such a relief to be close to him, to not feel panicked at his touch, to want more of it.

"Why do you want me?" Rainer's voice was almost pained.

Her eyes went wide. It was unlike him to be so forward.

As if reading her mind, his brow drew in with concern. "I'm sorry," he mumbled. "That was too frank. Truth be told, you make me nervous, and I can't seem to shut up around you."

She relaxed against him. "Really? Why is that?"

He chewed at his bottom lip. "I'm not sure. You do something to me that I can't explain."

"A good something, I hope."

He relaxed slightly. "A very good something." He glanced toward Xander. "You and the prince seem inappropriately close at times."

"Does that bother you? Are you a paragon of propriety?"

Rainer looked startled. "No, I just wonder about appearances and what the king will think."

"I don't care what the king thinks, and as for everyone else, they've made judgments on me long before now. I find trying to change hearts and minds tedious and wasteful of my somewhat fleeting energy. This Unsummoner bracelet does enough draining on its own."

Rainer's green eyes were radiant in the candlelight. "I know that the king told you to wear black and you defied him. I know that when you defy him, you pay a price."

"And tell me, Guardian McKay—what is the price of spirit? Of integrity? Is there a price that would cost you your allegiance to your post? Can you put a price on dignity?"

He studied her as if seeing her for the first time.

"I refuse to be a prisoner no matter how gilded my cage," she said hoarsely.

His gaze was heavy with admiration as he spun her away, and then back toward him.

"I aspire to be brave with my hand and brave with my heart," she rasped.

He winced as if the words tugged on a powerful memory.

Remember me. Come on, Rain. End this madness. Please.

She repeated the words over and over in her head like an incantation, waiting for him to look at her with true recognition.

Instead, his eyes narrowed on hers. "Who are you?"

"I'm Cecilia Juliette Reznik. I'm a fighter and a witch. I'm many things."

She grinned, drawing back as the song ended. She instantly missed the warmth and comfort of his arms.

Rainer bowed and kissed her inner wrist and her scar. She wondered if he noticed he'd done it or if it was muscle memory.

He met her gaze. "I think you're a thief."

Cecilia arched a brow. "Oh?"

"I suspect you've robbed many men of their good sense. Perhaps a few of their hearts."

She laughed as she pulled her hand from his. "A girl can dream."

Rainer's gaze dropped to the embroidery of her dress. "I hadn't noticed before because it shimmers like a star, but your dress..." He stared at it. "It tells a story."

She ran her hands down her bodice. "It does."

He brought a hand to her shoulder, running his fingers over the intricate stitching. "Will you tell it to me?"

She nodded, turning her back to him. "It starts just above the buttons on the back."

She was suddenly aware of how he'd slowly moved her toward the edge of the room as they danced. There were far fewer eyes on them, though she could feel Eloise's from clear across the room.

Rainer's fingers brushed over the embroidery. "Four hearts, two pink, one pink and gold, and one silver, and a baby between them." He met her eye over her shoulder. "You were adopted?"

She nodded. "Then there's the bow and arrow. After watching me the other day you must know I have a singular talent for archery."

Rainer's lips quirked up. "And you're so modest."

Cecilia shrugged. "Why would I be modest when I'm the best? My father taught me. It was how we bonded. He was very proud of how quickly I took to it."

Rainer's fingers moved higher. "These golden sparkles must be when your magic showed up. But what is this, where the two hearts have golden threads between them?"

His brow furrowed, trying to make sense of it, but when she opened her mouth nothing came out. She sighed in frustration. Of course he didn't recognize their bond represented on the dress.

"You were bonded with a guardian to pursue the Gauntlet? Is this supposed to be a soul bond?"

"How do you know about soul bonds?" Cecilia asked.

Rainer shrugged. "I'm not sure."

She held her breath, waiting for some sign he remembered.

The crease in Rainer's brow softened. "The fiancé you lost—was he your guardian?"

Cecilia swallowed hard and nodded, trying not to be crushed by the weight of disappointment.

"Is that what it feels like? Like your hearts are tied together by strings?" Rainer asked.

"Sometimes."

Rainer's fingers moved higher, stopping on the stitching on her right shoulder blade. "This cave must represent the Gauntlet, but there are these pale pink roses and lightning over a pink and gold heart."

"That's when I met Xander," she said. "Then there are the two rings from our marriage and the star flowers for the hope the union brought both of us."

Jealousy surged through their bond and she almost laughed. Rainer's instinct to still feel jealous of Xander was interesting.

"You married him?"

"I did."

"But it didn't work out?"

Cecilia wrung her hands. She wanted to explain herself but the burning in her blood reminded her of the boundaries of her bargain with Cato. There wasn't much she could say.

His hand rested on her left shoulder. "And this dagger through a silver heart?"

"That's when I killed the god of war after he killed my father."

Rainer walked around to face her to continue the story.

"The doves were for my power to bring hope." Her fingers traced over the stitching resting on two golden rings pulled apart by silver sparkles. "And this is where the trickster god pulled Xander and I apart."

Rainer's gaze drifted lower. "Then what are the two hearts stitched together with golden roots growing between them?"

A lump formed in Cecilia's throat. *That's where you anchored me to this world and dragged me out of the dark. That's where our love was stronger than death.*

When she didn't answer he pressed on. "And this spot with the stars?"

She waited for him to realize the stars were raining down, like the ones in his story.

He met her eyes looking crestfallen. "You can't say."

She nodded. "But this golden moon represents my oldest scar and I had it stitched just below my newest one." She held up her left palm with its crescent scar before running her fingers over the golden scar on her chest, displayed prominently with the daring neckline.

Rainer's gaze was riveted to the scar on her chest. She wanted him to say something about the fact that it matched his—though it wasn't as if she'd be able to say anything back.

Cecilia swallowed thickly. "I have always found comfort in stories, and I used to tell them every night. I had them stitched onto my dress so I don't forget who I am while I'm becoming who I need to be."

Rainer bowed to her as the song ended, as if they'd been dancing instead of storytelling. "Well, I think it's a masterpiece."

"The dress, the story, or the woman wearing it?" she asked as his lips brushed over her crescent scar.

"All three," Rainer rasped.

Cecilia's eyes burned. She turned away to compose herself, and came face to face with Cato.

"No," she said firmly before the trickster could open his mouth.

"Little Dove, let me explain." He reached for her hand.

She recoiled from his touch, bumping into Rainer's broad chest.

"Is everything all right?" Rainer asked.

"Yes, everything is fine. I'll just be taking some air," she huffed.

She brushed by a confused Rainer as Cato called after her. She didn't stop. She grabbed a glass of bubble wine from a passing servant and darted out into the courtyard. The cold air cut into her at the same time as the memory of Teddy covering her with his cloak when she shrunk away from her engagement ball years before. The thought of him was enough to punch the air from her lungs.

Cecilia threw back the effervescent wine and tossed the glass over the stone railing to the garden path below. It shattered there, chasing away the stony silence.

"It's considered a terrible offense to turn down the hospitality of a god, you know."

Cato's voice startled her. She turned to look at him. He held out a white fur cloak as a peace offering. She took it and wrapped it over her shoulders.

"Well, you turned down mine first when I introduced you to the pointy end of a Godkiller blade and you chose not to stay dead," she snapped.

Cato chuckled.

She tried to breathe evenly but the wine had gone right to her head; since she'd been unable to eat much after being cut off from her magic, she was dizzy.

"I came to check in on you," Cato said.

"You're a little late and I told you to leave me alone and I meant it. You have always had a lot of nerve, but after—" She couldn't bring herself to say the words. She squeezed her eyes shut and dug her nails into her palms to cut off the memory that needed no magic to be felt and relived every moment.

"You know I have to walk through the castle every day to ensure that my manipulations stick, but I'm here with you because I want to apologize," Cato said.

"I don't want to hear it and I don't want to see you," Cecilia snarled. "This is your fault. You finally got what you wanted. You broke me. Just not the way you expected."

Cato frowned at her. "I'm sorry. I didn't know. I don't expect your forgiveness, but I feel compelled to say it anyway."

"I have no absolution for you. You have no idea what it's like to feel that kind of terror and powerlessness. I wouldn't even wish it on you."

Cato looked surprised and wounded all at once. "I thought you a worthy adversary."

"And I thought you a common man. Only one of us was right," she said bitterly.

His quicksilver eyes studied her as if trying to determine if she was acting. He stepped toward her and she flinched.

"Don't think about putting a hand on me. I don't know what this new game is, but I don't want to play."

"Cece—"

Her eyes went wide at the tenderness in his tone. "No! Don't you dare! Don't you dare pity me! I'll not take pity from the likes of you. You created this. You cultivated it. You cared nothing for where the pieces would fall as long as you got what you wanted. You still don't."

"I do."

"I don't believe for one moment that you care—"

"I do," Cato insisted, his voice sharp and sorrowful. "Of course I like my games, but I like to play a worthy adversary. I don't believe in abusing a physical advantage to demean someone like that."

She laughed bitterly. "And yet I'm still here with him—a prisoner."

Cato blew out an exasperated breath. It ruffled a lock of hair that had fallen over his forehead. "Because of a deal you made. I did not orchestrate that; I simply bound it."

"So you think that absolves you from the circumstances I found myself in? You knew what I would choose. You found my weak spot and you used it. You let someone else break me. You let someone else mark me."

She clawed at her dress, hiking it up so Cato could see the glamour of Vincent's initials carved into her inner thigh. For his part, Cato looked genuinely startled. He didn't move, his eyes glued to the brand. The skin beneath the glamour had healed perfectly, but she wanted Cato to see the damage.

"Are you happy now? Do you feel victorious? Are you here to gloat?" she asked.

Cato paled. "This is not what I wanted—"

"If this wasn't what you wanted, it wouldn't have happened."

The truth sucked all the air out of the courtyard and left none for apologies. Silence hung heavily between them. Cecilia let it hang, hoping he'd make a noose of it. Unfortunately, he had the good sense —or perhaps the centuries of experience—to know when to keep his mouth shut.

"You can claim you're here to apologize, but you only show up when you want something, so spare me. I have nothing more to offer you because everything has been taken from me. I spend my days under the control of someone crueler than I could have ever imagined, within arm's reach of the man I love, who doesn't remember me and probably never will—the same man who is about to marry someone else."

Cato opened his mouth to speak, but she held up her hand.

"The only thing keeping me going is that we have to win," Cecilia said. "For Marcos, for Olney, for Xander—who, yes, before you taunt, I still love and always will. I didn't sacrifice my father, my ability to have children, and my life to lose now, so whatever you want, I don't care. I have no patience for it."

She didn't need to look to feel Cato's surprise.

"I have no forgiveness to offer you. I want you out of my sight. So, tell me, what will make you accomplish that as expediently as possible?"

She turned to meet his eyes again. She could have sworn she saw regret in them, but she refused to believe Cato was capable of feeling anything.

Cato's eyebrows shot up at the question. He looked startled, completely caught off guard for once.

She'd seen him. He didn't know what he was striving for anymore. Becoming mortal had shifted his priorities, but his awareness hadn't caught up yet. It would have surprised her if he wasn't so predictable. She would have cared if her heart wasn't broken.

She never expected him to protect her, but she'd been shocked he'd allowed Vincent to hurt her in that particular way after taking such a strong stance on consent himself. She was furious with him.

Now, Cato was human and subject to emotions and impulsivity and, most of all, time. He had one lifetime, and he hadn't yet realized that he didn't care about the same things he once had. It was so incredibly common she could have died laughing if it wasn't so sad.

All of them had suffered so much for his gains, and they weren't even worth it for him.

"Get out of my sight."

He looked like he wanted to say more, but he opened a fold in the air and stepped through, leaving nothing but the smell of pine and leather in his wake.

Cecilia's head spun. She was tired of being on her heels. Tired of keeping to herself. Tired of waiting for Rainer to come to her.

If she wanted him, she was going to have to push through her fear and go get him herself.

31

RAINER

Rainer paced his room. Eloise was expecting him, hoping they could start their family without delay. Even though it was untraditional, he trusted a woman to know what she wanted and Eloise had decided on him.

It should have been easy. He should have just marched down to her room and done exactly what she wanted. He didn't know what was wrong with him. He needed to get his head right. He was marrying Eloise in five days, and yet all he could think about was Cecilia.

All day he'd tried to write it off as lust from seeing her on her knees in front of him. But that wasn't on Rainer's mind now. Instead, he kept going over the story that was stitched into her dress and the golden scar over her heart that matched his. He was connected to her in a way he didn't fully understand. All he knew was that when he thought of Eloise, he felt nothing but mild affection. But when he thought of Cecilia, his whole body felt lit from within, her fire and magnetism drawing him in recklessly with not a care for his duty or his plans.

Until he had kissed Cecilia in the rain, he had not known that he could feel sweet relief and aching chaos at the same time. His body knew something his mind did not. It knew her taste, her rhythm, the way she sighed against his mouth.

Rainer tore out of the room and down the stairs to Eloise's room. As soon as he got to her door, he lost the will to do the right thing or even the ability to know what the right thing was.

He knocked on the door. Eloise opened it, leaning against the doorframe with a smile on her face.

She saw it in his expression immediately. "You aren't staying?"

"I'm sorry. I swear I will make it up to you, but I wouldn't feel right about it now."

She sighed and brushed a hand over his cheek. "You don't have to keep trying to win me over."

Rainer shook his head. "I'm not. I may not remember much from my life, but I know when I was younger I did not do things the right way and I regret that. I'm afraid rushing into this would make me too apprehensive to enjoy it or be fully present with you."

He was a little disturbed by how easily the lie came to him, but it wasn't as if he could tell her that he couldn't get Cecilia and her storybook dress out of his head.

Eloise sighed and parted her robe to reveal a delicate lace slip. "Are you sure I cannot change your mind and corrupt you for the evening?"

Rainer leaned in and kissed her cheek. "In a few days you can do all the corrupting you like."

She hid her disappointment with a tight smile as she nodded and closed the door.

Walking back to his room, he felt wretched, like his insides had been scooped out and replaced with brambles. Deep down he knew he'd feel worse if he'd gone through with what she wanted.

He closed and locked his bedroom door, leaning his head against the wood. A grinding sound on the other side of the room made him jump.

He blinked his eyes open as Cecilia stepped out from behind a tapestry on the far side of the room. She grinned at him, her face a mix of panic and relief.

"How did you—" Rainer cut himself off.

He knew the castle had passageways, but given that he could barely memorize the basic layout, he hadn't felt ready to learn them all. Clearly, Cecilia knew them well, and that was how she'd managed to do all of her sneaking around. He felt foolish for not realizing it sooner, but it was on Vincent for not warning him that she had another way to escape her rooms.

Cecilia stepped forward tentatively, tightening the sash on her crimson silk robe.

"Cece, what are you doing here?"

She let out a sigh. "I was worried you wouldn't be here. I was worried you'd be with her. I told myself if you weren't here, it would be a sign that I should give you up. But you're here."

He closed the distance between them, stopping himself before he touched her. It was a hard habit to get used to when the impulse to touch her was so strong.

Rainer ran a hand through his hair. "I couldn't do it. I just couldn't imagine being with someone else when the only one I'm thinking about is you. It wouldn't be right."

Her bright blue eyes met his and he felt her relief, which was as familiar as his own. "Why?"

"Can I touch you? Can I kiss you?" he asked. "I'll only touch your hair and your face and neck."

She nodded. He pulled out the pins holding her hair up and loosened her curls with his fingers. She smiled at him and he kissed her, soft and slow, like he'd done it hundreds of times.

It wasn't enough. They had so little time left.

The depth of his feelings for her was irrational. Rainer didn't understand it, but he also knew that it was remarkably different from how he felt for his fiancée.

He pulled away and met Cecilia's eyes again.

"Why?" she repeated. "Why can't you stop thinking about me?"

"Because you devastate me." He swallowed hard, all his love and terror stuck in his throat. "Because I *think* I loved you before...but I *know* I love you now. And I am condemned by my love for you."

She stood frozen in front of him as if she could sense every bit of the ragged agony of being torn between honor and duty. As if she could feel the way she's shredded the very essence of who he thought he was.

Then she pressed to her toes, took his face in her hands, and kissed him softly.

Cecilia stepped away and untied her robe. It slid open, revealing red lace against her pale skin. All Rainer could do was stare at her.

Finally, he got his mouth to move. "You're naked," he said dumbly.

She giggled. "Well, there are some strategically placed bits of lace, but mostly, yes."

"Why? I thought that—" He didn't finish.

He knew she didn't like to talk about whatever had happened to her. So he assumed she wouldn't be up for anything beyond kissing.

She looked at him with apprehension in her eyes as she unbuttoned his pants and shimmied them down his hips so that he stood before her in his underwear.

"Don't get me wrong. I am extremely pleasantly surprised," Rainer said. "I just thought you couldn't—"

She brought a hand to his chest. "I don't know what I can do, but I knew I would regret it if I didn't at least try to be close to you just once before I lose you."

"I don't want you to feel pressured."

"I don't. I want to try something."

Cecilia gently guided Rainer toward the bed and helped him out of his shirt. His heart pounded in his ears as she slid her hands over his skin. They trailed down his back, taking inventory of the scars there. Normally he couldn't stand to be reminded of them, but her touch was so soothing. She gasped as if feeling each one hurt her too.

She turned him around, continuing to explore his back. Apprehension twisted tight in his chest, but the desire to connect overcame his warrior's instinct to never give his back to someone who could hurt him.

Her lips replaced her hands. She kissed every scar, mapping the history of his pain with her mouth, trying to erase each ache with affection. She murmured words, her voice so soft he couldn't make out what she was saying until she reached the top of his back and whispered "I love you" to the scar across his shoulder blades.

Of all the things he'd been taught to fear, he'd never once considered that someone could break him with a kiss.

"Lay on your back," she said finally, satisfied that she'd thoroughly undone him.

He laid back, staring up at her. Before he could overthink anything, Cecilia straddled him. She laughed at his wide eyes. He couldn't believe she was in his bed, in just a red lace slip, on top of him. He could barely breathe.

She took his hands and guided them up to the pillow to frame his face. "Keep your hands here."

He nodded, unable to speak, eager to know what she was going to do.

She sat back and looked down at him. "I want you to touch me, but I don't know if it will frighten me, so I had another idea. I thought you could tell me where and how to touch myself while you watch."

Rainer stared at her, wide-eyed, breathless. It was the hottest thing he'd ever heard. She would be comfortable, and he could watch. It was a way he could bring her pleasure without ever touching her. His cock was already hard at the thought.

"Well at least part of you is up for it," she teased.

He finally spoke. "Sorry, I just was not expecting that. I would love to do that."

She grinned and leaned forward to kiss him. He shuddered as her breasts brushed over his chest, sending all the blood in his body south as he moaned against her lips. Warmth spread through his body and he felt lit from within with joy and excitement. He wished he could touch her, but he forced his hands into fists where they were framing his face. She kissed down his neck and chest, pausing to tease his golden scar with her tongue. He choked out a curse, arching toward her mouth.

She moved farther south, tracing her tongue down the lines of his abdomen. For a moment Rainer thought he might get off just from the suggestion of where she was heading. Just the thought of how good it felt when her mouth was on him might have been enough.

Instead of continuing, she sat back up again, settling herself over his cock.

"Gods, you are so beautiful," he sighed.

She ran her fingers over her collarbone. "Where would you start if you were touching me?"

"I'd run my hands through your hair and kiss you for as long as you'd let me." He smiled.

"Well, that you're allowed to do."

He sat and pulled her into a kiss, teasing and biting her lips until they were both breathless and he was struggling not to grab her ass and force her to grind against him. She pressed him onto his back.

"Now what?"

"Touch your neck and breasts and take off that lace."

Her hooded eyes stayed locked on his. She looked unbearably sexy. Rainer needed to calm down if he was going to last. Everything was making him much too hot.

She puffed her lips out in a pout as she brushed her hands over her breasts, her nipples pressing against the lace. She shrugged one shoulder out of its strap, grinning at what was surely a stupefied look on his face. Slipping out of the other strap, she rolled her hips against him. He lifted his hips to meet the movement as she pulled off the slip, freeing her breasts.

Rainer could only stare. The trust that she placed in him felt so sacred. He was the first person she was attempting intimacy with after whatever happened. She was putting him in the driver's seat in a way that felt safe to her.

Her body was incredible. She was petite, but her strength was obvious in the tone of her stomach and legs and her movements were fluid and sexy.

"Cup your breasts and play with your nipples," he said, his voice hoarse.

She smiled as she brought her hands to her breasts and rolled her nipples between her fingers. She let out a soft moan. Her movements were natural, as if she did it all the time.

"Show me how you like to be touched."

She paused before skimming her hands down her sides. Her fingers grazed up and down her inner thighs. She rubbed herself against his hardness and he gasped.

Her fingers dipped between her legs and she rubbed her clit. The friction worked her but also brushed against him as she moved. She rolled her hips as she rubbed.

Her breath grew shallow, her cheeks growing pinker as sweat beaded on her brow.

"Faster," he said, the word a command more than a request. Her eyes lit at the tone of his voice. "Yes, perfect."

Her lips parted in a soft, low moan.

"Slide a finger inside."

Her eyes locked on his as she followed his command. Her lower lip kicked out in a pout and he wanted to sink his teeth into it.

"How does it feel?"

"So good," she whimpered. "I wish it was yours."

"Good, now in and out and use your other hand to rub yourself."

She shifted so she could use both hands and he panted breathlessly as he watched.

"Rain." She said his name in such a desperate, breathy way that it stoked something primal inside him.

"Holy fuck, Cece," he groaned. "Can I sit up? I need my body against yours. I'll keep my hands behind me but I want you to touch me and kiss me while you make yourself come. Please."

"Yes," she said.

He sat with a start, keeping his hands behind him, propping himself up, and she wove her hands through his hair. She pulled him into a scorching kiss and her nipples pebbled against his chest. It just felt right having her pressed against him.

She rolled her hips and he met her movement. The only thing left between them was his underwear. She moved faster and he matched her pace as he kissed her neck.

"Yes, make yourself come," he whispered.

Her cheeks were flushed, her eyes locked on his in concentration. She panted as she matched his rhythm. He could feel her wetness through his underwear. He was so close. He felt like he was a teenager again, about to come from just making out with someone, but she was so unbelievably sexy he couldn't help it.

She moaned his name and her back arched, her chest pressing against his as she dug her nails into his shoulders and rode out her climax. He was so close, his body wound so tightly, pleasure coursing through his blood like fire.

Finally, she met his eyes again, increasing her pace for him this time.

He came undone with a groan he felt all the way down to his toes.

Cecilia leaned her forehead against his. They both struggled to catch their breath.

"Can I touch your face and neck and hair?" he asked.

She nodded breathlessly and he pulled her into a scorching kiss.

When he pulled away, her face was dazed. "That went even better than I thought it would."

"That was incredible. I don't think I've ever been more turned on in my life," he admitted. "How do you feel?"

"I feel great," she said. "I felt fine the whole time." She looked both relieved and triumphant.

He pressed her hand to his cheek. "Cece, I know that was hard for you and I'm just honored that you did that with me. I know someone hurt you. I can't imagine how hard it was for you to let me be so close to you—to let me touch you like that."

Her face softened. "You make it easier. I trust you, Rain."

"I know. And that's a privilege."

She grinned at him sleepily. "I would regret it if I didn't at least try with you. I love you."

His heart thundered at the words. She loved him. It was relief and also torture because in two days he would lose her.

"I love you, too. I know that I knew you before. I know I was in love with you. I wish I remembered more."

Cecilia smiled as she curled up under the blanket beside him.

"How do you imagine your future?" The question slipped out, the burn of it in his throat like poison he couldn't wait to spit out. He hated how afraid he was that this was a fleeting affair, that she'd move on to being queen and forget him completely. The sheer panic of losing her was so immense he could barely breathe as he waited for her to answer.

"I've imagined so many futures," she said softly. "It's funny how they shift and change. For so long I wanted great adventures and experiences, and now I think I would like a quiet life by the sea. I'd like to work in a healer clinic and help those losing their memories."

Rainer shifted onto an elbow so he could see her eyes better. "And you want to get married? Have a family?"

It was so irrational to want those things with her and yet he'd felt from the first moment he saw her stretching in the training room as if she already belonged to him, or perhaps that he belonged to her. And now, all the longing for status—all the worthless ambition in the hope of some sort of validation—had been replaced with longing for her.

She smiled, but her eyes were full of sadness that he didn't understand.

Rainer swallowed hard. "I'm sorry. I've upset you."

She shook her head. "You haven't. I've thought about it quite a bit. I would love to build a family. When I was with—" She paused as if struggling for the right words. "When I was with my love before, I was very foolish. We had been through a lot together and I worried that I wasn't ready to marry him, that I had too much hurt inside me —too much baggage that it wasn't fair to ask him to carry it around with me. Now he's lost to me and all the things that prevented me from taking the next steps seem so silly."

Rainer kissed her palm. "You can't blame yourself. The right answers are always clearer in hindsight. I'm sure you did your best."

She smiled weakly. "What about you?"

"I've never met a family member. Having children will be the first time I ever meet someone I'm related to. The man who raised me was not a good example of what a father should be, but I like to think he's at least taught me what not to do. I think I could do a better job."

When he met her glassy eyes, he felt like he'd shared too much—been too vulnerable too soon. But she placed her hand on his chest and a calm sensation wrapped around his heart.

"I have no doubt that you'd be the most wonderful father," she whispered.

"My adoptive mother was lovely, but I've never had that kind of connectedness that other people do. I was always alone."

Cecilia looked at him like his sadness was her own, her big cerulean eyes full of pain. "Loneliness is an awful burden to bear. I'm sorry you were alone."

She was quiet for a long time and Rainer had the distinct feeling he'd said something wrong, though he could not figure out what. He retraced his words. Perhaps it was just that she missed her late fiancé.

She traced the scar on his chest with her finger, her eyes clouded with unshed tears. "Oh, Rain, what are we going to do?"

"I don't know. I know what I'm supposed to do, but I don't know how to walk away from you." He rolled onto his back and scrubbed his hands over his face in frustration. "I need to remember. I hate that I can't."

Her small hand came to his cheek. "It's going to be okay. You'll remember. I know you will."

"I'm afraid to lose you when I just got you."

She smiled but there were tears in her eyes. "You'll always have me. You have my whole heart. No matter where you are, you'll still have it."

He wanted to believe her, but she was engaged to the king, and she hardly knew Rainer. In two days, he would marry Eloise. Rainer would no longer be beside Cecilia all day every day. Panic rose in his chest at the thought.

You don't have to marry Eloise.

The notion was like a splinter shoved into his mind. He couldn't stop picking at it, trying to get it out. If he didn't marry Eloise, he'd be going against the king—a king who was still engaged to Cecilia.

"Why are you engaged to Vincent?" Rainer asked.

She sighed, twirling her ring around her finger, a crease forming in her brow. "It was the best bad option available to me."

"But he hurts you."

"And I endure it."

"Why?" Rainer asked.

She frowned and squeezed her eyes shut like she was in pain. The silence stretched between them until, finally, her eyes snapped open. "To be close to you."

A potent mix of guilt and joy hit Rainer in the chest. She'd subjected herself to the king's wrath, to being dressed up and paraded around like a doll, to enduring whispers from the court, just to be close to Rainer.

"Don't marry him."

She sat up and looked at him with fierce conviction in her eyes. "Don't marry her."

Rainer rose to his knees and took her hands in his. "Run away with me. We can go back to Olney."

Her smile turned sorrowful. "I want to, but I can't. Not yet."

"What's holding you back?"

She squeezed his hands, brushing her thumb over his inner wrist. "Xander needs my help to rebuild after the attack."

"Don't you mean Vincent?"

She hesitated, looking down at their hands for a long moment before meeting his eyes again. "No, I don't. I mean Xander needs my help to fix things and as much as I want to run away with you and pretend it isn't my problem, deep down it is. There is nowhere we could go to outrun it."

Irrational jealousy settled like a stone in Rainer's stomach. Was she admitting that she was a traitor? Was she still in love with the prince? He was torn between envy and anxiety.

"Don't misunderstand," she said. "For all his flirting, Xander and I are just friends. He's a good man and I trust him with my life."

Rainer waited for her to say more, but she was studying him like she could read every emotion that slid across his face.

He couldn't bear the scrutiny. He didn't want her to assess him and come up short—to be disappointed that he cared she was working against the king. He owed Vincent his loyalty, but that loyalty felt like betraying her. And loyalty to her felt like betraying the man who had given Rainer his full support and every opportunity to make up for his mistakes since he'd awoken.

For that matter, how did Cecilia forgive him for failing her so completely during the rebellion?

"I'm sorry that I failed you."

A crease formed in her brow.

"During the attack."

Her face softened. "You didn't. You—" Her voice cut off and she huffed a frustrated sigh. "There was nothing else you could have done. I've never blamed you."

She was sincere, but it made him feel no absolution because he could not forgive himself. "Can I ask you something and you'll answer honestly?"

She laid back on the bed, her eyelids drooping as she snuggled into the blankets, pressing her cold feet to his leg. It was such a familiar, intimate gesture it bolstered his courage to ask the question.

"Did you tell me the story about the village where it rains stars?"

Her eyes remained closed and she held perfectly still. "No, you told me. In the library, remember?"

"I mean, did you tell me the story to lead me out of the dark? After the attack. I think it was your voice. I think it was this hand on my chest," he said, cupping her hand in his and placing it over his heart. "I think you knew how to get to me. Was it you?"

The question had been looming over him ever since Magdalena told him that Eloise hadn't told him the story or sat with him until he'd woken up. He desperately wanted to know who had made him feel safe and loved when he could not even find his way out of the dark of his own mind.

Cecilia slowly turned her head to look at him. She opened her mouth and the barest whisper slipped out. "Yes."

He hadn't expected that she'd be able to answer and, judging from her shocked wide eyes, she hadn't either.

"There is no darkness I won't follow you into," she said. "I will always come for you."

The words stirred an ache behind Rainer's eyes, like somewhere in the darkness those words connected to a memory. He waited, trying to force his mind to work—to connect the jagged ends of those words to some broader tapestry of memory. But the longer he waited, the more the ache abated until he was left with nothing but Cecilia's soft breathing.

"Thank you for saving me. I wish I could save you back," he whispered.

Her breathing grew soft and shallow. Just when he thought she'd drifted off to sleep, she whispered, "You save me every day."

32

RAINER

For once, the night seemed much too short. Though Rainer had fallen asleep briefly, he had spent the past hour watching Cecilia.

At first, he'd been afraid to touch her too much, worried that he'd wake her or, worse, make her panic. But she was a heavier sleeper beside him than she'd been the night he sat guard in her room watching her restlessly toss and turn. It was as if his presence beside her was enough to soothe her fear. Tentatively, he reached out, brushing his fingers over her collarbone. Her skin was soft and warm and smelled like summer.

Rainer ran his fingers down her side, as if tracing her over and over could imprint the moment on every one of his senses with sight and touch and smell. It was disorienting, the feeling of being cracked wide open, fully possessed by a beautiful woman who gave him so much of herself even when she was afraid.

He'd fallen in love with her perhaps the first moment he was sent to keep an eye on her and she'd bent over the table, giving him a glimpse of her perfect backside. Somehow it had happened without his permission or realization and now he was a helpless sap watching her sleep.

She let out a soft, contented sigh and rolled onto her back. Rainer drank in the sight of her, afraid at any moment she'd be ripped away from him. Her skin was so fair he could make out blue veins beneath the surface at pulse points like the spot on her wrist, marred by a pale scar she rubbed when she was nervous. He traced a finger over the three freckles that dotted her shoulder up her neck.

He tugged at the sheet, revealing her chest, and stared at the golden scar over her heart that matched his. They had two matching scars, though no matter how Rainer tried to call up a memory to explain the crescent scar on his hand or the golden slice over his heart, he found nothing but fog and darkness.

He wanted to press his heart against her chest, to leave an imprint there the way she'd left her mark on him.

Her waterfall of hair cascaded over the pillow. Something about the wildness of it unbound, seeing her so open and vulnerable, made him want to cling to her.

What little Rainer remembered about his life had made him pliant, desperate to prove himself, and yet Cecilia seemed delighted when he shirked his responsibilities. She never stopped asking him why he was so compelled to be what other people wanted. She asked what he wanted. Rainer was mortified that he had no answer.

He'd never considered what to want other than approval; hadn't bothered imagining what he'd do when he got it because Raymond McKay's had always been elusive.

But maybe Rainer had clung to it so tightly because as long as he was constantly chasing it, he'd never have to admit that he failed. It was a lie that allowed him to feel active in the pursuit instead of acknowledging that it was impossible. For Raymond there would always be more to gain—more money, more acclaim, more admiration. He could be king and still he'd never be satisfied. Rainer had known that since he was a boy, but to admit it meant that he'd have to forge his own path, and he already felt so alone in the world.

It left him with nothing but the very large boots of Zelden Novaris to fill, and his birth father was a legend and deceased—therefore incapable of giving his approval. Rainer was unsure how he could meet a higher standard, but for the first time, he realized how futile his endless pursuit of being better was.

He'd not been enough for the father who left him behind to go to battle. He'd been measuring himself against Raymond McKay's impossible greed ever since, ensuring that Rainer would always have something to do to blot out how terribly lonely he felt.

Cecilia was obviously lonely, but she clearly had friends in Xander and Jessamin. Rainer had no one.

He tried to pull up a memory from close to the attack but could only remember speaking with Xander's disgraced spymaster, Evan Farlan. But he hadn't felt in any way suspicious of Evan. If anything, Rainer had trusted him deeply. The only other memory was of sitting in Xander's room, drinking whiskey with the prince, and it was clear that what existed between them was more tolerance than genuine friendship. Even so, Xander had been so impatient and terse with Rainer since he'd woken from his coma. It made no sense.

Cecilia shifted, the light catching the emerald on her finger. Surely if Vincent found out what Cecilia and Rainer had been up to, she'd be hurt or thrown in the dungeon.

Rainer hadn't been thinking much at all once she'd taken off her robe, but now fear crept into his mind. He would not let the king put his hands on her again, and if that made him a traitor, so be it.

He'd surrender all progress he'd made in working with Vincent in the weeks since he'd woken if it meant keeping Cecilia safe. It baffled him that she could be on the side of the very people who had attacked her. It made no sense. If she was truly on the side of the rebels, that meant that Xander was as well, and they were both playing a dangerous game. Rainer couldn't bear the thought of her being hurt again. Her body was already a map of wicked-looking scars, and he could not see one more added. She'd suffered enough.

But he didn't know how to explain to her that they couldn't stay when she seemed to be intent on helping the rebellion. Perhaps if he had a little more time with her he could convince her the only real option was to run. If Rainer was honest with himself, he missed the sea and the sunshine. He wanted to go back to Olney, and he wanted to take Cecilia with him.

Guilt turned his stomach when he thought of Eloise. He'd go to her first thing in the morning and break things off. She was a good woman, but he couldn't marry her when his heart belonged to someone else. Surely, she'd prefer his honesty over entering into a marriage built on a lie.

Now that Rainer had been with Cecilia, no one else would do. He wanted time alone with her, away from the cold, away from that Unsummoner bracelet that took so much of her energy. She would probably light up in the warmer weather, and with access to her magic. Rainer would have the time to figure out what he actually wanted for himself instead of being crushed by the burden of endless striving.

Bolstered by the thought of it, he glanced at the first light of dawn creeping across the bedroom floor.

He leaned over and woke her with a gentle kiss. "Wake up, Cece. Daylight is coming and I need to get you back to your room."

She smiled, her eyes fluttering open as she stretched her arms overhead. There was so much he didn't know, but he knew the shape of her tucked against him. He knew the sleepy smile peeking through the mess of curls. He knew so many tiny familiar things despite the fact that he had no memories of them to call on.

"I didn't mean to sleep for so long," she mumbled.

Rainer shrugged. "It's fine. You were tired." He brushed her hair out of her eyes, grinning down at her. "I know you have things to do here still—but when you are finished with your work...run away with me. No more politics. No more court life. Just you and me and warmer weather and a home by the sea. We'll go back to Olney. I have plenty of money, but I can get a job somewhere. My family has land—"

"I have a cottage," she said. "On the sea."

Rainer grinned. "Is that a yes?"

She sat up, climbing into his lap and kissing him deeply. "Of course, it's a yes. As soon as I finish what I have to do here."

He pinned her body against his, kissing her like he was trying to bring her back to life, joy warming his chest and spreading through his whole body.

"Gods," he breathed between kisses. "How does it feel this good just to kiss you?"

She laughed, pulling away and winking at him. "Magic." She cocked her head to the side. "I need your help with something. I need Vincent to remove this Unsummoner bracelet. It's spelled so only he or the witch who created it can remove it."

Rainer frowned. "How do we do that?"

"Well, if you can take care of delivering my morning Godsbane today, I can avoid taking it and use my goddess power to give Vincent the memory of wanting to remove it for the day so that I can feel better. I just might need you to distract Grant while I do it."

The request made Rainer feel uncomfortable. He didn't like the idea of tricking the king. "Why are you on the side of the rebels?"

She frowned. "I'm not."

Rainer stared at her. She was so vexing. "But you're helping them."

"I'm helping Xander."

Rainer's frustration grew along with the buzz of anxiety in his chest. "Why do you care who is king?"

"Because one of those two men has only touched me with gentleness and the other has used his fists. I think you can learn a great deal about a man by how he loves. I do not wish to be ruled by a man who wields violence when compassion would be the more effective tool."

Rainer considered it. He loved her, but did he love her enough to betray the king who had given him nothing but support and encouragement?

"I swear that when you get your memory back it will all make sense," she said.

"Please, make it make sense."

She sighed and placed her hand over his heart. "You know that I can't, much as I want to. My tongue is bound by a bargain or I would tell you everything. Now can you bring my Godsbane or not?"

Rainer had seen her take a greenish-brown shot several mornings that Vincent referred to as some kind of nutrition, but usually Grant was the one who brought it to her.

"I will make that happen," he said.

Suddenly fear gripped him, his heart racing. Since he'd woken up, he'd never felt so much like he had something to lose.

He cupped Cecilia's face in his hands. "Please be careful not to tip your hand today. We have to act normal around each other."

She smiled at him. "I promise I know how to avoid trouble when I actually want to."

"And here I thought you made sport of hunting it down."

"Only when I want to get a rise out of you, Rain."

She kissed him again before rising from the bed, giving him a great view of her ass as she sauntered across the room to grab her robe. Before she could fasten it, he caught a glimpse of a scar on her right inner thigh, but she tied the robe and it was gone before he could see what it was. He had been too busy looking at the rest of her when she'd been on top of him, but now he desperately wanted to know what it was.

"What happened to your thigh?" he asked.

Her face hardened. "It's a scar from the attack."

"Can I see it?" Rainer asked.

She shook her head. "Not today."

Rainer understood. Even in asking about it, he could see the way her face clouded at the memory. They'd just had a beautiful night together. He didn't need to muddy it by dredging up bad memories.

"I'll show you the passageway to my room," she said with a grin.

Rainer just shook his head. He had no recollection of passageways, but that was clearly how she'd been getting around when he locked her in her room.

She pressed on the wall behind a tapestry on the far side of his room and the grinding of stone against stone revealed a dark corridor. Rainer trailed behind her, ducking his head to avoid the low ceiling joists. A moment later she paused in front of him, her pale fingers curling around a divot in the stone wall, and when she pressed it open, they emerged into her bedroom.

"Very tricky," Rainer said, trailing her into the room. "Go back to sleep. I will come wake you in a couple hours."

Cecilia tossed her robe on the chair next to her bed, giving him an eyeful as she slid under the blankets with a grin. "Good night, Rainer."

"Good night, Cece."

He made his way back to his room, careful to close the passageway behind him, and tried to prepare for a day of disappointing people.

————

Rainer's best attempts to fall back asleep were thwarted by the excited twisting in his stomach. He forced himself out of bed as bright sunlight cast the room in gold. He dressed quickly and was about to go speak with Vincent when a knock on the door startled him.

Opening it, he found a teary-eyed Eloise. Panic tore through him. There was no way she could know that Cecilia had visited him last night.

"What's wrong, El?" he asked.

She shook her head. "Will you come with me, please? I have something very important to tell you."

"Of course," he said, trying to give her an encouraging smile as he held out his arm, allowing her to guide him down the hallway.

The farther they traveled, the more tense Rainer felt. He fought to keep his pulse steady but his chest buzzed with anxiety that felt disproportionate to the threat.

Finally, they reached a sitting room in the corridor that led to the healer's suite, where Vincent was waiting with a woman whom Rainer struggled to place. He stared at her, searching his memories for her face. Her skin was pristine, free of wrinkles, her hair dark as night and without a hint of gray, but her violet eyes were knowing, almost ancient-looking.

"Rainer, we were sorry to disturb you so early this morning, but Eloise has brought something concerning to our attention," Vincent said. "I should have noticed it sooner, but it seems my fiancée has bewitched you."

Rainer frowned, shaking his head. "Your Majesty, I assure you that I find her very charming, but I would never presume—"

"I know you were with her last night," Eloise interrupted, her eyes narrowed at him.

Rainer stared at her, unsure what strategy to employ. He had been so careful, but it was possible someone had heard them through the door. "Just because I respected you enough to leave you alone last night doesn't mean that I was with someone else."

Eloise threw her hands up and turned to Vincent. "You see what I mean. He's under her spell enough to lie to me, his fiancée, and you, his king."

Vincent frowned, rubbing his chin. He looked less angry than concerned. "Rainer, have you felt anything unusual, like there's a connection to Cecilia? Like you're drawn to her inexplicably?"

Rainer's stomach dropped. How could they know how he felt about her? He shook his head but it was clearly unconvincing because Vincent looked at him with nothing but pity.

"Raven Whitewind is an ancient witch and seer," Vincent said, gesturing to the woman with the uncanny eyes.

That was how Rainer knew her. He'd met her when he was a boy. He could only barely remember it—a half of a memory about going to her house to possibly be paired with a memory witch, but nothing after that. Raven looked the same as she had eighteen years earlier.

"Raven, do you sense a magical connection in Guardian McKay?" Vincent asked.

Raven frowned and pursed her lips, looking from Rainer to the king like she was wholly unimpressed with both of them. "Yes."

Rainer shook his head. "No, I would know if Cecilia used magic on me, plus she's cut off from her power."

Vincent held up his hands. "I understand that this type of magic can feel very compelling. You're right that she's quite charming, but a spell like this makes it impossible for you to resist. You might not believe it now, but just wait until you see her. It will all be clear."

Rainer felt sick. Cecilia was the first bit of certainty he'd felt since the attack. Perhaps that was the point. If what they were saying was true, she'd known him enough to tell him what he wanted to hear. *"You are not a weapon."* He'd thought those words were an incantation giving him freedom, but now it seemed they were just the seductive manipulation of someone else who wanted something from him. He'd fallen for it so quickly.

They were going to bring Cecilia down here too. How could he protect her from whatever this was? Did he even want to?

Rainer's gaze darted around the room. Grant was notably absent. He must have been retrieving her.

Rainer wanted to deny everything they were saying, but even as he reached for the words to argue with them, he felt a stronger buzz of anxiety in his chest, like a life-form of its own.

All his certainty fled at once.

33

CECILIA

Cecilia followed Grant down the hallway. There was something ominous about his sudden appearance in her room this morning, especially when she'd been expecting Rainer. All she needed was to work her magic on Vincent and talk to Xander about getting Rainer out. Once Rainer was safe, she could handle the rest on her own.

Instead, Grant had handed her the daily dose of Godsbane and she'd been forced to drink it.

As she followed him down the corridor, she had the feeling of marching toward her death. Rainer's fear and anxiety buzzed in her chest and she was terrified of what she might be walking into.

She patted her pocket, comforted by the shard of mirror tucked away there. When they turned down the hall that led to the healer's suite, she cringed, instantly feeling an ache for Magdalena. She felt the healer's absence the moment she entered the room because the space felt claustrophobic instead of calm and welcoming.

It appeared she and Grant were the first to arrive.

"Who are we waiting for?" she asked.

Grant smiled in an unnerving way that made her stomach sink.

A moment later, Xander and Isla walked into the room looking equally anxious. They were quickly followed by Vincent and Raven Whitewind.

Cecilia hadn't laid eyes on Olney's seer since she was a girl, but she couldn't stop staring at the woman who had bonded her to Rainer. The witch met her gaze and a soft smile ghosted over her lips.

"What are you doing here?" Cecilia asked.

"Marcos sent her at the pleading of his good friend, Xander," Vincent said with a grin.

Cecilia whipped her head around to look at Xander, who didn't deny it. Why would he do such a thing? She tried to calm herself with the fact that the seer wouldn't be in Argaria with Vincent unless she wanted to be. And she would only want to be if it was for a reason that was for the good of both kingdoms. Still, Cecilia's palms grew sweaty and her chest tightened.

She was about to speak when Rainer walked in with Eloise Spellman on his arm. Cecilia smothered the knee-jerk desire to yank Eloise away from him. Rainer looked so handsome. His dark green tunic brought out his eyes and his too-long hair was swept back in waves.

Rainer met her eyes and his panic hit her in the chest. The crease in his brow was severe, his gaze darting from her to the floor to the king.

"I'll end the suspense for you all," Vincent started. "It's come to my attention that my lovely fiancée has somehow bewitched my top guard."

The words tilted the world on its side.

"What?" Cecilia laughed in stunned disbelief.

"It's true," Eloise said at the same time. "She put some sort of love spell on him and now he thinks he is in love with her."

"This is ridiculous," Xander said, taking a step toward Vincent.

Isla stayed at his right shoulder, hand skimming her thigh. Cecilia wanted to tell her to attack—to end this now. But if that happened, they couldn't be sure that they'd be able to get rid of all the traitors in their midst at once. If they missed even one, they might end up reliving this insanity in a few months or a year.

Rainer shook his head. "I know what you've all said, but this is impossible."

"Is it?" Vincent asked, turning to face Rainer. "We've already told you. Do you not feel a stirring in your chest? A pull toward Cecilia? Do your feelings not seem to mirror her expressions?"

Cecilia felt sick. Vincent's twisted game was so perfect in its cruelty. Rainer couldn't possibly understand their bond without his memory. She'd thought it would be an asset for her, but Vincent had turned it into a weapon in his game.

"No," she breathed. A revelation crashed down on her as she met Raven's eyes.

They were going to sever her bond to Rainer. She did not fear the pain of it, though she knew it would be substantial. What frightened her was the oblivion she'd face with the sudden severing of the thing that had tethered her for eighteen years. It was not enough for Vincent to steal her sense of safety and peace. He also had to rob her of her most precious possession.

"You can't do this," she rasped.

Vincent leaned close so that only she could hear him. "I warned you to fall in line, but you've done nothing but plot against me. There is a price to pay for treachery. Your talents are too useful to get rid of you but I will always find more to take from you. Now learn your lesson from this or you know what I'll do next time."

Cecilia shuddered at the words. Of course she did. She'd been waiting for it to happen since he first made the threat, but she was hardly willing to act as if he was being magnanimous.

"See how she doesn't even deny it," Eloise said. She turned to Rainer, taking his face in her hands. "Rainer, she has done something to you. To steal you from me. I know what you think you feel and I don't blame you for what you've done. She's very clever. But what you feel for her is only a product of magic. She's placed you under a love spell that makes you feel things that aren't real. You'll see. You'll know for sure once Raven does her work."

Cecilia turned to the seer. "Why are you helping him?" Even as she said the words, she knew Raven could see the future and would do whatever she wanted to achieve her desired end. The ancient witches of Olney had one master—balance. Severing a bond was a small price to pay if Raven thought it would somehow help Olney.

But, in that moment, Cecilia didn't care about her kingdom. She cared that the same woman who had linked her to Rainer eighteen years ago was about to rip out the roots of the bond wrapped around her heart.

Cecilia looked around the room for anyone who would help. Isla held a white-knuckle grip on Xander's arm. Xander looked helplessly from Cecilia to Rainer. Rainer crossed the room to her, his mouth a pinched line, his eyes wild as his hurt spread through her chest.

He took her face in his hands. "Tell me it's not just magic that ties us together." His touch and the desperation in his voice made her feel like she was about to shatter into a thousand little pieces.

"It's not a love spell," she insisted. "I told you before—in the market. There's no such thing."

"Tell me what I feel for you here is mine alone." Rainer leaned his forehead against hers and pressed his hand to his heart. His voice was so pained, and she understood.

Rainer had felt at home with her for the first time since waking from the attack—and now Vincent was going to take that from him and he would blame Cecilia for it.

Rainer would never forgive her and all his incentive to remember her would disappear.

Cecilia froze, closing her eyes. She couldn't actually say that. It would be a lie and Cato's bargain prevented her from telling the truth.

"Cece?" he rasped.

She met his gaze, her blood burning furiously with the reminder of her bargain. "I swear I would explain if I could, but I can't say."

"And you won't, right, love? Because you know that severing that love spell will be what's best for everyone," Vincent said.

Cecilia had learned to fight when she was old enough to hold a bow and she'd never stopped. How could she give up on Rainer now? But how could she do more?

Cecilia's mind could not keep up with this strategy. Vincent was acting like this was a punishment for what she'd done, but according to Evan, Raven had been in town before anything happened between her and Rainer. Perhaps Vincent had been planning this all along—to take the thing she held most precious and turn it into something ugly. To twist her fairy tale into a nightmare.

There was no end to his cruelty or his creativity in delivering misery. He enjoyed it, relished the opportunity to stun and silence his enemies with his viciousness. Cecilia could not fathom how to take on an enemy like that. With Cato, it was so clear that he saw attachment as weakness. But Vincent seemed to delight not in the winning, but in inflicting the pain itself. He did not just want to win; he wanted to annihilate the opposition.

She swallowed around the panic in her throat. "Rainer, I swear I did not cast a spell on you. If I could, I would explain what you feel, but I can't."

"It's very convenient the way this *alleged* bargain keeps you from explaining yourself and so efficiently cloaks your deception," he said curtly. He stared at Cecilia, looking utterly betrayed.

"Fortunately, I have the solution. I feel responsible for giving my lovely fiancée too much freedom. I won't leave you alone in this," Vincent said, placing a comforting hand on Rainer's shoulder. "We have brought in Raven here and she will be able to sever Cecilia's hold on you. You're a good man and your loyalty is commendable, but you'll see once the process starts." Vincent turned his gaze on Cecilia. "If it's truly a magical bond, it shouldn't hurt Rainer too badly. But you'll see—the results of her magic being used improperly will hurt Lady Reznik more. It brings me no joy to hurt her, but even my fiancée is not above being held accountable for her actions."

Cecilia shook her head. "It's all I have." She rubbed her sternum, her fingers skimming over her golden scar.

"Please lay down, Lady Reznik," Raven said, gesturing to two treatment tables at the center of the room.

Cecilia walked toward one as if walking to the gallows.

Raven patted the other table. "Guardian McKay, if I could have you here."

Rainer laid down as instructed. He stared up at the ceiling, ignoring Cecilia completely.

Raven stepped between their two cots and her violet eyes locked with Cecilia's.

"Please don't take this from me," Cecilia whispered.

"I'm sorry, my darling girl. Life takes with one hand and gives with the other," Raven said.

Cecilia sniffled loudly.

Raven stood over Rainer. "You might feel some discomfort in your chest, the same place you feel the magic. Try to stay as relaxed as possible."

Cecilia's breath grew shallow. She couldn't stay calm. It was one thing for Rainer not to know her, but she could hardly fathom not being able to feel him on the other end of their bond, especially now that she'd become accustomed to him not knowing how to close their connection. She'd found so much comfort in the bond throughout her life, but never more than in the last couple weeks when Rainer was so open to her. She couldn't bear to lose the connection that had held her together when her world was shaking apart.

The seer placed a hand on each of their chests.

Cecilia squeezed her eyes closed as the first magical hooks slid behind her breastbone. At first the tug was gentle, but Cecilia still bowed up off the cot, desperate to keep the bond exactly where it was. Out of the corner of her eye, she saw Rainer wince.

"Wait," he rasped.

Cecilia gritted her teeth. She could not stand for him to hurt so she squeezed Raven's hand. "Take it from me."

Raven nodded and the full strength of her power sank into Cecilia's chest.

An agonized scream burst from her mouth, her back bowing off the bed again.

It felt like someone had reached into her chest and was trying to yank out her heart. She instantly regretted her decision because it hurt so badly. Raven's magic spread through her chest, unstitching the connection around her heart.

"No, please," Cecilia groaned as the pain abated for a moment. "Please don't take it. Please—don't take him."

Rainer stirred restlessly, rubbing at the place below where Raven's hand rested on his chest. "I think something's wrong," he grumbled. "I feel a burning pain here, too."

"There might be some discomfort," Vincent said.

Cecilia's pain and her intense focus on Rainer made his voice sound far away. Her heart pounded, growing louder in her ears as if begging her not to let go.

Rainer met her gaze.

"Don't go where I can't go," she groaned.

He showed no sign of recognition.

Raven's power pressed into Cecilia again and she and Rainer went rigid in unison. It felt like someone had dug blazing talons into Cecilia's chest. Screaming echoed through the room, so shrill it took her a moment to realize it was her producing the wounded animal sound. She fought back against the magic as it slithered around her heart, tugging up the tangled roots of what was supposed to belong to just the two of them.

Their connection had always been private, but now there was another entity tangled in it and no matter how Cecilia screamed and pushed against it, she could not force it out.

The wave of magic relented and Cecilia groaned, her entire body aching from the effort of resisting. Sweat soaked her dress, her hair clinging to her neck and forehead, her head lolling to the side. Rainer's eyes locked with hers. She wished he could hear her thoughts as her view of him was blurred by tears.

How long have I known you? How long have I loved you? Forever.

He'd promised he would know her no matter what, but there was no recognition on his face now.

Did he still look at her and feel it like a pulse that beat through both of them, like a harmony that ran between them that only they could hear? That melody had made her certain Rainer was hers.

Even when she was young, she'd looked at him and known. Even when she was with Xander, no matter how she tried to ignore it, the melody played on. Even when she'd left her body and teetered on the edge of death, it lured her away. It was always bringing them back to each other over and over.

But Rainer's eyes showed no sign of hearing it—only betrayal and hurt.

"Rain, I would never trick you," she rasped. "I love you."

He looked away, and it felt like having a door slammed in her face.

"Enough. Sever this bond already," Vincent snapped.

Cecilia glared at him, wishing her eyes could shoot daggers. Beside him, Eloise sniffled, drying her eyes with a handkerchief like she was a victim in all of this. The woman deserved an award for her acting.

Raven sighed heavily. "She's fighting me. This is not simple work. It's heavily wrapped into them. I'll be happy to have someone retrieve you when it's finished."

Vincent scowled at her. "That's not necessary. I can be patient."

Cecilia wanted to believe that the seer's plan wasn't heartless, that she had good reason for doing this, but in her panic she couldn't think clearly of what reason that might be.

Raven locked eyes with Cecilia as if she could hear her thoughts. She leaned in close. "Sometimes a small victory makes a man careless. We are at a tipping point and I would not be here unless this was necessary. I bring tidings for the king of the unseen variety."

She backed away, allowing Cecilia to process what she was saying. Raven's gaze slid meaningfully to Xander. She had news for Xander. Perhaps she knew who they could trust and who they needed to oust as traitors. That was all they needed to finally push Vincent out, and perhaps this was the only way she could get close enough to deliver that information.

Cecilia bit her lip, trying to steel herself.

"You have to let go, girl," Raven chided. "If you hold on to it, it will only hurt worse. I'm trying to keep the hurt to you as you requested.

I'm trying to make it hurt him as little as possible, which means I have to dig out the roots from your side. I need you to let it happen. I know it's unbearable, but you must do this."

Cecilia met the seer's gaze and nodded, tears instantly streaming and blurring Raven from view as she continued the process. How many times had she endured unbearable things? The thought of *one more time* was exhausting, but for Rainer, she would do it.

The magic hit her all at once—like someone was prodding her heart with a hot poker. She'd literally been stabbed in the heart a year before and that pain had been nothing like this—this was coupled with a sense of losing something priceless and irreplaceable.

Each stitch that ripped free hurt more than the last. The loss flayed her.

Cecilia writhed in the bed, unable to stop screaming.

A hand clamped down on hers and when she turned her head she found Xander's grim face. The touch was enough to shatter her resolve.

"Breathe, love, breathe through it. You can do this. You can let go."

"I can't. I thought I could but I can't," she sobbed, her whole body shaking as sweat stung her eyes.

He leaned his forehead against hers. "You can. I have seen you do impossible things. You can do this too."

"I can't give him up. You don't understand," she gasped.

Xander's sad eyes met hers. "I'm not asking you to give him up. I'm asking you to trust what's between you. I'm asking you to trust that Raven wouldn't be here if it weren't for a very good reason," he whispered.

Her sobs grew hysterical. "How will I know I'm okay? How will I know he is? How will I learn not to feel that? How will I deal with the emptiness?"

Xander hushed her, holding her hand against his chest as she howled.

Raven's magic sliced through her, ripping out the connection root by root. Cecilia sobbed and screamed and cried as the witch who had given her the best thing in her life took it all away.

The agony went on for hours, or perhaps just a few moments. By the time the process was over, Cecilia's body was one raw ache and yet she felt completely empty.

She rubbed her sternum, trying to sense Rainer, trying to push through a bond that no longer existed. For the first time in her life, she couldn't feel him.

Cecilia curled onto her side to face him, trying to brace herself against the hollowed-out loneliness.

She had stood between Rainer and death. She'd gone into darkness in his place. She'd stolen herself from his mind, memory by agonizingly precious memory. But she did not know how to endure this loss.

Even when she'd been in between after she'd died, she'd still felt him. He had lost her but she'd never lost him and that realization brought on a fresh wave of tears.

She met Rainer's eyes. He rubbed his chest, looking betrayed.

"How could you?" he asked, his voice a hoarse scrape.

The words took all that was left of her hope. She crumbled, tucking herself into a ball and sobbing into the pillow until Xander lifted her and carried her back to her room with Isla close behind.

It felt like a funeral procession. Like she was both walking away from something, unsure how to let go, and walking toward a future that felt terrifyingly lonely.

Both Xander and Isla tried to whisper soothing words as they put her to bed. Jessamin stopped by and huddled in the bed beside her for a long time, just stroking her back, but there was no relief for Cecilia.

There was nothing that could fill the space around her heart that Rainer had vacated. She stared at the wall, tears streaming from her sore eyes. She had nothing left to give. She might have been the goddess of mind and memory and hope once, but now she was just a lonely girl who'd lost the thing that anchored her through every storm. The fight for peace had taken everything from her and she had nothing left to offer it but surrender.

34

RAINER

Rainer slumped into the red velvet chair, wishing it would swallow him whole so he wouldn't have to make excuses to Eloise. Her sitting room was tidy in a way that should have made him feel at ease but instead left him looking for anything that needed further neatening. Never had he craved a mess, and yet now, he felt useless with nothing to do with his hands.

She filled his teacup to the brim for the fourth time. He'd barely had more than a sip each time, but Eloise was clearly equally restless. She licked her lips, her green eyes fixed on him as if searching him for any remaining connection to Cecilia.

"How are you feeling?" Eloise asked.

Empty was the first word that came into his mind. *Wrong. Obliterated. Sore.* He resisted the urge to rub his sternum where a heavy ache had settled in. It wasn't just that he felt hollowed out; everyone acted like it was normal, but whatever Cecilia had done to him had burrowed deep inside his chest. Though he'd initially been happy to be free of it, it didn't feel like a broken spell. It felt like an agonizing loss. He felt robbed of something vital. When he was anxious now, there was no soft wave of calm that spread through his chest. There was only the climbing panic that choked him.

Rainer was so furious at Cecilia for tricking him into loving her. He waited for the fury to carry away the residual feelings, but the dregs of love for her remained. He was so heavy with guilt, haunted by the memory of the prince carrying her away as she sobbed.

Eloise was looking at him expectantly.

"A bit sore," he said.

She nodded, short and curt, looking out the window at the sky full of fluffy clouds. He knew he should apologize and say something comforting, but he was at a loss.

Beyond the physical ache lay a deeper wound. Rainer couldn't remember a time when his heart hadn't felt broken, but just when he'd realized it could be healed, Cecilia smashed it.

Even if their relationship was tense, she had the king of Argaria. What had she wanted from Rainer?

Perhaps he'd underestimated her boredom. He'd been fighting his whole life, but fighting with her had been exhilarating, and he had failed to see a tiny blue-eyed witch as a threat. He'd been entirely unprepared for how quickly her magic had brought him into her thrall, how real their history had felt to him even with no memory of it.

Still, as he thought of her smirk now, his heart kicked up.

He hated her for making him love her. Hated her more for making him realize he didn't feel what he thought he did. Now, the consolation was a fiancée he'd betrayed who would always doubt his love. He'd never be able to give up proving himself.

He couldn't be mad at Eloise. She'd done nothing wrong. She was just caught in the middle of Cecilia's magical game. Collateral damage in her scheme. Still, Rainer had a sense that Cecilia had somehow destroyed what he had with Eloise with her mere existence, but now he'd felt something for Cecilia—magical or not—that he knew he did not feel for the woman he was supposed to marry tomorrow.

Eloise sat rigidly, her hands fastened in her lap, ankles tucked beneath her chair. She was a lovely picture of hurt and he did not know how to begin to apologize. The first step in a lifetime of groveling would need to be a good one.

"Eloise," he said softly.

Her gaze locked with his and she looked as frightened by what he might say as he was.

"I owe you an apology. I was unfaithful when you have been nothing but true to me. You have been honest, and I've been weak, and you deserve much better. I take full responsibility for my actions."

"You have a good heart, but even you are not immune to magic's influence," Eloise said, with more anger than he'd expected.

"I'm afraid that I was more susceptible to it than I should have been as a man with a fiancée. I feel unworthy of your forgiveness." He ran a hand through his hair, trying to figure out how to explain himself. "I feel as though—and this isn't meant to be an excuse so much as an explanation—I've been struggling to place myself, to prove myself in so many different areas since I woke up. I didn't know how to prove myself as worthy of you or worthy of the king's trust, and it was easier to distract myself with someone who wasn't available."

"Why?" Eloise asked.

"Because if I failed with her, there was a good reason. She's engaged to the king, or at least she was."

Eloise huffed out a breath and rolled her eyes. "Yes, well, it seems she's still engaged. Gods know we should have the king checked for her meddling as well."

Her words brought to mind the one thing that nagged at him. Almost the entire time Rainer had been around Cecilia, she'd been cut off from her magic, with the exception of the time she'd been in the cell to search Reese Reynolds's memories. She was dosed with Godsbane each morning and wore an Unsummoner bracelet all day to smother her magic.

"What I'm still confused about, and frankly afraid of, is that Lady Reznik has been cut off from her power this whole time, so how exactly did she manage to cast a love spell on me?"

Eloise's eyes went wide. "She could have had another witch cast it. I'm not sure how spells work. Or perhaps she did not need access to her power to cast it. I'm not a witch, so I couldn't say, but they sell love potions in the market."

Rainer frowned, remembering how Cecilia had rolled her eyes at such a booth, saying that it was nonsense. She'd been adamant that there was no magic that could make someone love you. She'd said all magic required an exchange and nothing was valuable enough to grant love.

The memory of those words left him feeling gutted.

What if that was true? As much as he wanted to write off everything she'd said, he hadn't fallen in love with her all at once. It had happened slowly, in smaller moments. Watching her fearlessly shoot her bow to maim Vincent's guards. Lying beside him in the snow, calling him a fun-sucker. Gazing up at the night sky, looking for a star to wish on.

If she was able to cast magic, and if that magic could bring her something as potent as love, why had she needed wishes?

But it wasn't just that thought that made him uneasy. It was the fact that he remembered learning about exchange magic in classes while training for the Gauntlet. He knew for a fact that all magic had a cost and—much as he'd tried since the spell had been broken—he could not think of a single thing of equal value to love.

He cleared his throat and took a long sip of tea, trying to clear all the questions from his mind.

"El, what I'm trying to say is that I'm sorry. I am embarrassed of my behavior, ashamed that I let you down, and unsure how to fix things. If you want to break our engagement and find someone who knows what they have in you, I wouldn't blame you."

The words felt hollow and he wondered if Eloise could tell. He felt almost relieved by the opportunity to bail out. Things had moved much too quickly since he woke and he felt unable to keep up.

"I don't want that. I want to marry you, Rainer," Eloise said, sitting up straighter in her chair. "What we have is too important for this kingdom and too valuable to me to let a meaningless fling ruin it. I know you probably think that I won't be able to let this go, especially with that little bitch parading around as queen. But His Highness came to me this morning and offered his apologies for not keeping her on a tighter leash. He has offered a solution. They will be wed just a week after us. They are announcing it to the court today."

Rainer frowned. "Isn't she still in mourning?"

Eloise's face twisted in confusion. "For whom?"

"The fiancé she lost in the attack."

Eloise cocked her head to the side, and when she spoke, her words were slow as if she was being careful. "His Grace has agreed it's for the best to provide a happy occasion to lift her from the grief that has made her so restless. Plus, he's very eager for heirs."

Rainer looked away, a sick feeling settling in his stomach when he remembered the bruises on Cecilia's face and neck. Even if she'd manipulated Rainer, the thought of her forever tied to someone who hit her made him feel sick. It was idiotic to protect someone who'd tried to control him, but he felt compelled to anyway.

Eloise crossed the room to him, sitting on the arm of his chair. "Now, stop beating yourself up and go apologize to the king. It will make you feel better. I just want to put this all behind us so that we can have a lovely wedding and start our lives together."

She pulled him into a kiss that was nice but still felt somehow wrong. When he drew away, there was a question in her eyes, but she kept her mouth shut.

"Thank you, El. I don't deserve you. I will do better from now on," he said, bending to kiss her hand.

He knew she was waiting for more excitement and enthusiasm, but he just felt spent and he dreaded his conversation with Vincent. He turned and left her alone, cutting down the hall toward the throne room, where he was relieved to find Vincent and Grant alone.

"Your Majesty," Rainer said, bowing, looking to Grant and hoping he'd leave. When the guard remained, he turned his attention back to Vincent. "I came to apologize. I am embarrassed and ashamed of my behavior."

Vincent grinned at him, looking down his nose from his throne.

"Rainer, Rainer, Rainer, I would fault you if I did not understand the appeal. My fiancée is a stunning and very talented woman. It is I who should be apologizing to you for not keeping her well in hand."

Rainer nodded, feeling suddenly awkward, his gaze darting to Grant, who was always lurking and now was doing little to bite back a smug look of delight at Rainer's failure.

"Yes, well, I'm still sorry."

"For what exactly? For touching what belongs to me?"

Rainer tried not to grind his teeth together. Their culture might have embraced the notion that women belonged to their betrothed, but Cecilia always seemed so self-assured it was hard to imagine her belonging to anyone but herself.

"Yes," Rainer said, trying to sound light. "I should not have been tempted."

Vincent rubbed his chin as he studied Rainer. "Tell me. What did you do with my wife-to-be?"

Rainer's eyes went wide, darting around the throne room. The door was closed. It was just the three of them, but he was still uncomfortable discussing what went on behind closed doors. It only added further insult that it had felt so intimate and real to him.

Vincent waved a hand, urging him on.

Rainer cleared his throat. "We mostly just kissed, but she was naked."

"Were you?" Vincent asked.

Shaking his head, Rainer continued, "I was not, but I still—" He searched for an appropriate word.

"Finished?" Vincent offered.

"Yes."

Grant fought off a smile. "In your pants like a teenager?"

Rainer felt his cheeks heat from anger more than humiliation.

Vincent held up a hand to silence his guard. "Don't give him a hard time. Cecilia is a very passionate woman and he was compelled by magic. Is that all you did, McKay? I'm counting on your honesty here since I know she'll be selective with her account of events."

"No, sir, she also used her mouth on me the previous day."

Vincent's eyebrows shot up and Rainer had no idea what to expect from him. His eyes narrowed and then he burst out laughing.

"Well, no wonder you were so besotted. I half fell in love with the whore at your bachelor party," Vincent chuckled.

Rainer was disgusted but he needed Vincent's forgiveness before he could leave. As much as the king liked to make people squirm, Rainer knew it was little price to pay for such a huge offense.

Vincent's grin turned feral. "I appreciate how forthcoming you've been and I will see that Cecilia leaves you alone and is properly disciplined for her troublemaking. If I am honest, I'm quite desperate to get my lovely fiancée into the bedroom and get a chance at the hot little mouth that dazzled you right out of your duty. Obviously, she's quite a fiery woman and I'd be lying if I said I wasn't dying to make her mine."

Vincent studied him, waiting for a reaction like he was trying to test Rainer's loyalty yet again. When he got none, he tried a different tactic.

"I'll have to be careful, of course. I can be quite rough in the bedroom and that fair skin marks so easily."

Rainer bit the inside of his lip until it bled. He was careful not to react, even though the words made him want to throttle the king.

"Perhaps I'll go get a preview now," Vincent said, grinning at Grant. He turned his gaze back on Rainer, looking disappointed at his lack of affect. "Very well. It seems you are out of her thrall. I accept your heartfelt apology and I look forward to your wedding and mine so we can put this whole mess behind us."

Rainer nodded, bowing and turning to leave before what little self-control he had left abandoned him.

Back in his room, Rainer couldn't rid himself of the thought of anything but Cecilia, so he made his way down to his secret spot on the castle wall. The icy wind almost tore the door off its hinges when he thrust it open, but Rainer didn't care. The cold made him feel grounded as he wrapped his knuckles and faced the grain bag.

He punched furiously at it, ignoring the way each strike jolted up his arms and the ache that set into his knuckles immediately.

He tried to pull up any other memory. Unfortunately, the memories that he was left with—the ones that were the clearest—were all those sharpened by his father's cruelty.

Rainer punched the bag harder, his father's face invading his mind. The wind tore at him like it was trying to break him from his trance, but he was locked in.

Raymond McKay had built himself up from nothing, and so his eyes were constantly searching out some real or imagined imperfection in his son so that Rainer could do the same.

Rainer was eighteen when his mother died, old enough to know what it was to be willfully mean. When he was younger, she'd been a buffer of sorts, if not between them all the time then at least between Rainer and his pain. His father never hit him. He showed his disappointment in other ways.

It started with disparaging words, offhand comments to his instructors or other nobles when Rainer didn't rank at the top of the guardian class. But then it would spill over into breaking Rainer's favorite bow, burning his favorite histories or—worse—his mother's favorite things, most of which were irreplaceable pieces of art made for her by a friend. Rainer would come home and find his mother staring into the hearth at the remnants of a painting. She'd shake her head and tell him it was not his fault, but he knew it was how his father liked to get to him most.

After Maura died, it was like Raymond thrilled more in destroying what was left of her, and every hand-painted teacup broken and painting burned was like a barb in Rainer's heart. Like Raymond took joy in erasing what little memory his son had of kindness.

He might have stopped if it wasn't effective punishment. But each time Rainer came home and found the ruins, he'd run out for a workout before he even cleaned up the mess. Eventually, he trained himself not to care too much about anything that his father had the power to break.

His side spasmed in a sharp cramp. Finally, he stopped punching, leaning against the wall, breathless, his shirt clinging to his skin with sweat growing icy in the cold.

And though he'd woken with those memories as his only anchor, he'd forgotten the way that hurt grew inside him in every silence. Once again it felt like someone had broken something Rainer cared about to remind him how to focus, and he only had himself to blame for loving in the first place.

35

XANDER

Xander stood huddled outside the door to Cece's room with Isla and Jessamin at his side. Cece had been holed up inside for hours, rarely doing more than sleeping and occasionally swallowing a few spoonfuls of soup.

"When we get in there, just be gentle," Xander said. "She's had that bond with Rainer since she was six and she deserves time to mourn it."

Isla crossed her arms, glaring at him. He did not understand why she was mad at him. He'd gone along with what she said she wanted and had given her space.

"She needs to get it together," Jessamin said. "The rest of the group is counting on all of us to be ready for the wedding and we need her there. She's had a good sulk but she needs to get out of that bed and put one foot in front of the other."

Xander held up his hands. "But gently, right?"

Jessamin pushed into the bedroom. The heavy curtains were still drawn, just a slice of sunlight peeking through. The queen crossed the room and threw the curtains wide. Sunlight glanced off a tuft of dark, curly hair poking out among the blankets. The only sign of life was Cece's miserable groan.

Jessamin lifted her foot and gave Cece's body a light shove. "Get up."

"Don't be so rough with her," Xander said.

Jessamin rolled her eyes. "Darling, you're much too gentle with her."

"She needs that."

"She does not." Jessamin turned to look at her. "Is that what you need, Cece?"

"I need you to go away," Cece grumbled, peeking out from the blanket.

Jessamin yanked the blankets away and Cece groaned her discontent, hurrying to yank her twisted nightdress down to cover her legs.

Xander shrugged. "Nothing I haven't seen many times before."

Cece glared at him, but he grinned.

"I'll admit it's not the view of them I prefer," he continued. "My favorite view is when they were draped over my shoulders while I—"

Jessamin smacked her husband's arm. "That's enough. You're not helping."

"I thought she'd at least blush, but she's impervious to my charm now," Xander said with a shrug.

Isla glared at him from across the room.

"What?" he asked.

"Why are you like this?" Isla asked.

"Like what? Charming?" he challenged.

Her jaw ticked. He wished he could stop stoking her anger, but she'd hardly given him a second look despite his best efforts. "Why do you flirt with every woman you lay eyes on?" she huffed.

Xander feigned indignation. "I hardly think it's my fault that I surround myself with exceptional women."

"Yes, but must you bed them all?" Isla asked.

"Shouldn't it be admirable that I'm attracted to strong-willed, assertive women?" he said, trying not to grin at the way her fists balled.

"Then must you remind us that you've taken all of us to bed?" she asked.

Cece perked up. "To be honest, if that bothers you, Isla, you're going to be even more frustrated when everyone comes back to court and you realize how many exceptional women he's bedded."

Xander rolled his eyes. "I'm so glad you could rouse yourself to beat me down with your cutting wit, love."

A half-smile tugged at her lips—the first sign of life all day. "Well, Xan, there are simpler ways to tell a woman you like her than flirting with your ex-wife to make her jealous."

"Yes, but are those ways as much fun?" Xander asked.

"Come now, love, you're supposed to be brave," Cece said, a taunting edge to her voice as she lobbed the words he'd once used on her back at him.

"And you're supposed to be reckless," he countered, copying her response.

"She's got you shaking in your perfectly tailored breeches," Cece said, smacking his ass as she pushed out of the bed.

"He's afraid of all feelings except for lust," Jessamin agreed.

Xander looked back and forth from his wife to his ex-wife. "Really? This is what gets you out of bed finally? Ganging up on me when I'm just here to make sure that you're well."

Cece rolled her eyes. "You two should talk. And I do mean *talk*, Xander." She pinned him with a look that said she knew all his games and would not be impressed with any technique but honesty.

As if stringing together the perfect words was so simple. What he had with Isla wasn't like it was with Cece and that was the entire problem. Back then, he'd had so little damage, recklessness was a reflex. The greater the danger, the more thrilling the conquest. Now that he knew what it was to lose—now that he was aware what heartbreak could do—he was justifiably wary. How could Cece fault him?

Jessamin followed Cece into the washroom, closing the door behind them until there was only the muffled sound of the two of them chatting quietly and water splashing.

Xander cleared his throat. "I'll go first. Isla, I know I am bad at this—"

"Bad?"

"Fine. I'm terrible at this. I am—" The word was on the tip of his tongue but the fear in his chest was wild. "Afraid. I'm terrified, really. I know you feel a natural jealousy toward Cece. The truth is that loving her was easier—"

Isla huffed out a breath and he held up his hands.

"Just let me finish. What I mean is that it was easy because I didn't know to be scared. I didn't know I could fail. Gods, I had no idea what I had to lose, Isla. I was so naive and I thought I knew everything. What could be worse than a twenty-five-year-old prince who thinks he knows everything?"

Isla snorted, shaking her head.

"Exactly! I was ridiculous. I just had the benefit of not knowing it yet. But I spent most of my life in an enemy kingdom, doing the one thing I thought I was good at, the one thing that would make my family proud. I sacrificed all the good years with them to be a spy. Davide sacrificed his mind to keep me safe. My mother sacrificed her life so she wouldn't be used against me. My best friend sacrificed his life saving Cece. And even now I've had to surrender my regard for my father. But when I met Cece—well, really when I watched her from afar for a year—I didn't have any of that experience. I only had the experience of hearing 'yes.' I could throw myself into her full force because I didn't know what it was to lose, or to be used as a tool to torture the only person I had left."

Isla looked away.

"What I'm saying is that I had no idea how much it could hurt when I fell in love with her and it was easy to throw myself in with no regard for my safety."

"I don't want to hear any more about your love for her. You never godsdamned shut up about it," Isla snapped.

"I promise you do, darling. Please?" He gestured to the chair by the fire and Isla reluctantly slumped into it.

She looked adorable sulking. Normally she was so regal and alert, her spine straight, ready to spring into action, but now she was crumpled.

Xander knelt in front of her and her eyes went wide in surprise as he took her hands in his.

"What I'm trying to say—poorly—is that I know what I have to lose now, but I want to try anyway, because with you, even knowing how it could hurt, how you could flay me in a second both literally and figuratively, I simply cannot help myself."

Her face softened at last.

"I'm falling for you, and despite my terrible timing and the idiocy of my offer, I will take you in whatever way you'll let me. If you find my offer of consort insulting or not enough, I promise that I will understand and respect your wishes." The thought of it turned his stomach, indicating that he was in much deeper than he'd realized. "But if there is even a chance that you might want to stay here in Argaria and be with me in whatever position you choose, for however long you choose, I am putting myself entirely at your mercy."

Isla narrowed her eyes. "How do I know that you won't tire of me? That you won't simply be flirting with the next pretty girl you see with a bow in her hand?"

"Because I already swore off beautiful archers and I'll do it again," he said, trying for humor and failing.

"That's not good enough," she said.

Xander felt defeated. He had nothing else to offer. He was being honest about how he felt.

"What would feel like enough? I can assure you I'm quite single-minded when it comes to the things I want. If you give me another chance, one I know I don't deserve, I promise I will prove that you are a priority. Maybe it's unfair when I have an obligation to this kingdom first—"

"That doesn't bother me," Isla interrupted. "I would be expected to do the same, and there's no duty I understand better. But I cannot contend with your past."

Xander took a breath, trying to slow his swirling thoughts. He loved and loathed the adrenaline rush of this dance they were doing the same way he loved a good fight. "I can no sooner erase my past, nor would I. It made me who I am, Isla. Just as yours made you. I understand envy. Trust me. I was married to a woman whose heart was connected to the man she loved more than me and I knew it pretty much the whole time. Envy was my godsdamned best friend. But I cannot undo what was. I cannot retrieve the part of me that she has or give up the piece of her that's mine. To do so would be a betrayal of myself, and I can't do that, even for you."

Isla sat back, her arms crossed.

"Those are things I cannot give you. But what I'd like to give you is everything else. My heart has been broken. *I* have been broken," Xander said, trying to hide the waver in his voice with a cough. "But I'm still standing, still trying to put myself back together. And no one, not six beautiful princesses or any of the lovely ladies in this court, have made me want to try to be whole again until you. What I am offering you is what's left of me, and while I know it's unfair considering how exceptional you are, I'm hanging onto my last hope that it will miraculously be good enough."

For a moment she seemed to consider, her eyes taking on a glassy sheen before she looked away, blowing out a slow breath.

"It's not enough. I deserve better," she said. She stood abruptly, dropping his hands. "I'm not a stand-in."

"You're not."

"And I'm not a consolation prize."

Xander frowned. "Of course you aren't."

"And I'm not a place for a man to hang his last hope of love."

"And why is that?" Xander said, unable to hide his frustration.

Isla glared at him as if he'd been insulting her instead of pouring his heart out for her to eviscerate. "Because I cannot be a safety net and I deserve someone who can give me everything."

Xander swallowed hard. He'd tried his best. It just wasn't good enough. "I understand."

"Fight for her." Jessamin's whisper came only loud enough for him to hear through the washroom door. "She wants you to fight for her."

Xander climbed to his feet, searching for what more he could offer. He could not give Isla certainty, at least not this quickly. What he really needed was time. If he could at least bait her into staying, he had a chance of winning her over. He switched tactics.

"You're afraid."

Isla's eyes lit with fury. "How dare you!"

"I thought you Novumi warriors laughed in the face of fear, but it turns out your fears are just as common as the rest of us."

"Take it back," she huffed, drawing her blade and leveling it at him.

"I only recognize it because I've seen it in the mirror every day for the past year and a half," Xander said. "You can hide from yourself, but you can't hide from me. If you're too scared to be with me, that's okay, but I'm not going to pretend along with you."

Isla gaped at him for a full minute before charging at him. He barely drew his short swords fast enough to block her attack. They parried back and forth a few times, but he could tell she wasn't actually trying to hurt him. If she was, he would have let her—not to kill, but at least a gentle maim to prove his affection.

She met his eye as she swung, as if daring him to continue his proclamation. He was nothing if not a man who rose to every occasion to run his stupid mouth.

"You're afraid if you let me closer, if you hang around to see if I could love you, I might see all of you and not feel the same way. You're afraid that I'll see something I don't like and run away," he said. "But I won't because I won't find anything as ugly in you as what I've already found in myself, and it's all those sharp edges in you that have drawn me in anyway."

She shook her head and stepped away, sheathing her sword. Her dark eyes met his and she opened her mouth, then closed it before turning and leaving the room in a huff.

Isla couldn't do it. She couldn't risk loving him. Xander understood, but it didn't make it hurt less. Perhaps he was in much deeper than he thought.

The washroom door creaked open and Cece stood in her robe, her damp hair soaking through the fabric over her shoulders, suggesting she and Jessamin, who stood behind her, had been hiding in there, waiting for him to finish his groveling.

He shrugged, swallowing hard as the two of them crossed the room and pulled him into a hug.

"Oh, Xan, that was really good. I honestly thought it would work," Cece said.

"Would have worked on me," Jessamin said with a soft smile.

Xander shoved down the swell of grief and disappointment in his chest. "Yes, well, practice makes perfect. It was an excellent grovel."

Cece gripped his hand. "She will come around."

He shook his head. "That seemed definitive to me. It's never going to happen."

Cece grinned. "Never say never. Never is a challenge."

"Did you just quote Cato to me?"

"What is it you say? If we can't laugh about it, it's just sad?" She kissed his cheek. "Give her some time. She'll come around."

Jessamin nodded. "I know my cousin. She is stubborn and uncomfortable with affection. I suspect she'll come around, especially if you continue to be your charming self."

"What happened to letting her choose for herself and respecting her wishes?" Xander challenged.

Jessamin grinned, waving a hand dismissively. "That was just when I didn't know she was so content to lie to herself. And before I knew you were actually in love with her."

Xander stared at his wife and Cece nodding beside her. Apparently, he only successfully hid his heart from himself.

"Now I'm ready to see you win her over, and obviously, I'd prefer that she stay here in Argaria," Jessamin said.

Xander racked his brain for what else he could do. His eyes came to rest on the desk where an old letter sat unfolded. He could return to his roots, trace his story back to the beginning and play to his strengths by giving himself the time to think and write a well-crafted love letter.

Xander grinned as he sat down to write his best one yet.

———

It was only a couple hours later that Xander was sitting peacefully by the fire in his room, going over their plan of attack for the wedding, when Isla burst into the room, eyes blazing with fury.

"What the fuck is this?"

She tossed his letter into his lap and he picked it up as if seeing it for the first time.

"It looks like a love letter."

Her cheeks were flushed. "You said you loved me for the first time in a godsdamned letter."

He was exhilarated by her anger. "Well, you weren't interested in me saying it to your face and I refuse to go into such a dangerous plan without having all of my feelings on the table. It's not as if you gave me options."

Isla paced the room, fuming. "How dare you!"

"Love you?" Xander asked, trying not to laugh.

"You don't even know me."

"And yet I love you already."

"That's not love. It's infatuation," Isla said.

"Is that what you're afraid of? And here I thought it was just a general feeling of unworthiness."

Isla glared at him.

"Isla, you may be able to command whole armies, but you cannot command my heart any more than I can," Xander said.

"You are a stubborn, spoiled king," she grumbled, shaking her head. Xander could tell that she was trying not to smile.

"Anything could happen tomorrow and I would regret it if I did not tell you exactly how I feel." He took a tentative step toward her and, when she didn't back away, closed the space between them in a few quick strides. "You don't have to say yes. Just say you'll consider staying to see what this could be. Come on, Isla. Give me the best 'maybe' of my life."

She looked toward the fire, shaking her head.

He took her hands. "I know how you're feeling. You're thinking—what a foolish time to be weak. What a liability to have a heart."

A surprised laugh burst from her lips. "It's eerie how you do that."

"I only know because I feel the same," Xander said. "I've made the mistake of not being forthcoming in the past. I wish you'd see my past as an asset—as a series of mistakes I am trying hard to learn from. I'd spare both of us the chaos if I could, but even spoiled kings aren't free from love's influence. All I ask is that you stay after we finish this and give me a chance to prove this isn't infatuation. Give me a chance once the dust settles."

Isla met his gaze and he saw the same fear and longing he felt reflected in her eyes. "Maybe. That's the best I can do. I make no promises beyond that."

She turned away, retreating toward the door with his letter clutched to her chest.

"Isla? Is there anything you'd like to say to me?" he asked.

It was more a taunt than a real question, but when she froze in the doorway, Xander stopped breathing.

"Yes." She turned to look at him. "Your fly is unbuttoned."

She ducked out of the room, chased by the sound of his laughter.

36

CECILIA

Cecilia sat on the windowsill, her hip pressed against the cool glass. She traced the webbed frost on the corners of the window as she watched the snow swirl outside. The heavy wool blanket around her shoulders slipped and she pulled it tighter, rubbing her sternum.

She was still so unaccustomed to the void where their connection had once lived, finding herself trying to pull on the bond but finding nothing where the light between them used to glimmer.

She was almost relieved to have a physical pain that matched her emotions.

He'd looked at her like he hated her. Rainer had never looked at her like that. He'd been furious with her for fleeting moments, betrayed or hurt, but he'd never looked at her like she was the villain.

She was so lost in thought she hardly registered that the persistent thudding sound was a knock on the door until it cracked open and Xander's voice cut through the quiet room.

"Cece, someone wants to see you."

Cecilia sighed heavily, not bothering to turn and look at him. "I said I didn't want to see anyone."

Xander crossed his arms. "Yes, I understand you're having yourself quite a brooding session. You'd give Rainer a run for his money, but your visitor was quite insistent and I thought you should hear her out."

Raven Whitewind stepped out from behind him.

Cecilia narrowed her eyes at the seer. "Haven't you done enough?"

Raven held up her hands. "I'm sorry that I had to take something from you that you didn't wish to give up. It was brave of you to take on the pain yourself."

Cecilia shrugged. "Not really. It always hurts me worse when he's in pain."

Raven nodded, pursing her lips. "I promised Selene I would look out for you. Can we talk?"

Cecilia wanted to send the seer away—wanted to scream and rage at her—but her birth mother's name on the lips of someone who had known her stopped Cecilia in her tracks.

"Fine."

Xander looked between them. Satisfied that he didn't need to intervene, he started to close the door. "I'll be outside if you need me."

The seer sat in one of the chairs by the fire and gestured to the other. Cecilia begrudgingly crossed the room and slumped into the chair.

"You feel it now, don't you? The loss?" Raven asked. "I have never seen a bond rooted so deeply like that. I wasn't sure I'd even be able to sever it."

Cecilia brought her hand to her chest. Even when she'd died and hovered in between life and death, she'd still felt some semblance of connection to Rainer drawing her back. Now there was nothing.

"You know, there are some who believe even after a severing, a soul bond leaves a trail, a way back to each other," Raven said.

Cecilia perked up, meeting the seer's eyes. "I could get it back?"

"If both of you want it, it will form again, no intermediary like me required. It's a bit like planting cover crops to loosen soil for the main crop. Those roots leave a pathway and if both parties wish to cross it, they can find a way. Unfortunately, I cannot offer a guidebook on how to make it happen and I've never witnessed it firsthand. Your bond grew so strong over time through both of your willingness to share so much of yourselves—finding the way back to each other requires the same."

Cecilia shrunk back in her chair. That was hopeless. She didn't need her power to remember how wounded Rainer looked. He wouldn't be reaching out for their bond ever again. Cecilia was just finally winning him over and it only took a few tearful words from Eloise to wipe out all the progress she'd made.

"I doubt that will be happening," Cecilia sighed.

"You have very little faith in him, all things considered."

Cecilia shook her head, wringing her hands and rubbing her thumb on her inner wrist. "I have plenty of faith in him. It's me I don't trust."

Raven smiled, leaning toward her. "I knew your mother, you know. Knew his mother, too."

"You knew Rainer's birth mother?"

Raven nodded. "Aria Harron. She was bonded to Zelden Novaris, you know?"

Cecilia frowned. "How?"

Raven's violet eyes clouded. "Bonding is as old as the kingdom itself. It didn't start with the Gauntlet. In fact, those who were bonded tended to be guardians of the kingdom. Instead of protecting each other, they protected major points of conflict on our borders. It made it easier for them to communicate in battle if they could feel things from each other. It helped them work against both brute force and magical attacks."

Cecilia stared at her, trying to process the information.

"Aria and Zelden had a soul bond and were quite in love. Unfortunately, Aria had a very difficult pregnancy and a more difficult birth. The healers did the best they could. Zelden was out of his mind with fear and grief when they told him there was nothing more they could do. Her pressure wouldn't regulate, no matter how they tried. Aria made Zelden sit with her and the baby until the end. I think she tried to love Rainer enough in those few moments to make up for the lifetime she knew she wouldn't have.

"I think Zelden tried to love Rainer, too, but he didn't have that same gentleness as his son. He was so broken by the loss of Aria, he didn't know how to love a baby. So he did the next best thing and left Rainer with Maura McKay, a friend of Aria's who hadn't been able to have a child of her own. Some believe that losing Aria is what really brought Zelden down. He didn't have her there at the final battle, and he didn't have anything to come back for in his mind."

Tears burned in Cecilia's eyes, her heart aching for Rainer.

"All this to say that you wouldn't be the first person laid low by a broken bond," Raven said. "But there are many paths you can take and they entirely depend upon how willing you are to pick yourself up and soldier on."

Cecilia scowled at her. "Delightful. Did you just come to tell me about the love of my life's tragic past or was there something more?"

Raven grinned, not at all put off by her rudeness. "Good to see you've got a little fire left, girl. I knew the first time I laid eyes on you that you'd be a force. For what it's worth, your bond made you both stronger."

"I know that," Cecilia snapped. "Now what do you want?"

Raven placed a hand on Cecilia's. "I promised your mother I would keep an eye on you. When I told Selene how things would go for her, and how they'd likely go for you, she wanted to make sure you had someone in your corner. More than one someone, really. The future is a tangle of fate and free will and I have taught myself to see the most likely paths. You've doubted his love in the past—despite his assurance and that of your sister Aelish. You wanted to know that he would love you without the bond. Now you can find out for sure."

"I didn't think it would happen this way—with him having no memory," Cecilia snapped. "I am so tired. I've lost everything. I know Rainer is still alive and I'm so grateful for that, but I don't know how to lose him like this—how to let someone else have him." She shook her head, trying to take a breath around the pain in her chest. "How could I be so stupid before? I should have married him a year ago, grief or not. I was so foolish to push him away because I was so afraid to be loved. All of my hesitation seems so absurd now. I'm going to spend my life watching him with someone else. He'll never remember what we are to each other. Now, he doesn't even want to."

Tears poured down Cecilia's cheeks, dripping onto her dress in a percussive beat. She had learned enough to know that grief was just unspent love, but she'd never spend all the love she had for him. She'd spend her whole life grieving. Sometimes love just hurt, and Rainer had always been worth the pain.

Raven cocked her head to the side like she was reading Cecilia's thoughts. "There are many legends about soul bonds and the boundaries and limits of them, but most people misunderstand how they work. People are naturally selfish. They think that given the opportunity, they will fall into the trap of taking. I can tell even you think that. You think that Rainer has taken some part of you and you some part of him, and that makes you feel tied to each other and unable to know for sure what might exist between you without it."

Cecilia crossed her arms and leaned back in the chair, squinting at Raven through her tears. "Not anymore."

"Ah, but this is wrong. You give to each other. Those parts of him you felt in your chest were given, the same way the seeds you planted in his were gifted. You gave those things to each other. There was no stealing, no accidental theft. A true soul bond only grows into what the two parties allow. You grew love because that's what you gave to each other. You grew trust because you relied on each other. You chose to give the other parts of you that no one else could have. Magic did not require it. It was an exchange the two of you made freely."

Cecilia wiped her eyes. "This is supposed to make me feel better?"

"No, girl. It's supposed to make you feel *focused*. You wanted to know for sure that he wasn't compelled to love you—that he would have anyway if he could have chosen freely. He's told you so repeatedly, but you didn't believe him. I am telling you now what is true. It's not theft. It's generosity that brings you so close together."

Cecilia leaned her head back against the chair. "I doubt he's feeling generous toward me now."

Raven sighed. "Rainer McKay left you in those woods alone. Do you remember why?"

Cecilia swallowed hard. "To remind me that I could save myself—that I still had the will to do that."

Raven nodded.

"And that's why you decided to help Vincent?" Cecilia growled.

"My whole life has been about making hard choices that no one else understands, girl," Raven said. "I helped Selene create the Gauntlet. I rode from cave to cave with her and Clastor and Cato and two other witches. But it was only she and I and Clastor who knew that you were there, too. She hid her pregnancy well, but I have foresight. I knew you'd be before she and Clastor did.

"You are a lot like her, small and fierce and loyal. Selene had very high hopes for you, but most of all, she hoped that the wisdom of human love would guide you—and she was right. She hoped you'd be an embodiment of the principles of the Gauntlet. Wisdom to know that power is best when shared. Memory of our mistakes so as to not make the same ones again. Magic to restore peace and prosperity to the kingdom. You want to know why I'm here? There's still something unsettled in you; it was what unsettled your mother when we created the power trapped in the Cave of Longings. Go ahead and ask."

Cecilia wanted to ask so many things. "How could she let me give something up? How could she when I had no real choice?" she asked, all the hurt pouring out in a hiccupping sob. She could not call up this pain when she had nothing with which to anchor herself.

"At least you're asking the right questions. Exchanges do require consent. Whatever is traded must be given freely."

Cecilia threw her hands up. "But I didn't have the option to opt out. Once I walked into the Cave of Longings, I could not stop the exchange. If I hadn't accepted it—"

"Your soul would have been rendered from your body," Raven finished. A faint smile ghosted over her lips. "Makes you wonder—"

Cecilia barked out a disbelieving sound somewhere between a

laugh and a sob. "That! That is all you have to say? That exchanges require consent? Then why didn't this one?"

The seer paused, a maddening know-it-all look in her eyes. "Perhaps you should have paid closer attention in history classes."

Cecilia frowned. She could not recall ever learning about a magical exchange that was made without consent or how it worked out. She sighed and tipped her head back. The person who would know was Rainer and now that he didn't remember anything and hated her, he would not be the most reliable resource.

The seer stood and kissed Cecilia's cheek. "Selene was a woman of strong convictions, just like you. I bet her memories from the Gauntlet caves felt like home to you."

Cecilia placed her hand over her heart. The caves *had* felt like home. When she had access to her memory magic, she would call them up when she was sad and watch her mother's hands walk her through a spell, relishing the feeling of seeing, tasting, smelling, sensing what her mother did at that moment in time. But when the memory faded it always reminded her that she'd been robbed of the real thing and forced to settle for scraps of memory. Now she wished for so much more. She wanted to ask her mother so many questions and not be placated for asking the right ones. Raven was proving to be as cryptic as Cecilia's godly siblings.

"Selene would be happy to see you stand up for what you believe in. I must head home to Olney. I've done what I came here to do. I've delivered a message to the handsome king and now I must go. This is more excitement than my old bones can take."

Cecilia cocked her head to the side. Though she knew the woman had to be centuries old, Raven didn't look much older than forty. "That's all you have to say to me?"

Raven pursed her lips. "I've said plenty. Now, I know you're hurt and angry, but I need you to remember this next bit."

Cecilia glowered at the woman.

"You won't be trapped here forever." The seer's eyes clouded over and her body went rigid. *"Come and find me when you've reached dry land and the spinning won't stop."* Her voice was airier, frailer, and the moment after she said the words, her eyes sharpened and she grinned.

Cecilia shook her head. "What does that mean?"

Raven smiled. "Just another stitch slipping into place. You'll know when the time comes. You have this well in hand."

Cecilia held up the Unsummoner bracelet. "How do you figure? Between this and your cryptic rambling, I am not better off."

The seer laughed. "I'll see you soon. Remember—when you reach dry land and the spinning won't stop."

Raven crossed the room and opened the door to reveal Xander standing in the doorway. She patted him on the shoulder. "Don't look so serious, Your Grace. It will all work out."

Cecilia watched her go, torn between fury and helpless frustration.

Xander lingered outside the room.

"What do you want?" she asked, staring into the fire.

His footsteps crept closer and he lowered to his knees in front of her chair so she couldn't avoid his gaze. His hazel eyes were full of compassion and hope.

"I'm sorry you're hurting, but I want to tell you what you've bought with your pain." He took her hand in his. "Raven gave me the answer. We have him, love. We have all of Vincent's supporters. Raven confirmed that Corin is an ally and that means that we can put the plan into action tomorrow. That's where I've been. I sent a message to Evan and his reply came back almost immediately thanks to the new servants he installed in the castle. This time tomorrow—at the wedding, this will all be over."

Cecilia wanted to feel triumphant, but she settled for simply feeling ready for vengeance.

37

EVAN

The temple bustled with activity, the cacophonous din of voices grating on Evan's enhanced hunter's hearing. He looked around the cavernous space, waiting for the moment that Cato's magic failed and he'd be recognized, but no one even offered him a second glance.

Evan had never been one for prayer, even after meeting the gods, but he said a sort of prayer now. Perhaps it was more of a wish—that Vincent wouldn't even think of the fact that the temple was outside the castle wards and reachable by the gods, especially Goddess Aurelia for whom the temple was built.

Xander entered through the rear doors and the temple quieted as he cut down the aisle.

Evan told himself that if their plan worked, he'd finally be able to stop expecting the worst, but at times it felt he'd permanently stepped into the role of pessimist when Xander had taken the one of optimist. Being blessedly bored would be a nice change of pace, though it would take Evan a while to acclimate.

His gaze connected with Xander's across the room and his friend offered a half-smile.

"I like the gray hair, old man," he said so low that only Evan would hear.

"A disguise you'd never be able to pull off. You're much too vain," Evan countered. He was relieved for the break in tension.

Trying to corral a team of newly trained priestess warriors into the temple in a way that felt natural was a challenge. Trained spies were one thing, but these women lacked the instinct to hold still and pretend not to pay attention. They all kept looking around for each other, which he'd initially worried about. Luckily, men wrote off women who were whispering with their friends as gossips. They wouldn't make anything of the corsages of white roses on each of the women's wrists, marking them as allies.

Evan wore the same type of rose pinned to his tunic, as did Xander, Cato, Cal, Reese, and Chris, who were all similarly disguised thanks to Cato's help. Evan fixed his gaze on the god. He was still waiting for the last-second double-cross, but since Rainer and Eloise's engagement ball, he'd seemed strangely stoic and focused on their goal, even stepping in to train some of the priestesses.

To Vincent's guards, it appeared that a bunch of brainless women were all a-titter about the nuptials of the handsome and famous Rainer McKay. But Evan could see how the women flitted about the room, positioning themselves for an advantage as each of their targets took their seats of honor.

One thing went right when, in Vincent's attempt to torture Cecilia, he'd sent her to speak with Eloise. Cecilia had managed to memorize a copy of the temple seating arrangements in Eloise's suite. Thanks to Raven Whitewind and Cecilia, Evan knew both who and where to strike and had strategically placed their small army of women around the temple within arm's reach of the traitors.

It was hard to get used to everyone having a different face, but Evan had studied people long enough to recognize their gaits and mannerisms.

His gaze coasted casually up to the loft at the back of the temple where Maren and Jessamin were positioned with bows. Though he didn't catch a glimpse of either of them, there was a white rose sitting on the railing, indicating that they were in place.

He exhaled heavily as Sylvie sauntered over to him.

"Take a breath, Ev. We are ready and we have surprise on our side," she whispered.

She wove her arm through his and he led her to their seats toward the back of the temple. He was on edge being so far away from Xander, who stood at the front of the aisle talking to Mika, who was disguised as the temple's head priestess.

Mika had come such a long way from when she and Evan first met. She had sharpened her deepest wound into a deadly weapon and was focused solely on revenge. While her skill comforted him, he was a bit worried about how her anger might threaten her judgment in the moment. She'd promised she would be close enough to help defend Xander if something went wrong. She wouldn't have a weapon on her, but they'd hidden several different weapons on the altar, under certain pews, and even in some of the flower arrangements.

Cecilia appeared at the front of the temple and was immediately greeted by Xander. Side by side, Evan could see how much weight the two of them had lost being cut off from their magic. Both had dark circles under their eyes and a heaviness in their gaits. The sight of two of the most powerful people he knew looking so worn down was startling and stoked his anxiety into full force. He'd never realized how vital magic was to witches until he saw them look so lost without it.

Then Xander whispered something and Cecilia tipped her head back and laughed and the knot of anxiety in Evan's chest unwound. His friend had become better at not flirting with his former wife, but he could tell by the mischievous glint in Xander's eye that he'd said something inappropriate. Cecilia smacked his arm playfully.

The duo still made a formidable team and Evan had seen them both fight enough without magic to know what they were capable of. Beyond that, they thought so much alike that Cecilia was uniquely equipped to read Xander's reckless impulses. On top of her protection, Isla would also be at the very front of the room and she was perhaps the most fearsome warrior there. His best friend had a knack for surrounding himself with women who were as beautiful as they were deadly.

"This is always the worst part for you, isn't it?" Sylvie whispered.

Evan nodded. "The best-laid plans always have flaws. It's impossible to anticipate every single thing. Humans are too unpredictable, not to mention the fact that Cato is holding disguises for a lot of us at once."

They both glanced at the trickster god, who stood at the back of the temple handing out flowers to attendees based on their intentions. Red for those who were on Vincent's side and white for those on Xander's. It made Evan's skin crawl to trust Cato with such a monumental task, especially one where he could so easily ruin them.

But Cato was clearly contrite and it seemed he did have boundaries that could be crossed. He was also one of their only real assets, presenting the opportunity to tell the difference between friend and foe beyond what intel they'd collected. The god could still read intentions, so when he said, "Gods bless the king," he could ascertain the attendees' reactions and hand them the appropriate rose.

This plan was bound to be a bloodbath already and Evan didn't want to kill anyone they didn't have to. War was messy, but if he could avoid any unnecessary loss of life, he would do it.

Though most of the guards and noblemen normally would have turned down flowers, it was considered a terrible offense to turn down hospitality from a god, so despite their obvious discomfort, no one dared offend the trickster by doing anything but wear their rose prominently.

"He looks pretty relaxed for working hard," Sylvie mentioned.

"We'll see how he looks once this place is full."

As it stood, about two-thirds of the temple was occupied, the first few rows reserved for the most important folks still vacant.

Evan gave Sylvie's arm a squeeze. "Syl, I'm not stupid enough to ask you to run and hide now or even if things go wrong, but I—" He swallowed hard. "I know you are your own woman, but I cannot live with you being hurt as you have before, so if this goes wrong—"

"Don't even think of asking me to leave you," she said, her whisper harsh in his ear.

"I'm not. I'm asking you to get as many of the women out as possible and keep them safe. It's an impossibly unfair thing to ask, but I cannot think of that for you or Cece, or any of these women we've trained who have already endured so much. Use your magic. Use whatever you have to, but get out and I swear I will get back to you."

She turned to face him head-on. "You think I would not protect you in the same way? That it wouldn't break me to think of you tortured the way Rainer has been?"

"Of course I know it would hurt. I just also know that you're much stronger than me and that the one thing in this world that might truly make me a traitor is you being hurt, Sylvie. If Vincent had you, there is nothing I wouldn't do to keep you safe. I will get on my knees now and beg if I have to."

Her eyes shimmered with tears. "You cannot ask me to walk away from you."

"And yet, I must."

She looked away, her eyes passing over the women scattered throughout the temple. "For you, I will do that, but I will never stop trying to get you back after that."

Evan smiled. "That's fair."

He glanced around the room, looking for the groom, but Rainer was nowhere to be found. It was still early.

The ceremony was just under an hour away, but Evan was practically vibrating with nerves. All he could do now was wait and there was no worse task for a warrior. All he could do was worry that their timing would be off, or Vincent's guard patrols would be larger than they expected and easily overwhelmed their untrained allies, or that one of his friends would be killed. He took a breath and sat beside Sylvie, his palm itching for a weapon, anxiety twisting every muscle in his body tight as a bowstring as he waited for the wedding and their last stand to begin.

38

RAINER

Rainer darted down the Castle Savero hallway. He needed to get to the temple, but he'd forgotten the rings in his room and had to run back to get them.

As he stalked down the hallway, his mind spun through cycles from hating Cecilia to loving her to downright loathing her. He turned the corner toward the training room in the hope of burning off some of the nerves that had his hands shaking.

He rounded a corner and nearly ran into Michael.

The boy grinned up at him.

"No training today. I'm getting married," Rainer said.

The boy frowned and opened his mouth to speak. Before he could, an older woman with neatly braided dark hair, wearing an apron dusted with flour, stepped up behind Michael, resting a hand on his shoulder.

"Guardian McKay, I'm Michael's mother, Veronica. I wanted to thank you for taking the time to teach him so much."

Rainer grinned at the boy. "He's a good student."

"He is. As good in the kitchen as he is in here. He even learned how to make that pesto dish that you taught us a few months back—the one Lady Reznik loves so much," Veronica said.

Rainer frowned. "I taught you a pesto dish?" His mind pulled up a hazy memory in the castle kitchens, though he couldn't place the time period, just his hands gathering basil and pine nuts. An ache pressed behind his eyes. While he could not remember learning how to cook, he could easily call up a recipe now that he'd been told he knew one. "I'm sorry to say I don't seem to remember teaching you."

Veronica nodded. "Yes, it seems you're forgetting quite a lot. I wish I could tell you but—" She broke into a coughing fit when she tried to say more. "Damned trickster god made it impossible to say much about Lady Reznik."

Rainer frowned. What did the trickster god have to do with anything? He'd noticed that Vincent was especially wary about the trickster god's presence in the castle. But Vincent had said he was an ally and he made sure that Grant was available to escort him through the castle once a day for what he'd simply called "maintenance."

Rainer rubbed the back of his neck, feeling oddly chastened. "She cast a love spell on me."

Veronica tipped her head back and laughed in his face. "Love spells don't exist, you fool." Shaking her head, she turned toward the kitchen, corralling Michael along with her. "I hope you remember who you are before you break that poor girl's heart. It's already been broken enough."

The warm throbbing behind Rainer's eyes turned into a sharper pain. He waited for a memory to break through. He dug his mental claws into the scraps of memories with new desperation, but the pain didn't gain him any ground. All he could call up was the repeating glimpse of his hands cutting pasta.

Rainer rubbed his aching head and headed back toward the stables.

———

The temple was extravagantly decorated, the center aisle lined with enormous bouquets of bright red roses that filled the air with their sweet scent. Flower petals were scattered down the main aisles in such a thick blanket that it was impossible to see the white marble floors. A servant brushed him to the side so he'd avoid stepping on them. He cut down the side aisle, ignoring the heavy gazes of what seemed like everyone in the room. The temple was still half empty but it was clear everyone wanted to be there early for the spectacle. He didn't understand why they stared. Maybe they'd noticed he was pathetically alone.

Xander had begrudgingly agreed to be his best man since Vincent would be helping the high priestess with the ceremony and Rainer hated Grant. Truthfully, Rainer had no one else. The only other friend he'd made since waking was a young boy, which was truly pathetic.

He needed to make a point of making some new friends after the wedding.

The aisles were full of giggling girls in white rose corsages and nobles wearing red rose boutonnieres, including his future father-in-law, Edward Spellman. He was overbearing, opportunistic, and sought out conversations with Vincent whenever he could. He and Raymond McKay would be fast friends when they finally met.

Rainer ducked to the right, narrowly avoiding conversing with Spellman thanks to two priestesses in long golden robes who intercepted the father of the bride.

When Rainer made it to the front of the temple, he saw a blur of blue out of the corner of his eye. When he turned, he spotted Cecilia in the corner alcove of the side temple, right off the altar. She wore a light blue gown the color of Olney wedding dresses. It was an interesting choice, but it brought out her eyes in such a devastating way that Rainer was afraid to look at her up close.

He expected to feel less compelled by her, but nothing had changed except the lack of warmth in his chest. He was still drawn to her.

Cecilia closed her eyes, tilting her head back and talking aloud to herself. Rainer hesitated. Perhaps she was working a spell.

His feet carried him to her before he could stop them. He entered the side temple, out of view of the crowd.

When Cecilia opened her eyes and found him standing in front of her, she jumped back, her shoulder blade slamming against the wall.

She winced. "Sorry—you normally can't sneak up on me." Her face was full of such grief that he almost reached out to touch her.

Before he could overthink it, he grabbed her hand and yanked her into one of the private meditation booths. The rooms were not exactly hidden, but they were tucked into the side entrance of the temple, not visible from the main aisle. They were also made for one person. He and Cecilia had to stand so close together, their chests nearly touched. Her hands rested above his heart, less gentle caress than bracing herself. She looked up at him, her eyes full of confusion and hope.

He needed to get this out of his system. To be certain that he'd feel nothing at all when he touched her.

"I need to—"

He cupped her face in his hands and kissed her. Immediately her hands were in his hair, pulling him closer, taking on a desperate edge that made him feel out of his mind with longing. Goosebumps rose on his skin. He shoved the booklets of meditation practices off the small ledge lining the room and lifted her to sit on it, using his hips to keep her pinned.

She moaned against his lips. "Rain."

He pulled back, meeting her wide blue eyes.

"Why did you do that?" she rasped.

He didn't completely understand why. It was a desperate move. He saw her, knew in the moment he didn't hate her, needed to see if it felt the same to be with her as it had when he was bewitched. He still wasn't convinced that it wasn't some remnant of the spell.

He kissed her again and she let him.

Rainer swallowed her soft gasp as he hiked her dress to the tops of her thighs. Her body went rigid and he pulled back to look at her.

"I need to understand. I need to remember."

She studied him for a moment, chewing her lip. "Yes."

"Yes?"

She nodded, but a worried crease formed in her brow.

He slid his hands up her thighs and found the edge of her lace underwear. Hooking his fingers in the sides, he moved back as she lifted her hips and he helped her out of them. He stuffed them in his pocket, settling back between her thighs. He kissed her again, winding his hands through her hair, carefully unpinning and loosening her curls.

She smiled against his mouth like she knew some secret he didn't, and he supposed she did.

"What?"

"That's familiar," she whispered.

He held her gaze as he slid his hand up her inner thigh. She gave him a nod and he brushed his fingers over her, both of them sighing together.

"You're so wet."

She nodded. "Just for you."

He frowned. "Why are you letting me do this?"

"Because I love you."

Anger burned through his veins. "Then why did you trick me?"

She frowned. "I didn't."

Rainer froze. "Still lying."

"Lying and not being able to tell the truth are two different things," she said, her voice thin with exasperation. "When I reach the ends of what I can say, there's nothing more for me to do. I'm just waiting on you to remember."

"I want to. I want to remember you."

She worried her lower lip with her teeth, the movement mesmerizing.

"I need this. I just need to know what's real."

Gods, he sounded pathetic.

The crease in her brow returned and she let out a shaky breath. The silence stretched between them to the point where he was ready to storm out of the booth and never make eye contact with her again.

"Okay. Just go slow. I haven't done anything in months except for what I did with you."

She unbuttoned his pants with shaky hands. He couldn't tell if

440

she was scared or excited. There was no indication on her face. Before, he was certain he would have felt something in his chest. Something felt so wrong now, but he just needed that closeness, as if intimacy would reveal something he hadn't yet seen, uncover some new memory.

She pulled out his cock, spitting into her palm and taking him in her callused hand. He twitched at the touch.

She looked up at him, brushing the thumb of her other hand over the space between his brows. "I found a worry, but I'll fix it in a hurry."

The words sounded so familiar. He was so close to remembering. It was idiotic to think the key to his memories was fucking her, but some primal instinct for closeness spurred him on. Just this once, he could do this and get her out of his system.

She braced herself on his shoulders. "Brave with my hand. Brave with my heart," she whispered.

He kissed her again, rubbing himself against her as she whimpered. Her body was still so rigid.

He pulled back immediately. "I can't. You're scared. This isn't right."

Suddenly, the door swung open. Xander Savero appeared in the doorway, backlit by sunlight streaming through stained-glass windows. His eyes went wide.

"What the fuck are you two doing?" He stepped inside, closing the door behind him, making the space even more claustrophobic. He looked from Cecilia to Rainer to Rainer's cock.

"Want to put that thing away, McKay? You're going to take an eye out." Xander turned to Cecilia with mischief in his eyes. "Good for you, love. Now I see what all the fuss is about. Explains why he's such an expert swordsman."

She slapped Xander's arm, breathing out a startled laugh. Rainer tucked himself back in his pants as Cecilia pushed her dress down.

"McKay, get out of here," Xander said. "If you get caught in here with us, that's going to be harder to explain. I, on the other hand, have been known to have a serious weakness for my ex-wife."

Rainer didn't want to leave her—he had so many questions. Why had she let him touch her that way when she was so afraid? That was not the kind of trust born of obsession. It was born of intimacy.

He'd never been more certain that whatever had existed between them was not as fleeting as a spell. Much as he wanted to stay and ask questions, he knew they could not answer them and his presence would only get Cecilia into more trouble.

He met Cecilia's eyes and pulled her into a kiss.

Tears streamed down her cheeks. "Rain, if love was enough, I'd stay with you forever."

The words sparked a hint of a memory. For a split second, he swore he saw her on the beach in his arms saying those same words. It was there and gone so fast he thought he imagined it out of sheer desperation to remember.

"I'll take those," Xander said, swiping the lace underwear hanging out of Rainer's pocket and sliding them back up Cecilia's legs.

Rainer took one last look at her and left the booth. He smoothed his tunic and ran a hand through his hair as he walked back toward the altar, tugging at the words that laid a trail to the slice of memory he'd just seen. The throb in his head grew unbearable, but nothing else came save for a rush of fear and humiliation and an unbelievable sense of failure. Guilt and shame sent his stomach tumbling.

His head ached fiercely. At first, he thought it was some sort of magical sabotage or torture for walking away from her, but then an image surged through his mind.

———

Cecilia sat beside him on a beach, drawing swirls in the sand with her fingers.

"I don't want to be someone who is ruined by hurt. I want to be someone who's brave in the face of it."

———

His head pounded; it felt like someone was stabbing needles into his brain, and not just once, but again and again. The violence of his mind trying to right itself was all-consuming. He squeezed his eyes shut, gripping the altar railing to stay upright.

"McKay?"

He was vaguely aware of the prince beside him. He looked at Xander, expecting sympathy, but was met with narrowed eyes and barely contained anger.

"What?"

Xander shook his head, letting out a bitter laugh. "You're content to just leave her to remember alone. To leave me to remember with her. We were both there in that room while she suffered alone. If you don't remember right now I'll never forgive you for being such a fucking coward."

Rainer couldn't explain how he knew what Xander meant. He'd begun to suspect that as much as he had a compelling desire to remember, he had just as strong a reason to forget. He sensed the shame and failure that welled up whenever he thought of his life before, but he'd been too afraid to push past it and see what waited on the other side. It came to him in a flash when he'd killed Vincent's guards with his bare hands. Not the memory, but the furious rage that began with the empty dread connected to the blank space in his brain and never ended.

Lightning bolts exploded in Rainer's mind and he squeezed his eyes shut, afraid he might vomit all over the altar. When he opened his eyes, several nobles in the front row were looking at him, wide-eyed.

"Rainer?" Xander studied him.

"I'm fine. Just give me a minute." Rainer shoved away from the prince and made his way to one of the meditation rooms. He closed his eyes, leaning his forehead against the cool wood wall. "Come on."

He willed the memories to return to him. Something about those words Cecilia had mumbled when she was trying to summon the courage to be with him—"*Brave with my hand, brave with my heart.*" They seemed like the thread that, when tugged, would reveal what he'd lost, like throwing back the curtain on the darkness in his mind. He searched for the words, begged the memory to return.

———

Cecilia lay beside him in the dark, her gaze fixed on the night sky, eyes wide with wonder. She brushed tears from her cheek and looked at him. Her hand was warm in his and he'd never felt so at peace, so in awe, so utterly in love with someone.

"Thank you," she whispered.

Their gazes locked and held for too long.

"It's your turn to tell the story tonight."

———

Rainer's head throbbed but he held fast to the doorframe of the booth, breathing through the pain, begging for context, tugging at the thread of the memory for more. At first, his mind resisted, afraid of something dark lurking there. His mind seemed to be protecting him from a terrible knowing. Even without actually remembering, he could feel the dread.

He pushed beyond the fear, yanked hard, and the memory came in a surge.

Even though he was remembering it perfectly, his vision was hazy, his body a riot of pain.

———

Rainer's skin burned and ached, blood trickling from lash wounds down his back, stinging in every bit of broken skin. He could barely lift his head, but he sensed Cecilia's dread in his chest, making him feel cold and desperate.

He looked up as Vincent dragged her in front of him, her eyes red-rimmed, salty tearstains down her cheeks. She looked wrecked and terrified, but most of all, she looked worried about him.

With deadly precision, Vincent cut through the strap of her gown and the front folded down to her waist, revealing her lacy mauve bustier.

Vincent clicked his tongue. "Would you look at that? It's like she was expecting me."

Several of the guards laughed. He roughly palmed one of her breasts, and she curled away from him until he pressed his blade to her throat. "Move again, and I'll have my men break the bones in your fiancé's fingers one by one. Hold still."

Impotent rage surged through Rainer. He could do nothing but watch that animal manhandle his fiancée. Cecilia held still, a faraway look in her eyes.

Rainer willed her to look at him, but she tilted her head up to the ceiling as if waiting for the worst to be over. He squirmed but the guards next to him forced him down and he groaned as his ravaged back hit the chair.

"Please stop," she whispered.

Vincent grinned. "I'll stop when you tell me what I want to know."

Rainer knew she would never tell. He was ready to do it. Rage pulsed through him but it was nothing compared to his fear for her.

Cecilia's gaze flitted to Xander and Rainer could practically read how mad she would be if Rainer went through all that torture and then gave it up. She'd never forgive him. But if he let her be hurt like this, he'd never forgive himself.

"I don't know," she whispered. "None of us do. Only Marcos knows for sure. We compartmentalized knowledge for this very reason. I would have told you when you were brutalizing Rainer if I knew."

Vincent paused, considering. "Perhaps you all truly don't know. Only one way to know for sure." He stood straighter. "Enough games, Xander. Be a king for once in your life. Be a leader and make the right choice. Tell me now, or I'm going to take her to the other room and find out what all the fuss is about, and I'm not going to be gentle. I'm going to fuck the information right out of her, and if that doesn't work, I'll let my men take turns until the truth comes out. There won't be anything left of her."

Cecilia swallowed hard. Rainer shook his head violently. He felt her trying to soothe him through the bond and he almost burst into tears. She was in trouble but she still wanted him to be okay. It was too much.

"Wards. We used wards," Rainer mumbled.

The shame of confessing was almost too much. Rainer was supposed to be a warrior, but Cecilia was the love of his life and he was bound to protect her. He'd made the mistake of not putting her first once before and he wouldn't do it again. If she wouldn't be selfish enough to save herself, he would do it for her. If it had just been his body that was ruined, he could take it, but she was the most precious thing in his world and he would not let her be hurt like that.

Rainer looked up expectantly but no one reacted. No one had heard him.

"Trying to give me pointers, McKay?" Vincent taunted.

The guards laughed.

"Very well," Vincent huffed. He shoved Cecilia into the arms of two guards, who dragged her kicking and screaming into the other room.

Vincent looked from Xander to Rainer. "If you thought I was rough with Rainer, you haven't seen anything yet. You won't even recognize her when you see her again."

Fury rose up in Rainer and he yanked against the guards, only managing to tip his chair, landing with a thud on the floor. Pain burst like his back was on fire and his vision went dark as the guards yanked his chair upright and sat him back, making him black out.

Cold, unrelenting fear surged through his bond with Cecilia, waking him from the void.

"One last chance," Vincent shouted.

Rainer tried to speak—nothing came out but a grunt.

He tried to send love through their bond, but Cecilia was too terrified to send anything through but ice-cold fear. He wanted her to know that he was there, that he was with her the whole time, but she was fighting him, trying to close him out so he wouldn't feel her.

She was still trying to protect him. Something in Rainer broke. He couldn't breathe. His chest was so tight he thought his heart might stop.

Then the screaming started. Never in his life had he heard her scream like that. Rainer struggled, but every time he moved, he shifted in and out of consciousness, so weak from pain that the guards didn't even bother holding him in the chair.

Every scream that echoed from the other room was like a lash on his soul. He tried to get up but fell on the floor and couldn't rise again. He lay there, fading in and out of consciousness, for what felt like an eternity. Every time his vision went dark, he saw her resigned, terrified face.

The cold stone floor scraped at his cheek as he prayed, tugging at their bond, trying to send her love but only finding room for her fear and pain. Physical pain. He'd been connected to her long enough to know the difference. He tried to pull the pain away from her; it was so hard when his body was wrecked, but he would take it if it meant she wouldn't feel so alone in this. His vision went dark and then brightened again. He tried to send her love, then faded into unconsciousness and dreamt of all the ways he'd kill Vincent.

Finally, after an eternity, there was stirring in the other room and the guards yanked Rainer up and into his seat. Vincent dragged Cecilia back into the room. Her dress was in tatters, her eyes wet with fresh tears. He tried to make eye contact, frantically tugging at their connection. He looked her over for injuries and his eyes snagged on blood dripping down her legs. He went blind with grief and rage.

———

Pressure crested in Rainer's head as more memories surged, though he could not seem to let go of the first one. It was the crack in the dam of his mind and everything else flooded in on the heels of the memory of that failure. He leaned against the wall, riding it out as the lost memories reconnected.

Rainer finally knew who he was.

He knew who Cecilia was.

Most importantly, he knew who Vincent Savero was—a fucking dead man.

39

XANDER

A horn blared at the back of the temple, bringing the chattering crowd to a hushed silence.

The herald lowered his instrument and bellowed so the entire temple could hear, "His Majesty, King Vincent Savero."

Xander's blood boiled as he watched Vincent walk down the center aisle, crushing rose petals underfoot as he nodded to his bowing subjects. Many nervous glances darted from Vincent to Xander.

Xander hoped his people would not expect him to be vindictive that they were doing what they must to survive. Their contempt was quiet, just barely noticeable in referring to Vincent as "Your Grace" instead of "Your Majesty." But Xander had seen enough to know that people feared Vincent more than they respected him.

He waited until the last possible moment to join in the homage, vowing it would be the last time he bowed to a madman. He clenched his jaw as he rose to his feet.

Vincent offered a smirk. "Cousin."

Xander gave a curt nod. He was rigid with anxiety. If their timing was off, things could go very wrong very fast. If every noble they expected to be on their side wasn't, it would be a mess. There were too many points of failure in the plan, but they didn't have a better one.

He had to have faith in his wife and his friends. Once again, the women in his life were saving his ass and he hoped it wouldn't become a regular thing. He loved being surrounded by strong women, but he didn't love needing saving.

King Damian had been a man of violence. What would Xander's people think of him attacking Vincent and his men to regain power? Would they think he was the same as the man who raised him?

Xander had no right to be king over anyone else. But when he looked up to the loft and saw the white rose waiting there, he knew that he owed his people peace. He owed his and Jessamin's child peace. And they owed him a real chance to do better and make Argaria a kingdom worth being proud of for people of all classes.

Long ago, Xander had made a vow to his dying brother that he would make things better, and he did not intend to break it. He just needed the chance to move the exceptionally slow, stubborn attitudes of the aristocracy. With the obstructions removed, he hoped it would be easier.

Xander just needed to get through the next few minutes and hoped that the element of surprise was enough to save his friends and his kingdom.

The music changed and Cece appeared at the end of the long aisle. It was hard to see her face since she was backlit. Her light blue dress brought to mind the memory of their wedding. Her right leg peeked out from the slit as she walked. Xander tried to meet her eyes but they weren't focused on him. They were locked on Rainer.

Rainer—who looked frozen, awestruck, speechless. The same way Xander had looked when she walked down the aisle to him. Only she wasn't coming down to meet Rainer. She was preceding his fiancée, Eloise.

Rainer swallowed hard. "Xander."

It was a whisper so soft Xander thought he imagined it until he heard it again.

"Xander, does she have a weapon?"

Xander blew out a disbelieving breath. "You're the one that was just up her dress. Where do you think she'd hide a weapon?"

Panic seized Xander, and suddenly, he worried that they'd missed a more important point of failure in their plan. Rainer had already killed Magdalena. He was perhaps moments from ruining the rest of them.

Cece took her spot on the bride's side of the altar, and although Rainer's gaze was fixed on her, she glanced to the back of the temple, waiting for Eloise. Cece's lower lip trembled and she blinked rapidly, trying to clear tears from her eyes. Suddenly, her gaze caught on someone in the crowd.

Xander searched for what she might have seen and his gaze snagged on Grimon and Samson sitting halfway back in the temple. His eye was drawn to the loft, where he spotted Sayla, goddess of the hunt, who wore full leather armor and a scowl that brought to mind all the tales of violent men going missing in her woods.

They'd sent Grimon a message and he had come through for them. Although the gods could only help for a short time, Xander would take whatever advantage he could get.

The doors at the end of the aisle closed and the temple went unbearably quiet. The whole room rose to their feet and turned to face the closed doors—the whole room except Cece, whose gaze was fixed on Rainer, and Rainer, who was staring right back.

Xander glanced at Isla, who was seated in the front row. She gave him a regal and reassuring nod. She wasn't his true queen, but she definitely had the act down and looked downright sinful in a deep burgundy dress that hugged her ample curves. She was as tempting as she was absolutely sick of his nonsense.

The musicians began to play, the song swelled, and the doors opened. Eloise appeared in a ridiculously large red ball gown that was nearly too wide for the entryway. As she began to walk down the aisle, three attendants scrambled to adjust the dress's train.

Xander prayed to every god he could think of that their plan would work.

"Don't react," Rainer whispered. His eyes were fixed on Eloise and his mouth barely moved. Xander wouldn't have heard it without his enhanced hearing. "Xander. I remember." Rainer took a deep breath. "I remember everything and I'm going to fucking kill him."

Xander fixed his face into a stoic stare toward the back of the church, but out of the corner of his eye he could see Rainer's hands fisted at his sides.

"Don't do anything rash. We have a plan and I'm counting on you not fucking it up," Xander said, smiling as if nothing was amiss. "There's a sword under the first row of pews on the left. The signal is when the priestess hands the book of vows over to Vincent."

Rainer nodded, his gaze darting to Vincent on his throne at the back of the altar.

Vincent must have read his sudden shift in mood because he strode down from his seat of honor behind the altar and clapped a hand on Rainer's shoulder.

"Is everything well?" he asked, looking suspiciously between the two. "Not getting cold feet, are we?"

Rainer was not doing a good job of composing his face. He looked positively murderous.

"I was just saying how lovely Eloise's finer assets look in that dress," Xander said. "I'm afraid I've ignored McKay's delicate sensibilities."

The lie was easy. He'd spent so much time antagonizing Rainer over the past two years and that came with a unique understanding of how Rainer's mind worked.

Vincent clicked his tongue. "Now, now, I think you've picked his pocket of a woman one too many times for such a joke."

Eloise was halfway down the aisle, walking comically slowly, clearly relishing being the center of attention. Her gaze passed over each guest as if daring them to challenge her pending union. As if everyone in the room didn't know the story of the most romantic man in the two kingdoms.

Finally, Eloise reached the altar and took her place next to Rainer. Her attendants fluttered around her, adjusting her train until it lay perfectly.

Mika stepped forward in her disguise as head priestess. Thanks to Cato's help, she looked flawless, but the half-smile she offered Xander was a dead giveaway.

Vincent stepped up beside her. "Welcome, my loyal subjects. I am happy to be here for this special occasion. My finest swordsman is joining his hand with that of one of the greatest and oldest Argarian households. I am happy to be here to concelebrate this occasion."

He cast a mocking grin at Cece, who despite knowing their plan looked completely shattered. Xander caught her gaze and she forced a tight smile.

Vincent nodded to Mika. "Priestess, let's begin."

Mika opened the book of ceremony and began to speak. Xander could not concentrate on her words. The tension in his body was too profound. He repeated the steps of their plan in his head.

Grant lurked several paces behind Vincent, his gaze scanning the crowd for any sign of trouble. The guard glanced at Cece and smiled.

Xander hated that fucker. Vincent might have been the one who cut his initials into Cece's leg, but Grant was the one who held her down.

Xander forced his gaze not to stray to the post above the crowd where he hoped Jessamin was still hidden. If anyone moved too soon, their cover would be blown, but this was the hardest part of any surprise attack—waiting until the trap was sprung.

As soon as Mika handed the book of vows to Vincent, Xander would grab the short sword stowed in the giant bouquet of flowers on his side of the altar and Cece would grab her set from the one on her side. Mika would have her shot at Vincent, and Cece would have her chance at Grant. Isla would have Xander's back against Vincent's main contingent of guards. But there was a chance they'd underestimated how many guards Vincent would have patrolling nearby. If their timing was off, Xander's group of barely trained priestesses would not hold up against Vincent's army of battle-hardened hunters.

Xander reviewed the plan over and over in his mind, the way he had with swordplay techniques when he first started hunter training.

Sweat dripped down his back, his palms growing clammy. He itched for a weapon.

Isla shifted in her seat, running a hand down her knife-filled bodice. Just the sight of her centered him. He smiled at her and took a deep breath. Gods above, she was beautiful. He wished he felt certain that she wouldn't take her first chance to leave—that he hadn't blown his chance with her. Xander had taken his best shot and he could at least be at peace with that, but he was ever the optimist. Even after all the disappointment in his life, he held out hope that he could win her over.

Xander was so focused on her he nearly missed the signal.

Mika handed the heavy leather book to Vincent and yanked a dagger from her sleeve. Vincent's eyes went wide as she slammed it between his ribs, twisting with sadistic satisfaction in her eyes.

Mika pulled the dagger out and blood poured from the wound in Vincent's chest. "That was for Ivy." She plunged her blade in again. "And this is for Magdalena."

Before she could get the blade out, Vincent had unsheathed his dagger. He stabbed it into her side and fell back onto the floor, clutching at his chest.

Cece screamed and darted past Xander, her vengeance on Grant forgotten. She kicked Vincent's dagger from his hand and knelt on his chest, thrusting her wrist with the Unsummoner bracelet toward him.

"Take it off and I'll fix you," she said insistently.

Vincent narrowed his eyes at her.

"I'm the closest and I've healed wounds like this before," she said. "No doubt you've seen Xander's scar."

Xander knelt beside them, blades at the ready, afraid at any moment Vincent might toss her off.

"His first," Cece said, nodding to Xander's wrist.

Vincent hesitated, but Cece dug a knee into the wound in his side and he relented with a grunt. He wrapped his hand around Xander's bracelet and mumbled some words. A moment later, the bracelet slid free and landed on the marble floor with a loud clang.

Xander's magic rushed back to him all at once. His ears popped and his body buzzed with energy; he felt the soft hum of every storm coming through the mountain pass.

Vincent removed Cece's Unsummoner bracelet. She immediately punched him in the face and raced over to Mika, bringing her hands to her wound and pressing her power into it.

The room had erupted into full-blown chaos. Their small army sprang into action, resulting in mass confusion. Most of Vincent's guards were so shocked they didn't realize who was attacking until they'd been struck with a killing blow.

The tide seemed to be turning for Xander. Then, a group of Vincent's men poured in from the far side of the room.

Maren, Jessamin, and Sayla did their best to hinder the onslaught of men to help the rest of their friends regroup, but the priestesses weren't schooled in battle tactics. Once their initial tasks were completed, they stood wide-eyed, looking around the room.

Evan ran into the fray, trying to direct the priestesses, and Sylvie used earth magic to grow roots around their attackers' legs to slow them down.

The side doors of the temple burst open and another group of Vincent's guards charged in. Sylvie and Evan turned toward them, ready to cut them off before they met the crowd.

Xander's heart leapt into his throat. He wanted to back them up but was torn between going to help them and staying close to Isla.

Blinding golden light poured into the room, filling the whole front of the temple with a fierce glow that made Xander squint. When the brilliance receded, a tall woman with tawny skin and a wheat crown atop a head of dark curls stood at the center of the altar. Her golden dress shimmered in the light pouring through the temple windows.

The whole room seemed to have frozen, the entire group stunned to silence by the ethereal presence of Aurelia, goddess of fertility and the harvest.

Xander held his breath, afraid she might smite all of them, but then her gaze narrowed on the contingent of Vincent's guards standing shocked just inside the doorway.

"You dare to enter my temple with your filthy hands and your men who rape and pillage these lands and leave the fields barren and burned," Aurelia said.

She turned and locked eyes with Xander. She walked toward him slowly, her golden dress trailing behind her. Xander held perfectly still as she approached.

She nodded. "Your Majesty."

Xander's heartbeat kicked up. The goddess of the harvest, whose temple they were standing in, had just acknowledged him as the rightful king of Argaria in front of the most influential people in the kingdom.

She winked at him and turned her gaze on Vincent's men, who were in formation near the side doors. A guard at the front of the group frowned and winced. His hands flew to his groin and his eyes went wide.

"That which was fertile in you will decompose into nothing. Those among you who have stolen from the women who I shelter here—you are rotten and so you will rot."

The group began to writhe, all of them grabbing at their groins before doubling over. Their faces went purple, veins beneath their skin growing black, then green, as they collapsed one by one until all that remained was a solitary guard who turned and fled.

"I thought your power was about fertility," Xander said.

The goddess smiled a wicked smile. "It is. But I can also make things barren and rotten if I so choose."

Xander startled at a loud clap behind him. He spun, his short swords ready.

Samson leaned against the throne atop the altar. "Aury, you've outdone yourself," he said, crossing the altar and kissing Aurelia on the cheek.

She waved a hand as if it was nothing. "I'm saving my energy for the rest of his army. These ones just happened to come to me first in my house of power, and that was a slight I could not abide."

455

A new cluster of Vincent's men poured in the side door, stepping over the bodies of their fallen comrades.

Aurelia nodded to Samson. "Care to lend a hand, dear?"

Samson's grin grew wolfish. "It would be my pleasure." He strutted toward the guards, who drew their weapons and then, as if sensing the power of his aura, froze. Samson walked right up to the first man and poked his nose. "Boop."

Xander watched, waiting for the next horror to be unleashed.

The men shifted, waiting for Samson's magic to take effect, but there was no moaning, no crumpling to the ground. They stood tall, looking at each other and then at Samson as he tapped each of them one at a time.

Samson rounded on them and grinned. "Can you feel it? All that bloodlust is gone. So is the pleasure of enjoying good food, a good fight, a good fuck. You'll find no pleasure in anything ever again. That's what you get for being men who take what does not belong to you."

The men stared at him, looking almost apathetic. One by one, they dropped their weapons and stumbled out of the temple.

Samson turned toward Xander, placed a fist over his heart, and bowed. "Your Majesty."

Xander was too stunned to speak. Two gods had recognized him as the rightful king in a matter of minutes.

Samson winked and the edges of his body grew blurry before he disappeared.

Xander strained against the noise in the temple and heard pounding footsteps: another incoming contingent of Vincent's men. He turned back to survey the chaos on the altar. Cece had helped Mika to safety and was brandishing her short swords against two of Vincent's guards. Rainer was beating back two more on the far side of the altar.

Two men charged at Xander and he brought his short swords up to fend them off. This was a thing he knew—the choreography of a dance he'd done so many times. He loved this—not the violence so much as the way he learned to read a fighter, to see their subtle tells, and to win. It was good to show his people that he was not beat yet. That he was here to fight—for them and for his place as king.

Perhaps that was what separated him from the kings that came before him. They had fought to keep the throne, but Xander fought to earn it.

Xander blocked the first guard's blows and spun to shove his blade through a gap in the second guard's armor. The guard stumbled away and Xander spun back to fight the first.

He made short work of the men and then finally allowed himself a glance at the loft in the back of the room where Jessamin and Maren stood with their bows drawn. Beside them, a fearsome-looking Goddess Sayla had dark paint smeared around her eyes and looked more vengeful huntress than protector of the forest as she shot arrows with terrifying precision.

Xander waved to them and pointed toward the doors right as another group of Vincent's men poured in, stepping over the rotten bodies of their predecessors. Jessamin, Maren, and Sayla rained arrows on the men. Only a few slipped through their barrage and were quickly met with Isla's blades.

Xander watched, mesmerized, as she ducked and swiped and cut her way through the men two at a time. She was murderous and magnificent, her movements swift, vicious, efficient. She wasted nothing; her focus was uncanny and she cut through every man who came at her with a brutal efficiency that Xander had never seen anyone wield. He was grateful to have her on his side.

He started toward her to help when movement to his left caught his eye. Cece stumbled away from Grant. She blocked one strike and spun away from him, swiping her short sword along his side, leaving a long line in his leather armor.

She turned to face Grant again. He had the look of a cat playing with its dinner and Cece looked exhausted. On top of losing weight over the past month and the fatigue of being vigilant all the time, she'd used a lot of magic healing Mika and it showed in her form.

Xander took one last glance at Isla, who looked as fresh as if she'd just started fighting. Then, he charged toward Cece. Grant must have felt him coming because he blocked Xander's first blow with his gauntlet. Xander punched Grant in the face with his other hand and the guard reeled backward, hitting the back of his head on the arm of the marble throne and falling to the floor, unconscious.

A soft cry behind Xander made his blood run cold. He whipped his gaze to Isla. Blood dripped down her left side, but she was still fighting, surrounded by six of Vincent's men. She moved like she wasn't wounded, but Xander saw red.

He darted toward her, running his blade through two of the men in quick succession. Isla ignored him, continuing to fight off four men alone. Xander could tell she was growing tired, her movements slower, her breathing more ragged. Two more men came up behind her.

Xander didn't think. He jumped in front of them. The larger of the guards lifted his sword high and brought it down hard. Xander threw up his short swords just in time to break the blow.

It cost him; the second man sliced along his side. Xander winced. He countered, swiftly cutting the man's throat.

The move left him open a second too long, but Isla was there, breaking a wild swipe from the larger man and cutting across his throat with her curved blade.

She caught Xander's eye, looking a mix of shocked and furious, but he just kept fighting.

"I have it covered," she snapped. "Go help Evan."

He didn't want to leave Isla, but he didn't dare argue with her. He needed to trust her, so he shoved a guard back and set his sights on Evan and Sylvie, who were midway down the center aisle, trying to handle an onslaught of Vincent's men pouring in the back of the temple.

Xander had thought with Aurelia and Samson's help the tide might be turning, but it was impossible to tell and the element of surprise was gone now.

He was breathless when he reached Evan and Sylvie. They worked together, Sylvie ripping men apart with vicious thorny vines grown from the roses along the aisle and Evan and Xander cutting down anyone who made it past her brambles.

Xander's arms grew heavy and sweat slicked his back. He didn't know how many more men they could fight off.

A loud commotion broke out at the back of the temple, and at first, Xander couldn't see anything but smoke. When it cleared, Grimon strutted down the center aisle toward Xander. He came face to face with a bumbling Edward Spellman. The god of death grinned at the traitor and in quick motion Edward's skin went gray and cracked. He blinked rapidly as his body turned to dust before their eyes.

Xander stared in both shock and horror as the traitor became nothing more than a pile of ash. "You can turn people to dust?"

Grimon smirked. "Only a few at a time."

"I suppose I should stay on your good side," Xander said, cutting down a guard who charged at them.

"Bold of you to assume you've ever been on my good side," Grimon countered.

"I thought I was growing on you."

Grimon shrugged a shoulder. "Not *that* much." He touched another guard, who took two steps forward before he disintegrated. The god of death paused, his gaze locking with Aurelia where she stood in golden splendor on the altar.

"Don't give me that look," she said, but the hint of a satisfied smirk on her face suggested she didn't mind the attention.

Grimon licked his lips. "What look?"

"The look that says you're regretting your past foolishness," Aurelia said.

"Strange—I'm struggling to recall any foolishness when you look so stunning," Grimon replied.

"Good thing I have a good enough memory for both of us," the goddess said with a wink.

Grimon smirked at Aurelia. "Glad you have the reminder of what you're missing. I'm happy to remind you again—later."

"Can you focus, please?" Xander said, exasperated that the gods had time to flirt mid-battle.

The god turned and set his sights on a cowering Eloise, trembling behind the edge of a nearby pew. Her dress was in tatters, her hair wild, and her eyes full of tears.

"Please," she blubbered, falling to her knees.

Grimon studied her. "What do you think, Xander?"

Wisdom dictated that Xander should just have her killed. But he didn't want to be like Vincent or King Damian. He wanted to be better.

"I'll banish her. To the eastern wastes or Aldrena or anywhere beyond. She may go and make better of her life, but she won't do it with any of her family resources. The entire Spellman family will be stripped of their titles and their riches and banished from Argaria and its allies."

Eloise's eyes went wide and watery and he knew that the punishment was perhaps worse to her than death. Deep down, he'd known enough about Eloise to suspect she might feel that way, but maybe in time she'd see it for what it was—a generous gift from a man who had enough blood on his hands.

"You'll take care of the rest of the traitors on my council?" Xander asked.

Grimon's smile turned wicked and his eyes glowed with power. "With pleasure." He cast a glance over his shoulder at Xander. "Your Majesty."

He stalked past Xander toward the group of remaining nobles.

The army of priestesses had taken out most of the men, but a few more talented fighters still stood.

Xander began to assess the damage. It seemed they were making headway, but the room had erupted in such chaos it was hard to tell. From where he stood, Xander could see a few of the temple women were wounded, though none of them seemed to be in critical condition.

The temple finally settled. Most of the innocent bystanders had fled, but those who had cowered under the pews began to poke their heads out.

"Xander!" Cece's panicked voice cut through the din of the crowd. She ran to Xander, patting down his body, her wild blue eyes growing wide when she saw the gash on his forearm and side.

He shooed her away. "Just scratches, love. Save your energy."

The crease in her brow smoothed and she grinned. "Getting rusty, Your Grace?"

"Just being the reckless idiot you know me to be—"

His attention snagged on Isla and everything else faded away.

She looked like a goddess of war, the hem of her dress soaked in blood, a hand poised on the blade at her waist, and her murderous gaze locked on Xander. She closed the distance between them and slapped him across the face.

He rubbed his jaw. "That was not the thanks I was expecting."

"If you ever step between me and an opponent again, I'll gut you myself," she said, her voice wavering.

Xander threw his hands up in frustration. "You were fighting six men, Isla. Six! I do not doubt your ability, but that's excessive. I was protecting you."

"Protecting me?" She blew out a great, shuddering breath. "You would have broken me."

Then she grabbed him by the tunic and pulled his mouth to hers.

The kiss nearly took Xander's knees out with its fierceness. He dropped his blade, shoved a hand into her hair, and wrapped an arm around her waist. Isla felt so good there, bloody from battle, kissing him like she was a moment from absconding with him to some dark corner of the temple. Everything about it felt right. Because Isla wasn't kissing him like he was a casual fling or like they were only lovers—she was kissing him with the sort of mad desperation reserved for something far greater.

When she finally pulled away, he was breathless.

Isla leaned her forehead against his. "It would have broken me because I love you."

Xander grinned.

"Wipe that smug smile off your face or I'll stop," she said.

He smiled wider. "If you could, you would have already. I told you I would get you, darling, and I always hit my mark."

She shook her head, smiling despite herself. "As long as I get to hit mine back."

Xander rubbed his jaw. "Didn't think you'd be so literal." He drew back to meet her eye, the question on his tongue nearly too heavy to utter. He hesitated, afraid of the weight of it, afraid of her denial, afraid to fall once more with no one there to catch him. "Does this mean you'll accept my offer? Be my partner?"

"We can discuss it," Isla said.

A startled laugh burst out of him. There she was, negotiating for what she wanted.

A throat cleared behind them. Xander turned and came face to face with Cato. His hand flew to the dagger on his belt on instinct. The memory of the trickster god plunging a blade into his heart was as fresh as if it had just happened.

Cato held up his hands. "Easy there. I'm on your side, remember?" His shirt sleeve was torn, blood seeping from a wound on his forearm and his cheek was mottled with the first hint of a slow spreading bruise. "Congratulations on a battle well fought, *Your Majesty*."

When Xander didn't respond, Cato rolled his eyes. "My blessing has greater impact if you act as if you expected it." With that, he turned and walked back down the temple aisle and out the back doors.

Xander glanced around the room. Most of the fighting had ceased, since their friends and the gods had dispatched most, if not all, of Vincent's men. Aurelia had spirited away but he suspected she'd be back for the remainder of Vincent's men. All of them except Grant, who was standing face to face with Rainer.

Xander was pretty sure from the vicious look on Rainer's face that he didn't need or want any help.

Rainer swung his sword high and struck a brutal blow upon

Grant. Grant broke the strike, spinning to the side, but Rainer just kept walking toward him.

"You held down the love of my life so that Vincent could hurt her, and then you taunted her for months," Rainer barked, his voice unrecognizable with rage. "You took pleasure in her pain."

He swung again. Grant was fully on his heels. He slipped in a puddle of blood and stumbled backward.

Rainer plunged his sword into Grant's side, twisting the blade before pulling it out.

"You made her live in fear that the same thing could happen again," Rainer barked, plunging the blade into Grant's stomach.

Grant let out a wet gurgle as blood bubbled on his lips.

Rainer yanked his sword free. "Vincent is a monster and a manipulator. But you knew better and you let him hurt people anyway. And that makes you worse. You made her live in fear, but now, *you* get to be afraid."

Grant crumpled to his knees, fell sideways to the hard marble floor, and rolled to his back. Rainer towered over him, eyes full of menace, and pressed the tip of his sword to Vincent's crest at the center of his leather breastplate. He pushed the blade so slowly, making sure that Grant felt every painful inch, that he lived through as much pain as possible, until finally the tip of the blade hit the floor. Grant's eyes went wide and he gave one last wet, shuddering breath before he went still.

Rainer stood over Grant's body, panting, waiting, as if to make sure the guard didn't rise again.

"Well, that was definitive," Isla whispered from just behind Xander.

Several feet away, Vincent was crawling toward the marble throne, a smear of blood trailing behind him. Xander took a step toward him, ready to finish the job. But Rainer's hand came to his shoulder.

"Allow me."

Rainer marched over to Vincent and kicked his side. Vincent groaned and rolled onto his back, slashing at Rainer with his dagger, but Rainer just kicked it away. He stomped down, pinning Vincent's wrist to the ground.

"Is this the hand you used to hold her down? To hurt her?" Rainer growled.

Vincent was wheezing. His face was scrunched, body braced.

Rainer didn't wait for a response. He delivered a swift blow, severing Vincent's right hand from his body.

Vincent screamed in agony, dragging Xander's attention back to the bloody scene. Rainer was unmoved. He pressed a boot to the king's chest, ignoring the blood rapidly spreading beneath the usurper's body. Rainer dragged his blade to Vincent's groin and pushed it in slowly.

Vincent howled. The whole temple stilled, every gaze in the room narrowing on the false king and the guardian standing over him.

Rainer lifted his blade. "Enjoy your afterlife."

Vincent's face paled. Rainer's sword whistled through the air and beheaded Vincent.

Rainer blew out a breath, his hands shaking, cheeks still red with fury. He turned slowly and met Xander's gaze, his face splattered with blood and lit with the kind of anger that Xander had never seen in him.

"Feel better?" Xander asked.

Rainer wiped his face on his sleeve and searched the room for Cece. His eyes were manic. He pressed his hand to his chest and frantically surveyed the crowd.

"I can't feel her," he said. "I've never needed to look for her. I've always just known where she is."

Xander pointed to Cece and Rainer's shoulders relaxed when he saw her.

"The reunion will have to wait," Xander said, nodding toward the restless crowd. "Watch my back while I address the room?"

Rainer hesitated, his gaze locked on Cece. After a moment, he nodded, stepping up to Xander's left shoulder just as Jessamin shoved her way through the crowd. She tore free of the crush, a bow in hand, the quiver strapped to her back nearly empty of arrows. She ran to

Xander with Maren, Evan, and Sylvie on her heels. All of their disguises had worn off, leaving them with their true faces.

Xander pulled Jessamin into a hug before drawing away to look her over for injury. "Are you well?"

She frowned, clearly offended by the question. "I am a warrior. Of course I'm well and I'll not have you fussing as much as Maren, for goddesses' sake."

Xander bit back his smirk. "Well enough to address our people?"

Jessamin grinned and brushed her hand down her leather breastplate. "I'm hardly dressed for it."

"I must disagree. I think you look perfect," Xander said. He held out his arm and his wife threaded her hand through it. Together, they turned to face the crowd.

The murmurs of the survivors had reached a fever pitch, and no one seemed ready to settle.

Isla, poised at Xander's right shoulder, leaned closer. "You'll have to get their attention."

Xander smiled. For the first time in weeks, he stretched his power wide, reaching up into the sky and drawing down a storm. Joy crested in his chest at the return of the familiar magic that had been such a huge part of his identity for so long.

He feared the long absence of his power would make the work difficult, but it returned like muscle memory for a swordsmanship drill, the fronts bending to his command and threading together to form a swirling cloud. He could not see the storm, but the bright reflections the stained-glass windows cast on the walls turned darker and the crowd began to quiet.

A gust of wind blew the doors in and Xander unleashed a loud crack of thunder that shook the temple walls.

Xander was not just half royal blood. He was the sum of all his actions and intentions. He was the man who had risked his life behind enemy lines to find the Lost God. He was the man who'd drawn this kingdom back from the grips of war. He was the man who'd fought from the inside to keep his people safe and take back what was rightfully his not by blood, but by honor.

"I am Alexander Maxwell Savero, the rightful king of Argaria. Bend a knee now or leave my kingdom."

Another loud clash of thunder shook the temple and the crowd flinched. Then, slowly, in a ripple from the front of the room to the back, they lowered to their knees.

Evan looked like he might fall over from relief, but he was smiling a wide-open grin that Xander hadn't seen since his wedding. Sylvie was beside him, a hint of a smile on her face. She gave Xander a stern nod of approval.

Isla leaned forward and whispered in his ear, "It's about time, Your Majesty."

Xander smirked and eased the storm, unraveling the symphony he'd created as simply as one might tug a rogue thread on a scarf. The temple brightened as the storm lifted.

"You may rise."

The crowd slowly rose to their feet.

"We have a long way to go to rebuild, and change is never easy, but from here we rebuild. Jessamin and I vow never to forget who we serve—not just those in this room, but all of those in this land. We remain your humble servants in building a new, more equitable Argaria."

Some of the stunned guests slowly trickled out of the temple, leaving behind blood, bodies, and an enormous mess for the priestesses to clean up. But many of the people lingered to see what would happen between the fairy tale duo who remained at the front of the room.

Cece stood staring at Rainer and, no matter how much Xander might have wanted to fix this for his friends, what was left to be mended could only be tended by the two of them.

40

CECILIA

Rainer's sword hit the marble floor with a deafening clang.

Panic rushed through Cecilia's blood at the sound. He had never dropped a weapon like that. There were only two reasons a warrior laid down his sword: when he was dead, or when he'd lost the will to fight.

She was frozen in fear as she frantically scanned him for injury. But there were no wounds in need of tending.

Cecilia's heart pounded as he walked toward her with certainty in his eyes. That was when she knew. He hadn't laid down his sword because he could no longer hold it. He'd let it go because he'd fought his last battle.

The relief of knowing that almost brought her to her knees.

He looked like vengeance felt—monstrous and perfect. But Rainer had looked pain and loss in the face and hadn't let it turn him into a monster—or, rather, it had forged him into *her* monster.

Rainer's hands and forehead were speckled with blood. He pulled a handkerchief from his pocket and wiped his face with it. His green eyes settled on her, assessing, looking her over for injuries in such a painfully familiar way it made her chest ache. She knew that panicked, wild look, but was terrified to believe he was truly in full guardian mode.

Facing him after all this time—after he had hated her, after he'd dragged her into the meditation booth and twisted her in knots with fear and desire, after she'd fought a battle without feeling him in her chest—Cecilia was afraid to look too closely and know that he still didn't remember.

Because if Rainer didn't know her now, it meant that she'd done too much, gone too deep, and ruined his mind and years of beautiful memories for good.

The thought was unbearable. It felt like the entire temple was holding its breath, all of their friends poised to see if he was finally on their side.

"Cece." His voice was so gentle that she took a step back, putting distance between them, her knees suddenly weak.

She didn't want to be too close when he didn't remember. She didn't want to be within reaching distance when her heart was broken. The closer she was, the harder it would be to put on a brave face.

"I remember," Rainer said. "I remember you."

The words were a lightning strike. Her heart, already pounding from the adrenaline of the fight, beat harder, trying to escape the prison of her ribs. She was afraid she might not survive a fall from such perilous heights, afraid he would have a charcoal outline of their lives but never enough to fill in the color.

Tears blurred her vision. "Prove it."

"Three times."

"What?"

"Three times you've asked me what I wished for when we watched the Summer Firestorm meteor shower during our last Gauntlet run. But each time I've refused to answer."

Cecilia stared at him, hands trembling.

He smiled, his eyes looking brighter and clearer than they had in weeks. "I remember exactly what I wished for that night."

Cecilia couldn't breathe, certain that if she dared to feel relief it would be ripped away from her the moment she believed.

But Rainer looked *certain*. His face was full of love and fear instead of anger and confusion as it had been for weeks.

"That night I looked at you in the dark and I was so breathless with love for you, as always," he sighed, shaking his head. "You aren't supposed to be shocked by someone's beauty when you've beheld it every day for years. But you looked at that meteor shower with such wonder, even though we'd seen the same thing every year our whole lives. And I was struck by just how lovely and hopeful you were and I thought, *I will love Cecilia Reznik until the stars fall. And if all those stars rained down I'd use every one to wish for the same thing.*"

Several of the women in the front row gasped and Cecilia felt suddenly self-conscious that so many people were bearing witness to such an intimate moment.

Rainer took a step toward her. "That's where the idea for your story came from. I looked back up at the sky and I picked the brightest one. I repeated the wish I'd made every year since I knew what I wanted more than anything else. I wished to make all my wishes beside you. To weave all my stories with yours. I wished for all my good and bad days to be spent beside you, sharing the joys and burdens. I wished to spend every night for the rest of my life watching the stars blur while holding your hand."

Cecilia blinked away the burning in her eyes.

"I've wanted to tell you every day since, but I didn't for fear it wouldn't come true," Rainer continued. "But now there is no rule, no villain, no duty, and no magic that will keep me from you. I've known you were for me since the first moment I laid eyes on you and now I'd like to take you home and make it official."

Cecilia closed the space between them at a sprint and threw herself into his arms. The crowd in the temple broke into hushed murmurs.

"Please say that I can touch you," Rainer whispered into her hair.

"Yes," she mumbled. "But get me out of here because I don't want to cry in front of half the kingdom."

Rainer wrapped his arms around her and walked out the side door of the temple.

Outside, the rush of city noise felt far away, muted by the snowy temple gardens. The sugared greenery passed in a blur through her teary eyes as Rainer carried her. He ducked around the side of the building into the temple yard, hidden away from the door by trellises covered in ivy and a snow-covered willow tree. He ducked beneath the tree's shelter and sat on a bench with her in his lap.

"Is this real?" she rasped. Her chest was clotted with relief and grief and joy and she couldn't get any other words out.

"I'm sorry it took me so long. Cece, you've been so brave, but you don't have to be brave anymore," Rainer whispered, smoothing her hair.

Her whole body shook with sobs. Rainer was so gentle with her. Stroking her hair, tucking her face into his neck. He murmured in her ear, "I could never forget you, Cece. Not for long. I was afraid to remember because of what happened right before. I felt this aching guilt I didn't understand."

"I did that," she croaked. "I knew your guilt would bury it, but you really made me sweat it."

Rainer shook his head, his eyes bright with pain. "I failed you. I'm so sorry that I couldn't stop him from hurting you that day. I—"

"No." She made him meet her teary eyes. "You fought so hard. You were barely conscious but I felt you trying to reach me." She swallowed hard, not knowing how to explain herself.

No matter how Magdalena and Mika had tried to train it out of her, Cecilia still felt like she was having an extreme reaction to something that wasn't that bad. She'd done her best to unwind the thorny feelings, rip them from her insides to make it make sense, but Rainer could never fully understand, and she wasn't sure she wanted him to.

"Rain, he didn't do what you think. He just wanted you and Xander to think he did." She swallowed hard. "He just cut my thigh and broke my hand. He didn't—" The word had weight she was glad she didn't have to carry but was still hard to say. "He didn't hurt me that way. Just emotionally."

Fury tore over Rainer's face. "He touched you when and where you didn't wish to be touched, and while I'm glad it did not go that far, I won't downplay what you've been through or how it's affected you." He shook his head and the crease between his brows softened.

She loved Rainer so much for the way he understood her, for the way he could be both fierce and gentle at the same time.

"I was terrified," she whispered. "I've never felt so stupid and helpless and humiliated. My body didn't fight. I was just frozen."

He kissed her temple. "You were afraid. You can't blame yourself. You have nothing to be ashamed of."

Rainer tilted her chin up and she tried to keep her lower lip from trembling. It was such a relief to hear those words from his mouth. She could not feel him in her chest, but she felt the conviction in his words.

"I'm sorry I wasn't there," he said.

She met his gaze, his eyes glassy with unshed tears. "You were. You were with me the whole time. I felt you trying to tell me—" Her voice broke and she took a shuddering breath. "I felt you trying to tell me that I wasn't alone. I was so relieved and also I wanted to protect you from it."

The moment was burned in her brain. It was an act of love more profound than her placing the dagger in his hands on the beach and taking his place in death. She'd made that decision out of selfishness, but Rainer had been thinking only of her when he fought to keep their connection open. He'd been in so much pain, but still he fought to take hers—to remind her that he was there, that he always would be. He'd held her suspended, all her love and terror anchored through their bond. Rainer offered her something to hold on to when she was slipping away.

Cecilia clung to him, trying and failing to pull together words to express how much it meant to her that he'd done that and then relived it all over again to get his memories back.

"I'll keep you safe now. We're going home," Rainer whispered.

Cecilia collapsed against him, her relief so intense all her muscles went lax at once, his comfort soothing away her tension.

Rainer squeezed her tighter. "I missed you so much, even if I didn't know what I was missing. I'm taking you home and I'm not leaving your side for the next year. I don't care how annoyed you get."

She laughed, so relieved that she could finally talk about it—Rainer remembering on his own must have broken the bargain.

"I really thought you were going to marry someone else—that you wanted to. How do you remember?"

Rainer met her eyes. "I told you that I wouldn't be able to forget you and I couldn't. I told you I'd fall in love with you again and I did." He looked away. "I don't remember everything. There are holes in the story. But I remember the first time I saw you. I remember the day we were bonded and our first kiss. I remember the forest and the poison arrows, the beach and the dagger. I remember a hundred times your courage amazed me. Maybe in time I'll remember the rest little by little."

She kissed him frantically. "I'll help you remember. Every time we find a gap in your memory I will color it in. Can I ask you something?"

Rainer swallowed hard and nodded.

"Why did you never tell me who your birth father was?" she asked, cupping his face in her hands.

Rainer flushed and looked away. "I was embarrassed. He was so brave and I'm so terrified all the time. I couldn't even face the memory of you being hurt—I almost married someone I didn't care about because of it. I wanted to prove that I was worthy of Zelden Novaris's legacy. How could I face you, the most courageous person I know, and admit that I fell so short?" He shook his head. "When Vincent had you in his arms, I confessed how we avoided Cato's influence to save you, but no one heard me. I have always been weak. I didn't want to live in my father's shadow, but I still managed to put myself there in my own mind."

Rainer had always had such a warped view of himself, but his admission left Cecilia breathless. "You don't think Zelden—your father—would be proud? You've always protected me. You got me through the Gauntlet in one piece."

"Barely," Rainer said morosely.

"But you did. More importantly, you kept me together mentally, Rainer. You've collected all the pieces each time I've fallen apart and helped me put myself back together. You've been so gentle with me—loving me even when I made it difficult. I think he would be proud of your kindness—the way you know when to fight, when to push on, and when to surrender. Just because you're not standing on the front lines against the god of war doesn't mean you fall short."

"I didn't even save you today," Rainer said.

Cecilia smiled at him. "You save me every day. You're saving me right now."

She kissed him, soft and slow, and everything slid back into place. His hands cradled her face, trembling as he tenderly brought her back into her body one kiss at a time. When he touched her, she didn't want to wither up. She didn't want to run. She wanted more.

Little by little her body warmed. A stirring in her chest made her pull away. It was as if the frayed ends of the bond still wrapped around her heart were waking up.

She drew back leaning her forehead against his. "You laid down your sword."

Rainer nodded. "It was time I stop fighting for someone else's cause. If I'm going to fight, it will be for myself."

Pride swelled in Cecilia's chest.

Rainer looked relieved but still sad. "I know I'm still missing so much."

"Like what?"

He ran a hand through his hair. "I don't remember most of our last Gauntlet trip."

She placed a hand on his cheek and closed her eyes, brushing gently against his mind. At first he flinched, no doubt from the memory of the last time she'd taken so much from him. But then the fear passed and he let her in.

Cecilia pulled up the memory of their argument in the woods right before they split up, when she'd wanted him to love her so badly but he would not so much as kiss her. The next day they'd separated for the first time ever, which had led to Rainer's capture and her and Xander falling in love.

But it wasn't until she'd taken the memory from him months before that she'd felt his desperation in that moment. He'd wanted her just as badly, perhaps even more than she'd wanted him, but he was terrified of losing her.

They watched the whole event play out. Cecilia's advances, Rainer's rejection, and their eventual parting ways.

For so long Cecilia's magic had been in service to everyone else. Now it felt like she was reclaiming it. She had yet to fully reclaim her body and mind, but once again her magic felt like her own.

She'd forgotten what it felt like to watch a memory simply because it was dear to her. She'd forgotten the intimacy of sharing it with someone else until Rainer blinked his eyes open and looked at her with so much love.

"You kept me," he whispered.

"I did."

He swallowed hard. "It's a lot to hold."

"It's a gift to hold. What a joy to hold the memories of the one you love, the roots of their story."

"I hate that I can't feel you. It reminds me—" His voice broke. "It reminds me of when you died."

"I could still feel you then," she said. "I hate that I can't now."

The feeling stirred again in her chest, like leaves reaching toward the sun.

"Raven Whitewind told me it would come back," Cecilia said. "She said that it's believed that soul bonds can always find their way back to each other. Like the magic becomes second nature, so much a part of them that the outside world cannot touch it. She said it would come back if we both wanted it."

Rainer leaned his forehead against hers, sighing. "I didn't know. Gods, I let you suffer so much. You took all the pain so I would hardly feel it."

She ran her fingers through his hair, covering his face with kisses.

"I would do it again. But I miss our bond. I want it back. It's lonely without it."

Rainer lifted her hand to his mouth, kissing her engagement ring. "I'd make those vows again right here, right now."

"Do you remember the words?" Cecilia asked.

Those vows were private, but soon, she'd speak a different set of vows in front of all their friends and family.

Rainer nodded. He pressed his palms to hers the same way they had that day many years ago, holding her gaze.

"Today and every day for the rest of my life, I bind myself to you, Cecilia Reznik. I promise to protect and defend you and keep you safe from all threats. I pledge my sword and my life. I vow to be your partner in all things from this breath until my last. For the wisdom to know that power is best when shared." The corner of his lips kicked up in a half-smile. "For the memory of our mistakes, so as to not make the same ones again. For the magic to restore the peace and prosperity to the kingdom."

He nodded and Cecilia swallowed the lump in her throat. The last time she'd spoken those words, she was six years old and so unaware of the responsibility that came with them.

"Today and every day for the rest of my life, I bind myself to you, Rainer McKay. I promise to protect and defend you and keep you safe from all threats. I pledge my magic and my life. I vow to be your partner in all things from this breath until my last. For the wisdom to know that power is best when shared. For the memory of our mistakes, so as to not make the same ones again. For the magic to restore the peace and prosperity to the kingdom."

They waited, eyes locked, breath frozen in their lungs. She was afraid to believe and be let down again, afraid if it didn't return it would mean something in their love had been irreparably broken.

It started with a glimmer, like a cooling ember in her chest, starting to grow warmer again instead of burning out. It spread and grew until warmth flooded her whole chest and radiated down her arms, unspooling in familiar warm tingles, her whole body lit from within by their connection. The space around her heart felt incandescent, alive, the roots between their hearts reaching out and tangling around each other like the feral forest they were meant to be.

Cecilia let go of Rainer's hand and kissed him fiercely, pouring all of her fear and grief and anxiety into it. They passed things back and forth through the bond as if testing an injury after it healed, tentatively at first and then with great, sweeping rushes of love that left Cecilia sobbing in Rainer's arms once again.

Rainer held her as he always did when she felt too weak to hold herself, as she did for him. He placed her hand over his heart, cupping it between his palms, communicating with just their bond, with just the silent language they'd created.

That was how people held on to each other. Sometimes they just held pieces, sometimes the full weight. Sometimes, they shepherded each other along, helping one another avoid blind cliffs, and always finding their way back home.

PART IV:
BRAVE WITH
THE HEART

41

XANDER

Sitting in the grand dining room in Castle Savero with the light of sunset streaming through the window, Xander could hardly believe that just days ago they'd put an end to the war that had raged for his entire life.

The table was set in spectacular fashion, with delicately painted golden dishes, crystal wine glasses, and tall candelabras filling the air with the scent of beeswax.

Jessamin had taken to her first non-battle-related task as queen with relish, insisting that it was important to celebrate victories, especially those fought so hard for.

"Darling, it looks fantastic. Who knew you'd be as excellent a hostess as you are a warrior?" Xander said.

She smiled smugly. "You'll learn to never doubt me or I'll be forced to keep reminding you that you're foolish."

Jessamin was still dealing with morning sickness, but she absolutely glowed, her scarlet dress brilliant in the warm candlelight.

Xander turned to his other side, where Isla was equally resplendent in a burgundy gown with a plunging neckline that made him want to drag her into the adjoining sitting room for some alone time.

She caught him staring and her mouth twisted into a satisfied smile.

"You look stunning," he said.

"And you look in over your head," she countered, leaning over to brush his hair back from his forehead. He loved having her fuss over him. "I still think you should have worn the crown."

He waved a hand. "Not my style."

Xander hoped that within his lifetime perhaps there'd be no more need for crowns. No doubt there would always be opposition to his rule and to any change at all, but he hoped that his power could be shared, not just to bring more voices to the table but also to free him of the responsibility of trying to determine what was best for everyone when he was only one man.

He wanted more for the next generations. He wanted his children to have options he didn't, without the pressure of being impeccable or doubts about whether they were worthy. A new goal was beginning to form in his mind and, after all this time, he was finally surrounded by people who he truly believed could help him do it.

His friends slowly filed into the room. Cal, Reese, and Chris sat on the far end of the table along with Evan and Sylvie, who was dressed more like she was going to a formal ball than a celebratory dinner. The priestesses sat on the opposite side of the table with Maren and Jessamin's other guards. At the head of the table Xander sat with Jessamin, Cece, and Rainer beside her. Isla sat to his left and Mika sat on the other side of her.

At the center of the table, four seats sat empty for their fallen friends and family, white roses across their place settings along with glasses of bubble wine. One seat for Davide, one for Teddy, one for Leo, and one for Magdalena.

Once everyone was seated, Xander stood, tapping his knife on his glass to silence their chatter. His mouth went suddenly dry. It was overwhelming to see all of his friends' exacting gazes on him. Never in his life had he expected to be the one everyone wanted to hear speak, but they looked to him now.

Xander took a breath. "It's with both joy and sorrow tonight that I take in the faces of everyone here and all of those we've lost in this fight for equity and peace. I'd like to honor my older brother, who protected me as best he could. To Davide Savero."

He raised his glass and everyone toasted and drank.

Xander cleared his throat. "The mark of true friendship is the way you never stop feeling the loss. Teddy was my dear friend and I miss his warmth, his humor, and his relentless optimism. I feel his absence daily. To Teddy Reynolds."

He raised his glass and they all drank. Xander nodded to Cece and she stood.

"The huntmaster—" Her voice broke and Rainer reached out to squeeze her hand. "Leo Reznik was a good man and an amazing father. He trusted me to make my own choices, equipped me with the skills to ensure that no one took advantage of me, and loved me like I was his own flesh and blood. He died trying to save me, not because he didn't think I could make a hard choice, but because he didn't want me to have to. I miss him every day. To Leo Reznik."

She held up her glass and they all toasted again.

Finally, Mika stood. She still would not even glance at Rainer. "There is likely not a person in this room whom Magdalena did not help or heal at one time or another. She was kind and far too generous with her time and energy. She was also a terrible singer, though no one dared tell her. She raised the first woman I ever loved and she helped me heal more than once when I was certain grief would carry me away. I miss her, but I feel her in every hallway in this castle. I see her in all my friend's scars. And I hold her in my heart all day every day. To Magdalena Graves."

They all clinked glasses and drank as Xander stood again.

"Finally, to all those who have sacrificed their lives in this blood war and to everyone who risked and lost something fighting for what is right. To the fallen."

They clinked glasses one final time and Xander swallowed the lump in his throat down with the last of his wine.

"Now that we have tended to our dead, let us tend to the living and feast."

He sat back in his chair, watching his friends talk and laugh and enjoy their food. Plate after plate, from appetizers to dessert, their joy was in no way diminished by what they'd lost, and that was what he'd been fighting for to begin with.

He hadn't realized it until that moment, but it was the truth. When he'd set out for Olney as a teenager, hoping to find the Lost God, he'd not done it in the hopes of making war. In his own juvenile way, he'd done it for peace. It might have been foolish of him to not realize that bringing the Lost Goddess back to Argaria would have resulted in a war that crushed Olney, but that hadn't been on his mind when he was still so young and idealistic.

Now, as Cece met his eyes across the table, he finally believed that even if it was in the most roundabout way, he'd done what he set out to do so many years before.

There were plenty of snags to work through with the families of the traitors and in pushing toward a more equitable, less classist kingdom. If Xander had his way, he'd also try to make the monarchy as small a role as possible in ruling the kingdom so that someday his children would have the option to do what they wanted, instead of what was expected of them. Beyond that, he was well aware of the impossible task of trying to rule for an entire kingdom of people when he'd experienced one singular life of privilege.

As if sensing his overwhelm, Isla reached under the table and gave his hand a squeeze.

Xander smiled at her. There was so much he wanted to say to her. He was overflowing with relief that she hadn't left yet, but he was still afraid she might.

"Isla—" he started.

She shook her head. "There will be time to talk later when the dust has settled. Tonight let's just be present."

The words were not a guarantee, but they were enough to release the tension from his shoulders.

For the first time—possibly ever, but at the very least since he'd first set out for Olney at fourteen—Xander felt surrounded by people who truly cared about him and entirely at peace.

———

Isla stood on the balcony, looking down at the castle grounds and the city of Ardenis. Despite the cold, she wore the same dress she'd worn to dinner with no coat. Her arms were bare against the chilly breeze, her dark skin shining in the silver moonlight.

"You're staring." Her voice was just a whisper carried on the mountain wind.

"I've got to get all these longing glances in while I can," Xander said. He was trying to sound teasing but he knew by the way she turned to look at him that he'd failed.

"Have I given the impression that I'm going somewhere or is this just your incredible impatience?"

He crossed the balcony and ran his hands up her arms. Her skin was cold under his warm palms.

"I will always be impatient for you," Xander said. "I think it's what I was made for, just as you were made to make me wait."

"You like the suspense."

"I love and loathe it in equal measure. I like the chance to win you over—the thrill of a challenge, and also," he kissed her shoulder, "I know how crushed I will be if I fail. So please, Isla. Put me out of my misery. End the suspense."

She studied him, her fingers running over his cheek like she was tracing the moonlight on his skin.

His heart was in his throat. He didn't know if he wanted this dance between them to end or if he liked the rush of the suspense. The old hunter instinct was still so strong. He loved the chase—the adrenaline of a good fight. Victory felt like validation —but it was the fight itself that made him feel like he had earned it.

If Isla gave in too soon, before he believed she wanted to, he'd always be worried that she'd change her mind. But if he gave her time and she chose to stay, she'd be deciding it again daily and he'd be winning her over not just once, but thousands of times.

He pulled her into a kiss, his fingers lingering on her neck before sliding down her chest to rest between her breasts. He leaned his forehead against hers.

"What do you say, darling? Is today the day you accept my offer? Have I earned more than a maybe?"

She smiled, drawing far away enough that she could meet his eyes. "I have considered your offer—"

He braced himself, waiting for rejection, praying silently that she'd say anything else. She watched him, a ghost of a smile on her lips like she liked holding the power to break him.

"I want full autonomy to run the army training programs the way I wish," Isla said. "If I'm going to do this, I don't want to hear some ego-bruised hunter complaining about having to fight like a woman. I'll need your full support."

All the air rushed out of his lungs at once. "You'll stay?"

"To lead your army."

He couldn't help but smile. She was playing this for all it was worth—trying to maximize his suffering, yet it only made him love her more.

"And to be my consort?" he asked. "The position comes with a rather stunning heirloom ring."

She shrugged noncommittally but there was heat in her eyes. "That will take some convincing."

Xander wanted to sweep her into his arms and celebrate, but he forced himself to play it cool. "So it's still just a maybe?"

She ran her hand along his chest as she walked back toward the bedroom. She paused in the doorway, gilded in firelight as she cast a playful glance over her shoulder. "No, darling. It's the best maybe of your life."

———

A few days later, Rainer and Cece were finally packed and ready to go home.

Xander watched the two of them fall into the practiced rhythm of getting ready for a long journey, Cece teasing Rainer for triple-checking the buckles on all their saddlebags, Rainer pretending to be annoyed about it but smiling when she wasn't looking. The two of them had been inseparable since Rainer recovered his memories, but Cece watched him like she was worried he'd forget again.

The guardian rubbed his hands down Cece's arms and tucked her cloak around her tighter. Cece chided him for worrying and trotted over to Mika to help her finish packing her horse.

The biggest surprise was Mika's departure. With Magdalena gone, she had decided to leave Argaria. She wanted a chance to start fresh in Olney. Cece was delighted to have her and the two of them had caught Xander up on their plans for a women's clinic at the healing center.

Rainer turned to meet his eye. "Xander."

"Rainer."

"I think it's worth mentioning that the best man won." His tone was more teasing than barbed.

Xander burst out laughing. "I thought you put a fine point on that in my library. No need to rub it in." He nodded toward Isla and Jessamin. "I'd say I did all right for myself."

"Will she stay?" Rainer asked.

Xander shouldn't have been surprised that Cece had caught Rainer up on everything that had transpired, but Xander still felt protective of what he had with Isla. It felt so delicate and he didn't want anyone else to get too close or it could crumble before his eyes.

"Maybe," Xander said.

Rainer shook his head. "Truly, I don't understand your appeal, but you know how to make it work."

Xander grinned. "Well, luckily I don't need you to understand." He nodded to Isla. "Just her."

Rainer patted him on the shoulder. It was stiff, but perhaps all friendships started off a little awkwardly. "You've always been good at giving a woman the space and encouragement to trust her own mind. I think you'll be okay."

Rainer cleared his throat, his eyes darting to Cece, who stood chatting with Jessamin and Isla. "Thank you for keeping her together.

Even when I didn't know what was going on, I saw you watching out for her in subtle ways. Thank you for everything."

He pulled Xander into a hug. For a moment Xander stood uncomfortably before hugging the man who'd been his nemesis for two years.

"Are we friends now?" Xander asked.

Rainer laughed. "Let's just say that I'll enjoy you better in smaller doses."

Xander grinned as Rainer walked back toward the waiting horses. "I'm growing on you, McKay," he called after him.

"Like a fungus," Rainer quipped over his shoulder.

Xander would take it. They'd come a very long way from fighting over Cece's affection and his respect for Rainer had only grown. He hoped the feeling was mutual, but he wouldn't push his luck on the first try.

The snow crunched under Cece's boots as she closed the distance between them. Her eyes were bright and her smile was wide and tremulous.

The last time they had parted, Xander had walked away from Cece, leaving unfinished business between them and their kingdoms. This time, their business was settled, as was the chaos of the kingdom, and all that was left between them was history and a budding friendship.

"Xander," she said, cupping his face in her cold hands.

"Cece."

For a moment they were silent, their eyes speaking volumes in the way only two people who had suffered with and for each other could.

"I expect you to come back again and visit and finally get to enjoy my kingdom without threat of death or captivity," he said.

She shrugged. "Sounds boring."

"I promise I will find a way to make it more exciting. I'll take you on a proper hunt. We can go sledding."

"Sledding?" she asked, her eyes lighting up.

"Yes, speeding down the snowy mountainside on a piece of wood with steel rails. It's exceptionally fun and dangerous. You'll love it. Making Rainer worry himself to death is just an added benefit."

She giggled. "Sounds perfect." Her face grew serious. "Xan—" Her voice cracked and her eyes misted over. "I'm so proud of you. I know you're still doubting yourself, but you have already proved that you know how to be a great leader. It's the same as how to be a great partner—listening."

He pulled her into a tight hug. "I'm really going to miss you. Please say you'll keep writing. I swear I'll actually write back this time."

She nodded vigorously. "You better or I'll march back here and hunt you down. And Xan—"

He met her eyes.

"You're not King Damian. You're warm and kind and present. That baby is very lucky to have you and a gaggle of women who know how to keep you in line."

Xander laughed. "Yes, I expect I'll be bullied out of my doubts." He swallowed the lump in his throat. "We'll see you in a couple months for the wedding."

She grinned and kissed his cheek before finally letting him go.

This time, when Xander watched Cece turn to go, his heart didn't break; it surged with joy, knowing that all would finally be well.

42

RAINER

It was a relief to be back in Olney where winter was eager to surrender to an early spring. While it was still too cold for Rainer to swim in the mornings, he was happy to run in the fresh, salty air every morning.

The breeze hit him where he waited outside the Olney Healing Center for Cecilia to finish her shift. In the months following their return, she'd thrown herself into her work, as if the only way to heal herself was through her commitment to healing others. But unlike before, when she was running on guilt, now she seemed more focused, committed not to outrunning her grief and fear but to sitting with it each day like an old friend. Some days when he picked her up she was quiet and pensive, but little by little she came back to herself, her face brighter, her chatter livelier.

Twice a week she and Mika conducted a women's group to help victims of violence find comfort and support in each other's company. Originally it was under the guise of quilting, and slowly the women began to trickle in. Now there were more than twenty of them.

Rainer scanned the building down the street, trying to remember where each path in Olney City led. He couldn't stop testing himself.

His memory was better. Cecilia had done her best to gradually feed back in everything he'd lost, but it was slow work. If she gave him too much at once, he got headaches, so each day she told him their love story little by little.

Sometimes when he came across a blank spot, his anger still consumed him. He knew the rage might never fade completely, but he was trying to make peace with it and Cecilia was so patient with him.

Cecilia's pain was a love letter, bold and brutal and laid bare for him, so vulnerable that it hurt to look at. So personal it hurt not to.

What a beautiful thing to feel the cracks in someone else's heart, for them to let you try to glue them back together. It was humbling the way she opened up to him as if she'd never been hurt. The way she looked fear in the face and pressed on.

Some days she held the pieces together. Some days he did.

He longed to comfort her with physical touch. That intimacy had been so soothing to her before, but Cecilia wasn't ready yet. She'd been very attentive to him, but hadn't given Rainer the chance to return the favor. It was less about the physicality of it and more that he wanted nothing between them. He wanted to feel the comfortable intimacy of casual touch.

Mika had told him to be patient and he could feel his fiancée slowly coming back to herself.

Cecilia pressed through the front door of the Olney Healing Center, waving goodbye to Lyra and Mika.

"Those two seem...friendly," Rainer said, watching Mika thread her fingers through those of the other healer.

Cecilia smiled. "Yes, they do, and good for them. Mika deserves some happiness after all she's been through."

Rainer threw an arm around her, kissing the top of her head. "How was your day?"

"Productive. I'm tired, though. Looking forward to eating dinner and going straight to bed," she sighed.

"Well, that's a shame because Aunt Clara has been dying to talk to you about wedding plans—I have already answered about fifty questions about cake, but I know nothing about flowers."

Cecilia shook her head. "I know I should just let her enjoy this, but I could not care any less what kind of flowers are there. I just want to marry you."

He paused along the trail, pulling her into a slow kiss.

"What was that for?" she asked, blinking up at him.

"I am just always relieved when you say it. I thought maybe it would be how it was before, that you would want to wait until you felt more settled."

Cecilia smiled, brushing hair from his forehead. "I know enough now to know how ridiculous that is. I wanted everything to be neat and tidy before. Now I know that healing is long and messy and enjoying myself—settling in for a life I love—along the way is only going to help. I am—" Her voice broke, her eyes glassy. "I am all of these broken things. I am all of my wounds and fears, but I am also all of my love and joy. I can be all of those things at once. There's no clean slate and even if there was I wouldn't want to forget, not really."

Rainer swallowed hard. He knew what she meant. A clean slate was not all it was cracked up to be, him having had several months of it back in Argaria. He was so grateful she'd preserved the lost parts of him.

She gave him a quick hug before weaving her fingers through his. "Have you talked to Raymond?"

Rainer tensed.

"I know you think it's going to go poorly and I'm inclined to agree with you, but if you think there's any chance at all that you might want him at the wedding—"

"I don't. Cece, you of all people know he is the worst thing for me."

She sighed. "I know. I just thought maybe after everything you might have a thing or two to say to him yourself."

She looked suddenly nervous.

"What aren't you telling me, Cece?"

Her eyes flashed to the cottage door. "I may have invited him to talk with you tonight."

Rainer pulled away from her, feeling betrayed. Cecilia held her hands up in surrender. She had always been wary of Raymond McKay's influence in Rainer's life, yet now she was reintroducing him just as Rainer felt free of him.

"If you feel that strongly, I will ask him to leave," she said. "But if there's even a chance at healing what is between you, it might be worth trying. I keep thinking about how you were with Vincent, how under your skin there's this sense of not being enough, and I thought maybe you would want to stand up for yourself. And if you don't, I will tell him to leave and I will stand up for you because you're my love, and my hero, and you've saved me every day since we met."

Rainer lifted her into a tight hug.

"I'll be right behind you the whole time. Just like you always have been for me," she whispered.

He put her down and took a tentative step toward the cabin, pausing to collect his thoughts. What if it went wrong? What if his father was the same as always? It was pure insanity to expect otherwise, but he was accustomed to long shots, and Cecilia was always protecting him. If she didn't think there was a chance this might bring him peace, she never would have suggested it.

He pushed the door open and stepped inside, finding Raymond sitting on the window seat.

"Rainer?" He stood and closed the distance between them. "Son, you've been home for months but you haven't stopped to see your old man? I couldn't even get your attention at the commendation ceremony King Marcos had for you and that Reznik girl."

Rainer frowned. "That Reznik girl is a woman now. Cecilia is my fiancée and, being as you've known her since she was a child, the least you can do is call her by her name."

Raymond frowned at him, clearly unaccustomed to receiving correction.

"Why are you here?" Rainer asked.

"Can't a man visit his son—"

Rainer's laugh came out brittle. "A man can, but you have not been much of one so long as I've known you, and you've certainly never been a father. Just tell me what you want because that woman whose name you can't bother with is outside hoping that you're a man that both of us know you aren't. I'm here because I love her and she thinks that I need to make peace with you. But I think there is no peace to be had and nothing you can say will mend what is broken between us because you have only ever known how to shatter things; you've never learned to mend."

Raymond rubbed the back of his neck. "I did not know you felt that way. I only ever wanted to push you to be the best and you are. King's council. Friend to the king and queen of Argaria. Rainer, you have far exceeded my expectations, far exceeded the kind of recognition that would allow you to proudly take the Novaris name."

Rainer's stomach sank. There it was. The true reason Raymond was there. The man could not grant him peace. Rainer had finally reached the pinnacle and this man still managed to find a new height he could aspire toward. If Rainer let him, Raymond would break another beautiful thing, but this time it wasn't a toy or a book or his mother's prized possessions. This time it was Rainer's own story, which until that moment he had not realized was the deepest, most intricate part of himself.

If he let Raymond McKay have his story, he would take all the beauty, heartbreak, angst, and love and twist it into a hero's journey from orphan to renowned warrior. That was more than Rainer could take. It was his story and he would be the only one to choose the ending. It had taken twenty-seven years, but his father had finally crossed the line of no return. Rainer had well and truly lost the will to fight this battle anymore.

This wasn't a fairy tale as Cecilia had hoped it might be. It was a tragedy, and if Rainer had even expected for a moment that it wouldn't be, he might have felt grief. Instead, this was merely the grave marker on something already dead and buried. Rainer felt nothing but relief.

As if he could feel it too, Raymond stood and, for the first time in his life, looked aware that he'd lost something he couldn't get back.

For so many years, Rainer had swallowed Raymond's words like poison, thinking he deserved the burn and scorn. Now it was all coming back up—twenty-seven years of anger surging out of him like a dam breaking.

"I am grateful that you're not my real father—that it's not in my blood to be cruel and unfeeling. Someday Cece and I will have children and I will use your actions as a map of exactly what not to do. I'll love them in a way you aren't even capable of comprehending. You will never know them and their lives will be better for it. And if they ever ask about their grandfather, they'll only hear about Leo Reznik."

Rainer gestured to the door and Raymond stood frozen for a moment, a hint of hurt on his face.

Rainer was beyond caring and it felt good. "Goodbye, Raymond." He opened the door. "I hope you have a nice life."

Raymond opened his mouth to speak and then closed it before turning and making his way out the door. He paused in front of Cecilia before leaning over to whisper something in her ear. He didn't turn back as he walked down the trail toward town.

Rainer watched him shrink into nothing in the distance before turning and sitting on the edge of the kitchen table. He hung his head.

"I assume it didn't go well?" Cecilia said.

Rainer narrowed his eyes at her. "You didn't listen through the door?"

She gave him a sheepish smile. "I just wanted to be there if you needed me."

Rainer shook his head. Before he'd walked into that room, he'd been braced for impact, waiting for the heaviness in his chest that always arrived on the heels of his father, but now he just felt light.

"I'm so sorry," Cecilia whispered.

"No, I'm sorry to you. I'm sorry for you that he couldn't be good just for one godsdamned minute to be part of our lives. I'm sorry you didn't get your fairy tale."

Cecilia smiled at him. Her hand came to his cheek and she forced him to meet her gaze. "Rain, this *is* the fairy tale. This is what I wanted for you. You slayed the real dragon. You finally accepted that you were good enough without his approval and you told him. I am so proud of you."

Rainer let out a shaky breath. It was hard to express what it meant for someone to have seen all of his greatest struggles and still be proud. The lump in his throat threatened to choke him. She pulled him into a hug and he leaned his head against her shoulder, squeezing her until her ribs creaked.

"Do you think now you'll start using your birth father's name?"

Rainer swallowed hard. He'd been considering it since he dropped his sword on the temple floor.

His whole life he'd ignored the cracks in the illusion of his birth father. It was easier to make Zelden Novaris the good guy when Raymond McKay was the other option. For so long that had seemed the standard for heroics, but even heroes had their flaws. Much as Zelden might have been a savior to Olney, personally he had not been a hero to Rainer. He'd left his son alone in the world—traded responsibility for glory. True heroes were there for the people who counted on them, even when their hearts were broken.

As much as Rainer had looked up to Zelden, put him on a pedestal his whole life, it took forgetting who he was and being forced to stand up for who he'd become for Rainer to realize he no longer defined himself by someone else's standards. Now Rainer was a man who was worthy without having to prove it, who was loved for exactly who he was, both in his strongest and weakest moments.

Cecilia had fallen in love with Rainer McKay, and though he knew she'd love him no matter what name he had, his given name possessed folklore that had become more compelling and definitive of who he was now.

"I don't think so. I like being Rainer McKay—maybe for the first time ever. The name is more mine now than his anyway. I won't keep my lineage a secret anymore because I'm not ashamed, but I want to keep this name because I've made it my own."

Cecilia smiled, stroking his hair.

He was almost afraid to ask, but he had to know. "What did he say to you?"

Cecilia swallowed hard. "He said the best thing he ever did was bring you to the seer's suite that day. He said to love you better than he could."

For all their differences, at least Rainer and Raymond agreed on two things: the best thing he'd ever done and who could love Rainer best.

43

CECILIA

Home was hard for Cecilia in the way it was always hard to come back to a place that was the same when you'd been so permanently changed.

While they were gone, Marcos had married Ilani and he and his new queen had greeted them, along with a teary-eyed Aunt Clara, who had pulled both Rainer and Cecilia into hugs and refused to let them go until they pried her off. Now they were back in the cottage alone and as tentative with the space as they were with each other.

Before, they'd easily fallen into bed together, but Cecilia was still trying to get used to his sudden dark moods and brooding, and he was trying to accommodate her anxiety and fear as best he could. Both had improved remarkably, but still their experiences clung to them.

Rainer had been tentative with her at first, touching her only when he'd asked permission, constantly drawing a hand back from actions that had been reflexive for so long.

Every flinch frustrated her. Reminded her she was not yet well.

Part of her wanted to throw herself at him, tackle him into bed and not let him out for a week. It used to be that she never felt calmer and more grounded than when he was touching her skin—when she could be that close to him. But the other part of her still froze up when an unexpected memory invaded.

She berated herself when she was alone on the beach in the mornings. How could she be so wounded when Vincent hadn't actually done what he'd threatened?

But the fear was irrational. Her body had a mind of its own and it refused to be mastered by her will alone.

Before, Rainer had eclipsed everything. But even he could not blot out the fear from her body, could not ease the way she felt like what had happened was still happening. She couldn't stop brushing her fingers over her thighs to make sure no mark remained. But there was nothing physical save for the faint hint of the first slash Vincent had made, that cut a little too jagged for Magdalena to have healed cleanly.

Rainer's patience with her only agitated her further. He loved to tease her now, loved to stoke her desperation.

"Aren't *you* frustrated?" she snapped when for the fourth time in as many days she had frozen up in the middle of a kissing session.

He just smiled at her. "I am very satisfied."

She huffed out an exasperated sigh.

"Clearly I'm not as frustrated as you. Poor, sweet, horny Cece," he teased, hugging her from behind, kissing the freckles from her shoulder up her neck. "What do you need? My mouth on you?"

She shivered against him. She wanted it but was terrified it wouldn't go well.

She grabbed his hand, placing it between hers and her body as she slid it down her front, pausing between her legs. She prodded him to move his fingers against her, roughly through the layers of her dress. She moaned, tipping her head back against his shoulder.

"Mmm, what do you need, Cece? I'll give you anything you want," he murmured into her neck.

"Take your clothes off," she said, pulling his hand away and yanking at the ties of her dress until it pooled around her feet.

Rainer's eyes lit up, but she read the sudden shift in his body, still apprehensive of touching her too much. She hated it.

It had always been so easy between them but now it felt like they were in uncharted territory, fumbling their way through like it was the first time.

Rainer reached for her to help her out of her undergarments, only to draw his hands back before he could touch her.

"For the love of the gods. Touch me, Rain. I'll tell you if it's too much."

It was all the permission he needed. He was on her in a second, his hands in her hair, tipping her head back so he could kiss her before trailing down her body to squeeze her ass. She moaned against his mouth and he lifted her, her legs wrapping around his waist instinctively as he carried her to the bed, sitting on the edge with her in his lap.

For a long time they stayed like that, naked and kissing ravenously.

Finally she pulled back.

"I can keep my hands to myself," Rainer gasped.

She huffed out a breath. "I very much don't want you to. I want your hands all over me."

He smiled. "I know, but maybe we take it slow. Mika said it might help if you tied me to the bed."

A thrill pulsed through her at the prospect.

"Oh, would you like me powerless?" he asked, arching a brow. "I assure you I am already entirely at your mercy."

She kissed him, pushing him onto his back as she pressed her lips to his neck and the scars from old arrow wounds. "I love you," she whispered against each one as she always did. Like she was paying penance for not saying the words the day he received those wounds.

She guided Rainer's hand between her legs.

"Please, I need it."

His gaze locked with hers as he slid a finger inside her and she groaned.

"Fuck, you're tight," Rainer said, his hips flexing on instinct.

"Make me feel good," she sighed against his mouth.

He went slow at first, but she sat back, allowing him more control.

He pushed to a sitting position so he could kiss her while he worked her with two fingers.

She was right on the edge when the memory of Grant holding her down and Vincent behind her split present from past. She froze.

Rainer drew his hand back immediately.

"Cece." His whisper was so gentle, but Cecilia was furious.

She jumped out of bed, throwing a glass from the table against the wall with a frustrated scream. "I hate this. I hate that he's gone and yet he still manages to be here in this room. I hate that I cannot connect with you like this. I hate that I am held hostage by the perfect memory of the one thing I'd like to forget." She blew out a frustrated breath and turned to face Rainer.

"I know," he whispered, pulling her into his arms. "I hate it too, but it won't be like this forever. You don't have to push so hard."

She brushed a tear from her cheek. "I'm in ruins."

"I love ruins," Rainer said tenderly.

She rolled her eyes. The more calm he was, the more frustrated she felt.

"It's beautiful to see what's still standing after the storm," Rainer whispered, kissing the inside of her wrist and the crescent scar on her outer palm. "I look at ruins and see strength. They show that something important was forever changed, but still it stands. You're still standing, Cece."

She pulled away and twisted her hair up on top of her head, shoving in a few pins from the nightstand to hold it in place. Rainer was so good to her and so understanding but she was so impatient for the comfortable familiarity of being close to him. "I just want to feel safe in my own body. I'm not afraid of you."

He tilted his head to the side, smiling faintly. "You'll get there. Give it some more time. You know what might make you feel better?"

"Climaxing?" she said dryly.

Rainer chuckled. "Perhaps not *that* good, but still happy."

She crossed her arms. "What is it?"

"I don't think I ever told you the end of the raining stars fairy tale."

A thrill zipped up Cecilia's spine. She'd lost count of how many times she'd asked him how that story ended. "You'll actually tell me for real?"

He nodded. "I saved it because I knew you might need it eventually. How does the story start?"

"Once upon a time there was a village where for one night every year it rained stars." She took a deep breath.

"Go on," he whispered.

"The villagers ran outside with empty jars to collect them, because each star was worth one wish. One of the villagers, a man named Jack, was very in love with a fellow villager, June. Every year, after the stars fell, he'd use his wishes for very practical things: good crops for the village, safety for their people, and health for his parents. But he always saved one star for a special occasion."

Cecilia swallowed hard. The story made her so emotional now since it was tied to so many important moments in their lives.

She cleared her throat and continued. "June, on the other hand, was fast and often caught the most stars. She was also generous, blowing through her wishes within the first week of getting them. She wished for things to take care of everyone else in the community because she wanted everyone to love her. But as soon as they got something from her, they'd get too busy with their wishes coming true to make time for June. Except Jack. He would always ask her why she gave so much away when she lived in a tiny little cottage. And she told him she didn't want just any house—she wanted a home, and until she knew what kind, she wouldn't waste a wish. So, most of the year June would be without any wishes and every week she would ask Jack what he was saving his last wish for."

"What do you think he was saving it for?" Rainer asked.

Cecilia was certain; she just wanted Rainer to confirm it. "I think he was saving it so he could wish for June's dream home once she figured out what she wanted."

Rainer took a step toward her. "Jack didn't wish for a home because he didn't need one. To him, home was where his heart felt safe, so he'd already found one in June. Do you know what he wished for instead?"

Cecilia shook her head, trying to swallow the tightness in her throat.

"He wished that she'd finally see that she'd had a home in him all along." Rainer cupped her face in his hands. "I'll wait here as long as it takes for you to be ready, because your heart is already a safe place for me. I can wait until mine feels safe for you, too."

———

Cecilia flipped the clinic sign on the front door of the Olney Healing Center. She turned to face Mika, who appeared as fresh and golden in the late afternoon sunlight shining through the windows as she had when she arrived that morning. It was a little bit annoying how perfect she looked.

Cecilia crossed the room, removed her apron and tossed it into the laundry bin next to Lyra, and slumped into a chair.

"You seem off," Mika observed.

"I'm just frustrated, Mika. I want to be with him. We used to be so good together. I could not keep my hands off of him—wanted him to touch me everywhere. I can't stand this tentative thing. It does more to remind me what happened than make me feel better."

Mika sighed, shaking her head. "It's still not been very long. Be patient with yourself."

"I just want to be with him without bringing all this baggage into the bedroom with me," Cecilia said, wrapping twine around a bundle of rosemary and hanging it on a hook.

Mika rubbed the back of her neck and untied the kerchief holding her blonde hair away from her face. "You trust him completely, right?"

Cecilia nodded. "More than anyone in the world."

"Enough to let him be in control of everything?"

Cecilia hesitated. "In control?"

"Yes. In control of everything that happens in bed. Do you trust him enough to know what you want and need enough to surrender control?"

Cecilia considered it as she stood and swept loose bits of herbs off the floor and tossed them into the fire. "I would be willing to try it."

Mika nodded. "All right then. Send him to chat with me. I have an idea of something that might work to help you through this tricky spot."

"Thank you, Mika, you're a good friend." Cecilia leaned the broom against the wall, hesitating. "Did you learn all of this from Ivy?"

Mika's face softened. "Some. Some I learned from other women over the years. The idea I have for you will work better because of your bond with Rainer. Not many women have that benefit."

Cecilia hesitated. She knew it took a lot for Mika to offer to talk to Rainer, whom she rarely even made eye contact with. Much as she knew that Rainer couldn't entirely be blamed for killing Magdalena, Mika still could not forgive him. This offer was clearly entirely out of friendship with Cecilia.

"And how are you healing?" Cecilia asked.

"Some ends don't tie up easily. I expect it will take me some time to mend what still aches in me. The good news is that I finally have the time and space to do so and a life I enjoy enough to get better for." Mika's gaze darted to the counter where Lyra sat shuffling through the next day's schedule.

Cecilia had noticed the budding relationship between the duo but knew better than to pry. Mika would share if and when she was ready to and not a moment sooner. In the meantime, Mika had been happy to listen to Cecilia rant about her frustration, though her unresolved anger toward Rainer made Cecilia feel guilty for bringing him up so much.

"I won't hate him forever, you know," Mika said. "I just need some time to see him as someone other than the person who killed the woman who was like a mother to me."

"I know," Cecilia said.

Mika clasped her hands in her lap. "This program—what we are doing here—it matters. This is how I heal. I know you get it, but I expect at some point it will feel like enough—with enough distance and time and joy, I will be someone new. Grief is a crucible. I just haven't surfaced yet to see what it makes of me."

Cecilia nodded, placing a hand on her friend's shoulder. "I'll be here when you surface and I'll keep watch while you're under."

Mika nodded, a faint smile on her lips. "Now get home and eat dinner and tell that fiancé of yours that bringing me that delicious pasta for lunch a few times a week certainly doesn't hurt his cause."

Cecilia laughed. "I'll let him know."

44

EVAN

The trickster god waited for Evan outside of Death and Fortune Gambling Hall with a wide grin on his face. Evan was pretty sure it was supposed to be inviting, but it was more terrifying than anything else.

"Farlan, what a surprise."

Evan pinned him with a look. "Shouldn't be that much of a surprise since you've been tracking me the past hour."

Cato shrugged. "I prefer to think of it as watching your back."

"I can watch my own back. What do you want, Cato?"

The trickster fell into step beside him as he stalked toward the winter market. A sharp breeze lashed at his coat as he rounded the corner into the square. Though spring was fast approaching, winter was slow to surrender in Ardenis.

"While I know that I have historically remained on the outside of your crew and all the celebrations and such that being on the inside entails, I thought perhaps there might be more that needs doing other than just lying around and drinking wine like the lot of you."

Evan froze in front of a produce booth and turned to look at Cato. The god's nervous gaze darted to the booth and then back to Evan.

"You're bored, aren't you?" Evan laughed.

Never in his life had Evan expected to relate to or understand the trickster god, but it seemed that having a fleeting mortal lifespan had made Cato reconsider his antics.

Cato bristled. "I am trying to reform my ways and, as it turns out, many of my activities were what most of you would classify as *problematic*."

Evan crossed his arms. "You have no hobbies that aren't destructive?"

"You expect me to fall in love like the rest of these idiots?" Cato let out a long-suffering sigh. "What a preposterous waste of time and energy for the illusion of—"

"You protest it pretty hard for someone who thinks it an illusion," Evan countered.

Cato folded his arms, mimicking Evan's stance. "Whatever. The point is, I need something to do."

"Then I suggest you go get a job like the rest of the world. You've been around for centuries; shouldn't you know how this world works by now?" Evan taunted.

Evan had never had much desire for power, but he liked seeing their roles reversed for once, especially after he'd spent so much time trying to get ahead of Cato's plans.

Cato glowered at him. "You know what I mean. Common work is beneath me. I get too bored by it and the last thing you want is me bored. That's not a threat so much as a fact."

Evan held up his hands. "All right, I get it. Why not go to some other kingdom? See the world?"

Cato frowned. "I tried once. My power is strongest where people believe in me. When I tried to venture farther before, even when I was immortal, my power waned outside of Olney and Argaria. Everyone thinks being a god is so great, but it's not all it's cracked up to be. I guess my stories are less compelling around the world. There are bigger, badder gods to fear. Or more romantic ones—like how everyone just *loves* Goddess Cecilia." He rolled his eyes.

Evan sighed. "Why aren't you off bothering her?"

Cato's shoulders went rigid. "She said she appreciated my

penance but that what I'd done didn't begin to clear the debt between us. She asked not to see me for a very long time."

"And what compelled you to actually listen for once?" Evan asked, purely out of morbid curiosity.

Cato's hands held a white-knuckle grip on his biceps. "Because I did push it too far and I found a line I didn't like crossing. I told you before I find that strategy too brutish. I like to best an adversary on an equal playing field."

Evan arched a brow.

Cato shrugged and sighed. "A *slightly* more equal playing field."

If Evan hadn't seen Cato help so much firsthand, he might not have believed him, but after all they'd been through, Cato had held up his end and gotten them out of a very messy spot, albeit one he'd orchestrated.

Evan scrubbed a hand over his face. "I could use an adept spy."

While he'd never fully trust Cato with anything but to be self-serving, Evan knew the trickster could be crafty. It was better to have some idea of what he was up to than to let him run wild.

Cato's eyes narrowed. "To do what?"

"To keep a finger on the pulse of the city, see how the common people are feeling. To notice if Vincent and his allies are truly gone. To make sure the Spellmans stay banished to the eastern wastes or wherever else they wander. You have the unique ability to travel far and fast and that's an asset."

Cato rubbed his chin. "And you'd believe what I give you?"

Evan ran a hand through his hair, bracing against another frigid breeze. "I'd look into it. Perhaps over time, I'd come to believe you on your own. Perhaps you'd find a reason to settle down. I'd believe you were invested like the rest of us."

Cato frowned. "I prefer not having something to lose."

"Maybe it's time to reconsider that stance." Evan reached out his hand, unsure if he was making a mistake but for once unafraid that there would be people there to catch him if he did.

Cato shook Evan's hand, offering a curt nod before gazing deeper into the market. "Good enough. Don't make a big deal about it."

The god stalked away.

Evan watched him disappear into the crowd, then turned and walked home.

He wove through the streets of Ardenis, slowly making his way up the hill toward his estate just outside Castle Savero. It had technically belonged to his father, but Evan had kept it sealed up most of his life, visiting infrequently and startling the caretaker when he did. He paused outside the gate and stared up at the newly painted scarlet shutters on the house.

After a lifetime of feeling like a guest in someone else's home, he finally felt he had a home of his own.

Evan walked in the front door of the estate. Crates and trunks still lined the entryway since he and Sylvie had moved in just a few weeks earlier. Every night he helped Sylvie unpack more gowns and jewelry. Then he'd return the next day to find the foyer filled again. His wife was a prolific shopper.

He'd left the decorating to Sylvie and she'd been delighted to create her own space and do something other than spy and manipulate men of the court, though she was still a member of Xander's council and served as an Olney ambassador along with Cal. She'd stepped back and taken a more ancillary role since Xander had the support of both a wife with a sharp political mind and an almost-consort with a military mind.

Isla still had not agreed to the official title, though not for lack of Xander trying. He'd offered to change the name of it or simply not call her anything officially, but Isla seemed content not to be pinned down. Instead, she'd taken over army training and Evan had heard more than a few guards complaining about the new conditioning standards. She'd have the military whipped into shape in no time and Evan was glad of it.

He stilled, listening with sharpened hearing to sense where Sylvie was in the house.

He found her in the sitting room, facing the garden. She smiled warmly as he entered the room, hopped to her feet, and greeted him with a kiss.

Evan nodded to the freshly bloomed flowers out the window. "A bit early in the season for gardening, no?"

Sylvie shrugged. "I know, but I was a little homesick for the warm weather and I thought they'd make me happy even if they need a little more love."

"I see we got new furniture."

"Do you not like it? It was a gift from my mother, who is beside herself that we got married without her, deadly coup or not. She's expecting us to come visit and get married again in her garden in a few months."

"Months?"

"Why, do you have something better to do?" she asked.

Evan grinned. "Yes, my wife."

She tipped her head back and laughed. "That can be arranged, but surely after being the king's right-hand man you have more considerable ambitions."

"I promise I don't."

Sylvie laughed again, running her hands through his hair. "You're such a terrible liar. You don't know how to relax. I'm going to spend the next year teaching you how to have fun."

"I used to have fun. You don't have Xander Savero for a best friend and not know how to have at least a little bit of fun. I'm just a bit out of practice—" His gaze snagged on a new addition to the sitting room. "At the risk of being accomplice to a theft to the crown, I have to ask —is that Hank?" he asked, nodding toward the leafy green plant to the right of the window.

"It is. Hank the Houseplant," Sylvie said with delight. "I gave him a new pot and he seems to like it."

"I'm surprised he survived the invasion."

"He'll outlive us all," she deadpanned. "Did you think I would abandon our most staunch supporter and reliable spy? I had Cece water him so he would survive until I could go retrieve him after."

Evan narrowed his eyes, unsure if she was joking. "Have you figured out what kind of plant he is?"

"No, have you?"

"How do we take care of him?"

She rolled her eyes. "Evan, we have been caring for an entire kingdom for years now. You think a plant is outside of our abilities?"

"I've never cared for a plant before."

"You give him some water once a week and freshen up his soil every six months or so and I'll shoot some magic at him if he gets wilted. He'll be fine."

Evan frowned.

"I do think he may have developed a taste for fine wine, though," she said, arching a brow.

Evan laughed. "You love talking about magic because I can never tell if you're serious."

Sylvie crossed the room, drawing him along behind her. He sat in a chair and she perched on its edge. "I do."

Evan leaned back, sliding his hand up her ankle, tapping each of his fingers to his thumb, looking out the window. "So, what do we do now that Jessamin has taken over helping Xander run the kingdom and Isla has taken over helping Jessamin run Xander?"

Sylvie laughed. "Oh my gods, Evan."

"What?"

"You really don't know how to have fun."

He frowned. "Of course I do."

"No, you don't. You've been playing prince-sitter since you were old enough to hold a sword. I have never once seen you relax other than the few minutes after you climax."

Evan bit back a smile. "What would you suggest? Around court, they seem to think we should just be content to have children and settle down."

Sylvie rolled her eyes. "Of course—because the only happy resolution for a romance is for a woman to pop out babies. There are much better ways to have fun."

Evan grinned. "Fine. Then I suppose my wife will have to be in charge of all fun activities."

Her eyes lit up. "Fabulous. I just heard about a really excellent brothel."

45

CECILIA

Mika had explained everything to Cecilia and had also gone over rules and boundaries with Rainer. Still, Cecilia was a nervous wreck as they stepped inside the Reznik family's summer house. Set slightly farther north on the eastern coast of Olney, it was a smaller, breezier home away from the hustle and bustle of Olney City that they'd hardly visited since Cecilia was a girl.

The caretakers, Pierce and Liz Leiben, had been delighted to receive her letter requesting access and were awaiting her and Rainer when they arrived. Liz had hugged them both, having not seen them since they were children. Then she had smiled knowingly and winked at Cecilia, telling her to have fun and to be safe so that her wedding dress would fit.

Cecilia didn't have the heart to tell the woman she'd never need to worry about that particular problem. From time to time she still turned over the cryptic words Raven Whitewind had said about the unfairness of her exchange not truly being a choice and how Cecilia was asking the right questions. But those questions left her angrier and more confused when she so badly wanted peace.

Once the caretakers left, Cecilia pumped in water for a bath and took her time scrubbing her skin and hair as if soap alone could wash away her nerves. She tried not to think about the fact that Rainer was doing the same on the other side of the house, preparing for the evening.

She dried off and changed into a lilac silk dress before stepping into the kitchen and gazing out the glass doors that led onto the patio with wooden stairs that descended to the rocky beach.

Rainer's reflection appeared behind her in the glass. He wrapped his arms around her. "You look gorgeous in this color."

His gaze darted to the large dining table across the room. She swallowed hard, sensing his intention. Mika's instructions had been clear that recreating a similar set of circumstances in a safer environment would bring up maximum fear, but also the greatest opportunity to master it. If Cecilia could do this, it was possible that she'd get over the worst of her apprehension and be able to return to some semblance of normal intimacy.

"Are you sure you're ready?" Rainer asked, his voice taking on a sexy, authoritative edge that set her blood simmering.

She nodded. Cecilia loved Rainer enough to hand him all of her hurts and carry them with her. She trusted him enough to let him push her.

"You are giving me your trust, your pain, your fear. You believe I'll take care of you, don't you?" Rainer whispered. His lips brushed up the column of her neck and she shivered, pressing her back into his chest. "Mm, yes, you do. You're going to be a good girl for me, aren't you?"

She whimpered, her head lolling back against his chest, then laughed. "Why does something so patronizing make me so hot?"

He nipped at her earlobe. "Because you know I'll reward you for good behavior," he taunted. "Because you like when I'm in control. You like this darker side of me. I may have forgotten a lot, but I didn't forget the way those words affected you."

She was mesmerized by this new side of him—terrified and

turned on by the idea of what he might do. She wanted to feel every-thing only Rainer could make her feel.

"Say you trust me. Let me take control, Cece," he said.

"I trust you. You're in control."

"If I do anything you don't like, you know what to say to stop me."

Xander. That was the safe word Rainer had given her, knowing that her ex's name would stop both of them in their tracks.

"I'll keep you safe. I'll take care of you," he whispered as he pulled her into a kiss. His hands roamed down her body, caressing her curves through the silk of her dress.

Though Cecilia had struggled with touch since Vincent attacked her, Rainer's touch was easier to take. Perhaps it was because she loved him or because she was connected to him and could sense his proximity, but she was better able to let herself relax when she was with him.

"Gods, I have such exciting plans for you. Let's get you out of this dress." Rainer's fingers deftly unbuttoned her dress and he slipped her free of the silk so she stood in only midnight-blue lace. She turned to face him.

"You look incredible," he murmured, breaking his stern character for a moment.

She smiled at him and reached for the hem of his shirt.

He clicked his tongue. "Did I say you could help? Turn around."

She stuck out her lip in a pout and turned her back to him.

"Put your hands on the tabletop."

She hesitated only a moment. The fear was the same but the room was not. Still, she took a breath and flattened her hands against the cool wood. She tried to calm her breathing and ignore the memory that surged to mind.

Fingers brushed the back of her bare thighs and she gasped.

"Don't think about that, Cece. Think about this. This is real," Rainer murmured.

He dropped to his knees behind her and his breath danced over the skin he caressed. She froze for a whole different reason. Desire tore through her like wildfire.

"Do you like that?" he asked.

His hands brushed up and down her legs. The slow, tantalizing movements gave her chills. She was mesmerized by the feeling.

She was snapped out of her trance by the sharp slap of Rainer's palm on her backside. She sucked in a breath as his hand gently rubbed away the hurt from the spanking.

"I asked a question, Cece. You'll answer or you'll be reminded to answer." He kissed her inner thigh.

She shuddered as she pushed her butt out.

He chuckled. "Oh, I see—you liked that."

"Yes. I like what you're doing. All of it."

He smacked her ass again, smoothing away the sting with a gentle caress, the pain and comfort blending into something intoxicating.

"Good girl."

His hands slid higher, rising to the lace edge of her underwear. He was so close to touching her where she wanted him, so she pushed herself back, rubbing against his hand. He slapped her ass again and clicked his tongue.

"I'm in charge, Cece. You said you trust me. Now trust me to give you exactly what you need," he whispered. "Say it."

"You're in charge. I trust you," she rasped.

He rewarded her by rubbing her through the lace. She let out a soft moan.

"Good girl. Now hold still," Rainer whispered. His lips brushed up and down her inner thighs.

She dug her fingernails into her palms to try to keep from wiggling. She was so turned on. She shifted so his lips would go slightly higher, expecting a smack on the bottom, but instead was rewarded by a nip of his teeth on her inner thigh.

"Oh, fuck," she said, collapsing onto her forearms on the table. Rainer's tongue laved over the bite and she moaned.

"You're not doing a very good job of holding still," he scolded.

She shifted her feet slightly wider to give him more space.

"Please," she whimpered.

He rewarded her by nipping up and down her inner thighs and

kissing and licking away each hurt. She forced herself to hold still even though the sensation drove her crazy. She didn't want him to stop.

He slowly rose to stand behind her. "Stand up and turn around."

She obeyed and he chuckled when he saw her face. She was certain she was flushed and half-ruined for him already.

"I think you deserve a reward," he said, pulling her into a kiss and lifting her onto the edge of the table so that her legs dangled.

He pulled away and dragged a chair in front of her before sitting down. Rainer took her left foot in his hand, kissing the freckle on her little toe before placing it on the armrest of the chair as he kissed the freckle inside her knee. He placed her right foot on the other armrest. She stayed there, legs spread wide for him as he leaned back in the chair and smiled.

"Lay down," he said firmly.

Cecilia laid back and stared up at the ceiling. Flickering firelight made the shadows dance over the stone ceiling. She tried to contain her urgency.

"Stay still," Rainer whispered. His hands caressed her inner thighs, moving up and down in slow, languid patterns. It felt wonderful, but she was so turned on she wanted to yell at him to do more.

After what felt like an eternity of waiting, he broke the silence. "You're still okay?"

"Yes," she replied.

"Good, because I think you deserve another reward. Hold still," he whispered and his breath was hot through the lace.

He brought his mouth down on her, licking and sucking through the thin material. It took all of her concentration to not grab the back of his head and hold him right where she wanted him—to not moan and writhe all over the table. She thought the lace would be an obstacle but for some reason it made her even hotter that he could wring that type of pleasure out of her without even getting her naked.

He flicked his tongue against her and her thighs trembled from the effort of staying still.

"Rain," she moaned.

"Yes, sweetheart?"

"I need to move. I'm so—" She moaned as he sucked hard on her clit. "I'm going to—"

"You can move now. Be a good girl and come when I say," he murmured before continuing his ministrations.

She wound her hands through his hair and her legs clamped around his ears.

Rainer continued in earnest and the pleasure of his mouth on her through the damp lace, of his hands lifting her hips so he could feast on her, sparked her pleasure. Her whole body tensed, about to uncoil.

Cecilia arched her back, digging her fingernails into his scalp and moaning as the wave of pleasure crested and crashed down on her hard. Her thighs shook as the climax receded. Slowly Rainer lowered her back to the table and she untangled her fingers from his hair.

He kissed her inner thighs and stood tall. His smile lit up his whole face.

"Good girl," he whispered. "How do you feel?"

She laughed as she sat up. She felt triumphant. Now she knew it was possible. She wanted more. "I can't express it but maybe I can make you feel it."

Rainer's eyes lit up and he let her draw him into a kiss. For a moment, there was nothing but the two of them. No history of war and pain and fear. No blazing fire in the fireplace. No scored wood table under her that reminded her so much of the past. There was only Rainer's mouth on hers. Only his warm, rough hands on her skin. Only their shallow breathing as they pulled back and looked at each other.

Rainer cocked an eyebrow. "I think I can do better. Lay back."

She laughed but followed his command.

He kissed her stomach and hip bone through the gap in the lace of her bustier and underwear before catching the edge of her panties in his teeth and drawing them down. His fingers hooked on the other side, helping them along.

Cecilia cursed at the sight of it. Rainer was so sexy and he was finally hers again. She let her head fall back against the table and surrendered to the feeling of him as he pulled off the lace and began kissing up her legs.

He pushed her thighs further apart, and she gasped at how exposed she felt.

"It's just me, okay?" he soothed. He opened their connection, sending love through, and she relaxed.

"Yes," she whispered.

She moaned at the first brush of his tongue and lips, all her fear forgotten. He took his time with her. Any time he sensed her mind starting to drift, any time she felt a hint of fear, he'd brush his thumb over her inner wrist to remind her it was him until she fully relaxed and gave herself over. She writhed on the table and he gripped her hips, holding her in place. She let out a string of expletives as she went over the edge again, legs trembling with the intensity of it.

Rainer waited for her to come down, to relax back to the wood in a boneless pile. He kissed up her body until he finally met her lips and smiled against them.

"You're such a good girl."

She groaned at the affirmation and Rainer chuckled.

"Gods, if I knew that expression would wind you up so much, I would have used it long ago."

He pulled away abruptly and she let out a discontented whine.

"Stand up," Rainer commanded.

She stood up quickly and let Rainer unhook her bustier so she stood before him naked. Butterflies fluttered in her stomach as she waited for instructions.

"I missed you," Rainer whispered, turning her to face the table.

She sucked in a panicked breath as her hands settled on the tabletop. Her mind pulled her under. Out of nowhere, she drowned in the dark—imagining firm hands on her arms, the bones in her hand being broken one by one, a knife hacking at her dress, and—

"Cece." Rainer's arm wrapped around her, his lips brushing the shell of her ear, and she shuddered. "You are mine. It's just me and you right now. No one else can have you. I'm going to take care of you. You're safe."

He ground his hardness against her ass. She relaxed as his hand slid down her stomach, brushing her lightly between her legs. Pleasure snaked through her.

"Is there anything you need to say?" he asked.

Relief hit her. Rainer was waiting to see if she'd say her safe word. That alone was enough to make her relax.

"Keep going," she said.

"Good girl. Now, bend over," he whispered, kissing her neck.

Cecilia slowly bent forward, leaning far enough across the table that her feet dangled off the ground. The wood was cold against her breasts. She took a deep breath, focusing on Rainer's hands as they trailed down her back.

Her mind started to wander again. She was in this same position when Vincent—

A slap against her bottom jolted her right back to the present. She let out a whimper as Rainer soothed away the hurt with his palm.

"Focus. It's just me, Cece. It's just Rainer. Say it."

Cecilia fought hard against the torrent of memories warring with the desire to stay present. She hated that Vincent still took up space in her mind.

Rainer slapped her ass again, three times in quick succession, trying to obliterate the fear and focus her entirely on his touch.

"Are you afraid?"

"Yes," she said, blinking away surprised tears.

"And who does your fear belong to?" Rainer asked.

She hesitated. "You. It's yours."

"So why are you trying to keep it from me?"

Cecilia took a shaky breath. She thought it would be easy to surrender everything to Rainer, but now she was hesitating. She didn't want the fear hanging over her any longer. It would always be there in some way, but it felt like she was right on the edge of something critical.

"Do you want me to stop?" Rainer's voice softened.

She turned slightly, meeting his eyes. "No," she breathed. "Push me."

He nodded before spanking her several more times. The fiery sting grounded her almost as well as her desire. She pushed her ass out, hoping for more.

"Who does your fear belong to?" Rainer asked.

"You," she whispered.

"Good girl," Rainer said, rewarding her with two more hard slaps. He dropped to his knees behind her, kissing away the sting. "Gods, you're so wet. Do you like this?" he asked.

"Yes."

It was confusing and overwhelming, but Cecilia loved what he was doing. He stood, removed his shirt, and tossed it aside. Then, he bent over her body. His chest was warm against her back.

"You look so sexy like this. I could stare at you all night," he whispered in her ear. "But instead, I'm going to fuck you until you can't stop coming around my cock."

Cecilia groaned. He pulled away and she felt him press against her.

She tried not to tense, but Rainer was big and he normally spent a lot of time warming her up with his fingers.

"Do you trust me?" Rainer asked, reading her apprehension through their connection.

"Yes," she whispered.

He pressed into her slowly, inch by inch. Cecilia relaxed into the stretch, taking deep breaths as Rainer moved meticulously slowly. The slowness meant she felt everything. His hands flexed on her hips. The intake of breath when he bottomed out.

He held himself in place, both of them perfectly still.

"Fuck, you're so tight," Rainer rasped. He bent over her, kissing up her spine, and she shivered.

Cecilia could have stayed there just like that. So close to him, feeling how much he loved her through their connection. Feeling how hard he was, how he was holding himself back, how he wanted to take all her pain and fear and grief and hold it for her. She blinked away tears of relief.

"Are you well?" he asked.

"So good," she breathed.

"That's good because I need you now," he whispered.

He pulled out abruptly and thrust back into her as she groaned. There was the slightest bite of pain, but it was quickly swallowed up by pleasure.

Rainer moved faster, wrapping her hair around his fist and pulling her head back. Warmth pooled below her navel. Cecilia was already so close. Rainer knew her and her body, but most of all, he knew her heart and he knew what she needed. He moved faster, his lips and teeth nipping at her neck.

"Do you have any idea how many nights I fantasized about this? Taking you just like this? How many times I touched myself and thought of you when I couldn't even remember who you were to me? All while you were trying to drive me out of my mind. Gods, Cecilia, the fantasies don't do it justice. You feel so fucking good. There is nothing in the world like being with you."

Cecilia moaned. The dirty talk was going to send her over the edge.

"Do you like that? You like that I thought of you when I touched myself? That I couldn't stop? Gods, the way you made me ache for you. You were such a little tease. You feel perfect. You're so hot and wet for me." Rainer groaned. "Tell me how it feels."

"So full, almost too much. I thought about this so many times, but I was afraid. I wanted you to take me. I wanted exactly this." Her whole body trembled.

"That's right, and now you're going to come, aren't you?"

His hand came to her neck, holding her in place as his teeth dragged down the delicate skin where her neck met her shoulder. She cursed. He thrust into her harder and she dropped her head back against his shoulder and fell apart. Her legs shook violently, her whole body twitching with pleasure.

Rainer groaned. "Yes, good girl," he murmured into her skin.

She felt frenzied, manic with lust. Rainer didn't slow his pace at all. He thrust into her harder, drawing out her climax until she felt like she might black out. Her hand slapped against the table, fumbling for anything to hold on to, her heartbeat thundering in her ears.

"Fuck," he grunted into her shoulder. His hands flexed on her hips as he tried to keep himself from going over the edge with her.

She whimpered as he slid his hand between her and the table and began to rub her clit as he made shorter thrusts. She cursed, the words dissolving into incomprehensible nonsense. Rainer was entirely in control. Her body twitched and clenched under his ministrations.

"When we get home, I'm going to do this every day. I'm not even going to let you get out of bed for a week or two. I want you all to myself. I want this all to myself," he said, rubbing her harder. His teeth grazed her earlobe and she shuddered. "After that, I'm going to wake you up every morning with my tongue between your thighs. I'm going to make you get on your knees and take me in that hot little mouth. Then I'm going to fuck you until I'm late for everything. I'll give you anything you want, and I'll ask for everything back. Would you like that?"

"Yes," she moaned.

His fingers rubbed her furiously and she was so close to another climax she could hardly breathe.

"Tell me what you want me to do to you when we get back."

"Anything you want," she mumbled.

Rainer cursed, his fingers pressing hard on her clit, and she moaned. He pulled out and dropped to his knees, licking her as she shuddered.

"Rain, I want to see you," she gasped, her legs shaking so violently she wasn't even certain they would hold her if they switched positions.

He stood, turning her around to lay her back on the table. He slid back inside her.

"You feel so good," he whispered between kisses. "I love you."

He wrapped his hand around her neck, not to choke her but to remind her that he was in charge. Her whole body clenched in reaction.

Rainer's eyebrows shot up. "You like that?" he taunted. "You like when I hold you down and make you come all over my cock?"

"Oh my gods," she gasped.

She felt like she was burning from the inside out. How was he so good at this? He'd always been amazing in bed but never so commanding.

"Say it." His voice was so different, so demanding, and she wanted to do everything he said.

She knew exactly what he was looking for. The words that turned him on just as much as they comforted her.

"I'm just for you, Rain."

He gave her a lupine smile. "And what about this?" he asked, his hand sliding down to rub between her legs as he thrusted.

She was dizzy with lust, each possessive question ratcheting her pleasure higher. "Just for you."

His hand slid higher, coming to rest over her heart, his gaze softening. "And what about this?"

"It's just for you, Rain," she rasped.

He rewarded her by brushing his thumb over her golden scar. Every muscle in her body squeezed, her toes curled, her heels pressing into Rainer's back. She felt suspended in midair, separated from reality, so close to orgasm again. All the pent-up tension in her body made every feeling more intense.

Rainer smiled down at her, sweat dripping down his chest, his hair stuck to his temples. He looked so sexy and feral with desire for her.

"I want to be in control," she breathed.

Rainer's eyes lit up in surprise. He lifted her up and spun her so that he could lay back on the table, allowing her to lower herself on top of him.

"Fuck," he groaned. "Take what you need."

Cecilia did. She rolled her hips, moving with him. He sat up, folding her into his arms, meeting her rhythm.

Tears streamed down her face. She couldn't express the relief, the triumph she felt, the immensity of the love she felt for Rainer.

"You're so beautiful. So brave. So strong," Rainer murmured. His voice was warm, his lips full of praise as he kissed her.

She was right on the edge. It felt impossible, but the joy was going to send her over again.

The climax tore through her and Rainer opened their connection wide. She arched into him and his hands on her lower back held her in place as he pulsed inside her with a loud groan. Her whole body tingled with the sparkling starlight feeling she always felt when they were together.

Through it all, what existed between them stayed intact. Rainer still made her feel better than anyone ever had. He still loved her. She still loved him.

What they'd done didn't fix everything, but his plan worked because she no longer felt creeping dread. She felt relaxed, wrung out, pleasantly exhausted.

Rainer kissed the tears from her cheeks. "How do you feel?"

"Powerful. Loved," she said. "Like I just let out all the stress from the past few months at once and I'm going to sleep for days."

The concerned crease in Rainer's brow softened. They'd both gone a bit outside of their comfort zones.

"Thank you, Rain. I was scared, but you kept me safe. You pushed me just enough. Thank you for taking care of me."

"I can't believe you're thanking me," he said. "I'm honored that you trust me so much. That was so sexy I thought I was going to lose it right away."

"I like you bossy," she said, blushing.

He chuckled. "I noticed. We can do that anytime you like."

He pulled Cecilia into a kiss and she sighed in satisfaction.

It was hard to fathom the relief she felt taking back something she'd been afraid she lost. It didn't make it as if it never happened. Part of her would always carry that haunting fear. But in some small way, Rainer helped her heal over it by taking her fear and pain and letting her be in control of how it happened. It took tremendous trust, but she was relieved that he could give that to her. Relieved she was brave enough to try.

For a long time, they lay there in the rectangles of fading sunlight streaming through the glass doors as Rainer stroked her back and told her a story about a man who lost all the memories of the love of his life until she kissed him and his body remembered.

Cecilia snuggled into his side, nearly asleep by the time he reached the moral of his story: It was good to be a fool in love.

46

RAINER

R ainer stared out at the calm sea, breathing in the salty air
and tilting his head back in the sunshine. It was a beautiful spring day, as if the gods recognized that they owed
Rainer and Cecilia good weather for their wedding. He supposed
with so many of them related to the bride, and in attendance, that
might have been the case.

His stomach fluttered, though not with nervousness about
marrying Cecilia so much as nervousness about forgetting all the
heartfelt things he wanted to say. This day had been a lifetime in the
making and he wanted every single thing to be perfect for Cecilia
because she had fought so hard for him and for herself. She deserved
a wedding worthy of all she'd been through.

Healing was hard work. His mind was filled with holes still and
every time he found one, he was so angry with himself for forgetting
—so baffled how there could still be gaps. And she would patiently
place her hand in his and stitch his mind back together. The month
leading up to this day had been challenging for both of them, but
he'd found no better medicine than her love.

He looked out over the crowd, his gaze landing on the empty chairs placed in remembrance of all their lost family. Chairs for Leo and Rosalee Reznik, for Selene Carrick, for Teddy, and for Magdalena. Just looking at the Argarian healer's apron hanging over the seat made Rainer feel a pang of guilt. Finally, he looked at the chair for his mother, Maura.

He'd been thinking of her a lot in the days since he'd kicked Raymond McKay out of his life. He'd spent so much of his childhood angry at Maura for not leaving Raymond, for not doing more to protect Rainer. Now that he was grown, he could see how their life might have been if she'd left. Rainer's whole future would have been clouded by scandal. He never would have had any of the opportunities that opened to him because of Raymond's conniving. He probably would have never been bonded to Cecilia.

Rainer often thought of his mother's words: "*Someday you will be old enough to need those fairy tales again.*"

When Maura had said those words to him as a child, he'd felt so certain that he had outgrown them. But now, on a beautiful spring day, waiting for the love of his life, who'd stood between him and death and the oblivion of memory loss and loved him still, he finally knew what his mother meant. Those stories were the map that had brought him home to Cecilia over and over. He was finally old enough to need those fairy tales again.

He turned and caught Cal's eye. His friend threw an arm over his shoulder. "Finally doing what Sylvie and I always knew you would. It's about time."

Rainer rolled his eyes, and his gaze landed on Xander. The Argarian king crossed the sand to meet them.

"Nice crown," Rainer said, nodding to the jagged golden lightning bolt crown on Xander's head.

He rolled his eyes. "Jess insisted. Always trying to style me for the most drama."

"As if you've ever needed the help," Rainer said.

Xander grinned. "Exactly." He glanced out at the crowd before meeting Rainer's eye. "I'm sure you don't need me to tell you you're making the best decision of your life," he said. "She looks stunning, so just try not to get knocked over by the sight of her and you'll be okay."

Rainer felt an unexpected burst of affection for his old rival. He yanked Xander into a hug.

When Xander pulled back, he was grinning. "All right, don't fuss. Just take care of our girl."

He retreated to sit between Jessamin and Isla. The queen took his hand, but he and Isla stared at each other as she affectionately brushed his hair back from his forehead. It was good to see Xander so happy. It figured it would take not one but two exceptional women to rein in the king of Argaria.

The musicians began to play as King Marcos arrived with Queen Ilani. Queen Regent Elena followed them and placed an affectionate kiss on Rainer's cheek before taking her seat.

Marcos took his place at the center of the wisteria arch that Sylvie had constructed. Rainer stood beside him, the ocean at his back, his gaze focused beyond the smiling faces of their loved ones, waiting for Cecilia. They'd fashioned a curtain at the bottom of the cliff trail so Rainer wouldn't see her until it was time.

The music changed and Sylvie and Mika stepped out, pulling the curtains wide to reveal Cecilia arm in arm with Aunt Clara.

Cecilia was smiling, her eyes already locked on his, and the air punched out of Rainer's lungs at the sight of her walking toward him.

The closer she strode, the harder it was to breathe, his chest tightening to the point of lightheadedness. Cal tapped his arm and he finally took a startled breath.

As she made it to the end of the aisle, Rainer could finally take in the details of her dress. It started pale blue like the traditional Olney wedding color but grew darker and darker until it was a midnight-blue at the hem and all across it were beaded and embroidered stars. She looked like the Summer Firestorm meteor shower, stars pinned in her hair and cascading in all directions over the dress. The neckline plunged, revealing the golden scar on her chest, and each time she took a step forward, the silk billowed, showing a glimpse of her right leg through the slit.

Something inside of Rainer snapped, unstoppable tears streaking down his cheeks.

He bit back a laugh because, although he was falling apart, Cecilia smiled brightly as she closed the distance between them.

Cecilia, who was so known by everyone for extreme emotions, stayed very calm, shedding only a few gentle tears, while Rainer dissolved into an absolute wreck.

By the time Aunt Clara took her seat in the front row next to Mika, Lyra, and Sylvie, Cecilia was trying not to laugh.

She reached her hand up to cup Rainer's cheek.

"You look like a lifetime of wishes come true," he whispered, his voice hoarse.

Was it possible he'd spent his life trying to hold off lightning that was poised to strike every time he looked at her? Cecilia was a storm he'd never acclimated to. He felt just as stunned by her walking toward him in her beautiful dress as he ever did and he was struck by the intensity of his love for her, as he'd always been.

Cecilia sent a surge of calm through their bond, a wide, knowing smile on her face as Rainer fell apart. It should have been humiliating, but she was obviously charmed by it. He couldn't believe how wise and grown up she managed to look without the world-weariness that had weighed on her just months before.

Rainer had her, lost her, won her over, lost her again, and finally, *finally* they found their way back to each other. So he cried and she held it together and she squeezed his hand to anchor him. When he managed to clear his eyes, he almost started back up again at how beautiful she looked.

Their wedding felt both impossible and inevitable. In his heart, he'd always known this was where they were headed. There were many moments when he'd had reason to doubt, but now, holding her hands, it felt like they were meant to be. Through death and war and the grief that came after, their love endured.

Marcos started the ceremony. Rainer could hardly focus on the king's words. He was too transfixed by Cecilia's beautiful face.

When it came time to say their vows, Rainer desperately tried to hold it together and remember what he wanted to say, but when Cecilia started to speak she stole every thought from his head.

"Rainer Jordan McKay, this has been a very long time coming. What took you so long?" Cecilia said.

Everyone laughed and he fell in love with her all over again for making him laugh when he felt so overwhelmed.

"I was fortunate to have a lot of good examples of love in my life. My father taught me devotion, my mother taught me compassion, and Aunt Clara taught me how to make a fuss over someone. But you taught me to love myself. You believed in me when I didn't. You pretended to have courage when I was afraid. You reminded me who I was when I lost myself. You have been the one constant in a real whirlwind of a life. I have been so many things: a huntress, a witch, a princess, and a goddess. But by far, my favorite thing to be is your love. You have protected me, but more importantly, you taught me how to protect myself. You put your faith in me whether I deserved it or not. You're the best listener and my favorite storyteller."

Rainer squeezed her hands in his, trying not to crush her delicate fingers as he struggled to contain his emotions.

"I promise to do my best to abandon my on-again, off-again relationship with danger. I promise to make you laugh when you're taking things too seriously, to find each and every one of your worries and fix them in a hurry." She brushed her thumb over the crease in his brow and Rainer laughed. "I promise to never stop dreaming along with you because this story—our story—is worth telling."

Rainer kissed her fingers as she continued.

"We fought hard for this. It would have been easy to give up. Love is hard, even when it's as easy as loving you. But through a lot of hard-fought battles, I know the truth: Love is the last hard thing worth having—" Her voice broke, and a tear slid down her cheek. "I love you for way too many reasons to go into because I know we want to get on to the celebration, so I'll stick with this: you reminded me that love means loneliness is a matter of perception. You reminded me that no matter how lonely I feel, I am never actually alone because you're always right beside me when I need you. You've held on to my hurts along with me. You've made every burden of mine one you share. Your heart is wrapped around mine and no one has ever taken such good care of it."

Rainer swallowed hard, unsure how much longer he could keep even the smallest semblance of composure.

Cecilia squeezed his hands. "I promise to be brave with my hand and brave with my heart when it comes to you because you have always been worth the risk. Seventeen years ago, I promised you my magic and my life. Today, I promise you my heart and my soul because you've always had them anyway."

Rainer lost it. He couldn't pull himself together and Cecilia could barely contain her laughter. She cupped his face in her small hands and he leaned his forehead against hers.

"Is this how you feel all the time when I cry?" she whispered.

Beside him, Cal coughed to cover a laugh as Cecilia brushed away Rainer's tears, holding his face in her soft hands. He was a mess and he didn't care who knew it.

Raymond McKay had been so completely wrong. Love wasn't a fool's errand and it didn't make kingdoms crumble. It made Rainer strong, and it made Cecilia strong, too.

It was good to be a fool in love. In fact, it was the best feeling in the world. He was madly in love with Cecilia Reznik and he didn't care who knew it.

Rainer took a deep breath, took her hands, and spoke the words he'd been holding back their whole lives.

47

CECILIA

Cecilia couldn't decide if she wanted to laugh at how emotional Rainer was or cry along with him. In all their years side by side, she'd never seen him so undone. His verdant eyes scanned her face as he swallowed thickly, trying to push the emotion aside to speak. It was real and raw and so adorable. Her heart clenched in her chest.

She sent a gentle, soothing calm through their bond. Rainer's face softened and he smiled. His hands still shook in hers but he sucked in a shuddering breath and pulled it together finally.

"Cecilia Juliette Reznik. I'm sorry I'm late. Very late. I used to think you were the least patient person in Olney, but now I know better. You are the most maddening, beautiful, kind, brave, reckless person I have ever met. I fell in love with you a thousand times over the past few years. In little ways—like when I watched you shoot your bow for the first time, or when you told off a bully—and in big ways, like when you saved my life or the lives of our friends."

He squeezed her hands for dear life as if she was the only thing anchoring him to reality. He took a wobbly breath, barely containing his emotions until she sent another jolt of love through their connection.

Anyone who hadn't watched the way they silently communicated over the years might have missed it. It was the briefest of moments where Rainer's eyes fluttered closed and then a brilliant smile broke across his face.

"It's easy, much too easy today, in fact, to look at you and think the gods could never have made anyone more beautiful, but I know your heart is the real masterpiece. To be so compassionate, kind, loving, and so fiercely protective of the people you let in. I am so lucky to be the person with a direct connection to that heart, to know it like my own, to feel the ebbs and flows of your emotions like a language that's just for us."

Rainer squeezed her hands tighter still. "I have fallen for you over and over, all while trying to convince myself that it wasn't true. I am sorry it took me so long to get here. I should have given up on following the rules long ago and saved us a lot of heartache and trouble, but I don't regret it. I can't regret anything that brought us here to this day. I can't regret anything that let me see you as you really are: strong beyond any warrior I've ever known. Brave on instinct. And wise enough to stay hopeful and soft even with mountains of evidence to suggest otherwise. You make me hopeful in even the direst situations, just like you do for so many other people. You are truly the greatest gift of my life. I love you much more than I could ever put into these clumsy words, especially being this much of a mess."

Everyone laughed. Cecilia blinked rapidly, trying to keep tears at bay.

"I promise to be brave with my hand and brave with my heart. I promise that I will keep listening to you and encouraging you to tell your stories, to keep dreaming of big, impossible things. I promise to try to relax a little bit with the worrying and enjoy life more. I promise to cook so that you don't burn the cottage down. I promise to never wake you up before ten in the morning. I promise to love you as much when you are old and gray as I do right now...as I always have. I love you brave and exuberant, soft and tender, angry and raging, fierce and wild. I love all parts of you. I was made to love you, and I will never stop."

It was her turn to fall apart. Tears streamed down her cheeks as he spoke and she didn't care who saw. She didn't brush them away in anger or frustration. She just let them fall. She'd never again be afraid to bare her whole self to him.

Rainer was hers and she was his. It had always been that way. The ceremony only made it official to everyone else, but still, she felt as if something had shifted. She looked at him and saw a complete person. Someone with guilt and grief and longing. He saw her as someone who didn't need his protection as much as his love.

When Marcos bound their hands together and then untied them, handing each of them an end of the cord, she knew that neither of them would ever let go again.

———

After the dinner on the beach, musicians played so everyone could dance and celebrate the happy couple. Cecilia leaned against Rainer, swaying to the music more than formally dancing. She just liked the chance to be held and watch their friends drink and carry on after so much heartache.

Sylvie, Evan, and Cal sat huddled around the bonfire, drinks in hand. Reese and Christopher stood on the other side of the circle, regaling Aunt Clara with stories from their journey to Olney.

Cecilia smiled seeing them all there together safe and sound.

Samson stumbled across the sand with Cecilia's half-sister Desiree on his arm.

"Lady Cece, you sure know how to throw a party," Samson slurred.

Cecilia laughed at the exasperated look on Desiree's face. "Is he drunk?"

Desiree nodded, pursing her full lips. "Every party must be the best party and that lust for life and everything else makes him prone to overindulgence."

Samson grinned and winked at Rainer. "McKay, I told you stars would fall. You just needed a push."

"I did," Rainer said, kissing the top of Cecilia's head.

"Good thing I made you kiss her," Samson said, waggling his eyebrows. "Happy to watch you do more. Offer still stands."

Rainer's hands gripped Cecilia a bit tighter. "No, thank you."

"Come now, love. Let's get you home," Desiree said.

"But I haven't said good night to Evan," Samson whined.

Desiree smothered a smile. "Yes, darling, but you're already going fuzzy around the edges."

Samson grumbled something too low for them to hear as he and Desiree faded into smoke that smelled like tobacco, vanilla, and crushed rose petals.

"Will they be at every family party?" Rainer asked.

Cecilia burst out laughing. "As if I could control the gods."

She looked out over the godly guests who remained. Sayla, Devlin, and Aelish had left after the dinner. Clastor had stayed to dance with Cecilia and look gruffly at Rainer for a while, but he'd left shortly after the dancing started in earnest.

Grimon remained, flirting with Aurelia over plates piled with desserts. The goddess of the harvest did not look impressed—or was doing a convincing job of seeming such.

"What do you think, Lady McKay? Was the day up to your standards?" Rainer whispered into her hair.

She craned her neck to meet his gaze. "It was perfect. My only goal was for us to get married and for the only surprises to be good ones for once and I think we are safe on all fronts there."

Rainer's eyes lit with mischief. "Good, because I am more than ready to have some alone time with my wife."

A throat cleared, drawing their attention.

Xander and Jessamin stood beside them. "Sorry to interrupt, but I'm afraid to say that we should head out. My lovely queen has had more than enough partying for one evening."

Cecilia grinned at Jessamin, whose stomach was already swollen.

She'd spent most of the evening dancing anyway, despite both Xander and Maren's attempts to get her to relax.

"Before we go, we do have a wedding gift for you," Jessamin said, grinning at Xander. "Xander told me how much the two of you have always wanted to visit Estrellas during the summer auroras. I coordinated with my sister Karina, the princess and heir apparent, to organize a honeymoon for you. You'll get to go to the storytelling festival, at which you will, of course, be expected to share your story as it is quickly becoming a favorite among romantic story lovers. She'll show you around and act as tour guide and make sure you can stay at our family estate in the north to get the best view of the auroras."

Cecilia was jumping up and down by the time she finished, unable to hide her absolute delight. She threw herself into Xander's arms.

"Love, my wife is right there," Xander said, jerking his head toward Jessamin.

"Xander, I swear to the gods, if you hit on my wife at our wedding reception, I am going to have you thrown in the sea and drowned by my goddess sister-in-law. I don't care what you're king of," Rainer said, shaking his head.

"Relax, I won't flirt with your wife." Xander grinned and winked at Cecilia. "No matter how beautiful she looks."

Cecilia giggled and pulled away to lean back into Rainer. He wrapped his arms around her and it felt like coming home.

She gazed up at him. "We're going to the Moonrise City."

Rainer kissed her forehead. "I know. I am just as excited, though less eager to hug Xander."

"You'll leave just before Cece's birthday and be back by early September when Evan and Sylvie will be in Olney for their second wedding," Xander said.

"Congratulations to you both. We are very happy we could be here to see it made official," Jessamin said, kissing both of their cheeks. She reluctantly allowed Xander, Maren, and Isla to guide her up the cliff trail.

Cecilia turned and looked up at Rainer, bouncing from foot to foot with newfound excitement. "I'm your wife."

"You are. Finally."

"What do you say we go make it *really* official?" she asked with a wink.

Rainer didn't need to be asked twice. Before Cecilia could take another breath, he'd swept her into his arms and started toward their cottage and the rest of their lives together.

48

RAINER

Rainer and Cecilia's honeymoon in the Moonrise City of Estrellas was spectacular. Jessamin's sister Karina had gone all out to make sure they got to see everything that Novum had to offer. It was everything and more than they'd hoped for after reading stories of the beautiful landscapes and late summer auroras that colored the night sky.

They'd laid out under the stars each night, tangled together as they watched the auroras and their sweaty skin cooled. Though Cecilia still had her moments of panic, she seemed more at home in her body and more at peace with touch.

They'd learned that, despite having been out on the water often as children, Cecilia did not fare well on long ship rides. Most of their journey both there and back had seen her heaving over the side of the ship, barely able to keep down more than bread and water for days.

Even now, back on dry land, Cecilia was dealing with some left-over motion sickness and unrelenting dizziness, cutting back her clinic hours and spending more time in bed.

Today, though, she was on her feet, looking slightly less pale as she slipped into the blue dress Rainer loved so much. He met her gaze in the mirror as he buttoned up the back.

"You look lovely," he whispered.

"Thank you. You look quite handsome yourself with this new haircut. Is Sylvie going to have to come back every few months to do it or will you trust me to do it at some point?"

He laughed. "Aunt Clara took notes so she can do it. You have many talents, but I'm never letting you near my hair again."

"I only ruined it one time and I was sixteen," she grumbled.

Rainer shook his head. It was vain of him, but he loved his hair and he'd never forgotten what a mess Cecilia had made of it when she took over cutting it right after his mother died. Sylvie had come to the rescue then, shaping it into something decent, but he'd not make the same mistake again.

"Let's stick with the talents you've already cultivated and leave my hair to someone else." He pressed the back of his hand to her forehead. "Now, how are you feeling?"

Her gaze flashed to his and he could read her apprehension.

"Not as bad, but I'll still take it easy at dinner," she said.

Rainer nodded, holding out his arm. They walked down the trail, enjoying the early autumn day. The heat had relented, bringing a cool ocean breeze over town and making it the perfect day for Evan and Sylvie's wedding dinner.

Though Rainer had missed the couple's official ceremony back in Argaria, Cecilia had shown him the memory of the night. Now, months later, Evan and Sylvie were in town to have an official wedding dinner at the insistence of the Brett family.

Rainer and Cecilia greeted their newlywed friends along with Sylvie's family. The garden was decked out in ribbons and floral arrangements and the tablescape was woven with vines and wildflowers.

"What a show-off. I mean, we get it, Syl, you're very talented with earth magic," Cecilia teased.

"Your jealousy is unbecoming," Sylvie teased, touching her

friend's cheek. "I'm joking, though you do look quite pale. Are you well?"

Cecilia nodded. "Just some leftover ailment from our travels, but I promise I am well enough for a celebration."

Sylvie smirked. "Do you remember the first thing I ever said to you?"

Cecilia's hands flew up to her hair. She self-consciously patted her curls. "You said: Why does your hair look like that?"

Sylvie stifled a laugh and turned to Rainer. "You should have seen her. It was her first day of school. Aunt Clara was away and her father tried to braid her hair. It was a disaster."

Rainer couldn't imagine Leo Reznik braiding Cecilia's hair.

Cecilia rolled her eyes. "Six-year-old Sylvie was merciless. Never mind that my mother had just passed. She expected me to look impeccable."

"I mean do you remember the first thing of *substance* I said to you?" Sylvie asked. "We'd just learned about how different our schooling would be from the boys."

Cecilia's lips twitched into a grin. "Why should the boys have all the fun? I'm not letting some man decide my future." Cecilia's gaze slid to Evan. "Seems like young Sylvie was a visionary."

Sylvie squeezed Cecilia's hand. "I could not have done it without you." Her smile turned watery. "Thank you for helping me make a world where I have better choices."

Cecilia flushed with pride. "That was all you, Syl. Now let's go celebrate the future you chose for yourself."

———

The meal was joyful and involved another round of toasts, including one that had been written by Xander, who was expecting the arrival of his first child any day. He'd sent his toast with Evan to be read out loud in his absence.

After dinner, Rainer took Cecilia by the arm and walked her

around the garden. As they made their way to a row of tall sunflowers, she gripped his arm hard, leaning her head against his shoulder.

"Are you well?" he asked.

She sighed. "Just some dizziness."

Rainer frowned. "I'd thought that the spinning would stop now that we're back on dry land, but it's been a couple weeks."

Cecilia froze. "What did you say?"

"I said it's strange how the spinning hasn't stopped, even now that you're on dry land."

Cecilia's eyes lit up. "We have to go."

Rainer's body tensed, ready to fight off an invisible foe. "Where?"

"Raven Whitewind's."

The woman's name turned Rainer's blood to ice. The last time he'd seen the ancient witch, she'd been severing their bond. The memory of Cecilia's pain and the absence of their bond still haunted Rainer.

"The seer? Why—"

Rainer wanted to argue but he knew the determined look on Cecilia's face, so he took her hand and she practically dragged him down the trail. They walked by their cottage, continuing down the path as the foliage grew denser and the darkness of the early evening closed in.

Finally, when Rainer began to worry that they'd somehow missed it, a small, familiar cottage came into view. Just like he had eighteen years earlier when he first saw the cottage, Rainer took a bracing breath and pushed through the gate.

49

CECILIA

Cecilia's heart was in her throat as she pounded her fist on the seer's cottage door. She was terrified of what Raven's warning meant—of what might be wrong now.

She'd let her guard down. So much had gone well and now something was bound to be wrong.

The door swung open, revealing Raven Whitewind. She looked entirely unsurprised to see them.

"I take it the world has not stopped spinning," she said with a grin.

"Why am I sick? Is there something wrong with me? With my magic?" Cecilia asked.

Rainer's fear hit her in the chest.

"What's going on?" he asked.

Cecilia turned to look at him. "I didn't tell you, not for not wanting to, but because I was still trying to reckon with it myself. While we were in Argaria, just after Raven severed our bond, she came to me."

"And what did I say, girl?" Raven asked.

"You said that I was asking the right question—how could my

mother let me sacrifice something so permanent? How could I consent to an exchange that would have ripped away my soul?"

"That's right."

Rainer's jaw dropped as he looked from Cecilia to the ancient witch. He looked ready to throttle the woman.

Cecilia placed her hands on her hips, trying to steady herself for whatever bad news the seer was about to drop on her. "What's wrong with me?"

"You tell me," Raven said. "You're dizzy, nauseous, exhausted, and a newlywed. I wonder what it could be."

All Cecilia's bravado fled. Raven couldn't be implying what she seemed to be. "But you said—"

"I said you did exactly as your mother hoped you would," Raven said. "An exchange requires consent, but what happened to you was never really a choice, and as such, nature needed to balance it somehow. The only way to do that was to have the exchange be temporary."

Cecilia frowned. "My goddess power would have gone away?"

Raven shook her head. "Not exactly. The rules of magic say that something cannot be given without exchange, but that goddess power was always yours—it was just bound by your mother at birth. The Cave of Longings simply unbound the magic. You gave up your ability to bear children to release the binding spell, but that was only meant to buy you the time to defeat Cato and Endros and bring peace to the realm. It was supposed to keep Cato from using you in the way we suspected he wanted to."

Cecilia shook her head, her heart thundering so loudly in her ears she could hardly hear anything else beyond her own shallow breathing. "So that means—" She looked from the witch to Rainer, her hand coming to rest on her stomach.

Raven tracked the movement. "What do you feel?"

Cecilia closed her eyes, her brow furrowed in concentration as she tried to ground herself in her body, to scan her magic. She felt the pulse of her magic through her body like a heartbeat, but there was also something else—an entirely new rhythm.

Cecilia blinked her eyes open. "What is that?"

"What does it feel like?" Raven asked.

"Like a part of myself I can't fully sense," Cecilia said, her eyes suddenly glassy. "Am I—"

"Pregnant," Raven said. "Yes. I suspect a couple months along."

Cecilia felt weak in the knees, like she might collapse from shock or relief. She'd been especially exhausted in the last few weeks of their honeymoon, turning down wine because it made her too sleepy and eating every lemon cake she could get her hands on. She'd written the exhaustion and cravings off as sheer excitement of traveling and late nights in bed together, but now it all made sense.

"But I thought—"

"It was always a chance. You could have given in to Cato. But you became your mother's wildest dream for you," Raven said. "I'm happy that you had the faith to get here."

Cecilia was so stunned she could barely speak. After all her grief and frustration, after all her righteous anger about her choice being taken away... Every struggle and every choice had led her in a full circle to this moment.

Cecilia was afraid to believe it. "You're sure?"

Raven reached out a hand, placing it on Cecilia's stomach and grinning. "I'm certain. I suspect you'll be welcoming this little one in early May. I have a memory to show you before you go."

Raven took hold of each of their hands and Cecilia felt a gentle press on her mind.

She knew that face at first glance because it was so much like her own. She was looking at Selene Carrick.

———

Selene Carrick smiled and placed a hand on her swollen stomach. "My darling girl, I wish I could save you the heartache that Raven assures me awaits you. What an enormous blessing to be your mother, but also a curse to know I'll never meet you as a grown woman and won't have the opportunity to hold your hand through your struggles. I am already so proud of you and you aren't even here yet. Raven has been kind enough to share glimpses of you."

She cleared her throat. *"As you might have guessed, I planned this all along for you, Cecilia. There was only one path through that saw you get all the things you wanted, and it was so painful. I did not want that for you but I had to believe that you were strong enough to weather it, that you have the perseverance and fortitude or the sheer stubbornness to keep going until you got everything you wanted. Raven assured your father and I that the Rezniks were part of that, as was the guardian you'll one day be paired with. I hope that someday you'll be able to have the option to choose exactly what you want without apology. All I ever wanted for you is for you to be able to make your own choices. I love you and I'm very proud of you, my brave girl."*

———

The memory dissipated as they all blinked their eyes open.

"Why didn't you tell me before?" Cecilia asked.

"I couldn't risk that I'd influence the outcome," Raven said. "It is the curse of a seer to know what's best but have to contain it. Just like how Clastor could not tell you that making a selfless sacrifice for Rainer would allow you to come back to life. I could not tell you that the exchange would be temporary without it affecting how you reacted. The chances were so slim that with every turn you took down this path, I was afraid that any hints might interfere. Congratulations, Lady McKay. You'll make a wonderful mother."

Raven shooed the stunned duo toward the door. "You should be getting home before the sun sets and the woods get too dark. Remember lots of water and protein, Cecilia. Good luck."

Cecilia and Rainer wandered, dazed, to the picket fence around the seer's garden, staring at each other. The grief, gratitude, and overwhelm hit Cecilia all at once.

Her knees buckled and Rainer swept her into a hug. She sobbed against his shoulder, both of them utterly at a loss for what to say. Finally, he set her down.

"How do you feel?" Rainer asked.

She gave him a watery smile. "I would have been thrilled with me and you and adopted children. And I'm certainly not the sort of woman who believes she can only be happy with a child—" She shook her head as if she could shake off the flood of emotion. "But I felt robbed of the option. For so long, I thought I could stop wanting it when I knew it wouldn't happen and it never quite settled in. The wanting never abated and I didn't want to tell you because I knew how badly you wanted it too. Especially when you finally admitted it back in Argaria."

Rainer hung his head. "I'm sorry that you felt like you couldn't tell me. I meant that I would just be happy to be with you and adopt children, but obviously, I'm delighted with this also."

She blinked away happy tears as he lowered to his knees and pressed his mouth against her stomach.

"Hello, baby, this is your father. I am so excited to meet you, but please, for the love of the gods, stop making your mother so sick."

Rainer grinned up at Cecilia and rose to his feet, sweeping her into his arms and carrying her home.

PART V:
HOPEFULLY
EVER AFTER

50

RAINER

Rainer woke to the sound of waves crashing far below the cottage windows. Despite the chillier nights, Cecilia insisted on sleeping with a window cracked to bring in the fresh sea air. Gull calls and the faint sound of bells at the harbor swept in with the breeze.

Rainer smiled and rolled over, reaching for his wife.

Instead of finding Cecilia, he was met with a set of bright green eyes.

"Stella, what are you doing awake?" He smiled at his daughter as she kicked her pudgy legs and let out a soft gurgle.

He had a bleary memory of Cecilia stirring in the night, soothing a teething Stella in the rocking chair that now sat next to the bed.

"I know, little star. I know it hurts, but I promise you'll feel better if you go to sleep for a little bit," she'd whispered.

Rainer ran a finger down Stella's soft cheek as he glanced at Cecilia asleep beside her. His wife was splayed out on her back, her hair pinned up on top of her head and her cheeks rosy in the morning light. One of her arms was curled around the baby so Rainer wouldn't roll over and crush her. She didn't even stir as Stella bumped against her.

"Did you keep your mom up all night? Aren't you tired?" Rainer whispered.

Stella grinned and babbled.

He laughed. "Shh, don't wake her up."

He pulled Stella onto his chest, rubbing her back in the hopes that she'd lay down and go back to sleep. Instead, she pressed herself up onto her hands, blinking at him. Wisps of wild dark curls sprang out from her head in all directions.

"Not tired, huh? Want to go for a walk?"

Stella cooed softly.

"All right, let's go," he said.

It only took a few moments to get her changed, dressed in warmer clothes, and tucked into the sling on Rainer's chest. He tugged a hat over her head, which she instantly ripped off and threw on the floor.

He bent to retrieve it. "I know you hate it, but it's sunny and you have your mother's complexion, so you have to wear it."

She frowned as he placed the hat back on her head. Her legs churned in excitement as he ducked out of the cottage.

Rainer grinned. The first time he had felt his daughter kick, he was overwhelmed that he could love someone so much without ever meeting her. Cecilia had been equally in awe, though she was concerned that their little warrior was just going to try to kick her way out. Now that Stella was out in the world, her legs were always churning, as if he could set her down and she'd take off running.

Despite Rainer's upbringing, being a father came so easily to him. All the worry that he'd felt for years was replaced with the absolute joy of watching Stella develop a personality right before his eyes. Sometimes, she was fierce and quick to anger like her mother, and others, she was serious like him, an identical crease forming in her forehead like she was deeply concerned. Watching her learn and grow healed something in him he hadn't thought he'd ever make peace with.

Between fatherhood, finishing his apprenticeship, and starting to take on his own work, Rainer felt for the first time like he'd become something of his own making. While he still trained daily, he didn't push as hard, and the hands-on nature of woodworking and all the heavy lifting of building furniture kept him active enough to burn off his excess energy.

Rainer walked down the trail toward the beach, sand and pebbles crunching under his feet. Stella snuggled against his chest.

"See, I knew you were tired," Rainer chided. "Do you want to hear a story?"

Stella dropped her head back to look at him, her face brightening. He'd begun telling her stories from the moment they found out Cecilia was pregnant. He'd lay in bed each night with his head beside Cecilia's stomach, telling both mother and baby a bedtime story. Now, even at such a young age, Stella would sit still, listening attentively as he spun tales.

"How about one about your mom? You sometimes like to hear about her getting into trouble." Stella frowned and Rainer shook his head. "Okay fine, I'll tell you another one about *sharks*."

Stella barked out an approving screech and he laughed.

"I don't know why you like the scary stories the most, but whatever you want, Stell-bell."

He cradled her head as he walked and began to spin a tale about a mermaid escaping a vicious shark. Before long, Stella's head lolled against his chest and she fell asleep. He continued down the beach.

In sleep, Stella looked so much like her mother, her dark lashes fanned over rosy cheeks and her lips pursed in a soft pout. Rainer loved her more than words. The moment Lyra first placed the baby in his arms, he thought his heart would burst. Cecilia had been clinging to him, a joyful, sobbing mess. For perhaps the first time, he'd understood completely what it felt like to be so overwhelmed by emotions that it was impossible to settle on just one. The two of them had sat there for hours just staring at Stella's perfect face.

A stiff breeze blew in off the sea and he gazed tentatively into the waves, wondering if perhaps he was about to be joined by Auntie Adira, as Cecilia liked to call her now. But no goddess stepped from the surf, so he turned and strode back toward the cottage trail.

A few minutes later, Stella stirred and woke, looking at him expectantly.

A zing of love passed through his connection with Cecilia as if to say, *"Where did you go with my baby?"*

Rainer straightened Stella's hat. "I know you're hungry. We'll go find your mom. She's looking for us."

Stella let out a discontented whine of protest, looking longingly at the sea, reaching her pudgy hand toward it.

"It's going to be cold. Are you sure?"

She kicked her legs frantically in response as he lifted her from the sling. He loved that she seemed to share his love for the sea. He couldn't wait for her to be old enough to swim with him in the mornings.

He pulled off her tiny socks, tucking them in his pocket. Then he walked to the shoreline, bending low so Stella could dip her toes in the water.

She let out a squeal of surprise and he lifted her right away.

"I warned you, but you're as stubborn as your mother," Rainer said as he tucked her back into the sling, facing out this time so she could see the world—but she tilted her head back, looking up at him instead.

"Want to go see your mom?"

Stella smiled and cooed softly and he climbed the cliff trail toward the cottage.

After a lifetime of being regimented and eternally on time, Rainer was blessed to be joyfully and woefully late for everything. He could blame nothing but his happiness for it. He loved everything about his life. He was so stubbornly present and unconcerned about the future that he constantly lost track of just how much time had passed.

Rainer took the last few steps up the trail from his walk on the beach. As Cecilia came into view, standing in the cottage doorway, a hand on her hip, his daughter's tiny legs began kicking up a storm in excitement. Stella let out a happy babble at the sight of her.

"There they are—my two favorite people in the whole world," Cecilia said with a grin as she scooped the baby from the sling.

She held Stella high and the baby squealed in delight as Cecilia blew kisses on her stomach. Rainer had never had any doubt, but Cecilia was a wonderful mother—patient, gentle, and calm through fevers and teething.

"Have you ever seen anyone so beautiful?" Cecilia asked, smiling at Stella, who promptly ripped off her hat and threw it in the dirt.

Rainer grinned at Cecilia. "Just every day of my life."

She blushed and kissed him.

The older she got, the more Stella looked like Cecilia. It was an astonishing thing to see his wife's face reflected in his daughter, along with his own green eyes. She demonstrated more personality by the day, and he hadn't decided yet if they were blessed or doomed that she seemed to mirror her mother's swift temper and daring nature.

Stella cooed, looking quite seriously at Cecilia as if she was having a full conversation.

"I agree, your father is a shameless baby hog. Always finding excuses to wander off with you and hoard you to himself. I can't say I blame him. You are the most adorable baby in the world."

Rainer did tend to wander off with Stella, but it was only because he wanted their daughter to see everything. That and she was always hungry in the mornings and shared her mother's temperament, becoming incredibly cranky when she needed to eat. He took her for walks when she woke up so that Cecilia could have a few more precious moments of sleep.

Cecilia smiled at their daughter. "What's that?" She leaned in, pretending the baby was talking to her. "You're right, he does get more handsome every day and it's rather unfair." She winked at Rainer.

He felt the same way about his wife. If anyone had asked on his wedding day, he would have said with certainty that Cecilia never could have been more lovely than she was then, but somehow, each day she seemed to bloom progressively brighter. Perhaps it was the relaxation that came after a hard-fought battle. Maybe it was simply being happy but she grew more radiant daily.

"Perhaps we could leave Stella with Aunt Clara tonight and you could have some much-needed alone time with your very handsome husband. Let him remind you that he's not just a pretty face, but also a man of many talents," he whispered.

Lust fluttered through their bond.

She raised an eyebrow. "Oh really? I'm sure Clara would be delighted to have this girl to herself." She looked at Stella and her face changed. Worry creased her brow.

Rainer laughed. "Sweetheart, she will be right up the trail and it's just overnight. I'll go get her first thing."

When she met his eyes, he recognized the heat in them. "You've got a lot of ground to cover in just one night."

He kissed her neck and whispered against her skin, "I'm certain I'm up for it. The question is whether you're willing to give up a night of sleep because I have no intention of letting you get any rest."

They'd found their moments when Stella napped, but they hadn't had extended time together since she was born. They'd recently moved her into the additional bedroom he'd built onto the side of the cabin, which had offered them a bit more privacy, but being parents was exhausting.

Cecilia's appetites were still borderline insatiable and they were forced to find any moments they could to sneak away—in a frenzy bent over the kitchen table after dropping Stella at Clara's for the afternoon, or up against the wall while Rainer muffled Cecilia's moans with a hand during nap time, or in the moments before they gave into exhaustion in bed at night.

Rainer would be lying if he said he wasn't a little bit desperate to be with her. He missed their uninterrupted chats and not having to rush. He wanted to take his time, hold her close, remind her how much he loved her. He wanted to hear her moaning in his ear, desperately whispering how she was just for him. The words were possessive and archaic, but it drove him out of his mind when she said them. They'd been together so many times, but she still knew how to make him absolutely wild.

"It would be nice to have you to myself before I have to share you with our friends this weekend," she said.

Xander and all of their friends were visiting Olney for the winter holidays and his birthday and Rainer knew he wouldn't have his wife to himself until after they'd all packed up and headed back to Olney weeks later.

Her hand slid lower and she gave his butt a squeeze. "I'll stop by and talk to Aunt Clara on my way to the queen's garden this morning for me and Stella's girl talk. Now come inside and feed me so I can feed her before we both get cranky."

Rainer laughed and followed her into the kitchen.

———

Rainer didn't want to intrude. Saturday mornings were sacred to Cecilia, as they had been since her mother took her to the queen's garden as a child. He usually left Cecilia and Stella alone, but for some reason he felt restless, curious about their weekly ritual.

Instead of finishing the third commission he'd received this month for a table and chairs, he'd left his half-finished woodwork in his workshop. Now he was peeking through the hedges of the queen's garden, spying on his wife.

From this angle, he could see Cecilia's back, her lilac dress beautiful against her fair skin and her curls piled up on top of her head, out of reach of the baby, who loved to yank on them. Stella sat on Cecilia's lap, facing Rainer but staring intently at Cecilia as she spoke.

"I know it's hard," Cecilia said. "I know you're small and fierce and you can't do all the things you want to. I've been there too. But I want you to know that when you're bigger and stronger and older, I'm going to make sure you can do what you choose to do, that you can make your way in the world, no matter how different that way is from the norm."

Stella cooed, smiling up at her mother.

"I know it's hard to be little and have so much fire you think you might burn alive if you can't vent it, but I will be here to help you. So will your dad. He's good at it, too. He's so patient. I hope someday you find a partner like him. Someone who sees you even when you're terrified to be seen. Someone who loves you and knows how to push you. Someone steady and kind. We are a couple of very lucky ladies to have your dad to mellow us out—even when he spies on us. Don't you think?" She turned and smiled over her shoulder at Rainer. "You know, if you wanted to join us, you could just ask, Rain."

"I didn't want to intrude."

Stella let out a squeal of delight as she spotted him, her whole face lighting up.

"I think Stella speaks for both of us. You're always welcome," Cecilia said.

Rainer kissed both of their cheeks and sat next to Cecilia on the bench. "Is this what you do every Saturday?"

It was so sweet to watch the two of them together. The way Cecilia spoke to the baby like she understood, the way Stella stared at her mother, her eyes bright with intelligence.

For so long, he'd thought he needed to prove he was strong through force, that he'd feel satisfied once he fulfilled the legacy of his father, but the thing that he was most proud of was that he'd stayed himself no matter how the world had tried to change him. Hearing the way Cecilia spoke about him to their daughter, hearing her vision of his influence, solidified everything in his mind.

He had needed to prove to himself that he was worthy of his own dreams and wishes, that his value didn't come from someone else but was found in simply being himself. Rainer's legacy wasn't one of violence nor of greatness in battle—his legacy had become one of telling stories, of believing in long shots, of wishes that came true. His was a legacy of stars.

51

XANDER

Coming back to Olney was strange. Though Xander had been back once for Rainer and Cece's wedding, he was struck each time he entered the summer kingdom by how a place could go from being foreign to home and back to foreign again. Now, standing on the beach below Cece's cottage, he was drawn right back in time, though this time he had his wife, his consort, and his son beside him.

Xander's bare feet hit the cool sand and his eyes locked on Cece. He was struck by her stillness first. Restless, aimless Cece, who never seemed to stop moving, stood impossibly still at the water's edge. If ever there was a sign of her contentment, that was it.

She turned as if sensing his eyes on her and grinned. "Xander."

She looked tired but lovely in a simple light blue cotton dress embroidered with tiny flowers, the sleeves hanging off her slim shoulders and the bodice clinging to her curves, accentuating her slightly fuller figure. Her hair was pinned back save for a few stray curls that framed her face. Her cheeks were flushed from the ocean breeze and her eyes brightened with joy as she walked toward him. It was clear that motherhood agreed with her, not that he'd had any doubt.

Rainer must have been nearby, but Xander couldn't take his eyes off of Cece. He'd seen her transform before his eyes so many times. From uncertain huntress to terrifying goddess to sensitive mortal woman whose love had saved them all. This new transformation into someone calm and self-contained and so utterly at peace was the one he didn't know he needed to see.

"My love, every time I see you, I think it's impossible for you to be more lovely, and yet somehow here you are, more stunning than ever." Xander grinned and kissed her cheek.

"And you are as excessive a flirt as ever." She hugged him.

No matter how much time passed, having Cece in his arms felt good. His old love for her was like a splinter lodged in his heart, long healed over, the ache dulled by familiarity. That was just what it was to care. That pain was a remnant of unspent love and it was more distant than it had ever been. What existed now was grounded, tamer, and in some ways more real.

Long ago, she'd stoked a wild longing that he didn't know he possessed until she drew it out of him. She'd wedged something into the darkest part of his heart—a place he thought nothing could reach—and like a door propped open, he couldn't shut the world out anymore. Love got in.

And he was glad for it because he did not know until that light shined in just how much he'd withered in the dark.

Jessamin stepped forward to hug Cece.

"It is so good to see you. You look gorgeous as always. Now, where is he? I have been so excited to lay eyes on this handsome prince," Cece said, her eyes darting behind them.

Teddy toddled forward clumsily, gripping the back of Jessamin's dress and peeking shyly around her legs at Cece.

Xander's son had skin somewhere between his olive and his wife's brown, but his face and hazel eyes were just like Xander's. It was a wonder to behold Teddy's sharp mind and bubbling laugh every day. He had a joy so much like that of the late friend after whom they'd named him.

Cece knelt in the sand, her eyes wide with joy. "Oh my gods, look at him. He's going to be so handsome. He looks so much like both of you. Hello, Teddy, I'm your Aunt Cece."

She reached out a hand but Teddy buried his face in Jessamin's dress.

"He's in a shy phase. He'll warm up in a few minutes," Jessamin said.

Soon Rainer strode toward the group of them with a baby in his arms. "Your Graces," he said with a bow, holding up his daughter. "Meet Stella McKay."

Xander's chest warmed at the sight of her. "As if I wouldn't recognize that face," he said. "She looks just like her mother, thank the gods. No offense, McKay."

He expected Rainer to joust with him but he simply looked enamored with his daughter as he handed her to Xander.

Stella grinned at Xander and for a moment he could do nothing but stare. She looked so much like Cece with her fair skin and wild curls. She blinked up at him, her large green eyes curious.

"Goddess bless. She's beautiful, Rainer," Jessamin said softly.

"She is," Xander said.

Rainer laughed. "She's also incredibly smart and, gods help us, a bit daring like her mother. She's already trying to walk and extremely frustrated that she can't."

"You must love that," Xander chuckled.

"You'd be surprised to learn that one of us is quite used to worrying over a tiny, reckless brunette, and the other is brand new to the experience," Rainer said, his gaze flashing to Cece.

Sure enough, Cece looked on, her brow creased with concern.

Xander looked at Stella again. She let out a loud squeal and grinned at him.

"Stella, I expect you will lay the world at your feet like your mother," he said softly.

She chose that exact moment to spit up on him.

Xander chuckled. "Yes, it seems you're just like her. Won't have a man telling you what to do, king or not."

Stella grinned at him and giggled joyfully.

Rainer couldn't have looked prouder of his daughter's ability to vomit at such a convenient time. Cece rushed over with a cloth to clean him up, but Xander waved her off.

"It's fine. I got used to it with Teddy," he said, gesturing to his son, standing a few paces back with Maren and Isla, whom Xander's gaze lingered upon.

Though Isla had not agreed to be his official consort, Xander wasn't giving up. As far as pretty much anyone at court was concerned, Isla was the king's paramour and the Argarian huntmaster. No one had so much as batted an eye. Xander had made such little fanfare about it that the people who'd initially been eager for gossip about his and Jessamin's unconventional relationship lost interest entirely.

Life was certainly not easy, but it was peaceful. He'd settled into a love with Isla that was passionate but also steady and reliable. It was a grown-up love.

"I am shocked my husband gave her up!" Cece teased as she looked at her daughter in Xander's arms. "Rainer is an unbearable baby hog. I rarely get to hold her myself these days."

Rainer just wrapped an arm around Cece and kissed her in a way that was not wholly appropriate for public consumption.

Sylvie appeared behind them, rolling her eyes. "Gods, you two. Get a room, honestly," she said, giving voice to Xander's thoughts.

Cece giggled as she pulled away, her eyes still locked with Rainer's.

"You keep kissing her like that and we'll have a whole brood of these beautiful little green-eyed babies in no time," Sylvie huffed, stealing Stella from Xander's arms. "Come here, darling, let your Aunt Sylvie tell you how to work all of these poor suckers who can't stop looking at how cute you are."

Evan grinned at his wife as she walked the baby over to him. "Is Stella as bossy as her mother?" he called from where he sat in the sand.

Cece shot him a dirty look.

"I'm not even going to touch that one," Rainer said, kissing Cece on the top of the head before he followed Sylvie.

Xander met Cece's gaze. "Walk with me, love."

He held his arm out and she threaded hers through it.

"Teddy's getting so big. I can't believe he's already walking," she said.

"The time flies. I can't believe it myself and I see him every day. Jessamin has insisted we not just use nannies but it's stressful to run a kingdom and chase after a toddler. He is an absolute menace, but we adore him, even now that he manages to sprint around the castle," Xander sighed. "Stella is beautiful. She looks just like you."

Cece's eyes lit up. "She is. Gods, Xan, I never thought I'd get to have that. I can't believe I'm so wrecked and worried all the time about someone who can't even walk."

"You'll get used to it. She'll be fine because you made this world for her. You made a place where she could be safe," Xander soothed, rubbing a hand on her arm.

She nodded.

"Will you have more?" he asked.

Cece laughed. "If Rainer has anything to say about it. He's practically been begging me, but I refuse to relent so soon. I haven't even gotten my body back from this baby yet. Does it make me ungrateful that I'd like to have it to myself for a few months before I'm getting kicked by another of Rainer McKay's little warrior babies? I swear to the gods, I thought Stella was just going to fight her way out toward the end."

Xander laughed. "He just loves you. He seems very doting."

"Oh my gods, you have no idea. There has never been a more spoiled child in the two kingdoms. She can't even speak, and she already has him wrapped around her finger. He's so wonderful with her," Cece said.

"As if there was any doubt," Xander said.

She gave his arm an affectionate squeeze. "How are things at home?"

"Loud but very good. Trying to very slowly shift toward more collective governance. I think it could be really good. Evan and Sylvie keep me honest, but they do such great work and I have more free time than I ever expected. Though it's nice to have the family time with Jess and Teddy."

She smiled. "You two seem very happy."

"We are. She's an incredible friend and I love her dearly. Maren is also wonderful. And, of course, I have Isla."

She frowned. "And how is that?"

"I love her very much, though she makes me work for my daily maybe."

Cece laughed. "You're still doing that?"

Xander couldn't stop smiling. "I hope it never stops."

She drew him to a stop. "You don't want to know for sure?"

"I know for sure every day. Every day she chooses to stay with nothing tethering her to me—and did you see her hand?"

Cece whipped her head around to stare at Isla, who was speaking with Mika by the edge of the surf. He waited for her to see it. Isla pressed a hand to her chest, laughing at something Mika had said, and the ring on her left hand caught the sunlight.

Cece gasped. "Is that—"

"My mother's ring? Yes."

"So she said yes to being consort?"

He couldn't help but laugh at the sheer delight on Cece's face. "She's just trying it on."

Cece pursed her lips. "Oh, I see. Just giving it a test run."

Xander felt lit up by triumph. "I'm winning her over. There are so many ways to love, Cece. I have so much love in my life and I'm happy. You are, too. I can see it."

She grinned at him. "I am."

"The two of you are disgustingly in love as usual. I must admit I'm surprised to see you looking so relaxed with such a little one. It can be hard to find down time for personal *attention*."

She narrowed her eyes at him, her cheeks growing pinker. "I don't know what you mean."

"I'm quite certain you do," Xander teased. "Happy to see motherhood has done nothing to dampen your appetites, love. He's a very lucky man."

"Please continue to remind him," she laughed, looking over her shoulder at her husband.

Xander glanced at Rainer, whose eyes were trained on Cece's ass.

"Seems he already knows," Xander laughed.

"Xan, you should write more. You know I'm here for you. No pressure. But I'm happy to be a sounding board or to talk through things with you. Plus, I get a laugh out of making Grim play messenger."

Xander chuckled. A cool breeze blew in off the sea and he took a deep breath of the salty air, the scent tugging at a pattern in his memory. He knew if he pulled it up, he'd see all the interconnected memories of the Adiran Sea.

"All right, I promise I'll get back to it. I was giving you a break because I knew how exhausted you were after Stella was born," he said.

"I always have time for you, love. Don't forget it, okay?"

He nodded toward Stella. "I suppose this means I'm relegated to your second favorite person in the world now."

She burst out laughing. "You wish. The good news is that you are still in the top three."

"I'm afraid I have to bump you down to fourth favorite—what with my handsomeness and so many women vying for my attention," he taunted.

She stuck her bottom lip out into a pout. "I suppose I'll have to learn to live with it."

"Perhaps some lemon cakes will soften the blow," Xander said, gesturing to where Maren knelt on a blanket in the sand, reaching into a picnic basket.

Cece smirked. "You still know the way to my heart." She pressed onto her toes and kissed his cheek. Then she dashed across the sand toward the sweets.

Isla wandered over to him as if she hadn't been standing just far enough away to eavesdrop.

"Keeping secrets, darling?" she said, threading her fingers through his.

"I have no secrets from you. Your jealousy is thrilling, though unwarranted. We were talking about you," Xander said.

She tipped her chin up defiantly. "What about me?"

"She saw the ring and wanted to know if I'd made an honest consort out of you yet."

"And what did you say?"

He tugged her body against his, brushing his lips over hers. "I said that you make me honest and that is good enough for me."

Isla smiled and pulled him into a kiss.

Xander had married Cece out of reckless love and Jessamin out of necessity, but his relationship with Isla was a love that grew out of loss. It was trust that grew up through ground that had been slashed and burned, making more fertile soil for years to come. Theirs was a love that grew from *hope*.

He'd come through more trials than he ever expected and he'd learned the value of honesty. He had a wonderful wife, a sweet son, a love worth risking heartbreak for again, and a kingdom that was healing from old wounds. He'd done what he promised Davide he would. He'd named his fear and he'd made Argaria better, and it was so much more than he dreamed for himself.

Xander Savero was a man with no secrets left and that was how he liked it.

52

CECILIA

The cave mouth stretched before her, dark and wide like the mouth of a great beast waiting to swallow her whole, only this time, there was a cooing baby strapped into a sling on her chest.

"What do you think, Stella? Should we go in?" Cecilia asked as she wiggled her toes in the damp sand.

The baby tipped her head back, letting out a soft gurgle.

Rainer's warm hand came to Cecilia's back as he stepped up beside her. "Your mom and her caves." His tone was teasing as he brushed a kiss to Cecilia's temple before placing one atop Stella's head.

"This is actually your father's favorite sea cave. If I remember correctly, he used to sneak girls who were not me here to make out when he was a teenager—"

"I did that *one* time, Cecilia. You'll never let me live it down." Rainer rolled his eyes.

She grinned at her husband. She'd been so sad to say goodbye to their friends when they headed back to Argaria that morning, but she was happy to return to their everyday rhythm.

Rainer scooped the baby from the sling and sat in the sand with her in his lap as he pointed out sea life in one of the tide pools in the cave.

Cecilia's love for Rainer felt ancient and also brand new, a strange paradox that left her with the bone-deep familiar knowing of what he needed as well as the doubt that she could give it to him. Their love stretched and grew with them and she was used to the things she relied on being taken away. She was afraid to settle into life, but settle she did.

Sometimes she couldn't believe she was a mother, but she remembered the moment she'd first felt her daughter acutely, drawing it up in her memory and turning it over and over like an old, precious jewel.

———

It was Rainer's birthday. A beautiful spring day that seemed like a good omen.

But the labor was hard. Cecilia was exhausted and she'd been managing the pain for hours, having long burned off the lemon cakes Rainer had brought her from the bakery.

Worse, she could sense something was wrong in the way Lyra and Mika kept looking at each other and then looking at Rainer.

Her husband was oblivious. His full focus was settled on her as he pulled her pain into himself and rubbed her back.

"What aren't you saying?" Cecilia snapped.

Lyra held up her hands. "We don't want to worry you, but you've been laboring quite a while and we think you need to try another position to push or the baby might start to experience distress." Her tone was gentle but serious and Cecilia had worked with her long enough to know when the healer meant business.

She turned to Rainer, terrified to lose this thing that she wanted so badly. She'd been afraid to even really admit how badly until that moment. She was still afraid.

"What do you need, sweetheart?" Rainer took her face in his hands. She couldn't focus, her wild eyes panicked and darting around the room. "Cece,

it would be okay if you wanted something just for yourself. Even if you needed it."

She blinked away tears. In that moment, she wanted that baby fiercely.

For so long, she'd blamed Rainer's desire for a child, but now that the baby was practically here—now that Cecilia could feel the truth in her bones—she wanted to have a child for herself.

She'd taken what was given. She'd felt it was tempting fate to hope for more than survival and happiness with the love of her life. But now she wanted this with every beat of her heart and every breath of her lungs.

Cecilia closed her eyes and tried to sense a connection between herself and the baby. She pressed a hand to her stomach, the muscles sore, exhausted from effort. Between one breath and the next, she felt her daughter's emotions swell around her.

The baby was frightened.

"Okay, baby. I know you are scared, but you are already so loved and so very much wished for. I know change is hard and you're worried about what comes next. I am, too. But I am willing to be scared with you and your dad is here and ready to be brave enough for both of us and he wants to meet you so badly."

She pulled on her goddess power and tried for the first time to use it on the baby, sending the familiar hopeful sense of peace into the life inside her. Slowly, the tension and fear eased.

Lyra leaned in. "Ready to try again."

Cecilia nodded. Lowering to her knees, she took Rainer's hand and pushed. She stayed calm through the pain, focused on Rainer's voice, on his eyes, and only a few moments later, a muffled cry broke through the silence and Lyra placed a red-faced baby girl in her arms.

In that moment, she believed for the first time that it was okay to need other people. It was okay not to just give all the time but to want things for herself, and she looked at her daughter's scrunched-up face and broke down in sobs.

———

Cecilia's consciousness returned to the cave and Rainer caught her eye.

"Where'd you go?" he asked.

"Just remembering the day she was born."

Rainer grinned. "That was a top-three day."

"Top three?"

"Impossible to pick between you saving my life and coming back from the dead, the day we got married, and the day Stella was born." Rainer smiled at her, then scooped the baby up and wandered down the beach to their picnic.

With Stella's arrival, Cecilia had worried she'd have to split up her love and give the baby what had once belonged to Rainer. Instead, her heart seemed to grow and stretch to accommodate both of them with ease. She was hopeless to the sweet baby with big green eyes and a smile that made Cecilia's world stop.

Cecilia grinned as Rainer did pushups over Stella on the blanket, kissing her button nose each time he lowered. Stella giggled a deep belly laugh each time.

Rainer was the kindest, most loving man she'd ever known, and sometimes simple scenes—like when he pretended Stella was tackling him or when they had what he called "their chats," where she would babble and Rainer would speak to her as if they were having a whole conversation—brought tears to Cecilia's eyes.

Rainer grinned at her.

"Are you happy with your life?" she asked.

Rainer laughed. "My life is amazing. I get to spend my days with this happy girl and cook every night. We are going to travel the world several times a year. We have friends in high places. I'm surrounded by beautiful girls." He punctuated each word with kisses on Stella's belly and she giggled each time. He met Cecilia's eye. "And my wife is a gorgeous goddess who I'd like to get on my knees and worship right now."

"Rainer!" Cecilia scolded.

He shrugged. "What? Stella doesn't know what I mean."

"You don't know that. She could be the most powerful memory

witch of all time and once she has context, she'll come back to this memory and know how inappropriate her father was and she'll be horrified. I cannot believe I have to say this—don't dirty talk in front of the baby."

Rainer grinned as he hopped to his feet and pulled her into a long, slow kiss. When he drew back, she couldn't help but grin.

Rainer was right. Their lives were pretty perfect. She'd feared domesticity would dull her, that she'd feel trapped by it, but she felt inspired, overwhelmed, expansive, and so very at peace with the variability of her days.

She'd had a lifetime of adventure in a short period of time, and now she was ready to be still. The clinic was busier than ever. Cecilia and Mika were helping people. It was a lot to manage, but Rainer made sure she had time for it and encouraged her when she felt guilty for leaving Stella with him for long stretches. He visited her sporadically so she could feed the baby and assuage her guilt for giving her time and energy to other people. And twice a year, they would take long trips to Novum or Argaria and visit their friends.

They ate in quiet, watching the waves crash rhythmically against the sand.

After dinner, Cecilia laid on the blanket next to Rainer as the sun set and the first stars lit the sky. Stella slowly nodded off to sleep on her chest.

Even in sleep, Cecilia could feel the restless wildness in her daughter—the same endless longing she'd always felt as present as her heartbeat. Cecilia watched it in her every day. The way Stella's bright green eyes studied their movements. The way her brow furrowed in concentration that reminded Cecilia of Rainer so much that she laughed out loud the first time she saw it. The way the baby let out frustrated, startled cries when her body wouldn't cooperate with the speed at which she wanted to move.

Her daughter was a force, and Cecilia promised she'd try to always encourage her to hold onto that fire. The world was dull without it. She would do what her father and mother had done and embrace every reckless, wild thing about her daughter, even when she was afraid. Cecilia knew what it was to be caged in a life too small for her and to have responsibilities much too large. The only thing she wanted for her daughter was for her to get to choose her way in life.

Staying wild was a blessing.

The bravest thing Cecilia had ever done was let Rainer love her. It took a lot to allow someone to be so gentle with her. It was hard to stay soft and open to him, but she did it each day. Some days it was easy. Some days she had to grit her teeth and repeat their silent prayer over and over in her head.

Brave with my hand. Brave with my heart.

On those days, Rainer always seemed to read her, taking the green ribbon from their bedpost and tying it around her wrist as a reminder.

Cecilia laid back and looked up at the stars shooting across the sky.

"Would you look at that—sugared with stars," Rainer said.

A smile tugged at her lips. "Sugared with stars. Well said."

She racked her brain, but the truth was she wasn't sure what there was left to wish for. She had the love of her life, a beautiful daughter, amazing friends who'd become family, and a kingdom that was rebuilding for the better. They were all complicated and flawed people, but they understood each other. They healed with and through each other. They allowed for those flaws without judgment. They loved each other not in spite of their weaknesses but often because of them.

They'd all loved and lost and fought hard for what they had. They were people who understood what it was to be lost and found and lost again. They'd helped her rebuild when she'd been broken. They fought hard for freedom and won. They were all strong in the weak places.

Cecilia had earned her freedom, and the price had been steep, but there was never a day she didn't look at her husband and daughter and know it was worth it.

She'd raged over the ruins of so many versions of herself. She'd likely be reborn again often, but she feared it less.

She'd asked for more than the small life she'd left behind three years earlier, and more than once, she'd regretted that wish. But now, with a job that helped her put herself and others back together, with a husband who took such good care of her, and in seeing their friends happy and satisfied, she'd come full circle, back home to the very place that had once felt so unsuitable.

She'd saved the two kingdoms, saved her love, and then saved herself. Her life was like a shattered mirror, impossible to perfectly piece back together but beautiful in its breaking.

Cecilia carried many hearts within her own. She carried many memories. And she no longer feared the power in them.

Now, when the sea whispered, "*Remember,*" she whispered back.

She reached out her hand, intertwining her fingers with Rainer's.

"Make a wish," she whispered with a smile on her lips. So far, she was two for two with these wishes. She liked those odds.

Cecilia picked a star and sent one more wish out into the world.

A wish to keep writing a long and happy story that was uniquely their own. Some stories tied people together. Some stories saved. Their stories had done both, leading them back to each other as often as they led them home to themselves.

The best tales weren't the ones written in a storybook or marked in a language of scars on a body. The best stories were the ones written in the history and love between people—in the hope that allowed those who'd lost so much to keep dreaming.

She kept their story close at heart so they could continue it forever, adding to it nightly, living in between.

DEAR READER,

A profound thank you to everyone who has made it this far. Thank you for passing the trauma of this series on to all of your reader friends. I'm humbled by your commitment to see this story through. I hope that I did these characters and this story justice after four books of heartache.

This series was drafted in its entirety during the pandemic. In many ways, this story and these characters carried me through a dark time. They gave me purpose, direction, and a place to escape to when the world was chaotic and terrifying. I will always be grateful for the way isolation forced me to slow down and remember what it was like to chase something for the simple joy of it. What a powerful thing.

I can hardly believe we are here at the end. Three and a half years of work. 633,631 words published (though there were a lot more in the many, MANY revisions I did). These books are truly the books of my heart and a labor of immense love. I chose to self-publish because I couldn't bear to trust anyone else with something so dear to me. But that meant it all rode on me.

There were times when I thought this moment would never come, or when I thought that no one but me would be there to witness it. Now that it's here I can't stop crying as I write this because it's so bittersweet to see it come to an end.

It's hard to believe that a nagging idea about generational memories combined with one sharp visual between dreaming and waking can be the seed that grows into an entire series. This story was born out of imagining magic that would perfectly preserve memories, and it turned into a group of characters that leaped off the page and demanded I tell their tale.

I spent a lot of my reading life looking for characters who felt things intensely the way I do. The fantasy genre was full of heroines who seemed so cool and unaffected, and heroes who were stoic in the face of immense danger. I wanted to write characters who were messy and human.

I need to take a moment to acknowledge my POV characters because I've spent these last three and a half years in their heads.

To Evan - my steady, strategic single parent to this chaotic found family. You really took charge and kept everyone on course through these last two books especially. I loved watching you learn to choose your heart over your responsibilities for once. I hope your journey will teach readers that they are worth more than their productivity and it's okay to find someone who can teach you how to have some fun.

To Xander - my intense, chaotic, charming prince turned king. You got your maybe. You took charge of your story right from the start and turned yourself from a villain into a hero. I am grateful for the absolute chaos you made of this series and that you found love on your own terms. I loved watching you grow and learn to break the patterns that were holding you back from happiness. Thank you for teaching me how to push boundaries. I hope your journey will teach readers that they deserve to be loved exactly as they are and it's okay to take big risks to find that love.

To Rainer - my steady and anxious people pleaser. You took a lot of heat but I think it's because you represent some of the parts of ourselves we don't particularly like to look at. I loved getting to write your journey from self-sacrificing and rule-following to going after

Dear Reader,

what you want and staking claim to what you need. Thank you for teaching me about taking care of myself. You and I will always have a special bond because of that. I hope your story will teach readers to make home a safe place for dreaming.

To Cece- my fierce and sensitive heroine. I think the whole world tells us that being careful, strategic, and cynical will save us, but my hope is that your courageous vulnerability, emotional fortitude, and compassion will make every other fierce heroine out there feel seen and understood. Sometimes strength looks a lot like being honest with yourself and letting someone else teach you how to love your rougher edges. I hope your journey will bring readers home to themselves and teach them to be brave with their hands and brave with their hearts.

Now Reader, I don't say this to be self-deprecating, or to downplay how much work it is to write a book or a series, but I believe that if I can do this, anyone who has that same quiet storyteller's voice tugging on their heart, can do it too.

Sometimes you weave a story out of the few fragile threads of hope you can find alone in a room and away from your family and friends for months. Sometimes stories anchor the author and whisper to the reader. The truth is that sometimes stories save us, and sometimes sharing them saves someone else. They rescue us from overthinking, they deliver us from boredom, or they make us feel less alone. I hope THE LOST GOD series has done that for you in some small way, and I'm so grateful for your support over the fourteen months it took to get these books out into the world.

This series deals with so much loss—losing loved ones, losing hope, losing parts of yourself—but it's also about what grows out of that loss. So my hope for you, Reader, is that you'll grow a wild garden out of your heartbreaks, that you'll surround yourself with friends who teach you how to love yourself better, and that someday you'll be old enough to need those fairy tales again.

Love,
Sheila

573

Thank you for reading

THE G☉DLESS KINGD☉M

Did you like it? Love it?
Read it because you needed to prove you're
not afraid of commitment?

✷ ✷ ✷ ✷ ✷ ✷ ✷ ✷ ✷ ✷ ✷ ✷ ✷

However you feel about it, I would be so grateful if you
would **REVIEW** it on Amazon.

Reviews help indie authors like myself reach new readers
and they help readers determine if this book is for them.

Please take a moment to write a short review.
THANK YOU!
Scan the code to review

✷ ✷ ✷ ✷ ✷ ✷ ✷ ✷ ✷ ✷ ✷ ✷ ✷

You can also get a BONUS EPILOGUE
by following this link:

https://starsagespirit.ck.page/tgkbonus

or scanning this code

ACKNOWLEDGMENTS

It truly took a village to make this series happen so allow me to not cut this short, if you will.

To Tanya- You were the first cheerleader for The Lost God and your steadfast support has seen me through an entire series. I can hardly believe we are here but it's safe to say we wouldn't be if you hadn't given me that push in early 2021. Thank you for being my first and safest stop with this series. I am so grateful for your unwavering support and for all the hours on the phone working through all things writing and life. How lucky I was to meet someone at fourteen whom I could share all my stories with.

To Liz - Thank you for being a top-notch writing wife and for lovingly rolling your eyes when I text "this book is trying to kill me", instead of writing divorcing me. Thank you for helping to reflect this story back to me, for critiquing The Storm King and The Godless Kingdom back to back, and for treating these characters with the same love and care you bring to your own. You worked through so many snags with me over voice memos and in weekly writing babysitting sessions. Thanks for keeping me sane.

To Mike - You listened to me talk about these characters and this world for the past three and a half years. Thank you for making me laugh when I wanted to cry and give up. Thank you for making sure I don't sell myself short. Thank you for sending me flowers from Rainer, Cece, and Xander when I was afraid I'd never finish this book. Thank you for investing your time and energy in this series to make it the best it can be. You have been behind me this whole time, *just in case*.

To Erin - Thank you for seeing this series through to the end and for putting your whole heart into it.

To Andrea - For the purple and for making this series of covers your own down to the tiniest details.

To Tabs - Thanks for being my extra set of eyes to close this out.

To my beta readers - Fil, Michelle, and Lauren. You followed me through this whole series and I am so incredibly grateful for all of your insights and suggestions.

To my sensitivity readers - Thank you for helping me me handle the most harrowing parts of this story with as much grace as possible.

To all my fellow indie authors who have shared their wisdom and celebrated alongside me - Em, Helen, Kara, Les, Nicole, Penn, Tay, and Vanessa. Thank you for riding along in the passenger seat of this journey with me. It's easier to find my way through the chaos alongside you.

To my business witches - Thank you for sharing your spells with me and for giving the best advice through all my rough patches. Your magic has helped shape this story from start to finish.

To Megan - Since day one you have been the kind voice in my ear trying to help me protect my peace. Thank you for your wisdom.

To my friends and family - Thank you for supporting this series by shouting it from the rooftops. I'm lucky to have your support.

To my amazing ARC team - You're the most creative, supportive, hilarious team I could've asked for. You took this series and ran with it in the best way and I truly couldn't have done it without you.

To my readers - What a beautiful, sad, terrifying thing to do—bring a series to a close. It's a huge responsibility when so many of you are invested in this journey. Thank you for loving these characters so much. Thanks to all of you who have shared kind words about how these books touched you. Your encouragement is the fuel that kept the creative fire burning so I could finish.

I hope that I did your favorite characters justice but most of all I hope that you let yourself love along with them. I hope you carry their stories with you always, like a memory witch.

SONG OF THE DARK WOOD

A standalone gothic fairytale romance coming September 20, 2024

Never stray from the main trail. Never meet the eyes of the dead or the monsters that lurk in shadows. Never bleed in the Dark Wood. And above all ... keep the Wolf happy.

For centuries, the people of remote Ballybrine have kept the peace with their gods by sacrificing a Red Maiden to ferry souls from the Mother's realm of the living, through the Dark Wood, to the Wolf's realm of the dead. Soon it will be Rowan's turn.

Ripped from her family as a young girl, Rowan Cleary has been forced into a cloistered life learning to please the wolf and wield her spirit-enchanting voice. Though none of the previous maidens have survived their five-year term, Rowan is determined to beat the odds and protect the women who have become family to her.

When a deathly blight breaks out in the Dark Wood, and the acting maiden is murdered, Rowan vows to strike a new bargain with the god of death to ensure her survival. The Wolf has always been someone to fear—even more so now that the townspeople blame him for the blight—but he's far from the vengeful death god she expects.

To unravel the mystery, Rowan must seduce the Wolf. Soon, the attraction between them grows into a relentless magical force, threatening to shatter the delicate balance between realms and unleash a darkness eager to swallow their world.

Order here:

https://www.amazon.com/Song-Dark-Wood-Sheila-Masterson-ebook/dp/B0D1M81771

or scan the code to order:

ABOUT THE AUTHOR

THE GODLESS KINGDOM is Sheila Masterson's fourth novel. When she's not writing fantasy romance novels, you can find Sheila practicing yoga, or curled up reading tarot or a book. She lives outside of Philadelphia with her fiancé and way too many houseplants. Keep up to date on new releases by visiting her website sheilamasterson.com or following her on instagram.

instagram.com/sheilareadsandwrites

ALSO BY SHEILA MASTERSON

Made in the USA
Columbia, SC
08 June 2024

36862724R00357